William Pynchon, Mass., Springfield, Henry Martyn Burt

The First Century of the History of Springfield

the official records from 1636 to 1736, with an historical review and biographical

mention of the founders - Vol. 1

William Pynchon, Mass., Springfield, Henry Martyn Burt

The First Century of the History of Springfield
the official records from 1636 to 1736, with an historical review and biographical mention of the founders - Vol. 1

ISBN/EAN: 9783337377519

Printed in Europe, USA, Canada, Australia, Japan

Cover: Foto ©Andreas Hilbeck / pixelio.de

More available books at **www.hansebooks.com**

THE FIRST CENTURY

OF THE

HISTORY OF SPRINGFIELD

The Official Records from 1636 to 1736

WITH AN HISTORICAL REVIEW AND BIOGRAPHICAL
MENTION OF THE FOUNDERS

By HENRY M. BURT

VOLUME I

SPRINGFIELD, MASS.:
PRINTED AND PUBLISHED BY HENRY M. BURT
1898

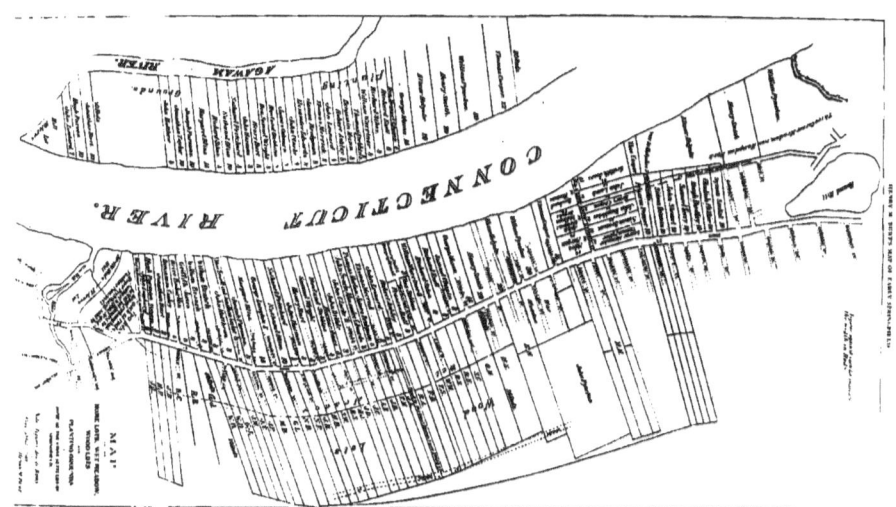

A people which takes no pride in the noble achievements of remote ancestors, will never achieve anything worthy to be remembered with pride by remote descendants.

—MACAULEY.

It is in the town records of Massachusetts that the American historical unit is to be sought. The political philosopher can there study the slow development of a system as it grew from the germ up. The details are trivial, monotonous, and not easy to clothe with interest; yet the volumes which contain them are the most precious archives. Upon their tattered pages the hardly legible letters of the ill-spelled words are written in ink grown pale with age, but they are all we have left to tell us of the first stages of a political growth which has ripened into the dominant influence of the new world; nor is it too much to imagine that when the idea of full human self-government, first slowly welded into practical form in New England towns, and as yet far from perfect, shall have permeated the civilized world and assumed final shape, then these town records will be accepted as second in historical importance to no other description of archives.

—CHARLES FRANCIS ADAMS.

INTRODUCTORY NOTE.

The many difficulties which have hitherto attended a careful and exhaustive reading of the early Town Records of Springfield have deterred even those who have given considerable thought and attention to the history of the founding of the town, from making a thorough study of the events which occurred during the formative period, or more than briefly mentioning individuals who made up the community in this pioneer undertaking in Western New England. It is with no small degree of satisfaction that I am now able to present the first volume of this work to the public, which will, with the second volume, to be issued a few months later, embody the official acts of the town during the first hundred years.

In addition I have given a brief review of some of the leading events, and a chronological summary from which the dates of occurrences can be readily obtained, which otherwise could be learned only by a more exhaustive reading. The index will also be found unusually full. This will bring to the reader a more accurate knowledge of the various transactions which originated here, some of which concern the beginnings of other settlements, and also a clearer view of the circumstances and motives which gave them birth, and will enable the individual reader to find that which is of most interest to him without spending hours in fruitless search.

The writers of our early history have made mention of William Pynchon's book, which was the cause of his departure from Springfield sixteen years after founding the town, and of his return to England, but no one has given an adequate idea of what it contained. The book was printed nearly 250 years ago in England, and what was then regarded as a heresy by the leading ministers and officials in the Colony, was a protest against certain Calvinistic beliefs. The book, or nearly the whole of it, has been printed in this volume, and will be found interesting as relating to the religious beliefs of the first settlers of New England and in comparison with the progress of religious thought which has taken place within the last two or three centuries.

William Pynchon was without doubt the ablest reasoner and the best scholar residing here during the first century. The drift of his mind was towards abstract discussion of theological questions, which he treated with an independence of thought rare for his time. Viewed in the light of the present it lacks that importance which he attached to them, inspired as they were by others who were feeding on the dry husks of dogmatic theology and placing more importance upon the letter than upon the spirit, which latter pervades the understanding and the beliefs of the present generation.

The official records have been followed literally in orthography, punctuation, and capitalization, in the printed volume, as well as the abbreviations common in all records of that time. It will no doubt facilitate the reading of those who are not familiar with the customs of the time to know that ye stands for the, y^t for that, y^m for them, y^r for their, w^t for what or white. Used in this connection the letter "y" represents the Saxon character for "th." These contractions were never found in the printed books of that period, and were in use only in written records or other writings of the time. To explain what may be misleading as to dates it may be well to keep in mind that the new year began with the 25th of March, consequently where double dates appear, like 1651-2, the last figure represents the correct year, as we reckon at present. In the chronological summary changes have been made in the dates of the years to conform to present reckoning, but no change was made in the dates of the month to correspond with New Style. While March 25 was the beginning of the new year, March was always considered as the first month, hence where "2d mo." appears it stands for April. With these explanations even the casual reader will find no difficulty in understanding the records.

In all the early New England settlements "Goodman" was in use as a prefix to surnames. Mister was applied to ministers, or some distinguished person. In the official records of Springfield "Goodman" was often contracted to the letter "G." If the reader in turning from the index to the records finds, for example, G: Parsons, or G: Ashley, he will understand that the letter "G" is not the initial of the given name, but refers to the title of "Goodman."

The recorders are also responsible for the different ways of writing the name of Thomas Merrick. It appears as Mirick, Myrick, and Merrick. Whether the original Thomas, the founder of the family, was Merrick or Mirick, no one can tell. The division of this family name comes from the lack of knowledge on part of the recorders, whose incorrect orthography have in other New England families made many branches from a single family tree.

The map which accompanies this volume shows the location of the homelots of the first settlers, and will be useful in establishing this interesting fact to their many descendants. The grants were made at various times, but mainly between 1636 and 1646.

I have given much time to the preparation of this work, including making the transcription from the records, and I hope it may prove to be acceptable and of permanent value.

HENRY M. BURT.

SPRINGFIELD, Mass., May 10, 1898.

CORRECTIONS.

In list of Town Recorders on page 47, the date of service of William Pynchon, Jr., given as from 1628 to 1636, should read from 1728 to 1736.

The toll-road mentioned on page 53, was across wet meadow on what is now State Street,—not in West Springfield, as stated in the 16th line.

In last line on page 63, "coming to England" should read "coming to New England."

On page 90, 11th line, instead of "Christ did suffer," should read "did not suffer."

On page 53, line 17, the statement relative to the location of the toll bridge in 1660, over Mill River, is incorrect. The bridge was established farther west of that point, on the road which crosses the river, turns southerly and leads over Long Hill.

On page 343 "Joseph Chapin" should read "Japhet Chapin."

February 1664.

Here followes a Record or List of y' Names of the
Townesmen, or men of this Towne of Springfield
that is to say of the allowed admitted Inhabitants
who they are this present ffebr: 1664.

Rowland Thomas	Cap' John Pynchon	John Harman.
Henry Chapin	Leiu' Elizur Holyoke	Nath: Pritchard.
William Brookes	ffrancis Pepper	Benjamin Parsons.
John Bagg	Timothy Cooper	Widdow M: Bliss
William Hunter	m' Pelatiah Glover.	Sam'll . Bliss.
Peter Swinck	Diacon Sam' Chapin	John Matthewes.
Griffith Jones	Japhet Chapin	Anth: Dorchester.
Obadiah Miller.	John Stewart	Rich: Sikes
John Henrisson	Thomas Noble	Jonathan Burt
Richard Excell	William Warriner	John Lumbard
John Dumbleton.	Serj: Tho: Stebbins.	Thomas Bancroft.
Jonathan Taylor	Benjamin Mun.	Benjamin Coley.
Hugh Dudley	David Ashley	John Bliss.
John Baker	Abell Wright.	John Keepe.
John Scott	James Warriner	Nathaneel Burt
John Riley	Jeremy Horton.	Widdow Burt
Joseph Crowfoote.	Symon Bemon	George Colton.
Edward Foster.	Thomas Day .	Sam'll Ely.
Thomas Miller	Charles Ferry .	James Taylor.
John Lionard :	Thomas Mirick	Jonathan Ball
Ens: Tho: Cooper.	Sam'll Marshfield	John Horton
Alex Bedortha.	Nathaneell Ely.	
Sammuell Terry	John Clarke	
John Lamb	Rowland Stebbin	
Robert Ashley	Lawrence Bliss.	
Serj: Miles Morgan.	James Osborne.	
William Branch.		

HISTORICAL REVIEW.

That spirit of unrest, which has marked the progress of every age and country, and which even in our own time we contemplate with grave concern, plainly foretold long before Massachusetts was settled,the coming condition of the mother country. Intolerant and corrupt rulers, favoritism, and misgovernment were developing that opinion which was to be the source of constitutional liberty, the very foundation of that freedom of thought and action which have made all progress possible, and that high attainment in modern thought, the consummation of a purpose which might not have been fully comprehended when the assertion of individual rights began. Out of that conflict of opinion which distracted England came the men who laid the foundations of New England. If results have been greater than were the first conceptions, those pioneers caught the glimmer of that fundamental truth which has grown brighter as the years have come and gone.

The founders of New England were earnest and devout. They came fully imbued with that conviction which was antagonistic to the dominant spirit then governing England. If they now seem to us to have been over-zealous in their opinions and narrow and contracted in their religious views, we should not overlook in our judgment of them the conditions out of which they had come, and the conflicts which had beset them before putting foot on these shores. From the standpoint of to-day, all Europe at that period seems but little more than half civilized. There was no freedom of thought, no right of private judgment. Power made right with the administrators of law, and to it the humblest and the highest must yield obedience. While it is true that, viewed in the light of the present, our New England ancestors are open to the charge of bigotry and intolerance, we must not forget that bigotry is the limitation of knowledge, and that the higher the education in every thing that concerns the moral and spiritual welfare of man, the broader become the views of right and duty. Earnestness of purpose, steadfastness of conviction, were the ruling motives of the men who laid the foundations of civil and religious liberty in this country. Out of those early beginnings came a fuller development of that fundamental principle which has, like a reflex tide, set back upon the shores of the Old World, while their example has been an inspiration to those who were striving for light in the country across the sea, as well as to us who have succeeded them.

Two and a half centuries ago Springfield did not promise much to our ancestors beyond the simplest living, and those who came here must have had their reward in the feeling of independence of the conditions which had beset them in their English homes. Freedom of thought and purpose were sufficient in themselves to make the plainest life attractive. Notwithstanding the long lapse of time since the aboriginal inhabitants of this land passed the title to the soil to the people of Anglo-Saxon blood, the struggles and hardships of the pioneers are not forgotten, and each year there is an increased interest in what our ancestors accomplished. The beginnings of New England must be of interest to every thoughtful person, for then and there was born the belief that man is capable of self-government. Much of that purpose which marked our early settlements has broadened as it has adapted itself to new conditions, but that spirit which came here at the beginning has made New England conspicuous among the great Commonwealths of our country.

Springfield was the first town west of Boston, Cambridge, and Watertown, to be settled in Massachusetts. A few Connecticut towns are of slightly earlier date, Wethersfield and Windsor, having been settled a little more than a year prior to Pynchon and his small company's first location on the Agawam meadows. Roger Ludlow and William Pynchon, both patentees in the Massachusetts Bay Company, began an almost simultaneous movement towards the Connecticut, the former to Hartford and the latter to what is now Springfield. The Rev. Thomas Hooker's company set out for Hartford a month after the arrival of Pynchon's company of eight persons in this then far-away wilderness. In the years 1634 and 1635 movements looking toward permanent settlements in the Connecticut valley had begun, but it was not until 1636 that there was anything like a concert of action to found towns so far to the westward of Boston. Hooker and his company made a toilsome journey through the wilderness to Hartford, and it is probable that Pynchon's company did the same when it came to Springfield, although they left no description of their route to the Connecticut. The settlers' household goods probably came by sea from Boston to the mouth of the Connecticut, and thence up the river to the falls above Warehouse Point, so named from the fact that Mr. Pynchon subsequently established a place for the storage of freight. Very little in the way of description of those overland journeys between Springfield and Boston has come down to us. John Winthrop, son of the first governor of Masachusetts Bay, and afterwards himself governor of Connecticut, briefly described his journey from the Bay to visit Mr. Pynchon at a later period in Springfield. His route was from Boston to Lancaster, and thence up the valley of the Nashua river, much of the way along the Central Massachusetts railroad. He traveled on horseback and was a part of three days on his way to Springfield. The journey was without incident, save an encounter with a few Indians at or near Brookfield.

The eight men who signed the agreement for the settlement of Springfield were these: William Pynchon. Mathew Mitchell, Henry Smith, Jehu Burr, William Blake, Edmund Wood, Thomas Ufford, and John Cable. It is dated May 14. 1636, and is in the handwriting of Henry Smith. and is in a good state of preservation in the office of the City Clerk.

Pynchon, in his own hand, concluded the agreement with the the following words just before the signatures: "We testifie to the ord^r above said, being al the first adventurers and subscribers for the plantation." Not one of the subscribers spent his life in Springfield; most of them, on the contrary, abandoned the enterprise within a few months. William Blake returned to Dochester; Jehu Burr, the ancestor of Aaron Burr, went in a few years to Fairfield, Ct., John Cable to a Connecticut town, in or near Fairfield, while it does not appear that either Mitchell, Ufford, or Wood, remained more than a few months. Pynchon went back to England in 1652, and his son-in-law, Henry Smith, the year following, where both died.

In these far-away days from the beginning of the settlement there remain comparatively few scattered threads with which to weave the story of the pioners; but it is not difficult to construct a picture of the scene that must have been presented to them as they approached their destination, and, emerging from the great wilderness through which they had traversed, looked down for the first time upon the wide-flowing Connecticut, the broad meadows which skirted the great forest beyond. Save a few scattered wigwams of the Indians there could have been no signs of human life. These virgin acres along the great river needed only intelligent cultivation to make them capable of supporting those who came, and those likely to join them in the near future. This entrance of Pynchon and his company brought a new era and at once opened new opportunities to those who had lately come from over the sea to found homes and rear families and train their children in the duties of good citizenship. It must have been a period of earnest endeavor, and those who settled down to the work before them must have grown strong in their determination to convert uncultivated fields and primeval forests into a land of plenty. It was no light task to which they had come, and it must have required no small degree of heroism to grapple successfully with the difficulties before them. While some faltered and turned away, the leadership of the founder held the settlement together, and it slowly grew into importance. Each subsequent year there came others to unite their lives and their fortunes to those who had been steadfast in their purpose to found this far-interior settlement within the jurisdiction of the Massachusetts Bay Company.

PYNCHON'S ENGLISH HOME.—THE CHARTER GRANTED.

Before entering upon the detailed history of the new settlement let us glance briefly at the background across the sea, looking for a moment at William Pynchon's home in the parish of Springfield, in the County of Essex, and inquiring into some of the transactions which led to migration from Old England to New England. Twenty-nine miles northeasterly of London is Chelmsford, the shire town of Essex. Across the little river, the Chelmer,—not unlike our own Mill river,—a mile to the northwestward, stands the ancient Parish Church of Springfield. It crowns a gentle eminence and near it are several residences of gentlemen of fortune and leisure. The view down the valley, along the Chelmer, which winds its way toward the sea, presents a lovely rural scene. The wide valley, the well-rounded outlines of distant gently sloping hills, presents in some slight degree the picture we get from the various eminences which skirt our own Connecticut. In this Parish Church William Pynchon worshiped, and for a time was one of its wardens. He and another warden had charge of making the repairs of the edifice in 1624, six years before sailing for New England with Winthrop's fleet.

Under date of March 4, 1629, King James gave a grant of land from the Merrimack on the north to a line three miles south of the Charles river, and extending westward "from the Atlantick and western sea and ocean on the east parte, to the south sea on the west parte," to twenty-seven persons, of whom Pynchon was one, styling themselves "The Governor and Company of the Massachusetts Bay in New Eng-

land." As a consideration for the grant the king reserved
one-fifth of all the gold and silver ores found within this do-
main. This was largely a commercial enterprise, and included London and other capitalists, who were styled "the adventurers," those going out to New England being called the
"planters," hence our settlements came to be known as
"plantations," and this is the origin of the term as early used
in New England.

Meetings for organization and for perfecting arrange-
ments for transportation and settlement were held several
times a week for a year or more, until the 8th of April, 1630,
when the Arbella, the Talbot, and the Jewel, weighed anchor
and sailed out of the harbor of Cowes for the then far distant
New England. On the 12th of June they arrived at Salem,
whither Gov. Endicott had previously gone. Gov. Winthrop and his company soon settled in Boston and vicinity,
Pynchon making his home in Roxbury.

After the charter was granted perhaps the most important
metings of the company in London were those held on the
28th and 29th of August, 1629, when on the first named day
the question arose as to whether the government of the
Colony should be continued in England, or be transferred to
New England. After considerable discussion the question
was postponed until 7 o'clock of the morning of the 29th,
at which time there was a full attendance, 27 members being
present, including William Pynchon. Debate followed the
convening of the meeting at that early hour, and a vote was
finally taken "by the erection of hands, and it appeared that
by general consent of the company that the government and
patent should be settled in New England." This saved to
the colonists home rule, and the settling of their own concerns without interference from those in England, who could
know but little of the situation and of the hardships to which
the immigrants would be subjected.

The price of passage for Winthrop's company was fixed
in England at "five pounds for a person, and 4 pounds a ton
for freight. Sucking children not to be reckoned; such as

are under 4 years of age 3 for one; under 8, 2 for one; under 12, 3 for 2, and that a ship of 200 tons shall not carry above 120 passengers." It would appear by this that our ancestors in crossing the ocean more than two and a half centuries ago paid about the same amount as is now charged for steerage passengers in our ocean steamers.

The First Settlements on the Connecticut.

In 1636 the General Court having granted the right to make settlements upon the Conecticut river, Roger Ludlow and others went to Connecticut, and William Pynchon and others to Springfield. Pynchon coming as one of the patentees of the Winthrop colony, obtained some special privileges concerning trade with the Indians, and it was this that brought him hither, and it was the fur trade which gave him a special interest in founding Springfield. It was this feature in the settlement of New England which led the London "adventurers" to embark in the enterprise of founding settlements in America. There is no doubt that the prospects of large returns induced Pynchon to seek a home on the banks of the Connecticut. At that time there was an abundance of beaver inhabiting all the streams which flowed into the "great river," and it proved a profitable venture for Pynchon, for he and later his son shipped many thousand dollars' worth of skins to England. The open spaces along the Connecticut, which became our fertile meadows, made farming comparatively easy, and while Pynchon bought and sold, the others generally confined themselves to the cultivation of the earth, thus securing a living, if not great wealth.

No other single feature of our early history excites so much admiration as the capacity which the first settlers displayed at the very beginning, in constructive and orderly government. While it was but natural that they should bring with them the habits and opinions acquired before landing upon these shores, they began life in the new country on an entirely new model. In England there was law and order

based upon the principle that the few were born to govern
the many. Here there was neither law nor opinion other
than that which was evolved from their own inner conscious-
ness. They did not stop to wander in the wilderness of
doubt and fear, but set out with the supreme conviction that
they were able to govern themselves, and that government
was something in which all, even the humblest, should take
part. The land in the old home, which should have been
in the ownership of those who tilled it, was possessed by the
few who had been the favorites of kings and courts. There
were no free homesteads like those our ancestors created, and
there was no equal distribution of the burdens and the benefits of government. Here, immediately after possessing
the soil, there began an equal distribution of responsibilities
of government, and the humblest had equal voice in public
concerns. In England there were no taxes on lands, and no
general registration of titles, and whatever laws in that
regard were adopted here, they had no parallel in England.
As we look back to the beginning it is that genius which
shaped the destiny of this country, which builded so differ-
ently and so wisely for the future, that excites our admiration, and it must ever remain as the supreme example, and
the foundation for philosophic study of the men who crossed
the ocean in peril and in poverty, to found a new system of
government.

The commonplace affairs which may seem unimportant
to us, who are now under different conditions, were incident
to the beginning of this settlement on the Connecticut. We
get here the picture of the everyday life of the founders. After this long lapse of time it opens to our view the character
and the purposes, as well as the habits, of those who came
here at the beginning, and valiently, against great obstacles,
worked out the new problems which were presented to them.
While they brought with them from England the habits,
and to a great extent the beliefs of their old homes, they
proved that they were equal to the new duties which were
presented to them under entirely new conditions. It was

no one-man power, the strong oppressing the weak, that they found dominating the new settlement. They all walked and lived, and toiled on a common level, and nothing short of superior education or intellectual acquirements, gave any one advantage over another, or placed any one in the front rank in directing the affairs of this little community. It was as pure a democracy as dreamers in our own time have pictured, in which there was a gradual but constant ripening of faith in the higher duties, which have come down to the race as the view has broadened.

The Lands Purchased of the Indians.

Two months after the agreement of the eight persons to found the settlement, William Pynchon, Henry Smith, and Jehu Burr, made an agreement with the Indians for the purchase of the lands on both sides of the Connecticut. The price paid, "eigheen fathoms of wampum,18 coats, 18 hatchets, 18 hoes, and 18 knives," was not much of a burden to the settlers. Mr. Pynchon's payment was assessed on the lands as they were subsequently granted to the settlers. The Indian deed is given below:—

"Agaam, alias Agawam, This fifteenth day of July, 1636.

It is agreed between Commucke and Matanchon, ancient Indians, & in particular for & in ye name of Cattonis, the right owner of Agawam & Quana, & in the Name of his mother, Kewanusk, the Tamaham, or wife of Wenawis, & Niarum, the wife of Coa, to & with William Pynchon, Henry Smith & Jehu Burr, their heirs & associates for ever, to trucke & sel al that ground & mucke of quittas or medow, accomsick, viz: on the other side of Quana; & al the ground & muck of quittas on the side of Agaam, except Cottiwackesh or ground that is now planted, for ten fatham of Wampam, Ten coates, Ten howes, Ten hatchets & Ten knifes: also the said ancient Indians with the Consent of the rest & in particular wth the Consent of Menis & Wrutherna & Napompenam, do trucke & sel to Willam Pynchon, Henry Smith, & Jehu Burr, & their successors for ever, al that

ground on the East side of Quinneticut River called Usquasok & Nayasset, reaching about four or five miles in Length,
from the north end of Masaksicke up to Chickuppe River,
for four fathoms of Wampam, four coates, four howes, four
hatchets, four knifes: Also the Said ancient Indians Doe w^th
the Consent of Machetuhood, Wenepawin, & Mohemoos,
trucke & sel the ground & muckeosquittas, & grounds adjoining, called Masaksicke, for four fatham of wampam, four
Coates, four hatchets & four knifes.

   And the said Pynchon hath in hand paid the said eighteen
fatham of wampam, eighteen coates, 18 hatchets, 18 howes,
18 knifes to the said Commucke & Matanchan, & doth further condition wth the said Indians, that they shal have and
enjoy al that Cotinackeesh, or ground that is now planted;
And have liberty to take Fish & Deer, ground nuts, walnuts,
akornes, & sasashiminesh, or kind of peas, And also if any of
our Cattle spoile their corne, to pay as it is worth, & that
hogs shal not goe on the side of Agawam but in akorne time:
Also the said Pynchon, doth give to Wruththena two Coates
over and above the Particulars expressed, & In witness hereof
the two said Indians, this present 15th day of July, 1636."

   This deed was signed by the marks of Menis, Kenix, Wesai
alias Nepinam, Winepawin, Cominuk, Macossak, Wenewis,
Cuttonis, Wrutherna, Coa, Keckusnek, and "that they under-
stod al by Ahauton, an Indian of the Massachusetts," who
came from the Bay to act as interpreter.

   The witnesses to the signing of the deed by the Indians
were John Allen, Richard Everet, Thomas Horton, Faithful
Thayeler, John Townes, Joseph Parsons, and Ahauton.

   Ahauton, Everet and Townes signed by making their
marks.   Allen, Thayler and Townes have no mention in subsequent records.   This was the first mention of Joseph Parsons and his name does not appear again for many years.

   This deed was entered in the records of the county July 8,
1679, and is in the handwriting of John Holyoke, who was
then the recorder.   At a court held at "Northampton, March
1661-62, Joseph Parsons testify on oath that he was a witness

to this bargaine between Mr. Pynchon & the Indians."

John Holyoke when he entered the deed, wrote the following underneath it:—"Memoranda.—Agaam or Agawam, It is the medow on the South of Agawam River, where ye English did first build a house, wch now we comonly cal ye house medow, That peice of ground is it wch ye Indians do cal Agawam & where ye English kept ye residents who first came to settle and plant at Springfield now so called: & at ye place it was (as is supposed) that this purchase was made of the Indians. Quana is that middle medow, adjoining to Agawam or house medow: Masacksick is y^t ye English call the Longmeadow below Springfield. on ye East side of Quinneticut River. Usquasok is the Mil River wth the Land adjoyning. Nayasset is the lands of Three Corner medow & of the plains." Three Corner meadow is our present Hampden Park, and the plain refers to the lands north of it, later known as Plainfield and Brightwood.

Were it possible it would be interesting to trace the sources of the emigration from the mother country which ultimately found its way to Springfield. Most of those who came here within the first ten or fifteen years after the arrival of Pynchon from Roxbury, were young unmarried men. Of these, and a few who were married, several were from Wales, or were of Welsh descent, including Thomas Merrick, Alexander Edwards, Roger Prichard and perhaps others, but the great majority were English in birth and training, and all possessed that element in character which triumphs over obstacles. They were the yeomanry of the mother country, who held that all labor was honorable and ennobling.

It was several years after the settlement was begun before many additions were made to those first arriving here. A few came and a few went away, and it was not till 1640 that there began to be any perceptible change for the better. Less than twenty of those who came brought families. Of those who were married prior to their arrival, and who brought children with them were: William Pynchon, Henry Smith, John Cable, Samuel Hubbard, Rev. George Moxon, Henry Burt,

Benjamin Cooley, Robert Ashley, John Harmon, Samuel
Chapin, Samuel Wright, Richard Sikes, James Bridgman,
George Colton, Rowland Stebbins, Roger Prichard, Griffith
Jones, and Obadiah Miller. All of these, with the exception
of Pynchon, Stebbins, and Prichard, had children born here.

Among the young men whose marriages were recorded
here were the following: Elizur Holyoke, William Warriner,
Thomas Merrick, John Leonard, Alexander Edwards, Francis Ball, Thomas Cooper, Edmund Haynes, Thomas and
John Stebbins, John Pynchon, Reice Bedortha, Samuel, Lawrence and John Bliss, Joseph and Benjamin Parsons, Rowland Thomas, John Lombard, George Lancton, Hugh Parsons, James Osborn, John Clark, Benjamin Munn, Thomas
Miller, Richard Exell, Samuel Marshfield, John Bagg, William Brooks, Hugh Dudley, Samuel Terry, Morgan Jones,
Richard Everett, John Searle, Charles Ferry, Thomas Bancroft, Thomas Day, Thomas Noble, Judah Gregory, John
Mathews, Simon Beaman, Jonathan and Nathaniel Burt,
Samuel Ely, and possibly a few others.

Nearly all the above have descendants in Springfield or its
vicinity at the present time. Several of these married young
widows, whose husbands had died soon after their arrival.
Others married the daughters of the older settlers, or found
wives in some of the Connecticut towns, or in the eastern
part of the Colony.

Before proceeding farther it may be of interest to know
what constitute the first records of the town. They extend
over the first hundred years, from the foundation of the town
in 1636, and include the doings of the first settlers in public
meetings, the transactions of the selectmen in ther official
capacity, and the record of births, marriages and deaths. For
many years town government included church government,
until early conditions and opinions were outgrown. The
first two books cover nearly the first half century of the existence of Springfield, including what may be termed the legislative acts of the town, the granting of land to the settlers,
and bringing all public concerns of the community into har-

mony with the enactments of the "Great and General Court."
The pages of the two first books are six by eight inches and
bear marks of their long usage. They are more or less ink-
stained, and their pages have grown yellow with age, and yet
considering the mutations of time and the careless hands
through which they have some times passed, they are in a
fair state of preservation. They are difficult to read unless
one has become familiar with the names of the settlers, the
idiom of the times, and the peculiarities of each recorder,
easily understood in some instances and exceedingly difficult
in others. When the recorder turns his h's bottom end up,
makes the letter "s" in at least four different ways, and adds
the peculiar custom prevalent in his day of contracting many
words, follows an orthography of his own, and oftentimes
inconsistent with himself, the task of transcription becomes
slow and difficult.

The third volume is more than double the size of the two
that precede it, and the three bring the record down to 1736.
These records open in the handwriting of Henry Smith, under date of May 14, 1636, being the agreement of the eight
persons to found the settlement. The handwritings of several of the early recorders are particularly noticeable for ele-
gance, and as the original pages are noted in the transcript
as printed in the records which form the larger part of this
volume, they can be easily found in the manuscript volumes,
in the possession of the city clerk.

The entries made by the selectmen are in the handwritings
of Thomas Cooper, Henry Burt, Samuel Marshfield and several others. While Deacon Samuel Chapin was for a long
time one of the selectmen his hand does not appear in any of
the town records. A recently discovered deed of his lands
to his son Japhet Chapin, which is entirely in his hand, indicates that he had received a better education than many of
the early emigrants to New England.

The records of births, marriages and deaths are in the
handwriting of Henry Smith, from the beginning to 1649,
when Henry Burt, by virtue of his office, as Clerk of the

Writs, became the recorder for that purpose. He continued
to make the entries until his death in 1662; the last entry by
him was that of Susannah Swink, whose death occurred nine
days before his own. After the death of Henry Burt, Thomas Cooper was chosen Clerk of the Writs, but the entries appear to have been made for some time by John Pynchon, and
later by Elizur Holyoke, his son John Holyoke, and Jonathan
Burt, the three last as town clerks.

THE EARLY MINISTERS OF SPRINGFIELD.

The regularly settled ministers during the first century in
Springfield, were George Moxon, Pelatiah Glover, Daniel
Brewer, and Robert Breck. Mr. Hosford, Thomas Tomson,
Mr. Hooker, and John Haynes severally officiated for a short
time, but appear to have gone away on their own desires.
Mr. Moxon's pastorate was from 1638 until his return to
England in 1652. He was succeeded by Mr. Hosford, whose
given name and previous residence are not stated in the records, and whose stay was not long. He evidently came
from Connecticut. John Pynchon made this entry in his
account book: "February 10, 1653. Mr. Hosford's maintenance and bringing up his goods."

Next came, in 1655, Thomas Tomson, who remained a
year or more. He was given grants of land and the homelot
which afterwards went to the ownership of Widow Margaret
Bliss. He went to Connecticut when he left here, and was
succeeded by Mr. Hooker. At a town meeting held February
7, 1659, "there was full and unanimous acceptance of Mr.
Hooker to dispense the word of God. He will not engage
longer than 3 months. He agrees to stay three months
for £20." It does not appear that he remained longer, although efforts were made to have him make a permanent settlement. Pelatiah Glover, son of John Glover, who was one
of the Assistants in the General Court, came next, in 1660,
and continued in active service until his death in 1692, and
he was greatly esteemed. John Haynes filled the position
after Mr. Glover's death for a few months, and he was suc-

ceeded by Daniel Brewer, who served nearly 40 years. He was followed in 1734 by Robert Breck, who saw a half century in the pastoral office in Springfield. The dates of service of each minister, so far as can be stated, are given in the following table:—

George Moxon,	1638—1652.
Mr. Hosford,	1653.
Thomas Thomson,	1655—1656.
Mr. Hocker,	1656—three months.
Pelatiah Glover,	1660—1692.
John Haynes,	1693—a few months.
Daniel Brewer,	1694—1733.
Robert Breck,	1734—1784.

THE SELECTMEN—FIRST AND SUCCEEDING BOARDS.

While Springfield was without a distinctive name for four years, it being known as "the plantation," it was eight years before authority to govern was delegated to a board of selectmen. Leading individuals were at an early date chosen to allot planting grounds and make grants of land to the inhabitants, but town affairs appear to have been discussed for a long time by the whole number in general town meetings. The selectmen and all others when placed in charge of any affair touching the interests of others, paid regard to dealing justly with them. There could have been no greater regard for equity as between man and man. There was no disposition manifested to overreach a neighbor or any member of the community in any transaction, and differences were settled in the most equitable way. This feature of those early days stands out in bold relief, shedding honor and respect upon those plain people, to whom every descendant can turn with honest pride. The men who were chosen by the town to manage its public affairs, were sometimes designated "Select Townsmen," but more generally "Selectmen."

William Pynchon, who wrote the record of the names of the first board of selectmen, laid down the rules to govern them in brief and plain language: "They shall have power,"

says the record, "to order in all prudential affairs of the
town, to prevent anything that they shall judge to be to the
damage of the town, and to order anything they shall judge
to be for the good of the town." And the five, or any three
of them, shall be given full power to hear complaints, to arbitrate controversies, to lay out highways, to make bridges,
to repair highways, specially to order the making of the way
over the Muxie meadow, to see to the scouring of ditches,
to the killing of wolves, to training up children in some good
calling, or any other thing they shall judge to be of profit to
the town." The "way over Muxie meadow," refers to the
road from Main street across what was then a meadow, to
the Bay Path, which is now our State street. The first mention of the "Bay Path," by that designation, in the records,
was in 1647, in connection with building this road over the
Muxie meadow, which was alluded to as "a horse-way," and
subsequently mentioned as the "causey," or causeway.
"Scouring of ditches," refers to the keeping of what has been
known in later years as the "Town Brook," clear, and to prevent an overflow of its banks.

September 4, 1646, William Pynchon, whose handwriting
is seen in the town records on only three or four pages, lays
down the rules to the board of selectmen that year, as follows:—

"They shall reach to reconcile disagreements & disputes
between neighbor & neighbor.

They shall take care to find out some convenient way to
separate oxen from cows in their daily feeding.

They shall judge where bridges & highways are to be
made or mended, how it may be done & they shall call upon
the surveyors, it to be their affair.

They shall also advise about some course about destroying
of meadows, & how hogs may be kept with most profit &
least damage to the plantation.

They shall have power to see that men's chimnies be kept
clean, and to fine them for their neglect, the fine to be under
five shillings a tyme.

They shall have power to higher a cow-keeper for the keeping of cows of the plantation.

The making of all rates for the plantation shall belong to their affairs, & in general for the making of rates for the Smith.

They shall have power to fine such persons as carry fire uncovered, providing it be under 5 shillings a tyme, & whosoever shall refuse to pay the fines shall be complained of to the magistrate who will grant his warrant to distraine for ye said fines."

"Making rates for the plantation," refers to what we now call taxes, to meet the expenses of the town. This term long since obsolete here, is still in common use in England. In the above rules we see many of the simple customs of the people of the town at the beginning. The want of fences made the cow-keeper a public necessity, and whatever was regarded as a benefit to the whole was held to be a legitimate public charge.

John Pynchon and Deacon Chapin were elected on the board of 1652, but having been appointed commissioners,—magistrates,—they could not serve, and Thomas Stebbins and Joseph Parsons were chosen in their places. In 1653 the town adopted, among other rules, the following:—

"It is ordered, that when any many shall be fairly and clearly chosen to any office, & place of service, in and to the Towne, if he then refuse to accept the place, or shall afterwards neglect to serve in that office to which he shall be chosen, every such person shall pay 20 shillings fine for refusal unto the Town Treasurer, unless he had served in that office the year before, no person being compelled to serve two years together in the same office, except Selectmen, two whereof if chosen again are to stand two years together, so there may be always some of the old Selectmen who are acquainted with the Town affairs."*

In 1655 the town chose Thomas Cooper, Miles Morgan, Benjamin Cooley, Robert Ashley and John Dumbleton selectmen. Some dissatisfaction was created and Thomas

Cooper, Robert Ashley and Benjamin Cooley promptly refused to serve.   The town recorder took notice of the refusal
and in his record says: There was a choice made of five
Townsmen," naming them, "and Thomas Cooper, Robert
Ashley and Benjamin Cooley refused to serve in that place,
being fairly chosen by a vote of the town, for which refusal
they are liable to the fine of 20 shillings apeice."   The records do not show that it was collected, but if the authorities
were as zealous in respect to this infringement of their rules
as they were in others, the probabilities are that it was.   The
breach in the board was filled by making choice of George
Colton, Thomas and John Stebbins.

That it may be readily seen who were the "Fathers of the
Town" during the first century, the entire list of selectmen,
from the first board chosen in 1644, to that of 1737, is here
given.   It may be of interest to the many descendants of
those worthy men, to know when their ancestors served and
who were their associates in the management of town affairs.   The government of the town was handed down from
father to son through many years, as will be seen in the list
which follows:—

1644.—Henry Smith, Thomas Cooper, Samuel Chapin,
Richard Sikes, Henry Burt.

1645.—No record of election. The old board held over.

1646.—Henry Smith, Elizur Holyoke, Samuel Chapin,
Henry Burt, Benjamin Cooley.

1647.—Henry Smith, Samuel Chapin, Thomas Cooper,
Henry Burt, Benjamin Cooley.

1648.—Henry Smith, Samuel Chapin, Thomas Cooper,
Henry Burt, Benjamin Cooley.

1649.—No record of election. The old board held over.

1650.—John Pynchon, Henry Smith, Samuel Chapin,
Henry Burt, Thomas Cooper.

1651.—John Pynchon, Samuel Chapin, George Colton
Henry Burt, Thomas Cooper.

1652.—John Pynchon, Samuel Chapin, George Colton
Henry Burt, Benjamin Cooley, Thomas Stebbins, Joseph

Parsons.—Seven were chosen this year, but John Pynchon and Samuel Chapin, being commissioners, were "discharged from Townesmen & so ye worke rests upon ye last five."

1653.—George Colton, Robert Ashley, Thomas Cooper, Benjamin Cooley, Thomas Stebbins.

1654.—Thomas Cooper, George Colton, Robert Ashley, Henry Burt, Benjamin Cooley.

1655.—Thomas Cooper, Miles Morgan, Benjamin Cooley, Robert Ashley, John Dumbleton.—Thomas Cooper, Robert Ashley and Benjamin Cooley refusing to serve, George Colton, Thomas Stebbins and John Stebbins were chosen.

1656.—Thomas Cooper, George Colton, Thomas Gilbert, Benjamin Cooley, Robert Ashley.

1657.—Robert Ashley, Miles Morgan, John Dumbleton Jonathan Burt, Thomas Gilbert.

1658.—Thomas Cooper, Benjamin Cooley, Jonathan Burt, William Warriner, Robert Ashley.

1659.—The day for choosing town-officers was changed from the first Tuesday in November to the first Tuesday in February. The board of 1658 held office till the election in February.

1660.—Thomas Gilbert, Benjamin Parsons, John Dumbleton, Miles Morgan, John Pynchon.

1661.—Elizur Holyoke, Samuel Chapin, Thomas Cooper, Benjamin Cooley, Robert Ashley.

1662.—John Pynchon, Nathaniel Ely, Elizur Holyoke, George Colton, Miles Morgan.

1663.—John Pynchon, Benjamin Cooley, Robert Ashley, Thomas Cooper, Samuel Marshfield.

1664.—Samuel Chapin, Nathaniel Ely, George Colton, Rowland Thomas, Elizur Holyoke.

1665.—John Pynchon, Benjamin Cooley, George Colton, Samuel Marshfield, Lawrence Bliss.

1666.—Ensign Cooper, Robert Ashley, John Dumbleton, Benjamin Parsons, Elizur Holyoke.

1667.—George Colton, Nathaniel Ely, Benjamin Cooley, Rowland Thomas, Samuel Marshfield.

1668.—Thomas Cooper, Miles Morgan, John Dumbleton, Benjamin Parsons, Elizur Holyoke.

1669.—John Pynchon, George Colton, Nathaniel Ely, Samuel Marshfield, Lawrence Bliss.

1670.—Elizur Holyoke, Thomas Cooper, Benjamin Cooley, Benjamin Parsons, Henry Chapin.

1671.—John Pynchon, George Colton, Samuel Marshfield, Rowland Thomas, John Dumbleton.

1672.—Nathaniel Ely, Benjamin Cooley, Benjamin Parsons, Anthony Dorchester, Elizur Holyoke.

1673.—George Colton, Samuel Marshfield, Thomas Cooper, John Dumbleton, Henry Chapin.

1674.—Nathaniel Ely, Thomas Cooper, Benjamin Parsons, John Keepe, Elizur Holyoke.

1675.—George Colton, Samuel Marshfield, John Dumbleton, Henry Chapin, Jeremy Horton.

1676.—Benjamin Cooley, Jonathan Burt, John Keepe, John Hitchcock, Elizur Holyoke.—Holyoke died a few days after election and Samuel Marshfield was chosen on the 23d in his place. John Keepe was killed by the Indians near Pecowsic on the 26th of March and Anthony Dorchester was elected in his place. This was five months after Springfield was burned by the Indians.

1677.—George Colton, John Dumbleton, Benjamin Parsons, Henry Chapin, John Dorchester.

1678.—Samuel Marshfield, Japhet Chapin, John Hitchcock, Nathaniel Burt, John Holyoke.

1679.—John Holyoke, George Colton, Benjamin Parsons, John Dumbleton, Henry Chapin.

1680.—Benjamin Cooley, Samuel Marshfield, Jonathan Burt, Japhet Chapin, John Hitchcock.

1681.—Daniel Denton, John Holyoke, George Colton, Benjamin Parsons, John Dumbleton.

1682.—Cornet Joseph Parsons, Deacon Jonathan Burt, Thomas Day, John Hitchcock, John Holyoke.

1683.—Samuel Marshfield, Benjamin Parsons, John Dumbleton, Japhet Chapin, James Warriner.

1684.—Jonathan Burt, Henry Chapin, John Hitchcock, Samuel Ball, John Holyoke.

1685.—George Colton, Samuel Marshfield, Benjamin Parsons, John Dumbleton, Samuel Bliss.

1686.—Japhet Chapin, John Hitchcock, Samuel Ball, Thomas Stebbins, John Holyoke.

1687.—Jonathan Burt, Benjamin Parsons, Henry Chapin, John Dumbleton, Luke Hitchcock.

1688.—Samuel Marshfield, Japhet Chapin, John Hitchcock, Samuel Ball, John Holyoke.

1689.—Japhet Chapin, John Hitchcock, Samuel Ball, Thomas Colton, James Warriner, Thomas Stebbins.

1689.—John Dumbleton, Jonathan Burt, Benjamin Parsons, Henry Chapin, Abel Wright.—This board was chosen on the 3d Monday in May, in accordance with an Act of the General Court, which changed the day for holding the annual town meetings from February to May.

1690.—Japhet Chapin, John Hitchcock, James Warriner, Thomas Stebbins, John Holyoke.

1691.—Jonathan Burt, Henry Chapin, John Dumbleton, Isaac Colton, John Holyoke.

1692.—Japhet Chapin, Thomas Colton, Samuel Bliss, Thomas Stebbins, John Barber.

1693.—John Hitchcock, Eliakim Cooley, Joseph Stebbins, Jonathan Ball, John Holyoke.

1694.—Pelatiah Glover, John Dorchester, Joseph Stebbins, Nathaniel Bliss, David Morgan.

1695.—Thomas Cooper, Thomas Colton, Daniel Cooley, Charles Ferry, Senr., John Holyoke.

1696.—John Pynchon, Jr., James Warriner, Luke Hitchcock, Edward Stebbins, Benjamin Leonard.

1697.—Jonathan Burt, Henry Chapin, James Warriner, Sr., Samuel Bliss, Sr., John Warner.

1698.—John Hitchcock, Benjamin Stebbins, Pelatiah Glover, Abel Wright, John Warner.

1699.—Isaac Colton, John Hitchcock, Samuel Bliss, Sr., Joseph Stebbins, John Myrick.

1700.—Joseph Stebbins, Edward Stebbins, Japhet Chapin, James Warriner, Sr., Thomas Colton.

1701.—Henry Chapin, Pelatiah Glover, John Barber, David Morgan, Ebenezer Parsons.

1702.—John Pynchon, Jr., Pelatiah Glover, John Barber, John Warner, Samuel Ely.

1703.—Eliakim Cooley, Joseph Stebbins, Edward Stebbins, John Warner, Nathaniel Munn.

1704.—Luke Hitchcock, Sr., James Warriner, Sr., Edward Stebbins, Benjamin Leonard, Joseph Williston.

1705.—John Pynchon, Jr., Joseph Stebbins, Luke Hitchcock, Sr., Joseph Cooley, Sr., John Merrick.

1706.—John Pynchon, Jr. Eliakim Cooley, Ebenezer Parsons, John Miller, Nathaniel Burt, Jr.

1707.—Thomas Colton, John Merrick, Samuel Bliss 3d Henry Burt, John Holyoke.

1708.—John Hitchcock,Sr., Edward Stebbins, John Ferry, Benjamin Leonard, John Holyoke.

1709.—John Hitchcock, Sr., John Merrick. John Day, Pelatiah Bliss, John Holyoke.

1710.—John Pynchon, Jr., Edward Stebbins. John Burt, Sr., Nathaniel Munn, Samuel Bliss 3d.

1711.—Joseph Cooley, Sr., Tilly Mirick, John Miller, Thomas Horton, John Holyoke.

1712.—Luke Hitchcock, Sr., Joseph Stebbins, Sr., John Mirick, Samuel Bliss 3d, John Ferry.

1713.—Pelatiah Glover, Ebenezer Parsons, Nathaniel Burt, Jr., Henry Burt, John Day.

1714.—Pelatiah Glover, John Mirick, Joseph Cooley, Sr., John Ferry, Thomas Terry.

1715.—John Pynchon, James Mirick, Samuel Bliss 3d, Luke Hitchcock, Pelatiah Glover.

1716.—John Ferry, Sr., James Warriner 2d, Capt. John Pynchon, Joseph Stebbins, Samuel Ely.

1717.—Joseph Stebbins, John Mirick, Samuel Bliss 3d, John Ferry, Samuel Day.

1718.—John Ferry, Samuel Bliss 3d, Henry Burt, John

Worthington, Joseph Parsons.—Worthington was the father of Hon. John Worthington, of Revolutionary notoriety, whose loyalty to the Colonies was questioned.

1719.—Samuel Day, Samuel Ely, Ebenezer Parsons, John Day, James Mirick.

1720.—Luke Hitchcock, John Ferry, Samuel Bliss 3d, Henry Burt, James Warriner, Jr.

1721.—Joseph Stebbins, Joseph Cooley, Samuel Bliss 3d, Thomas Bliss, Sr., Increase Sikes.

1722.—John Mirick, John Ferry, Ephraim Colton, John Worthington, Increase Sikes.

1723.—Samuel Bliss 2d, Joseph Stebbins, Ephraim Colton, Samuel Day, John Day.

1724.—John Ferry, James Warriner, Samuel Bliss 2d, Nathaniel Sikes, Increase Sikes.

1725.—Luke Hitchcock, John Ferry, Ephraim Colton, Samuel Bliss 2d; Joseph Williston.

1726.—James Warriner, John Bagg, John Hitchcock, Joseph Williston, Henry Burt.

1727.—Samuel Bliss 2d, John Ferry, Ephraim Colton, John Day, John Worthington.

1728.—Samuel Bliss, Ebenezer Warriner, Ephraim Colton, John Day, John Ferry.

1729.—James Warriner, John Day, Ebenezer Warriner, John Burt, Ephraim Colton.

1730.—James Warriner, Ebenezer Warriner, John Burt, Thomas Colton, Thomas Stebbins.

1731.—Samuel Bliss, Joseph Williston, James Warriner, Thomas Colton, Thomas Stebbins.

1732.—Joseph Williston, John Worthington, Pelatiah Bliss, Thomas Stebbins, John Day.

1733.—John Burt, Luke Hitchcock 2d, John Ely, James Warriner, Ebenezer Warriner.

1734.—Pelatiah Bliss, John Burt, Luke Hitchcock 2d, Ebenezer Warriner, John Ely.

1735.—Pelatiah Bliss, Ebenezer Warriner, John Burt, John Ely, Luke Hitchcock 2d.

1736.—John Burt, Luke Hitchcock 2d, William Pynchon, John Day, Benjamin Chapin.

GRANTS OF LAND TO THE SETTLERS.

The division of lands, which was begun in 1636, soon after the arrival of Pynchon's company, was continued yearly, as fast as new comers arrived, or the older ones needed more land. These grants were in larger quantities after the first twenty years than they were prior to that time. Then, too, there were the boys growing to manhood; they were to be provided with separate estates and came in for a share. The grants were made upon the condition that the settler should remain in the town five years. If he left before that time had expired he must resign it into the town's hands. In some instances the improvements were sold to a new arrival. In each case the "chapman," or buyer, must be acceptable to the authorities. When Henry Gregory, who was the first owner of our present Court Square, submitted his "chapman," in the person of Richard Everett, the selectmen objected, and the estate passed into the hands of Thomas Stebbins, who continued to abide there until his death. Everett had almost from the beginning been an inhabitant of the town, coming immediately after the arrival of William Pynchon, in whose employ he continued for some time, and what objection the selectmen had to him does not appear. Not long afterward he returned to the eastern part of the Colony and finally settled in Dedham, where he was a prominent citizen, and the ancestor of many who bare his family name in that part of Massachusetts.

The desire of each individual for land was made known at the annual town meetings, in the earlier days of the settlement, and the grant was made at the time of the application, "provided there be so much there to be had." At a subsequent meeting the granting of lands was left with the selectmen, and it was decided that no grant would be made on the day of application, but it must go over to the next meeting. This evidently was with the view to give the selectmen op-

portunity to consider the propriety of making the grant.
While the granting of lands was for many years in the exclu-
sive control of the selectmen, at a still later period two commissioners were chosen annually to join with them in considering and making the grants. Those to whom grants were
made were obliged to pay Pynchon a share of the Indian
purchase, but this in no instance was a hardship, as the sum
seldom exceeded more than a few shillings. The conditions
of the grants were always plainly set forth. The needs, or
the possibilities of highways being laid through them, were
specifically stated. Frequently in the Longmeadow region
there was this condition, "providing that the Indians be not
wronged in their pease." On the west side of the Connecticut river in 1652, there was this grant to Thomas Miller:
"that vacant parsel of planting ground over the great river
by the higher wigwam, provided hee bee not an occasion of
troble and disturbance to the Plantation by an unwis clashing
with the Indians; if so he shall forfeit the sayd land into the
Towns hands." In this way the rights of the humblest were
protected in every instance, and any possible disturbance
of the public peace prevented.

Following the grants of land came also the disposition to
let them easily slip from the possession of those who had
received them; more frequently was this the case in relation
to the homelots at the extreme upper and lower parts of the
town. Outlying lands were frequently sold or exchanged,
and it soon became apparent that there would follow insecurity of titles, unless each sale or exchange was recorded.
The General Court in 1648 passed a law requiring transfers of
lands to be put on record, and from this our form of registration sprung. Such a system was unknown in England, except as to a single class of conveyances, and even to the present time there is no compulsory registration of titles in the
mother country, save only in the counties of Yorkshire and
Middlesex. The General Court fixed the penalty of neglect
to record at 20 shillings. Our authorities reduced the fine to
five shillings. The fee for registering was 2d for each piece.

The selectmen and the committee acting with them for making grants, were confronted in 1664 by an unusual condition. Three of their own number, George Colton, Benjamin Cooley and Thomas Miller, had failed to comply with the law, not having either measured or recorded their grants within the required six months. They were not only liable to a fine, but had forfeited their grants. To overcome the conditions they acknowledged their liability to be confronted with fines, and resigned their grants into the town's hands, whereupon they, in joint action with the other members of the board, immediately proceeded to regrant the same pieces to themselves, thus making their titles good, but no mention is made relative to the fines.

SPRINGFIELD'S DEPUTIES IN THE GENERAL COURT.

The first Deputy, or Representative, sitting for Springfield was John Johnson of Roxbury, the Surveyor General, who was present at the May meeting of the General Court in 1649. The next year, 1650, Edward Holyoke, sat for Springfield. He was the father of Elizur Holyoke, and was succeeded by Henry Smith, and the latter by William Davis of Boston, both of whom were sons-in-law of William Pynchon. In passing it is noteworthy how often the office fell to the relations, either by blood or marriage, of Mr. Pynchon. There are, for example, the third son-in-law, Elizur Holyoke; the son, John Pynchon; and four grandsons, John Holyoke, Joseph Pynchon, John Pynchon and Benjamin Davis. In fact, office holding for many years after the settlement of Springfield was largely a family affair. John Pynchon, the first, was elected a Deputy in 1662, and after that date was elected by the Deputies as an Assistant in the Council. His last term of service was in 1701, two years before his death.

William Pynchon was chosen an Assistant in England and attended the meetings in London of the Massachusetts Bay Company. He continued to be elected to that office after his arrival in this country, up to 1650, when the publication of his book resulted in his being summoned before the General Court, and his return to England in 1652.

The Deputies were elected by the qualified voters of the various towns, and, upon assembling in Boston, procceded to choose Assistants who constituted the upper branch of the General Court. Upon the Assistants there devolved judicial as well as legislative functions, for they sat with the Governor and Deputy Governor as a court for the trial of causes appealed from the county magistrates and of such criminal cases as were beyond the jurisdiction of the lower courts.

In 1694 the Governor objected to Benjamin Davis, who appeared as Deputy for Springfield, on the ground of his being a non-resident. Nathaniel Bliss served in his place.

Towns not having more than 30 freemen were obliged to pay the expenses of the Deputy while serving, but he was sometimes excused from attending the October sessions. The first sessions were in May, and as the General Court was hindered in legislation it was voted in 1654: "That the Deputies of the General Court should dyet together, especially at dynner, it is therefore ordered that the Deputies of the General Court, the next year ensuing, viz: 1655, shall be provided at the Ship Tavern at Boston in respect of dynner, and that they shall all accordingly dyne together, & that Lieut. Phillips, the keeper of the said tavern, shall be paid for the same by the Treasurer for the tyme being, by discounting the same in the custom of wyne, payable by the said Phillips, & that the Treasurer shall be repaid by the several towns, according to the charges of their respective deputies with the next country rate & in the same kind of payment."

The record further says:—"An agreement made with Lt. Phillips by the Deputies now assembled in General Court, that the Deputies of the next Court of Election shall sit in the new court chamber, & be dyeted with breakfast, dynner, & supper, with wine, & beer between meals, with fire and beds, at the rate of three shillings per day, so many as take all their dyet as aforesaid at the said house, but such as only dyne, & not supp, to pay eighteen pence for their dynners with wine, & beer betwixt meals, but by wine is intended a cupp to each man at dynner & supper, & no more. Lieut. Phillips did accept of this, & agreed thereto, with this proviso, that only such as had all their dyet should have beer between meals, & also uppon extraordinary occasions he might have the use of the great court chamber."

In some instances Springfield paid the expenses of its Deputy directly to him, as will be seen by the town records.

Boston was reached by the Deputies traveling on horseback. Springfield, Northampton and Hadley were for many years the only towns represented from the western part of the Colony. Our town records show what was paid on account of Lieut. Thomas Cooper in 1668, in the following items:—

To Timothy Cooper for his horse into the Bay 20 shillings, & his pasturing there, 10s 6d, this for ye Deputy, £1 10s 6d; for ye Deputyes Dyet at ye Corte in May '68, £3 10s 0d; for his tyme at Corte & travellinge, £1 10s 0d,—£6 10s 6d.

Timothy Cooper, who furnished the horse, was the son of the deputy, who was absent from Springfield a little more than a month. The expense of legislation,—less than $35, was not a very great burden to Springfield in those remote days. Nearly at the close of the session Lieut. Clarke of Northampton and Lieut. Cooper of Springfield, "on their request, having been long absent from their homes, are dismist the service of this Corte." Peter Tilton of Hadley, was also given leave at the same time to return home, but Capt. Aaron Cook, the other Northampton deputy, remained until the close of the session. The three horsemen, Cooper, Clarke and Tilton, might have been seen following the trail through the woods, slowly wending their way from Boston toward the Connecticut, conscious of having faithfully discharged their public duties. It must have taken nearly three days to make the journey from Boston to their homes.

It was required that all deputies must be orthodox in religion, and it was "ordered that no man, although a Freeman, shall be accepted as a deputy of the General Court, that is unsound in judgment concerning the many points of the Christian religion, as they have been held forth & acknowledged by the generality of the Protestant orthodox writers, or that is scandalous in his conversation, or that is unfaithful to the government."

The names of those who represented Springfield up to the close of the first century are given in full, so far as can be ascertained, as follows:—

1650.—Edward Holyoke.
1651.—Henry Smith.
1652.—William Davis.
1653.—Capt. Humphrey Atherton.
1654.—Not represented.
1655.—Not represented.
1656.—Elizur Holyoke.
1657.—Not represented.
1658.—Not represented.
1659.—Capt. John Pynchon.
1660.—Edward Holyoke.
1661.—Elizur Holyoke.
1662.—Capt. John Pynchon.
1663.—Capt. John Pynchon.
1664.—Not represented.
1665.—Not represented.
1666.—Capt. William Davis.
1667.—Elizur Holyoke.
1668.—Lieut. Thomas Cooper.
1669.—George Colton.
1670.—Capt. Elizur Holyoke,—one session.
1671.—Capt. William Davis and George Colton.
1672.—Capt. William Davis.
1673.—Capt. Elizur Holyoke.
1674.—Capt. Elizur Holyoke.
1675.—No record of an election.

1676.—No record of an election.

1677.—George Colton.

1678.—No record of an election.

1679.—No record of an election.

1680.—Samuel Marshfield.

1681.—Joseph Pynchon.

1682.—Joseph Pynchon.

1683.—Samuel Marshfield.

1684.—Samuel Marshfield,—one session.

1685.—No record of an election.

1686.—No record of an election.

1687.—No record of an election.

1688.—No record of an election.

1689.—Henry Chapin.

1690.—No record of an election.

1691.—John Holyoke.

1692.—John Holyoke.

1693.—Major John Pynchon, chosen and afterwards elected an Assistant. Succeeded by his nephew, Benjamin Davis of Boston.

1694.—Benjamin Davis of Boston. Objected to by Gov. Phipps, on the ground of being a non-resident. Succeeded by Nathaniel Bliss.

1695.—Abel Wright.

1696.—Luke Hitchcock.

1697.—Luke Hitchcock.

1698.—Luke Hitchcock.

1699.—John Hitchcock.

1700.—John Pynchon 3d.

1701.—John Hitchcock.

1702.—John Hitchcock.

1703.—John Hitchcock.

1704.—John Hitchcock.

1705.—John Hitchcock.

1706.—Joseph Parsons.

1707.—Lieut. Joseph Stebbins.

1708.—Joseph Parsons.

1709.—Maj. John Pynchon.
1710.—Col. John Pynchon.
1711.—No record of an election.
1712.—Col. John Pynchon.
1713.—Luke Hitchcock.
1714.—Col. John Pynchon.
1715.—Luke Hitchcock.
1716.—Luke Hitchcock.
1717.—Lieut. Joseph Stebbins.
1718.—Capt. Luke Hitchcock.
1719.—Capt. Luke Hitchcock. .
1720.—Capt. Luke Hitchcock.
1721.—Lieut. Joseph Stebbins.
1722.—Capt. Luke Hitchcock.
1723.—John Pynchon.
1724.—William Pynchon.
1725.—Lieut. William Pynchon.
1726.—Samuel Day.
1727.—Samuel Day.
1728.—Samuel Day.
1729.—Samuel Day.
1730.—William Pynchon.
1731.—William Pynchon and William Pynchon, Jr.
1732.—Capt. John Day.
1734.—William Pynchon, Jr.
1735.—William Pynchon, Jr.

EARLY INHABITANTS.—WHEN THEY CAME.

The years in which the early inhabitants of Springfield were supposed to have settled, have been variously stated by writers of local history, but, except in a few instances, the dates so given have been largely conjectural. The date of the first mention of a settler's name in such records as the writers had consulted would be stated as the time of his arrival, but later investigations have shown an earlier period in many instances than that given, and in a number of cases the precise year of settlement has been established. Mr.

Thomas B. Warren, to whom I am greatly indebted for the following table, has made a more extensive research than any predecessor, and he has been able to make many corrections, as well as additions, to what has been published. He has also added the date of removal or death, which is given in this table for the first time. Where the precise date of any settler's arrival could not be ascertained, the year given in connection with his name refers to the first mention of it in the records, but his coming here could not have been long prior to it. The list embraces all who came here previous to 1663 who remained long enough to become in some degree identified with the settlement, even if they did not take up a permanent abode, but a majority remained, and their descendants are still numerous in and about this region:—

1636.—William Pynchon. Returned to England in 1652.

1636.—Matthew Mitchel. Did not remain here.

1636.—Henry Smith. Returned to England in 1652 or 1653.

1636.—Jehu Burr. Removed to Fairfield, Conn.

1636.—William Blake. Removed to Dorchester.

1636.—Edmund Wood. Removed.

1636.—Thomas Ufford. Removed.

1636.—John Cable. Removed to Fairfield, Conn., in 1641.

The above signed the agreement dated May 14, 1636.

_____

1636.—Thomas Woodford. Removed in 1639.

1636.—Samuel Butterfield.

1636.—Jonas Wood.

1636.—John Reader.

The preceding were granted land May 16, 1636.

_____

1636.—Richard Everett. Witnessed Indian deed. Removed to Dedham.

1636.—Joseph Parsons. Witnessed the Indian deed to Pynchon. Appears here next in 1645. Removed to Northampton; afterwards returned and died here in 1683.

1636.—John Allen. Witnessed Indian deed to Pynchon.

1636.—Thomas Horton. Witnessed Indian deed, and died here, 1641.

1636.—Faithful Thayler. Witnessed Indian deed. Did not remain.

1636.—John Townes. Witnessed Indian deed. Did not remain.

1636.—John Pynchon, son of William. Was 14 years old when he came here with his father. Died here, 1703.

1637 or 1638.—Rev. George Moxon. Returned to England 1652.

1638.—John Searle. Died here, 1641.

1638.—Thomas Merrick. Died here in 1704.

1639.—William Warriner. Died here in 1676.

1639.—Rowland Stebbins. Removed in 1656 to Northampton, where he died in 1671.

1639.—Thomas Stebbins, son of Rowland. Died here in 1683.

1639.—John Stebbins, son of Rowland. Removed to Northampton in 1656; died there in 1679.

1639.—John Leonard. Killed by the Indians in 1676.

1639.—Robert Ashley. Died here in 1682.

1639.—John Woodcock. Went to Connecticut. Died 1642.

1639.—John Allen.

1639.—John Burt. Rated, but never came here.

1639.—Henry Gregory. Went to Connecticut in 1642.

1639.—Samuel Hubbard. Went to Newport in 1648.

1639.—Samuel Wright. Went to Northampton in 1656 and died there in 1665.

1639.—Benjamin Wright, son of Samuel. Went to Northampton.

1639.—Samuel Wright, Jr., son of Samuel. Went to Northampton.

1639.—James Wright, son of Samuel. Went to Northampton in 1656.

1640.—Henry Burt. Died here in 1662.

1640.—Jonathan Burt, son of Henry. Died here in 1715.

1640.—David Burt, son of Henry. Removed to Northampton in 1655 and died there in 1690.

1640.—Nathaniel Burt, son of Henry. Died here in 1720.

1640.—Elizur Holyoke. Died here in 1675.

1640.—John Dibble. Died here in 1646.

1641.—John Noble. Died here in 1641.

1642.—Samuel Chapin. Died here in 1675.

1642.—Henry Chapin, son of Samuel. Died here in 1718.

1642.—Josias, son of Samuel. Died at Braintree, 1683.

1642.—David Chapin, son of Samuel. Went to Boston.

1642.—Japhet Chapin, son of Samuel. Died here in 1712.

1642.—Richard Sikes. Died here in 1676.

1643.—Alexander Edwards. Went to Northampton in 1656 and died there in 1690.

1643.—John Dover.

1643.—Morgan Jones. Died here in 1643.

1643.—Francis Ball. Drowned here in 1648.

1643.—Thomas Cooper. Killed by the Indians in 1675.

1643.—James Bridgman. Went to Northampton in 1655 and died there in 1676.

1643.—Roger Pritchard. Died at New Haven in 1671.

1643.—Judah Gregory. Died in Connecticut.

1643.—William Branch. Died here in 1683.

1643.—John Matthews. Died here in 1684.

1643.—John Harmon. Died here in 1661.

1644.—Benjamin Gooley. Died here in 1684.

1644. Miles Morgan. Died here in 1699.

1644.—Abraham Munden. Drowned at Enfield Falls in 1645.

1645.—William Vaughan.

1645.—William Jess. Drowned at Enfield Falls in 1645.

1645.—Francis Pepper. Died here in 1685.

1645.—John Burrhall.

1645.—Griffith Jones. Died here in 1676.

1645.—James Osborn. Died at Hartford in 1676.

1646.—George Colton. Died here in 1699.

1646.—John Clark. Died here in 1684.

1646.—Thomas Reeve. Died here in 1650.

1646.—Richard Exell. Died here in 1714.

1646.—Margaret Bliss, widow of Thomas of Hartford. Died here in 1684.

1646.—Nathaniel Bliss, son of Margaret. Died here in 1654.

1646.—Lawrence Bliss, son of Margaret. Died here in 1676.

1646.—Samuel Bliss, son of Margaret. Died here in 1720.

1646.—John Bliss, son of Margaret. Died here in 1702.

1646.—Edmund Haynes. Died here in 1646.

1646.—Thomas Thomson. Removed.

1646.—Reice Bedortha. Drowned here in 1683.

1646.—Hugh Parsons. Tried in Boston for witchcraft and found not guilty. Went to Watertown and died there in 1675.

1646.—John Lombard. Died here in 1672.

1646.—George Lanckton. Went to Northampton and died there in 1676.

1647.—Rowland Thomas. Died here in 1698.

1648.—Thomas Sewell. Took the oath of fidelity on 6th of February, 1649.

1648.—Samuel Marshfield. Died here in 1692.

1649.—Anthony Dorchester. Died here in 1683.

1649.—Henry Walkley. Went to Stratford, Conn.

1649.—Nathaniel Brown. Went to Middletown in 1650.

1649.—Benjamin Munn. Died here in 1675.

1649.—Thomas Miller. Killed by the Indians in 1675.

1649.—Jonathan Taylor. Lived here but died in Suffield in 1683.

1649.—William Brooks. Went to Deerfield and died there in 1688.

1650.—John Dumbleton. Died here in 1702.

1650.—John Stewart. Died here in 1690.

1650.—Edward Foster. Died here in 1720.

1650.—Samuel Terry. Died at Enfield, Conn., in 1731.

1650.—Hugh Dudley.

1650.—Richard Maund.

1651.—Benjamin Parsons. Died here in 1689.

1651.—Nathaniel Pritchard. Went away after 1691.

1651.—John Lamb. Died here in 1690.

1653.—Mr. Hosford.

1653.—Thomas Bancroft. Was dead in 1684.

1654.—George Alexander.

1654.—Simon Beamon. Died here in 1676.

1654.—Obadiah Miller. Date of death unknown.

1654.—Abel Wright. Died here in 1724.

1655.—Simon Sackett. Died here in 1659.

1655.—Thomas Gilbert. Died here in 1662.

1656.—John Gilbert, brother of Thomas, desired grant of land at Westfield but it was never taken.

1656.—Jonathan Gilbert, brother of Thomas, desired grant at Westfield but did not settle there.

1656.—Thomas Noble. Went to Westfield and died there in 1704.

1656.—William Morgan. Drowned here in 1663.

1656.—John Riley. Died here in 1684.

1657. John Bagg. Died here in 1683.

1658.—John Wood. Removed 1660.

1658.—John Stiles. Died at Windsor in 1683.

1658.—Joseph Crowfoot. Supposed to have died at Northampton in 1678.

1658.—Thomas Day. Died here 1711.

1658.—Richard Fellows. Died at Hatfield in 1663.

1659.—Rev. Pelatiah Glover. Died here in 1692.

1659.—John Scot. Died at Suffield in 1690.

1659.—Tahan Grant.

1659.—Nathaniel Ely. Died here in 1675.

1659.—Samuel Ely, son of Nathaniel. Died here in 1692.

1659.—Peter Swinck, negro. Died here in 1699.

1660.—John Keep. Killed by Indians in 1676.

1660.—Quince Smith. Given liberty to stay two months in town from December 18, 1660, when he was warned to depart the town.

1660.—Mr. Hooker. Preached here a short time and went away.

1661.—Charles Ferry. Died here in 1699.

1661.—Elizabeth Hitchcock, widow of Luke of New Haven, died here in 1696.

1661.—John Hitchcoock, son of Elizabeth. Died here in 1712.

1661.—Luke Hitchcock, son of Elizabeth. Died here in 1727.

1661.—Jeremy Horton, son of Thomas. Died here in 1782.

1661.—John Horton, son of Thomas.

1661.—John Harmon, son of John. Died here in 1712.

1661.—Samuel Harmon, son of John. Died at Suffield in 1677.

1661.—John Dorchester, son of Anthony. Died here in 1705.

1661.—James Dorchester. Died here in 1732.

1662.—John Petty. Died here in 1680.

1662.—John Henryson. Went to Haddam, Conn., and died there in 1688.

1662.—William Hunter. Killed by Indians in 1676.

1662.—James Taylor. Died here in 1720.

1662.—Thomas Mascall of Windsor, admitted.

1663.—Hugh Mackey. Had seat in church.

1663.—Thomas Thomson, a boy, had seat in church. Belonged in Windsor.

1663.—John Barber. Died here in 1712.

CLERK OF THE WRITS.

The Clerk of the Writs was an official which the General Court required each town to elect, subject to confirmation at the next session of the County Court. It was his duty to issue summonses and grant writs of attachments in civil suits,

and to enter in the town books a record of all births, marriages and deaths.   For a summons he received a fee of two-
pence; for a writ of attachment, threepence; for recording a
birth, marriage or death, threepence.   Henry Burt was the
first Clerk of the Writs chosen for Springfield, having been
elected by the town on the 29th day of the third month, 1649.
The records of births, marriages and deaths are in his handwriting from his appointment in 1649 to 1662.   The following are the names of the persons, with their terms of service,
who held that office in Springfield:—

Henry Burt, 1649—1662.   Died in office.

Thomas Cooper, 1663—1676.   Killed by the Indians when
Springfield was burned.

Samuel Holyoke,1676.   Died in office.

John Holyoke, 1677.

Town Recorders.

Every one who has had occasion to search the early records in various New England towns has noticed the difference in their completeness and intelligent statement of the
various transactions which occurred, and how much is due to
the recorders for a careful statement of those events which
have become of the greatest interest to thousands of descendants in tracing the part which each inhabitant took in founding the towns and in making that history which now stands
forth as a bright example of intelligent and conscientious endeavor.   The records of Springfield are much more complete
than any other in the first settlements on the Connecticut
River, and much is due to Henry Smith, the first Recorder,
who served from 1636 until his return to England in 1653.
Elizur Holyoke, who soon succeeded him, appears to have
been equally painstaking, but his duties were more perfunc-
tory in their execution and reflect less of the feeling and
opinion of the townspeople in their doings when assembled
in public meetings.   The following are the names of the recorders and their terms of service from 1636 to 1736:—

Henry Smith ....1636—1652

John Pynchon....................1652—1655
Elizur Holyoke...................1656
    In the absence of John Pynchon.
John Pynchon....................1657—1660
Elizur Holyoke..................1661—1676
    Died in office.
John Holyoke....................1677—1680
Daniel Denton....................1681
John Holyoke....................1682—1695
John Pynchon, Jr................1696
Jonathon Burt...................1697—1700
John Pynchon, Jr.................1701
John Holyoke....................1702—1711
Pelatiah Bliss..................1712—1715
Joseph Warriner.................1716
Pelatiah Bliss..................1717—1727
William Pynchon, Jr..............1628—1636

THE GOOD SENSE OF THE COMMON PEOPLE PREVAILED.

Looking backward from this period of time we find but
little in the town records to indicate that William Pynchon
had an active part in the administration of the town's affairs.
Undoubtedly he was looked to for counsel and suggestion,
but after the first few years the details were entrusted to others, who appear to have been fully equal to their various duties. Returning to England in 1652, he left nothing except
the record of his duties as magistrate and the transactions
connected with the publication of his book and the burning of
it by the authorities in the market place at Boston, to show
from our present point of view, any impression which he
made upon the life of the community. That he was a man of
ability and one who exerted a powerful influence in the earlier
work of the Colony, there can be no doubt. But after the
settlers had once secured a foothold, neither the withdrawal
of a few nor the death of any single individual, would have
broken up the settlement. The law of average prevailed,
and there was sufficient cohesive force in the leading spirits

to have successfully worked out the problem of self-government, and brought any question that might have arisen, to a successful issue. The sternest problem which at any time, with perhaps a single exception, confronted them, was simply one of food and clothing,—material subsistence. When the Indians in treachery came down upon the settlement it was the average opinion and the average courage which saved the inhabitants and it was this spirit which rebuilt the town.

Transferring the business of the town from the whole body to a chosen few, the selectmen, did not relieve the inhabitants of responsibility. It was the duty of every man in the settlement who was an "admitted inhabitant" to be present at the annual town meetings and to take part in its affairs, to either agree or express dissent. May 7, 1645, this vote was passed:—

"It is voted and agreed upon by y° generall consent of the Plantation that if any inhabitant shall absent himself from any town meeting upon any sufficient warning given them, or shall withdraw from the meeting before there be a full discharge, without a sufficient excuse or leave, he shall be liable to pay half a bushel of Indian corn for every such defect. It was voted to be a sufficient warning if publik noticement is given after a lecture to meet in the afternoon."

It would appear that even this vote did not produce the desired effect, for the fine was increased the next year to one bushel. The inhabitants were required to be present "when the blessing is desired," indicating that town meetings in the early years were opened with prayer. This law, as laid down by the town, was kept in force for many years, but the fine was finally reduced to sixpence. At the town meeting in April, 1665, there were no less than fifteen voters absent, but the majesty of the law was sustained. The founders swerved not from the decrees which they had laid down for the governing of the town. The foremost as well as the humblest, from Deacon Chapin down to John Matthews, who used to beat the drum for Sunday meetings, came in for his share when delinquent.

Location of the First Meeting House.

There is nothing in the town records to show where religious services were first held. In the absence of a meeting house it is probable that they were conducted at the residence of some of the settlers,—at the house of William Pynchon, at Mr. Moxon's, or possibly elsewhere. The first mention of a meeting house is under date of January 10, 1645, when it was voted that every inhabitant should give 28 days' work toward such purpose, no man to be required to work over six days at a time. It was first voted to take forty rods of land from the lot of Thomas Stebbins, but later six rods square was deemed sufficient, and for the remainder of the forty rods Stebbins was to allow a rod in breadth for a way to the training field. February 28, 1645, a bargain was made with Thomas Cooper to build the meeting-house. It was to be 40 feet long, 25 wide, nine feet between joints, to have four large windows, two on each side and one on each end. There were to be two turrets, one for the bell and the other for a watch-house. It was to be completed by the 30th of September at an expense of 80 pounds. On the 26th of March, less than one month, the town acknowledged that Cooper had fulfilled his bargain. He was to receive in payment, "wheate, pease, pork, wampum, debts and labor." It stood, as is generally known, on the south side of our present Court square, a few feet back from Main street, near what is now Elm street, on which it faced. This lot was originally Henry Gregory's, but when he withdrew from the town and went to Connecticut, Thomas Stebbins, son of Rowland, purchased it. On this spot was erected the first building devoted to religious worship in this State west of Boston and vicinity, and the first public building for any purpose in Springfield. This was the beginning of our present First church. Thomas Cooper, the builder of the meeting-house, came with John Stiles' company from England to Windsor, removing thence to Springfield when still a young man.

In 1650 John Pynchon appears to have driven an advantageous bargain to make a chamber in the meeting-house:—

"February 6, 1650. It is agreed by the towne that if mr John Pynchon will make a chamber over the meeting howse and board it he shall have the use of it Intirely to himself for Ten years, and then if the Town need it they may have it, provided they alow the s^d mr John Pynchon the charge that he hath been about it, or else he is to have the use of it longer till they do alow him the charge that he layed out about it."

Evidently this gave dissatisfaction when the voters re-flectd upon what they had done, and two years later it came up in town meeting again for consideration, when this action was taken:—

"There falling out some disputes betwixt mr John Pynchon and the towne in reference to the above mentioned bargain, about the meeting-house chamber, it was put to vote whether the Inhabitants be willing to take the chamber into theyr hand again presently, promising to pay mr. John Pynchon his wholl charge that he hath bin at about it, for the time past; and he to have the use of the chamber till October next, pro-vided he lay not above 400 bushells of corne in it; if he exceed that quantity he is to underprop ye floor at his own charge, as Rich: Sykes and Thos: Cooper shall judge meete. It was voted affirmatively to all the particulars, whereupon George Colton and Robert Ashley were nominated by mr. John Pynchon, and appointed by ye vote of ye Inhabitants, to gather in ye rate that shall be made by the Selectmen for the charge layed out about this floor, and see it payd into mr. Pynchon by ye 20th of February next, in marchantable wheate at 3s 10d per bushell."

The chamber, coming into the hands of the town, was let for many years to different individuals as a place for storing grain, though John Pynchon does not appear to have occu-pied it again after giving it up to the town.

THE BURYING-GROUND AND TRAINING-FIELD.

West of the meeting-house, on the banks of the Connecti-cut, William Pynchon and Henry Smith, by order of the town, bargained with Francis Ball and Thomas Stebbins, ac-

cording to a report made to the town February 26, 1645, for
2 1-2 acres of land for a burying ground and a training-field.
Here were the home lots of the two; Ball on coming here
from Connecticut bought the improvements of the lot owned
by John Woodcock, on which are now located the Chicopee
bank building, the Hampden County court house, and the
Elm-street grammar school building. The town took an
acre of Ball's lot and an acre and a half of the Stebbins lot, for
which it gave in payment double the number of acres elsewhere. A street had been previously opened from Main
street to the meeting-house, and this was continued two rods
wide to the training-field. After Ball's marriage, and four
years after his settlement in Springfield, he was drowned in
the Connecticut. His widow married Benjamin Munn, who
continued to reside on her home lot until his death. In 1645
Thomas Cooper, who was then one of the selectmen, made
this entry in the town book:—

"It was voted that Thomas Stebbins and Benjamin Munn
should have use of the trayning place for pasture for the term
of ten years, for certayne, and for the term of their own personal living, if they live longer, upon condition that they
keepe it cleare of offensive matter, as wood and brush, or the
like and they are now to sow it with inglish grass seed."

This lot was used for exercising the military company, and
for a burying-ground for about 200 years. When the first
settlers came from England to this country, both France and
England were little more than a military camp, and evidently
the first impulse of the settlers was to arm for defence; but
where the enemy was to come from to make the attack was
not explained. Nevertheless they set about preparing for
defence by training the youth as well as the elder men in the
manual of arms. They evidently cherished their military
titles, regarding them as tokens of honor. Under the date
of November 14, 1639, is this record:—

"It is ordered y^t the exercise of training shall be practiced
one day in every month, and if occasions do sometymes hinder, then ye like space of tyme shall be observed another tyme

though it be 2 dayes after one another. And y^t this tyme of trayning is referred to ye discretion of Henry Smith, who is chosen by mutuall consent to be the Serjant of ye Company, who shall have power to choose a Corporall for his assistant, and who soever shall be absent himselfe with out a lawful excuse shall forfeit 12 pence, & y^t all above 15 yeares of age shall be counted for soldiers, and the tyme to begin the first Thursday in December next."

An Early Adoption of Referendum.

Referendum, or the submitting of certain public measures to the people for approval, after having been enacted by the Legislature has been discussed at considerable length in recent times, and no doubt it has been considered in the light of a new discovery,—certainly as something never practiced in this country.   In Springfield it is more than 250 years old. When the selectmen were elected in 1646 this vote was adopted:—

"By mutual consent it is agreed to refer into theyr the Selectmen's hands the ordering of all prudential affayers of the town, and whatsoever they so order in reference to the good of the towne shall stand in force as ye act of the towne, provided that what orders or conclusions they shall agree upon, be openly published before the generality of ye towne after a lecture, or at any trayning day, or any other public meeting: and in case there be no negative vote by the generality of the towne within 7 days after, then it shall stand and be taken for granted that the towne by such silence doe confirme and establish theyr orders."

The "generality of the town" is understood to mean a majority of those having right to vote.   This practice was maintained for many years.   The second volume of records shows by frequent statement that measures adopted by the selectmen were read on public occasions, with the date of reading affixed to the selectmen's decree.

A Toll Road Established.

The making of public roads was one of the early duties to

which the selectmen were called, and the first toll road was authorized in 1648. The selectmen were allowed liberty to set a certain toll on carts that shall pass any highway which shall appear more than ordinary chargeable in the reparation of it." At a town-meeting held November 7, 1648, it was voted as follows:—

"It is agreed that those who will joyne to make a cartway over ye meddow against Robert Ashley's shall have liberty to barr up ye Cartway, and to take 4 pence per load of any others that shall cart over said way, who have not Joyned in making of it. Those who have given in their names to make ye cartway are as followeth: Thomas Merrick, Thomas Stebbins, James Bridgman, John Clarke, William Warriner, Rowland Stebbins, Samuel Wright Samuel Marshfield, Widow Ball."

This road was at some point north of the present village of West Springfield. In 1660 a toll bridge was established over Mill river, where the street railway now crosses the river on the way to Forest park. The town voted:—

"The lower end of the Towne have Liberty to make a cart Bridge over ye mill river, above ye old mill, & such as Joyne not in making of it, if they shall make use of it they shall allow or pay to ye makers of it 3 pence per Load for Three years."

This establishes the locality of Pynchon's grain-mill nearer than any other record in the first volume; it must have been at or near the site of the mill which is still in existence there.

EXCLUDING UNWORTHY PERSONS.

Unworthy persons or those liable to become a town charge, were not admitted for settlement, the founders thus undertaking to guard at the beginning against all undesirable characters. As early as 1642 this vote was passed:—

"It is agreed with the generall consent and vote of the Inhabitants of Springfield: That if any man of this Township shall under the Colour of friendship or otherwise intertayne any person or persons here, to abide or continue as inmates, or shall subdivide theyr house lots to entrtayne them as tenants or otherwise, for a longer tyme than one month, or 31 days, without the generall consent & allowance of the inhab- itants (children or servants of the family that remayne single persons excepted) shall forfeit for the first default xx shil- lings, to be destrayned by the Constable of their goods, cat- tell or chattails, for ye publique use of the Inhabitants: And alsoe he shall forfeit xx shillings per month for every month that any such person or persons shall soe continue in this township, with out the generall consent of the Inhabitants: and if in ye tyme of theyr abode after ye limitation they shall neede releefe, not being able to mayntayn themselves, then he or they that entertayne such persons shall be lyable to be rated by the Inhabitants for ye releife & maintenance of the said party or parties, as the Inhabitants shall think meete."

In 1659 John Wood was called to account for giving enter- tainment to Isaac Hall for the space of two months, and was fined 40 shillings. Quince Smith was regarded as another undesirable person. He was given liberty to tarry in town "2 months from ye 18th of December, 1660; if he tarry long- er it must be by a new liberty from ye selectmen." On the 18th of February he was warned by the selectmen to depart the town. The sons of even the first settlers were not admit- ted as inhabitants, to be voters and assume the responsibili- ties of citizenship, without giving bonds to the town to se- cure it against any charge which might possibly arise on their account. Deacon Chapin gave bonds of 20 pounds each when two of his sons were admitted, Henry in 1660, and Josiah in 1663. At the time of Henry's admission Elizur Holyoke gave bonds in the sum of 20 pounds to the town treasurer for the admission of Samuel Ely, "to secure the town from any charge which may arise to the town by the admission of the said Ely or his family," the same as had been imposed on Deacon Chapin.

BEFORE THE SELECTMEN AND THE COUNTY COURT.

Looked back upon in the light of the present, the first set- tlers of Springfield formed almost a spotless community, not entirely unlike some of the remote rural communities of recent times. There were no thefts, little drunkenness, and no brutal assaults. The breaches of the public peace were mostly of a trival nature, and with rare exceptions would not now call for consideration. The shortcomings of the first settlers consisted mainly in not living strictly up to "town orders," such as failing to ring the swine, not maintaining suitable fences, and occasionally omitting attendance at town meetings. Possibly there might have been some neighborhood gossip and occasionally departures from the standard set by the "fathers of the town," but there were no crimes committed that would shock the community, such as breach of public trust, assault or murder. The offenses of our ancestors were mostly of a nature which would now, rarely, if at all, be heard of in our courts. There was no lack of vigilance and no lack of public officers to enforce what was then held as a public offense. At a very early day "Two wise and discreet men" were chosen annually at the town-meeting, "to present on court days all breaches of Court or Town orders, or any other misdemeanors as shall come to theyr knowledge, either by their own observation or by credible information of others, and they shall take out process for the appearance of such as are delinquent, or witnesses, to appear on sayd days, when all presentments shall be Judicially heard and examined by the magistrate. . . . . These to stand in this office for a year or till others be chosen in their roome."

The cases of breach of town orders came before the selectmen, and the graver offenses before the county court, held twice a year, which was at Northampton in March and in Springfield in September,—for which 12 jurymen were summoned, selected mainly from the jurisdiction of the two towns, but from other settlements in part at a later period. The first trials, when William Pynchon was the magistrate, were before a jury of six, all residents of Springfield, as no other settlements had been made hereabouts prior to his departure in 1652 for England.

One of the breaches of town orders relates to a defective

fence in what was later West Sprinfield. Reice Bedortha and John Bagg had been chosen fence-viewers on the west side of the "Great River," and they discovered that John Scott had a very defective fence, to which they called his attention. They found "20 rods altogether deficient & 20 defects in other places. Having given him warning and yet upon a 2d view a month after they found the aforesaid defects; & a 3d tyme they found ye defects a fort Night after." The selectmen considered his case and summed up his great neglect as below:—

"The Select men doe Judge that after ye first warning to the 2d view should be accounted but one defect. But the 20 rod is now 20 shillings, & ye 20 other defects 20 shillings more. After ye 2d warning when ye viewers went the 3d tyme to see it a fortnight after being 12 days at 12 pence per Rod, makes 20 shillings every day, which comes to 12 pounds the 12 days; togither with y^e 40 shillings aforesaid makes y^e whole 14 pounds, one half wherof y^e Towne order gives to y^e viewers, & y^e other halfe to y^e Towne."

This fine of 14 pounds, nearly equivalent to $70, would probably have bankrupted John Scott, and on a training day the town voted to remit its half, undoubtedly taking this view of the situation. At the same time, when Bedortha and Bagg, the two viewers, had presented Scott, there came another complaint:—

"John Bagg complaining against Reice Bedortha, his partner, for one rod defective. Reice disowning it to be his fence the Selectmen Judged that ye fence must first be determined his before he can be concluded defective, or Lyable to ye fine." But this was not the end. It being shown that Bedortha and Bagg had been remiss in their public duties as fence viewers, they two were brought to justice, as the record shows:—

"It is ordered that ye viewers of fences, viz: Reice Bedortha and John Bagg, for neglecting their Charge in not viewing fences according to order, shall pay a fine of 10 shillings to ye Towne, that is 5 shillings apeice."

Fines for having defective fences were not imposed upon the white settlers alone. The viewers at a later date, Edward Foster and Thomas Miller, complained of the "Indian Catonis & his company for not doing up the water fence belonging to their land in the field, they having had warning, about 4 or 5 rods being defective upon the land next to the river, besides ye securing of the river, for which neglect they are fined to pay 2 and 1-2 bushels of Indian corne." The Indians were neither prompt menders of fences nor in payment of fines. At the next meeting of the selectmen they entered their decree in this case:—

"The Indian fence into Agawam river being still defective it is ordered that ye viewers shall amend it & have double compensation according to law, & have warrant to ye constable to Levy it, & also to Levy the 2 and 1-2 bushels of Indian corne, which they were fined at the last meeting of ye Selectmen."

INDISCRETIONS OF OUR PURITAN YOUTH.

The sons of our Puritan ancestors could not have been entirely unlike the boys of our present time, but they had the law laid down to them in a summary manner when they transgressed. The selectmen, Deacon Chapin, Nathaniel Ely, George Colton, Rowland Thomas and Elizur Holyoke, in 1664, made observation and recorded this decree:—

"The Selectmen considering the great damage done to ye glass windowes in ye meeting house by childrens playing about ye meeting house. They do order that if any persons children or others, shall be found playing at any sports about the meeting house, whereby ye glass windows thereof may be endamaged, such persons shall be liable to a fine of 12d a peece for each tyme they shall be found soe playing, which fine is to be paid within 3 days after such default, and if the Governors [fathers] of any youth that soe offend shall refuse to pay the said fyne, such youths shall be liable to be whipt by the Constable before 3 or more of ye Selectmen, who shall determine ye number of stripes to be inflicted,

& if any other persons so offending shall refuse to pay ye said fyne as aforesaid, they shall be liable to ye punishment as aforesaid, & all such fines shall go one half to the informers, & the other half to ye Selectmen, for the use of the town in bearing publik charges."

This had the desired effect as no record was made of the boys being whipt under the direction of the benign Deacon Chapin and his fellow-members of the board. But the spirit of youth was evidently abroad and if they could not throw stones at the meeting-house windows they could do some other things even at the risk of being punished. The argus eyes of the conservators of the public peace were not unmindful of improprieties by whomsoever committed, as the following indicates:—

"It being observed & complayned of that Persons do frequently take liberty to ride very swiftly with their horses in the streets to ye endangering of children and others, it is therefore ordered that if any person be observed to Run his horse or to ride faster than an ordinary gallop in ye streets of this town, except upon such urgent occasions as shall by ye Selectmen be judged warrantabel so to do, he shall be liable to a fine of 3s 4d, to be paid, one shilling to the Informer & the rest to ye Towne. This order not to extend to Troopers in tymes of their exercise."

"Troopers," were the members of the cavalry company, who might be out for exercise on a training day. The first to transgress this order were Thomas Stebbins, Jr., Timothy Cooper, John Hitchcock, Samuel Bliss, Jr., and Jonathan Ashley, all young men. On notification to appear, Stebbins went before the selectmen, who for "fiersely galloping & running his horse last Wednesday forenoon, in ye street from Goodman Miracks upwards, acknowledged it and was sentenced to pay 3s 4d." The others not appearing, their trial was continued till the next lecture day, when they were fined 2s 4d each.

Youthful indiscretions began to show themselves about this time within as well as without the meeting-house. At a meeting of the selectmen April 7, 1669, it was voted:—

Miles Morgan and Jonathan Burt are ordered to sit in ye Gallery to give check to the disorders in youth & young men In tyme of Gods worship. Anthony Dorchester is to sit in ye Guard Seate for ye like end."

The preceding are not the only instances in which the youth of that time were transgressors of the established customs. Even Elizur Holyoke's sons were subject to disciplin and were brought into court with others. In the Pynchon Magistrate Book is the following record:—

"Thomas Noble, Constable, presenting Thomas Thomson and John Horton for the last Sabbath, June 7, 1664, in the evening about 1-2 hour after Sunset, Samuel and Elizur Holyoke, being accessories in sayd fray; the Commissioners upon examination of the case do find that the said four persons did profane the Lord's day and therefore determine that they all shall be admonished thereof, and that Thomas Thomson, John Horton and Samuel Holyoke shall pay a fine of 5 shillings apeice to the County, or be whipt by the Constable on the naked body with three stripes apeice, whereupon they were all admonished and the three former desiring to pay their fines than otherwise, were ordered to pay them to the County Treasurer."

The Justices, or Commissioners, as they called themselves, who sat in this case, were Deacon Samuel Chapin and Elizur Holyoke, the latter the father of the Holyoke boys. Thomas Thomson was a Windsor youth who resided here for a short time.

JOHN PYNCHON'S EXPERIENCE IN PORK RAISING.

In 1656 John Pynchon set out on a pork-raising speculation, on Freshwater river, now in Enfield, Conn.,—at that time within the jurisdiction of Massachusetts. He procured a grant of land, 20 acres for himself, and 10 acres each for George Colton and Benjamin Cooley. When granted it was with the agreement that "if they doe not make use of it themselves it is to return into the Townes hands agayne—

they are not to sell it to any other." The sequel was not recorded until October 8, 1660, when it appeared that Cooley
had withdrawn, Pynchon taking his portion. The record
gives the conditions and the results:—

"According to order by the Selectmen there was granted
parsell of land at fresh water brook, to Mr. Pynchon, George
Colton and Benjamin Cooley, in proportion as they carry
on their design of keeping swine there. In all forty acres of
upland, ten acres to each quarter part, and this upon condition that they doe within two years carry on the design of
keeping swine there. If they fail in carrying on that design
within two years, or such of them as doe faile, they forfeit
the land, & it remains to the other or them that do keep
swine there; or else falls to the town, if none carry on that design of keeping swine. The design of keeping swine there
was accordingly caryed on & within the tyme limited, and
continued until Windsor corne fields eat up ye swine."

This quotation is in the handwriting of John Pynchon, and
what he probably intended to say was, that the swine ran out
of the Enfield woods, in which they were fattening on acorns,
and other nuts, into the Windsor corn-fields, and ate so much
that they consequently died from the effects, and not by
being eaten up by the fields.

In the grants of land at Woronoco were sixty acres on
the request of Thomas Merrick and David Ashley to Timothy
Mather of Dorchester, and forty acres to his father, the Rev.
Richard Mather, the first minister of that town. The family of the Rev. Mr. Mather were of more than ordinary ability. His sons, with the exception of Timothy, were ministers. Two went back to England and preached there during
their lives. Another, Eleazer Mather, was the first minister
of Northampton, and it was his daughter Eunice, who became the wife of the Rev. John Williams, and was killed by
the Indians after the burning of Deerfield, on the way to
Canada. From her is descended Mrs. Elizabeth Storrs
Mead, president of Mount Holyoke college at South Hadley.
Timothy, the father of the family, is the ancestor of all who

bear the name of Mather in New England. This grant at Woronoco remained in the family for a considerable period.

ROUND HILL GIVEN TO PYNCHON FOR BRINGING SHEEP TO TOWN.

The name "Round hill," applied to the elevation between North Main and Plainfield streets, is nearly as old as Springfield itself. The hill is mentioned in the record by that name not many years after the settlement was begun. In 1654, it was, with adjoining land on the west, given to John Pynchon by the town on condition that he would bring 40 sheep into the town and offer them for sale to the inhabitants. This, too, was the introduction of that important domestic animal into this region. Among the "Several particulars which was voted unto by the Towne upon a trayning day, May 29th, 1654, was the following:—

"In consideration of this said land the said John Pynchon doth promise to purchase 40 sheep within the space of six months, and he to use his best indevoure to bring them into Towne and there to dispose of them as he shall see cause, provided he sell them not to any out of town in case any in towne will buy them.

The 15 acres of land was laid out to him, part of it under the round hill next to his 3 corner meddow, & part of it upon ye round hill: It goeth over ye round hill and leaving a part of it. John Pynchon desired the rest of ye land on that hill & so down to ye brooke called Endbrooke, or 3 corner meddow brook, being about six acres, so that in all Mr. Pynchon hath about 21 acres."

At a later day this grant to Pynchon was increased to 23 acres, on account of his introducing the 40 sheep. "Three-corner meddow" is now Hampden park, and Endbrook in later days came to be known to Springfield as North-end brook. The level region, on part of which stands Brightwood, was known to the first settlers as the "Plaine," and has not the name of Plainfield street, of the present time, come down to us from that fact?

OUR VILLAGE BLACKSMITH CAPTURED BY CROMWELL AND FORCED TO MIGRATE.

The blacksmith was an important and useful citizen in all the New England settlements. In the early days his work was needed by every one who was tilling the earth and clearing the forests. In many communities unusual efforts were made to secure a competent workman in this craft, who was given valuable grants of land to make a permanent abode in the town and perform such work as was most needed; in fact, it was a calling that came nearer and was in closer touch with the people of those early times than any other. Longfellow's picture of the smith in later days might apply to him of ancient Springfield:—

> Under a spreading chestnut tree
>   The village smithy stands;
> The smith, a mighty man is he,
>   With large and sinewy hands;
> And the muscles of his brawny arms
>   Are strong as iron bands.

Our smith was John Stewart, a thrifty and bustling Scotchman, whose early adventures made him an interesting character, though he appears to have embarked in a failing cause, which brought to him deportation from his native land to the wilds of America, where he served more usefully and with greater credit to himself than when he was fighting the battles of Charles I in his own Scotch Highlands. But let us go back to the record here prior to his advent in Springfield. The town was without a permanent smith and might have had none, for nearly 10 years after the beginning of the settlement. Under date of January 8, 1646, this record was made: "George Colton and Miles Morgan are appoynted to doe theyr best to get a smith for ye Towne." Eight months later, September 4, this entry in the records was made:—

"A bargaine was driven the day above said betwixt the towne of Springfield and Francis Ball for a Shop for a Smith, which is to be 12 foote wide, 16 foote in length, six foote stud

betwixt Joynts, a chimny for the forge, runged, to be boarded
both roofe and sides, to make a doore and windowe in the
end, with a beam in ye middist, for which work to be sufficiently accomplished by September 28th, next, the towne
doth condition to pay him five pounds either in wheate at 3s
8d per bushel, or in worke as he shal need it, to be payd in
unto him ye 10th of march next, at the house of Henry Smith.
He doth also agree to find boards for ye covering and sides,
with nayles & hinges, &c, and what he wants else, and he is
to bring in his account what boards he useth and what other
charges he is at, for which he is to be payd as before in wheate
at 3s 8d per bushel, or in worke as he and they shall agree.
It is agreed that this house shall remayne in the hands of the
towne till they se cause to dispose otherwise of it."

What success George Colton and Miles Morgan had in getting a smith, is not known, nor the date of John Stewart's
coming to Springfield, but he is the first one mentioned and
probably was the first to take up his residence here.   His
quitting Scotland was enforced by Cromwell after the battle
of Dunbar, he having been engaged on the side of the van-
quished.   Prior to this event, the marquis of Montrose, who
began his career as a covenanter, went over into England
and there came under the influence of Charles I, whose cause
he espoused in opposition to his former declarations.   He
returned to the Highlands of Scotland and there raised the
royal standard, around which he gathered an army and then
waged war in behalf of the king.   Into this service went our
John Stewart, who was, as he says engaged in five battles till
the tide turned against   the   cause which he was serving.
The royal army was then under David Leslie, and had more
than double the numbers of that commanded by Cromwell.
Confident of success, Leslie left his entrenchments at Dunbar
and marched to the open plain, when Cromwell seized the op-
portune moment and won the day, capturing the entire army
not already slain in the engagement.   Many of the prisoners were deported and John Stewart was among the number.
On coming to England he was sold to service and John

Pynchon was the buyer.   As he was a capable smith he was
put to work in the smithery, which had been built by the town
and in Pynchon's accounts appear credits to various ones for
"your helping John in the Smithery."   November 29, 1653,
before Elizur Holyoke and William Warriner, was made this
agreement between Pynchon and Stewart:—

"I agree with John Stewart to allow me yearly 12 shillings
in Smithery work for 3 years, which is for my staying [wait-
ing] so long for that 30 pounds which is due to me from him
for releasing him from my service.   And he ye said John
Stewart consented & promised to allow me for three years
twelve shillings per year in mending or making of Iron work.

John Pynchon."

In 1658 the shop was given to Stewart by the town, and he
pursued his calling many years.   One of his public duties was
to see that all swine above three months old were ringed,
and the selectmen appointed him "to goe twice every week
through the town, from March to November, to take notice
what swine are unrung and to demand of the owners for every
such swine, and in case any shall refuse to pay him 6d for
ringing them, warrant will be granted to the constable to
distraine, who shall have 3d for his pains."

Stewart prospered for some years and received various
grants of lands.   In his old age he became infirm and finally
bedridden, and among other misfortunes a horse was taken
from him for use in an expedition in pursuit of Indians and
died from hard usage.   When Sir Edmund Andros came into
power as governor of New England Stewart sent him a petition, now in the State archives at Boston, wherein he re-
counts his service under the king and what he had suffered
here.   It is in the handwriting of James Cornish, of Northampton, who was clerk of the courts for Hampshire county
under Andros's administration, and is as follows:—

"To His Excellency Sir Edmund Andros, Knight, Governor & Captain General in Chief of all His Majesties Territory: in New England: Whereas, your poor petitioner was

in service in five battles under the noble Marquis of Montrose, in Scotland, for His Majesty, King Charles the First, & thereby suffered & received many dangerous wounds, having escaped with his life through mercy, yet his health has been and is likely to be deeply impayred whilst he lives, being altogether left uncapable of getting a livelyhood in this world for himself and family; that although having a trade which might afford him a comfortable living, he through Gods providence was layd about three years last past bedrid, and so continues uncapable to gaine any reliefe in his sad condition, and never received one penny towards all his service, wherein he was engaged. Was afterwards taken by Lord Cromwell in the fight at Dunbar, & after sent into this land where I was sold for eight years service to purchase my future freedom.

"God having bestowed some small estate on your poor petitioner whilst he gave him ability to labour, may it please your excellency, I had lately a horse pressed from me for service in this country, in pursuit of Indians, which dyed in the service by the wrong he received before he came home. Your poor petitioner was greatly disappointed by his loss, which was all the team he had, & having bin constrayned to buy another, which cost 6 pounds 10 shillings, for supply of his familys present want, although he is very doubtful whether this will prove so serviceable as the former did.

"Your humble petitioner most humbly craves that your Excellency would vouchsafe to order a just & due satisfaction to him for his so great damage, & your petitioner shall daily pray for the best of blessings on your Excellency, & remayne your most unworthy humble servant, John Stewart.

Springfield, 19th September, 1688."

As Andros was not looked upon at that time with greater favor than was his royal master in England, our Puritan ancestry did not honor John Stewart's draft. The poor man quitted this world's troubles April 21, 1690, and two days later his will was presented for probate, Samuel Marshfield and Obadiah Miller making oath that they were present and saw him sign it.

The battle of Dunbar took place September 3, 1650, when 4,000 of the Scotch army were slain and 10,000 taken prisoners by Cromwell. Deportation of the prisoners must have begun very soon afterwards. The ship John and Sarah cleared from London and passed the search office at Gravesend on the 8th of November, 1651, for Boston, with 272 Scotch prisoners, who were consigned to Thomas Kemble of Charlestown. John Stewart probably came in a previous ship as his name is not in the list. Rev. John Cotton, in a letter to Cromwell, under date of Boston, July 5th, 1651, wrote:—

"The Scotts whom God delivered into your hands at Dunbarre and whereof sundry persons were sent here, we have been desirous (as we could) to make their yoke easy. Such as were sick of scurvy or otherwise have not wanted for physic or chyrurgery. They have not been sold for slaves to perpetual servitude, but for 6 or 7 or 8 years, as we do our own; and he that bought the most of them (I heare) buildeth houses for them as their owne, requiring 3 days in the weeke to worke for him (by turns) and 4 days for themselves, and promiseth as soon as they can repay him the money he laid out for them, he will set them at liberty."

John Stewart was not the only one who gave service to Pynchon under like conditions or for payment of passage. It appears to have been a common custom for young unmarried men to pay for their passage in labor, after their arrival, and John Pynchon must have secured them personally, or by an agent in Boston.

HAMPSHIRE COUNTY CREATED.

The movement for creating a county organization in this part of the colony of Massachusetts Bay, which resulted in the formation of the County of Hampshire, was begun in a special town-meeting held February 26, 1662, which declared:—

"Upon conference & serious consultation, the Town by vote concluded it convenient & necessary that there should be all due consideration concerning Setling the Townes in this Western part of the Collony into the forme of a County: In order whereunto Capt. Pynchon, Lieut. Holyoke & Ensign Cooper"—

Here the record, which is in the handwriting of Elizur Holyoke, ends, but we find that at the next meeting in May of the General Court, the proposition was presented by John Pynchon, who was present as the deputy from Springfield—his second year's service. The county organization was perfected, thus signalizing an important event in the progress of our local government, and almost the first entry of John Pynchon into public life, beyond the confines of the township. He was now in his 36th year, and for more than 40 years after this he was an important figure in the history of the Connecticut valley, of which Springfield was the central point of action. The creation of courts and the settlement of towns, all eminating at suggestion from this central point, gave Springfield a foremost rank among the places outside the settlements along the eastern seaboard, and marked an era in the little settlement, founded 26 years before under difficulties which to spirits less courageous might well have seemed too great to overcome.

MINOR EVENTS, BUT NOT WITHOUT INTEREST.

Our selectmen must have had regard for financial responsibilities, and sometimes returned the offenses against their commands to profitable sccount. In 1660, Richard Fellows, having sold his land by promise contrary to order, whereby it was forfeited to the town, they took off the forfeiture on condition that he "supply the Towne with a sufficient horse for a journey to ye Bay this next Spring or Summer, when ye Towne shall please to call for it." This might have been with a view of supplying the transportation for the deputy to the General Court when he went to Boston.

Monopolizing official positions was not confined to the General Court. In 1660 John Pynchon was selectman, town clerk, town treasurer, and moderator of all town-meetings for the year, which with his numerous business interests must have kept him well occupied.

The annual town-meetings, after the town's affairs were placed in the hands of selectmen who were elected by the people, were at first held on the first Tuesday of November of each year. At a special meeting in January, 1660, it was voted that henceforth the "Generall Towne meeting for the choice of Towne officers shall be on y⁰ first Tuesday in February." The town was called together at the usual time in November, and after much deliberation it was concluded to adhere to the former vote. At the February meeting it was voted that "Hence forward yearly at y⁰ Generall Towne meeting there shal be a moderator chosen who shall stand as moderator not only for that day but for all town meetings the year ensuing." At this meeting it was voted that the moderator shall always be "chosen by papers,"—that is by ballots,—which is the first mention of a vote being taken other than "by the erection of hands."

The town constable was an important officer in early times, and was selected with more than ordinary care, regard being had to those qualities which would make him an acceptable and efficient official in maintaining order, and in collecting town rates and fines. At the meeting in 1660 it was voted:—

"That henceforth y⁰ choice of y⁰ Constable shall be after this manner: The Constable whose tyme is expired before he goes out of his place, shall Nominate two men, and y⁰ Towne commissioners or chiefe civil power in Towne, shall Nominate one more, or two, which they pleas. The Three men, or 4, if 4 be Nominated, shal be put to vote, & y⁰ that hath most votes shall be constable the yeare ensuing, who by Country Law [law of the General Court] is lyable to Five Pound fine for refusal of y⁰ office."

At this meeting Robert Ashley was chosen constable, "& had his oath given him, which he took y⁰ same day. Lawrence Bliss was chosen Constable Deputy for supply of y⁰ Constables place in his absence."

Toil in its hardest aspect must have been expressed in the

faces of those who wrestled with the difficulties which beset every one on the banks of the Connecticut at the beginning, and toil was alike honorable to all.. Every one labored in the fields and in the woods, or in following such other work as the settlers required. We find Richard Sikes, who was on the first board of selectmen, not only following the vocation of a farmer but doing whatever came to him, and while he had stood as one of the foremost of "discreet men," we note his public service in sweeping the meeting-house and in ringing the bell for meetings, marriages and funerals. The record under the date of February 10, 1653, says:—

"Richard Sikes hath covenanted to ring the Bell and to sweep the meeting house according to former terms, namely 12d the week, provided he will have his liberty to leave the work at a months warning. His pay to be payed halfe merchandable Indian corne and halfe merchandable wheat, to be payd at one intire payment at the end of June next, ending the date hereof, but if he leave the work after the payment is made he is to abate 1 shilling the week.

"There is granted to Richard Sikes for ringing the Bell for marriages and Burials 1 shilling a time. This pay to be payd by those who shall imploy him for such service."

He continued to serve the town in this office for several years, for which he received 52 shillings a year.

Taxation does not appear to have aroused much if any hostility concerning town affairs, during the first 30 years. Whatever charge of a public nature was held to be necessary was cheerfully met. John Pynchon, Elizur Holyoke and John Dumbleton were the only ones that were even in a single instance, dissatisfied, and that relates to an early reservation in which they simply fell back upon a prior exemption as a right. In the first compact "Three-Corner meadow," our Hampden park, was divided between William Pynchon, who had 20 acres, Jehu Burr and Henry Smith, who had 10 acres each. It was mutually agreed at the time that these three individuals should have 40 acres granted to them, to be free of all charges forever, as compensation for their continued prosecution of the settlement at great expense, while others fell off. William Pynchon's interest went to his son, Jehu Burr's and Smith's went to Holyoke and Dumbleton. In 1656 the question of taxing these lots came up and after considering the original agreement, they were declared to be free of all taxes by the town.

With a boundless wilderness at hand, the founders nevertheless guarded the possibilities of a much greater demand for lumber, when some settler pleaded for liberty to transport boards and planks to other settlements,—probably down the Connecticut, and the town adopted this order:—

"It is ordered that any person that desires to transport boards or planks, shall first Tender such to the Selectmen, & if they provide an chapman in ye town within 21 days, at an Indifferent price, then ye owner thereof have liberty to transport or re-sell them out of ye Towne."

"Indifferent" was intended to convey what we should mean by using the word impartial. "What indifferent persons shall judge," is an expression frequently found in all early records. With such limited opportunities for acquiring even the means of living, and such an ample supply of timber, it would seem that a broader view might have been taken, without endangering the wants of the little hamlet. At that time all boards not riven were sawed by hand, and there was not much danger of overstocking the market or exhausting the forests.

Killing wolves now and then brought money to depleted pockets. The town paid a bounty for many years of 10 shillings to any one who would kill a wolf within five miles of the town, and payments on this account often swelled the town's indebtedness, in which the youths as well as the older persons had a share in creating.

These minor events which have been recorded with considerable minuteness are the side-lights of early days in Springfield. They may seem trival and to some unintresting, but tle by little they reveal to us the conditions and the surround-they help to form the picture of life here at the outset, and lit-

ings of those who brought civilization and a higher conception of the needs of humanity to the western world. We may regard them as narrow and contracted in many of their views, but they lived up to the divine light within, and whatever may have been their failings in some respects, in the light of our greater liberality of thought, they held firmly to the purpose for which they had come, and they never deviated from the convictions which led them from home and country. In this we have a grand example of faith united with patience, born in the hearts of a simple people, whose achievements have been greater than that of the courts and kings they so willingly left behind them to found a state and a government resting on the consent of the governed.

At a town meeting February 18, 1656, "it was voted by consent that whosoever within this township shall kill any ffox or ffoxes shall be allowed 3s ffor any ffox so killed pvided they bring here the body or head unto any of the Selectmen." Subsequently this was reduced to "only 12d apeace for every two ffox killed in ye bounds of ye Towne."

On May 10, 1698, it was "Voted to allow Mr. Mackcranny Twenty shillings out of the Rates for his killing of four Cattamounts, itt was also further voted that if any Inhabitants of this Towne shall hereafter kill or destroy of the forementioned wild creatures within the Bounds of this Towne & bring the head & Tail of every one soe killed unto the Selectmen or Towne Treasurer, they shall bee allowed for soe doeing five shillings for every such creature so destroyed." On November 22, 1716, "It was voted to raise Ten pounds in money for Wolves."

The first mill erected not being adequate, on February 6, 1665, "This being the Genll Town meeting, It was considered that there is great necessity of a Corne mill that shall be serviceable for a mor comfortable supply of this than there late has been." A committee was appointed "to consider what course they judge best be taken for the supply of the Towne." They were to report whether it is best to continue the present mill or build a new one in some other place, "and the said persons are desired and earnestly entreated by the Towne to consider seriously & speedily what they judge behoofeful in ye case; who also have power to call the Towne together as need shall require to declare w^t they apprehend requires in the case."

This committee called a town-meeting on February 26, 1665, and reported in favor of a new mill, and Capt. Pynchon agreed to spend 200 pounds in erecting the mill if the town would disburse the additional amount necessary to complete it. "But the Plantation being not cheerful to engage therein, Tryall was made what would be disbursed by particular persons; and Divers Psons did thereupon promise to allow Capt. Pynchon towards ye worke certain sums." Thirty one townsmen subscribed money and labor to that end.

At the same meeting on February 26, 1665, the town made a grant of fifty acres of upland, thirty acres of meadow, "if he would build a saw mill on fresh water brook or on the old Mil Stream," within three years, otherwise "this grant to be voyd."

This offer not being attractive, on August 11, 1666, the town voted Capt. Pynchon "for his encouragement," and in addition to the former grants, thirty acres on "Old Mill Streame," "the free use of ye said streame for ye said Worke, as also free liberty for felling and Sawing what trees he shall please that are upon the Comons belonging to ye Plantation except such trees as are between ye Bay path & Chicuppe River."

Great attention was given to highways, those necessary means of communication. The method of determining them is shown by the order of the Selectmen on "October ye 12th, 1650. It is ordered there shal be a high way of 5 or 6 rod broad from ye way that Leads to ye mill up to the cart bridge that is over the mill River & Soe from that bridge up into the Pyne plaine on ye South side of ye mill River to be laid in place most convenient by Benjamin Parsons, Jonathan Burt & Nathaniel Pritchard."

WITCHCRAFT IN SPRINGFIELD.—HUGH AND MARY PARSONS.

Certain shadows from the Dark Ages still cast a gloom over the New World in the seventeenth century, and it is not strange their malign influences should have fallen upon the little settlement of Springfield. The belief in witchcraft had prevailed throughout the world from the earliest times, and in even the most enlightened countries of Europe, the lives of thousands upon thousands of innocent persons had been sacrificed to the delusion. With the Puritan settlers this belief came to New England, but during the first sixty or seventy years of our history there were only a few isolated cases that found their way into court. Some forty years before the terrible outbreak of 1692, at Salem Village, Springfield had what was practically its sole visitation of the witchcraft craze. It came under strange and sad circumstances, only a part of which are disclosed by the record, but enough appears to make a distressing story, in which the alleged killing of an infant child by its insane mother is the central event.

Hugh Parsons, a sawyer and bricklayer, and Mary his wife, were the unfortunate principals in the sad case. They were married at Springfield October 27, 1645, her name before marriage being Mary Lewis. Three children were born to them: Hannah, b. August 7, 1646; Samuel, b. June 8, 1648, d. about the last of September, 1649; and Joshua, b. October 26, 1650, and said to have been killed by his mother March 4, 1651. Parsons seems to have been a roughspoken fellow, quick to engage in a quarrel, and both he and his wife appear to have shared the general belief in witches. Some trouble occurred in 1649 between them on the one hand and Reice Bedortha and his wife Blanche on the other, in which the Widow Marshfield, who nursed Mrs. Bedortha in confinement, took part. The result was a suit by Mrs. Marshfield against the Parsonses for slander, she alleging that Mary Parsons had called her a witch. Mr. Pynchon, as magistrate, found Mary guilty, and sentenced her to receive twenty lashes or pay £3 damages, which amount was paid in 24 bushels of Indian corn. This affair, together with other troubles, apparently affected Mary Parsons's health, and finally her mind gave way. Hugh fell under the suspicion of witchcraft, and the most absurd and childish stories were told of him. In February, 1651, Hugh and Mary Parsons were arraigned before Mr. Pynchon upon formal charges of witchcraft. The special complaints against Mary were the bewitching of Martha and Rebecca Moxon, children of the minister, while her husband was accused of practicing devilish arts upon perhaps a dozen persons. The records are not altogether satisfactory as to details, but it appears that the examination of Hugh Parsons was adjourned from time to time, beginning February 27, and ending about April 7, some of the witnesses giving their testimony. His wife was one of his accusers.

The testimony heard by the magistrate was nonsensical in the extreme, but no more so than such as was received in England in all seriousness by so great a judge as Sir Matthew Hale about this period. Here are some specimens of it: Hannah Lankton several times found the pudding cut from end to end when she took it from the bag, and on one such occasion Hugh Parsons came to her door about an hour after. He did not satisfactorily explain his errand to the court, which thereupon infers "that the spirit that bewitched the pudding brought him thither."

Thomas Miller joked Parsons about the pudding while eating dinner in the woods with a number of men engaged in lumbering. Parsons said nothing, but a few minutes later, when the men resumed work, Miller cut his leg.

Blanche Bedortha, having had some words with Parsons, suffered from unusual cutting pains after her next confinement. Parsons had trouble with Mr. Moxon about making bricks for the latter's chimneys, and threatened to "be even with him." The same week Mr. Moxon's children began to have fits. Then there were stories of bewitched cows, a strange disappearance of an ox tongue from a boiling kettle, and other queer doings about town. For one and all of these there was but one explanation,—the devilish doings of

Hugh Parsons. Mrs. Parsons also complained of rough treatment at her husband's hands, and of his frequent absences from home. There was evidence that he was at Longmeadow at the time of the death of his child Samuel, and that he received the news with no display of natural grief.

On March 4, 1651, before Hugh's examination was concluded, occurred the death of his youngest child, Joshua, an infant five months old. Mary at some time during March declared herself a witch, telling of her own misdoings in words which demonstrated her insanity, and either at the same time or later confessed to the murder of her baby She was sent to Boston for trial, as was her husband at the close of his long examination. Mary Parsons was dangerously ill at the sitting of the General Court in May, but was tried on the 13th upon an indictment for witchcraft and was acquitted. To the charge of murder she pleaded guilty and was sentenced to death. She was reprieved until May 29, and from the absence of any record of further action it is believed that she died in prison before that date.

The full record of Mary Parsons's case, as found in the Records of the General Court, is as follows:—

"The Court understanding that Mary Parsons now in prison. accused for a witch, is likely through weakness to dye before trial if it be deferred, doe order, that on the morrow, by eight of the clock in the morning, she be brought before and tried by, the Generall Court, the rather that Mr. Pynchon may be present to give his testimony in the case." —[This paragraph appears under date of 8d., 3mo., 1651.]

"May 13. 1651.—Mary Parsons, wife of Hugh Parsons, of Springfield, being committed to the prison for suspition of witchcraft, as also for murdering her oune child, was this day called forth and indicted for witchcraft: By the name of Mary Parsons you are heere before the Generall Court chargded in the name of this comon-wealth, that not having the feare of God before your eyes nor in your hart, being seduced by the divill, and yielding to his malitious motion, about the end of February last, at Springfield, to have familiarity, or consulted with a familiar spirit, making a covenant with him, and have used diverse divillish practises by witchcraft, to the hurt of the persons of Martha and Rebeckah Moxon, against the word of God, and the laws of this jurisdiction, long since made and published. To which indictment she pleaded not guilty: all evidences brought in against her being heard and examined, the Court found the evidences were not sufficient to prove hir a witch, and therefore she was cleared in that respect."

"At the same time she was indicted for murdering her child, by the name of Mary Parsons: You are here before the Generall Court, chardged in the name of this comon-wealth, that not having the feare of God before your eyes nor in your harte, being seduced by the divill, and yielding to his instigations and the wickedness of your owne harte about the beginning of March last, in Springfield, in or neere your owne howse, did willfully and most wickedly murder your owne child, against the word of God, and the lawes of this jurisdiction long since made and published. To which she acknowledged herself guilty."

"The Court finding hir guilty of murder by her own confession, &c., proceeded to judgment: You shall be carried from this place to the place from whence you came, and from thence to the place of execution, and there hang till you be dead."

A marginal note states that she was reprieved to the 29th of May.

Hugh Parsons's trial was put off for a year, probably from the difficulty of bringing witnesses to Boston. He was tried at a Court of Assistants May 12, 1652. Besides calling witnesses upon certain facts, the prosecution undertook to use in evidence the written testimony of most of the Springfield witnesses, which had been forwarded to the Bay by Mr. Pynchon; the accusation of the persons supposed to be bewitched were also offered, together with Mary Parsons's confession implicating her husband. The jury returned a remarkably discriminating verdict, declaring that "by the testimony of such as appeared in court" they find so much against the prisoner "as gives them ground not to clear him," but that if the General Court should hold that the written testimony, the "impeachment" or accusation of the alleged victims and the confession of the wife were "authentic testimonies according to law," then the jury find him "guilty of the sin of witchcraft."

Upon reviewing the case the General Court reversed the verdict and acquitted Parsons. The grounds of their action are not set out, but can readily be inferred from the verdict. The introduction of the depositions of absent witnesses, the hearsay evidence of the wife's confession and the ravings of the afflicted was too gross a violation of the prisoner's rights to be overlooked by a court which undertook to follow the forms of established law, and Parsons's life was saved. Had the court exercised such appelate jurisdiction in the Salem cases, forty years later, the colony would in all probability have been spared the disgrace of the barbarous executions that then took place.

Hugh Parsons never returned to Springfield. John Pynchon sold his lands and effects and sent him the proceeds. He, according to Bond's History of Watertown, went to that place, was married again and died there. The records relating to his case are as follows:—

"October 24, 1651.—It is ordered, that on the second Tuesday in the 3d month next, there shall be a Court of Assistants held at Boston, for the trial of those in prison accused of witchcraft, and that the most material witnesses at Springfield be summoned to the Court of Assistants. to give in their evidence against them accordingly."

May 31, 1652:—

Whereas Hugh Parsons of Springfield, was arrained and tried at a Court of Assistants, held at Boston, 12 of May, 1652, for not having the feare of God before his eyes, but being seduced by the instigation of the divill, in March, 1651, and divers times before and since, at Springfield, as was conceived, had familiar and wicked converse with the divill, and hath used diverse divillish practises, or witchcrafts, to the hurt of diverse persons, as by several witnesses and circumstances appeared, and was left by the grand jury for further triall for his life."

"The jury of trialls found him guilty. The Magistrates not consenting to the verdict of the jury, the cawes came legally to the Generall Court. The Generall Court, after the prisoner was called to the barr for triall of his life, perusing and considering the evidences brought in against the said Hugh Parsons, accused for witchcraft, they judged he was not legally guilty of witchcraft, and so not to dye by law."

Historians who have studied the case of Mary Parsons as narrated in the records have differed in their conclusions as to her guilt and as to whether or not she suffered the death penalty. Some have come to the conclusion that her confession of the murder of her child was only an insane delusion, no more to be relied upon than her self-accusation of familiarity with the devil, or the story which it is recorded she told Constable Thomas Cooper to the effect that she with her husband and two women, all under the spell of witchcraft, had passed a night prowling about Stebbins's lot, being, she said, "sometimes like cats, and sometimes in our own shape." Be that as it may, the townspeople unquestionably believed her guilty. The entry in the town records of deaths, in the handwriting of Henry Burt, sets out that: "Josua Parsons, the sonn of Hugh Parsons, was kild by Mary Parsons his wife, the 4 day of ye 4 mon. 1651." While this does not prove the fact of her guilt, it establishes that it was regarded as sufficiently proved to be made a matter of official record.

Whether the death sentence was carried into effect would seem to be a question of more doubt. She was doubtless just lingering betwen life and death, a mental and physical wreck, at the time of her trial before the General Court. Unfortunately the records of deaths in Boston at that period in question were very imperfect, and while her name does not appear therein we can draw no inference one way or the other from its absence. Charles W. Upham, in "Salem Witchcraft," sums up as follows all that we can justly infer as to the outcome of the sad case:—

"We are left in doubt as to the fate of Mary Parsons. There is a marginal entry on the records to the effect that she was reprieved to the 29th of May. Neither Johnson (author of "Wonder Working Providence") nor Hutchinson (in his "History of Massachusetts Bay") seem to have thought that the sentence was ever carried into effect. It clearly never ought to have been. The woman was in a weak and dying condition, her mind was probably broken down,—the victim of that peculiar kind of mania—partaking of the character of a religious fanaticism and a perversion of ideas—that has often lead to child murder."

No other case of witchcraft attended with serious results was ever brought to trial in Springfield after the Parsons prosecutions. It is not unlikely that the sad results of these cases opened the eyes of the people to the folly of the current belief,—and the Connecticut Valley was too far removed from Boston for the influence of the Puritan clergy to be as effective in the stimulation of witchhunting as it was yet to prove in the tragedies of Salem. We can easily condemn our ancestors for their superstition and folly, yet we should remember that only a few generations separated them from the darkest years of Christendom, and they rather deserve praise for so speedily throwing off under their new conditions the yoke of bondage to fear of supernatural influences.

PYNCHON'S HERESY.—HIS BOOK BURNED IN THE MARKET PLACE AT BOSTON.

William Pynchon's career in New England was brought to a sudden termination about the year 1651, under circumstances which reveal a side of his character that we should not have looked for in the enterprising merchant and pioneer and the stern magistrate. In 1650, after fourteen years residence in Springfield, he published a book entitled "The Meritorious Price of Man's Redemption, Justification, &c."

This work was a protest against the Calvinistic theology as preached by the clergy of that day, and proves Mr. Pynchon to have been a profound scholar, a logical writer, and an independent thinker. He read his Bible in the original tongues, and while a sincere believer in the literal truth of the Scriptures and in the exact fulfillment of prophecy, he was his own interpreter and he would not accept as a part of his faith the system which Calvin had framed in all its terrible details. In his book he condemned specially the doctrine that Christ suffered the wrath of God and the torments of hell to pay man's debt to his Creator. His theory of the atonement was that, inasmuch as sin came into the world through Adam's disobedience, so Christ by his perfect obedience, paid the full price of our redemption." The killing of Jesus was not the display of God's wrath, but was the work of the devil through his instruments, the Jews and the Roman soldiers. The theory that the guilt of the world was laid upon or imputed to Christ he denounced unsparingly. "If Christ bare Adam's sin," he says, "by God's imputation, and his curse really, then you make Christ to be dead in sin." Again:—

"If our Mediator had stood as a guilty sinner before God by his imputing of our sins to him, Then he could not have been a fit person in God's esteem to do the office of Mediator for our Redemption."

A large part of the work deals with the subtleties and abstractions of now by-gone theology, but the one thought stands out strongly that God the Father is a God of Justice, and the writer burns with indignation at the unworthy conceptions of the Almighty which the old theologians taught. Quoting Ezekiel's words, "One man shall not die for another's sin," he adds:—

"By this rule of justice God cannot inflict the torments of hell upon an innocent to redeem a guilty person.

"I hold it a point of gross injustice for any Court of Magistrates to torture an innocent person for the redemption of a gross Malefactor."

On another page he writes:—

"There is no need that our blessed Mediator should pay both the price of his Mediatorial obedience, and also bear the Curse of the Law for our redemption.

"I never heard that ever any Turkish Tyrant did require such double satisfaction of any Redeemer for the Redemption of Galley slaves. I never heard that ever any Tyrant did require to pay both the full price that they demanded for their redemption of their Galley-slaves, and to bear their punishment of their curse and slavery also in their stead. Therefore, I cannot choose but wonder at the common doctrine of imputation, because it makes God the Father more rigid in the price of our Redemption than ever Turkish Tyrant was, and to be a harder Creditor in the point of satisfaction than ever any rigid Creditor was among men."

The book is written in the form of a dialogue between a tradesman, who is seeking for light, and a minister, who replies to his queries in accordance to Mr. Pynchon's views. It is of great rarity, only three copies being known to exist at the present time. One copy is in the Congregational library in Boston, one is owned by Dr. Thomas R. Pynchon, of Hartford, and the other is in the British Museum. Beginning on page 89 of the present volume is reprinted substantially the whole of Mr. Pynchon's book, omitting the questions, the answers to which are sufficiently complete in themselves for an understanding of the scope and purpose of the work.

In view of the rigid adherence to the established doctrines enforced by the Massachusetts clergy, at that time, it is not to be wondered that Mr. Pynchon's book should have aroused a storm of wrath and indignation. The book, which was printed in London by James Moxon (very likely a kinsman of the Springfield minister), was received in Boston early in October, 1650. Copies of it were laid before the General Court, which was then in session, and were read by the members with undisguised horror. Such a heretical publication, in their view, tended to undermine the very foundations of the colony. The following vote was passed:—

"October 16, 1650.—The General Court now sittinge at Boston in New England, this sixteenth of October, 1650. There was brought to our hands a book written, as was therein subscribed, by William Pynchon, gent, in New England, entitled The Meritorious Price of our Redemption, Justification, &c., clearing it from some common Errors, &c., which booke, brought over here by a shippe a few days since, and contayninge many errors & heresies generally condemned by al orthodox writers that we have met with, we have judged it meete and necessary for vindication of the truth, so far as in us lyes, as also to keep and preserve the people here committed to our care & trust in the true knowledge & fayth of our Lord Jesus Christ, & of our own redemption by him, as likewise for the clearing of ourselves to our Christian brethren and others in England, (where this book was printed and dispersed,) hereby protest our innocency, as being neither partyes nor privy to the writing, composing, printing, nor divulging thereof; but that on the contrary, we detest and abhorre many of the opinions & assertions therein as false, eroneous, hereticall; yea, & whatsoever is contayned in the said book which are contrary to the Scriptures of the Old and New Testament, & the generall received doctrine of the orthodox churches extant since the time of the last and best reformation, & for proof and evidence of our sincere and playne meaning therein, we do hereby condemn the said book to be burned in the Market Place, at Boston, by the Common Executioner, on the morrow immediately after lecture, & doe purpose with all convenient speed to convent the said William Pynchon before authority, to find out whether the said William Pynchon will owne the said book as his or not; which if he doth, we purpose (God willing) to proceed with him according to his demerits, unless he retract the same, & give full satisfaction both here & by some second writing, to be printed and dispersed in England; all which we thought needful, for the reasons above aleaged, to make known by this short protestation & declaration. Also we further purpose, with what convenient speed we may, to appoynt some fitt person to make particular answer to all materiall and controversyall passages in the said book, & to publish the same in print, that so the errors and falsityes therein may be fully discovered, the truth cleared, & the minds of those that love & seek after truth confirmed therein."

It being put to vote in the House of Deputies six of its members voted in the negative, viz: Capt. William Hathorne, the Speaker, and Henry Bartholomew of Salem; Joseph Hills of Malden, Richard Walker of Reading, Stephen Kingsley of Braintree, and Edward Holyoke, sitting for Springfield,— the father of Elizur Holyoke.

The following was also adopted immediately after the passage of the preceding:—

"It is agreed uppon by the whole Court that Mr. Norton, one of the reverend elders of Ipswich, should be entreated to answer Mr. Pynchon's book with all convenient speed."

"It is ordered that the foregoing declaration concerning the book subscribed by the name of William Pynchon, in New England, gent, should be signed by the Secretary, and sent into England to be printed there."

"It is ordered that William Pynchon shall be summoned to appeare before the next General Court of Election, on the first day of their sitting to give his answer for the book printed and published under the name of William Pynchon, in New England, gent., entitled the Meritorious Price of our Redemption, Justification, &c., & not to depart without leave from the Court."

The books were accordingly burned forthwith in the market place, a few copies presumably being saved for the use of the authorities and the clergymen who were interested in bringing the author either to justice or to a more orthodox frame of mind.

Mr. Pynchon's disappointment and grief at the cruel destruction of the fruit of his labor must have been intense. He had published the book, undoubtedly, as a labor of love, hoping to spread among his people a more wholesome religious spirit than that inspired by the old theology, and probably without realizing that he was to be reproached with attempting to overturn Christianity and to be summoned to court like a common criminal.

He attended the May session of the General Court in 1651, both in the capacity of a witness against the unfortunate Mary Parsons and to answer to the complaint as to his book. He was detained a fortnight or so in Boston, and at the request of the Court he conferred with the leading clergymen of the colony about his alleged heresies. One layman even with Mr. Pynchon's learning, could hardly compete in argument with three eminent divines skilled in the discussion of the metaphysical niceties in which the schools of that day delighted. As a result of a prolonged conference he practically acknowledged himself in error on a single point—that Christ's sufferings were more than mere trials of obedience, as he said, but were appointed as the "due punishment for our sins." He did not admit, however, nor did he ever afterward, that Christ actually suffered the torments of hell. Still, it was a great concession and was so regarded by the Court, as will be seen by the record:

"May 22, 1651.—Mr. William Pynchon, being summoned to appear before the Generall Court, according to their order, the last session, made his appearance before the Court, and being demaunded whether that book which goes under his name, and then presented to him, was his or not, he answered for the substance of the book, he owned it to be his.

"Whereuppon the Court, out of their tender respect to him, ordered him liberty to conferr with all the reverend elders now present, or such of them as he should desire and choose. At last he took it into consideration, and returned his mind at the present in writing, under his hand, viz:—

According to the Court's advice, I have conferred with the Reverend Mr. Cotton, Mr. Norrice, and Mr. Norton, about some points of the greatest consequence in my booke, and I hope I have so explained my meaning to them as to take off the worst construction, and it hath pleased God to let me see that I have not spoken in my booke so fully of the price and merrit of Christ's sufferings as I should have done, for in my book I call them but trials of his obedience, yet intending thereby to amplifie and exalt the mediatorial obedience of Christ as the only meritorious price of man's redemption. But now at present I am much inclined to think that his sufferings were appointd by God for a farther end, namely, as the due punishment for our sins by way of satisfaction to divine justice for man's redemption.

Subscribed your humble servant in all dutifull respects,

WILLIAM PYNCHON.

Boston 9: 3mo., 1651.

"The Court finding by Mr. Pynchon's writing, given into the Court, that through the blessing of God on the paines of the reverend elders to convince him of his errors in his booke conceive that he is in a hopeful way to give good satisfaction, and therefore at his request, judge it meete to grant him liberty, respecting the present troubles of his family, to return home some day the next week if he please, and that he shall have Mr. Norton's answer to his booke up with him, to consider thereof, that so at the next sesion of this Court, being the 14th of October next, he may give all due satisfaction as is hoped for and desired, to which session he is hereby enjoyned to make his personall appearance for that end.

"It is ordered that thanks be given by this Court to Mr. John Norton for his worthy paynes in his full answer to Mr. Pynchon's book, which at their desire he made, & since presented them with: & as a recompence for his paynes and good service therein, doe order that the Treasurer shall pay him twenty pounds out of the next levy."

What Mr. Pynchon's family troubles were, to which the Court refers, we do not know, but it is not unlikely that their existence made him less firm in resisting the urgent arguments of the clergymen than one would have expected. He must have returned to Springfield saddened and disheartened, having found his faithful work of fifteen years in the wilderness and his success in building up the chief settlement of the Connecticut valley all set at naught by his old associ-

ates in Boston in view of what they felt to be his almost un-
pardonable sin, the writing of the truth as he believed it.

During the summer which followed William Pynchon's
plans for the future were formed.   He was in no mood for a
contest; he was an old man and he knew that the outcome
would be disgrace, confiscation of his property, ruin, and
the destruction of his hopes and plans for the career of his
son.   He had retracted all that he could conscientiously do;
the theologians were not satisfied, and if he remained in the
colony a conflict must surely come, and with it ruin.   He
would return to England.   The country which had perse-
cuted the Pilgrims would now shelter him from New England by the Puritans and there he could pass his closing days
in peace.   It is a sad commentary on the extremes to which
the Bay authorities proceeded.

In pursuance of his plans he conveyed to his son John
Pynchon, as a gift, on September 28, 1651, all his lands and
buildings on both sides of the Connecticut River at Springfield.   At this time his land grants from the town aggre-
gated about 280 acres, and the   conveyance   made   John
Pynchon the largest land owner in the town.   He also succeeded to his father's business and later to his position as
magistrate.

The Court met according to adjournment on the 14th of
October, but Mr. Pynchon did not appear.   Ten days later,
on the 24th, the following was entered on the records:—

"The Court doth judge it meete and is willing, that all patience be exercised toward Mr. William Pynchon, that, if it
be possible, he may be reduced into the way of truth and that
he might renounce the errors and heresies published in his
book, and for that end, doe give him time to the next Generall
Court, in May, more thoroughly to consider of the said errors and heresies in his said book, and well to weigh the judi-
cious answer of Mr. John Norton, and that he may give full
satisfaction for his offence, which they more desire than to
proceed to so great a censure as his offence deserves.   In case
he should not give good satisfaction, the Court doth therefore

order, that the judgment of the cawse be suspended till the honorable Court in May next, and that Mr. William Pynchon be enjoyned under the penalty of one hundred pounds to make his personall appearance at and before the next Generall Court, to give full answer to satisfaction if it may be, or otherwise to stand to the judgment and censure of the Court."

"It is ordered by this Court that the answer to Mr. Pynchon's book written by Mr. John Norton, shall be sent to England to be printed."

Here ends the record history of this remarkable case. Mr. Pynchon and his wife, and Rev. Mr. Moxon and family, left Springfield and returned to England, but the date of departure is not known. His son-in-law, Henry Smith, followed him early the next year. Whether the prosecution was quietly dropped, or whether he went in defiance of the authorities, there is nothing of record to show. In the rural village of Wraysbury, England, not far from Windsor, Mr. Pynchon passed the rest of his life in tranquility. He published several theological works, among others a rejoinder to Mr. Norton's reply to his former book. He died October 29, 1662, aged 72.

The Rev. John Norton, who wrote the reply to Mr. Pynchon's book, was a clergyman of marked ability, and became soon afterward minister of the First Church in Boston. It was from his home estate that his widow gave, years afterward, the land on which the Old South Church was built. He was a vigorous writer and one of the most skilful defenders of Calvinistic theology. In his reply he took up Pynchon's book, paragraph by paragraph and combatted his unanswerable logic. The book he declared contained three "damnable heresies," the results of which would be these:—

"The first holdeth us in all our sin, and continueth the full wrath of God abiding upon us.

"The second takes away our saviour.

"The third takes away our righteousness and our justification.

"What need the Enemy of Jesus, grace and souls add more?"

Mr. Norton's earnestness in the matter and his kindly personal feeling for Mr. Pynchon are well expressed in the concluding paragraph of his book, in which he expresses the hope "that truth may look down from heaven........preserve the Reader from every false way, and lead him into all truth; magnifie his compassion in the pardon and recovery of the Author, a person in many respects to be very much tendered of us; in so saving of him (though as by fire) as that his rising again may be much more advantageous to the truth, comfortable to the people of God, and honourable to himself, than his fall hath been scandalous, grieving or dishonorable."

William Pynchon's book, literally and figuratively, was "the voice of one crying in the wilderness." The details of his theology are of less importance to us than the fact that he alone in all New England dared to proclaim the faith that was in him when that faith was opposed to the lawfully established religion. It was a marked step forward in the evolution of religious truth, and we see in it a glimmering of the great light which many years later was to break over New England and dispel the gloom of an antequated and cruel theology. When he tests the rules of divine justice by the common standard of man's justice, he makes a bold departure from Calvinism, and one recognizes the same spirit which has inspired others in later times.

Several of Pynchon's friends in England addressed appeals to the Governor and Council and the clergy in his behalf. The first which is printed in Mr. Norton's book, is a signed reply by five of the leading Massachusetts ministers to the appeal of certain English clergymen, and the second is the reply of the Governor and Council to a letter from Sir Henry Vane, both of which follow Mr. Pynchon's book.

On page 90, eleventh line, which reads, "Though I say that Christ did suffer," should read "did not suffer."

THE
MERITORIOUS PRICE
O F
Our Redemption, Iuſtification, &c.

Cleering it from ſome common Errors;

And proving,

Part I.
1. That Chriſt did not ſuffer for us thoſe unutterable torments of Gods wrath, that commonly are called Hell-torments, to redeem our ſoules from them.
2. That Chriſt did not bear our ſins by Gods imputation, and therefore he did not bear the curſe of the Law for them.

Part II.
3. That Chriſt hath redeemed us from the curſe of the Law (not by ſuffering the ſaid curſe for us, but) by a ſatisfactory price of attonement; *viz.* by paying or performing unto his Father that invaluable precious thing of his Mediatoriall obedience, wherof his Mediatoriall Sacrifice of attonement was the maſter-piece.
4. A ſinners righteouſneſſe or juſtification is explained, and cleered from ſome common Errors.

By *William Pinchin*, Gentleman, in New-England.

The Mediator ſaith thus to his Father in *Pſal* 40.8,10.
I delight to do thy will O my God, yea thy Law is within my heart: (viz.) I delight to do thy will, or Law, as a Mediator.
I have not hid thy righteouſneſſe within my heart, I have declared thy faithfulneſſe, and thy ſalvation: Namely, I have not hid thy righteouſneſſe, or thy way of making ſinners righteous, but have declared it by the performance of my Mediatoriall Sacrifice of attonement, as the procuring cauſe of thy attonement, to the great Congregation for their everlaſting righteouſneſſe.

L O N D O N.
Printed by J. M. for *George Whittington*, and *James Moxon*, and are to be ſold at the blue Anchor in Corn-hill neer the Royall Exchange. 1650.

I hold that Jesus Christ our Mediator did pay the full price of our Redemption to his Father by the merit of his mediatorial obedience, which according to God's determinate counsel, was tried through suffering, inflicted upon his body as upon a Malefactor, by Satan and his Instruments.

I put as much worth and efficacy in Christ's Mediatorial obedience so tried, as they do that pleade most for our redemption by his suffering God's wrath for us.

They place the price of our Redemption in his suffering God's wrath for us in the full weight and measure, as it is due to our sins by the curse of the Law: I place the price of our redemption in the merit of his Media-torial obedience, whereof his Mediatorial sacrifice of Atonement was the Master-piece.

I agree with others in this, that divine wrath is fully satisfied for the sins of the Elect, by the merit of Christ's Mediatorial obedience. I differ from others in this, namely, in the manner of his satisfaction; I say that Christ did suffer God's wrath for our sins, by suffering the extremity of his wrath; neither did he suffer the torments of hell, neither in his body, nor in his soul, nor any degree of God's wrath at all.

Secondly, Though I say that Christ did suffer his Father's wrath nei-ther in whole nor in part; yet I affirm that he suffered all things that his Father did appoint him to suffer, in all circumstances, just according to the predictions of all the Prophets even to nodding of the head, and the spitting of the face, as these Scriptures do testifie.

1. Peter told the Jews that they had killed the Prince of Life, as God before had showed by the mouth of all the Prophets, that Christ should suffer, and fulfilled it so. Acts 3.17, 18.

2. Christ did expressly by his disciples tell that he must go to Jerusalem and suffer many things of the Elders and chief Priests and Scribes, and be killed and raised again the third day. Mat. 16.21.

3. After his resurrection he said to the two Disciples, O fools, and slow of heart to believe all that the Prophets have spoken: Ought not Christ to suffer these things and to enter into his glory? Luke 24.25, and in verse 44.46 he said thus to all his Disciples: These are the words which I speak unto you, that all things must be fulfilled which are written in the Law of Moses, in the Prophets and in the Psalms concerning me; thus it is written, and thus it behoved Christ to suffer and rise again from the dead on the third day.

4. Paul told the men of Antioch that the Rulers of the Jews condemned him because they knew not the voices of the Prophets concerning him, and therefore though they found no cause of death in him, yet they desired Pilate that he should be slain, and when they had fulfilled all things that were written of him, they took him down from the tree, and laid him in a sepulchre. Acts 13.27, 28, 29,—mark this phrase, They fulfilled all things that were written of him; if they fulfilled all his sufferings, then it was not God's wrath that he suffered.

5. The Lord told Adam not only that the promised seed should break the devil's head-plot, but also that the devil should crucifie him and pierce him in the foot-sole. Gen. 3.15. The devil did it by his instrument, the Scribes and the Pharisees, by Pilate and the Roman soldiers.

The Vindication of Gen. 2.17.—In the day thou eatest thereof thou shall die the death.

You say that the term Thou is thou in thine own person, and thou in thy posterity; thus far I approve of your exposition; but whereas you extend the term Thou unto the Redeemer, this last clause I dislike; for the death and curse here threatened cannot extend itself unto the Redeemer in the manner of his working out our redemption.

This Text doth not comprehend Jesus Christ within the compass of it, for this Text is a part of the Covenant only that God made with Adam and his posterity, respecting the happiness they had by Creation.

Death here threatened concerns Adam and his fallen posterity only therefore Christ cannot be included within this death.

God laid down this rule of Justice to Adam in the time of innocency, Why should the Mediator be comprehended under the term Thou? The nature of death intended in this Text is such as it was altogether impossible the Mediator should suffer it.

The death here threatened must be understood primarily of a spiritual death in sin.

Calvin in Gen. 2.17, demandeth what kind of death it was, that God threatened to fall upon Adam in this Text; he answereth to this purpose. It seemeth to me (saith he) that we must fetch the definition thereof from the contrary: Consider (saith he) from what life Adam fell, at the first (saith he) he was created in every part of his body and soul with pure qualities after the image of God, therefore on the contrary (saith he) by dying the death is meant, that he should be emptied of all the image of God, and possessed with corrupt qualities as soon as ever he did but eat of the forbidden fruit.

If there be any good and necessary reason (as there is) to exempt our Mediator from the first cursed spiritual death, then there is good reason also to exempt him from suffering any other curse of the Law whatsoever.

Examine the particulars of any other curse of the Law, and they will be found to be such as Christ could not suffer Diseases, natural death, putrefaction of body after death, eternal death, are curses of the law. Christ did not bear diseases and bodily infirmities, yet by common doctrine of imputation you must affirm it; nor suffer natural death in our stead, nor see corruption, nor suffer eternal death, therefore he did not suffer the cursed death meant, Gen. 2.17.

My reasons why Christ could not suffer eternal death for our redemptions therefrom, are first, Then he must have suffered all other curses of the Law to redeem us from them, but I have shown that utterly impossible immediately before. 2. Then he did descend locally into hell itself to suffer it there: for no man can suffer death eternal in this life: no man can suffer the second death after this life is ended.

If Christ bare Adam's sin by God's imputation, and his curse really, then you make Christ to be dead in sin.

Consider the true force of the word Impute in the natural signification thereof, and then I believe you will acknowledge that it cannot stand with the justice of God to impute our sins to our innocent Saviour; for to impute sin to any is to account them for guilty sinners, and to impute the guilt of other men's sins to any is to account them guilty of other men's by imputation.

If our Mediator had stood as a guilty sinner before God by his imputing of our sins to him, Then he could not have been a fit person in God's esteem to do the office of Mediator for our Redemption.

The common doctrine of imputation is I know not what kind of imputation; it is such a strange kind of imputation, it differs from all the several sorts of imputing sin to any that ever I can meet withal in all the Scriptures.

———————————

The Vindication of Isaiah 53.4.—Surely he hath born our griefs, and carried our sorrows.

He saith not only (saith M. Jacob) that he sustained sorrows but (our) sorrows: yea, the Text hath it more significantly (our very) sorrows themselves, that is to say, those sorrows that else we should have born.

The Evangelist Mathew hath expounded this text in a quite contrary sense, Mat. 8.17, saying that this Text was fulfilled when Christ did bear our infirmities and sickness from the sick, not as a Porter bears a burthen by laying them on his own body, but bearing away by his own power.

Isa. 53.5. But he was wounded for our transgressions, he was bruised for our iniquities. The chastisement of our peace was upon him, and with his stripes we are healed.

These words I confess do plainly prove that Christ did bear divers wounds, bruises, and stripes for our peace and healing: but yet the Text doth not say that he bare these wounds, bruises, and stripes of God's wrath for our sins.

1. It was Satan by his instruments that wounded and bruised Christ, according to God's prediction, Gen. 3.15.

2. Christ bare these wounds, bruises and stripes in his body only, not in his soul; for his soul was not capable of bearing wounds. Satan could not wound his soul: the Jews fulfilled all his sufferings, Acts 13.27, 29. Peter expounds the Text of his bodily sufferings only, 1. Pet. 2.24. If Peter's Phraise, He bear our sins in his body on the tree, had meant anything of his bearing God's wrath for our sins, the case of his sufferings had not been a fit example to exhort to patience, his appeal to God had not been suitable. 3. The end was a trial of his mediatorial obedience and our peace.

I hold it necessary often to remember this distinction, namely, that Christ suffered both as a malefactor and as a Mediator at one and the same time.

He bare our sins in his body upon the tree. 1 Peter, 2.24. Peter means he bare the punishment of sin (inflicted according to the sentence of Piltae) in his body on the tree: sin is often put for the punishment of sin.

I will show you how Christ did bear our sins divers ways, in several senses.

1. When he bare our sins as I have expounded, Isa. 53.4.

2. As our Priest and sacrifice, as I have expounded. Isa. 53.5.

3. As a Porter bears a burden, as I have expounded. 1 Peter 2.24.

4. When he patiently bear our sinful imputations, and false accusations and imputations of the malignant Jews. Psa. 40.12. Psa. 69.5. In these words Christ doth not complain or grudge against his Father for his im-

puting of our sins unto him as the common doctrine of Imputation doth speak.

The Vindication of Isaiah, 53.6.—All we like sheep gone astray, we have turned every one to his own way, and the Lord hath laid on
him the iniquity of us all.

The Lord laid not the sin of the Elect upon Christ by imputation. The true manner how the Lord laid all our iniquities upon Christ, was the very same manner as the Lord laid the sins of Israel upon the Priest and sacrifice and no other.

The Priest bare the iniquity of the holy things by his Priestly appearing before Jehovah with his priestly apparel, especially with the golden plate. Exo. 28.30, he bare the iniquity of the Congregation by eating the people's sin-offering in the holy place to make atonement. Lev. 10.17. The Lord laid all our sins upon Christ as upon our sacrifice, Isa. 53.12, where dying, sin intercession, are Synonimas. He bare the sins of men, namely, by his Mediatorial sacrifice. God laid all our sins upon Christ as our sacrifice of atonement. In this sense Paul explaineth the Levitical bearing of sin. IIb. 9.26, 28.

If you will build the common doctrine of imputation upon this phrase, The Lord laid all our iniquities upon Christ, then by the same phrase you must affirm that the Father laid all our sins upon himself, for the Father is said to bear our sins as well as Christ, Paul 25.18 & 32.1, and elsewhere.

Those three terms, Blessed is the man whose transgression is born, whose sin is covered, whose iniquity is not imputed, are Synonimas and they do sweetly expound each other, and they do also set out the true manner how sinners are made just and blessed, namely, where their sins are born away, covered, and not imputated by the Father's merciful atonement, pardon, and forgiveness.

The word [in Hebrew] which is translated in verse 6, hath laid upon, is translated in the 12 verse of this 25 chapter hath made intercession and therefore the Verb signifying both incurrere fecit and intercessit, is to make a foundation for the doctrine of imputation, and of Christ's suffering God's wrath.

The Vindication of Exo. 20.10, Lev. 1.4, & 4.29, Lev. 8.14 & 16.20,21.

Every owner must impose both his hands upon the head of the sin-offering, this imposition of hands did (as the asserters of the doctrine of imputation say) typifie the Lord's laying our sin upon Christ by imputation: and so godly expositors do understand it. See Exo. 20.10, Lev. 1.14, and 4.29, 8.14, 16.20, 21.

A private man's imposition cannot represent God's act, the imposition of the hands of the Elders cannot, for the Elders' actions represent the Churches action: neither can the imposition of the Priests and High Priests, they were types of Christ's Priestly nature, and not of the Father.

Imposition of hands with confession of sins upon the head of the sin-offering, signified the owner's faith of dependance.

If you make the act of laying on of hands on the sin-offering, to signifie God's laying our sins upon Christ by imputation, then the same act
of laying on of hands with confession of sins upon the Scape-goat must
also signifie that God did impute our sins to Christ as well after he was
escaped from death by his resurrection, as when he made his oblation here
upon earth, and then by this doctrine Christ is gone as a guilty sinner
into heaven.

But the Hebrew Doctors did not understand this imposition of hands
with confession of sins of God's imputation: but they understood it to
be a typical sign of the faith of dependance upon Christ's sacrifice of
Atonement; and so much the prayer of the High Priest imports. See
Ainsworth, Lev. 16.21.

If God's imputing of the sins of the Elect to Christ was the cause of
God's extreme wrath upon him, then by the same reason Christ doth still
bear the wrath of God, for Christ doth still bear our sins in heaven as
much as ever he bare them upon earth.

The Vindication of 2 Cor. 5.21.—God made him to be sin for us which
Knew no sin.

The meaning of these words is not that he was made of sin for God's
imputation, but that he was made sin for us, that is to say, a sacrifice for
our sin; sin is often used for sin-offering, sacrifices for sin are often called
sin: the word Made is a word of Election and Ordination.

The Apostle doth explain the word Sin. Psal. 40.6, thus for sin, Heb.
10.6, therefore seeing the Apostle doth explain in the word Sin by the
particle for, I may well conclude that Christ was not made sin by Imputation.

The water of purification from sin is called sin, Numb.19.9. The money
employed to buy the publique sacrifice for sin, is called trespass-money,
2 King 16, and in this sense God made Christ to be sin.

The Vindication of Mat. 26.37, Mark 14.33, Luke 2.53.

Mathew saith that Christ was sorrowful and grievously troubled, Chap.
26.37. Mark saith, that he was sore afraid and amazed. Chap. 14.33.
Luke saith that Christ was in agony, Chap. 22.53. Christ made all this
adoe about a bodily death only.

Only do but consider what a horrid thing to human nature the death
of the body is, then consider that Christ had a true human nature, and
therefore why should he not be troubled with the fear of death as much
as human nature could be without sin?

All mankind ought to desire and endeavor to preserve their natural lives
as much as lies in them in the use of means, and therefore seeing Christ
as he was true man, could not prevent his death by the use of means:
he was bound to be troubled for the sense of death as much as any
other man.

These were the true causes why Christ was so much pained in his mind
with the fear of death not only that night before his death, but at other
times also long before.

But Mathew and Mark in the place cited speak only of these sorrows which fell upon him in the night before his death: Mathew saith, he began grievously to be troubled, i.e. he began afresh to be troubled with a nearer apprehension of his death than formerly: M. Calvin in his Harmony upon those words, speaks to this effect: We have seen (saith he) our Lord wrestling with the fear of death before; but now (saith he) he buckleth his hands with the temptation. Mathew calls it the beginning of sorrow.

By these sentences of M. Calvin, we may see, that Christ was deeply touchd with the fear of death, for he wept and groaned in spirit, and troubled himself for the death of Lazarus.

I cannot apprehend that he was afraid of the wrath of God for our sin in the night before his death; for then he could not have said as he did, I have set the Lord alwaies before my sons, he's at my right hand, Psa.16.8, therefore I shall not be moved. I cannot apprehend that his troubled fear exceeded the bounds of natural fear.

These sentences of M. Calvin may advise us how we do attribute such a kind of fear to Christ as might disorder his pure, natural affections, which doubtless would have fallen upon him, if he had undergone the pain of the loss for our sins, such as the damned do feel in hell, as the common Doctrine of Imputation doth teach.

And if he had died without manifesting fear of death, it would have occasioned wofull heresie; yea, notwithstanding the evident proof given of his human nature, sundry hereticks have denied the truth of his human nature; it was necessary therefore that he should be pinched with the fear of death as much as his true human nature could bear without sin, as Calvin well observeth.

If fear of death which he expressed to his Disciples in the night before his death, had risen on the sense of his Father's wrath inflicted upon him for our sin, then you must say that he suffered his Father's wrath for our sins six days before this, for six days before this he spake those words, Luke 12.50, where our Saviour doth express as much distress of mind as here: yet I know no expositor that ever gathered so much from this place of Luke.

Our Saviour tells the two sons of Zebedee they must drink of his cup and be baptised with his baptism, by these two expressions which are Synoniams or equivalent, our Saviour doth inform the two sons of Zebedee what the true nature of his sacrifice should be, viz: no other but such only as they should one day suffer from the hands of tyrants.

His son was not touched with any suffering from God's wrath at all, except by way of sympathy from his bodily sufferings only.

If the circumstances of his agony be well weighed, it will appear that it did not proceed from his Father's wrath but from his natural fear of death only: because he must be stricken with the fear of death as much as his true nature could bear; he must be touched with the fear of death in a great measure (as the Prophets did foretell.) Add to these pains of his mind, his earnest prayers to be delivered from his natural fear of death: the fear of death doth often cause men to sweat and earnestly pray; as he was man he must be touched with the fear of death, as he was Mediator he must fully and wholly overcome his natural fear of death by prayers; therefore there was no necessity for him to pray, and to strive in prayer until he overcome it, as I shall further explain the matter by and by, in Hebrews 5.7.

We must observe the due time of every action, the manner, the place and all other circumstances to fulfill every circumstance just as the Prophets had foretold nothing must fail; if he had failed in the least circumstance he had failed in all; and his human nature could not be exact in these circumstances without the concurrence of the divine nature: in all these respects his natural fear of death could not chuse, but be very often in mind, and as often to put him unto pain till he had overcome it.

Scanderberg was in such agony when he was fighting against the Turks, that the blood hath been seen to burst out of his lips with very eagerness of spirit only. I have heard also from credible persons, that Alexander the Great did sweat blood in the courageous defence of himself and others. The sweating sickness caused many to sweat out of their bodies a bloody humour, and yet many did recover and live many years after, but if their sweating blood had been a sign of God's wrath upon their souls (as you say it was in Christ) then I think they could not have lived any longer by the strength of nature.

Do but consider a little more seriously what a horrid thing to nature the approach of death is; see in how many horrid expressions David doth describe it, Psa. 116.3, & 18.4, & 55.4,5.

Suppose Adam in his innocency had grappled with the fear of death: like enough it would have caused a violent sweat all over his body.

It's no strange new doctrine to make the natural fear of death to be the cause of Christ's agony, seeing other learned men do affirm it. Christopher Carlisle in his treaties of Christ's descent into hell, p. 46, saith thus. Was not Christ extremely afflicted when he for fear of death sweat drops in quantity as thick as drops of blood? John Fryh a godly Martyr saith thus in his answer to Sir Thomas Moor, B. 2: Christ did not only weep but he feared so sore that he sweat drops like drops of blood running down upon the earth, which was more than to weep. Now (saith he) if I should ask you why Christ feared, and sweat so sore? what would you answer me? was it for fear of the pains of purgatory? he that shall so answer is worthy to be laughed to scorn, wherefore then was it? Verily even for the fear of death, as it appeareth plainly by his prayer, for he prayed to his Father, saying, If it be possible, let this cup pass from me.

It passeth my understanding to find out how an Angel could support our Saviour under the sense of his Father's wrath. Can Angels appease God's wrath? or can Angels support a man's soul to bear it? It's absurd to think so. God will not afford the least drop of water to cool any man's tongue that is tormented in the flames of his wrath: therefore that cannot be the reason.

But on the contrary it's evident that God doth often use to comfort his people against the fear of death, by Ministry of Angels.

The Father's sending of an Angel to comfort his son in his agony, was not an evidence that the Father was angry with him for our sin, but it was a sure evidence to him that his Father was highly well-pleased with him even in the time of his agony.

Good reasons there were why Christ should be more afraid of death than many Martyrs have been, namely, for the clear manifestation of his human nature, and also for the accomplishment of the predictions that went before him touching his sufferings, if he would he could have suffered less fear of death, and showed more true valour than ever any Martyrs have done, but then his death, which for fear of death were all their life time subject to bondage.

The Vindication of Hebrews 5.7.

Hebrews 5.7.—Christ in the days of his flesh when he had offered up prayers and supplications with strong crying and tears unto him that was able to save him from death, and he was heard in that which he feared.

I reverence your Authors who expound the word Fear to mean Fear of Astonishment at the feeling of God's wrath for our sin, but I must tell you, that there are other Learned and Godly Divines that are contrary to them in their interpretation of the word Fear. King James his Translators do read it thus in the margent, He was heard for his reverence. And the Geneva in other places translate the same Greek word Godly fear, as in Luke 2.25, Acts 8.2, Heb. 12.8, and in this very sense must this Greek word be translated in Heb. 5.7.

The Greek word doth properly signifie such as makes a man exceedingly wary, and heedful how he touch any thing that may hurt him.

I come now to explain the very thing it felt from which Christ prayed to be saved, which was that he might be delivered from death, and this petition was the masterpiece of all his prayers.

But for the better understanding the very thing itself that he did so often and so earnestly pray to be delivered from, we must consider him with a twofold respect.

1. As he was true man, so he prayed to be saved from death conditionally. Mathew 6.39.

2. We must consider him in this Text as he was our Mediator, and so he prayed to be saved from death absolutely, namely, to be saved from his natural fear of death when he came to make his oblation; for he knew well enough that if there had remained in him but the least natural unwillingness to die, when he came to make his oblation, it would have spoiled the mediatorial efficacy of his oblation.

For he had from eternity covenanted with his Father to give his soul (by his own active obedience) as a mediatorial sacrifice of atonement for our sins. John 10.17, 18, therefore he must die a positive death by the power of man, but he must die as a Mediator by the actual and joynt concurrence of both divine and human nature; no man could force his soul out of his body by all the torments they could devise, but he must separate his own soul from his body by the joint concurrence of both his natures.

Christ made his oblation an exact obedience unto God's will, both for matter, manner, and time, and this mediatorial action of his was the highest degree of obedience that the Father required, or that the son could perform for man's atonement and redemption.

His obedience in his death was not Legal but mediatorial.

2. He prayed also to be delivered from the domination of death after he had made his oblation, and God heard him and delivered by his resurrection on the third day. Acts 2.24, 27.

Neither doth the word Fear in this Text signifie such an amazed natural fear of death as the other word Fear doth signifie, Mar. 14.33, which word I have expounded to signifie our Saviour's troubled death, and no more.

And therefore it caused him in the days of his flesh to offer up many prayers and supplications with strong cries and tears unto him that was able to save him from death, namely, from his natural fear of death, and he was heard because of his godly fear.

The Vindication of Psalms 22.1.—My God, My God, why hast thou forsaken me?

Many Divines conclude from this Text that God did forsake his son in his anger, because he had imputed to him all our sins; but yet other Divines differ from them. M. Broughton saith, My God, My God, showeth that Christ was not forsaken of God, but that God was his hope. 2. Saith he, The word forsaken is not the Text, but Why dost thou (leave) me? namely, why dost thou leave me to the griefs following from the malice of the Jews? as they are expressed in the body of the Psalm 3. Saith he, None ever expounded one matter, and made his amplification of another; but Psalm 22 hath amplification of griefs caused by men, and not from God's anger. Therefore the Proposition in the first verse is not a complaint to God that he forsook his soul in anger for our sins. M. Robert Wilmot, showeth at large that the term forsaken is not so proper to this place as the term leave, and he doth parallel it with the word leave, in Psalm 16.10. M. Ainsworth saith the Hebrew word which we translate forsaken may be translated, why leavest thou me? And he saith in a Letter to myself that there is no material difference between leaving and forsaking, so as the meaning be kept sound. Therefore it followeth by good consequence that Christ doth not complain, Psa. 22, that God had forsaken him in anger for our sins.

Our Saviour's complaint must run thus, Why hast thou left me into the hands of my malignant adversaries, to be used as a notorious malefactor? It's not so fit a place to say, Why hast thou forsaken me into the hands of my malignant adversaries, as to say, Why hast thou left me into the hands of my malignant adversaries:

God forsakes the damned totally and finally, because there is no place of repentance left open to them, but he did not so forsake his son, neither did he forsake his son by any inward desertion, as he does sometimes forsake his own people for the trial of their grace; but he left his son only outwardly when he left him into the hands of Tyrants to be punished as a malefactor without any due trial of his cause.

Therefore the complaint of Christ lies far and round thus, Why hast thou left me in my righteous cause unto the will of my malignant adversaries, to be condemned and put to death as a wicked Malefactor?

John Hus appealed to Jesus Christ for justice, saying, My God, My God, why hast thou forsaken me? Ammond de la Roy, Martyr, in the time of his torments said, Lord, Lord, why hast thou forsaken me?

Christopher Carlisle upon the Article of Christ's descent into hell, saith not a word of the suffering of his Father's wrath, yet he makes use of Psa. 22.1, and of M. Calvin's judgment in other points, though he differ from him in his exposition of Ps.22.1. The Holy Ghost hath indited this Psalm by the Prophet David in the Person of Christ. If so, then all the words of this Psalm must have relation to the person of Christ. The Psalm itself hath two principal parts, the first is ver. 1 to 21, in all which Christ doth complain to his Father of his unjust usage by his malignant Adversaries; the 2d part of the Psalm is from the 22 verse to the end. Therefore seeing Christ in this place doth double the term of his affiance in God, saying, My God, My God; it proves evidently that God had not forsaken his Son in anger for our sins, but that God was still his hope; and that he would at last turn all his sufferings but not unto the tryal of his perfect obedience.

Why art thou then so far from my help, and from the words of my roaring? Why dost thou leave me unto the will of my malignant adversaries, notwithstanding my prayers, and my righteous cause?

My heart is melted in the midst of my bowels, that is to say, the evil spirit that is in my malignant Adversaries, and their doctors, do make my human affections to melt in the midst of my bowels.

Thou hast brought me unto the dust of death, ver. 15. God doth not so bring Christ unto the dust of death, as he doth other men, namely, not so as death is laid upon man for sin. Gen. 3.19.

But for the better understanding of the true difference, I will distinguish upon the death of Christ; for God appointed him to die a double death. 1. As a Malefactor, and 2. As a Mediator, and all this at one and at the same time.

1. He died as a Malefactor by God's determinate counsel and decree; he gave the devil leave to enter into Judas to betray him, and into the Scribes and Pharisees, and Pontius Pilate to condemn him, and to do what they could to put him to death, and in that respect God may be truly said to bring him into the dust of death. Gen. 3.10.

2. Notwithstanding all this, Christ died as a Mediator, and therefore his death was not really finished by those torments which he suffered as a Malefactor, for as he was our Mediator he separated his own soul from his body by the power of his God-head. All the Tyrants in the world could not separate his soul from his body, John 19.11; no, not by all the torments they could devise, till himself pleased to actuate his own death by the joint concurrence of both his natures. John 10.18.

Thus have I showed unto you the dependance of the first part of this Psalm; by which you may see how the scope of this Psalm doth set the sufferings of Christ to proceed not from God's wrath but from man's only. Neither do I find anything of God's wrath either in this or in any other

Psalm, and yet Christ doth make as dolefull complaint to God of his sufferings both in this Psalm and in Psalm 69, as any can be found in all the
Bible.

_____

The Vindication of Galatians 3.13.

Gal. 3.13.—Christ has redeemed us from the curse of the Law, being
made a curse for us, as is written, Cursed is every one that hangs on a tree.

In this Text the Apostle speaks of a twofold curse. 1. He speaks of the
eternal curse in ver. 10.2, of an outward temporary curse, in ver. 14. such
as all men do suffer, who are hanged upon a tree; the Apostle brings in
this latter curse in a Rhetorical manner only, saying thus, Christ hath
redeemed us from the curse of the Law, namely, from the eternal curse at
the very self-same time, when he was made, not that curse, but a curse
for us according to Deuter. 21.25.

I confess that D. Luther was a rare instrument in the Church of God in
his days, and he hath expounded the Epistle to the Galatians better than
many others; but yet I believe he is far from the Apostles' meaning in this
matter, and it seemeth to me he had some doubt also about his Exposition.
But he thinketh that the latter curse may well be expounded of his sacrifice for the Curse (and yet that Exposition is not right neither) for this
latter Curse is no other than an outward temporary curse. For the Text
in Deuter. runs thus, If there be in a man a sin worthy of death, and thou
hang him upon a tree, &c., then he that is hanged is the curse of God.

This latter curse is no other than an outward temporary curse; for the
text in Deut. 21.22, runs thus, If there be in a man a sin worthy of death,
and thou hang him on a tree, &c., then he that is hanged is the curse of
God. What curse of God is it, that is meant? I answer, that may be
discerned by taking notice of what kind of persons, and for what kind of
sin this curse of God doth fall upon any, The persons, the Text describes
them thus, namely, he that is put to death as a Malefactor, by the Magistrate. The kind of sin that are said to deserve this curse of hanging
upon a tree, are described by this general term, a sin worthy of death,
namely, of this death; hence it is evident, that not every sinner that deserved death is here meant, but as such as deserved a double death, namely,
1. Stoning to death . 2. Hanging up of their bodies upon a tree, after
they were stoned to death.

M. Calvin in Deut. 21.23, saith, That the hanging of Christ upon a tree
was not after the manner that is here spoken of; for such as were stoned to
death among the Jews, were also hanged upon a gibbet after they were
dead.

M. Goodwin and M. Ainsworth from the Hebrew Doctors reckon 18
particular capital sins, for which men were first stoned to death and after
hanged, and M. Ainsworth doth also say, that the Hebrew Doctors do
not understand this hanging of being put to death by hanging, but of
hanging a man up after he was stoned to death, which was done for the
greater detestation of such henious malefactors.

The Rebelious son, Deut. 21.21, is brought in as an instance of this
double punishment, he was first stoned to death, and then hanged upon a
tree.

Thus shalt not let his carkass remain all night upon the Tree , but thou shalt surely bury him in the same day at the going down of the sun, and the reason is added, because he is the curse of God, namely, because such sinners are more eminently cursed of God, because they were punished with the heaviest kind of death that the Judges of Israel did use to inflict upon any Malefactors.

I think I have sufficiently proved that God did appoint the hanging upon a tree to be a type of the temporal curse.

If hanging upon a tree had been appointed by God to be a type of the eternal curse, then every one that is hanged upon a tree should be eternally cursed, and then divers Martyrs that were crucified, as Christ was, are eternally cursed, and the penitent thief was eternally cursed.

But if the circumstances of the Text be well marked, they will tell you plainly, that this hanging upon a tree be a type of the eternal curse, for 1. This Law of Moses must not be understood of putting any man to death by hanging, but of hanging a dead body upon a tree after it was first put to death by stoning: but Christ was crucified whilst he was alive. 2. This hanging in Moses time was done by Judicial Law and civil Magistrates, and not by the ceremonial Law nor the Priests. 3. This hanging in Moses was commanded to be practiced by the Magistrates of the Jews' Commonwealth, but the death which Christ suffered was a Roman kind of death.

When the Romans did put Christ to that kind of death which they used to inflict upon their base fugitive slaves, they made him cursed in his death in the highest degree they could and yet at the self-same time Christ did redeem us from the curse of th Law, even from the eternal curse, because Christ died not only as a Malefactor by the Roman soldiers, but he died also as a Mediator by his own Mediatorial obedience.

This act of Christ was an everlasting act of Mediatorial obedience, it was no legal obedience, nor was it any human act of obedience as all legal obedience, it was no less than a Mediatorial oblation, and therefore it was the meritorious procuring cause of our Redemption from the curse of the Law even at that very same time when Christ was made a curse for us by hanging as a Malefactor upon a tree. Therefore the Tree on which Christ was crucified as a Malefactor cannot be the Altar, neither were the Roman soldiers the Priests by whom this mediatorial sacrifice was offered up to God, but it was his own Godhead that was the Altar, by which he offered up his soul to God, a mediatorial sacrifice for the procuring of our redemption from the curse of the Law.

Christ redeemed us not from the curse of the Law, by his soul-sufferings only. And of the meaning of Haides.

Good Divines do affirm that Christ hath redeemed us from the curse of the Law, not by his bodily but by his soul-sufferings only, which God inflicted upon his soul when his body was crucified upon the Tree.

This kind of reasoning is very absurd, for as M. Broughton well observed, if Christ suffered the wrath of God in his soul only, to redeem our souls, and not to redeem our bodes, then our bodies are not redeemed.

If Christ suffered the wrath of God in his soul to redeem our souls from the eternal curse, he must also suffer the wrath of God in his body to redeem our bodies from the eternal curse, or else our bodies must still continue under the eternal curse, though our souls be redeemed by his soul-sufferings: Is not this to make Christ an imperfect Redeemer, and to leave a doubting conscience in a Labyrinth of queries?

The truth is, I find much uncertainty amongst Divines what to affirm in this point, for first, some affirm that Christ suffered the wrath of God in his soul only. Secondly, Others affirm the wrath of God as well in his body as in his soul, to redeem our bodies from God's wrath as well as our souls.

Of the Dialogue's arguments taken from the description of the torments of hell; and from the place of suffering the torments of the damned.

By describing the torments of hell you shall be the better able to judge whether Christ did suffer the torments of hell for our redemption, or not. The torments of hell are usually divided into two parts. 1. Into the pain of loss. 2. Into the pain of sense. The pain of loss is the privation of God's favor, by an everlasting separation.

For as the favour of God through Christ is the fountain of life, because it is the beginning of eternal life. Psa. 36.9, so on the contrary to be totally separated from God's favor by an eternal separation, must needs be the beginning of hell-torments or of death eternal.

God doth not forsake the Reprobates so long as they live in this life, with such total forsaking, as he doth after this life; yea, the very Devils themselves as long as they live in this world (being spirits) in the air, are not so forsaken of God as they shall be at the judgment; for as yet they are not in hell, but in the air, and therefore they have not their full torments as yet.

And yet this pain of loss may a little further be explained by opening the term Second death, which may be in part described by comparing it with the first death, which I have at large described to be our spiritual death, or the loss of the life of our first pure nature; I may call it a death in corrupt and final qualities, as I have opened, Gen. 2.17, yea, all other miseries which fall upon us in this life till our bodies be rotten in the grave, I call them altogether the first death, because they do all befall us in this world; therefore on the contrary this second death must needs imply a deeper degree of sinful qualities than did befall us under the first death.

And this term Second death doth plainly tell us that it is such a degree of death as surpasseth all the degrees of death in this life, and that the full measure of it cannot be inflicted upon any man till this life is ended, and then their end shall be without mercy. Jam. 2.13.

The Second part of the torments of hell is the pain of sense, or the sense of all tortouring torments.

As God's rejection is the principal efficient cause of their damnation, so Jesus Christ the Mediator is the principal instrumental cause thereof, because they believed not in him that was promised to be the seed of the woman.

Now come we to examine the particulars, and whether Christ did suffer the torments of hell for our Redemption. 1. Did Christ suffer these torments of hell for our Redemption? Did Christ suffer the second death? Was he spiritually dead in corrupt and sinful qualities without any restraining grace? and did God leave him to the liberty of those corrupt and sinful qualities, to hate and blaspheme God, for his justice and holiness, as inseparable companions of God's total separation, for these sinful qualities are inseparably joined to them that suffer hell-torments, as the effect is to the cause. Did Christ suffer this pain of loss when he said, My God, My God, why hast thou forsaken me?

Did Christ at any time feel the knawing worm of an accusing concience? Was he at any time under the torment of despiration? truly if he had at any time suffered the torments of hell, he must of necessity have suffered these things: for they are as nearly joyned to those that suffer the torments of hell as the effect is to the cause.

Did Christ suffer the torments of hell in his body as well as in his soul, to redeem our bodies as well as our souls from the torments of hell?

How long did he suffer the torments of hell? Was it forever? or how long did he suffer them? and when did the torments of hell first seize on him? and when was he found freed from them? or did he suffer the torments of hell at several times or in several places, or but at one time or place only?

Was he tormented without any forgiveness, or did Abraham deny him the least drop of water to cool his tongue?

Did Christ inflict the torments of hell upon his own human nature? or did his Divine nature forsake his human nature in anger? or did his Divine nature forsake his human nature in anger as it must have done if it had suffered the torments of hell? if so, then he destroyed the personal union of his two natures, and then he made himself no Mediator but a cursed damned sinner.

These and such like gross absurdities the common doctrine of imputation will often fall into.

Christ could not suffer any part of the torments of hell as long as he lived in this world, because the very devils as long as they lived in this air do not suffer the torments of hell, as it is evident by the fearful crying out to Christ, Mat. 8.29.

M. Broughton in a Manuscript saith thus: No words in all the Bible do express anything that Christ suffered the wrath of God for our sins, therefore it is no small impiety for men from general metaphorical terms to gather such a strange particular: none that ever spake Greek (Spirit of man) gathered hell torments for the just from Haides, or from any other Greek or Hebrew Text. Again, the same Author affirmeth in Rev. 11.2, that hell-place and torments are not in this life.

And truly it seems to me that the holy Scriptures do confine hell torments to the proper place of hell itself, which is seated on high before the Throne of the Lamb, and Solomon doth tell us that all men's souls both good and bad do ascend, Eccl. 3.21. and the Hebrew Doctors hold generally that hell is above as well as heaven: and Learned M. Richardson doth probably conjecture in his Philosophical Annotations on Gen. 1, that hell-place is seated in the Element of fire, and may it not be so, seeing its place is next before the Throne of the Lamb where John doth place it, Rev. 14.10. And it is certain by Luke's Parable that hell is seated near unto heaven, or else the comparisons that Luke useth to describe their nearness, were absurd.

1. He describes their nearness by two persons talking together, the one in heavenplace, and the other in hellplace.

2. He describes their nearness by seeing each other's case, Luke 16, and so doth Isaiah in Chap. 24.

3. Hence we may see the reason why Haides is put as a common name to both places; both places are usually called Haides in sundry Greek Writers, as if they were but two Regions in the same world of souls: one Region for the godly, and the other for the wicked, where the godly and the wicked may see each other's condition, and talk together in their next adjacent parts, Luke 16.23.

It is evident that Christ did not suffer the torments of hell in this world, because there was no necessary use of such sufferings, for such sufferings are no way satisfactory to the justice of God for our sins; for the rule of God's justice doth require that soul only to die with sins, the soul that sins shall die; one man shall not die for another man's sin, Ezek. 18. By this rule of justice God cannot inflict the torments of hell upon an innocent to redeem a guilty person.

And as God doth tye himself to this Rule of Justice touching the ever-lasting state of men's souls, so he doth appoint civil Magistrates to ob-serve this Rule of justice touching the bodies of sinful Malefactors, they may not punish an innocent for a guilty person, but that man only that sins must die, as 2 Kings 14, doth expound the meaning of the judicial Law in Deut. 24.16. I hold it a point of gross injustice for any Court of Magistrates to torture an innocent person for the redemption of a gross Malefactor.

––––––––––

Of the nature of Mediatory obedience, both according to the Dialogue and the Orthodox.

1. That Christ hath redeemed us from the curse of the Law, not by suffering the said curse, but by a satisfactory price of Atonement, namely, by paying or performing unto his Father that invaluable precious thing of his Mediatorial obedience whereof his Mediatorial sacrifice of Atonement was the master-piece.

2. A sinner's Righteousness or Justification is explained and cleared from some Common Errors.

That which Christ did redeem us from the curse of the Law, was not by bearing of the said curse really in our stead, (as the common doctrine of imputation teach) but by the procuring his Father's atonement by the invaluable price or performance of his own Mediatorial obedience whereof his Meditorial sacrifice of atonement was the finishing master-piece, this kind of obedience was the rich thing of price which the Father required and accepted as satisfactory for the procuring of his atonement for our full Redemption, Justification and Adoption.

And according to this tenor the Apostle Paul doth explain the matter, he doth teach us to place the obedience of the Mediator in a direct opposition to the first disobedience of Adam, Rom. 5.19, he makes the merit of Christ's Mediatorial obedience to countervail the demerit of Adam's disobedience; for the disobedience of Adam was but the disobedience of a mere man, but the obedience of Christ was the obedience of God-man, and in that respect God the Father was more highly pleased with the obedience of the Mediator than he was displeased with the disobedience of Adam.

It is necessary to distinguish between Legal and Mediatorial obedience; Legal or natural obedience is no more, but human obedience performed by Christ as a Godly Jew unto the Law of works, all actions of Christ from his birth until he was thirty years of age, must be considered but as natural or but legal acts of obedience: I cannot see how any of these actions (which yet it somewhat corrects, as we shall find in due place) can be called Mediatorial obedience.

Of the Divers ways of Redemption.

If so, then there is no need that our blessed Mediator should pay both the price of his Mediatorial obedience, and also bear the Curse of the Law for our Redemption.

I never heard that ever any Turkish Tyrant did require such double satisfaction of any Redeemer for the Redemption of Galley-slaves. I never heard that ever any Tyrant did require to pay both the full price that they demanded for their redemption of their Galley-slaves, and to bear their punishment of their curse and slavery also in their stead; I think no cruel Tyrant did ever exact such a double satisfaction therefore I cannot choose but wonder at the common doctrine of imputation, because it makes God the Father more rigid in the price of our Redemption than ever Turkish Tyrant was, and to be a harder Creditor in the point of satisfaction than ever any rigid Creditor was among men.

The way of Redemption are ranked into three sorts. 1. By exchange of one captive for another; but we are not the redeemed, for God did not give his Son into the hands of Satan to redeem us from under the power of Satan. 2. There is a Redemption by force and strength, but this may be called a deliverance rather than a Redemption, but however Christ did not thus redeem us from God's wrath; for then Christ must be stronger than his Father, John 14.28. 3. Therefore Christ hath redeemed us from the curse of the Law, and so consequently from his Father's wrath, by no other way or means, but by that rich and invaluable price or merit of his Mediatorial obedience.

And this way of Redemption is often taught and confirmed by the holy Scriptures, as in 1 Cor. 6.20, 1 Pet. 1.19, and in this sense only we have atonement, Rom. 5.11, and redemption through the blood, Eph. 1.7, and in this sense he gave his life a Ransom for many, Mat. 20.28, and in this sense he gave himself to redeem us from all iniquity, and to clens us to himself, Ti. 2.14.

It is evident by another typical ceremony of Redemption that Christ hath redeemed us by a price only, and not by bearing the Curse of the Law for us, Lev. 25.25, 39.

It is a dangerous error in the tenet of the Lutherans to say, that one drop of the blood of Christ is sufficient to redeem the whole world.

Of that wherein the true meritorious efficacy of the blood of Christ lieth.

The true meritorious efficacy of the blood of Christ lies not in this, that it was a part of the corporal substance of the Lamb of God without spot; nor in this, that he suffered his blood to be shed by the Roman soldiers in a passive manner of obedience, but it lieth in this, that it was shed by his own active priestly power, by which means only it became a Mediatorial sacrifice of atonement.

Christ at one and the same time died both as a Mediator actively, and as a Malefactor passively, as I have explained the matter, Gal. 3.13, and in other places also.

But for your better understanding of the meritorious efficacy of the blood of Christ consider two things. 1. Consider what the Priestly nature of Christ, and 2. Consider what was his Priestly action. 1. His Priestly nature was his Divine nature, for he is said to be a Priest for ever after the order of Melchisedeck, of whom it is witnessed that he liveth, or that he ever liveth. Heb. 7.8.

But yet withall take notice that the term He, Gen. 3.15, doth comprehend under it his human nature as well as his divine; yea, it doth also comprehend under it the Personal union of both his natures.

Consider what was his Priestly action, and that was the sprinkling of his own blood by his own Priestly nature, that is to say, by his divine nature, Isa. 53.12, namely, by the active power of his own divine Priestly nature, Heb. 9.14, that is to say, he separated his soul from his body by the power of his Godhead when he made his soul a trespass-offering for our sin, Isa. 53.10, and the manner of sprinkling of blood by the Priests upon the Altar, must be done with a large and liberal quantity, and therefore it is called pouring out, and this sprinkling with pouring out did typifie the death of the Mediator; a large quantity of bloodshed must needs be a true evidence of death.

And secondly, In this respect the blood of Christ is called the blood of God, Acts 20.28, not only because his human nature was united to his Divine nature, for by the communication of proper ties that may be attributed to the Person which is proper to one nature only; but secondly, it is called the blood of God in another respect, namely, because he shed his blood by his own Priestly nature, that is to say, by the actual power of his divine nature, for he offered himself by his eternal Spirit, Heb. 9.14.

In like sort he is called Jehovah our Righteousness, Jer. 20.3, because his Mediatorial obedience (whereof his oblation was the masterpiece) was actuated by Jehovah, that is to say, by his divine nature as well as by his human.

So then I may well conclude that the death of Christ was a Mediatorial sacrifice of atonement, because it was the act of the Mediator in both his natures, in his human nature he was the Lamb of God without spot, and in his Divine nature he was the Priest to offer up his human nature to God as a Mediatorial sacrifice of atonement for the full Redemption of all the Elect.

It was the holiness of his Divine nature that gave the quickening power to the oblation of his human nature, John 6.63.

In this answer John 6.63, our Saviour declareth two things.

1. That the gross and carnal substance of his flesh and blood considered by itself alone had no meritorious efficacy, and therefore his legal obedience cannot profit us.

2. Our Saviour in his answer declared wherein the true force and efficacy of his sacrifice did lie, namely, in these two things.

1. In the Personal union of his human nature with his divine nature.

2. It lies in his Priestly offering of his human nature by his own divine nature.

Whether the Jews and Romans put Christ to Death.

Neither did he die a passive death by the power of the Roman soldiers, as the Jews thought, and as the Priests and other carnal Protestants do think: All the men and devils in the world could not put him to death by their power, I mean they could not separate his soul from his body, till himself pleased to do it by his own Priestly power, John 10.17, 18, his soul was not separated from his body by the sense of those pains which the Roman soldiers inflicted upon him, as the souls of the two thieves were crucified with him, for Christ died no sooner nor later than the very punctual hour in which God had appointed to make his oblation.

The Centurian did plainly see a manifest difference between the manner of Christ's death, and the death of the two thieves that were crucified with him, for as yet they did still continue alive in their torments till after the time that Joseph of Arimathea had begged our Saviour's dead body of Pilate, at the Sun-set Evening: for Joseph did not go to Pilate to beg our Saviour's body until the Evening was come, Mat. 27.57, Mar. 15.52, 53, and that was at Sun-set, it could not be when the first Evening was come but Christ was dead long before this, for he gave up the ghost at the ninth hour, and yet by the course of his nature he might have lived in his torments as long as the two thieves did, for the Roman soldiers did crucify all three alike.

What then was the true reason why Christ died three hours before the thieves? had he less strength of nature to bear his torments than they? or did the Roman soldiers add more torment upon his body than upon the two thieves? or did the Father's wrath kill him sooner than the two thieves as some think? Surely none of all these things did hasten his death before the two thieves, but the only true reason was because he did actuate his own death as a mediatorial sacrifice of atonement (at the just hour appointed by his Father) by the joint concurrence of both his natures.

Of the Dialogue's Distinction of Christ's dying as a Mediator and as a Malefactor.

I have already showed you that Christ died a twofold death: for he died both as a Malefactor at one and at the same time; as a Malefactor he died a passive death, but as a Mediator he died an active death, and the Scriptures doth often speak of both these deaths, sometimes jointly and sometimes severally: when the Scriptures doth mention his passive death then it saith that he was put to death, killed and slain.   But secondly, the Scriptures doth sometimes speak jointly of his passive death and of his Mediatorial death together in one sentence, as 1 Romans 8.13, and in Galatians 3.13, (which Scriptures I have opened at large in the first part,) Luke 22.19, compared with 1 Cor. 11.24, Luke 22.20, so Isa. 12, with Rom. 4.25. The Scriptures doth sometimes speak of his Mediatorial death only as Isa. 53.10, he gave his soul to be a trespass-offering himself by his eternal spirit, Heb. 9.14, and he laid down his own life, John 10.17 and 18, and he sanctified himself, John 17.19, therefore seeing the holy Scriptures doth teach us to observe this distinction upon the death of Christ, it is necessary that all God's people should take notice of it, and engrave it in their minds and memories.

When I speak of Christ as a Malefactor, then the Scribes and Pharisees must be considered as the wicked instruments thereof, yet this must be remembered also, that I do no mean that they by their torments did separate his soul from his body, in that sense they did not put him to death, (himself only did separate his own soul from his body by the power of his Godhead) but they put him to death, because they did that to him which they thought sufficient to put him to death: and men are often said to do that which they endeavor to do, as in the example of Abraham, Heb. 11.7, Haman, Esth. 8.7, Amelek, Exod. 17.16, Saul, Psa. 143.3. The Magicians, Exo. 8.18. The Israelites, Numbers 14.30, as the matter is explained in Deut. 1.14, and in this sense it is said, that the Jews did kill and stay the Lord of life, because they endeavored to do it.

He laid down his life by the same power by which he raised it up again, John 10.17, 18.

Yea, his Mediatorial death may well be called a miraculous death.

Christ died not by degrees (saith M. Nichols in his Day-Starr) as his Saints do, his sense do not decry, &c.

Austin saith thus, Who can sleep (saith he) when will, as Christ died when he would? Who can lay aside his garment, so as Christ laid aside his flesh? Who can leave his place as Christ left his life? his life was not forced from him by any imposed punishment, but he did voluntarily render it up as a Mediatorial sacrifice: in his life time he was often touched with the fear of death, but by his strong crying out unto God with daily prayers and tears he obtained power against his natural fear of death, before he came to make his oblation: as I have expounded, Heb. 5.7.

Again, it is evident that his death was miraculous, because at that instant when he breathed out his soul into the hands of God, the veil of the Temple (which typified his human nature) rent itself in twain from the top to the bottom; and at the same time also the graves of the Saints did open themselves, and many of the dead Saints did arise, Mat. 27.51.

Hence we learn that the doctrine of the Papists and the Lutherans in transubstantiations and consubstantiations is very erroneous; for they place the meritorious price of their Redemption in the gross substance of Christ's flesh and blood, and in the passive shedding of it upon the Cross by the Romans.

The cleansing virtue of his blood lies in his own Mediatorial shedding of it, for though he did not break his own body, and pour out his own blood with nails and spears, as the Roman soldiers did, yet he break his own body in pieces by separating his own soul from his own body by the power of the Divine nature: and then he did actually shed his own blood when he did pour out his own soul to death, Isa. 53.12, as a Mediatorial sacrifice of Atonement for the procuring of his Father's Atonement for our full Redemption, Justification and Adoption, and in this sense only the blood of Christ doth purge us, Tit. 2.14, and cleanse us, I John 1.17, and wash us from our sins, Rev. I.

Obedience of Christ to the Moral Law, Whether for our Justification, or by way of Imputation.

Before I can speak anything touching Christ's obedience to the Moral Law, it must be understood what you mean by this term moral Law: By the term Moral Law you mean the Decalouge or Ten Commandments, and call it Moral Law, because every one of these Ten Commandments were engraven in our nature in time of innocency: but in my apprehension in this sense the term Moral Law is very ill applied, because it makes most men look at no further matter in the Ten Commandments but at moral duties only: or it makes them look no further but at sanctified walking in relation to moral duties.

But the truth is, they are greatly deceived, for the Ten Commandments do require faith in Christ as well as moral duties, but faith in Christ was not engraven in Adam's nature in time of his innoceney, he knew nothing concerning faith in Christ, till after his fall; therefore the Ten Commandments in the full latitude of them were not given to Adam in his innocency: they were not given till after Christ was published to be the seed of the woman, to break the devil's head-plot, therefore the Ten Commandments do require faith in Christ as well as moral duties.

If the whole Law and the Prophets do hang upon the Ten Commandments as the general heads of all that is contained within the Law and the Prophets, then the Ten Commandments must needs contain in them rules of faith in Christ as well as moral duties.

And this is further evident by the Preface of the Ten Commandments, which runs thus, I am Jehovah thy God, which brought thee out of the Land of Egypt: Christ was that Jehovah which brought them out of the Land of Egypt: So it was Christ that gave the first Commandment, Thou shalt have no other Gods but me, that is to say, Thou shalt have no other Gods but the Trinity, and no other mediator but me alone to be thy Redeemer and Saviour. In like sort Christ in the second Commandment doth require obedience to all his outward worship and in special to all his Levitical worship, and the observation of that worship is especially called the Law of works, though the Ten Commandments also must be included.

But the right application of the typical signification of the Levitical worship to the soul, is called the Law of faith, the third Commandment doth teach holy reverence to the person of the Mediator: Faith in Christ is also typically comprehended under the fourth Commandment.

Arguments Against the Imputation of Christ's Obedience.

I cannot see how the common doctrine of Imputation can stand with God's justice; God cannot in justice impute our Saviour's Legal obedience to us for our just righteousness or justification, because it is point blank against the condition of the Legal Covenant so to do: for the Legal promise of eternal life is not made over to us upon condition of Christ's personal performance, but upon condition of our personal performance.

It is evident that God never propounded the Law of works to the fallen sons of Adam, with any intent that ever any of the fallen sons of Adam should seek for justification and atonement in God's sight by Legal obedience , but his intent was directly contrary, for when he propounded the Legal promise of life eternal to the fallen sons of Adam, he did propound it upon condition of their own personal obedience, to allure them thereby to search into their own natural unrighteousness, by this perfect rule of Legal righteousness, so by this Law of life God intended chiefly to make the soul of fallen sons of Adam to be sensible of their own spiritual death in corruption and sin, thereby to provoke our souls to seek for life some other way, viz.: by the mediation of the Mediator promised: So it follows by good consequence that God did never intend to justifie any son of Adam by Legal obedience done by his own person, nor yet by our Saviour's obedience imputed as the formal cause of a sinner's justification or righteousness.

God cannot in justice justifie sinners by our Saviour's Legal obedience imputed: because Legal obedience is altogether insufficient to justifie a corrupt son of Adam from his original sin; for our corrupt and sinful nature did not fall upon us for the breach of any of Moses his Laws, but for the breach of another Law of works, which God gave to Adam in his innocency by way of prohibition, In the day thou eatest thereof thou shalt die the death: so God cannot in justice impute our Saviour's Legal obedience to any corrupt son of Adam for his full and perfect righteousness, because it is altogether insufficient to make a sinner righteous from his original sin.

If Christ's Legal obedience imputed were sufficient to justifie a sinner from all kinds of sin both original and actual, then Christ made his oblation in vain, for it had been altogether needless for him to give his soul as a Mediatorial sacrifice of atonement for the procuring of our justice in God's sight, if his Legal righteousness performed by his life had been sufficient to justifie us from all sin in God's sight; for if righteousness could have come to sinners by the Law, then Christ died in vain, Gal. 2.21.

Christ's Legal obedience was but the work of his flesh or of his human nature; therefore it could not be the procuring cause of God's atonement for justification; for no obedience is meritorious but that obedience which is mediatorial. I never heard that the Father required the Mediator to perform Legal obedience as a proper condition of his Mediatorial office, nay, our Saviour himself doth testifie, that his flesh (alone considered) doth not profit us to life and salvation, John 6.63, therefore not his Legal obedience: for that was but the work of his flesh or human nature.

There was great jarring among Divines about the right stating of the doctrine of imputation.

1. Some affirm, that God the Father doth impute Christ's Legal obedience to sinners as their obedience for their full and perfect justification.

2. Others do affirm that Christ's Legal obedience imputed is not sufficient to make sinners righteous, and so they do affirm that God doth impute another kind of Christ's righteousness to sinners for their full justification, viz: the purity of his nature to justifie us from original sin.

3. Others go further in that point of imputation, for they affirm that God imputes another kind of righteousness to sinners for their full justification, viz: the passive obedience: and so by necessary consequence they do make sinners to be their own Mediator, because they do make Christ's Mediatorial obedience to be a sinner's obedience by God's imputation.

The actions of Christ's obedience neither active nor passive can be made ours by God's imputation, no more than our sinful actions can be made his by God's imputation; as I have at large expressed in the opening, Gen. 2.17.

If God do make sinners righteous by the active obedience of Christ imputed, then Christ must perform all manner of obedience for us that God doth require of us, or else God cannot in justice make us perfectly righteous by the active obedience of Christ imputed; but Christ did not perform all manner of acts of obedience for us that God requireth of us, because he was never married, &c. and yet we have as much need to be made righteous in such like actions as in any, therefore God cannot in justice make us perfectly righteous by the actions of Christ's active obedience imputed.

Distinction Between Legal and Mediatorial Obedience.

It is a necessary thing to observe a right difference between Christ's Legal and Mediatorial obedience, which we have in part distinguished already, but for your further satisfaction I will again distinguish already between them.

I grant that God required the Mediator to fulfill all righteousness, but yet his obedience to the Law of works, and his obedience to the Law of Mediatorship must be considered as done for several ends and uses.

First, God appointed the Mediator to fulfill the Law of works, I mean so much of it as fell within the compass of his human course of life, not as a proper condition belonging to the Law of Mediatorship: (as Mediator) but as true man only, for he was bound to observe the Law of works as he was true man, as much as any other Jew, by a native right, Gal. 4.4.

Secondly, Though I make this Legal obedience to be no more but human obedience, yet I grant that he was thereby qualified, and fitted to make his soul a Mediatorial sacrifice, for he could not have been the Lamb of God without spot, if he had not been exact in the performance of so much Legal obedience as fell within the compass of his human course of life, Heb. 7.26.

Thirdly, The rewards which his Father did promise him for his Mediatorial obedience, do far exceed the rewards which he doth promise to Legal obedience: for I cannot find that ever the Father did promise to reward any man's Legal obedience with such special rewards as he doth promise unto Christ's Mediatorial obedience.   I will give thee the end of the earth for thy possession, Psal..2.   And he shall see his seed, and prolong his days, when he shall make his soul a trespass-offering, Isa.53.10

Fourthly, Christ was not bound to fulfill personal obedience to every branch of the Law of works (for he had no wife and children to instruct, &c.) but he was bound to fulfill every branch and circumstance of the Law of Mediatorship, he must not be wanting in the least circumstance thereof, if he had been wanting in the least circumstance he had been wanting in all.

M. Calvin observeth rightly, that some of the actions of Christ were proper to his God-head only; and some of his actions were proper to his human nature only, and some of his actions were common to both his natures, and this observation (saith M. Calvin) shall do no small service to assoyl many doubts, if the Reader can but fitly apply it.

It is absurd to affirm that all the acts of Christ's obedience were Mediatory, because his person consisted of both natures; for then his natural Actions should be Mediatorial as well as any other. You may as well say, that all actions of the Son, and of the Holy Ghost are the actions of the Father, because they are united into one Godhead, as say that the acts of Christ's Legal obedience were Mediatorial, because his person consisted of two natures.

As for example all the Actions of Christ from his birth until he began to be thirty years of age, must be considered as natural actions, or as Legal acts of obedience: for till he began to be thirty years of age, he led a private life with his parents.

Secondly, When he began to be thirty years of age he did then begin to declare himself to be the Mediator, for when he was baptized of John in Jordon, the Holy Ghost lighted upon him in visible manner before all John's Auditory, and the Father by his voice from Heaven declared that he was the Mediator.

Thirdly, In the upshot of his life, as soon as he had fulfilled all things that were written of him he sacrificed himself and sacrificed his oblation by the joint concurrence of both natures; and this was the masterpiece of his Mediatorial obedience. Having thus distinguished the actions of the Mediator, we may and must rank his acts accordingly: his obedience to the Law of works must be ranked among the actions of his human nature, and his obedience to the Law of Mediatorship must be ranked among his Mediatorial actions, which he performed by the personal union of both his natures.

It may be you think (as many others do) that Christ began to pay the price of our redemption from the very first beginning of his incarnation, for many affirm that he was conceived by the Holy Ghost without any original sin, that so he might thereby justifie us from our original sin, which opinion I have confuted: but the open History of the Evangelists do speak nothing at all of his Mediatorial actions till he was publicly installed into the office of the Mediator by John's Baptism.

Yet the Apostle testifieth that Christ himself saith by the Psalmist, wherefore when he cometh into the world he saith, sacrifice and offering thou wouldst not, but a body hast thou prepared me: in burnt offering and sacrifice for sin thou hast had no pleasure; then said I, Low I come (in the volume of thy book it is written of me) to do thy will, O God: Coming into the world, his incarnation, doing his will, is the fulfilling the Law for our Redemption.

Yea, when Christ began to be thirty years of age, he was publicly installed into the Mediator's office, by the joint consent of all the Trinity; and so our Saviour doth explain the matter unto John, saying. Thus our Desire is (or thus it becometh us) to fulfill all Righteousness, Mat. 3.14. The two terms, 1. our desire, 2. our fulfilling all righteousness, had need to be explained : the term us or our desire must have relation to some other, namely, to the joint desire of the Trinity: all the Trinity desired to fulfill all that righteousness which appertained to the Mediator's person and office: at this time they desired to fulfill that part of righteousness which appertained to his public Installment.

Further Reasoning against the influence of Christ's Obedience unto Justification by way of Imputation.

The Apostle in the text, Rom. 8.4, that the Righteousness of the Law might be fulfilled in us, doth not speak of that part of Legal obedience which God requires of every man that looks to be saved thereby: but in this place he speaks only that part of righteousness which the Gospel-part of the Law taught and tipified by their sacrifices of Atonement, which sacrifices are called sacrifices of righteousness, becuse they taught sinners how they might obtain the Father's Atonement by the Mediator's sacrifice of Atonement for their full and perfect Righteousness.

Did Christ condemn sin in the flesh by his Legal Obedience? no; but by his Mediatorial Obedience only, Rom. 8. 3,4.

God sent his Son for sin, when he sent him to make his soul a sacrifice of Atonement for sin, as I have opened the phrase at large in Cor. 5.21.

In brief the meaninig of the Apostle lies thus, when God sent his Son to die as a Malefactor in similitude of sinful flesh, Christ did at the same time condemn sin, because he did at the same time die as a Mediator, and make his soul a Mediatorial sacrifice of Atonement for sin, and so procured his Father's Atonement to poor sinners, and by this means he condemned sin in the flesh, and made sinners sinless, that is to say Righteous. But this distinction of the double death of Christ I have opened more at large in Gal. 3.13, and Luke 22.19, and in Psa. 22.15.

And in this very sense all sacrifices of Atonement are called sacrifices of Righteousness. Deut. 33.19, Psa. 4.5, 51.19.

And in this sense Christ is the end of the Law for Righteousness to every one that believeth. Rom. 10.4.

And thus I think I have explained the true nature of a sinner's right- cousness, justice, or justification, which I have described to be nothing else, but the Father's merciful atonement, pardon, and forgiveness, so that I may more fitly call a sinner's righteousness a merciful justice put upon poor believing sinners, by God's Fatherly pardon and forgiveness, than a strict Legal righteousness imputed to us from Christ's Legal obedience, as our actual righteousness, as the common doctrine of imputation doth teach.

And indeed the righteousness which God the Father bestowed upon poor believing sinners in making them sinless by this Atonement, is an example of the highest degree of mercy.

The Geneva note on Psalm 130.3, is excellent, and speaketh thus, he declareth that we cannot be just before God, but by forgiveness of sins, for God's forgiveness is a part of his merciful Atonement.

Hence it is evident that God's Atonement, pardon, and forgiveness communicated to poor believing sinners must needs be the formal cause of a sinner's righteousness.

Whether the Justice and Righteousness of a Sinner doth lie only in God's Merciful Atonement.

The justice and righteousness of a sinner doth not lie in his own righteous nature, nor in his own just actions, nor yet in the righteousness of Christ imputed, but it doth lie only in the Father's righteous atonement pardon and forgiveness, procured by the meritorious Sacrifice of atone- ment, and conveyed by the Father through the Mediator to every believ- ing sinner, as soon as they are in the Mediator by faith.

This doctrine of a sinner's righteousness hath ever been well known, and witnessed among the godly in all ages from the beginning of the world.

1. It is witnessed by the practices of all sacrifices of Atonement before the Law.

2. It is witnessed by the practices of all sacrifices under the Law.

3. It is witnessed by the doctrine of the Prophet.

4. It is witnessed by the doctrine of the New Testament, and it was never so much obscured as it hath been of late days by the doctrine of impu- tation.

It is evident that our first Parents were well acquainted with the doctrine of a sinner's justification by God's Atonement: for as soon as ever God had told them, that the seed of the woman should break the devil's head-plot, he explained unto them the manner how the seed of the woman should do it, namely, by his Mediatorial sacrifice of Atonement.

After the flood when Noah offered sacrifice of Atonement, Jehovah smelled a smell of Rest, Gen. 8.21, and to that resting of God in the promise, the sweet smell of rest, which God smelt in Noah's sacrifice did look. The word Rest impleth that now God's Spirit was quieted, and that he did rest satisfied and well pleased in the sacrifice of Christ, which was thereby typified: confer to this Eph. 5. the fathers by faith saw Christ's sacrifice.

By this means Noah knew and believed that he was made righteous or sinless by God's merciful Atonement procured by Christ's Mediatorial sacrifice of Atonement.

For the God of Glory Jesus Christ appearer to him (that is, to Abraham) whilst he dwelt at Ur of the Caldees, Acts 7.2, no doubt but Jesus Christ did then tell him in what miserable lost condition he was, and how he should be that seed of the woman that should break the devil's head-plot by his sacrifice of Atonement, and how he should thereby procure his Father's Atonement to all broken-hearted sinners. All which Abraham believed, and so his sins were done away by God's Atonement, which he received by his faith, and so he was made perfectly just and righteous in God's sight.

The doctrine of a sinner's justification or righteousness was abundantly taught under the Law by their sacrifices of atonement, namely, by their burnt-offerings, sin-offerings, trespass-offerings, in Lev. 1. Lev. 4 Lev. 5, &c., as I have explained their use above.

The doctrine of a sinner's justification or righteousness by the Father's Atonement was taught, and explained by the Prophets. The Prophet David saith in the Person of Christ, I have preached thy righteousness to the great Congregation, Psa. 40.9, what righteousness was it that he by himself and by his Officers preached to the Church of the first born? Was it his Legal Righteousness made theirs by his Father's Imputation? no, the Text denieth that, and saith, that it was such a righteousness, as he obtaineth by his sacrifice of Atonement, saying, Sacrifice and offering thou didst not desire, and then said I, Lo I come, I delight to do thy will, O my God, Ps. 40.8, By the doing of which will, saith Paul, we are sanctified from sin, or made perfectly righteous.

Or thus, Christ purchased or procured such a righteousness of his Father for sinners, as shall last to all Eternity by the same way and means by which he purchased their eternal redemption, but he did not purchase their redemption and freedom from sin by his active Legal Obedience, but by his active Mediatorial Obedience, when he made his soul a Mediatorial Sacrifice of Atonement for poor sinners. Compare Heb. 9.12, 14, with Dan. 9.24, therefore Christ purchased and procured such a righteousness for sinners as shall last to all Eternity by no other way or means, but by his Mediatorial Sacrifice of Atonement, therefore his Father's Atonement is a sinner's Righteousness.

The New Testament doth also bear witness to this doctrine. St. Paul the Apostle doth tell us Rom. 8.4, that the Righteousness of the Law, (namely, the righteousness which was taught and typified by the sacrifices of the Law) might be fulfilled in us, that walk not after the flesh but after the Spirit; as I have explained this Text a little before.

Secondly, The Apostle Paul doth in another place confirm this doctrine, saying, God made him to be sin for us (that is to say, God ordained him to be a Sacrifice of Atonement for our sins,) that we might be made the righteousness of God in him; that is to say, that we might be made righteous or sinless by God's Atonement.

How Abraham's Faith was imputed to him for Righteousness.

Abraham's faith was imputed to him for Righteousness, because by it he did receive the Father's Atonement for his full and perfect Righteousness, because he believed all this both in Gen. 11.31, and again Gen. 12, therefore God imputed that faith to him for righteousness, for by that faith he apprehended and received the Father's Atonement, and applied it to his own soul, as an effectual remedy to acquit him from the guilt of all his sins, and so by that means he became sinless, that is to say, justified and righteous in God's sight.

And in this sense the Apostle Paul doth prove that Abraham's faith was accounted to him for righteousness, by a Testimony taken from David, Psa. 32, saying, even as David also describeth the blessedness of that man unto whom God imputeth righteousness without works; saying, Blessed are they whose iniquities are forgiven, and whose sins are covered, Blessed is the man to whom the Lord doth not impute sin. What other reason can any man else render, why the Apostle should interlace this testimony in this place, but to describe unto us the true manner how Abraham's faith did make him righteous, namely, because by faith he did apprehend and receive the Father's atonement, by which his sins were forgiven, covered, and not imputed.

And thus after this sort the Apostle doth bring in forgiveness of sin as an effect of justifying faith: for faith is the only instrument of the Spirit, by which sinners come to the Mediator in and through whose Mediation they apprehend, and receive the Father's Atonement, pardon and forgivness, for their full and perfect justification.

This was the only true reason why God imputed Abraham's faith to him for righteousness, namely, because he believed in God's Atonement, through the mediation of the seed promised.

And it is further evident that this doctrine of a sinner's righteousness by faith was taught and preached by all the Prophets as Peter affirmeth, for all the Prophets, (saith he) do witness that through the name of Christ, whosoever believeth in him shall receive remission of their sins, Acts 10.43, that is to say, they shall receive remission of their sins for their justification by the Father's atonement, procured by Christ's sacrifice of atonement.

And to this tenor the Apostle Paul doth explain the use of faith in the point of a sinner's justification, Phil. 39, and in Rom. 10.4, 6.10, With the heart saith he man believeth unto righteousness. He doth not say faith is a sinner's righteousness, but that by it a sinner believeth unto righteousness.

And in this sense all Sacrifices of Atonement are called Sacrifices of Righteousness, not only as they are the procuring cause of the Father's Atonement for a sinner's righteousness, but also because they must be offered in righteousness, Mal. 3.3, that is to say, in faith, because poor believing sinners do by faith receive the Father's Atonement for their full and perfect righteousness.

And it is further evident that faith doth not otherwise justifie a sinner but as it is that grace or instrument of the Spirit, whereby a sinner is enabled to apprehend and receive the Father's atonement, by the Apostle's discourse in Rom. 3.21,22,23,24,25, all which verses I will briefly expound unto you: Firstly, the Apostle in these words doth teach us the nature of a sinner's justification he calls it the righteousness of God. He doth not call it the righteousness of Christ, but the righteousness of God the Father, because the formal cause and finishing act of a sinner's righteousness or justification doth come down from God the Father upon all believing sinners. A sinner cannot be made righteous by the works of the Law, as the former verse doth conclude: For by the Law come men to know themselves to be sinners and they that are sinners are ever sinners in themselves, therefore if ever sinners can be made righteous they must be made righteous by such a kind of righteousness as it pleaseth God the Father to bestow upon them, and that can be no other righteousness than a passive righteouness proceeding from God's merciful atonement, pardon and forgiveness.

But the Apostle doth further describe this righteousness of God, ver. 21, by two other circumstances, 1. Negatively. 2. Affirmatively. 1. Negatively he saith that this righteousness is without the works of the Law. He doth plainly affirm that the works of the Law have no influence at all in the point of a sinners justice or justification.

He doth affirm that this righteousness of God whereby sinners are made righteous, is such a righteousness as is witnessed by the Law and the Prophets. It is witnessed by the Law, namely, by that part of the Law which did teach and typifie unto sinners how they might be sinless by God's atonement through their sacrifice of atonement, as the procuring cause thereof, as I have opened the matter more at large already.

Faith itself is not a sinner's righteousness, and therefore it cannot be accounted as a sinner's righteousness, instead of the righteousness of the Law, as some would have it. For if faith were a sinner's righteousness no otherwise but in the place or stead of the righteousness of the Law, then faith could not justifie a sinner any further than the Law would do, if it could be supposed that a sinner could by any means attain to the righteousness of the Law, and then truly faith would be but a poor righteousness to cover a sinner's nakedness. For if a sinner could keep the whole Law in every circumstance of it, from his birth unto his death, yet it would not be sufficient to justifie his orginal sin.

The true manner how the Law taught sinners to get righteousness by faith: When a poor humble sinner brought his sacrifice of atonement to the priest to be offered for him upon the altar, he must lay both his hands with all his might upon the head of the sacrifice of atonement. This kind of imposition was ordained by God to teach and tipifie unto sinners how they must by faith rest and depend upon the sacrifice of Christ as the only meritorious procuring cause of the Father's atonement for their full and perfect righteousness.

Vers. 25. Whom God hath foreordained to be a propitiation (or a sacrifice of atonement) through faith in his blood. The Apostle explains the
matter by another sentence, Rom. 5.11, by whom we have received the
atonement. The Apostle doth imply three things in this sentence.

1. That Christ is the Mediator by whom sinners do receive.

2. The main thing which they do receive by him is the Father's atonement.

3. That the means or manner by which they receive the Father's atonement, is the grace of faith.

Vers. 25. To declare his righteousness by the passing over sins that are
past, through the forbearance of God.

1. God declared his righteousness towards sinners by ordaining Jesus
Christ to be a propitiation.

2. By ordaining the grace of faith as the instrument of the spirit, whereby
poor sinners might be enabled to believe in the Mediator's propitiatory
sacrifice, and receive through him the Father's atonement for their righteousness.

And therefore justified persons have need of new justice to their con-
sciences every day.

Enumeration of the Causes of Justification.

And now for a conclusion I will sum up the Doctrine of Justification
in six heads.

1. The subject matter of Justification is, believing sinners of all sorts
both Jews and Gentiles all the world over.

2. The formal cause of Justification, or of a sinner's righteousness, is
the Father's atonement, pardon, and forgiveness.

3. The meritorious cause of the Father's atonement for a sinner's Justification, is, Christ's Mediatorial Sacrifice of atonement.

4. The next instrumental means by which a sinner doth receive and
apprehend the Father's atonement for his Justification, is faith in Christ.

5. The only efficient cause of all the former causes and effects, is God's
free grace and mercy in himself.

6. The end of all is the glory of God's free grace and mercy in the believing sinner's justification and salvation.

Examination of Arguments Propounded by M. Forbes for proving Justi-
cation by the Imputation of the Passive Obedience of Christ in
his Death and Satisfaction.

I pray you produce some of his arguments that they may be tried and
examined whether there be any weight of truth in them or no.

Nothing (saith M. Forbes) is made of God to be a sinner's righteousness, but Jesus Christ alone and his righteousness, and this he proves by
1 Cor. 1.30, Jer. 23.26, with other places. The Apostle saith that Christ
was made of God unto us righteousness, but how? not as the doctrine of
imputation speaketh, but thus, God made him to be our righteousness in
a Mediatorial way, by ordering him to be the only meritorious procur-

ing cause of his atonement, which is a sinner's righteousness. Christ is not a sinner's righteousness any otherwise but in a Mediatorial way only, as I have oft warned. Christ is called Jehovah our righteousness, but still it must be understood in a Mediatorial way, and no otherwise.

And thus Christ is our Righteousness in one respect, the Father is another, and the Holy Ghost in another. Each person is a sinner's righteousness in several respects. The manner how Christ should justifie the many was by bearing their iniquities, and how else did he bear their iniquities but by his sacrifice of Atonement? and in this sense Christ is said to justifie us with his blood, Rom. 5.9, that is to say, by his Sacrifice of Atonement; therefore his righteousness cannot be the formal cause of a sinner's righteousness; it is but the procuring cause of the Father's atonement which is the only formal cause of a sinner's righteousness.

The Father is a sinner's righteousness. 1. Efficiently. 2. Formally. His Atonement so procured must needs be the formal cause of a sinner's full and perfect righteousness.

The Holy Ghost also doth make sinners righteous, instrumentally by fitting, preparing and qualifying sinners for the Father's Atonement, by quickening their souls with the lively grace of faith, by which grace sinners are enabled to apprehend and receive the Father's Atonement.

It is well that your Author will grant remission of sins to be righteousness in effect: if remission of sins be a sinner's righteousness then I pray consider whose act it is to forgive sins formally. I have already proved it to be the Father's act to forgive sin formally, and not Christ's; he doth forgive sin no otherwise but as a Mediator by procuring his Father's pardon and forgiveness.

M. Forbes is put to his shifts to declare that Christ's passive obedience is the matter of a sinner's righteousness, by a distinction between Christ as he was our Lamb for Sacrifice in his human nature, and as he was our Priest in his divine nature; for else he did foresee that he should run into an exceeding gross absurdity, if he had made any action of Christ's Godhead or Priestly nature to have been a sinner's righteousness by imputation: Therefore to avoid that absurdity he doth place a sinner's righteousness in his passive obedience only. His distinction between Christ as he was a Lamb for sacrifice in his human nature, and as he is our Priest in his Divine nature, is very ill applied, because he makes Christ's passive obedience to be meritorious and satisfactory, excluding him as he is our Priest.

From all the premises I think I may well conclude that your Author is in a great error, to ascribe the whole matter of a sinner's righteousness to Christ's bloody Sacrifice only. Neither was his bloody sacrifice the only procuring of his Father's atonement, but his Priestly nature must concur thereunto; he made his oblation by his divine nature as well as by his human nature.

The blood of Jesus Christ doth clense us from all sin, 1 John 1.7, by a Synecdoche; for the Apostle doth not say that his blood alone without anything doth clense us from all sin (as M. Forbes would have him speak) but he names his blood as a Synecdoche of his death or as a Synecdoche of his Mediatorial obedience, which also he sealed with his blood, when he made his soul a Mediatorial Sacrifice.

I grant that all mankind are one with Adam by a natural union, as proceeding from the same root and fountain of nature; but I fear your Author doth stretch our natural union with Adam unto a personal union (I mean M. Forbes doth so by consequence) to the end that he might make Adam's personal action to be ours by imputation.

Adam's disobedience had this effect, that it procured a corrupt and sinful nature to himself, and to all his posterity, which otherwise had continued righteous and sinless.

In like sort Christ's Mediatoril obedience had this effect, that it procured God's fatherly atonement and acceptance of all his posterity and seed that should be born of the same promise. Gen. 3.15.

By one man, namely, Adam's sin in eating the forbidden fruit, death entered into the world, and death by sin, namely, spiritual death in sin fell upon Adam and his posterity for his sin; and so death passed upn all men for all men had sinned.   That is to say, in whose loins all men have sinned (by receiving from his loins his corrupt nature which is sin) and also is the punishment of Adam's sinful eating; not whose act of obedience in eating the forbidden fruit, all men have sinned in eating the forbidden fruit, for then we must have been united to Adam as one person with him.

But it passeth my understanding to conceive how God in justice can impute the act of Christ's Mediatorial Sacrifice of Atonement to us as our act, unless he doth first make us one with Christ in the personal unity of both natures, neither can I see how any of the actions of Christ can be imputed to Believers as their actions.

In like sort our blessed Mediator (as he is the mystical head of all believers in the Covenant of grace) did take care to do all and every act of Mediatorial obedience that might procure his Father's Atonement for the good and benefit of every member of his mystical body, as fully and effectually as if every member could have performed those acts of Mediatorial obedience themselves.   And in this sense God doth impute the efficacy of all Christ's Mediatorial obedience to all believers as the only meritorious price of his Father's atonement for them.

Of Atonement or Reconciliation.

The Father's Atonement comprehendeth under it justification and adoption.

These two parts of the Father's atonement or reconciliation are evident by the effects, which all the sacrifices of atonement under the Law did procure to poor believing sinners (for all the sacrifices of atonement under the Law did typifie Christ's Sacrifice of atonement) and they procured the Father's atonement, which hath a threefold effect towards poor believing sinners.

1. All Sacrifices of Atonement in general were ordained to procure a savour of rest unto Jehovah, namely, to procure a savour of rest to God the Father.

2. The sin offerings (which were sacrifices of atonement) were ordained by God to procure God's merciful atonement, pardon, and forgiveness to poor believing sinners, by which means only sinners are made sinless, that is to say, just and righteous in God's sight.

3. The burnt-offerings (which also were sacrifices of Atonement) were ordained of God to procure his favorable acceptance towards poor believing sinners, by receiving them into special favor as Adopted sinners.

Therefore his forgiveness of sin is not only a bare acquittance of the fault, but it doth comprehend under it his receiving of sinners into favor. And I do also grant that his receiving of sinners into favor must be distinguished as another part of God's Atonement.

This also must be remembered, that no other person in the Trinity doth forgive sins formally but God the Father only, Mar. 2.7, Col. 2.13, he of his free grace did ordain the Mediator as the meritorious cause of his forgiveness, and therefore it is said that he doth forgive us all our sins for Christ's sake, Ephes. 4.32. Sometimes Christ is said to forgive sins, Col. 3.3. but still we must understand his forgiveness to be in a Mediatorial way, not formally.

And whereas I have often in this treatise made God's atonement to comprehend under it our Redemption from sin, as well as our justification and adoption; I would have you take notice that I do not mean that God's atonement doth contain under it Redemption as another distinct point differing from justification; but I make our redemption and freedom from sin by the Father's atonement to be all one with our justification from sin.

The Father's Atonement or Reconciliation is the top-mercy of all mercies that makes poor sinners happy.

But the truth is, a sinner's Atonement must be considered as it is the work of all the Trinity.

1. The Father must be considered as the efficient and as the formal cause of a sinner's atonement.

2. The Mediator must be considered as the only meritorious procuring cause of the Father's Atonement. Rom. 5.10.

3. The Holy Ghost must be considered as the principal instrumental cause of the Father's Atonement, by working in sinners the grace of faith, by which sinners are enabled to apprehend and receive the Father's atonement: or thus, The Father must be considered as the efficient cause, the Son as the Mediatorial cause, and the Holy Ghost as the principal instrumental cause of all blessings, that poor believing sinners do enjoy, Eph. 1.13.

To conclude, If thou hast gotten any spiritual blessing by anything that I have said in this Treatise, Let God have all the Glory.

Answers to Letters from England.

Copy of a Letter written from New England, in Answer to a Letter which they have Received from some Brethren in Old England, in the behalf of Mr. Pinchon.

Reverend and Beloved Brethren in our Lord Jesus:—

We see by your Letters you have thought it meete to address yourselves to us (the Elders of these Churches) in behalf of Mr. Pinchon and his Book, to incline us to a favorable construction of the Tenents held forth in it as Disputable, and (to some of note) probable; and for himself to move us to intercede with our Magistrates to deal favorably with him as a Gentleman pious and well deserving. In both which we shall give you a just account of our Proceedings.

When Mr. Pinchon's Book came to us it was the time of the sitting of our General Court, wherein both Magistrates and Deputies of every Town in the Country, do assemble to consider and determine of the chiefest affairs which concern this Colony: At the same time a Ship in the Harbor was ready to set sail for England. Now the Court (both parts of them, the Magistrates and Deputies) perceiving by the Title Page that the Contents of the Book were unsound, and Derogatory, both to the Justice of God and the Grace of Christ, which being published in England might add to the heap of many errors and Heresies already too much abounding, and this Book being published under the name of a New English Gentleman, might occasion many to think that New England also concurred in the allowance of such Exorbitant Aberrations: They therefore judged it meet, not to stay till the Elders could be gathered together but whilst the Ship yet stayed, to declare their own judgment against the Book, and to send a Copy of their Declaration to England by the Ship, then ready to depart: Had the Tenets therein seemed to them to be matters, either of doubtful disputation, or of small moment, we doubt not, they would either not at all have declared themselves against the Book, or if they had, they would have stayed for some opportunity of previous consultation with the Elders: but some of the Tenets seemed to them so directly to shake the Fundamentals of Religion, and to wound the vitals of Christianity, that they being many of them well versed both in Dogmatical and Controversial points of Divinity, thought it their duty to profess their Orthodox faith against all destructive Paradoxes, and dangerous Innovations vented from amongst ourselves; for according as they believe, they do also profess (as ourselves likewise do.) That the

Obedience of Christ to the whole Law, which is the Law of Righteousness, is the matter of our Justification; and the Imputation of our sins to Christ (and thereupon his suffering the sense of wrath of God upon him for our sin) and the Imputation of his obedience and sufferings are the formal cause of our Justification and that they that do deny this, do now take away both these, both the matter and the form of our Justification (as this Book doth) and take away also our Justification, which is the life of our souls and of our Religion, and therefore called Justification of life. Rom. 5.18. As for the Notion which you conceive he declineth, of Infinite wrath, we readily conceive with you, that though God's wrath be (as himself is infinite, yet no creature can bear infinite wrath) but be swallowed up of it; and therefore the wicked are put to suffer finite wrath in an infinite time; yet this suffering in an infinite time is accidental, in regard to the finiteness of the creature, but Christ being infinite God, as well as finite man, his manhood suffering, though in a finite measure, the sense of God's wrath both in soul and body, the infiniteness of his Godhead (whereto his manhood was united in one person) made his finite suffering, in a finite time to become of infinite value and efficacy, for the satisfaction of God's Justice and transaction of our Redemption. (Thus much for the Book.)

Now for the Author of the Book; before your letter came to our hands the Court dealt favorably with him, according to your desire. Before they knew your desire, they appointed three of our fellow Elders and Brethren, all of them his friends and acquaintances (such as himself chose) to confer with him, and finding him yielding in some main points (which he expressed willingly under his own hand) the Court readily accepted the same, as a fruit of his ingenuity, and a pledge of more full satisfaction; withal they gave him a Book penned (at their appointment by our Reverend Brother Mr. Norton) in way of answer to all his grounds, which he thankfully accepted, and promised upon due perusal & consideration thereof, to return further Answer. All which, though it pleased God to have done, before your letter came to our hands; yet we acquainted our Magistrates with the contents of your Letter, whereto they reurned this Answer. They doubted, either you had not read the Book throughout, or that having seriously weighed it (as the matter required) you would find some Fundamental Errors in it, meet to be duly witnessed against: For ourselves we thankfully accept of this your labor of love in advertising us of what you think behooful; wherein though we differ, and (as we believe) justly differ from you, yet if we did not lovingly accept advertisement from our Reverend Brethren sometimes when there is lsss need we might discourage ourselves and other Brethren from sendng us due advertisement when there is more need. Now the Lord Jesus Christ, the God of Truth and Peace, lead you by his Spirit of Truth into all Truth; and support you with a Spirit of faithfulness and holy zeal, to stand in the gap against the Innundation of all the Errors and Heresies of this present Age; and by his Spirit of Peace, guide and bless your Studies and holy Labours, to the advancement and establishment of Peace with

Truth throughout the Nation: So desiring the fellowship of your prayers, we take leave and rest.

Your loving Brethren in the Lord Jesus and in the Fellowship of his Gospel,

John Cotton.

Richard Mather.

Zech. Symmes.

John Wilson.

Will. Thompson.

Sir Henry Vane wrote from England to the Colonial authorities at Boston, his former associates, asking them to deal lightly with Mr. Pynchon, to which they replied:—

Honoured Sir:—

We received your letter bearing date the 15th of April, 1652, written in the behalf of Mr. William Pincheon, who is one that we did love and respect. But his book and the doctrine therein contained we cannot but abhor as pernicious and dangerous; and are much grieved, that such an erroneous pamphlet was penned by a New England man, especially a Magistrate amongst us, wherein he taketh upon him to condemn the judgment of most, if not all, both ancient and modern divines, who were learned, orthodox and godly in point of so great weight and concernment, as tend to the salvation of God's elect, and the contrary, which he maintains to the destruction of such as follow it. Neither have we heard of any one godly orthodox divine, that ever held what he hath written; nor do we know of any one of our ministers in all the four jurisdictions that doth approve of the same; but all do judge it erroneous and heretical. And to the end that we might give satisfaction to all the world of our just proceedings against him, and for the avoiding of any just offence to be taken against us, we caused Mr. John Norton, teacher of the church of Ipswich, to answer his book fully, which, if printed, we hope it will give yourself and all indifferent men full satisfaction.

Mr. Pincheon might have kept his judgment to himself, as it seems he did above thirty years, most of which time he hath lived amongst us with honour, much respect and love. But when God left him to himself in the publishing, and spreading his erroneous book here amongst us, to the endangering of the faith of such as might come to read them (as the like effects have followed the reading of other erroneous books brought over into these parts,) we held it our duty, and believed we were called of God to proceed against him accordingly. And this we can further say, and that truly, that we used all lawful Christian means, with as much tenderness, respect, and love, as he could expect, which we think he himself will acknowledge. For we desired divers of our elders such as he himself liked, to confer with him privately, lovingly and meekly, to see if they could prevail with him by arguments from the scriptures, which accord-

ingly was done, and he was then thereby so far convinced that he seemed
to yield for substance the case in controversy signed with his own hand.
And for the better confirming of him in the truth of God, Mr. Norton
left with him a copy of the book he writ in answer to him; and the Court
gave him divers months to consider both of the book, and what had been
spoken unto him by the elders. But in the interim (as it is reported) he
received letters from England, which encouraged him in his error, to the
great grief of us all, and of divers others of the people of God amongst us.
We therefore leave the author, together with the fautors and maintainers
of such opinions to the great Judge of all the earth, who judgeth right-
eously and is no respector of persons. Touching that which you honoured self doth advise us unto, viz. not to censure any person for matters
of a religious nature or concernment, we desire to follow any good advice
from you, or any of the people of God, according to the rule of God's
word. Yet we conceive, with submission still to better light, that we have
not acted in Mr. Pincheon's case either for substance or circumstance, as
far as we can discern, otherwise than according unto rule, and as we believe in conscience to God's command, we were bound to do. All which
we hope will so far satisfy you as that we shall not need to make further
defence touching this subject. The God of peace and truth lead you into
all faith, and guide your heart aright in these dangerous and apostatising
times, wherein many are fallen from the faith, giving heed to errours, and
make you an instrument (in the place God hath called you unto) of his
praise, to stand for his truth against all opposers thereof, which will
bring you peace and comfort in the saddest hours, which are the prayers
of, Sir, your unworthy servants,

John Endicott, Gov'r
Tho Dudley Dep'ty
Rich. Bellingham
Increase Nowell
Wm Hibbins
Sam. Simonds
Robt Bridges
John Glover

20 October, 1652. Past by the Council.

Religious Services Conducted by Laymen.

After Mr. Moxon's departure, there being no regular minister to take his place, the services were conducted by the leading members of the church. At a town-meeting held February 18th, 1656, "It was voted that Mr. Hollyoke and
Henry Burt should carry on the work of the Sabbath in this
plase, but in case that through any providence of God part
of the tyme (they) should be disenabled that Deacon Chapin

should supply that present vacansy; more over the town voted to allow them also 50 pounds a year, that is to say from
the 4th of November last the time they began and to continue till the town have another suply or shall so cause to alter they are to in that particular, but they would accept but
of 40 pounds unto which the Town assented."

"it was also voted that they would allow to Decon Wright,
decon Chapin, Mr. Hollyock, Henry Burt 12 pounds for their
labours the last summer which they spent in that work."

"At a town meeting, November 9th, 1657, Mr. Holyoke
is made choice to cary on ye worke of ye Sabbath once every
Sabbath day which he accepts of. Mr. Pynchon is made
choise of one part of ye day once a fortnight which he will
endeavour to attend sometimes by reading note and sometimes by his own meditations till March next. Deacon
Chapin and Henry Burt are made choice of to carry on y^e
other part of ye day once a fortnight for which these persons
they are allowed forty pounds a year."

SEATING THE PEOPLE IN THE MEETING-HOUSE.

The selectmen and the deacons, or a committee appointed
by the selectmen, determined the order in which the seats
in the meeting-houses in New England, in the early settlement, should be occupied. Ability and general regard, as
well as wealth, had much to do with the order of selection.
The women, as a rule, do not appear to have been assigned
to particular seats, but occupied, in another part of the
house, such as suited their own preferences. The lists still
preserved, which give the order of seating the men and boys
in Springfield, do not indicate any great regard for those
having the largest possessions. At Northampton, "age and
estate" determined the order, and to some extent that might
have prevailed here. The first list, still of record, bears the
date of December 23, 1659, and reads:—

"The order which persons now seated in the meeting-
house by the Selectmen and Deacon Chapin. The select-

men are as followeth: Robert Ashley, Benjamin Cooley, William Warriner, Jonathan Burt, Thomas Cooper.

Henry Burt in the little Seate by the Deacon's seate.

First Seate.—Robert Ashley, Thomas Cooper, Rowland Stebbins, George Colton, Benjamin Cooley.

2d Seate.—Richard Sikes, Thomas Merrick, William Warriner, Richard Fellows.

3d Seate.—Thomas Stebbins, Miles Morgan, John Harmon, John Leonard, Benjamin Munn, Anthony Dorchester.

4th Seate.—Thomas Gilbert, Jonathan Burt, Benjamin Parsons, John Dumbleton, William Branch, Samuel Marshfield.

5th Seate.—John Matthews, Rowland Thomas, Reice Bedortha, John Clark, John Lamb, Thomas Day.

6th Seate.—John Lombard, Lawrence Bliss, Griffith Jones, Thomas Miller, Nathaniel Pritchard, Richard Excell.

7th Seate.—Thomas Bancroft, Jonathan Taylor, John Stewart, John Scott, William Brooks, James Osbourn.

8th Seate.—Simon Beamon, Thomas Noble, James Warriner, Francis Pepper, Obadiah Miller, Nathaniel Burt.

9th Seate.—Abell Wright, Hugh Dudley, John Bagg, John Sacket, David Ashley, Samuel Bliss, John Riley.

And for order sake there were placed in the

10th Seate.—Japhat Chapin, John Harmon, Samuel Harmon, James Taylor, John Henrison, Edward Foster, Peter Swinke.

The rest of the younge persons that want years, are to sit on the other side of the alley in the seate next to the stayers.

The order of seating, bearing date of February 23, 1662, in the records,—1663, according to present reckoning, the year at that time beginning March 25th,— was as follows:—

By Deacon Chapin & the Selectmen. Thomas Cooper, Robert Ashley, Benjamin Cooley & Samuel Marshfield.

In ye first Seate.—Robert Ashley, Benjamin Cooley, Thomas Cooper, George Colton & Rowland Stebbins.

In ye 2d Seate.—Nathaniel Ely, Richard Sikes, Thomas Merrick & William Warriner.

In ye 3d Seate.—Serja Stebbins, Miles Morgan, Benjamin Munn, John Leonard, Anthony Dorchester, Samuel Marshfield.

In ye 4th Seate.—Benjamin Parsons, Jonathan Burt, William Branch, Reice Bedortha, John Dumbleton, Rowland Thomas.

In ye 5th Seate.—John Matthews, John Clarke, John Lamb, Lawrence Bliss, Thomas Miller, Thomas Day.

In ye 6th Seate.—John Lombard, Griffith Joanes, Nathaniel Pritchard, Richard Exell, Thomas Noble, Samuel Ely.

In ye 7th Seate.—Jonathan Taylor, Thomas Bancroft, John Scot, Nathaniel Burt, John Stewart, William Brooks.

In ye 8th Seate.—Jeremiah Horton, John Bagg, John Riley, Simon Beamon, Abell Wright.

In ye 10th Seate.—Joseph Crowfoote, Edward Foster, Charles Ferry, James Osborn, William Hunter, Peter Swinke.

In ye foreseate of ye Gallery.

In ye upper seate above ye Pillar on ye North side.—Henry Chapin, John Bliss, John Keepe.

In ye upper pt above ye Pillars on ye South side.—Francis Pepper, James Warriner, Samuel Bliss.

Below ye Pillars on ye North side.—Samuel Holyoke, David Ashley, Jonathan Ashley, Japhat Chapin, Timothy Cooper, Isack Colton, Obadi Cooley.

On ye South side below ye Pillars.—Thomas Cooper, Jun., Joseph Warriner, John Leonard, John Harmon, Samuel Harmon, Increase Sikes, John Dorchester.

In y^t seate in ye Gallery wch faces agt ye minister.—Ephraim Colton, Eliakim Cooley, Jonathan Morgan, Samuel Stebbins, James Dorchester.

In ye Backer seate of ye Gallery on the North side at the upper end of it.—James Taylor, John Horton, Hugh Mackey, William Morgan.

In ye South side at ye upper end of the Backer seate.—
Jonathan Ball, Samuel Ball, Joseph Harmon, Nathaniel
Sikes, Thomas Thompson.

In ye Backer seate above the Pillars on the North side.—
John Hitchcock, John Clarke, John Lombard, Samuel Bliss.

On the South side.—Joseph Thomas, Thomas Stebbins,
Joseph Dorchester.

Goodwife Chapin is to sitt in the seate along with Mistress Glover and Mistress Hollyoke.

BURNING OF SPRINGFIELD BY THE INDIANS.

The burning of Springfield by the Indians October 5,
1675, nearly forty years after its settlement, was the most
startling and important event in its early history. King
Philip had begun open hostilities which had spread to the region of the Connecticut valley. Hadley, Deerfield, and
Northfield had suffered. Captain Lothrop and his brave
men had been slaughtered at Deerfield, and terror reigned
in every town and hamlet. Major John Pynchon had gone
to Hadley with a small force on the 4th of October, leaving
Springfield unprotected.

On Long Hill in the south part of the town, overlooking
the valley, a fort had been constructed for the protection of
the friendly Indians, who were dwelling in peace in the
neighborhood. Into this a large number of hostile Indians,
including some who had previously been on terms of intimate friendship with the whites, had secreted themselves.
Toto, a friendly Indian, who was living with a white family
in Windsor, revealed the plot, and that night a messenger
rode swiftly to Springfield, who roused the inhabitants and
warned them of the threatened danger. Every one was notified who had not gone to Hadley, with Major Pynchon, and
immediately took refuge in the three fortified houses.
Among the numbers were some of the older men of the community, including Deacon Samuel Chapin, Rev. Pelatiah
Glover, Jonathan Burt, Lieut. Thomas Cooper, Thomas
Miller, and others. Mr. Glover at once carried his library

to Mr. Pynchon's house for safety. A messenger was dis-
patched to Hadley to notify Major Pynchon of the great danger that was impending, but the morning of the 5th opened
without any indications of an attack upon the town, and
Toto's statements began to be discredited. Rev. Mr. Glover,
confident that there was no danger had carried his library
back to his house, and Lieut. Cooper, long engaged in
trade with the Indians, and who well knew every Indian in
this region, set out on horseback for the fort. Thomas
Miller accompanied him. They had approached Mill river,
within less than a half a mile of the fort, when they were
fired upon by the Indians. Miller was instantly killed and
Cooper severely wounded. The latter's horse galloped back
to town and stopped in front of Major Pynchon's house,
when Lieut. Cooper fell dead to the ground. The Indians
then followed up this attack, and soon the dwellings, which
had been temporarily deserted by the occupants, for places
of greater safety, were set on fire and destroyed. Pentecost
Mathews, wife of John Mathews, was shot and killed in the
south part of the town, and her house set on fire and con-
sumed. The work of destruction, now fairly begun, the
prominent actors in this most startling frontier drama, no
longer continued their disguise. They proved to be some
of the hitherto friendly Indians,—one of them an old sachem
who had been on the most intimate terms of friendship, almost
from the first settlement. The house of correction, some of
Pynchon's mills, and many dwellings and barns, were burned
to the ground. Various accounts differ as to the actual
number. Major Pynchon, who hurried back from Hadley as
soon as informed of the contemplated plot, but did not arrive
until the town was in ashes, stated that about thirty houses
were burned. Capt. Samuel Appleton, who was at Hadley,
in a letter put the number at thirty-three house, and twenty-
five barns, while Jonathan Burt set down the number at
"twenty-nine houses and barns." He was chosen one of the
Selectmen the next February and entered a brief account in
the third volume of the town records, which now occupies a

fly leaf of that book, and this is the only account that has been preserved in Springfield.

During the attack Edmund Pryngrydays and Nathaniel Brown were severely wounded, and both died soon afterwards. Major Treat, of Connecticut, who had been stationed at Westfield with an armed force, and Major Pynchon and Captain Appleton with their two hundred soldiers prevented further destruction.

Mr. Glover's valuable library shared the common fate and was entirely destroyed with his dwelling. Fifteen houses on the street, and twenty or more in the outskirts of the town were saved.

Major Pynchon's letter to Rev. John Russell of Hadley, his letter to the Governor, both of which are on file in the State Archives at Boston, and one to his son then in England, contain some interesting statements concerning this entirely unexpected and startling event. His letter to Rev. Mr. Russell is given in full below:—

SPRINGFIELD, Oct. 5, 1675.

REVEREND SIR:—

The Lord will have us ly in ye dust before him; wee y^t were full are emptyed. But it is ye Lord & blessed be his holy name: we came to a Lamentable & woefull sight. The Towne in flames, not a house nor Barne, except old Goodman Branches, till we came to my house, & then Mr. Glovers & John Hitchcocks & Goodman Stewarts, burnt downe with Barnes, corne & all they had: a few standing about ye meeting house, & then from Miricks downward, all burnt; two garrison houses at the Lower end of ye Towne, my grist Mill, & corne Mill, Burnt downe; with some other houses & Barnes I had let out to Tenants: All Mr. Glovers library Burnt with all his corne, so y^t he hath none to live on as well as my selfe, & Many more y^t have not for subsistence; they tell me 32 houses ye Barnes belonging to y^m are Burnt & all, ye Livelihood of ye owners & what more may meete w^{t}h ye same stress ye Lord only knowes; many more had there estates Burnt in there houses, So y^t I believe 40 familys are utterly destitute of subsistence; ye Lord shew mercy on us. I see not how it is possible for us to live here this winter, & If so the sooner we were holpen off ye Better. Sir, I Pray you acquaint our Honored Governor with this dispensation of God. I know not how to work, neither can I bee able to attend any Public service, the Lord in mercy speake to my heart, & so all our hearts is this Reall desire of

Yours, etc.,

JOHN PYNCHON.

Under date of October 8, Major Pynchon wrote Governor Leverett:—"I desire to give you an account of the sore stroke upon poor distressed Springfield, which I hope will excuse my late doing of it. On the 4th of October our soldiers which were at Springfield I had called off, leaving none to secure the towne because the Commissioners' orders were so strict. That night a post was sent to us that 500 Indians were about Springfield intending to destroy it on the 5th of October. With about 200 of our soldiers I marched down to Springfield where we found all in flames, about 30 dwelling houses burnt down and 24 or 25 barns, my corn mill, saw mill and other buildings. Generally men's hay and corn are burnt, and many men whose houses stand had their goods burnt in other houses which they had carried them to. Lt. Cooper and two more slain and 4 persons wounded. That the town did not utterly perish is cause of great thankfulness. As soon as said forces appeared the Indians drew off, so that we saw none. Our endeavors here are to secure the houses and corn that are left. Our people are under great discouragement and talk of leaving the place. We need your orders and directions about it. How to have provisions, I mean bread, for want of a mill, is difficult. The soldiers here already complain on that account, although we have flesh enough. Many of the inhabitants have no houses, which fills and throngs every room of those that have, together with the soldiers; indeed it is very uncomfortable living here. But I resolve to attend what God calls me to and to stick to it as long as I can. I hope God will make up in himself what is wanting in the creature, to me, and to us all.

JONATHAN BURT'S ACCOUNT OF THE BURNING OF SPRINGFIELD

on the 5th day of october in the yeare 1675 a day to be kept in memory by posterity when the Barborus heathen made an assalt on this poore towne filled two men and a woman and wounded severall: on of which dyed soone after Burned downe 29 dwelling howses and Barns much Corne and hay but god god wonderfully preserve us or we had been a prey to these teeth god in his good providence so ordered it that an Indian gunns Brutlyganes of the enemis designs to fall on this downe where by we escaped with our lives for which we should give god the glory

Jonathan Burt being an eye witness of the same

To speak my thoughts—all these towns ought to be garrisoned, as I have formerly hinted. To go out after the Indians in the swamps and thickets is to hazard all our men, unless we know where they keep, which is altogether unknown to us."

Major Pynchon, referring to Mr. Glover's loss, says: "He had all his books burnt; not so much as a Bible saved; a great loss, for he had some choice books and many."

This was Springfield's first baptism in fire and blood, and although the settlers must have been greatly disheartened, they immediately set about repairing their broken fortunes. During this year, 1675, according to Judd, in his history of Hadley, 145 persons were killed within the limits of what was then Hampshire county, as follows: At Brookfield August 2, 13; above Hatfield, August 25, 9; at Deerfield, Sept. 1, and after 2; at Northfield, Sept. 2, 8; near Northfield, Sept. 4, 16; at Muddy Brook, (Deerfield) Sept. 18, 71; of Capt. Mosely's company, Sept 18, 3; at Northampton, Sept 28, 2; at Springfield, October 5, 4; at Hatfield, October 19, 10; at Westfield, October 27, 3; and at Northampton, Oct. 29, 4. This great destruction of life in a single year brings to us some realizing sense of the danger that attended the early settlements, and the great insecurity of life.

On the preceding page is Jonathan Burt's account of the burning of Springfield, reproduced from the original record in the town book.

Longmeadow.—The First Location.

The rich alluvial lands at Longmeadow early attracted the attention of those who settled here, and grants of land were soon made in that locality. As is generaly known the first settlement in Longmeadow was on that stretch of lowland in the region through which the railroad passes. Subject to inundations in every high freshet the residents experienced much discomfort and damage. Action was finally taken looking towards a new location of the street and the home-lots upon the high ground to the eastward. At a town meeting held in January, 1703, the question of removal was brought up, when a petition was presented asking for a new grant of land on the hill. They desired room sufficient to lay out some sixty or eighty homelots, each to be twenty rods in width and eighty rods in length. The petition is here given in full:—

"We, the Inhabitants of Longmeadow in Springfeild do make our Address to this Town of Springfeild, as followeth:

We declare our difficult circumstances.

1. Our living in a general field we are thereby forced to be at great charge to make lanes or outlets for our Creatures.

2. By reason of floods our lives have been in great danger, our housing much damnified, and many of our cattle have been lost..

3. A third difficulty, which we shall mention in the last place, not that we count it a matter of least concern, but because in reason it will be helpt in the last place, and that is our living remote from public worship of God, as to hearing the Word preached, &c., and also our children are thereby deprived of the benefits of instruction by the schoolmaster in the Town.

Now for our relief we do suppose our best way is to move out of the general field, and build on the hill against Longmeadow; and we have been at the pains to measure what lands we thought might be convenient to build on, and we do find land indifferently convenient to build upon for three score lots and to be twenty rods in breadth, and about eighty rods in length. We therefore desire the Town to grant us said Lands as homelots to build on; also that the Town would order those lands to be laid out and modeled in such way and manner as may be most comfortable for settling thereon. We desire not this that the Town by granting this our desire should be brought into any snare or inconvenience hereafter, but for our own benefit and comfort and our posteritys. We subscribe, Nathaniel Burt, Senr., Thomas Colton, Eliakim Cooley, Samuel Stebbins, Samuel Bliss, 2d, Nathaniel Bliss, Joseph Cooley, John Colton, Nathaniel Burt, Jr., George Colton, Samuel Keepe, Daniel Cooley, Benjamin Cooley.

Thereuppon the Town did vote that Major John Pynchon,

Japhet Chapin, Lieut. John Hitchcock, to be a committee to
go upon the place and view the lands, who are to make return of what they find to the Town."

At a general town meeting held March 9th, 1703, the committee made their report, and the record states:—

"At this meting the petition of the inhabitants of Longmeadow presented at the Town meeting January 29, was
considered and it was voted to give the liberty to build upon
the hill Eastward of said Longmeadow.

It was further voted to give the land from Pecowsic to
Enfield bounds, and from the hill Eastward of the Longmeadow half a mile further Eastward into the woods unto
the said Longmeadow inhabitants, and unto such others as
a Committee appointed by the Town shall allow, in all which
they shall be ordered and modeled in such way and manner
as may be most comfortable to settle on, reserving liberty for
convenient highways. And Major John Pynchon, Japhet
Chapin, and Lt. John Hitchcock, were appointed to be the
Committee to see to the modeling and ordering of those said
lands, and the charge of this work to be borne by the Longmeadow inhabitants and such others as shall be added to the
Longmeadow inhabitants. Luke Hitchcock, Senr., desired
his dissent hereto entered."

This was the beginning of the work of settling in that portion of Springfield which now constitutes the beautiful village of Longmeadow, the most delightful suburb in proxim-
ity to the original town, and what it seems must at some future time return and become an integral part of the Springfield that is to be, coming back to the house from which it
left at a time when circumstances were greatly different from
the present.

Nathaniel Burt, who headed the petition for removal from
the meadow to the uplands, was the youngest son of Henry
Burt, and he and his sons and grand-sons, were for many
years prominently identified with the interests of the place.
He made donations of land to the town in support of the
church and schools of Longmeadow, and eighty years after

his death his benefactions were recognized by the erection of a monumental tablet at his grave by the town, bearing this inscription: "Mr. Nathaniel Burt, a respected and worthy Father of the town of Longmeadow, was born A. D. 1636, and died Sept. 29, 1720. This monument is erected to his memory by the said Town as a token of gratitude for donations in land made by him to them for the support of the gospel and public schools. Is. 32.8 'The liberal deviseth liberal things and by liberal things shall stand.' Erected by the votes of the Town, passed 1796 and 1797." This was the first public gift in support of popular education made in this part of the colony.

SPRINGFIELD'S FIRST SCHOOL HOUSE.

While no doubt it was adequate for the needs of that time, Springfield's first school house presented a marked contrast with the palatial edifice which is now being erected. It was 22 feet long and 17 feet wide, and the contract price for building was £14, unless the builder should have "an hard bargaine," and in that event he was to be paid "10 shillings more." It was located on what is now Cypress street, then known as "the lane to the upper wharf." It was built in 1679, more than forty years after the settlement was begun, and its builder was Thomas Stebbins, Jr., son of Lieut. Thomas and grandson of Rowland Stebbins, the ancestor of the large number who bear this family name.

The record of this transaction is of sufficient interest to be repeated in this place: "At a town meeting, being a legal meeting, May 7th, 1679, it was voted & concluded, 1st, that there should be an house erected for that noble design & use of Learning the youth in those necessary peices or parts of Learning Videl: reading & writing. & 2ly, That this house should be twenty & two foot in length & eighteen foot in breadth. & 3ly, That the Select men should be appointed or trusted to agree with any meet person or persons to frame this said building, & when ye town shall have deliberated & determined where to sit it, viz: ye school house, ye same appointed persons are likewise to finish it for school use."

The Selectmen proceeded to carry into effect the vote of the town and on the 2d of June, at a meeting of the board, Deacon Benjamin Parsons, John Dumbleton, Henry Chapin, and John Holyoke, being present, they voted: "It having been formerly at a Town meeting propounded to ye Town that they should set up a school house for the Town, they concluded that such a school house should be erected, & appointed the Selectmen to bargain with any meet person to build such a house for such use: accordingly they have bargained wth Thomas Stebbin Junr to get timber for such a building & frame it, whose length is to be 22 foot; & breadth 17 foot; & stud 8 foot half; & he the said Thomas Stebbin is to carry the frame to place & to nail the clap boards close on both sides & ends & to lath & shingle the roof, & to make three light spaces [windows] on one side & two lights on one end, & to set up a mantletree, & set up a rung chimney, & to daub it, & the said Thomas is to have for his work so done fourteen pounds paid him by the Town, & in case it so prove that the said Thomas have an hard bargaine it is hereby agreed that he shal have 10s more of the Town."

It does not appear that prior to this that the public school had an established place, but that such quarters were used as could be conveniently had. After the new meeting house was built at a town meeting held on the 9th of October, 1678, "it was voted and agreed that the watch house to ye New meeting house should be, or serve instead of a school house, until such time as the Town shal see cause to order otherwise."

The location of the first school house did not give satisfaction and two years after it was begun, at the annual town meeting, it was voted, "that if any persons appear that will remove the school house without any charge to the Town & bring it into ye Middle of ye Town, & set it in such place as ye Selectmen apoint, without damnifying ye house by the 1st of March next ensuing they shall have liberty to do it. But if no such persons appear the house shall be finished & Continued where it is now by ye Select men."

FORMATION OF COUNTIES AND TOWNS.

For many years Springfield continued the central point of operations relating to the territory which is now embraced in the four western counties; and also in Brookfield in Worcester, and Enfield and Suffield in Connecticut. Out of Springfield have sprung counties and towns of no small importance. Out of the old county of Hampshire have come Berkshire, Franklin, and Hampden, while the old name was retained in the territory in the central limits. The towns which have gone either directly from Springfield or have been subdivisions of those which were established out of Springfield in the earlier years, include what is now within the county of Hampden. Hampshire and Berkshire were named for the corresponding shires in England, while our Hampden has come from the brave and patriotic Puritan leader, John Hampden, and our neighbor on the northern border, from the statesman and philosopher, Benjamin Franklin, one of the best and wisest of New England's sons.

The formation of the present counties of Hampshire, Hampden and Franklin, grew out of an act of the General Court passed March 1, 1787, which created three districts for registering deeds. The towns which now practically constitute the county of Hampshire, were made a district with the office at Northampton. The towns north of them constituted another district, with the office at Deerfield, and those towns which comprise the present county of Hampden a third district, with the office at Springfield. When Hampden County was set off from Hampshire the real estate records for this district remained in Springfield, and also all real estate records for Hampshire County previous to the passage of the act of March 1, 1787. All records of the County Court and Probate Court previous to 1812 remained at Northampton.

THE EARLIEST IMPORTANT COUNTY HIGHWAY.

After the settlement of Northampton and Hadley, there was need of a better highway between the upper and lower settlements. As Hadley was settled from Connecticut towns, mainly from Windsor, communication betwen the older and newer towns became frequent. The first road that was traveled between Windsor and Northampton was through what is now within the limits of Westfield and Easthampton. Travel between Springfield and Northampton in early times was by this route. In 1664, ten years after the settlement of Northampton, a movement was made for a road on the east side of the Connecticut, mainly with the view of providing a shorter road to Hadley. The County Court took action and the report which follows is from the records at Northampton. In this is the first mention of Mount Holyoke by that name. "Scannunganuck," (variously written in other records,) refers to a locality now within the limits of Chicopee. "Munhun" is now Manhan, the name given to the mill stream in Easthampton. After the east side road was built travel between Hadley and Windsor passed through Springfield, and the town records show that there was complaint made of the Hadley men doing much damage with their carts to the road in Longmeadow. The action of the County Court and the report of the Committee to lay out the road is given in full, as follows:—

"At the county corte held by Adjournment at Northampton, October ye 3d, 1664: The County Corte at Northampton in March last past haveing made choyce of a Committee viz: Capt. Cooke & Quartermr Woodward of Northampton, Cornett Allys & Andrew Warner of Hadley, & Ens Cooper & George Colton of Springfield, to make a survey & to lay out high wayes between Hadley & Windsor, giveing to ye sd Committee or the majoryt of them full power to determine anything concerning ye highwayes both ye place & places where such highwayes shall ly, & the manner how & by whom & when they shal be repayred: Ens Cooper being not cheerefull to attend the work the Towne of Springfield according to the said Corte, chose another in his roome, which choyce fell on Benjamin Cooley. And the said Committee haveing done what in their judgments concerned them for effecting their said work did under the hands of ffive of them make returne to this Corte of what they had done in ye busyness: This Corte doth approve & allow of the said Returne, ratifying & confirming ye work: A Coppy whereof here followes the Originall being on file:

Northampton May ye 21st, 1664.

Whereas wee whose names are underwritten were chosen & appointed a Committee, by ye County Corte at Northampton ye 29th of March last past, to survey & lay out the highwayes of ye County, as namely, betwen Hadley & Windsor, being ordered by the Corte to take the first opportunity thereof, have on ye 16th day of this present May begun to attend our said work in surveying & considering ye same & doe agree & determine.

That ye highway from Hadley Townes end on ye East side of ye great River to ye fort meadow gate, running as it now lyes, be in breadthe six rodds: and from thence to ye towne end of ye sd meddow in breadth two rodds: and from thence (ye way lying still as it doth) to ye end of Mount Holyoke, in breadth ten rodds, & from thence to Scanunganunk, as ye cart way now runs, in breadth Twenty rodds, & from thence to Springfield to the upper end of ye Causey going down into ye Towne, Six rodds: & from ye lower end of Springfield to long Meddow gate, running where it now doth, in breadth ffour rods, & from ye long Meddow gate to the bridge ye lower end of by the Rivers bank shal be in breadth two rods, & from ye lower end of the Said Meddow into fresh water River, soe called, as the way now runs, ffourr rodds, & from thence to Namerick, where John Bissell had a barne standing, as now ye way runs twenty rods, & from thence to Namerick brook where will best suite for a bridge, two rodds, & from thence to ye dividing lyne betweene the Collonyes, where ye house way now lyes, two rodds: And from the said dividing lyne on the West Side of ye River, towards Waranoak in ye way that is now improved, comonly called ye new way, (that is to say) to two miles brooke, fourty rodds, & from thence to Waranoak hill, where the trading house stood, twenty rods, & from thence to ye passage of ye River where ye way now lyes, Six rodds, & from thence thorough ye other Meddow to ye great hill ,as the way now lyes, Six rodds, & from thence to Munhan River, forty rodds, & from Munhan River to ye lotts now laid out neere ye Mill River, fourty rodds, & from thence to the Town of Northampton ffoure rods, & from Northampton along

by the comon fence side unto ye great River, Six rods in
breadth, & from ye River side just opposite on ye last side,
to run cross to ye middle way y^t leades to ye Centre of Hadley Towne, two rodds, & soe to Hadley Town two rodds;
allowing for the conveniency of landing places an acre of
land on each side of the River, to be in length twenty rods
& in breadth eight rodds, viz: on Northampton side opp. y^e
River from ye fence, & on ye other side up & down the
River each town to make its own landing place, The ferry
to be appoynted by the next County Corte, & in ye meane-
tyme y^t the way through Northampton may be improved
accordingly.   And further we judge & determine that the
Towne of Hadley shall make & maintayne all ye high wayes
& bridges from their Towne to Scanunganunk to ye foot
of the falls, & in case it appeares to be our Collonyes right
over Namerick brooke, that the way be made & maynteyned
by this County, & the wayes & bridges from the Landing
place at the great River unto the top of Waranoak hill, to
be made & maynteyned by Northampton, & from thence unto Windsor to be made & maynteyned by Hadley & Northampton mutually: And further wee determine y^t if Hadley
& Northampton either or both of them shall at any tyme
hereafter see cause to dissert ye highway they now use, &
shall make the way through Springfield their comon roade
to Windsor for carting, then either or both shall contribute
to ye mending the bridge at Longmeddow: And for these
Severall wayes & bridges to be made & repaired sufficient
for travell with carts, wee determine that they be done by the
Severall Townes respectively, at or before ye Sixth day of
June next, as also y^t such Stones as are moveable in Scanun-
ganuck river be turned aside out of the Cart way & ye charge
thereof to be paid by the County Treasurer.

> Aaron Cooke
> Henry Woodward
> x Andrew Warners mark
> George Colton
> Benjamin Cooley.

CHRONOLOGICAL SUMMARY.

A brief summary of interesting events in the history of Springfield, and to some extent that of other localities, which have a contemporaneous interest, will be found in the following pages. The early settlement of Springfield followed so closely the first founding of the towns in New England, that it has a wider historical interest than those towns which have a much later origin. That the dates of settlement of other towns may be brought into connection and more readily kept in memory, the following table is here inserted:—

Plymouth, settled in........................1620
Salem, under Endicott......................1628
Charlestown 1629
Boston, Dorchester, Roxbury and Water-
    town, from Winthrop's Massachusetts Bay
    Company 1630
Cambridge 1631
Wethersfield. Ct., from settlers at Water-
    town 1635
Windsor, Ct., in October, from Dorchester...1635
Springfield, under Pynchon, from Roxbury..1636
Hartford, Ct., in June, under Hooker and
    Stone, from Cambridge.................1636
New Haven, Ct............................1638
Northampton, from Windsor, Hartford and
    Springfield 1654
Hadley, from Hartford and Wethersfield....1659

May 14, 1636.—Settlement of Springfield begun by William Pynchon, Matthew Mitchell, Henry Smith, Jehu Burr, William Blake, Edmund Wood, Thomas Ufford and John Cable. May 16, 1636.—The agreement under which the settlement was made signed this day by the above named persons.

July 15, 1636.—Lands in and about Springfield purchased of the Indians.

January 13, 1638.—A rate of £40 agreed upon to build a house for the minister, George Moxon.

March 30, 1638.—Ordered that future inhabitants should bear a share of the cost of the minister's house.

January 3, 1639.—It was agreed at a general meeting that William Pynchon, Jehu Burr, Henry Smith, John Cable, Richard Everett and Thomas Mirick, should set the bounds of the Plantation up the river on both sides of it. On the West side the bounds were fixed at a brook above the great meadow, a quarter of a mile above the mouth of Chicopee river.

March 26, 1639.—John Cable and Samuel Hubbard were given power to lay out the lots in the Plantation on both sides of the Connecticut River. For "theyr payns they are to have 2d an acre for homelots and 1d for greater lots."

November 14, 1639.—The exercise of training shall be practiced one day in every month.

April 16, 1640.—"It is ordered that the Plantation be call-ed Springfield."

January 26, 1642.—Henry Smith, Elizur Holyoke, Henry Burt, Samuel Chapin, Richard Sikes, and Thomas Mirick, shall have full power to lay out the lands both of upland and meadow on the west side of the Connecticut.

February 2, 1655.—Land was purchased by the town of Thomas Stebbins, and Francis Ball, in "theyr homelots next to the river," for a burying ground,—an acre and a half of Stebbins and an acre of Ball. This was the first cemetery in the town, which was also used as a training field.

September 26, 1644.—First board of Selectmen chosen, consisting of Henry Smith, Thomas Cooper, Samuel Chapin, Richard Sikes, and Henry Burt.

January 10, 1645.—Six rods square having been reserved, out of the lot which was Henry Gregory's, then owned by Thomas Stebbins, now that part of Court Square which faces

Elm Street, "it was mutually agreed by the inhabitants for the speedy carrying on of a meting house, and that every inhabitant shall afford 28 days' work, when he shalbe required by him who shal undertake the building of it, providing he shall not require but 6 days at a tyme."

February 28, 1645.—An agreement was made with Thomas Cooper to build the meeting house. "It is to be 40 feet long, 28 feet wide, 9 feet between joints, have 4 large windows, two on each side, and one small one at each end, one door at the south side and two small doors as shall be thought convenient." This was the first building devoted to religious meetings and public uses, erected within this State west of Boston and its vicinity.

March 26, 1645.—This bargain with Thomas Cooper was acknowledged by the town to have been fulfilled.

May 7, 1645.—It was voted that all the inhabitants who shall absent themselves from town meetings shall be lyable to a fine of a half bushel of Indian corn.

January 8, 1646.—It was agreed with John Matthews to beat the drum for the meetings at 10 of the clock on lecture days and at 9 of the clock on the Lord's days, in the forenoon only, from Mr. Moxon's to Rowland Stebins—from near Vernon Street to Union Street, and for which "he is to have 6 pence in wampum, of every family, or a peck of Indian corn, if they have not wampum."

January 8, 1646.—George Colton and Miles Morgan were appointed "to do theyr best to get a smith for the town."

September 4, 1646.—A bargain was made with Francis Ball for a shop for the smith, which "is to be 12 feet wide, 16 feet long and six feet stud between joints."

January 29, 1647.—It was voted that the £30 due to Mr. Pynchon for the purchase of the lands from the Indians shall be raised by a rate on lands.

March 11, 1647.—It was voted that any man who shall kill a wolf within five miles of the town shall have 10 shillings, to be raised by a rate on cattle.

January 2, 1648.—It was ordered that every inhabitant

shall repaire to the Recorder and have all his lands recorded, and that if any man neglect to have his lands recorded for six months he shall be liable to a fine of 20 shillings.

December 27, 1649.—It is ordered that no inhabitant shall sell or in any way pass away his house or lot to any stranger before he has made the Selectmen acquainted who his chapman is, and they allow of his admission, under penaity of 20 shillings.

1651.—Hugh and Mary Parsons examined before William Pynchon in Springfield for witchcraft.

1651.—Hugh and Mary Parsons appeared at Boston for trial for witchcraft.

1651.—William Pynchon appeared before the. General Court to answer the charge of heresy. His book burnt in the market place by the order of the General Court.

1652.—William Pynchon and wife, and Rev. George Moxon, the first minister of Springfield, and family, returned to England.

September 14, 1652.—John Pynchon, Henry Burt, Samuel Chapin, and Thomas Cooper, appointed a committee to treat with Mr. Moxon for the purchase of his house and lands, and accordingly they did agree with him for his house and lands, to remain for the use of the ministry forever.

1653.—Henry Smith, William Pynchon's son-in-law, returns to England.

February 20, 1656.—It was voted that the toll of the miller shall be the eleventh part of a bushel.

November 4, 1656.—"It is agreed that these four men, Deacon Wright, Deacon Chapin, Mr. Holyoke and Henry Burt should be allowed £12 by the town for their labors spent among us in the Lord's work on the Sabbath. It was further voted that the inhabitants would allow £50 per year to such as did labour in the same work amongst us, in the future, till such times as we shall have a settled minister."

November 9, 1657.—Mr. Holyoke is made choice of to carry on the work of the Sabbath once every day, which he accepts of. Mr. John Pynchon is made choice of for one part of the day once a fortnight, which he will endeavor to attend sometimes by reading notes and sometimes by his own meditations, till March next. Deacon Chapin and Henry Burt are made choice of to carry on the other part of the day once a fortnight, for which their payns they are allowed forty pounds a year."

January 10, 1658.—It is ordered that all sorts of cattle belonging to this town shall be marked with some distinctive mark, which every owner shall repair to Mr. Pynchon and from time to time to the recorder to take and keep on record each man's particular mark.

January 19, 1660.—It was agreed that the town meetings which have been held on the first Tuesday in November shall be held on the first Tuesday in February.

December 31, 1660.—It is ordered that every proprietor of land which is not fenced, but lies in common with others, shall before the last of April next set on each side of his land two good stones, full one foot above ground, or in their stead make a trench three feet long and two feet deep, near the front and rear of his lot.

February 12, 1661.—It was voted that the raising of rates for bearing public charges shall be raised on houses, lands and live stock, according to their worth.

February 15, 1661.—It was voted to petition the General Court to settle the bounds of the town which desires that the northerly bounds meet the bounds of Northampton on the west side of the river, and New Town (Hadley) on the east side. The southerly bounds to extend 20 poles below the place where Mr. Pynchon had a warehouse,—to run east five miles from the Connecticut river and west as far as Woronoco is from Springfield.

February 26, 1662.—More room for seating in the meeting house being needed it was voted to build a gallery.

January 9, 1663.—The Selectmen having agreed with Goodman Buell to "set up the gallery," Capt Pynchon engageth to defray all the charges for which he shall be paid by such as shall be seated there,—4 shillings a person.

February 3, 1663.—It was ordered that there shall be three days warning given to all inhabitants for holding ordinary town meetings, and that Hugh Dudley will leave word at men's houses or places of usual abode, and if not at home he is to leave word for them at the next neighbor's.

May 11, 1663.—It was voted that if any persons entertain an inmate after he has been in town one month without consent of the selectmen they that so entertain shall be liable to a fine of 20 shillings. An inmate was one who had no established abiding place, and had not been admitted by the selectmen as an inhabitant.

December 8, 1664.—The bounds of Enfield fixed by the town and to be accounted a part of Springfield until the General Court otherwise order.

January 14, 1670.—Settlement of Suffield begun by the grants of land to Samuel and Joseph Harmon, Benjamin Parsons and others.

October 5, 1675.—Springfield burned by the Indians. Three persons killed, Thomas Cooper, Thomas Miller, and Pentecost Mathews.

April 15, 1674.—At a town meeting it was decided to build a new meeting house, and it was "voted that Serjant Stebbing should be treated with that it might be sett up in his house lott on the hill by his pasture," and that "the house shalbe made fifty foot long, & fourty foote & halfe wide, & that the house shall be underpind with Stone two foot & halfe above ground." It was "voted & concluded that the house shalbe built soe high as that it may be accomodated for galleryes when the town shall see need." It was further voted "that Major Pynchon, Elizur Holyoke, Nathaniel Ely, Anthony Dorchester & Jonathan Burt shall be a committee to agree with a workman or workmen for the building of such a new house."

May 13, 1674.—This being a lecture day the committee chosen to build a new meeting house asked "that there might be liberty allowed by the town that the work might lye till October next in respect to felling timber for the work, and liberty for that was granted." It was further voted, that "Lieut. Thomas Cooper shalbe added to the committee chosen to order matters for building a new meeting house."

February 2, 1675.—Voted to give Serjeant Stebbins four acres of land, "meddow & upland which lyes on the North side of ye round hill," in exchange for the land taken for a meeting house, out of his homelot.

August 24, 1676.—At a town meeting it was "ordered that Ensign Cooley & Samuel Marshfield be added to ye Committee for ye meeting house affaires, some of them being dead." Lieut. Cooper had been killed on the 5th of the previous October by the Indians, and Elizur Holyoke had died a few days after the town meeting in the preceding February.

February 6, 1677.—At a town meeting held this day the committee for building the meeting house reported that Thomas Stebbins, Senio^r, and Thomas Stebbins, Junr, have granted five rods square to "set ye new meeting house on, & having added a rod more in breadth to the way that leads up to ye new meeting house, now ye committee have granted them ye said four acres," on the north side of Round Hill. "And it being further considered about ye townes land where ye old meeting house yet stands, how easily by exchange with Thomas Stebbins, it may ly together up to the new meeting house, wch being propounded to ye said Stebbin, he also agreed to give him the land which lies next to him, two house & ye new meeting house unto the town. The town also agred to give him the land which lies next to him, two rod in breadth where it fronts on ye street Easterly, the town reserving to themselves four rod broad at ye front or highway, or Street, Eastward, & from thence to run back westward through ye said Stebbin, his land, up to ye new meeting house land aforesaid, a little aslant, so as to range strait with ye outside or north side of ye second stud beyond or to the northward of ye East door of ye new meeting house, whereby this four rod broad of ye towns land, where it fronts on ye street Eastward will & is to gain a little more in breadth by

it, running a little aslant into Tho: Stebbin his land as aforesaid, so y^t the breadth of it toward ye Westward end next y^e
meeting house will be full four rod & an half there & something better.   In full satisfaction the town granted to Stebbins out of the Town land in the training field one rod &
half of ground next to Stebbin's lot and in rear of it, all that
breadth of his lot."   This location of the second meeting
house must be the site, or near it, of   the   present   First
Church.   The builder was John Allis, and the last acounts
concerning the building of the meeting house were approved
in February, 1683.   The cost of the building was £400 5s.

June 2, 1679.—A bargain was made with Thomas Stebbins
Jr., to build a school house, to be 22 feet long, 17 feet wide
and 8 1-2 feet stud, for which he is to have £14.   This was
the first building to be used exclusively for school purposes.
Location, on the lane to the upper wharf, now Cypress Street.

———————

The dates relative to the formation of the four western
counties and of the towns in Hampden County are given in
the following, as found in the manual of the General Court:—

Hampshire County....Incorporated May 7, 1662
Berkshire County....Incorporated April 21, 1761
Franklin County....Incorporated June 24, 1811
Hampden County....Incorporated Feb. 25, 1812

———————

Springfield, founded in....................1636
Westfield......................May 19, 1669
Brimfield....................August 16, 1722
Blandford....................April 10, 1741
Palmer, "The Elbows,"............Jan. 30, 1752
Granville......................Jan. 25, 1754
Monson......................April 28, 1760
Wilbraham....................June 15 ,1763
Southwick....................Nov. 7, 1770
West Springfield...............Feb. 23, 1774
Ludlow....................Feb. 28, 1774
Montgomery....................Nov. 28, 1780

Chester..........................Feb. 21, 1783
Holland.........................July 5, 1783
Longmeadow....................Oct. 13, 1783
Russell..........................Feb. 25, 1792
Tolland.........................June 14, 1810
Wales...........................Feb. 20, 1828
Agawam.........................May 17, 1855
Chicopee.......................April 29, 1848
Holyoke......................March 14, 1850
Hampden......................March 28, 1878
East Longmeadow................July 1, 1894

Governors Chosen Under the First Charter.

John Endicott..................April 30, 1629
John Winthrop.................May 18, 1642
Thomas Dudley...............May 14, 1634
John Haynes...................May 6, 1635
Henry Vane...................May 25, 1636
John Winthrop.................May 17, 1637
Thomas Dudley...............May 13, 1640
Richard Bellingham.............June 2, 1641
John Endicott..................May 29, 1644
Thomas Dudley...............May 14, 1645
John Winthrop.................May 6, 1646
John Endicott..................May 2, 1649
Thomas Dudley...............May 22, 1650
John Endicott..................May 7, 1651
Richard Bellingham.............May 3, 1654
John Endicott..................May 23, 1655
Richard Bellingham.............May 3, 1665
John Leverett (act'ng)........December 12, 1672
John Leverett...................May 7, 1673
Simon Bradstreet.........May 28, 1679—1686

Governors Appointed by the King Under the Second Charter.

Sir William Phipps..............May 14, 1692
William Stoughton..........November 17, 1694

Richard Coote, Earl of Bellomont..May 26, 1699
William Stoughton.................July, 1700
The Council.....................July 7, 1701
Joseph Dudley..................June 11, 1702
The Council................February 15, 1714
Joseph Dudley................March 15,1714
William Tailer..............November 9, 1715
Samuel Shute................October 4, 1716
William Dummer...........December 27, 1722
Willam Burnet..................July 13, 1728
Willam Dummer............September 7, 1729
William Tailer..................June 30, 1730
Jonathan Belcher..............August 8, 1730
William Shirley...............August 17, 1731
Spencer Phips.............September 11, 1749
William Shirley...............August 7, 1753
Spencer Phips.............September 25, 1756
The Council....................April 4, 1757
Thomas Pownal...............August 3, 1757
Thomas Hutchinson.............June 3, 1760
Sir Francis Bernard...........August 1, 1760
Thomas Hutchinson...........August 1, 1769
Thomas Hutchinson.............March, 1771
Thomas Gage...................May 13, 1774

English Sovereigns During the Colonial Period.

James I 1603-1625
Charles I 1625-1649
The Commonwealth.................1649-1653
Cromwell, as Lord Protector.........1653-1660
Charles II 1660-1685
James II.........................1685-1688
William (III) and Mary (II).........1688-1702
Anne 1702-1714
George I 1714-1727
George II.......................1727-1760
George III......................1760-1782

RECORDS OF THE TOWN OF SPRINGFIELD.

The official records of the Plantation, and later of the Town of Springfield were opened on page 9 of the original book, and were continued in regular order. The blank pages at the beginning were at a later time used for various entries without regard to chronological order. Under date of 28th of March, 1638, thre is this record: "There was a free choyce according to an order from mr Ludloe by the plantation of two Goodmen, Committys for the Generall court to be at Hartford the 4th of April, 1638. The partys chosen are Mr. George Moxon and Jehue Burr." This election took place when it was supposed that this plantation was to be under the jurisdiction of Connecticut.

Here follows the estimate of the value of Goodman Gregory's estate which the town purchased, and subsequently sold to Thomas Stebbins:—

3 acres broken up	£3		
11 rod fencing at 2s 6d	1	7	6
29 rod fencing at 14d	1	14	0
ye house	3	00	0
	9	01	6

When John Cable was about to leave Springfield he sold his house and lands to the town. The agreement is as follows:—

These P'sents doe witness the tenor of a bargaine betwixt John Cable on the one party and the Inhabitants of Springfield on ye other party, touchinge the sale of ye sd John Cables Lott to the Inhabitants abovesd or theyr Assigns in forme & manner followinge.

The sd John Cable doth by these P'sents sell and pass over all his right in his lott house & grounds broken up or unbro-

ken up, alsoe all his right in future dividents. In concidera-
tion wherof the s^d Inhabitants doe agree & covenant to
pay unto ye s^d John Cable or his assigns the some of £40 at
3 severall payments, viz: ten pounds in hand already payd,
and £20 more at ye 29th day of ye 7th month followinge, &
£10 more the first day of the 3d mo. 1642, wch 2 payments
the s^d Inhabitants do covenant & P'mise to pay in money if
they can P'cure it, if not, then in such goods or comoditys
as ye s^d John Cable & ye s^d Inhabitants can agree uppon: In
case they differ in price about ye goods or comodities then
two Indifferent men are to Judge between————In witness of the P'sents above s^d the s^d Inhabitants (— — excepted) & ye s John Cable have set to theyr hands — —
Memorandum: it is agreed that if the s^d John Cable doe conclude to take corne for payment above s^d, then he is to have
it delivered at Windsor, as the ordinary price at that tyme
shall be of——in the Plantation uppon the River.

JOHN CABLE.

Aprill 2d 1641.

January 27th 1642

It is agreed between the Inhabitants of Springfield on the
one party and Thomas Cooper of Windsor on the other party
viz: The Inhabitants of Springfield doe sell all the Land and
housinge wch they bought of John Cable to the sayd Thomas
Cooper his heyres and assigns for and in consideration of
£25 to be paid as followeth: the first yeare after the date her-
of the s^d Thomas Cooper doth binde himselfe & executors to
pay £10 in Corne. and the second yeare £15 in corne or
worke as the Inhabitants shall desyre, and the s^d John Cable
doe at this P'sent asigne and set over to the s^d Thomas
Cooper the dwellinge house and fouer acres meddow, more
or less appertayning to the house. and foure acres & about
halfe of the wet marish before his house. and one acre and
a halfe of the [three] corner meddowe fenced. and seven
acres Just over agaynst it on the other side of the river. and
in future dividents acording to a single lott of 4 akers to a

house lott. In witness wherof the s^d Thomas Cooper hath here set to his hand, the daye and yeare above sayd.

THOMAS COOPER.

————————to the assignment

————in ye behalfe of the

————————inhabitants.

WILLIAM PYNCHON
HENRY SMITH.

———

The town sold the above property to Thomas Cooper. The agreement of sale according to the record bears date of "January 27th, 1642." According to present reckoning the year should be 1643. Both of these agreements as entered in the record, are in the handwriting of Henry Smith. The signatures as principals, Cable and Cooper, and of the witnesses, Pynchon and Smith, are autographs in the original.

The transcriber of the records has preserved the original page numbers which are here inclosed in brackets; for instance, [I—20] will be understood as volume 1, page 20.

The abbreviations in the records which have been preserved were in general use in all records for many years, but not in printed books of the same period. The letter "y" which stands for the is said to be a contraction of the Saxon character for "th." Bearing this in mind the casual reader will easily understand that y^e is the, y^t that, y^m them, y^s this, y^r their, w^t what, or white. Which is often written "w^{ch}." Other contractions will be easily understood. Contractions, orthography, punctuation, and capitalization, have been literally followed in this volume. It has been the purpose to preserve the custom in this regard which then prevailed and also the archaic character of the period. The completeness of all records in every particular, depended very largely upon the qualifications of the various recorders, and to them we are indebted for the facts which bear upon the first settlements of New England.

The opening of the original record of the plantation of Springfield begins with the following:—

[I—9]

[In the handwriting of Henry Smith.]

May the 14th, 1636.

Wee whose names are underwritten beinge by Gods p'vi-dence ingaged to make a Plantation and over agaynst Agaam uppon Conecticot, do mutally agree to certayne articles and orders to be observed and kept by us and by our successors, except wee and every of us for ourselves and in our owne p'sons shall thinke meete uppon better reasons to alter our p'sent resolutions:

1ly. Wee intend by Gods grace as soone as wee can wth all convenient speed to p'cure some Godly and faithfull min-ister with whome we purpose to Joyne in Church Covenant to walke in all the ways of Christ.

2ly. We intend that our towne shall be composed of fourty familys, or if we thinke meete after to alter our pur-pose yet not to exceede the number of fifty familys, rich and poore.

3ly. That every inhabitant shall have a convenient ppor-tion for a house lott as we shall see meette for every ones quality and estate.

4ly. That every one that hath a house lot shall have a pportion of the Cowpasture to ye North of Endbrooke lying Northward from the towne: and also that every one shall have a share of the hasokey Marish over agaynst his lott if it bee to be had, and every one to have his pportionably share of al the wood land.

5ly. That every one shall have a share of the meddowe or planting ground over agaynst them as nigh as may be on Agaam side.

6ly. That the long meddowe called Masacksic lyinge in the way to Dorchester shall be distributed to every man as wee shall thinke meete except we shall find other conven-iency for some for theyer milch cattayls and by other cat-tayle also.

7ly. That the meddowe and pasture called Nayas toward Patuckett on ye side of Agaam lyinge about foure miles above in the river shall be distributed to foure five or six at most of them that are likely to improve it in tillage and pasture, thereby to ease the towne of the greate stocks that soe there may be the better conveniency for them that have lesser stocks as we shall see meete, and it is agreed that Matthew Mitchell shall have 50 acres layd out together at the farther end of this ground as above said in ye former order, and this was altered with consent before ye hands were set to it.

[I—9]   8ly. That all rates that shal arise upon the towne shall be layed upon lands accordinge to every ones pportion aker for aker of house lotts and aker for aker of meddowe both alike on this side and both alike on the other side and for farms that shall lye further off a less pportion as we shall after agree, except we shall see meete to remitt one halfe of the rate from land to other estate.

9ly.   That wheras Mr. William Pynchon, Jehu Burr and Henry Smith have constantly continued to p'secute this plantation when others fell off for feare of the difficultys, and continued to p'secute the same at greate charges and at greate personall adventures: therefore it is mutually agreed that fourty acres of meddowe lyinge on the South of Endbrooke under a hill side shall belonge to the s^d partyes free from all charges forever: that is to say twenty acres to Mr. William Pynchon and his heyrs & assigns for ever, and ten acres to Jehu Burr, and ten acres to Henry Smith and to theyr heyrs and assigns for ever: which s^d 40 acres is not disposed to them as any alotments of towne lands, but they are to have theyr accomodations in all other places not wth standinge.

10ly.   That wheras a house was built to a comon charge which cost £6: and alsoe the Indians Demannd a greater some to buy theyr right in the s^d lands and also 2 greate shallops which was requisite for the first plantinge: the valew of which engagements is to be borne by each inhabitant at theyr first entrance as they shall be rated by us, till the s^d disbursements shall be satisfyed: or else in case the s^d house and boats be not soe satisfyed for, then soe much meddowe to be sett out about the s^d house as may counter vaylr the sayd extraordinary charge.

11ly. It is agreed that no man except Mr. William Pynchon shall have above 10 acres for his house lott.

12ly. It is alsoe agreed that if any man fell any tymber out of his lot in any comon ground, if he let it ly above three months before he worke it out, it shall be lawfull for any other man to take it that hath p'sent use of it.

13ly. It is agreed that Mr. William Pynchon shall have thirty.—Wheras there are two Cowe Pasturs the one lying towards Dorchester [Windsor] and the other Northward from End brooke. It is agreed that both these pasturs shall not be fed at once, but that the towne shall be ordered by us in the disposinge of it for tyme and seasons till it be lotted out and fenced in severalls.

May 16th, 1636.

14. It is agreed that after this day we shall observe this rule about dividinge of plantinge ground and meddowe in all plantinge ground to regard chiefly persons who are most apt to use such ground: and in all meddowe and pasture to regard chiefly Cattell and estate, because estate is like to be imp'ved in cattell, and such ground is aptest for theyr use: and yet we agree that noe p'son that is master of a lott though he have noe cattyle shall have less than three acres of mowinge ground: and none that have cowes, steeres or yeare olds shall have under two akers apiece and all horses not less than fower akers and this order in dividing meddowe by cattyle to take place the last of May next: soe that all cattyle that then appeare and all estate that shall the truly appeare at 20s a cowe shall have this pportion in the medows on Agawam side, and in the long meddowe Masacksic, and in the other long meddowe called Nayas, and in the pasture at the North end of the towne called Endbrooke.

15. It is ordered that for the disposinge of the Hassaky marish and in the grantinge of home lotts these five men under named or theyr deputys are appointed to have full

power, namely, Mr. Pynchon, Mr. Mitchell, Jehu Burr, William Blake, Henry Smith.

[I—12] It is ordered that William Blake shall have sixteene polle in breadth so abuttinge at the end of it to the next high land and three acrs more in some other place.

Next the lott of William Blake Northward lys the lott of Thomas Woodford being twelve polles broade and all the marish before it to ye uplande.

Next the lott of Thomas Woodford lys the lott of Thomas Ufford beinge fourteene rod broade and all the marish before it to ye upland.

Next the lot of Thomas Ufford lys the lott of Henry Smith beinge twenty rod in breadth and all the marish before it, and to run up in the upland on the other side to make up his upland lott ten acres.

Next the lott of Henry Smith lys the lott of Jehu Burr beinge twenty rod in bredth, and all the marish in bredth abuttinge at the end of it, and as much upland ground on the other side as shall make up his lott ten acres.

Next ye lott of Jehu Burr lyes the lott of Mr. William Pynchon beinge thirty rod in bredth and all the marish at the east end of it, and an adition at the further end of as much marish as makes the wholel twenty fouer acres, and as much upland adjoyninge as makes the former house lott thirty acres in all together fifty fouer acres.

Next the lott of Mr. Pynchon lyes the lot of John Cable foureteene rod in bredth and fouer acres and halfe of marish at the end of his lott.

Next the lott of John Cable lys the lott of John Reader beinge twelve rod in bredth and fouer acres and a halfe in marish at the fore end of his home lott.

[I—13] The lotts of Mr. Matthew Mitchell Samuel Butterfield, Edmund Wood, Jonas Wood, are ordered to lye adjoinning to mill brooke, the wholl beinge to the number of twenty five acres, to begin three of them on the great river, and the fouerth on the other side of the small river.

It is ordered that for all highways that shall be have liberty and power to lay them out where they shall see meete though it be at ye ends of mens lotts giveinge them a alowance for soe much ground.

[In the handwriting of William Pynchon.]

We testifie to the ordr above said being al of the first adventurers & subscribers for this plantation.

William Pynchon
Math Mitchell   The marke of Thomas
Henry Smith   Ufford
The mark of Jehu Burr   John Cabel
William Blake
Edmund Wood

[I—14]

[In the handwriting of Henry Smith.]

The Disbursements of the 3^d £40 P contra as followeth:

ffor a frame of a house 35 foote longe and 15 foote wide wth a porch five foote out and 7 foote wide wth a shady over head wth stayrs into cellar & chamber making doors & laying bords for fouer roomes wth duble chimnys. ye sides of ye cellar Planked.

	£	s	d
To Good: Burr for the thatchinge of ye house	18	00	00
to John Allen he to undertak the getting of ye thatch and all other things belonging to it wth lathing & nayls only ye cariadge of thatch excepted	03	00	00
for ye sawinge of all ye boards & slit worke 4 locks wth nayls & hooks & hinges for ye doares to John Cable at	11	00	00
for ye daubing of ye house & chimnys underpinning ye frame making ye stack & oven 7 foote high wth laths & nayls, to Henry Smith at	08	00	00

[I—15]

The 13th of January 1638.

A voluntary rate agreed upon the day above s^d for ye rays-

ing of ffourty pounds toward ye building of a house for Mr
Moxon

John Searle	01—00—00
Thomas Horton	
Thomas Mirack	01—00—00

ye 12s pd him for ye rent John Leonard 02—00—00
of his house for robrt Robert Ashly 01—00—00
John Cable to pay
for J. w.

John woodcock	00—12—00
Richard everit	01—10—00

Hen: Smith to pay John Alline 01—00—00
Mr Pynchon will pay it John Burt 00—10—00

Henry Smith	05—00—00
Jehu Burr	07—00—00
william Pynchon	21—00—00
John Cable	01—12—00
	41—04—00

ffor Mr Moxons maintenance till next michaellmas.

	£	s	d
Mr william Pynchon	24	06	08
Jehu Burr	08	03	04
Henry Smith	05	10	00
John Cable	02	00	00
	40	00	00

John Searle	01—00—00
Rich: Everit	01—00—00
John Alline	01—00—00
Tho: Horton	01—00—00
John woodcock	01—00—00
Robrt Ashly	00—16—00
John Leonard	00—10—00
Tho: Mirack	01—05—00
	07—11—00

[I—16 Blank.—I—17]

March 20th 1637

It is ordered that in consideration of certayne charges wch the P'sent inhabitants have been at for mr Moxons house and fencing his lott, such as shall for future time come to inhabite in ye place shall beare a share in the like charges in pportion with or selves.

It is ordered that a high way is to be reserved out of the marish ground of Thomas uffords lott.

It is agreed y^t John Searle and Rich: Everitt shall measure out twenty foure acres of mowing marish ground afore ye house of mr william Pynchon and soe much upland ground adjoyning as shall make his house lott wth ye s^d marish fifty and fouer acres according to an order in ye first devision of house lotts.

October 17th, 1636.

It is ordered wth ye consent of ye Plantation that from this day forward noe trees shall be cut downe or taken away by any man in ye compass of ground from ye mill river upward to John Readers lott wch parsell of ground is appoynted for house Lotts, and in case any man shall trespass contrary to y^s order he shall be lyable to ye fine of five shillinges.

[I—18 Blank—I—19]

September 3th, 1638.

There is granted to John Searle by ye consent of the rest of the inhabitants an house lott of 8 rod broade & in length from the brooke to the greate river wch lyes neere ye pyne swamps wth ye meddow before his lott of the same breadth y^t his house lott is: Next to ye Lott of John Searle upwards lyes the lott of Thomas Horton 8 rod in breadth wth the meddow over agaynst of ye same breadth & ye length of it as the former. Also on ye other side of Conecticot river over agaynst the s^d lott is granted him a lot of meddowe of 8 rod broade and 80 rod in length reserving through y^t & all other lotts there a cart way of two rod breadth when it may be seene convenient.

November 23th, 1638.

There is granted unto mr Pynchon wth the consent of ye Plantation a lott of upland ground adjoyninge to ye mill of ten acres, and alsoe seven acres more in Lew of the marish ground y^t is before every mans lott. it is alsoe agreed y^t this lott is to lye in breadth from the mill river upwards in breadth twenty rod and in length upwards by ye mill river till the nombr of ye acres be up. and for ye layinge out of this Lott there is appoynted Jehu Burr and Henry Smith to doe it wth as much conveniency as may be, only reservinge liberty to lay out high wayes wher they shall be thought fittinge.

It is alsoe ordered that a foote path and stiles be allowed through every mans lott and next ye greate river.

January 3th, 1638.

It is agreed by ye Plantation at a generall meeting that these six men undernamed shall set out the bounds of ye Plantation up ye river on both sides of ye river and to marke ye trees for ye clering of it. ye P'sons apoynted are mr w: Pynchon: Jehu Burr: Hen: Smith: John Cable: Richard Everit: Tho: Mirack.

January 8th, 1638.

According to the order above s^d these six men layd out ye bounds of ye Plantation up the river on ye other side of ye river & ye bounds are at a brooke above ye greate meddowe wch is about a qrtr of a mile above ye mouth of Chiccapee river.

[I—20]

May the ffirst 1645

It is agreed by ye Plantation y^t Thomas Stebbins who is the P'sent owner of the lott wch was Henry Gregorys shall accordinge to ye order P contra, allowe for ye meetinge house 6 rods square, & what is remayninge of ye 40 rod in y^t order mentioned on ye other side he is to allowe a rod in breadth for a way to ye trayninge place lately purchased of him & ffrancis Ball, & what ground is overpluss he hath liberty to appropriate it to his owne pper use.

The Brooks in y[e] longe meddow at y[e] lower end is y[e] bounds Southward & y[c] Brooke a little below on y[e] other side and the bounds y[t] is set for gathering candlewood into y[e] woods.

This order P contra for putting over cattell on y[e] other side is voted to be at y[e] 20th of October.

[I—21]

It is ordered that the three rod of ground y[t] lies betwixt John Woodcocks pale and Goodman Gregorys Lott shall be appropriated 2 rod of it to Goodman Grigory & one rod of it to Rich: Everit, reserving 40 rod for a pale for a meeting house w[ch] is to be alowed out of Goodman Grigorys Lott.

ffebr 14th 1638.

It is ordered y[t] it shall be lawfull for any inhabitant to fell any Cannoe trees and make y[m] for his owne use or for y[e] use of any inhabitant y[t] grow on y[e] Common but not to sell or any ways pass away any Cannoe out of y[t] Plantation untill it be five years old, and in case any shall transgress this order after this day he shall be lyable to a fine of twenty shillings.

It is alsoe ordered y[t] shall be Lawfull for any man to put over horse Cowes or yong cattell on y[e] other side of y[e] river at the first of novembr, and to take y[m] away thence on the 14th of Aprill, and if any shall trespass y[s] order he shall be lyable to pay any damages y[t] shall appeare to be done by his cattayle.

January 24th 1638.

It is ordered and voted wth y[e] Joynt consent of y[e] Plantation y[t] no man y[t] is posessed of a lott by y[e] dispose of y[e] Plantation, shall after sell it to another, of y[e] Plantation, y[t] hath a lott already: neyther shall any man posess two mens Lotts, wth out y[e] consent of y[e] Plantation or such as shall be appoynted, till they have been inhabitants 5 years in y[e] Plantation: But If any desire to sell his Lotts, he may to a (stranger,) p'vided y[e] s[d] Plantation shall not disalowe of y[e] s[d] Stranger. But in case they shall not alowe y[e] admission of y[e] s[d] stranger then y[e] Plantation shall bye the s[d] lotts as indif-

ferent men shall apprise y^m: But if ye Plantation shall delay
ye s^d purchase twenty days then ye s^d seller shall have his Liberty to take his chapman, And ye Plantation shall be bound
to take notice of such a purchase y^t is ppounded to fower of
the chiefe Inhabitants to geather: If ye s^d 4 men shall hold
theyr peace and not oppose it in ten days then It shall be esteemed y^t ye Plantation doth allowe of ye s^d purchase.

2.   It is ordered y^t if any man in ye Planta: shall be at y^e
charge of fencing his neighbour y^t hath alotments lye next
him: he shall be forced to beare the one halfe of ye fence & to
mainteine it: soe y^t one man shall not damage his neighbour.

[I—22 Blank]

3.   It is ordered y^t all y^t have a ditch by ye high waye before theyre doores, shall keepe it well scowred for the ready
passadge of ye water y^t it may not be pent up to flowe the
meddowe.

November 14th 1639.

1.   It is mutually agreed on by ye Plantation y^t the sealed
peck wch mr Pynchon hath, shall be the ordinary peck to bye
& sell by in ye Plantation, and who ever will may repayer to
ye Constable & have his peck sealed paying him 2d for his
labor, with this seall H. S.

2.   It is alsoe agreed y^t the exercise of trayning shall be
practised one day in every month, and if occasions doe some-
tyms hinder, then ye like space of tyme shall be observed
another tyme though it be 2 days after one another: And y^t
this tyme of trayning is referred to ye discretion of Henry
Smith who is chosen by mutuall consent to be ye Seriant of
ye Company, who shall have power to choose a Corporall for
his asistant.   and who soever shall be absent himselfe wth out
a lawfull excuse shall forfeit twelve pence, & y^t all above 15
yeares of age shall be counted for soldiers and the tyme to
begin the first Thursday in Decembr next.

3.   It is also mutually agreed on y^t no P'son in ye Plantation, shall trade give or lend to any Indian any quantity of
powder, little or great, under ye penalty of 40s for any tyme
y^t any P'son shall be found a transgressor in this kind.

4. It is alsoe agreed for ye ordering of Laborers wages yt carpenters shall have for 9 months 2s 6d P day & for 3 months from ye 10th of November to ye 10th of ffebr: 2s P day: mowers shall have 2s 6d P daye. Sawers 6s 6d P C they to fall & hewe & the owner to bring to ye pitt; alsoe for husbandry or any ordinary labor to have 2s P day for 9 months, only from ye 24th Aprill till the 24th June they are left to theyr liberty as men can agree wth them, and for the other 3 months, viz: from Novembr 10th till febr 10th to have 18d P daye.

disanulled by generall vote.

[I—24 Blank I—25]

March 26th 1640.

It is ordered by ye Plantation that John Cable and Samuell Hubbard shall have power to measure and lay out all lotts in the Plantation both on this side and on the other side of ye river, and for theyr payns they are to have 2d an acre for home lotts, and 1d an acre for greater lotts.

It is ordered that an high way shall be left and layed out in ye hassekey meddowe betwixt Richard Everits lott & yt wch was Thomas woodford lott, the way to be 2 rod in breadth.

It is agreed yt John Leonard shall be the surveyer for the yeare followinge to see ye high ways cleerd and kept in repayr of all stubs sawpitts or tymbr & if any man shall not amende on sufficient warninge what is amiss all things yt are Judged offensive betwixt this & michaelstide shall forfeite 12d for every such default; & If it remayn after yt tyme 6 dayes, he shall forfeite 2s.

disanulled.

April 16th: 1640:

It is ordered yt Henry Smith & Th: mirack shall have power to restrayne ye Indians from breaking up any new grounde or from planting any yt was broken up ye last yeare, alsoe for ye Swampe yt is in ye neck they are to pitch up stakes yt soe ye Indians may be limited & restrayned from enlarging ym selves in yt Swampe. Mr Moxon is desired to Joyne wth ym in this acte.

It is ordered y^t no man shall fall any Cannoe tree y^t shall be wth in ye bounds of ye Plantation wth out ye generall consent of ye Plantation, under Penalty of 20s for every such default.

It is ordered y^t ye Plantation shall be called Springfield.

December 24th 1640

It is ordered & voted that wheras Henry Grigory John Leonard Robert Ashley have contrary to an order formerly made sold or pawned away theyer cannoes, they shall have therfor liberty granted them to redeeme & bringe y^m into the Plantation agayne untill the 15th of may next, & in case of defect herin they shall be lyabel to the forfeture y^t is expressed in the order Dated ffebr: 14th 1638.

[I—26]

It is ordered that these persons underwritten shall have theyr Lotts for ye 2^d division of plantinge grounde, granted them according to ye number of acres and order of place as is underneath written, wch is to be measured out by ye first of Aprill next: P'vided that those y^t have broaken up ground there shall have alowance for it as 2 indifferent men shall Judge equall. Single P'sons are to have 8 rod in bredth, maryed P'sons 10 rod in bredth, bigger familys 12 rod, to begin upward at ye edge of ye hill.

```
John woodcock.....1.. 8 rod in bredth.
Wid: Searle.........2..10
Robert Ashly.......3..08
John Deeble........4..08
Rowl: Stebbines ....5..10
Tho: Stebbines .....6...8
Sam: Hubbard .....7..10
Tho: mirack........8..10
Sam wright ........9..10
Hen: Burt ........10..12
Hen: Smith.......11..20    10 of w^ch is for mr Moxon
will warener.......12..10
Rich: Sikes........13..10
wid: Horton.......14..14
```

John Leonard .....15..10
Hen: Grigory......16...8
Eliz: Holyoke.....17..10

December 24th 1640.

There is leave granted mr Hollyoke, william wearrener, & Henry Burt to seeke out for yᵉ use of them a Cannoe tree. Samuell Hubbard is alsoe appoynted by a generall vote to Keepe an ordinary for yᵉ entertaynment of Strangers.

December 24th 1641.

It is mutually by vote agreed for yᵉ orderinge of wages for Severall labourers, viz for husbandmen or ordinary laborers frᵒ yᵉ first of Novembr to yᵉ first of march to worke at 18d P'day, for yᵉ other Pt of yᵉ yeare not to take above 20d P day, for carpenters for yᵉ first 4 months 20d P day, for yᵉ other Pt of yᵉ yeare 2s P day: for mowers 2s P day for taylers 10d P day, wᶜʰ severall laborers are to worke 8 hours in yᵉ winter Pt, & 10 hours in yᵉ Somer Pt, besides eatinge & sleepinge, taylors to worke 12 hours: It is alsoe for teames that they shall worke 4 cattell & one man at 6s P day, fro. may till October to worke 8 hours, & yᵉ other Pt 6 hours, & if they carry by yᵉ loade to worke pportionally, this order to continue for one wholl year followinge on till order be taken to yᵉ contrary.

It is ordered yᵗ every trayned man shall have his peice fixed fit for service, & each peice 1 lb of powder & 20 bullets to ly by them, besides what they use in dayly service, wᶜʰ they are to get in readyness by yᵉ 8th of January next and on defect herin to be lyable to what fine shall be imposed.

It is ordered yᵗ every householder shall have in readyness about his house a ladder about 16 rungs or steps at least to P'vent ye danger of fire.   Penalty 5s.

It is ordered yᵗ no P'son shall carry fire in yᵉ street wᵗʰ out coveringe, under penalty of payinge 5s for every offence in this kind.

It is ordered yᵗ every inhabitant shall scoure & make a ditch yᵉ bredth of his lott before his doore wᶜʰ is to be done by ye last of may next, on ye penalty of 5s for every default y^t way.

[I—28 Blank I—29]

March 17th 1641.

It is agreed with the generall consent and vote of the In-habitants of Springfield: That if any man of this Township shall under the Coulour of friendship or otherwise, Intertayne any P'son or P'sons heere to abide or continue as inmates, or shall subdevide theyr house lotts to entertayne them as ten-nants or otherwise for longer tyme then one month or 31 days wthout the generall consent and alowance of the In-habitants (children or servants of the family that remayne single P'sons excepted) shall forfeite for the first default xx ^s to be destrayned by the Constable of theyr goods cattell or chattailes, for ye publique use of the Inhabitants: And alsoe he shall forfeite xxs P month for every month that any such P'son or P'sons, shall soe continue in this township wthout the generall consent of the Inhabitants: and if in ye tyme of theyr aboade after ye limitation abovesayd they shall neede relcefe, not being able to mayntayne themselves, then he or they that intertayne such P'sons, shall be lyable to be rated by the Inhabitants, for ye releife & maintenance of the s^d P'ty or P'tys soe entertayned as the Inhabitants in theyr dis-cretion shall thinke meete.

November 17th 1642.

It is ordered by ye Joynt consent of ye Inhabitants of ye Plantation for the orderinge of Sayers [Sawyers] wages, that workmen of y^t nature shall sawe henceforth at 3s 8d P C for boardes, & 4s 4d P C for slitworke ye tymber to be brought home to ye pit hewn and made ready, & if ye s^d workmen shall sawe tymber & sell ye boardes they shall not exceed ye price of 5s 6d P C, P'vided y^t if ye Pit be made wthin ye space of distance y^t is betwixt mr Pynchons house & Sam: wrights it shall be accounted as in ye towne.

There is leave granted to Samuel Hubbard to sell his Cannoe.

[I—30]

March 14th 1642.

Henry Gregory beinge purposed to sell his lott and ppoundinge it to ye Plantation by his sonne Judah accordinge to order, Richard Everit beinge his chapman. The Plantation gave ye voate wherin they disalowed ye chapman ppounded and resolve to buy ye lott accordinge to ye conditions expressed in a former order, Dated January 24th, 1638.

January 26th 1642.

It is agreed upon by ye generall vote and consent of the Plantation that these six men undernamed shall have full power to lay out the lands both of upland and meddowe on ye other side of ye greate river where ye Indians live, and all ye meddowe on Aggawam, so far as shall amount to an hundredth & fifty acres, allotinge to every P'sent Inhabitants his pportion of these meddowe grounds, and ye uplande for 30 familyes of plantinge grounde, to be distributed to every P'son his pportionable quantity as shall be by ye chosen P'sons thought sutable to ye P'sons & estates of ye P'sent Inhabitants, soe far as ye discression of ye s^d P'sons shall leade y^m. Y^e P'sons are as followeth:—

Henry Smith, Elitzure Holyoke, Henry Burt, Samuell Chapin, Richard Sikes, Thomas mirack.

It is alsoe voted y^t £20 of ye purchas shall be layd on ye P'sent Inhabitant & ye other £10 on those Inhabitants y^t are yet to come, p'vided y^t if ye Indian purchase be payd, & no man to have any benefit by ye land undivided in case of sale till y^s tyme 12 months, then every man to possess his land.

March 9th 1642.

It is ordered that there shall be a bridge & high way made to ye mill, for ye passadge of Carts & cattell, those y^t were wantinge in ye worke of ye former bridge to make it up in y^s, & then to goe through ye towne every man his day, & what is done by every man to be kept on account, & to be made even when they make ye way over ye meddowe. Henry Smith & Richard Sikes are appoynted overseers of ye worke.

ffebruary 22th 1643

whereas ther was a clause in a former order dated December 24th 1641 alowinge husbandmen or ordinary laborers for 4 months in ye winter Pt of ye yeare 18d P day, it is therfore y^s day aboves^d ordered by ye generall voate y^t all such husbandmen or laborers shall not exceede 16d P day for tyme to come & to worke 8 howers as in ye former order expressed.

Ordered alsoe y^t morgan Johnes shall have 4 acres of ground layd out for plantinge next above ffrancis Ball up ye river.

[I—32]

Aprill 6th 1643

A list of ye Alotments of Plantinge lotts as they were cast wth ye order how men doe fall, begininge at ye ends of ye 80 rod lotts y^t face to ye greate River. mr moxon is to have ye first by consent of ye Plantation.

			acres	
	Mr Moxon		18 acres	
	·Tho: Coooper	1	5	
	Tho: Stebbins	2	7	3-4
2 lott	Tho: Stebbins	3	7	1-2
	Good: Bridgman	4	11	0
	Sam: Chapin	5	10	1-2
	Rich Sikes	6	8	0
	Rowl: Stebbins	7	11	0
2 lott	Sam: Hubbard	8	5	0
	Ell: Hollyok	9	34	0
	Hen: Burt	10	15	1-4
	mr Pynchon	11	80	0
	Robt Ashly	12	17	0
	Jno Leonord	13	9	0
	Sam: Hubbard	14	10	3-4
	will warener	15	8	1-2
	Alex: Edwards	16	11	0
	Hen: Smih	17	45	1-2
	Tho: mirack	18	12	3-4

Rich Sikes	2	I	
Jno Dover	19	5	0
Sam: wright	20	13	3-4
Jnº Deeble	21	6	3-4
Roger Pritchard	22	5	0

disanulled agayne.

[1—33]

Lots cast for meddow ground on Agawam side, wher is 2 Pts of yᵉ quantity to be divided.

			acres	
	mr moxon	I	8	
	Ell: Holyoke	2	14	
	mr Pynchon	3	32 alowance 8 acres.	
	will warener	4	02	
2 lot	Sam: Hubbard	5	01	
	Rich: Sikes	6	01	
	Hen Smith	7	17	
	San: ,wright	8	02	1- 2
	Tho: mirack	9	04	
	Rowl: Stebbins	10	02	1-2
2 lot	Th: Stebbins	11	02	1-2
	Jnº Dober	12	01	
	G: Bridgman	13	03	
	Alex: Edwards	14	03	
	Jnº Deeble	15	01	
	Jnº Leonard	16	02	
	Hen: Burt	17	02	
	Sam: Chapin	18	01	
	Ro: Ashly	19	04	1-2
	Tho: Cooper	20	02	
	S. Harmon			
	Tho: Stebins	21	02	
	Sam: Hubbard	22	02	
			108	

Lotts on ye other side of yᵉ great river for meddow

Rowl: Stebbins	I	I	I-2
wil: warener	3	I	
Robt Ashly	4	2	I-4
mr Pynchon	5	16	I-2
Tho: Cooper	6	0I	
Hen: Burt	7	I	I-2
Alex: Edwards	8	0I	I-2
Sam: Hubbard 2 lot	9		I-2
Tho: Stebbins 2 lot	10	00	3-4
John Leonard	11	0I	I-4
Sam: Hubbard	12	0I	
Hen: Smith	13	09	
G: Bridgman	14	02	I-2
Jnᵒ Deeble	15	0I	
Tho: mirack	16	0I	3-4
Jnᵒ Dober	17	00	I-2
Sam: wright	18	0I	I-4
Tho: Stebbins	19	00	I-2
Ell: Holyoke	20	07	
Sam: Chapin	21	00	I-2
mr moxon	22	04	
		57	I-4

[I—34]

ffebruary 23th 1643

It is ordered yᵗ Samuell Chapin shall have his 2d lottment to Elitzur Holliokes & John Dober next to him downward. Thomas Cooper is to have his 2d lott next yᵗ he hath already & Roger Prichard to have his 2d lott next above him.

It is ordered and voted yᵗ ther shall no Barnes nor any other housinge be set up or built in yᵉ high way betwixt yᵉ streete fence & the Brooke, except they have 4 rod for yᵉ high way. Se ffebr 5, 1649, order 5th.

April 3th 1644

It is ordered yᵗ Henry Smith, Sam: Hubbard, Robt Ashly shall have power to dispose of the Swampe grounde for this

P'sent yeare to whom they shall Judge most to be in neede.

It is ordered yᵗ those Lotts from Roger Pritchards down-ward shall have theyr 2d alotments below Aggawam River mouth, every man to have 5 acres a peice to runn in length 80 rod, theyr lotts to abutt agaynst yᵉ greate river.

ffebruary 26th 1643

Accordinge to trust imposed on us the partys undernamed by yᵉ Plantation: we have treated with Thomas Stebbins and ffrancis Ball for the purchase of a parsell of ground of them in theyre home lotts next the river, wᵗʰ ffrancis Ball we have agreed for one acre of ground, and to give him two acres for it in recompense in his second lott on the other side of the river: with Thomas Stebbins we have agreed for one acre and a halfe, of wᶜʰ we have conditioned to have 2 rod in breadth to yᵉ meeting house: and in recompense of this acre & halfe we agree to give him 3 acres of land adjoining to his third greate lott on yᵉ other side of yᵉ greate river.   By us

william Pynchon
Henry Smith

[Note.—On the margin of the preceding, in the hand of Henry Smith, the town clerk, is written: "It is accom-plished." In the hand of another and subsequent clerk is: "See in the new Town Booke page 159 satisfaction for it; in the new Town Booke page 159 Jonathan Bell had land on his own account."]

[I—35]

A rate made the 6th of may, 1664, for the raysinge of £20 in part of payment for yᵉ Indian purchas of yᵉ land of the Plantation.

	£	s	d
James Bridgeman	0	12	06
mr Pynchon	4	08	08
mr moxon	1	01	08
Ell: Holyoke	2	00	00
Tho: Cooper	0	11	00
Hen: Smith	2	06	06

Sam Chapin	o	o8	10
John Doben	o	07	04
Rich: Sikes	o	09	02
will: warener	o	10	oo
Tho: Stebbins	o	o8	09
ffra Ball	o	07	o6
Robt Ashly	o	05	oo
Jno Leonard	o	10	04
Tho: mirack	o	13	03
Alex: Edwards	o	11	10
Sam: Hubbard	o	10	09
Jnº Deeble	o	o8	05
morgan Johnes	o	03	oo
Rowl: Stebbines	o	11	o6
Sam: write	o	12	05
Henry Burt	o	12	07
Jnº Harman	o	o8	10
Rodger Pritchard	o	o8	o6
Tatall is	19	18	04

This rate is made voyd by an order made the 26th January 1646.

[I—36]

[In the handwriting of William Pynchon.]

Springfield the 26 of the 7 m. 1644.

It is this day agreed by. generall vote of yᵉ Towne that Henry Smith Tho Cooper Samuell Chapin Richard Sikes & Henry Burt shall have power to order in all the prudential affaires of the Towne, to prevent anythinge they shall judge to be to the dammage of the Towne or to ordr any thing they shall judge to be for yᵉ good of yᵉ Towne: & in these affaires they shall have power for a yeere space & that they, 5, or any three of them shall also shall be given full power & virtue, alsoe to here complaints, to Arbitrate controversies, to lay out High ways, to make Bridges, to repayr High wais, specially to order yᵉ making of yᵉ way over the muxie meddow, to see to the Scouring of Ditches, & to the killing of wolves, & to training up of children in some good caling, or any other thing they shall judge to be to ye p'fitt of ye Towne.

[In the handwriting of Henry Smith.]

January 10th 1644

By ye Joynt consent of ye Plantation there is leave granted (notwth standinge a former order Dated March 17th 1641 to ye contrary) unto william vaughan to lett out his land to Rise Burdondon for ye space and terme of six yeares, to be imp'ved by him.

[I—37]

It is mutually agreed by the Inhabitants for the speedy carryinge on of a meeting house that every inhabitant shall afford 23 dayes worke when he shall be required by him who shall undertake ye building of it, P'vided he shall not require above 6 dayes worke at a tyme, and if ye carpenter shall imploy them about any kind of worke they are to attend to it as if they were in the carpenters worke, and to be accounted as worke done to ye meeting house.

ffebr 28th 1644.

The conditions of a bargaine made by ye Inhabitants of Springfield wth Thomas Cooper for the buildinge of a meeting house is as followeth. The s^d Thomas Cooper is to build ye house in length 40 foote. in breadth 25 foote, 9 foote betwixt Joynts, double studded, 4 large windowes, two on each side, & one smaller windowe at each end, one large doare at ye south side, and two smaler doars as shall be thought convenient: to lay justs for a floore above, to shingle ye roofe wth two turrets for a bell and a watch house, to underpin ye house with stoane, to dawbe ye wales, to p'vide glass for ye windows (if ye pay he hath of the Plantation will p'cure it) alsoe to find nayles and Iron works for ye ful compleating of ye buildinge, wch is to be finished by ye 30th September, 1646. In consideration of which worke ye Plantation doe Covenant to pay him fouer score pounds as money:

to be payed quarterly If he desires it, wch is to be payd in wheate, pease, porke, wampam, debtes, labor.

The 26th of March, 1644, this bargaine wth Thomas Cooper was acknowledged by ye Towne to be fulfilled & he discharged by vote.

[I—38]

ffebr 20th 1644.

It was by ye generall voate of ye plantation referred unto ye five men to pitch a prise on such comoditys as are payable to Thomas Cooper for his worke about ye meeting house, and accordingly we have Joyntly agreed, that wheate shall be p^d in at 3s 4d P b. pease at 2s 8d P b, porke at 3d 1-2 P lb, the first payment beinge to be £30 to be payed march next.

There is alsoe power given to ye 5 men to pportion to each men of ye new inhabitants y^t have not yet had theyr devisions of plantinge land & meddowe what they shall Judge competent to each man & suitable to his condition.

Revoked.

Wheras there is notice taken of a greate neglect in many of the Inhabitants for want of seasonable sweepinge of ye chimnys, wch may p've very p'judiciall to y^m & others, therof: in consideration hereof we have mutually agreed & ordered y^t fro: this p'sent day forward every householder doe carefully attend ye sweepinge of his chimny once every month for ye winter tyme, & once in two months for ye somer tyme. this order to be in force fro: this p'sent day, and in case any man shall be found defective heerin by ye p'son appoynted by us to see ye execution, it shall be in ye power of that man to apoynt another to doe it & ye p'son soe neglectinge shall be lyable to pay 12d to him y^t shall doe ye worke.

It is alsoe agreed by us to meete ye last Thursday in every month when all p'sons y^t have any busynes to us may resort.

march 28th 1645

It is voted y^t Samuell Hubbard, John Leonard, william Jess. shall take an accovnt of ye cattell & stock of ye Plantation & apprise y^m for the raysinge of a rate for mr moxons maintenance of £55.

may 1. 1645.

It is voted alsoe may ye first, 1645, y^t ye rates shall be made only upon the house lotts & all other alotments wch are already layde out shall be exempted.

It is alsoe voted y^t mr Hollioke, Tho: mirack, ffrancis Ball Tho: Stebbins shall speedily take a view of ye long meddow & what other grounds they shall thinke meete and light to ye Plantation for future divisions.

There is a remission of all fines y^t are due for defect of making & scouringe ditches, untill ye last of y^s month & if any be then defective ye penalty is to be executed of 5s to goodman Pritchard.

[I—40]

may the ffirst 1645.

It is voted with ye Consent of ye plantation that whosoever shalltakeany mans Cannoe or vessell without his leave shall be lyable to ye fine of 2s 6d for every such default.

william warrener Robert Ashly is to be accountable to ye towne for 5s each of y^m for breach of an order for selling y^r Cannoe wthout leave ye rest of ye fine being remitted y^m, wch they are to pay in to Samuell Chapen ye Constable.

william warener is to be accountable to ye towne for 10s for breach of an order for sellinge his cannoe wch he is to pay in to Samuell Chapen, 10s more is remitted to him.

may the 7th 1645

It is voted and agreed upon by ye generall consent of the Plantation that if any Inhabitant shall absent themselves from any towne meetinge upon any sufficient warninge given them, or shall withdraw themselves from ye meetinge before there be a full discharge without a sufficient excuse or leave, shall be lyable to pay halfe a bushell of Indian corne for every such defect. It was voted to be sufficient warninge if publik noticement given after a lecture to meete in the afternoon.

[In the handwriting of William Pynchon.]

ma y. 7. 1645

It is voted and agreed that six men that wanted their third

Allotments of planting ground on ye other side of Quinnette-
cot River viz: Jo: Dober Sam: wright Alexander Edwards Jo
Dible Tho Mirack & Roger Pritchard shall have the said
quantities of planting ground formerly granted in this
Booke: in the Long meddow.

And Henry Smith has his 3d allotment of planting ground
wch he wanted on the other side of ye River wch was 45 akrs
to have it in the upper end of ye plaine above ye 3 corner
meddow brook, & in exchange for his 2d lott of planting
ground on ye other side of ye River he is allowed 6 akrs
more adjoyning to ye said 45 in ye upper end of the said
plaine, in all he is allotted to have 51 akrs.

disanulled wth consent

[I—41]

Moreover it is granted to miles morgan Abraham munden Francis Pepper John Burrhall & 4 other lottes next
John Burrhall that they shall have each of them a convenient
portion of planting ground in the said plaine above the 3
corner brook next adjoyning to Henry Smith.

Moreover it is agreed that ye said 3d allotments wch are
granted to the lower end of the Towne shall have their
allotments in the long meddow & that they shall lie in this
ordr Mr Pynchons mill lott allotted to his mill shall be laid
out about the——or knapp of pines by the River side & so
all the other alotments are to lie in ordr upward as the house
lotts lie in ordr, except the 5 men now assigned to pportion
the said lotts shall see cause to alter it: & the six men above
named shall have their allotments in ordr this side them. It
is also ordered that 5 men viz Elitzur Holioak Serjant merick: Samuell Chapin: Robert Ashly & Henry Burt shall consider what pportion of planting ground shall be allowed to
each house lott according to ye former rule leaving some
things to their discretion for inlarging ye quantie: & besides
ye 3d allotments to Alexander Edwards, no 2 is 11 akrs, there
is 7 akrs now granted to him at his request as a free gift:
in all he is to have there 18 akrs, he requested ye said 7 akrs

in recompense of a house lott which he thought was due to him when he married the widdow Searles.

disanulled wth consent

[I—42]

[In the handwriting of Henry Smith.]

may the 19th 1645

It is ordered wth ye Joynt consent of all ye Plantation at a publique meetinge after sufficient warninge: That whereas there was formerly a 3d Alotment of Plantinge grounde granted to all ye Inhabitants fro: Roger Pritchards lott & upwards, The s^d Inhabitants are now freely content to lay downe ye s^d 3d alottments, and are all content to stand to ye determination and alotment of seven men chosen by ye wholl assembly for ye appoyntinge of 3d & 4th alotments to ye wholl Town: viz: Henry Smith: Elizur Holyoke: Sam: Chapin: Tho: Cooper: Tho: mirack: Rich: Sikes: Hen: Burt: who are to divide ye towne in eqall parts for estates and persons: and soe halfe ye Towne downward accordinge to an equall division of estates, and as in discretion they shall Judge fit and Just, are to have theyr third and 4th alotments in ye Longe meddowe, and on ye other side of the River over agaynst ye long meddowe: And ye upper part of the towne are to have theyr third and 4th Alotments in ye playne above ye 3 corner brooke, and one ye other side of the greate river at ye end of ye five acre lotts. And all wth one consent doe freely pmise to stand to ye afores^d determination and allotment; and all former orders about the 3d alotments to be nullified.

[I—43]

September 23th 1645.

wheras the Plantinge of Indian Corne in ye meddows & swampe on ye other side of Agaam river, hath occasioned a longe stay after mowinge tyme before men can put over theyr cattell thither: Therefore it is ordered wth the consent of all those that have plantinge grount there That no more Indian corne shall be planted neither in ye meddow nor in ye Swampes, That soe the cattell of all those that have alot-

ments there may be put over by ye 15th of September, P'vided they take a sure course to keepe theyr cattell from goinge
over ye river by a Keeper in ye day tyme, & by Keeping y^m
in some fenced place in the night tyme: only calves may be
put over thither by the 14th of August. & if any shall put cattell there bef: ye days expst he shall forfeite 2s 6d P ye head
for every default & be lyable to pay all damage y^t his cattell
shall doe on either side ye river.

Complaynt beinge made that divers that keepe teames on
the other side of ye River in ye Springe tyme to plough
there, have formerly much damnified other men by theyr
Cattell, in eating the greene corne, and ye first sprout of
mens meddows: It is ordered therfore y^t ye s^d teames of Cattell shall be kept in some house or yeard till ye first of may
and if any keepe theyr longer, they are to pasture them uppon theyr owne ground or uppon ye Comon, or uppon ye 3d ,
lotts, not beinge meddow nor impved to tillage, soe they tend
y^m wth a sufficient keeper: And in case any shall neglect this
order, they shall be lyable to py ye five shillings for ye breach
of it: Besides other damages fro: feedinge upon other mens
corne or meddow ground, as Indifferent men shall award y^e
vewe therof.

whereas divers neighbors between ffrancis Ball his lott and
Benjamin Coolys lott have complayned that some of y^t
Neighbor hood refuse to Joyne wth y^m in makinge a fence
to save theyr neighbors harmeless: Therefore it is ordered
that all the sayd Inhabitants shal Joyne together in a sufficient generall fence, every man brakinge a pportionable share
accordinge to each mans quantity of acres: and in case any
cattell brake in through any part of ye s^d generall fence:
Then two indifferent men shall be chosen by ye partys in
Controversy, to vew ye s^d fence and trespass, and he whose
fence is found defective shall beare ye damadge as two indifferent men shall award: And in case y^t any cattell breake in
out of mens particular yeards, they shall pay such damadges
as ye two indifferent men shall award, and they shall amend
theyr fences as the s^d indifferent men shall order and appoynt

And if ye partys in Controversy doe not agree in ye choyes
of ye two Indifferent men, then uppon complaynt ye magistrate shall appoynt them: And this generall fence is to be
finished by ye first of Aprill next, or else they will be lyable
to pay damages as ye s^d two Indifferent men shall award: alsoe ye end next ye River is to be rayled: Leaving out a sufficient high way next the River.

[I—44]

It is alsoe further ordered, That if any neighbor from ffrancis Balls lott to Goodman Coolys shall desire to Inclose his
yard wth a garden or an orchard: If his next neighbor refuse
to Joyne for ye one halfe of the s^d fence he may compell his
neighbors on each side of his lott to beare ye one halfe of his
fence, p'vided he compell them not to Joyne for above 20
rodds in length, and in case his neighbor shall refuse to doe
his share of the fence wthin 3 months after demands: He shall
be lyable to pay damages as two Indifferent men shall award,
wch shal be chosen by the partys in Controversy: or in case
they agree not then upon Complainte ye magistrate shall
appoynt them: P'vided alsoe y^t ye s^d fence exceede not y^e
charge of a sufficient five foote pale, or 5 rayles, as ye two indifferent men shall order in case of disagreement betweene
ye sayd neighbors.

wheras divers Inhabitants have alotments of Plantinge
ground in ye longe meddowe, and some of these have manifested theyr desire to brake up theyr alotments the next
Springe, and to defend it with a sufficient fence agaynst all
Cattell: But others of that company are not willinge as yet
to brake up theyr alotments nor to fence, wherby ye former
company will be hindered of theyr intentions or put to an
excessive charge to fence in particular wch was never intended in ye first layinge out of those lotts: Therefore it is ordered that all those whose allottments lye within the others,
y^t have manifested theyr desires to breake up theyr ground
and to fence this next Springe, shall be forced to beare a
pportionable share in a Comon fence, agaynst all Cattell,
accordinge to ye severall quantitys of theyr alottments: And

in case any cattell breake in through any part of the s^d generall fence: Then two Indifferent men shall be chosen by
ye partys in Controversy, or by ye magistrate if they agree
not, to vew ye defects of the sayd fence, and he whose share
it was to make the fence, & is ye owner of it shall beare y^e
damage as ye s^d Indifferent men shall award, and shall be
compelled to mend all ye defects as ye s^d two Indifferent men
shall order, and in case any P'sons shall refuse to Joyne in
ye s^d generall fence then such P'son or persons, shall pay as
ye s^d Indifferent men shall award. It is alsoe ordered y^t
every man shall cut his fencinge stuff upon his owne grounde
(I—45.) except he first have ye consent of his neighbor to
fell uppon his: and except it be ye fencinge of the two out-
sides, then it shall be lawfull for such as fence ye two out-
sides to fell in any mans lott y^t is next to hand: and it is alsoe
P'vided y^t those yet set out every mans pportion of fence,
shall as neere as they can place every man to doe ye reare of
his own lott.

January ye 8th 1645.

It is agreed by ye Plantation wth John Matthews to beat
the drum for the meetinge for a yeares space, at 10 of y^e
clock on the lecture days and at 9 a clock on the Lords days
in the forenoon only, & he is to beate it fro: Mr. Moxons to
R: Stebbins house & ye meetinge to begin w^thin halfe an
houer after, for wch his payns he is to have 6d in wampam of
every family in the towne or a peck of Indian corne if they
have not wampam.

George Colton and Miles Morgan are appoynted to doe
theyr best to get a Smith for ye towne.

Thomas Cooper is chosen measurer of ye lands of ye towne.

Thomas mirack and Joseph Parsons are chosen surveyors
to make ye way fro: ye mill river to ye Longe meddowe who
shal have power to call to ye worke, & in case any P'son
shall refuse to come to ye worke havinge had 3 days warninge before hand, shall be lyable to pay 2s 6d fine except they
can alledge such an excuse as ye magistrate shall Judge to be
sufficient, alsoe they are to see this way finished by ye end of

may next: alsoe if they give 3 days warninge to teames and they come not to yᵉ worke they shall be lyable to a fine of 5s for defects except yᵉ magistrate shall allowe of theyr excuse.

Nov: 2th 1646. The same surveyers voted to continue yᵉ worke and finish it by yᵉ last of may, 1647, & in case yᵉ sur-veyers be defective In finishing by yᵉ day they are to pay 10s Pᵉ weeke for every weeke after yᵉ day appoynted.

Lieftenant Smith Rich: Sykes: Sam: Chapen Tho: Cooper Henry Burt are discharged of yᵉ office in looking to yᵉ af-fayrs of yᵉ Towne.

[I—46]

January 8th 1645.

It is ordered yᵗ if any Trees be feld having no other worke bestowed on yᵐ above 6 months from this day forward in yᵉ Comons, it shall be lawfull for any man to take them. But any tymber yᵗ is cross cutt, or fire wood yᵗ is cut out & set on heapes, or rayls, or clefts for pales, no man may take any of these till it have lyen twelve months after it is soe cross cut or cloven and in case any P'son shall be found to cary away or convert to his use any tymber or fire wood, before yᵉ tyme above limited he shall be lyable to make satisfaction to yᵉ owner in kinde or otherwise to his content, & shal alsoe forfeite 10s to yᵉ Towne use for every such parcell of tymber rayls bolts or fire wood, yᵗ he shall soe disorderly take away & convert to his owne use.

March 12th 1645.

It is agreed on by the vote of yᵉ Plantation that a rate shall be made for yᵉ remayninge £40 due to Thomas Cooper for yᵉ completinge of yᵉ meeting house, £30 of wᶜʰ is to be payed into him by yᵉ last of this month yᵉ other £10 to rest in yᵉ Towns hand till opportunity appeare for P'curinge glass or till ye house be finished.

It is alsoe voted yᵗ a rate shall be made for £55 for mr moxons maintenance for yᵉ P'sent yeare ensuinge, 1646.

It is alsoe voted yᵗ these 2 rates above sᵈ shall be made upon all uplands (meddows excepted) and livinge stock in towne. mr Holyoke ffra: Ball, Thos Stebbins are chosen to valew goods, who alsoe are to make up y[e] rates.

September 4th 1646

A bargaine was driven the day aboves[d] betwixt the towne of Springfield and Francis Ball for a shop for a Smith w[ch] is to be 12 foote wide, 16 foote in length, six foote studd betwixt Joynts, a chimny for the forge rungd, to be boarded both roofe and sides, to make a doore and windowe in the end, wth a beam in y[e] middest, for w[ch] worke to be sufficiently accomplished by September y[e] 28th next, the towne doth condition to pay him ffive pounds either in wheate at 3s 8d l' b. or worke as he shall neede it, to be payd in unto him y[e] 10th of March next, at the house of Henry Smith.

He doth alsoe agree to find boards for y[e] Coveringe and sides wth nayles and hinges &c. and what he wants else, and he is to bringe in his account what boards he useth & what other charges he is at, for which he is to be payd as before in wheate at 3s 8d p b: or in worke as he and they shall agree.

It is agreed y[t] this house shal remayne in the hands of the towne till they se cause to dispose otherwise of it.

This shop [for the Smith] was by Joynt consent given to John Stewart Jan: 10th, 1658.

[In the handwriting of Elizur Holyoke.]

Septembr 4, 1646.

It is likewise agreed by the vote and Consent of the Plantation that Robert Ashley shall keep the ordinary:

[In the handwriting of Henry Smith.]

It is ordered that Thomas Cooper shall measure out the playne for w[ch] he is to have 1d P acre.

[I—48]

[In the handwriting of William Pynchon.]

September 23 1646

It is agreed by the joynt consent and Generall vote of the Townsmen that this 5 men are chosen for the orderinge of all the prudential affaires of this Plantation viz: mr Henry Smith Elitzur Holioak, Samuell Chapen Henry Burt & Benjamin Cooly to be for a year or untill new be chosen in their places.

2.   They shal reach to reconsile disgrements & disputes between neighbor & neighbor.

3.   They shall take care to find out some convenient way to separate oxen from Cowes in their daily feeding.

4.   They shall judge where bridges & high ways are to be, made or mended & how it may be done and they shall call uppon the surveyers it to be their affair.

5.   They shall also advise about some course about destroying of medows: & how hogs may be kept with most p'fitt & least damage of ye plantation.

7.   They shall have power also to see that mens chimnies be kept clean or else they shal have power to fine men for their neglect so that their fine be under 5s a tyme.

8.   also they shall have power to higher a cow keeper for the keeping of cowes of the plantation.

9.   & the making of all Rates for the Plantation shall belong to their affaires & in genrll for the making of the Rates for the Smith as it is understood on the other side of the leaf.

10.   They shall have power to fine such persons as carry fire uncovered provided it be under 5s at a tyme & whosoever shal refuse to pay the said fines they shal complaine to the magistrate who will grant his warrant to distraine for ye said fine.

[I—49]
[In the handwriting of Henry Smith.]

November 3th 1646

It is agreed by ye generall vote of ye Plantation that if any inhabitant shall absent themselves from any towne meetinge upon sufficient warninge given them or shall w^th^draw y^m^-selves before there be a full discharge w^th^out a sufficient excuse or leave granted, or shall no be Psent when ye blessinge is desired, shall be lyable to a fine of a bushell of Indian Corne, or the valew of it, to be Levyed by ye Constable on such as shall transgress.

It is alsoc agreed by ye Plantation that the first Tuesday in

November shall be a generall towne meeting for all y⁰ In-habitants, on wᶜʰ day orders are to be published & towne officers chosen, &C.

There is choyce made by yᵉ generall vote of the Planta-tion of five men who have by mutuall consent agreed to refer into theyr hands the orderinge of all yᵉ Prudentiall affayers of the towne, and whatsoever they shall soe order in reffer-ence to yᵉ good of yᵉ Towne shall stand in force as yᵉ Act of the towne: P'vided yᵗ what orders or conclutions they shall agree upon, be openly published, before yᵉ generality of yᵉ Towne after a lecture or at any trayninge day, or any other publique meetinge: and in case there be no negative vote by yᵉ generality of yᵉ Towne wᵗʰin 7 days after, Then it shall be taken for granted that the Towne by such silence doe con-firme and establish theyr orders. The men chosen are as fol-loweth: Henry Smith, Elizur Holyoke, Sam. Chapen, Henry Burt, Ben: Cooley.

It is alsoe voted by yᵉ Plantation yᵗ yᵉ abovesᵈ 5 Towns-men shal have power accordinge to theyr discretion to give a pportion of meddow ground to those that yet have none in yᵉ longe meddow, and in case any other shall manifest theyr want of meddow ground, they shall have power to give an addition of meddow to yᵐ as they in theyr discretion shal see fitt & competent for yᵐ.

[I—50]

November 3th 1646.

Thomas Stebbines and william warrener are chosen sur-veyers for this next yeare ensuinge, and till another be chosen in yʳ roome.

Robt Ashly and miles morgan are chosen by yᵉ towne to yᵉ oversight of yᵉ fence of yᵉ house lotts and the greate playne accordinge as they shall be directed by yᵉ townsmen.

George Colton and James Bridgeman are likewise chosen to yᵉ oversight of yᵉ fence in yᵉ long meddowe.

It is likewise agreed and voated by yᵉ Plantation that Jnᵒ Clarke or those that shall Joyne wᵗʰ him in yᵉ burninge of Tarr shall have liberty to gather candlewood in ye playne

in ye Bay path: p'vided they come not togather on this side
the greate pond, and the swamps that poynt out from it to
Chicopee river and the mill river wch is Judged to be about
five miles from the towne. And in case the say^d Jn° Clarke
or any of his partners shal be found to transgress and gather
w^{th}in these limits they shall be lyable to a fine of 20s for every
loade they shall soe gather: This grant to stand to them for a
yeare this P'sent.

To draw an order for candlewood 6 miles East.

Thomas Cooper is appoynted to measure out ye meddow
ground in ye Longe meddowe.

performed accord to order.

January 29th 1646.

It is voated y^t a rate shal be made for mr moxons maintenance of £55 for ye P'sent yeare ensuinge 1647, to be payd
the first halfe at ye 25th march next & ye rest at michalstide
next. The rate to be made on all lands & goods.

[1—51]

It is alsoe voted that y^e £30 wch is due to mr Pynchon
shall be raysed on all ye alotments in ye towne, wch is due to
him from each inhabitant for ye purchas of the lands of the
Plantation, of the Indians, to be raysed wholly on lands, and
by y^s order a former order for raysing £20 is made voyd.

January 29th 1646.

It is agreed by a genrrall vote that all Swine that breake
into any mans corne ground or meddows y^t is sufficiently
fenced agaynst yoked hogs: In case men let y^r Swine abroad
unyoked if they breake in and doe any man Trespass, then y^e
master of the say^d Swine shall be lyable to pay all damadges
as two indifferent men shall Judge ye damadge to be: But if
Swine be yoked and runge then they are free from damages.

This order is repealed by ye Joynt consent of ye Inhabitants the first of Aprill 1647.

This ffirst of Aprill 1647, at a Towne meeting by a Joynt
consent of the Towne there is power given to ye Townsmen
to make an order according as they shall thinke meete about

yokinge and ringinge of Swine y^t are kept about mens howses, alsoe they are to endevore to make a bargayne wth some P'sons for ye keeping of Swine in ye woods, & ye Towne doth p'mise to stand to wth the conclutions they shall soe agree upon, as alsoe they have power to rayse a rate for his paymt.

March 11th 1646.

At a publipue Towne meeting It was agreed to give to any man y^t shall kill wolves wthin five miles of ye Towne 10s for every wolfe, to be raysed by rate upon all sorts of Cattell. And if by accident any P'son shall by setting of gunns, or trapps kill any Cattell they shall be free from damages, p'vided it be done fro: halfe an houre before sunsett, till halfe an houre after sun risinge, provided alsoe that they doe give ye owner word that he may have the flesh. But if any Cattell be killed fro: halfe an houre after sun rise till it be halfe an houre before sun set, he y^t sets ye gun or trap shal be liable to pay damage as two indifferent men shall Judge meete.

[I—52]

By the Townesmen, march 6th 1646.

wheras there are Surveighors chosen yearely by ye Towne for ye oversight and amendinge of high ways bridges or other defects of y^t nature: we have therfore ordered that ye surveighors shall give sufficient warninge to any man to attend such workes who shall attend such warninge soe given: And in case any man shall be defective and not attend such warninge he shall be lyable to a fine of 2s 6d for every days absence: Alsoe if any P'son shall neglect to cutt downe his stubbs or cleere ye high way before his Lott of timber wood, or other offensive matter w^{ith}in 6 days after he is soe warned he shall be lyable to a fine of 12d, & in case he neglect it 7 days longer, then ye fine to increase to 2s, & soe to increase 12d for every weeke it shall be soe neglected to be amended.

wheras there is observation taken of the scarsity of tymber about the Towne for buildinge sawinge shingles or such like: It is therefore ordered that no man shall hence forth transport out of the town to other places, any buildinge tymber

board loggs or sawne boardes or planks or shingle tymber or
pipe staves, wch shall be growinge in ye Towne, to the p'judice of the Plantation, viz: fro: chickopy river to freshwater
brooke & six miles East from ye greate River. And if any
man shall be found to transgress this order, he shall be lyable
to a fine of 20s for every fraught of such tymber, boards, shingles, or such like by him soe transported.

wheras it is Judged offencive and noysome for flax & hemp
to be watered or washed in the Brooke before mens doores,
y^t is of ordinary use for dressinge meete: Therfore it is ordered that noe P'son shall hence forth water any flax or hemp
in the sayd brooke or any where neere adjoining to it, & if
any shal be found transgressing heerin he shall be lyable to a
fine of 6s 8d for every such default.

[I—53]

A rate for ye raysinge of £30 for the purchase of the lands
of the Plantation 1646.

	acres		£	s	d
Rowland Thomas	29	1-2	00	08	02
John Stebbins	27	1-2	00	07	08
miles morgan:	34	1-2	00	09	06
James Osburne	40		00	11	04
Tho: Cooper	41		00	11	04
Mr will: Pynchon:	237		03	05	06
mr: Elitt: Holyoke:	125		01	14	06
Hen: Smith:	148		02	00	08
mr moxon	67		00	18	08
Sa: Chapen	43		00	12	00
Tho: Reeve	32		00	08	10
Rich Sykes	39	1-2	00	11	00
will: warener	40	1-2	11	11	02
Tho: Stebbin	34		00	09	05
ffra: Ball	33		00	09	05
Robt Ashley	51		00	09	02
John Leonard	34	1-2	00	09	06
Tho: mirack	46		00	13	00
Ja: Bridgeman	41		00	11	04

Alex: Edwards	60 1-2	00	16	09
Jnº Clarke	36	00	10	00
Wid: Deeble	22	00	06	00
Katterine Johns.	19	00	05	04
Rowl: Stebbin	38 1-2	00	10	08
Sa: wright	41 1-2	11	11	06
Hen: Burt	47 1-2	00	13	04
Jnº Herman	33	00	09	02
Roger Pritchard	28	00	07	09
Nat: Bliss	51 1-2	00	07	09
wid: Haynes	40 1-2	00	11	02
Tho: Thomson	56 1-2	00	15	10
Rich: Exell	40 1-2	00	11	02
Jos. Parsons	42 1-2	00	11	09
Jnº Matthews	31	00	08	08
will: Branch	27 1-2	00	07	08
Geo: Colton	61	00	16	09
Grif: Jones	36 1-2	00	10	00
Reice Bedortha	20	00	05	06
will: Vahan	06	00	01	08
Benj. Cooly	40 1-2	00	11	02
Hugh Parsons	37 1-2	00	10	04
Jnº Lumbard	25	00	06	10
2 vacant Lotts	40	00	11	00
vacant lott	25	00	06	10
vacant Lotts	40	00	11	00
3 vacant lotts above	60	00	16	06
	2178 1-2	30	11	02

[I—54]

Aprill the first 1647. By yᵉ Townesmen.

It is ordered that all Swine that any person shall keepe about his house or neere any corne ground belonginge to the Plantation and not under the hand or custody of a keeper: shall be sufficiently yoked and runge, accordinge to the age and bigness of the Swine: And in case any Swine that are above the age of six months shall be found in the Streete or

about any of ye Comon fences of the corne fields wthout yoke
& ringe: It shall be lawfull for any person soe finding them,
to drive them to the pound (wch may be any mans private
yard or out house in ye present defect of a Comon pound)
P'vided alsoe y^t he give the owner of the sayd Swine notice
of his impoundinge them wthin 24 hours after it is soe done
who shall be Lyable to pay to the party that hath soe impounded them 6d for every Swine before they be set at Liberty: But if any Swine shall be found in corne unyoked or
unrunge, then ye owners of the s^d Swine shall be Lyable to
pay any damages done by them, as 2 indifferent men shall
Judge it to be. besides the 6d on every head for impoundinge
them.   And in case any shal neglect to redeeme his Swine
in 24 hours after he hath warninge of theyr impoundinge:
It shall be lawfull for the party that hath impounded them
to take two neighbours to apprise one or more of the sayd
Swine, & to sell it or them, satisfyinge himselfe of the damages done in his corne, as the s^d 2 indifferent men shall Judge
it to be. as alsoe for the impoundinge of the Swine, and to
returne the overpluss to the owner.

This order to take force fro: the 20th of Aprill next, 1647.

[I—55]

ffebr 10th 1647.

At a towne meetinge It is agreed by ye generall vote of y^e
towne y^t £55 shall be raysed by a rate on goods & lands for
mr moxons maintenance.

The persons under named have agreed to add £5 more
soe y^t ye wholl some is £60.

mr Pynchon, mr Jno Pynchon, Hen: Smith, Elitzur Holy-
oke, Sam: Chapen, Rich: Sykes, Tho: Cooper, ffra: Ball,
Sam: write, Hen: Burt, Tho: Reeve, Ro: Prichard, will:
Branch, Rice Bedortha, Nath: Blis, Jno Matthews, Griffith
Jones, Tho: mirack.

November 2th 1647.   at a generall Towne meetinge, The
names of the persons chosen for orderinge the prudentiall
affayres of the Towne to whom the Towne by a Joynt con-

sent have conferred full power to order and determine all the prudentiall affayers of the Towne.

Sam: Chapin.   Hen: Burt.

Henry Smith.   Tho: Cooper   Benj: Cooly:

The Surveyers chosen at the same tyme.

ffrancis Ball   Jnº Clarke

　　　　　for the upper pt.   for the lower pt of

miles morgan   Jnº Harman   yᵉ Towne

[I—56]

The surveyers are not to call any person to the high way worke above 6 days in a yeare.   Every family is to work his dayes and those that have Teames are to come wᵗʰ theyr ｉeames if they are required.   If a family have 2 or 3 men in it and a Teame, If the surveighor call not for the Teame he shall send 2 men in place of the Teame if he have yᵐ.   If any man refuse to come to yᵉ worke havinge 3 dayes warninge he shall forfeite 2s 6d, & each Teame 5s a day, to be implyed to the use of yᵉ highwayes.

The Speciall works to be attended this yeare are, a Horse way over the meddow to yᵉ Bay path, a Bridge over the 3 corner Brooke into the playne, &c.

September yᵉ 8th 1647.

It is ordered yᵗ no person shal gather any hops that grow in yᵉ Swamps or in the comon grounds untill this P'sent day yearly, upon payne of forfeitinge what they shal soe disorderly gather, & 2s 6d for breach of order.   The forfeiture to yᵉ Informer, & yᵉ penalty to the Towne treasury.

[I—57]

January the 2d, 1647.

wheras it is Judged needfull in Sundry respects that each inhabitant should have the severall parcells of theyr land recorded, Therfore for prevention of future inconveniences It is ordered that every particular Inhabitant of this Township shall within six months after the date of this P'sent order, repayre to the Recorder who is chosen and appoynted by yᵉ sᵈ inhabitants for that purpose: who uppon information given him by each person of his severall parcells of Land, the number of acres, wth the breadth & length of the s^d alottments, and who are adjoyning on each side of them, shall by virtue of his office fairely record each parcell of land wth ye limits, bounds, and situation of them, in a booke for that purpose: for which his paynes, the owner of the s^d lands, shall pay unto the Recorder two pence for every parcell of his land soe recorded.   And if any inhabitant shall neglect to have his lands thus recorded accordinge to the tyme above limited of six monthes, he shall be lyable to a fine of 20s for every such parcell of land as he is possessed of which remaynes unregisfeild.

Henry Smith is chosen Register for ye Towne of Springfield.

[I—58]

March the ffirst 1647.

It is ordered y^t all P'sons that have any interest in generall fences shall carfully attend to repayrs & sufficiently close up theyr severall fences in ye comon feilds by ye 25th day of march yearlly, & to see y^t they be kept in sufficient repayre till the last day of September, in wch interim it shall not be lawfull for any P'son to put in any cattell to pasture or any way lay open ye Sayd Comon feild to his neighbors pridjce: wthout ye Joynt consent of the wholl y^t have interest in ye s^d feild.   But after that tyme it may be lawfull for any P'son to put in his cattell y^t hath interest in ye s^d generall feild, & If any shall be found to lay open his fence or turne in any cattell Into any comon feild before ye day above limited he shall pay all ye damages & a fine of five shillings for contempt of order.

It is ordered y^t ye P'sons who are yearly chosen overseers of ye generall fences shall at least 2 severall tymes in the yeare, viz: march 29th & July 20th & as often as they se cause diligently vew over ye fences under theyr trust that they be fuly closed up and repayred as they shall in theyr wisdome Judge to be sufficient: And if upon theyr vew of

them they shall find any insufficient fences, they shall give
the owners of ye s^d fence warninge to amend it within 2 days:
If ye pty so warned shall neglect to amend his s^d fence accordinge to ye tyme appoynted by vewers he shall be lyable
to a fine of 12d for every defect, and for every day that it re-
mayns unamended after to encrease 12d upon every such defect, besides all damages y^t may fall on him by the Insuffi-
ciency of his fence, ye one halfe of ye fines to fall to the overseers of the s^d fence, & ye other halfe to ye use of the Towne
and if any Just complaints shall be brought against the s^d
officers for neglect of theyr charge they shall stand accountable to ye Towne at ye generall metinge or when they shall
be thereunto called.

Chosen for long meddow, Geo: Colton Tho: mirack, for
ye home lotts, James Bridgeman Hugh Parsons, for ye
Plaine, will: warener Tho: Reive.

[I—59]

At a generall Towne metinge the 6th of Novembr 1648

The same power that the last year was conferred upon the
Townsmen for orderinge of ye prudentiall affayres of y^e
Towne is at this tyme committed into y^r hands for this next
yeare ensuinge, & till others are chosen in theyr places. The
ptys chosen are, Henry Smith Sam: Chapin Hen: Burt Tho:
Cooper Benj: Cooly.

It is ordered that there shall from henceforth fouer Courts
be kept in this Township yearly, viz: The first Tuesday in
Novembr, the first Tuesday in ffebruary, The first Tuesday
in may, The first Tuesday in Septembr, except some speciall
occasions to alter ye day, and then seasonable notice shall
be given of it. The first Tuesday in Novembr is appoynted
to be a generall Towne meetinge for all the Inhabitants when
Towne officers are to be chosen & orders published.

It is alsoe ordered y^t on ye first Tuesday of Novembr there
shall be yearly chosen by ye Inhabitants two men in y^r stead
of Grand Jury men who shall by virtue of an oath imposed
upon them by ye magistrate for that purpose, faithfully P'sent
on such Court days all such breaches of Towne orders or

Court orders, or any other misdemeners as shal come to theyr knowledge either by theyr owne observation or by credible information of others, and shall take out p'cess for ye appearance of such as are delinquents, or witnesses to appeare the s^d day, when all such P'sentments by ye s^d partys shall be Judicially heard and examined by ye magistrate and warrants for distresses granted for ye Levying of such fines or penaltys as are anexed to ye orders violated, or wch shall seeme meete or reasonable to ye magistrate to impose or inflict accordinge to ye nature of the offence.   These two men to stand in y^s office for a yeare or till others be chosen in theyr roome.

[I—60]

Novembr 7th 1648.

It is agreed that those who will Joyne to make a cartway over ye meddow against Robrt Ashlees shall have liberty to barr up ye Cartway, and to take 4d P load of any others y^t shall cart over s^d way, who have not Joyned in making of it. Those who have given in y^r names to make ye Cartway are as followeth Tho: mirack, Tho: Stebbin, James Bridgeman, Jno Clarke, will: warrener, Rowl: Stebbin, Sa: wright, Sa: Marshfield, Wid: Ball.

James Bridgeman and will: warrener are chosen Surveyors for the high ways for the yeare followinge.   Overseers for ye fences in Long meddow, Geo: Colton, Alex: Edwards. For ye home lotts & ye Plaine, Nath: Bliss, Tho: Stebbin.

By the Joynt consent of the Inhabitants there is granted to mr Pynchon a parcell of meddow ground about 4 or five acres more or less lyinge at the lower end of ye Longe meddow adjoyninge to his mill Lott.

It is alsoe voted that all those that have alottments over ye greate river agaynst the longe meddow as theyr third divident, who have desired to resigne up those Lotts into ye Townes hands: p'vided they might have in Lue therof a parcell of land in the longe meddow behinde the meddow Lotts there: It is wth ye Joynt consent of the Towne granted that

those who are posesors of such lands, shal have appropriated
to them lands in the Longe meddow suitible thereto in quantity if it will reach. If it fall out that they have a less portion there then they had on ye other side: then the Inhabitants of ye upper end of ye Towne y^t have no alotmts there,
are to be abated soe many acres of land in thyr rates, to make
it pportionable to y^m of ye Lower end.

[I—61]

By the Select Townsmen Aprill 7th 1649.

wheras there is notice taken of a disagreement amongst
severall of the neighbours who have lands lyinge in the longe
meddowe, wch they have ingaged themselves to fence by the
15th of this month, and by reason of this difference the
fenceinge is neglected to the aparent damage of many in the
s^d feild, Therfor for the better setlinge of this difference, It is
ordered and appoynted that this fence be carryed on by the
s^d proprietors accordinge to theyr former agreement amonge
themselves. And for avoydinge of all contentions y^t may
arise about the setting or pportioninge of the s^d fence: It is
ordered, that the wholl number of Acres y^t every man hath
in ye s^d feilds be taken, whither plantinge land or meddow, as
alsoe the number of rods or quantity of fenceinge to be done,
and that each P'son doe make his share of fence pportionable to his number of acres, such as shall be Judged sufficient
for the security of the s^d feilds, from George Coltons side
fence to the Brooke. The fence to run at ye reare of the
plantinge lotts there layed out, and fro: thence to cross over
East to ye high way (wch is marked out) and soe South to the
Brooke. All the Swampes at ye reare of those plantinge
lotts to lye in comon: Alsoe for ye fence by ye Brooke It is
ordered that every person that hath Land in the side fields,
shall make and maintaine a pportionable share of fence accordinge to the number of his acres, such as shall be sufficient for turninge off Cattell in the Judgment of those that
are chosen for that purpose: And further to avoyde confu-
sion in ye carryinge on of this fence, we order that those
plantinge lotts that lye uppermost, shall set up theyr share

of fence at theyr owne reares, if it soe fall out, & after them
Jn⁶ Leonard to begin & soe successively as men live in order:
And the like order is to be followed in the fence by ye
brooke, Jn° Leonard to begin at the upper end and soe every
one to fall in successively wth his share of fence as they dwell
in order.

[1—62]

Decembr 27th 1649

There is (wth ye Joynt consent of the Inhabitants) power
given to the Select Townsmen and Deacons for the tyme beinge and such as shall hereafter succeed them: to order the
seatinge of P'sons in ye meetinge howse as they in theyr discretion shall Judge most meete.

It is alsoe ordered y^t ye Select Townsmen wth ye Deacons
shall in the behalfe of the Towne draw up & send downe to
ye Elders a letter desiring y^m to explaine ye cleere meaninge
of our voates concerninge mr moxons maintenance.

ffebr 21th 1649.

There is granted to Samuell wright Senior 1 acre & halfe
of planting land in lue of soe much due to him in his lot in
ye neck, wch is to be layd out as conveniently as may be at his
5 acre lott in ye 2d division.

It is ordered y^t Geo: Colton and Thomas Cooper who is y^e
Towne measurer should wth y^r best discretion lay out the
severall parcells of meddow granted ye last yeare, to Henry
Burt 4 acres, Tho: mirack 4 acres. Alex: Edwards 4 acres,
Jn° Harman 4 acres, In ye Longe meddow over ye Brooke.
Henry Burt & Tho: mirack is to have an acre & halfe more
each of y^m, of upland in y^t place in lue of an acre & halfe due
to them in ye neck.

There is granted to Deacon Chapin a parcell of Land by
Agawam falls where he hath 1 acre & halfe already, adjoyninge to mr moxons meddow ground, wch acre & halfe is to
be made up 6 acres.

There is granted to Jn° Stebbin 2 acres of land at ye end of his ffather Stebbins 5 acre lot, in ye 2d division, wch is due to him in lue of soe much wanting in ye neck.

[I—63]

There is granted to Thomas Stebbin 5 acres of meddow ground over Agawam river in ye 2d meddow on ye west side under the hill: p'vided he resigne into the Towns hands a meddow lott of 1 acre & halfe wch was formerly granted him. ordered that every person that hath Land in the side feilds, ground over agawam river lyinge at ye reare of a meddow lot of Rowland Stebbins over a little brooke there, wth an acre & halfe of meddow ground that his brother Thomas Stebbins hath resigned into ye Towns hands, P'vided he resigne his former 5 acres into the Towns hands.—[Not accepted.]

[In the handwriting of Thomas Cooper.]

There beinge granted to Henry burt divers years agoe 5 acars and halfe of land as pr contra on the other side longe meddow Brooke and finding it lye inconveniante in respect of fensinge by reason of the greatnes of charge: and there beinge a parscell of land lyinge in comon adjoyninge to itt. which if granted to him would much safe his charge in fensinge, Therefore in 1659 the Townsmen takinge into consideration his request saw good to grant the same (vide) all that land to the vallew of 3 acars, more or less, lyinge betwixt his land formerly granted and long meddowe brooke and allsoe a small parsell at the frontt of Thomas merricke his lott lyinge next unto him which here hath compassed in by a ditch to the vallew of 3 quarters of an acar: provided that he doe not pregidiss the high way but that hee doe leave at the bridge two rod betwixt the brook whear the bridge now is and his fence for the conveniante of the passadge. by the Townsmen,

Thomas Cooper,
Jonathan Burt,
william warriner,

The mark of   Robbert Ashley.

[I—64]

ffebruary 6th 1649.

It is agreed by the Towne that if mr John Pynchon will make a chamber over the meeting howse and board It: he shall have the use of it Intirely to himselfe for Ten yeares, and then if the Towne neede it and require it they may have it, P'vided they alow the s^d mr John Pynchon the charge y^t he hath been at about it, or else he is to have ye use of it Longer, till they doe alow him the charge y^t he layed out about it.

At a Towne meetinge assembled ffebruary 5th 1651. There fallinge out some disputes betwixt mr John Pynchon and the Towne in reference to the above mentioned bargaine about the meetinge howse chamber. In conclusion it was put to ye vote: whither the Inhabitants be willinge to take the chamber into theyr hands agaayne presently, promis-inge to pay mr John Pynchon his wholl charge that he hath bin at about it for ye tyme past; And he to have the use of the chamber till October next, p'vided he lay not above 400 bushells of corne in it, if he exceed that quantity he is to un-derprop ye floore at his owne charge as Rich: Sykes and Tho: Cooper shall Judge meete. It was voted affirmatively to all ye particulars. whereupon George Coulton and Robt Ashly were nominated by mr Pynchon, and appoynted by ye vote of ye Inhabitants to gather in ye rate y^t shall be made by the Select men for the charge layed out about this floore, and to see it payd in to mr Pynchon by ye 20th of ffebruary next, 1652, in marchantable wheate at 3s 10d P bushell.

The Select Townsmen are to take care for ye securing of these men.

P' mr Henry Smith.

[I—65]

ffebruary the 5th 1649.

A copy of such orders as are made and confirmed by the Inhabitants of Springfield the day and yeare above written.

1. ffor the prevention of disorders in puttinge Cattell to Pasture on the other side of the greate river to the prejudice of mens Corne: And yet that men may have the benefite of

the Pasture there for theyr Cattell in seasonable tyme: It is therefore ordered that no person shall put over any Cattell on the other side of the greate River to Psture there untill the feilds there are to be cleered of Cattell of all sortes: And if 25th day of March they may continue there, by which day the fields there are to be cleered of Cattell of all sortes: And if any Cattell shall be found there goinge at Liberty and not under the hand of a keeper, or in an inclosed piece of ground, before or after the days above sayd the owners of the s^d Cattell shall be lyable to a fine of 12d a head for all that shall be found within 100 rods of any corne or meddow halfe of ye fine to ye Informer & ye other halfe to y Towne, and alsoe shall make good what ever damadge shall appeare to be done by theyr s^d Cattell in that tyme.

Nov. 2d, 1658. It is ordered y^t noe man shall keep or allow his cattle to feed on other mens grounds wthout Consent, noe man beinge to keepe his cattel over ye River but on his owne ground or on any Common fro: October till 25th March yearely: this order above written is repealed at ye genll meetinge on the 3d day of ffebr 1661.

2. wheras the planting of Indian Corne in the meddows and Swamps on the other side of Agawam river hath occationed a longe sty after mowinge tyme before men can put theyr cattell thither to pasture: Therfore it is ordered, (wth the consent of all those y^t have Planting ground there) that no more Indian corne shall be planted there, either in the meddows or Swamps, that soe the Cattell of those y^t have allottmnts there may be put over by the 15th day of Septembr yearly, P'videde they take a sure course to p'vent theyr Cattell from goinge [I—66 Blank—I—67] over the River, either by fencing, or by a keeper in the day tyme, and by securinge them in some inclosure in the night: But there is Liberty for Calves to be put over thither by the 14th day of August: And in case any P'son shall put Cattell there before the days expressed, he shall forfeite 2s 6d for ye head for every such default, and alsoe be lyable to pay all damadge that his Cattell shall doe on either side of the river.

[Note.—On margin of page 65 against article 2 is this:]
"Revoked, Jan ye 29, 1651, & noe liberty to put over cattle
but at such tyme as they may be put over ye greate River."

3. It is ordered that if any Inhabitant shal desire to make
a Cannoe, he may have liberty to feel any tree or trees in the
Towne Comons, and make it or them into Cannoes for his
owne use or the use of any Inhabitant: But no such Inhabitant shall have liberty to sell or in any kinde pass away any
Cannoe soe made out of the Towne, untill it be full five years
old, or if he lend his Cannoe it shall be returned with in a
month: And in case any shall transgress this order he shall
be Lyable to a penalty of 20s for every default.—Repealed
Dec. 30, 1664.

4. It is ordered that whosoever shall take away or make
use of any mans Cannoe or boate w^{th}out his Leave shall forfeite unto the owner 2s 6d for every such default.

5. It is ordered that there shall be no barns or any other
howsinge, built or set up in the high way betwixt the Street
fence and the brooke: Except ther be soe much roome, as
they can leave 4 Rod for the Street or high way, and then
men may make use of that side next the brooke for what
building they please: And if any shall transgress this order,
It shall be lawfull for the Select men to appoynt men to pull
downe and demollish such buildings.

[Note.—On margin of clause 5 is this:] "See ffebr 25
1643. Se ye 2d book of the Select mens acts mar. 3, 1664."

[I—68 Blank—I—69]

6. For the prevention of sundry evils that may befall
this Townshipp ill disposed persons, that may thrust themselves in amongst us, agaynst ye likeinge and consent of the
generality of the Inhabitants by purchasinge a lott or place
of habitation &c. It is therfore ordered and declare that no
inhabitant shall sell or in any kind Pass away his howse lot
or any part of it, or any other of his alotmnts to any Stranger, before he have made the Select Townsmen acquainted
who his chapman is, and they accordingly alow of his admission, under penalty of paying Twenty shillings for every

p'sell of land so sold or passed away: But if the Select Townsmen see grounds to disalowe of the admission of the s^d chapman, then the Towne or Inhabitants shall have 30 days tyme to resolve whither they will buy the s^d alottmnts, which s^d alotmts they may buy as indifferent partys shall apprise them. But in case the Inhabitants shall delay to make a purchase of the s^d lands above 30 dayes after the ppounding of it to the Select Townsmen, then the s^d seller shall have his Liberty to take his chapman, and such chapman or Stranger shall be esteemed as entertained and alowed by the Towne as an Inhabitant.

7. It is ordered that if any man of this Township or any pprietor of land here or any y^t shall or may dispose of land he shall under the Colour of friendship or other ways, entertaine any P'son or persons, heere to abide as Inmates, or shall subdevide theyr howslotts to entertaine them as Tennants or other ways for Longer tyme then one month or 30 days, wthout the consent or allowance of the Select Townsmen (children or servants of the family that remaine single P'sons excepted) shall forfeit for the first default 20s to the Towne, and alsoe he shall forfeite 20s P month for every month that any such person [I—70 Blank.—I—71] or persons shal so continue in the Township without the consent of the Select Townsmen: And if in any tyme of theyr abode after the Limitation aboves^d they shal neede releefe, not beinge able to maintain themselves, then he or they that entertained such persons, shall be Lyable to be rated by the Select men for the releife & maintenance of the s^d partys so entertained as they in theyr discretion shall Judge mete. And it is further ordered y^t no man shal be entrtained wthout leave longer then a month or 30 days, y^t if he have bin a Month in Towne noe Inhabitant may entertaine him a day Longer wth out leave on Penalty.

8. ffor the regulating of workmens & Labourers wages, It is ordered, 1. That all workmen shall worke the wholl day, alowinge convenient tyme for foode and rest. 2. That all Husbandmen and ordinary Labourers, from the first day of

November to ye first of march, shal not take above 16d by the day wages, for the other 8 months they shall not take above 20d by the day, except in tyme of harvest for reapinge and mowinge, or for other extraordinary works such as are sufficient workmen are allowed 2s P day. 3. That all Carpenters, Joyners, wheel wrights, or such like Artificers, from the first of Novembr to the first of march, shal not take above 20d P day wages: And for the other 8 months not above 2s P day. Tailors not to exceed 12d P day through the yeare. 4. That all Teames consistinge of 4 Cattell wth one man shall not take above 6s P day wages: ffrom may till Octobr: to worke 8 howers, and the other part of the yeare 6 howers for theyr days worke. And it is further ordered that whosoever shall either by givinge or takinge exceede these rates he shall be Lyable to be punished by the magistrate accordinge to the quality and nature of the offence.

[Page 72 was left blank by the clerk, Henry Smith, in 1649. In 1661 in the hand of John Pynchon was written the addition to the preceding clause which is here inserted.]

ffebr 4th 1661. At a Generall Towne Meeting.

It is ordered that whosoever of this Township shall fall any Trees in ye Towne Comons: His falling of them though he hath bestowed noe other worke upon them, shall give him right to them for worke six months, soe y^t noe other p'son shall meddle wth any such fallen Tree or Trees till 6 months are expired after ye falling of y^m. But for tymber that is cross cut, or firewood y^t is cut out and set on heaps, or Rayles or clefts, or Pales, these may lye 6 Months more after they are so cross cut or cloven (by ye first faller) besides ye first 6 Months before y^t any other man shall meddle wth them. And it is declared y^t he wch felled ye Trees may take his owne tyme for cross cutting of ye tymber or Cleaving Bolts, Rayls & Pales, or setting ye firewood on heaps, p'vided he doe it before ye first 6 Months be expired, and ye ffaller having bestowed such worke on the trees he felled, though he did it at ye tyme of falling them. Such worke as afores^d

shall give him right to such tree for twelve months from his first tyme of falling them: & after ye tyme Limited it shall be Lawfull for any man to take them. And for such Timber as becomes forfeited as afores^d at 6 M^o after falling, for want of Such further worke bestowed on it as is before exp'essed: who ever shall seaze upon it as forfeited, if he fetch it not p'sently away hom, But bestow worke upon it in ye woods by cleaving it out into Rayls, Pales or ye like, such worke shall give him right for one whole month after so it shall not be Lawfull for an other man to take it or any pt of it till one month after & then it may be Lawfull for any p'son to take it: And in case any p'son shall be found to take away or Convert to his owne use any Trees, Timber or firewood &c: as afores^d before ye tyme above Limited he shall be Lyable to make satisfaction to ye owner in kind or otherwise to his Content: And shall also forfeite Ten shillings To ye Towne Treasury for every p'sell of Timber Rayls, bolts firewood or Trees that he shall so disorderly take away & convert to his owne use. It is ordered to take place fro: henceforth forward & so it reaches not to trees already fallen but such shal not be forfeited till they have lyne according as the former order alowed them.

November 2, 1652. Upon ye pleading of many for liberty to transport Board & Planks: It is ordered y^t any p'son y^t desires to transport boards & planks, shal first Tender such board or Planks to ye Select Townsmen, & if they p'vide noe chapman in ye Towne wthin 21 days to take off such boards or Planks at an Indifferent price then ye owner thereoff have Liberty to transport or Re-sell y^m out of Towne, Notwthstanding ye order P Contra. Repealed Dec. 30 1664.

[In the handwriting of Henry Smith.]

13. To the end that such Candlewood as lyeth neere the Towne may not be wasted, by such as burne Tarr & to ye p'judice of the Inhabitants. It is therfore ordered that no person shall have liberty to gather, or having so gathered to burne any Candlewood for the making of Tarr, Pitch, or Coale, wthin the Compass of 6 miles East from the greate

River, and soe extending fro: Chickuppe river to ye Longmeddow brooke: And if any shall be found to burne any Candlewood soe gathered wᵗʰin the Limites or bounds above expressed, he shall forfeite 20s for every loade of Candlewood
soe gathered and burnt for Tarr, Pitch, Cole, or ye like use.
Provided notwᵗʰstandinge that every Inhabitant may gather
Candlewood for his owne family use where he pleaseth.

[On the margin of clause 13 is written:] Nov. 3d, (58) It
is ordered yᵗ whosoe shal gather any candlewood together in
heapes in the Town Comons If he shall let it ly above one
Month it shall be lawfull for any man to take it unless ye Select men shall allow Longer tyme to such as burne Tarr &
Coles.—The order No. 13 is repealed Dec. 30, 1664 & yᵗ on
yᵉ Margens was agreed to by a full vote & is to be Transcrib-
ed into yᵉ New Booke.

14. wheras it is Judged offensive and noisome for flax
and hempe, to be watered or washed in, or by the Brooke
before mens doores which is of ordinary use for dressinge
meate: Therfore it is ordered that no person hence forth,
Shall water or wash any flax or hemp in the Brooke either on
yᵉ east or west side of yᵉ street, or anywher neere adjoyninge
to it and if any p'son shall be found transgressinge heerin, he
shall be Liable to a fine of 6s 8d for every such default.

15. It is ordered that no p'son shall gather any hopps
that grow in the Swamps or any Comon grounds untill the
ffith day of September yearly, upon payne of forfeiting what
they shall soe disorderly gather, and 2s 6d for breach of order: The forfeiture to the Informer, the 2s 6d to the Towne
Treasurer.   Repealed Dec. 30th 164.

[I—76 Blank—I—77]

16. wheras it is Judged needfull in Sundry respects that
each Inhabitant should have the severall parsells of his land
recorded, Therfore for prevention of future inconveniences,
It is ordered, That every particular Inhabitant of this Township shall repayre to the Recorder that is chosen and appoynted by the Towne, for that end and purpose: who upon Information given him by each person, of his severall parcells

of Land, the number of Acres, wth ye Length & breadth of the s^d alotments, and who are borderinge on each side of him: Shall by virtue of his office fairely record, each parcell of Land, with the Limits, bounds, & situation therof in a Booke for that purpose: for which his paynes, the owner of the s^d Lands shall pay unto the Recorder Two pence for every parcell of his Land soe recorded. And if any person shall neglect ye Recording of his Lands longer then sixe Months after ye grant of it he shall be Lyable to a fine of 5s for every p'cell of his Land that is not then recorded: And if after that he shall neglect to record his Land he shall pay 12s P month for every months neglect of any parcell. And ancient grants are all to be Recorded by ye last of May next upon like Penalty.

17. It is ordered That if any person whose howse Lott lyes Inclosed in a generall fence, shall desire to inclose a part of it for yards gardens or orchard, his neighbor on each hand of him shall be Compellable to make and sufficiently maintaine the one halfe of the s^d fence from tyme to tyme: P'vided his share of fence amount not to above Ten rods: P'vided alsoe that the s^d fence exceede not the charge of a sufficient five foote pale or 5 rayles: And in case any neighbour shall refuse to doe his share of the s^d fence within 3 months after due notice given him of it, he shall be lyable to pay what damadge his neighbour shall sustaine through his default: and alsoe 5s P month soe long as he shall neglect it, for contempt of order.   Repealed Dec. 30, (64.)

[I—79]

18th. It is ordered that all persons that have any interest in generall fences shal carefully attend to repayer and sufficiently close up theyr severall fences in the Comon feilds by the 25th day of march yearly, and to see that they be kept in sufficient repayre till the last day of September: In which Interim, It shall not be lawfull for any person, to put in any cattell to Pasture, or any way Lay open his part of fence in the s^d comon feild, to his neighbours prejudice: wthout the Joynt consent of the wholl that have Interest in the s^d feild: But

after that tyme it shall be lawfull for any p'son to put in his
cattell that hath Interest in ye s^d Generall feild. And if any
shall be found to lay open his fence, or have in any Cattell, into any part of any Comon feild before the day above
limited he shal pay all damages that shall be done through
his default, and a fine of 5s for breach of order. There is liberty granted for men to baite theire workinge cattle on theire
owne ground in ye tyme of their workinge of y^m p'vided they
secure y^m fro: doinge damadge to any.

19. wheras there are persons yearly chosen by the Inhabitants to view the Comon fences of every theyr Corne
feilds, It is therfore ordered that the p'sons soe chosen by the
Towne to that worke, do from tyme to tyme as neede shall
require take due notice of the reall defects and insufficiencys
of the s^d fences under theyr charge, And shal forthwith acquaint the owners therof with the same: And if the s^d owners doe not w^{th}in 3 days tyme sufficiently repayre theyr s^d
defective fences, then the afores^d viewers shal forthwith repayer and renue them, and shal have double recompence, for
all theyr labour, care, cost and trouble, to be payed by the
owners of ye s^d insufficient feince or fences, and shall have
warrant from the Select men directed to the Constable to
Levie the same either upon the Corne or other estate of the
Delinquent: Provided the defect of ye fence or fences be sufficiently proved by two or three..........

[I—78 originally left blank, on which John Pynchon entered an amendment to Clause 19]

December 30th 1664. The order here below & the other
Repealed And ye Select men (according to Countrey Law)
are to make orders about ffencing, &c.

This order confirmed by the Townesmen in 1653.

19th. Wheras there are p'sons yearely chosen by ye Inhabitants to view all ye Generall and particular fences: It is
therefore ordered y^t ye ptys so chosen by ye Towne for y^t
service, shall two severall tymes in ye yeare at least, viz:
March 29th & July 28th, take a survey of all ye s^d fences be-

longing to their care & circumspection, To ye Intent they
be fully closed up & kept in repaire, as ye s^d viewers shal allow
to be sufficient: And in case they shall find any Reall defects
& Insufficiencys upon their view of ye s^d fence, they shall
forthw^th give notice thereoff, unto ye owners of ye s^d defective fence or fences: warning him or y^m to amend ye same
w^thin 2 or 3 days at furthest: And in case ye pty so warned
shall delay to amend his s^d defective fence according to y^e
tyme limited, to ye satisfaction of ye viewers: He shall be
Llable to a fine of 12d for every such defect, & so to increase
12d for every days neglect till he doe fully amend ye same:
Besides all damadges y^t accrew to any through ye Insuffi-
ciency of his s^d fence: The one halfe of ye fines to fall to y^e
Towne & the other halfe to the overseers of ye s^d fences: who
on complaint made shall have warrant fro: ye Select men directed to ye Constable to levie what fines are due accordinge
to order, upon ye estate of ye delinquent. If he refuse to sat-
isfie ye s^d fines, being of him demanded, And it is further ordered y^t if ye s^d overseers of fences shall Rec: Information
fro: others, or by theyre own observation at any other tyme,
besides ye forementioned tymes above expressed, shall understand of any defects or Insufficiencys in ye fences under theire
care, they shall take due notice thereoff & seasonably attend
ye aboves^d direction for amending of y^m: And in case any Just
Complaint so Judged by ye Select men shall be brought ag^t
ye s^d veiwers for neglect of theire charge, they shall be lyable
to a fine of 5s & in case fur: neglect of 10s according as they
shall be thereunto adjudged by ye selectmen for every neglect.

[I—80 Blank—I—81]

20. ffor the better carryinge on of Towne meetings: It
is ordered that whensoever there shall any Publike notice
be given to the Inhabitants, by the Select Townsmen or any
other in theyr behalfe of some necessary occation wherin the
Select men desire to advise wth the Inhabitants, and the day,
tyme, and place of meeting be appoynted: It is expected that
all the Inhabitants attend p'sonally such meetings soe ap-

poynted. And in case the tyme and hower of meeting be come, Though there be but nine of the Inhabitants asembled, it shall be Lawfull for them to p'ceede in agitation of what ever busyness is then ppounded to them and what the major part of the Asembly then mett shall agree upon, It shall be Taken as the act of the wholl Towne & binding to all.

21. The ffirst Tuesday in November (November is altrd to ffebruary) yearly is mutually agreed on and appoynted to be generall Towne meetinge for the choyce of Towne officers,, making confirming and publishing of orders, &c. on wch day it is more especially expected y^t each Inhabitant gives his p'sonall attendance and if any shall be absent at ye tyme of ye major part, he shal be lyable to a fine of 2s 6d. This clause was added Nov. 4th (51).

22. It is alsoe ordered that on the first Tuesday in November there shall be yearly chosen by the Inhabitants Two wise discreete men: who shall by virtue af an Oath imposed on them by the magistrate for that purpose, faithfully p'sent on the Court days, all such breaches of Court, or Towne orders, or any other misdemenors as shal come to theyr knowledge, either by theyr own observation or by credible information of others, and shal take out p'cess for the appearance of such as are delinquents: or witnesses to appeare [I—82 Blank—I—83] the sayd day: when all such presentments by the sayd partys shal be Judicialy heard and examined by the Magistrate, and warrants for distresses granted, for the Leavyinge of such fines or penaltys as are anexed to the orders violated, or which shal seem meete and reasonable to the magistrate to impose or inflict according to the nature of the offence. These to stand in this office for a yeare or till others be chosen in y^r roome.

23. It is ordered and declared that when any men shall be fairely and cleerly chosen to any office, & place of service in and to the Towne. If then he refuse to accept the place or shall afterwards neglect to serve in that office to which he shal be chosen, every such person shal pay 20s fine for refusall unto the Towne Treasury: unles he had served in that

office ye yeare before; no person being to be compelled to serve two yeares to gither in ye same office except Select men, Two whereoff if chosen agayne are to stand 2 yeares together, so ther may be always some of ye old Select men who are acquainted wth ye Towne affaires. This change added by ye Towne ffebr 12th 1660.

24. It is ordered that such swine only as shall doe trespass (in Corne feilds meddow or gardens) shall be lyable to satisfy damadge: And for that end, if any man shall find any Swine damadge feisant in his Corne feilds, meddow, or garden he shall drive them to the pound, and shall take two or more neighbours to veiw the damadge done by them: And the owner of the s^d Swine, shall be lyable to pay such damages as the s^d indifferent men shall appoynt. But in case Swine that are sufficiently yoked and rung shal doe any Trespass, then the owner of the Insufficient fence where they went in shall pay the damadges to ye party damnified as Indifferent men shall Judge to be equal, or such as are appoynted to be viewers of the fences.

[I—84 Blank—I—85]

25. To the end that the common High ways of the Towne may be Layed out where they may be most convenient and advantagiose for the generall use of the Towne: It is therefore ordered that the Select Townsmen shal have full power and authority to Lay out all common Highways, for ye Town where and how they shall Judge most convenient and usefull for the Inhabitants, Though it be through or at the end of mens Lotts, p'vided they give them reasonable satisfaction, accordinge to equity: But if the party like not therof, then it shall be referred to the Judgment of Indifferent partys, mutually chosen by the partye one and the Select Townsmen one & if those 2 indifferent pty doe not agree they shall pitch upon a 3d p'son to Joine with^m se & determine it:

26. It is ordered that all such Common Highways for ye Towne which are or shall by the Select Townsmen be Judged needful to be made or repayred by the Towne, the wholl

Towne shall Joyne in the makinge or repayringe of them, when the are required by the Surveyors, accordinge to orders, And the Select Townsmen are alowed Liberty to set a certain Toll on carts that shall pass any High way which shall appeare more than ordinary chargeable in the reparation of it.

[I—86 Blank—I—87]

27. ffor the equall and Indifferent carryinge on and bearing the charge, of makinge and repayringe, such Comon High ways and Bridges, as are or shall be thought needfull to be made or repayred from tyme to tyme, with in this Township: It is ordered that every householder that hath or keepeth in his use or possession a Teame consistinge of 4 Cattell, shall on due warninge given him by the surveyor, send at every day and place appoynted, his s^d Teame wth his Cart and such necessary tooles as the Surveyor shall alowe of, and an able man therewith: To doe such worke as the Surveyors shall appoynt him, for the space of eight howers in a day, besides the tyme of rest and refreshinge, p'vided they be not required above 6 days in a yeare: The like is to be done by those that have but halfe Teames: But in case such Teams or Carriages shall not be thought needfull to be made use of by the Surveyors, then every such person whose Teame is exempted, shall send two able men, for his Team so spared, and every halfe Teame to send a man a day & a halfe in steed of his Teame so spared. And it is herby declared that 2 oxen & a mare or horse is to be esteemed a full Teame.—Repealed.

And it is further ordered that every other howsholder (who hath no Teame) shall by himselfe or some other able Labourer, attend the works appoynted him by the Surveyors for the space of 8 howers, (besides tyme of rest and refreshinge) on every day y^t he shall be called or required soe to worke, p'vided he be not called to worke above six days in a yeare.

[I—88 Blank—I—89]

And it is also ordered that all persons Inhabitinge in the

Towne who are above £100 estate in other rates and yet have no Teame: every such P'son shall be compelled to send one sufficient Labourer to ye high way worke on every day he shall be duly warned therunto, accordinge to his pportion of the 6 days wth other men.

It is alsoe further ordered that every person shall cutt downe his stubbs and cleere the high way before his lott, of tymber wood, standinge trees, (wch are heerby declared to be a mans owne) or any other offensive matter, that the surveyors shall warn him of, within three days after notice given him, or else be lyable to a fine of 12d for every defect.

28. wheras ther are surveyors chosen yearly for the oversight and amendinge of Highways, Bridges, and other defects of that nature, that soe the Comon highways of the Towne may be kept in continuall reparation: To that end, and for the regulatinge of Surveyors in the discharge of theyr office; It is ordered y^t the Surveyors for the tyme beinge shall take care

1. That all Highways, Bridges, wharfs &c, belonging to their care be made, repayred, and amended sufficiently, accordinge to theyr discretion or as they shall be directed by the Select Townsmen.

2. That all Highways be kept cleer from trees Timber wood, earth, stone, or any other offensive matter, y^t shall anoye the Highway, within a mile of any dwelling house.

3. That if any person upon notice given him by ye Surveyor shall neglect to move or cleere away, any such anoyance to the high way, or offensive matter by him caused, longer than 3 days: Then ye Surveyor shall doe it and have double recompence for all his labour cost and charge from the party soe neglectinge, besides the 12d wch the party is to pay in way of fine for neglect accordinge to the order forementioned.

[I—90 Blank—I—91]

4. That the Surveyour shall give three days warninge to such as they call for and require to come to the Highway worke. viz: the day of warninge and a day more: soe y^t men

must come the 3d daye after warninge: unless the surveyors give them longer tyme.

5.   That they shall   require no howseholder to worke
above 6 days in a yeare, nor more of those 6 days than shall
in a due pportion fall to his share.

6.   The Surveyors shall require no man to worke above
2 days in a week, nor above 8 hours in a day besides tyme for
refreshing.

7.   That they call for these 6 days (or as many of them as
shall serve) Within the compass of time betwixt ye 20th of
may and the 20th of June yeerly, and not at any other tyme,
unles by the consent of the major pt of ye Select Townsmen
it be agreed unto.   Yet in as much as some times ways may
suddenly become defective that they may not be too long
neglected it is declared the Three of ye Select men meeting
& any 2 of y^m agreeing may appoint & allow the surveighors
to repare such defective ways.

8.   That they duely present to the Select Townsmen at
the weeks end, all defects of persons or Teames, that on lawfull warninge given, neglect to come to the work appoynted,
who shall give warrant to the Constable for p'sent distress of
2s fine, for a man and 5s for a man and teame, to be imployed in the next worke, that is to be done about Highways.

9.   That they give in theyr accounts yearly, to the Select
men, at the generall meetine in ffebruary, when they yeild
up theyr office, or in theyr neglect therof to remaine in theyr
office another yeare.

[I—92 Blank—I—93]

[In the handwriting of John Pynchon.]

March 28th, 1650.

wheras there appears to be a defect in the former order
about Highways, wherby some p'sons take advantage to
exempt themselves from such publique works wch in equity
they should attend with others pportionably: It is therfore
ordered that all single persons or unmarried (though liveinge in another mans family) who are possessed of a lott,

either by the grant of the Towne (after 3 months) or by Purchase or otherwise, they shall from hence forth be Lyable
to attend the worke of the Highways, pportionable with
other howseholders accordinge as they shall be duely warned
thereunto by the surveyors.

And it is alsoe ordered that if any Inhabitant shall have in
his use and possession, two or more distinct alottments
either by way of purchase or by way of rentinge: Every such
person shall be Lyable to send one sufficient man to the
Highway worke, on every day he shall be duely warned therunto for every such alottment as shall be in his possession.
And if any man shal keepe two Teames for the improvement
of such Lands, his s^d Teames shall Likewise be compelable
to the worke, as in the former order is required of other men
that have Teames.

[I—94]

March ye 13th 1653-54.

Whereas there hath bin a p'sell of land over ye greate
river at ye lower end of Chickkuppy plaine, reserved for y^e
Townes use, & yet notw^{th}standing some of ye land hath bin
disposed off to p'ticular p'sons so y^t there is now but about
Thirty acres thereoff left, some p'sons desiring y^t ye s^d Thirty
acres may also be disposed off & distributed to severall
p'sons: The Towne took it into consideration whether to
yeild thereunto, & ye Major pt of ye Towne for severall reasons doe resolve not to dispose of ye s^d Thirty acres of land
to any p'ticular p'son or p'sons as theire ppriety: But doe
here by order y^t ye afores^d Thirty acres of land at ye lower end
of Chikkuppy plaine over ye grt river shall be reserved in y^e
Townes hands, as ye Townes land for ye Townes use, either
for ye helping to maintaine a scholemaster or ruling Elder or
to help beare any other Towne charges accordinge as it shall
hereafter be concluded on. But not to be disposed off fro:
ye Townes ppriety.

And further it is ordered y^t ye Select Townsmen shall have
liberty to let out ye s^d land for yeare or yeares to bring in
some yearly rent to ye Towne if they can find any to take it.

It is also further ordered y^t all p'sons whomsoever that

have any land granted y^m fro: ye Towne they shall wthin Sixe
months at ye furthest after such grant get ye s^d land measured & Recorded upon penalty of Ten shillings fine or for-
feiting ye s^d land for neglect either in getting it measured or
recorded wthin ye tyme so fixed: & if any man y^t choose to
pay ye 10s fine, shall afterward neglect to record his land, he
shall pay 12d P month for every months neglect: If ye pty
choose to pay 10s rather than forfeite his land, it is to be understood 10s for every distinct p'sell of land one halfe of
wch fine shall goe to ye recorder & ye other halfe to the
Towne.   Repealed by the Towne.

   [I—95]

   And for any land formerly granted if it remaine unrecorded above 3 month after this p'sent day, they shall pay 10s for
every p'sell of ye s^d land, & when the 3 months are expired,
12d P Mo so long as it is unrecorded.   Also if any p'son shall
sell or any ways pass away any of his land to any other man
he shall wthin one month record such sale or alteration of
land, & in case of his non recording ye seller & purchaser
shall each of y^m pay 10s a p'sell for neglect when taken notice off ye one halfe to ye Recorder, & the other halfe to
the Towne.   The Recorder is allowed 4d P p'sell for record-
ing all alterations of land: or exchanges for every p'sell he is
to be allowed 4d for his paines.

   [I—96 Blank—I—97]

   [In the handwriting of Thomas Cooper.]

march 30th (1665)

By the Selecktt men:—

   itt is ordered all Swine within the Township from 3 months
ould and upward shall be sufficiently Roonge by the 20 day
of Aprill nextt insuinge: and for the well persorving of the
same wee have apointed John Steward to make Rings and
to see to Sett them on and wee apointt thatt hee shalle have
3d for every Swine soo Roonge paid him by the owners of
the sayd swine with sufficient help for the worke and if any
Swine above the adge of 3 months shall be found to goe att

liberty abroad in the streett or comons unRoonge att any time betwixt the first of march unto the last of november yearly they shall be lyable to a fine of 12d for every such deffecktt which fine of 12d shal be payd to the informer by the owner of the swine and in case any shall Refuse to pay the sayd fine being of them demanded upon complaintt made the seleckt men shall dyreckt a warrantt to the constable to levy the same but if any be minded to Ringe there swine themselves they shall be adjudged to be sufficiently Roonge by the sayd John Steward or else they shall be lyable to the fine notwithstandinge.

[I—98, 99 and 100 Blank—I—101]

[In the handwriting of Henry Smith.]

November 5th 1650.

At a Towne meetinge there was a choyce made of five Townsmen, John Pynchon, Henry Smith, Samuell Chapen, Henry Burt, Thomas Cooper—To whom by ye major vote of the Inhabitants was comitted power to order all ye prudentiall affayers of the Towne agreeable to wht is expressed in the Court order, wch power is given y^m for a yeare or till men be chosen in theyr roome.

Mr. John Pynchon is chosen to be the Towne Treasurer for the yeare ensuinge & till another be chosen in his roome.

George Langton and Jno Stebbine are chosen Surveighors of the high ways of the Towne for the yeare ensuinge.

william warrener and Robt Ashly are chosen overseers of fences for ye feilds p^{r}tayninge to ye upper pt of the Towne from ye meetinghowse upward.

. Joseph Parsons and John Clarke are chosen overseers of the fences from ye meeting howse downeward who are to take direction from ye Townsmen for ordering these fences.

[I—102]

By the Townsmen: January 30th 1650.

It is agreed that these rates are heere under expressed shall be gathered this p'sent yeere, viz: March 25th.

mr Moxons maintenance   £70   00

mr will. Pynchon for the Bell	05	00
for mr Moxon wᶜʰ he pᵈ for yᵉ Towne upon yᵉ close last yeare	10	00
	15	00

mr John Pynchon for a barrell of powder for a towne stock	07	12	6
p 1 lb 1-4 & 11 lb of musket bulletts & yᵉ caske	01	17	6
p 50 lb of match at 8d	01	13	4
p to yᵉ cartway to yᵉ foot of yᵉ falls	10	00	0
	21	03	4

p for charges about repayringe the meeting howse, hanging the bell & other charges	18	00	00
for killinge 5 wolves	05	00	00
Totall	129	03	04

It is agreed and ordered that the prices of corne for payments of all these rates shall be wheate, at 3s 6d P b, pease
at 3s P b, Indian at 2s P b, only mr Moxons rate we are to
agree wᵗʰ him.

The persons appoynted to take account of mens estates &
price cattell are, mr Hollioke, Nathaniell Bliss, Juᵒ Stebbin.

The rate for wolves is to be raised only on Cattell.

[I—103]

May 19th 1651.

mr Elitzur Holyoke was chosen to yᵉ office of a Constable
for yᵉ towne of Springfield for yᵉ yeare ensuinge and till another shall be chosen in his roome, & hath accordingly taken
his oath, yᵉ day & yeare above sᵈ

[I—104 Blank—I—105]

[In the handwriting of Elizur Holyoke.]

Nov: 4th: 1651.

At a Towne meeting there was a choyce of five Townsmen

vist: mr John Pynchon, Samuell Chapin, George Colton, Henry Burt, Thomas Cooper, to whom by yᵉ Major vote of yᵉ Inhabitants was Comited power to order all yᵉ Pruden- tiall affayres of yᵉ Towne, agreeable to it is expressed in yᵉ Court Order wᶜʰ power is given yᵐ for a yeare or till new be chosen in yʳ roome.

It was also voted yᵗ mr Henry Smith shall have full power wᵗʰ yᵉ Townsmen to act in yᵉ distribution of what lands are to be Laid out this yeere:

Richard Sikes was chosen to p'sent such breaches of Or- ders as he shall take notice of or yᵗ shal come to his knowl- edge by information: to wᶜʰ office he is sworne for yᵉ yeare insuinge.

Robert Ashly & Nathaniell Bliss were chosen surveyors of yᵉ high wayes for yᵉ yeare ensuinge.

James Bridgman & Benjamin Parsons are chosen viewers of yᵉ fences for yᵉ lower end of yᵉ Towne: And Miles Mor- gan & Richard Exell for yᵉ upper end of yᵉ Towne.

[I—106]

[In the handwriting of John Pynchon.]

Decembr yᵉ 25th 1651.

Agreed wᵗʰ Richard Sikes for ringing yᵉ Bell & sweeping yᵉ meeting howse & for the yeare ensueing: viz fro ye 1st of January, 1652; he to carry on ye work according as he hath done yᵉ yeare Past: In Recompence whereoff wee In- gage to see him pd yᵉ Sum of 12d P weeke yᵗ is to say fifty two shillings for yᵉ yeare.

By yᵉ Select Townsmen.

ffor yᵉ yeare past by agreement he was to have but 40s. By the Selectmen, January yᵉ 9th, & Jan yᵉ 22th 1651. Mr Henry Smith also concurring wᵗʰ them (according to order) in yᵉ distribution of Land:

There is granted to Antho: Dorchester a p'sell of planting land, over yᵉ greate River, at yᵉ Lower end of chikkuppy plaine on this side of the 60 acres for the ministry, adjoyning to yᵉ brooke, of about 8 acres, wᶜʰ he is to get measured, & Record the quantity, be it more or less.

There is granted to Sam Wright Junior 7 acres of planting land over Agawam River If it will hold out.

Ther is granted to Tho: Mirack on ye other side Agawam River, all the planting land, fro: his meddow to the Brow of the Hill, being guessed at neere 4 acres.   [Erased.]

There is granted to Tho: Cooper, upon Mill River, below Rich Sikes his meddow, a p'sell of about an acre & 1-2 of meddow, in 2 or 3 lotts, wch is due to him in lew of 1 acre & 1-2 wch he falls short of on ye other side of ye River.   this he accepts though it hold not out 1 acre & 1-2.

There is granted to Rowland Thomas 6 acres of meddow lying Remote upon ye Northerne branch of ye mil River, in a psell of meddow Judged to be 16 to 17 acres, wth liberty to make a choise at wch end to begin.

There is granted to ffraunces Pepper 4 acres of meddow adjoyning Rowlands.

Also to Tho: Stebbins & Jno Stebbins, each of y^m 3 acres. But if ye meddow hold out 7 acres & but 7 (Besides Rowlands & ffraunces) then to devide it between y^m.   In case it pve more then 7 then all above 6 acres to be at ye Towns dispose:

There is granted to Tho: Miller one acre & halfe of meddow ground over Agawam River, wch formerly Tho: Stebbins resigned up into the Towns hand.

[I—107]

Jan ye 22th 1651.

The names of such as have medow granted y^m, & how they are to ly by lot.

On Pacowsick beginning at ye lower end

		acres	
Benjamin Cooley	1	3	
Anthony Dorchester	2	4	
Widdow Bliss	3	3	
Roger Pritchard &			
John Lumbard	4	1	1-2
Nathan Pritchard	5	4	
John Harmon	6	2	1-2

On ye Mill River beginning lowermost on ye South east branch, & so going up ye little brooke & then upward to ye 16 acres, & so over to ye North branch at ye upper end & then Come downeward & lastly to ye lake or pond

		acres
Jn° Clarke	1	4
Nath Bliss	2	2
Miles Morgan	3	2
Jn° Leanord	4	2
Rich Exsell	5	1 1-2
Jonathan Burt	6	1 1-2
Sam Marshfield	7	1
Benja Mun	8	1
James Bridgman	9	2
Mr Moxon	10	2
Jn° Dumbleton	11	4
Henry Chapen	12	4
Robert Ashly	13	3 1-2

But one acre of it is given in relation to his keeping ye ordinary; he is to leave it in ye Towns hands, when ever he shall cease to keepe ye ordinary.

John Lamb	14	5
Tho Mirack	15	3
Henry Burt	16	3
Rice Bedortha	18	1
Wm Wariner	17	1

Upon condition he allow a sufficient cart-way through ye medow he hath already.

Rice Bedortha	13	1
Tho Cooper	19	1
Jonath Taylor	20	1
Sam Chapen	21	1

which sayd acar was exchanged with the Towne for a parcell of meddow of about an acar or an acar and halfe lyinge below the lott which was mr moxons below

[I—108]

By ye Townsmen ffebr 13th, 1651.

It is agreed that these Rates underwritten shall be gathered this p^{r}sent yeare, viz: by March 25th.

£

Impr: ffor Mr Moxons maintenance.........70
ffor killing 5 Wolves.....................05
ffor lapbording of ye meeting howse, cleaning it
   & Ringing Bell, & some other charges......11

                —

In all......82

This Rate of £11 was never gathered in: ye worke not beinge done, & ye Rate not p^d in, except by 3 or 4 p'sons: It
was concluded by ye Select Townsmen, Ano 1652, y^t those
3 or 4 y^t had pd should have it allowed y^m back againe, w^{ch}
was accordingly done, & so ye Rate is Void.

[I—109]

At a Towne meeting, Septemb^r ye 14th 1652: There being
Consideration had of how necessary It was for the Towne to
Purchase Mr Moxons howse & Land to Remaine for ye vse
of ye Ministry to Posterity: There uppon by ye Joynt Con-
sent of ye Towne it was concluded to treate wth him about y^e
Purchase of it & Jno Pynchon, Hen: Burt, Sam: Chapen &
Tho: Cooper, were appointed & deputed by ye Towne to
Bargaine for ye s^d Purchase, who accordingly did agree wth
ye s^d Mr Geo. Moxon for his howsing & all his Land in
Springfield to Remaine for ever to ye vse of ye Inhabitants of
Springfeild: as is more fully expressed in ye Towne Booke
for Recording of Land.

And ye 15th Novemb^r 1655. It was agreed & concluded
by the Towne y^t all ye s^d allotmts of Land bought of Mr Geo
Moxon wth ye howsing theretoe belonging should for ever
belong to ye ministry in Springfeild & not be otherwise disposed off Being hereby appriated & given by ye Towne to
ye vse of ye ministry afores^d for ever & not otherwise to be
disposed off:

[I—110 Blank—I—111]

Novemb^r 2d 1652.

At a Towne meeting it was concluded to make choise of Seven Townsmen for ye yeare ensuing: viz: John Pynchon, Sam Chapen, Geo: Colton: Hen: Burt: Benja: Cooly: Tho: Stebbins: Joseph Parsons. Novb^r 22, 1652. Two of these Townsmen being sworne Commissioners for ye Towne of Springfeild were discharged fr: Townsmen & so ye worke rests upon ye last five. To whom by ye Joynt Consent of ye Plantation is Given full power to order all ye prudentiall affaires of ye Towne & to distribute Land this yeare & to act according to what is expressed in ye Court orders: These to continue in this place for a yeare or till new be chosen:

The Surveyour of ye Highways Chosen for y^c prsent year ensueing are, Robert Ashly Jonathan Burt:

Wm Warriner & Griffith Joanes are chosen veiwers of fences for ye upper end of ye Towne, fro: ye meeting howse upward: Alex: Edwards & Sam Wright Junior are chosen overseers of fences from the meeting howse downe ward.

John Pynchon is chosen Recorder for ye Towne, both to Record Lands, & Towne orders & what is ye Publike occasions of ye Towne:

[I—112 Blank—I—113]

[In the handwriting of Henry Burt.]

Dated the 22 of December 1652

It is granted to Thomas Mirrick by the Select men sixe ackers of planting ground over agawam next to Samuell wright planting lot.

It is also granted at the same tyme to Samuell Marshfield

It is granted to John Lambe 16 ackers of planting ground at Chickapee next in order to his lot formerly given him.

It is also granted to John Lamb 4 ackers of meddow uppon the mill river lying on the lower Branch.

It was covenanted him and pmised by the sayd John Lambe that in case hee removed from Springfeild within 5 yeers after the date heerof hee should resigne up these two lots agayne in to the towns hand pvided hee be payd for what necesary Charges hee shall be at as two indifferent men shall Judge.

It is also granted to Thomas miller that vacant parsell of planting ground lying over the great River by the higher wigam pvided hee bee not an occasion of troble and disturbance to the plantasion by any unwise Clashing with the Indians if so he shall forfitt the sayd land in to the Towns hand freely agayne.

[I—114]

Dated the 10 of February 1652.

By the Select men:

There is granted to Richard Sikes this yeere all the new ground Broken up in the home lot that was mr moxons for 8s the acker to bee payd in wheat or pease the 10th of this month next ensuing the date hereof.

It is also granted to Richard Sikes to have the said land at the same termes the yeere next ensuing the former provided the Select men that shall be chosen for that yeere approve it.

[I—115]

Dated the 10 of February 1652.

By the Select men

Richard Sikes hath covenanted to ring the Bell and to sweep the meeting house according to former termes, namely 12d the week pvided hee will have his liberty to leave the work at a months warning this pay to bee payd halfe merchandable indian and half merchandable wheat to bee payd at on intire payment at the end of June next ensuing the date here of but if hee leve the work after payment is made he is to abate 1s the weeke.

There is granted to Richard Sikes for ringing the Bell for marrages and Burials 1s a time this pay to bee payd by those that shall imploy him for any such service.

[I—116]

[In the handwriting of John Pynchon.]
ffebr 10th 1652

By ye Select men

It is agreed y^t these Rates here under written shall be gathered this p^rsent yeare viz by March 25th.

Impr. ffor ye Purchase of Mr Moxons Land, ye one halfe to be p^d this yeare is...................... £ 35 00 00

ffor Mr Horsfords maintenance.... 50 00 00

To John Pynchon for flooring ye meeting howse chamber........ 10 18 00

To John Pynchon for what he p^d to Thomas Stebbins for cleaning y^e   s
meeting howse formerly.........0 10

for Benches in ye Alleys..........0 10
  08 00 00

for Ringing & sweeping Ano 1652..2 12
ffor bringing up Mr Horsfords goods.......................4 08
To Miles Morgan............... 02 8
To G: Colton Due of old for 2 Journeys 5
ffor his Journey downe to Mr Horsfords 6
To G: Branch for his Mare........ 4 6 03 14 05
To G: Ashly for his Mare......... .3 0
for an houre glass to Jos Parsons.. 1 3
To G: Sikes for Ringing ye Bell & sweeping &c ye yeare to come Ano 1653....................2 12 0

ye whole is.... 107 12 06

The Persons appointed to take care of mens estates & Prize Cattle are

Tho: Cooper:
Jn° Dumbleton:
Alexander Edwards:

[I—117]

[In the handwriting of Henry Burt.]

Dated the 10the of February 1652

By the Select men:

There is granted to Rowland Thomas liberty to carry away those stones hee hath dudgd in powscowsack river by the end of June next ensuing the date heerof no man to molest him in the mayne tyme but in case hee leve any after that tyme it shal be free for any man to take them.

There is granted vnto John Dumbleton by reason his other lot proved barren that he cannot subsist on 14 ackers next to John Lambe at Chickepey provided in case hee remove the towne within five yeers hee shall resigne it up agayne in to the towns hand the sayd 14 ackers pvided the towne give him for the charge hee hath bin in breaking of it up as two indifferent men shall judge.

Dated the 10th of febuary 1652

There is granted unto John Stebbin on quarter of the meeting howse chamber at the north side next to the Brook till the first day in november next ensuing the date here of and for this roome hee is to pay—7s 6d ether in merchandable wheat or merchandable wampum this pay to be brought in the first of october next.

There is also granted to william warriner halfe of the meeting howse chamber next to the great river till the first day in november next ensuing the date here of and for this roome he is to pay 15s to be payed either in merchandable wheat or merchandable wampum on the first of october next.

[I—118]

The 10 of the first mon: 1652

By the Select men:

There is granted vnto David Burt two ackers of meddow lying next adjoyning to his father Henry Burts meddow pvided hee abide in the Towne five yeers but if hee remove before five yeers be expired he shall yield it up in to the Towns hands pvided the Towne pay him for what cost hee shall be about the sayd lot as two indifferent men shall judg.

this grant fell into the Towns hand againe. This 2 acars of meddow was given to Henry Burt at a towne meetinge 8th february 1654.

[I—119]

[In the handwriting of John Pynchon.]

Novemb^r 1st 1653.

At a Towne meeting it was concluded to make choise of five Townsmen viz Geo: Colton, Robert Ashly, Tho: Cooper, Benja Cooly, Tho: Stebbins, who are to order ye prudentiall affaires of ye Towne for ye yeare ensuing: & same power is conferred upon y^m as formerly only ye Towne reserve to y^mse. ye liberty of disposing of their lands:

Joseph Parsons & Miles Morgan are chosen surveyours for ye highways ye yeare ensuing:

Rowland Thomas & John Lamb are chosen veiwers of fences for ye upper end of ye Towne fro: ye meeting howse upward, & Wm Branch & Anthony Dorchester are chosen veiwers of ye fences fro: ye meeting howse downeward: for ye yeare ensuing.

December 28 1653 By ye Select men

itt is granted to Benjamin Cooly to have the use of the west end of the meeting howse chamber from the inermost side of the pillers to the end of the house and to injoy itt the first tuesday in november next and in consideration whereoff he is to pay 7s in good wheat or wampom by the 1st of november next ensuinge.

[I—120]

[In the handwriting of Thomas Cooper.]

December 28 1653

itt is granted will: warriner the use of the west side of the meetinge house chamber from the first tuesday in november nextt and in consideration whereoff hee is to pay 7s in merchantable wheatt or wampom by the first of november next insuinge.

it is granted unto John Stebbins the east end of the meet-

December 28: (1653)

inge house chamber from the pillars to the end of the house
and to injoy itt till the first tuesday in november next and in
consideration whereoff hee is to pay 6s in merchantable
wheate or wampom by the first of november next ensuing.
By the Townsmen march 7th 1653-54

itt is granted nathaniell Prichett the meddow upon the 2
springs that lyeth eastward upon the northern branch of
pacawsack which is to make up his 4 acars which was grant-
ted him in the division of meddow upon pacawsack.

By the Selecktt men

whereas there is complaintt made of a greatt defecktt for
wantt of a fence at the both ends of the longe meddow betwixt the topp of the banks downe into the River for the securinge of the saide ffeeld it is thereffor ordered by the Se-
lectt men thatt George Coulton and Benjamin Cooly shall
have full power to indentt with any person or persons for
the makinge and maintaininge of the saide fence or to do it
themselves and that they whole propriotors of the saide
ffeeld shal be lyable to contributte to the saide charge and
if any man shal Refuse the same there shal be a warrant
granted to the constable [   ] forthwith to distraine for any such Just charge.

By the Townsmen march th7 (53)
[I—121]

it is ordered that the overseers of the highways chosen for
this yeare namely myles morgan and Joseph parsons shall
make or cause to be made a convenientt foott bridge over the
mill River in some conveniantt plass petwixt the plasse wheer
the mill now standeth and the mouth of the River as they in
there wisdome shall see meet and that itt be doone by the 25
of this presentt month.

The Rates that are to be Raised this yeare:

1st. £50 for the ministry.

2dly. £35 for the purchase of mester moxons house and
land.

3dly. £06 for killinge of woolves.

4th £03 18s for the Secrutary in the bay.

agreed with Richard Sikes for Ringinge the bell and sweepinge the meetinge house hee doth it as formerly for 52 shillings the yeare previded he may be att his liberty upon a months warninge if his occasion soe Require.

By the Townsmen march th7 1653

It is ordered that noe inhabitants dwellinge in the longe meddow shall att any time suffer any of there Swine to go att libertty in the medow with outt beinge sooffitiently Roonge upon the penalty of 5 shillings for every severall swine soo found which fine shale be levied by the constable who shale have warrant from the selecktt men to make distraintt upon the owners Refusal to pay.

[I—122 Blank—I—123]

wheeras there is complaintt made against the dwellers in the longemeddow that much spoyle is done both in medow and corne land by there swine going at liberty; march th7 1654 by the Select men it is therefore ordered that noe householder in the longe meddow shall att any time from the middle of february untill the ffeeld be broken open suffer any of theare swine to goe att libertty in the saide ffeld uppon penalty of 5 shillings a swine which is soo found and for the execution of this order the constable upon true information given shall hand a warrant from the Seleckt men to distraine the same 3 shillings to the Towne and 2 shillings to the informer.

March 9th it was voted by the towne that the order above expressed concerninge long meddow inhabitants such reach likewise to the Towne Swine as well as theare.

[I—122]

March 14th 1653-54.

Tho Cooper & Tho Mirack are ordered by ye Towne to rectifie ye defects in ye lots right over the grt river wch want measure, & to se yt Mr. Pynchons lot be 30 rod broad ac-

cording to yᵉ Townes grant so there could not be land found
to make it.

It is ordered yᵗ yᵉ pprietors of yᵉ feild in yᵉ long meddow
shall make a sufficient Cart gate at yᵉ Bridge over yᵉ long
medo brook at thaire own pp charge for yᵉ p'sent, & by yᵐ
to be maintained unless yᵉ Generall Cort shall determine yᵗ
yᵉ Towne ought to Join in yᵉ charge of it.

It is ordered that hence forward there shall be given to him
yᵗ shal be found able & willing to undertake yᵉ making of yᵉ
Rates for this Towne, The Sum of Twenty shillings P annum
for making all yᵉ Rates belonging to yᵗ yeare.

Richard Sikes hath a little spang of meddow granted him
by his meddow on yᵉ Mill River of about halfe an acre wᵗʰ
Liberty if he shall fence to take in some of yᵉ upland for
straightning & fencing.

There is granted to Mr. Holyoke to have what land is
betweene his 11 acre lot over yᵉ river & yᵉ highway without
yᵉ front of yᵉ 3d devision.

There is granted Tho:Bancraft foure acres of wet meddow
about 6 miles off beyond Mill river next yᵉ Mill River &
Pacowsick

Also to Benja Cooly two acres next to Tho Bancraft, But
Two acres there.

Also to John Mathews Three acres if it will hold out.

There is granted to Mr. John Pynchon what land there is
between his meddow lot over yᵉ grt River & yᵉ brow of yᵉ
hill on yᵉ upland wᶜʰ is at yᵉ east end the rest.

It is granted to Henry Burt That his wet meddow on yᵉ
back side of yᵉ medow shall abut on yᵉ brooke runing nere
yᵉ west end.

There is granted Jonath: Burt that little psell of meddow
adjoyning to his meddow wᶜʰ llyes on yᵉ litle brooke runing
into yᵉ east branch.

Whereas Mʳ Jnᵒ Pynchon hath about 50 acres of land on
fresh water River, or between fresh water river & Grape
Brooke, & also a portion of meddow on fresh water branch
suitable thereunto.

It is ordered that Tho Cooper, Geo Colton & Rowland Thomas shall [   ] yᵉ sᵈ land & Judge where it is convent where yᵉ Grant should ly.

March 14th 1653-54.

There is granted to Rowland Stebbins one acre and halfe of meddow on yᵉ Northerly branch of yᵉ Mill River between Benja Munn & Deacon Chapins meddow.

There is granted to Tho Mirack 4 acres of swamp over Agawam River between yᵉ howse meddow & Agawam River.

Likewise to Lawrence Bliss 4 acres in yᵉ same swamp.

There is granted to Deacon Chapin on yᵉ other side of yᵉ Northerly branch of yᵉ Mill River a litle psell of meddow of about one acre more or less, about a qʳ of a mile his meddow.

There is granted Tho Cooper to have yᵗ little ppsell adjoyning his med. on yᵉ N branch of yᵉ [   ] on yᵉ other side of those three acres.

[I—124]

Mr. Holyoke hath yᵉ wet meddow by his 3 corner meddow side Granted to him, pvided he set his fence halfe a rod fro: yᵉ foote of yᵉ hill into yᵉ wet meddow. also there is granted him yᵉ wet meddow before Mr Smiths 3 Corner meddow fro: Mr Smiths 3 corner meddow to wᵗʰ halfe a Rod of yᵉ foote of yᵉ hill, pvided he allow a sufficient Cart way ther on it into Mr Smiths 3 Corner meddow, & all to Mr Pynchon so much as yᵗ he may have pt of it at yᵗ side next to yᵉ still & next to Mr. Pynchons.

The 15 acres of land (P Contra) granted to John Pynchon was laid out to him, pt of it under yᵉ round hill next to his 3 corner meddow, & pt of it uppon yᵉ round hill: It goeing over yᵉ round hill & leaving a pt of it: John Pynchon desired the rest of yᵉ land on yᵗ hill & so downe to yᵉ brooke (called Endbrooke or 3 corner meddow brooke,) whereuppon this 26th of March, 1656. There is granted to John Pynchon wᵗ land is remaining upon yᵉ round hill, being about 6 acres more or less: all yᵗ hill, fro: yᵉ hither end of it, he is to run on yᵉ North side of yᵉ hill all along uppon yᵉ brow

Northward & so downe at ye further end to ye 3 Corner meddow brooke: So that in all Mr. Pynchon hath about 21 acres.

[I—125]

[In the handwriting of Thomas Cooper.]

Severall Particulars which was voted unto by the Towne upon a trayninge day may 29th 1654

1st itt was voted that the persell of land which the Towne bought of mester moxon lyinge in the plaine beyond the three corner meddow brooke should bee Laid to the Comon and thatt the Towne woulde be att noe further charge aboutt itt maintaining of the fence about itt.

2ly itt was Likewise voted thatt Thomas Stebbins and Benjamin mun should have the use of the trayninge plase for pasture for the terme of Ten years for certaine and for the terme of thare owne personall Living if they live Longer upon condition that they keepe itt cleare of offensive matter as wod or brush or the like and thatt they sow itt with inglish grass seed:

3ly itt was voted to Samuell marshffeeld thatt he should have all the overplush of Land in the farther medow where Samuell wright and Thomas merrick have grantt of allottments and all the rest of the saide parsell of land is granted to Samuell marshfeeld provided that itt exceed nott the quantitye of fouretteene acars, & Three acres of it (being all y^t it holds out) he keep himselfe

4ly it was granted to mestr John Pynchon 15 acars of the plaine adjoining to his three corner meddow and soe to be alayd outt by the Townsmen as they shall see conveniantt: and in consideration of this saide land the saide John Pynchion dothe promise to purchase 40 sheepe within the space of Sixe months and he to use his best endevoure to bring them into Towne and there to dispose of them as hee shall see cause provided hee sell them nott to any outt of towne in case any in towne will by them.

P contra is an addition to this grant of about 7 acres So ye whole is about 23 acres taking in all ye round hill.

[I—126 Blank—I—127]

5ly it was granted to Thomas merricks a parsall of Land adjoyninge to his meddow Lott over agawam previded it exceed nott two acars.

6ly itt was voted thatt Thomas Stebbins should be the Towne mesurer.

These sixe particulars were propounded by voatt to the Towne and allsoe granted.

Novemb 21, 1654

Liberty is granted to Benja Cooly for Conveniency of fencing his meddow on Pacowsick river to Run a fence straite under ye hills & ye land betweene y^t & his meddow to be his ppriety

The like liberty is granted to Antho Dorchester & to Nath Pritchard.

There is granted to Mr Holyoke all y^t land, meddow and swamp wch lyes betweene his meddow in ye middle meddow & ye howse meddow, togither wth y^t Nooke that lys betweene ye Pond & hill at ye higher end of the howse meddow

[I—126]

[In the handwriting of John Pynchon.]

Novemb^r 21th 1654.

At a Towne meeting there was granted to John Dumbleton Tho: Miller Jn° Lamb, Reice Bedortha & Griffith Joanes to each of y^m 3 acres of wet med opposite to their homlots also each of y^m a wood lot of foure acr Tho Miller to ly first & so in order. Only ye wood lot agt Reice Bedorthas lot bought fro: Geo Alexander is to belong to Symon Beamon who purchased Reice his land there.

There is granted to Mr John Pynchon for a farme: all ye land on ye other side of Chikkuppy River by ye grt River side upward & at the mouth of Chikkuppy River:

Also there is granted at Skepmuck a farm to Mr Pynchon & Mr Holyoke betwixt y^m

And Tho Coop: Tho Stebbins, Rowld Thomas & Tho

Miller are appointed by ye Towne to veiw ye land at Skepmuck & at ye mouth of chikkuppy River, & up by ye grt
River over chikkupy river, & to determine what may be convenient for Mr Pynchon & Mr Holyoke farmes there & to
make report what land may be left for ye Towne to dispose of

The returns of the aforesaid Comittee.

[In the handwriting of Elizur Holyoke.]

Wheras Thomas Stebbin Rowland Thomas Tho Miller &
Thomas Cooper were made choyce of by the Towne for the
bounding of two Farmes given by the Towne in 1654 the
one farme given to Mr John Pynchon Lying over Chickuppe River wth ye Islands in ye Said River below the place
comonly called the wading place wth a meddow at the mouth
of ye Same River on the South side ye s^d River, as also a
Swamp betwixt the meddow & the river. This farme is by
us thus bounded vis^t, to run from chickappe river up the
great River northward to the brook called Wullamansep &
soe up y^t brooke to ye foot path y^t goeth to Squannunganuck
& Soe to follow the path down to Squannunganuck & from
Squannunganuck downe to ye mouth of Chicuppe river. And
this is the conclusion of us above mentioned. As witness
our hands March 6, 1659.

Thomas Stebbins.   Rowland Thomas his m^rke
Thomas Cooper.   Thomas Millers m^rke.

The other farme wch was given by the Towne was at Skeepnuck given to Mr John Pynchon & Mr Elizur Holyoke w^ch
wee the s^d Tho: Stebbin, Row: Thomas, Thomas Miller &
Tho: Cooper by the Townes Order, bound on this manner
as followeth: Chicuppe river is to be the bounds by the South
fro: Squannunganuck to the brooke one mile above the
comon passage over ye river, wch is about two miles & halfe
above Squannunganuck: & on ye West bounded by Mr Pynchons farme or ye foot path wch goeth from Squanunganuck to
Wullamansepe & on ye North up Wullamansepe & fro: y^e
head of Wullamansepe upon a Square line over to the brooke
wch cometh unto Chickuppe river about a mile above Skeep-

muck, & Soe to follow y^t brooke down to Chickuppe river: And this is to be ye bounds of this farme. witness our hands march 6, 1659.

Thomas Stebbins Rowland Thomas his mark.
Thomas Cooper: Thomas Miler his mark.

[I—128]
[In the handwriting of John Pynchon.]

Octob^r 31th, 1654, this day being made choise of by ye Towne instead of ye 1st tuesday in Novemb^r:

At this Towne meeting it was concluded to make Choise of 5 Townsmen for ye yeare ensueing: viz Tho: Cooper Geo Colton Robt Ashly Henry Burt Benj Cooly. To whom by ye Joint consent of ye Towne: There is ful power given to order all ye prudentiall affaires of ye Towne & to act according to what is expressed in ye Court orders: only ye giving out of ye land belongs to ye Towne:

Benja Parsons & Miles Morgan are chosen Surveyors of ye Highways the yeare ensuing.

John Dumbleton & Rich Exell are chosen veiwers of fences for ye upper end of ye Towne fro: ye meeting howse upward:

John Harmon & Sam Marshfeild are chosen veiwers of fences fro: ye meeting howse downewards for ye yeare ensuing.

Griffith Joanes is chosen to p'sent such breaches of orders as he shal take notice of, or y^t shal come to his knowledge by information.

[I—130]
[In the handwriting of Thomas Cooper.]

ffebruary 8th (1654) thease parsells of meddow comonly called by the name of wattchuett was granted these inhabitants as ffollowethe vid

	acres
John Harman	3
Rich Syeks	4
Lawrence Bliss	4
will Brooks	4

Anto: Dorchester	3
Jonath Burt	3
John mathews	2
Deacon wright	6 previded hee stay in towne
James Osbourne	3

and to Jonathan Burt it was granted a small parsell about 2
acars adjoyninge to the meddow lott formerly granted lyinge on the little Brooke at the east branch of mill river

alsoe to miles morgan in the house meddow provided it
did nott hinder the Townes lott which is to be 9 acars.

To John Dumbleton at the could springe at the Rear of
the 3d divission about 1 acar

allsoe The grantt of homelotts to the parsons folowinge

                                                 acars

first francis pepper a house lott..............3
        hassaky meddow......................3
        with a wood lot of....................4
Next Symon Beamon a house lott............3
        hassaky meddow......................3
        a wood lott.........................4
John Steward a homelott of...................3
        hassaky meddow......................3
        a wood lott of......................4
John Stewart hath sold & fully passed away to Mr
    Jo Pynchon his assigne for ever: & Mr Pynchon
    hath exchanged ye homelot wth Rich Maund for
    Richs Lot next to Mr Pynchons sheepe pasture.
Sam Terry a homelott......................3
        hassaky meddow......................3
        a wood lott of......................4
Hugh Dudley a homelott of.................3
        hassaky meddow......................3
        a wood lott of......................4

alsoe there was granted to Anth: Dorchester the upper
end of the lott which is myles morgans in chickpee playne
about 5 acars.

    [Bottom I—130]

The homlot P Contra wch was John Stewarts Mr Pynchon bought it & exchanged it wth Richard Maund so y^t it became Richard Maunds lot: & so is forfeited to ye Towne But by ye Select men ffeb^r 15 1659 it is Granted to Mr Pynchon: who hath sold it to Deacon Chapin so y^t it is now Deacon Chapins lot & ly next that lot wch Symon Beamon sold to Mr Pynchon.

[I—132 Blank—I—133]

ffebruary 8th (1655) the grant of meddow lyinge on fresh water River viz:

	acars
To mr John Pynchon	20
george coulton and	
Benjamin Cooley each of them	10

if they doe not make use of itt themselves it is to Returne into the Townes hands agayne they are not to sell it to any other.

[I—134]

[In the handwriting of John Pynchon.]

June 1654. There was granted to Obadiah Miller a homlot of Three acres lying in ye plaine next above Hugh Dudley, also Three acres of wet meddow & a woodlot of 8 rod broad & 80 rod long next above Hugh Dudly as aforesd.

Novemb^r 1655. There is also granted to Symon Sacket a homlot of Three acres, in ye plaine next above Obadiah Miller wth Three acres of wet meddow: & foure acres of wood lot, upon condition he stay 5 yeares in ye Towne & if he remove wthin 5 years it is to returne to ye Towne.

[I—135]

Jan 2d 1665. There is granted to Abell Wright a homlot containing Three acres, in ye plaine, next ye round hill & it is to ly next above.

The Towne lots wch Mr Thomson if he continue in Towne 5 yeares is to have else it is ye Townes. Three acres of ye wet meddow & ffoure acres woodlot. This is granted him upon condition he stay 5 years in ye Towne, after this grant or else to forfeite it to ye Towne in case he remove wth in 5 yeares: This was p^rsently made over to Mr John Pynchon & Possessed by him.

Jan 2d 1665. Also There is granted to Mr John Pynchon & Mr Elizur Holyoke a woodlot to theire Mill lot, conteining Sixe acres and a quarter wch is to run eastward 50 rod long fro: ye end of ye Mill lot up ye mill river, & to run the whole breadth of ye mill lot y^t is to say 20 rod broad, & 50 rod long

There is granted to Robert Ashly ffoure acres of wet meddow & other land wch he is to take as it fals wet meddow & other land togither one wth another; which is to ly next above Abell Wright, & to run fro: ye highway y^t goes up to ye round hill eastward to ye brow of ye further Hill viz to ye litle end of the woodlots this is granted upon condition he continue 5 yeare in Town or else to leave it.

There is also granted to Tho Cooper foure acres next above Robert Ashly & to run to ye brow of ye Hill & woodlots as Robert Ashlys is to run, & this upon condition he stay 5 years in Town.

These grants are not to hinder a Cartway but y^t is to take place where it shall be most convenient over ye meddow & ye low land.

[1—136]

January 30th 1655.

There is granted to Tho Stebbins one acre of land in ye wet meddow next above Symon Sackett, to run ye whole length y^t others do: & this upon condition he continue five yeares in Towne & further y^t he shal not desire any more share in ye meddow if it come to be given out.

There is granted to Hugh Dudly about 8 acres of land by ye greate riverside in chikkuppy plaine next above John Stewart upon condition he continue five yeares in Towne.

There is granted to Wm Brooks a peice of land on this side ye cold Spring at ye reare of Goodm: Miricks 2d devision being about seven acre pvided he continue 5 yeares in Towne or else he is to leave it.

There is granted to John Lamb y^t little strappet of land

over ye river at ye hay place, betwixt Rowland Thomas & Thomas Miller if any land be there & it doe not come in lots formerly granted, it is turned over to Wm Brookes.

There is granted to Symon Beamon a psell of wet meddow about two or three acres lying about foure miles off ye towne on ye North side ye Bay path, pvided he continue 5 yeares in Towne. This Grant Symon Beamon sold & made over to Rowland Thomas for ever.

There is granted to Jonath Taylor a strappet of medow about two acres wch lyes beyond ye mill river in ye way to Goodm: Harmons meddow pvided he continue 5 y in Towne.

There is granted to Griffith Joanes a psel of wet meddow on ye South side of ye Bay path about halfe a mile on this side ye 5 mile pond being about 2 or 3 acres pvided he continue 5 y in ye Towne.

whereas there was formerly a peice of ground granted Rich Sikes for a homlot over ye brook y^t goes to ye Mill, upon his request there is granted him all ye land betwixt Tho Bancrafts lot & John Lumbard & to run fro: ye way to ye Mill eastward, as far as other mens Lotts doe run.

[I—137]

There is granted to Tho Miler liberty for mowing of ye wet meddow over ye great River beyond ye cold Spring under ye greate hil, pvided he doe not fence it but let it ly common for free feed of cattle to any pson, & not to molest any psons cattle in feeding there on these termes he is to have ppriety in it for mowing: & none to molest him in mowing of it.

There is granted to John Stebbins (who desires to build beyond ye long meddow) a lott off ffive acres upon ye hill over ye bridge on ye most convenient place there, wch is to be 20 rod broad, & 40 rod long: and this is granted on condition he continue 5 yr in Towne else to resigne it to ye Towne.

There is also granted to Geo: Colton ffive acres of land there by John Stebbins on condition he live 5 yeares in Springfeild.

There is also granted to John Stebbins ffive acres of land

a little beyond yᵉ long meddow, on yᵉ lower side of the litle miry brooke by some called Potbrooke, betwixt yᵉ great river & yᵉ swamp there & to come up to yᵉ cartway, so yᵗ yᵉ way be not straightened by him & fro: thence downeward yᵉ ffive acres is to be made up: & this grant is upon condition he continue 5 y in Springfeild.

There is granted to Rich Sikes for a wood lott ffive acres of land, on yᵉ further side of yᵉ mill river on yᵉ east side of the way yᵗ goeth up grt hill on condition he stay 5 years in Towne: this lot is to front upon yᵉ mill river & so to run back along by yᵉ cart way yᵗ goeth up yᵉ long hill

[I—138]

January 30th 1655.

A grant of land in yᵉ wet meddow, & Low Land over yᵉ meddow, beginning a litle on this side yᵉ round hill: & so goeth upward in what order men ly, as was cast by lots, is as followeth

Sam Terry 1st next to RobertAshlys & Thomas Coopers land the grant whereoff is 2 leaves backward who hath 1 acre.

Wᵐ Brooke 2d 2 acres, this 2 acres Wᵐ Brooks sold to Sam Terry so that Sam Terry hath 3 acres.

Hugh Dudly 3d 3 acres. And this 3 acres to Mr Pynchon: he sold this Symon Sackett to Tho: Stebbins.

Towne lot 4th 3 acres.

Griffith Joanes 5th 2 acres.

Richard Exsell 6th 2

Reice Bedortha 7th 2

John Lamb 8th 2

Deacon Chapin 9th 3

David Chapin 10th 2

Miles Morgan 11th 3 1-2

W Warriner 12th 3

Tho Miller 13th 2 his 2 acres Tho Miller hath sold to mʳ Holyoke.

John Dumbleton 14th 3

Mr Pynchon 15th 6

Benja Mun 16th 3

Obadiah Miller 17th 1   This is now Mr Pynchons

ffr: Pepper 18th 1

John Stewart 19th 1 this John Stewart hath sold to Mr Pynchon

Hugh Dudley 20th Now Mr Pynchons

Mr Thomson 21 4 Now Towne Land

Abell Wright 22 1

Symon Beamon 23 1

Tho Noble 24 1 1-2

Mr Holyoke 25 4 this 4 acres Mr Holyoke sold to Tho: Noble

The whole is 56 acres.   This land above s^d is given upon condition these men doe continue 5 years in Springfeild, & if any pson doe remove before y^t tyme he is to loose his land, & it is further agreed y^t a cartway over ye meddow & also thorow ye low land cross the lots should be laid out in ye most convenient place before these lands

A grant of land over ye mill river, ye first lot being to ly next ye mill river, & fro: thence goes downward, ye lots are to run fro: ye brow of ye hill (viz) from the top of ye hill wch the cart way goes up, back to ye grt river.

John Lumbard 1st 2 1-2 acres

Thomas Mirick 2d 2

Wid Bliss 3d 1 1-2

Sam Marsfeld 4th 1

Rich Sikes 5th 4

Deacon Wright 6th 2

Lawrence Bliss 7th 1

Tho Bancraft 8th 2

Benj Cooly 9th 3

Tho Gilbert 10th 2 this is sold to Rich Siks

Benj Parsons 11th 1 this sold to Rich Siks

Rowland Stebbins 12th 1 1-2

Jonath Burt 13th 2

James Osborne 14th 1 to Rich Sikes

Nath Pritchard 15th 1 to Richard Sikes
Anthony Dorchester 16th 3
John Harmon 17th 3
John Mathews 18th 1
John Clarke 19th 2
Jonath Taylor 20th 2 sold to Jh Mathews
John Leanord 21th 3 who hath sold to Jn° Mathews
Mill lot (Mr Pynchon or Mr Holyoke) 22th 3

It was concluded before these grants were made, that ye Comon way shal not be barred out, But y^t it shal still goe all along thorough these lots & severall mens Lands It is also given them on condition they continue 5 yeares in Towne or else to forfeit it.

[I—139]

Novemb^r 6th 1655.

There was a choise made of 5 Townsmen, viz: Tho: Cooper: Miles Morgan Benj Cooly & Robert Ashly John Dumbleton: Tho: Coop: Robert Ashly & Benja Cooly refused to serve in y^t place being fairly chosen by ye vote of ye Towne for wch refusall they are lyable to ye fine of Twenty shillings a peice: & Geo: Colton: Tho: Stebbins & John Stebbins were chosen in there roome To whom by ye Joynt consent of ye Towne there was ful power given to order all ye prudentiall affaires of ye Towne & to act according to what is expressed in ye Court orders & for ye giving, or disposing of land these 5 men wth Mr John Pynchon & Sam Chapin have full power to act therein.

[In the handwriting of Elizur Holyoke.]

Jonathan Burt and John Lamb were chosen for overseers of the High wayes for ye yeare ensuinge:

Griffith Jones & Rice Bedortha are chosen for veiwers of the fences for the higher end of the town, from the Meeting house upwards: And Thomas Bancroft and John Lumbard were chosen for veiwers of the fences for the Lower end of the Towne fro: the meetinge house downwards for the yeare ensuinge.

Likewise at the same Town Meeting John Leanord was chosen p^rsenter for yeare ensuing: And he took his oath accordingly.

Likewise Thomas Mirack was chosen to be measurer for such Lands as are to be laid out: for the yeare ensuinge.

[I—140]
[In the handwriting of John Pynchon.]

At a Towne meeting Novemb^r 15th 1655. It was voted & Concluded, y^t Mr Thomson during his continuance a preaching minister in Springfeild Should Possess & injoy ye Towne house lot, & housing (lying between ye lot of Tho: Coop: & Deacon Chapin) wth all the land there too belonging (wch formerly ye Towne bought of Mr Moxon,) ye sais^d howsing & all ye severall psells of land theretoo belonging wth all ye pfits there off, are hereby given to Mr Thomson for ye tyme he shal continue amongst us in dispensing ye word of God & caring on ye place of preaching Elder, & when he shall cease to be our preaching minister then ye s^d howsing & land to returne into ye Townes hands: It is also further voted y^t ye Towne will require ye s^d howsing & ffencing & set it in a Comfortable condition & so Mr Thomson is to keepe it, & leave it in like good repaire.

As also they intend by ye help of God to Continue Mr Thomsons maintenance £50 p annum & to give him a psell of land (by reson of the Inability of ye Towne to increase his maintenance) viz Thirty five acres (as is over ye leafe)

[I—142]
It was further voted ye 15th Nov 1655: To give Mr Thomson for his own ppriety Pvided he now continue 5 yeares in Towne as followeth viz:

A homlot of ffoure acres, ye neerest land wch is undisposed of viz The Townes foure acres on this side ye round hill as also Six acres of wet meddow before it with a woodlot of six acres adjoyning to it at ye east end of it.

Mr Thomson lost this grant by removing fro: this Towne soone after, & so ye land remaines to ye Towne.

likewise Twenty acres of land in Chikkuppy plaine over ye great river, lying next above Anthony Dorchester.

this grant void, ye Towne resuming ye land to its apointmt by order March 13th 1653-54

Jan. 7th 1655. There was granted by ye Towne to Sam Terry ye Ten acres of land in Chikkuppy plaine over ye greate river next below John Dumbleton y^t betwixt John Dumbleton & Mr Thomsons pvided he continue in Towne 5 yeares.

At a towne meeting Decemb^r 23 1655. There being a question ppounded to ye Towne by ye Select men (in regard of Mr Thomsons not making use of ye Townes land for the p^rsent) whether it were ye minds of ye Inhabitants y^t they should notw^thstanding goe on with ye repairing of s^d howse as formerly was agreed on: And it was by vote agreed in ye affirmative viz That ye repairing of ye house should be caryed on as was formerly agreed on notw^thstanding.

At ye same Towne meeting it was voted, & agreed to, by ye whole, to increase Mr Thomson his maintenance £10 P annum viz £60 P annum so much at least for this p^rsent yeare beside former advantages by ye Howse and land.

[I—143]

It was further voted & agreed upon this 3d Decemb^r 1655 That hence forward ye land of ye plantation shalbe rated (not according to the number of acres as formerly) but according to ye vallue & worth of ye land, as it is at p^rsent, or as it shall be vallued fro: yeare to yeare: & so all land is to be brought into all rates, as so much estate of ye plantation viz Living stock is to be rated to all rates as formerly but now ye land is Joined wth it according to its vallueation. It is also further ordered y^t howsing shall be vallued, & brought in wth ye land & stock of ye plantation as so much estate, wch every pson is posessed off, & so pportionably to each mans estate every pson is to pay to all rates whatsoever.

And it was agreed y^t ye Townsmen for ye p^rsent, & fro: yeare to yeare if need be shall set ye price on ye lands of ye plantation to vallue what land every man is posessed off according to ye true worth of it, wth other men in an equall pportion: As also to prize & vallue every mans howsing in an equall pportion.

And further it is concluded y^t it is meete & requisite, y^t every pson should allow some maintenance to ye ministry, though not Posessed of land or estate to rate him theretoe & therfore it is agreed y^t every person being at his own hand & not a son or servant who hath noe land or estate or whose land & estate doth not amount to 5s a yeare in the rates: That every such pson shall be liable to pay to ye ministers maintenance, five shillings P annum, & ye intent of this order is not to free any howseholder whose estate may not reach to pay 5s P annum but much rather are to be set down to ye minister by virtue of this order.

[I—144]

At a Towne meting Jan. 7, 1655. It was agreed & concluded y^t ye land at Woronoco, (being laid to this Towne by ye Court) should be disposed off: To wch end John Pynchon Mr Holyoke Geo: Colton Benja Cooly & Tho: Cooper were appointed & desired by ye Towne to y^t work, to whom power was given to dispose of ye land at Woronoco to such men as they Saw fit, & what quantity they should give to any pson whomsoever they in theire best discretion saw fit: it should be esteemed as theire ppriety & ye act of ye Towne.

2. Whereas uppon ye making of y^t Order over ye former leafe Dec. 3d (55) That all land should be vallued as so much estate, & so accordingly be lyable to pay all rates; Some dispute hath bin thereuppon concerning ye land in ye 3 corner meddow, on this side end Brooke, wch Mr John Pynchon Mr Holyoke & Jno Dumbleton is Posessed off whether though it were first granted y^m free fro: all charges for ever as on page 2 at ye beginning of this Booke, yet whether there owne voting to ye order over ye leafe y^t all land should be vallued & so pay to rates did not cut y^m off fro: theire first priviledge of Injoying y^t land rate free, It was concluded by ye Towne y^t ye first grant of it free fro: charges for ever to y^m theire heires & assignes stand firme & [I—145] good, & y^t ye Towne would not take any advantage agt y^m of theire not excepting agt it, in theire votin; but would notwthstanding, (& doe hereby) allow y^t land to be free from all charges for

ever: viz: Twenty acres to Mr John Pynchon his heires & assignes for ever, Ten to John Dumbleton & Ten to Mr Holyoke theire heires & assignes for ever, to be free fro: all Towne
charges y^t is to say fro: all charges wch may any ways arise
upon, or be to Springfeild for land; This land afores^d stands
exempted there from for ever.

3. It is agreed y^t ye price of Indian corne for this yeare
shall be abated as well as other graine, & y^t hence forward
till ye Towne se cause to alter it Indian Corne shall pass & be
accepted at ye price of Two Shillings p bush. fro: man to man
in Springfield.

4. There being some question ppounded about ye bounds
of land whether men shall Injoy all ye land w^thin ye bounds
laid out to y^m though it were more number of acres than
were granted y^m It was voted & concluded y^t where any mans
first & pp bounds of his land was cleare & manifest & w^thout
alteration he should have & injoy all ye land wth in such
bounds though more number of acres than was recorded to
him were w^thin such bounds, pvided he did noe ways intrench
upon or wrong his neighbor y^t lay next him of his due quantity & portion of land. And w^t overplus is any mans land it is
to be brought into Rates.

[I—146]

ffeb^r 1655.

It is agreed y^t these Rates here vnderwritten shall be made
& gathered this p^rsent yeare viz by march 25th.

£

Impr. ffor Mr Thomsons maintenance.............60
ffor mending ye glass of ye meeting howse ringing ye
 Bell & Sweeping ye house shingling, & other reparation of ye Towne howse & for ye maintenance of old Katherin £4 till next march, & some
 other things in all.........................40

It is agreed y^t for ye gathering in of these Rates, & for
future of all Towne Rates There shall be some one man or
men appointed and who shall give warning to every man to
bring in his Rate at ye day & place appointed; & if any man

having had due warning shall refuse or neglect to bring in
his rate to ye pson appointed to receive it ye day Set: Then
such pson so failing to bring in his rate shall pay as a fine
over & above his rate 12d overpluss, for ye least rate & if
ye rate be above 10s then 1s as overpluss & for all rates above
20s 2s in ye pound & wch overpluss togither wth ye rate. the
pson appointed to gather in ye rate shall demand of ye pty
at his howse & if distrained for it in case of non payment
calling ye constable to his assistance: who are also to demand
or distraine in fetching ye rate & forfeiture over and above.

This order was repealed and made void by ye Towne
March 3d 1655-56.

[I—147]

[In the handwriting of Thomas Cooper.]

Att a Towne Meeting February 20th 1655 itt was voted
by the Towne, that for the Settlement of the Toulle of the
miller it should be the eleventh partt of the bushell, for all
Sorts of graine that shall be heere ground, and to this rate
mr Pynchon with mr Hollyock who were the owners of the
sayd mill doth consent.

[In the handwriting of Elizur Holyoke.]

March 24th 1656

It is voted by Joynt consent of the Plantation that seeing
Mr Thomson hath deserted this Plantation & soe wee are
left destitute in respect of any whom we would call to yt ministry of ye word for continuance that therefore these persons
underwritten shall take councell among themselves wt course
may be taken for a supply in yt work and that they shall take
wt course that to them shall seem good by sending abroad for
advice in this matter: & so accordingly they shall give information to the Towne wt they have done or think convenient to
be done. The persons here unto chosen are mr Pynchon,
Deacon Chapin George Colton, Benjamin Cooley, Deacon
Wright & Elizur Holyoke.

[I—148]

It was further voted and agreed this 24th march, 56,
that whereas yesterday being the lordsday Deacon Wright

was chosen to dispense the word of God in this place till some other should be gott for ye worke, y^t Deacon Wright shal have for his labor in ye employment 50s P month for such tyme as he attends on the said work:

[In the handwriting of John Pynchon.]

May 17th 1656. There is granted to Rich Maund for a homelot Three acres of ground on this side ye round hill, next above Abell Wrights lot the breadth 10 rod length 50.

This Three acres Rich Maund hath passed away to Mr. Pynchon by exchange, Mr. Pynchon having peured him y^t lot wch was John Stewarts. This Lot of Richard Maunds (^{ch}w was John Stewarts) being forfeited to the Towne, it is granted to Mr Pynchon ffeb 18 1659 and by him sold to Deacon Chapin.

[In the handwriting of Thomas Cooper.]

There is granted to Rowland Thomas and Symon Beamon neere Skepmuch on this side of chikkuppy river. To Rowland Thomas first in ye Neck 18 acres, & to Symon Beamon 12 acres And w^{ht} out ye neck first to Rowland Thomas 4 acres & to Symon 4 acres. This land in ye Neck fell short & so is abated to each of y^m as in ye Record.

There was granted to Benjamin Cooley 10 acars of land adjoyning unto the parsell of land formerly granted to John lenard adjoyning to the hither end of sayd meddow previded the said Benjamin doe alow a cartt way of 4 rod broad and that he continue in town 5 years.

Sept 10th (1656) there is granted to John lumbard the remainder of the land betwixt greate hill and benjamin Coolys his lot above upperside previded he be noc detrymentt to the highway and that he continue 5 years in towne

[I—149]

[In the handwriting of John Pynchon.]

Whereas Wee: John Pynchon: Elizur Holyoke: Geo. Colton: Tho Cooper. & Benja Cooly, were appointed by ye Towne to dispose of ye land at Woronoco wch ye Cort hath laid to this Township: Having made a View of ye land there we Judge it may be devided into foure pts, & so distributed

to foure severall psons: The first pt of it lyeth on this side y^e
river next to Springfield up by ye river side: & opposite agt
it on ye further side of the river lyeth another pt or portion:
& then further up ye river lyeth the other 2 pts or portions
of land togither on this side ye River.

These severall pts of land lying remote fro: our Towne, &
there being noe appearance of any at p^rsent, y^t will make use
there off: we thought good to ppound it to ye Towne to allow
some priveledges for incorridgement to such as would appeare to live so remote: Where uppon this 2d of June 1656,
By ye Joint Consent of ye Plantation it is agreed & ordered
That for Six yeares ensuing fro: ye date hereoff: The land
at woronoco wth such ratable estate as ye owners thereoff
shall have there, Shall be rated but half so much as other
land & estate in Springfeild, And for ye Incoridgm^t of Jonath
& John Gilbert, they shall be freed fro: Paying any Rates to
ye Towne for one whole yeare after ye 29th day of Septemb^r
next.

August ye 9th 1656. Jonath Gilbert & John Gilbert desiring a grant of Land at Woronoco Wee who were appointed by ye Towne to act in ye disposall thereoff. Considering
theire desire doe Judge meete to bestow upon them mutually one of ye foure pts of land there: vix This 9th of August
1656. There is granted to Jonathan Gilbert & to John Gilbert Jointly That first pt of ye land at Woronoco by river
[I—150] on this hither side of Woronoco river next to
Springfeild (wch is ye Northeast side) uppon condition they
doe build uppon it, & make some impvent of it, by Michalstide come 12th Month & further upon condition they carry
on some Impremt thereoff for 5 yeares togither & y^t they doe
not sell it or pass it away till they have injoyned it 5 yeares
in case they doe it is to be forfeited to ye Towne upon these
tearmes they pforming y^m, That first portion of land lying
by woronoco river on this side of it being about is granted to
Jonath & John Gilbert Jointly to them & theire heirs for
ever: They are (wth w^t convenience they can) to get it measured & record it in ye Book of records also they are to pur-

chase out yᵉ Indians right & to treate wᵗʰ the Indians for the purchase of yᵉ rest.

Decembʳ 10th (58) Jonath & John Gilbert having forfeited theire right to land aforesᵈ, renew theire request & desire advantage may not be taken agt them of forfeiture wᶜʰ is yeilded to pvided they build there & also make Impvmnt of yᵉ land before Midsummer next, & continue it 5 yeares fro: this tyme: And we desire a full & sufficient cartways thorough theire land wᶜʰ shall be most convenient for Passadge fro: yᵉ further farmes as we shall Judge most fitting & by us theire portion to be bounded & set out.

The 2d Portion of Land on this side of woronoco River granted to Tho Coop: pvided he build & make Impvmᵗ of the land there by yᵉ end of Aprill next come 12 Mo & continue so to doe 5 years reserving Highways throu it & this portion of land to be set out & bounded by us Jo Pynchon Eliz Holyoke Geo Colton: Benja Cooly.   Granted Decembʳ 10, 1658.

John Clarke, Wᵐ Brooks & Jno Sackat have yᵉ land yᵉ further side of woronoco wᶜʰ is granted yᵐ pvided they each of them build & make impvment of the land by Aprill come 12 mo. & continue so to doe 5 y.   else to forfeit it.   Granted Jan: 10th 1658.

[I—151]

[In the handwriting of Thomas Cooper.]

Att a town meetinge november the fourth, 1656, it was agreed by the inhabitants that thease 4 men, vidz Deacon wright, decon chapin mr hollyocke, Henry Burtt, should have twelve pounds alowed them by the towne for there labour formerly spent amongst us in the lords worke on the Sabothe and the sayd twelve pound to be disposed of to each particular by the Seleckt men.

it was further voted that the inhabitants would alow of these £50 pr yeare to such as did labour in the same worke amongst us for future till such time as we should have a settled ministry amongst us and the sayd £50 likewise to be disposed of by the seleckt men answerable to quantiety of each mans particular labours.

[In the handwriting of Elizur Holyoke.]

[I—152]

At the same Town Meeting Nov. 4th 1656. There was a choyce made of Select men for Ordering the Prudentiall affaires of the Towne vizt Thomas Cooper, George Colton, Thomas Gilbert, Benjamin Cooley and Robert Ashley.

William Warrener is chosen and desired to continue in his office of a Constable and thereto aggreed.

And Samuel Marshfeild doe continue as Deputy:

David Chapin was chosen to ye Office of a Sealer for weights and measures: who took his Oath accordingly.

Elizur Holyoke was chosen for the Recorder till mr Pynchons returne or for the yeare insuing:

John Harman was chosen to ye office of a Presenter to p^{r}sent breaches of ye Lawes of the Countrey or of Town Orders & to wch service he took his oath:

Samuell Marshfeild and Nathaneel Pritchard were chosen surveyers of the Highwayes for ye yeare ensuinge: And for veiwers of the fences for the yeare ensuing were chosen Anthony Dorchester and Lawrence Bliss for the Lower end of ye Town from the Meeting house downward & from the meeting house & upward being the Hyer end of ye Town were chosen Thomas Miller and Benjamin Munn:

At this Same Town Meeting there was granted to Rowland Thomas a peece of meddow Land on the Mill River on ye further Branch thereof a little above the falls wch are above the 16 acres, which peece of meddow contaynes about an acre:

[I—153]

[In the handwriting of Thomas Cooper.]

Att a meetinge of the Select men Desember 5th (1656) itt was granted to Ben: coley the use of the westt end of the meeting house chamber for the sayd yeare painge 7s

Alsoe it was granted to Tho: Cooper the north syde and the east end of the same chamber painge 13s

ffebruary 13th 1656.

it was granted to Abell wright alattmentt of 20 acars

which hath formerly beene in the hand of Rowld Thomas lyinge in the great plaine over the greate river called chick-pee plaine providen he continue 5 years in towne.

Likewise there was granted unto Anto: Dorchester 10 acars of upland on the Sowwest side of chickepee plaine begininge att the litle springe and soe to run South east till it make up 10 acars previded hee continue 5 years.

Likewise there was granted to lawrance Bliss liberty to exchange the lott of meddow in his presentt possession for that which was formerly decon wrights but now fallen into the hand of the towne and likewise 2 acars over the mill river amonge the small lotts which formerly was given to decon wright: previded he continue 5 years.

Likewise there is granted to george coulton a persell of land lyinge by the great river side on the east side about 3 quarters of a myle below longe medow bridge all betwixt the brow of the hill wheare the carttway now goeth and the great river downe to the brow end of the swampe neere about a dozen acars previded hee continue 5 years in towne.

[I—154]

by the Select men desember 5th (1656)

it is ordered that noe person within this township shall suffer any of his Swine above 3 months ould to goe abroad out of his yard from the first of march next unto the last of november exceptt they be sufficiently runge upon penalty of 6d pr time for any swine soe found that is above 3 months of adge exceptt such swine as are under a constant keepers charge abroad in the woods: and for the well execution of this order wee have appointed John Steward twise every weeke duringe the sayd time that is to say betwixt the first of march and the last of november to goe thorough the towne to take notiss what swine are unrunge accordinge to the intent of this order and to demand of the owners for every such swine and in case any shall refuse to pay upon his complaints warrant be granted by the seleckt men to the constable to distraine who shall have for his pains upon every distress soe made 3d and nott withstanding wee have apointed him to goe thorough the towne but twyse a weeke yett hee is nott thereby prohibited to goe as often hee seethe good but less than twyess he is not to goe.

by the Seleckt men december 5th (1656)

Itt is lykewise ordered that noe Swine shall goe at libertye on the other side of the greate river above two months in the yeare vidz from the middle of december to the middle of february upon penaltye of 12d for every Swine so found and for every time hee is soe found which sayd 12d shale be demanded by the grand jury man whose care it is to see to the breach of this order and if any shale refuse to pay warrant shale be granted to the constable to make distress who shale have 1s syxe pence for his paines for every such distress and hereby is declared that good information by any shall bee of equall forse as if the grand Jury man had seene it himselfe

[I—155]

by the Selecktt men december 5th (1656)

it is ordered that during and all the inhabitants betwixt mr John Pynchons and to the brow syde of Ben: parsons who are proprioters of any partt or parsell of the wett medlow before our doares shale take course to cleare and scoure the brooke soe far as their lott or lottments is in breadth in the same medow and that it be done sufficiently to the aprobation of the Seleckt men and that by the last of June next upon penalty of 3s 4d per weeke for every parsell that is found undone at that time and soe to continue 3s 4d pr weeke till the worke be ffullye donne the which fines shale be dulye levied by the constable and im......for publique use.

[I—156]

Att a Towne meetinge ffebruary the 18 (56) it was voted that mr Hollyock and Henry Burt Should carry on the work of the Sabboth in this plase but in case that thowrough any providence of god other of them should be disenabled that decon chapin should supply that presentt vacantye:

more over this Towne voted to allow them £50 a yeare
that is to say from the 4th of november last the time they be-
gane and to continue till the towne have another Suply or
shale see cause to alter theyer acts in that particular but they
would acksept but of £40 unto which the Towne assented.

it was alsoe voted that they would allow to Decon wright
decon chapin mr Hollyocke Henry Burt £12 for there labours the last soomer which they spentt in that worke.

[I—157]

at a Towne meetinge ffebruary 18th 1656 it was voted by
consentt that whosoever within this Township shale kill any
ffox or ffoxes within the bounds of this Township shall be
allowed 3s ffor every foxe soe killed prcvided they bring
either the body or head unto any of the Seleckt men.

This order was afterward repealed & only 12d apce allowd
for every fox killed in ye bounds of ye Towne.

march 9th (1656) it was voted that for the cornefeilds
whensoever any towne meetinge is warned by the Seleckt
men or by towne apointmentt there shall be the major partt
presentt before any ackt that passeth shall be byndinge to
the whole but when the major partt is assembled they shall
have liberty to ackt in what concerns those presentt meetinge and the rest shall stand to such ackts soe pased: and it
was further voted that is to say 3 days warninge and was
likewise voted that of those 3 days the Towne meetinge day
is one of the three: and the day before is another, and the day
before that is understood to be the three days: and if any person which is an inhabitant shal nott be presentt when the
clossing is desired provided the major part of the inhabitants
be presentt before the moderator doe begine the meetinge
then any such inhabitant shal be lyable to a fine of 3s 6d or if
any shale withdraw without leave or departt before the meetinge be concluded by the moderator shale be lyable to the
same fine which sayd fine shale be distrained to such as doe
atend the meetinge in due time previded they are the major
partt which shale attend by there constable who shall have
6d for his pay for every particular fine

[I—158]

march 6th (1656) it was voted that for the cornefeilds here about the Towne that if they be well fensed at each ends of the severall feilds downe into the greate river it was accounted sufficient fense for such parts of the feilds the intent of this order is to free men from fensinge alonge the river bank from the lower wharfe to the head of the plaine

it was likewise voted that for every swine that is scene in any inclosed ground about the towne as the home lotts meddows before the doores 3 corner meddow or the plaine above shal pay 1s for every swine soe found besides all damadge that may be done by such swine the which 1s is is to be paid by the owner of the swine to the informer provided this order take plase before the 10 of Aprill next.

it was likewise voted that for swine over the greate River should be for to goe at liberty from the time that Cattle are at liberty to goe there provided they be sufficiently runge & in case they are found unrung from the 1st of March to ye 1st of Decemb^r yearly to pay 2s 6d apeice halfe to ye Informer & halfe to ye Towne they are to be Rung sufficiently to pvent Rooting. This clause added by ye Select men Decemb^r 31, 1660.

[I—159]

[In the handwriting of John Pynchon.]

At a Towne meeting Novemb^r 3d 1657.

There was a choise of five Select men for ordering ye prudentiall affaires of ye Towne, viz,

Robert Ashley, John Dumbleton Thomas Gilbert:
Miles Morgan, Jonathan Burt:

Sam Marshfeild was chosen Constable for this yeare & was sworne by ye commissioners ye day aboves^d according to ye order: Anthony Dorchester was chosen his deputy:

Tho: Bancraft & Tho: Miller were chosen p^{r}senters to p^{r}sent breaches of laws of ye Country or Towne orders to wch service they tooke theire oaths:

John Lumbard & Reice Bedortha are chosen Surveyours for repairing of ye Highways for this yeare ensuing.

The veiwers of fences chosen for ye yeare ensuinge are Benja Parsons & John Mathews for ye lower pt of ye Towne fro: ye meetinghouse downeward, & Wm Wariner & Symon Sackut fro: ye meeting house upwards.

[I—160]

Novemb^r 9th 1657. At a Towne meeting there was granted to Mr John Pynchon in lew of his want of land ni his lot over ye grt river wch upon measure now appeares to be but 26 rod broad, when as it was 30 rod, in lew of his want the s^d 4 Rod of ground in breadth: there is granted to him what vacant ground is at ye west end of y^t his s^d lot betwixt it & ye 3d devission flank & ye brow of ye hill, as also all the common ground at ye west end of Mr Holyokes lot & at ye west end of Mr. Smiths lot fro: ye reare of theire lots to ye brow of ye hill agt ye meddow, & Joining agt Mr Pynchons meddow, being foure or five acres more or less.

At ye same meeting it was agreed y^t the Select Townesmen for ye yeare ensuing shal have power to give out, & dispose of land, as in theire best discression is fitt:

There is liberty granted to Symon Beamon to dig a sellar to worke in for this winter in ye Towne lot pvided he fill it up againe in ye spring:

Mr Holyoke is made choise of to carry on ye worke of ye Sabbath once every Sabbath day wch he accepts of. Mr Pynchon is made choise of for one p^t of ye day once a fortnight wch he will indeavor to attend sometimes by reading notes & some^t by his owne meditations till March next: Deacon chapin & Henry Burt are made choise of to carry on ye other p^t of ye day once a fortnight ffor wch theire Paines they are allowed after forty pound a yeare for ye disposing whereoff to each pty: Tho Coop: wth ye Townesmen are to act therein

[I—161]

at a meeting of the Townesmen the 18th of December Robert Ashly was chosen Sealer by the Towns men and the Constable for this year.

it is agreed upon by the Townsmen having taken in to

Consyderation the great damig that acrue to the towne by
swine it is therfor ordered that if any swine shall be found
in any Corne feilds or meadows or any inclosed ground
the said swines not being rung the owners shall be lyable to
pay two shillings for every such default besides paying all
damyges that may be done by such swine Also if any swine be
found in any inclosers the swine being rung the owners of
such swine shal be lyable only to pay the damige theare of
that such swine may doe but al swine going in the Street
shal not be lyable to any fine also if any mans swine be in his
own inclosed ground whear as no man is wronged but him
selfe he shal not be lyable to breach of order of tow shillings.

March 4th 1657. There is a dispensation for this yeare of
ye order y^t cattle shall not goe at liberty after March over y^e
river, allowing Liberty for all cattle (except swine) to goe
at liberty there, till ye first of Aprill pvided in case any shall
be damnified due satisfaction be allowed him.

[I—162]

[In the handwriting of Thomas Cooper.]

November 2d: 1658: There was granted by the Towne
unto Rowland Thomas a parsell of woodland at the rear of
mr Hollyocks woodlott: not exceedinge six acars the breadth
whereoff was to be the breadth of mr Hollyocks and to run
in length soe far as to the rear of mr Pynchons.

[I—163]

[In the handwriting of John Pynchon.]

At a Town meeting held the 4 of January 1657 thes highways which followeth: being agreed upon, & laid out (formerly) by ye Select men were publikely declare, & setled:
Impr: Ordered & agreed, that there shall be a highway on
ye west side of ye greate River fro: Agawam river mouth on
ye South along by ye grt River side Northward untill it come
into ye Common conteining Three rod in breadth fro: the top
of ye Bank by the greate River side: Also y^t at ye Common
Landing place usually called ye Hay place against Miles Morgans, Wm Brookes, & Symon Sackcuts lots: The Highway

shall be at least five rod broad there, for a place to set hay on for yᵉ use of any pson: it is to be a common Hay place.

2. Ordered & Agreed That there shall be a highway fro: yᵉ Comn Hay place aforesᵈ, to yᵉ flank of yᵉ third devision conteining two rod broad, one rod of it to be taken out of Wᵐ Brookes Lot & yᵉ other rod out of Rowland Thomas Lot wᶜʰ now Symon Sackcut posesseth (Satisfaction being already made yᵐ by allowance of Land in other places) This Highway when it comes to yᵉ flank of yᵉ 3d devision is then to turne & run southward at yᵉ reare of yᵉ 2d devision lots & by yᵉ flank of yᵉ 3d devission: & This Highway is to run southward downe to yᵉ front of yᵉ Third devission & then to turne westward & run yᵉ front of yᵉ 3d devission, between yᵉ 3d devission & yᵉ further side of Mr Smiths 3d devission wᶜʰ now Mr Pynchon Posesseth:

3. Ordered & agreed that there shall be a highway [I—164] of one rod & halfe broad run fro: yᵗ Highway at yᵉ front of yᵉ 3d devission, all along yᵉ Towne Lot downe South-ward into Agawam river, this Highway to be taken out of yᵉ Towne lot wᶜʰ lyeth betwixt Mr Holyoke & Sam chapin, & to ly on yᵗ side of yᵉ Towne lot wᶜʰ is next to Sam Chapin: This rod & halfe of ground aforesᵈ is still to belong to yᵉ Towne lot so as yᵗ whosoever hath it of yᵉ Towne shal have yᵉ grass or what ever may grow upon it allowing liberty for a Passable highway; noe other man being to claime any other priveledge here, but only for a Passable way of one rod & halfe wide:

4. Ordered & agreed that there shall be a highway allowed of a rod broad, at yᵉ end of Rowland Stebbins, Thomas Mill-ers Jonath Burts & Robert Ashlys meddow lots by Agawam river (viz) at that end of theire meddows next to Mr Smiths Pikle meddow, & so to run at yᵉ end of Mr Pynchons med-dow that Joines to Mr Smiths & betwixt Mr Smiths & John Clarks straight to yᵉ highway at yᵉ front of yᵉ sᵈ devissions:

[I—165]

At a Town Meeting Novembʳ 2d 1658. There was a choise made of ffiveSelect Townesmen, for ordering yᵉ prudentiall affaires of ye Towne for this yeare ensuing. The psons chosen are

Tho: Cooper
Benj Cooly
Jonath Burt
Wm Warriner, &
Robert Ashly:

John Harmon & John Lamb are chosen Survyours for reparing of ye Highways y^t belong to ye Towne: for ye yeare ensueing.

Serjant Stebbins & Serj Morgan are chosen veiwers of fences for ye upper pt of ye Towne fro: ye meeting house upwards. Lawrence Bliss & Nath Pritchard are chosen veiwers for ye lower p^t of ye Towne fro: ye meeting house downward.

[In the handwriting of John Holyoke.]

Nov. 2d There was granted by the Towne unto Rowland Thomas a parscel of wodland, at the Reer of m^r Holyokes wood lot, not exceeding six acres the breadth wheroof was to to ye Reer of m^r Pynchons (viz) woodlot.

[I—166]

[In the handwriting of John Pynchon.]

At a Town meeting Jan. 10 1658. It was fuly agreed & ordered That the Gate at the higher Wharfe shall be set in repaire agt ye Spring of ye yeare: & y^t ye s^d Gate shall be kept in repaire & well hung fro: yeare to yeare & after fences be made up in ye Spring yearly the s^d Gate shall be always kept shut till all feilds about it be broken up: & if any pson shall throw open or leave open ye s^d Gate fro: ye tyme of making up fences in ye Spring till liberty of laying all feilds Comon, such pson shall forfeite five shillings to be p^d to him y^t shall take notice thereoff who is to call for it & Receive it, one halfe to himselfe & ye other halfe for ye use of ye Towne & toward keeping ye s^d Gate in repaire

It is further agreed & ordered That ye Great River is & shall be accounted a fence, & shall stand for a fence, both for us on this side, & also for ye Land Meddows, & Cornefeilds on ye other side of ye grt river, And the People shall not be compelled to fence in theire meddows & cornefeilds any where on yᵉ west side of yᵉ great River, by any other fence, But yᵗ yᵉ sᵈ River shal serve for yᵗ end to preserve cornfeilds & meddows & to prevent & ease yᵉ greate charge of fencing. Only there is liberty granted to yᵐ yᵗ dwell on the west side of yᵉ greate River: That if [I—167] they will secure all yᵉ Cornefeilds & meddows on yᵉ west side of yᵉ grt river, from receiving any dammadge by any of theire Cattle: They shall have liberty to Impve yᵉ Common there (for feeding of theire cattle) by fencing it out fro: mens allotmts there & those yᵗ live on this side of yᵉ River are not to put over theire Cattle to feed on yᵗ Common & to opprss yᵗ Common wᶜʰ they shall be at charge to fence out, without theire Consent unless they will Joine wᵗʰ yᵐ in theire charge of fencing it, or allow yᵐ for there Cattles feeding as indifferent men shall Judge And this priveledge & liberty is granted yᵐ for 12 yeares fro: this yeare 1658.—Repealed Dec. 29th 1664.

It is ordered yᵗ Cattle of all sorts belonging to this Towne, shall be marked wᵗʰ some distinct knowne marke, for wᶜʰ end every owner of any cattle shall repaire to Mr Pynchon & fro: tyme to tyme to yᵉ Recorder: to take a keepe upon record each mans particular mark, & this to be done by yᵉ 1st of March next or else yᵉ owner of such Cattle shall forfeit 5s to yᵉ Towne: And every man is to marke all his cattle accordingly by yᵉ March next And it is further ordered that fro: tyme to tyme hence forward every mans Cattle shall be marked by yᵗ tyme they are 3 months old, & If any psons cattle shall be found unmarked at or after Three months old he shall pay 12d apce to him yᵗ shal Informe agᵗ him There is Liberty granted to Tho Cooper to keepe a fferry at yᵉ Lower wharfe & to land people below yᵉ mouth of Agawam river, & none are to carry over any psons, horses, or cattle over yᵉ [I—171 Error in number] great River to take any pay except they allow & pay it to yᵉ sᵈ Tho Cooper, unless it be such as Pass over yᵉ River to theire worke & in theire owne & neighbours vesseles. And the Priveledge of this ferry is granted to him for 21 yeares fro: this yeare 1658:

And ye s^d Tho Coop is to pvide a good boate & cannoes &
to carry over persons at the Rates following: a single pson at
3d a tyme: all above one 2d a peice: horse & man at 8d y^t is
to say 6d a horse, only the Inhabitants of this town are to be
caryed over when they pass wth a horse, for 6d horse & man,
& when ye Inhabitants of this Towne put over cattle a Yoake
of oxen are to be caryed for 6d & any of this Towne y^t shall
pass as troopers are to go free when upon trooping occasions.

There is granted to John Leanord 40 acres of land on y^e
highland adjoyning to Tho Miricks meddow over Agawam:
also Two acres next to it is granted to Tho Mirick pvided it
pve noe inconvenience to Jno Leanord grant.

There is granted to Mr John Pynchon over Agawam
River upon ye upland ag^t ye howse meddow & middle meddow 40 acres of land, adjoyning to ye howse meddow & middle meddow upon ye highland on ye South side thereoff to
Run towards ye grt River.

There is granted to Benja Cooly y^t his land at ye hither end
of ye long meddow shall run to ye Brow of ye hill on the east.

Tho Noble & James Warriner have liverty to Posess &
injoy ye Two acrs of wet meddow on this side of ye round hill
formerly granted David chapin & forfeited to ye Towne.
This 2 acres by agem^t betweene James wariner & Tho Noble
is wholy to belong to Tho Noble & is absolutely his ye s^d Tho
Nobles to dispos off.

The Smiths shop was given to John Stewart as his own forever.

[I—172]

At a Towne meeting ffeb^r 7th 1658

There was a ful & unanimous acceptance of Mr Hooker
to dispense ye word of God to us, & whereas he at p^rsent will
not certainely ingage to us longer than 3 Months the Towne
doe agree & ingage to give & allow him £20 for ye s^d Three
months & w^thall manifest theire desire & hopes of his further
continuance among us, being willing to continue ye like
further allowance upon his further Continuance with us.

And Mr Pynchon Mr Holyoke & Deacon chapin were appointed to signifie ye Townes mind & desires to Mr Hooker, who accordingly did it. & Mr Hooker manifested his willingness to help us Three Months as afores^d, & for p^rsent could resolve noe further but his coming to a resolution should take rise from this tyme.   It was further agreed y^t there shall be a Rate of £20 made and gathered for Mr Hooker in Satisfaction for his paines till May next, And in case for allowance for ye next quarter there shall be occasion to allow him (or any other) another complete £20.   That it shal then be raised & gathered according to this first rating w^thout new prizing of estate & making of new rate.   And this to stand good by virtue of this Towne act.   It was further agreed y^t Town Rates shal be made in ye same manner as formerly w^thout any alteration: further it was agreed by ye Towne, That for them who have Caryed on ye worke of ye Sabbath hithertoo, they shall be allowed after £40 a yeare.

There being some consideration about Ten acres of land in chikkuppy plaine over ye grt River wch was granted to Sam Terry about Three yeares agoe: It appearing by an order made in March 1653-54 That y^t land was otherwise disposed of & y^t it ought not to have bin given away; & besides ye land being otherwise forfeited: The Towne conclude y^t grant void & doe reasume ye land to its former use & appoint for the Townes use according to ye afore recited order: And that Sam Terry may have noe wrong by any Rates wch he may have p^d for ye land, it is ordered & agreed y^t what Rates he hath p^d, that hath bin raised on ye s^d Land, The Townesmen shal take notice thereoff, & pay ye same back againe to Sam Terry:

[In the handwriting of Thomas Cooper.]

1658-1659   Samuell Marshfeild desired of the Townsmen liberty to purchase a peese of the Indians on the other side the great river to the vallew of 4 or 5 acars adjoining to mr Pynchon his ditch at the South end of his orchard and runeth west alonge by his meddow lott and east bounded by ende of the lotts that runeth from the greate river; which sayd desire of his wase granted by the sayd Townsmen: y⁰ purchase of his alowed off.

[I—173]

may 10th 1659 Agreement made between Tho: Stebbins and the Townsmen about the setting up off the Towne pound the sayd Thomas doth condition with the said Townsmen that the pound shale bee sett the one halfe of the breadth of itt upon his land that is to say wheare they shale see most convenientt and so to stand during the Townes pleasure previded that duringe the time of its standinge theare the saide Thomas is to have the spare land that shale bee lost betwixt the corner of the pound next to his howse and his owne land at his own disposall for his proper use: provided allsoe that the Townsmen from yeare to yeare shale secure the sayd Thomas from any damadge that may acrew unto his land by reson of the insuftiency of the sayd pound previded alsoe that the pound doe nott exceed tow rod and halfe in length toward Thomas Stebbins.

December 24 (59) Grants off land by Tho: Cooper Rob: Ashly Ben: Cooly will: warriner Jonath Burt Selecktt men for that yeare.

Granted to John Clarke a parsell off meddow on the other Syde off the mill river opositte off med formerly granted him by the Towne provided that the parsell amount nott above the quantitye of one acar.

Granted to Abell wright 3 acars off meddow Lyinge South of pacowsucke towards or upon a branch of longe meddow brooke previded he Settle in Town 5 years

[I—174]

Granted to Laurence Bliss 3 acars off meddow lyinge South of pacowsucke toward one of the branches off longe meddow Brooke begininge where Abell wrights doth end and in case there is nott 3 acars to be had then to bee made up where it can conveniently be found: In reference to this there was granted to L: Bliss 3 acars of Swampe over Agawam River together with wch there was 4 acres more added, being 7 acres all in one peice: for this grant see further march 12th 1661-1662.

Decemb 23 (59) John wood being called before the Seleckt men and questioned for the breach of a Towne order in givinge intertainmentt to Isacke Hall the Space off two months hath liberty granted him: for which acordinge to order we find him to transgress the order to the vallew of 40s

At a Towne meetinge January 19 (1659) itt was unanimoesly agreed uppon by the Towne that the Towne meetinge which had heretofore beene usually keptt on the 1st tuesday in November for the chusinge of Townsmen and other offisers for Towne devision shoulds hense forward bee keptt on the 1st tuesday in ffebruary yeerly.

att the Same meetinge in January 19 (59) itt was concluded that the killinge of foxes should henceforward be att 12d apeese.

Alsoe at the Same meetinge in January 19 (59) it was agreed upon that the Townsmen then in presentt beinge should make a rate off Two and thirty pounds for the defrayinge such debtts as was dew from the Towne to particular persons and that: that prizinge of the Towne stock shold stand for the makinge of the rates the yeere ensuinge.

[I—175]

January 27 (1659) there is granted by the Seleckt men a parsell off land lyinge on the other side agawam river to the quantitye 5 or 6 acars more or less previded itt be noe detriment to the landinge for the ferrye or to a Suffitientt high way that shale be thought convenientt to be layd outt there: wee Say this is granted to mr Pynchon on the South syde agawam river at the mouth of the river and by the greate river syde:

January 27th (1659) there is also granted to mr Pynchon that the wood lott which he bought of william Branch lyinge next to Mr Pynchons owne woodlot on the other syde of the muxxy meddow, should have soe much added at the farther end in length the same breadth vid of 14 rod wide as should parrelell the equall length of his owne wood lott: viz at ye

Reare to run even with Mr Pynchons owne woodlot, wch 14 rod broad being added to Mr Pynchons 54 rod broad make ye whole bredth 68 rod: in all his woodlot is now 68 Rod Broad.

January the 27th 1659 there is granted Thomas Cooper a parsel of swamp land lying by agawam river side at the South end of the meadow lots at the hither wigwams side all that swampe with what land thear is as yet undisposed of as also lyberty to purchas any land of the Indians adjoining unto it bounded by agawam ryver on the south and the meadow lots on the north.

[I—176]

[In the handwriting of John Pynchon.]

January 27th (1659) there was granted by the Select men unto Richard fellows 20 acars of land vidz an adition of 20 rod in breadth to John Lenards lott which land lyeth at the hyer end of the plaine comonly called chickopee plaine on the other side of the greate river beinge 30 rod in breadth as it was granted to John Lenard now to Richard fellows there is 20 rod more added which maks 50 rod in breadth and alsoe an inlardgmentt to the lott which Richard ffellows bought of Hugh Dudley to make it alsoe 50 rod broad anserable to the lott which was granted to John Lenard and to increase the length of these two lotts up the river 32 rod and 50 rod broad anserable to the other land above specified soe that the whole land of Richard fellows there what by purchase from John Lenard and Hugh Dudley with this addition of the grantt of the Select men makes the parsell of land 50 rod breadth and 115 rod in length up the road

[I—177]

The Towne according to theire order met togither on Tuesday ye 1st of Novemb^r 1659, being ye Day fformerly appointed for the yearly choise of all Towne officers: But pceeded to noe choise. Judging it best in Sundry respects, that at p^rsent all officers should Continue in theire Places till ye 1st Tuesday in ffeb^r next The Towne resolving & mutually agreeing then to pceed to a new choise & soe yearly hereafter to meete on ye first Tuesday in ffebruary To make choise of Towne officers & order ye General affaires of ye Towne, hereby repealing ye former order wch appointed ye day to be on ye 1st Tuesday in Novemb^r And determining That ye first Tuesday in ffebr yearly shal be Generall Towne meeting day: This was concluded at ye meeting in Novemb^r And also at a Towne meting in Jan 19th 1659 it was unanimously agreed that yearly ye Generall Towne meeting day for choise of Towne officers should be on ye first Tuesday in ffebr.

At the Generall Towne meeting, on ye first Tuesday in ffebruary, being the 7th day of ffebr: 1659: And ye day appointed for election of Towne officers, & ordering Towne affaires:

There was a choise made of five Select Townesmen for ordering all ye Prudentiall affaires of ye Towne for this yeare ensuinge: (viz)

Tho: Gilbert	Miles Morgan: &
Benja: Parsons:	John Pynchon:
John Dumbleton	

Select men are to take care what they may for ye welfare of ye Towne: & according to theire wisdome to order the hearding of cattle, making of Rates, To dispose of Single psons & inmates as they shall se cause in ye Towne, To admit Inhabitants & To settle ye Comon highways of ye Towne, & determine any difference about y^m. To Dispose of any of ye appropriated land, unless That is to let it out wch they may doe for Twenty one yeares or less tyme, as they shall se cause, & Judge most advantagious to ye Towne: And alsoe any of the estate of ye Towne wch lyes dead. (if y^t any doe so) they may let it out for a yeare or yeares if they shall Judge it best for ye good of ye Towne. And what ever they Judge concerning to ye welfare of ye Towne they are to act therein & order ye same according to theire best wisdome: And in theire making of orders they are to heed ye Generall good of ye Towne, & such orders made by y^m as they apprhend for ye Generall good, they may anex penaltys thereunto according to Law wch Penalty they are carefully to exact & Recover for the

Townes use fro: such inhabitants, as shall neglect or refuse
to observe them:

It is ordered that hence forward yearly at ye Generall
Towne meeting in ffeb^r there shall be a Moderator chosen,
who shal stand as Moderator not only that day But for all
Towne meetings ye yeare ensueing: And ye Moderator shall
always be chosen by Papers, & first at ye beginning of y^e
meeting before any other Towne officers, whose worke shall
be to order tymes of Speech & silence, to put things to vote,
& to regulate all proceedings in Towne meetings that
disorders as much as may be p^rvented. And in case of his
absence at any tyme fro: any Towne meeting, the Select men
to agree who among themselves shall supply his place at such
meeting as he shall be absent fro: And at p^rsent Mr John
Pynchon is chosen Moderator for ye yeare ensueing.

It is ordered that hence forward the Select Townsmen
shal yearly be chosen by Papers.

It is also ordered that yearly hence forth there shall be
one meet man chosen at ye Generall meeting in ffeb^r To y^e
place of Clarke or Recorder for Recorder for ye Towne,
whose worke shal be [I—178] faithfully & truly to Record &
Enter Towne orders, Grants of Lands, & all agreemts & acts
of the Towne or Select Townsmen who also shall observe to
keepe & enter in a booke for that purpose a true accot of all
dues arising to ye Towne by Penaltys anexed to ye breaches
of Towne orders or otherwise, And also keepe a true acct of
all the Just expences & debts of ye Towne that fro: him y^e
Towne or Select men may know how to act in making Rates
& shall dlr. to the Select men a true Transcript thereoff out
of his booke y^t so all dues & Penaltys payable to ye Towne
may be Seasonably Looked after: And he shall be chosen....

It is also Ordered That there shall Annually be some one
meete pson chosen to ye place of a Towne Treasurer who
shall carefully receive & gather in all dues belonging to ye
Towne, either by penaltys for breaches of Towne orders or
otherwise, & keepe a Tru acco^t thereoff: And what Stock
he shall have in his hand of ye Townes, he shall not pay it out

to any pson, but to such, to whome he knowes ye Towne are really indebted too, & in any doubtfull case to suspend payment on Penalty of satisfiing ye Towne out of his owne estate what he shall so pay out, if ye Towne or Select men shall not allow of such his payment, all his disposing of ye Towne stock & paym^{ts} out, to be by order fro: ye Select men or Towne, unless some express order doe allow & warrant his disbursing it. And for this yeare ensueing: Mr John Pynchon is chosen Towne Treasurer.

[I—179]

John Pynchon (also) for ye present yeare is chosen Clarke: or Recorder for ye Towne.

Ensigne Tho: Cooper & John Lumbard are chosen Surveighours for ye highways to carry on ye repairing of y^m the yeare ensueing.

Tho: Mirick is chosen Measurer for Land.

Robt Ashley chosen Constable & had his oath given him, wch he took ye same day:

Laurence Bliss was chosen Constable Deputy for supply ye Constables place in his absence.

It is ordered that henceforth ye choise of ye Constable shall be after this manner: That constables whose tyme is expired, before he goes out of his place shall Nominate Two men And ye Towne commissioners or cheife civill power in Towne, shall Nominate one more (or two wch they please) The which Three men or 4 if 4 be Nominated shall all be put to vote & he y^t hath most votes shall be Constable the yeare ensueing who by Country Law is lyable to five Pound fine for refusall of ye office.

It is ordered that at ye Generall Towne meeting on ffeb^r yearly, at ye beginning of ye meeting next after ye choise of Moderator there shall be chosen a Committee of two able psons to examen ye aco^{ts} that ye Select men bring in about publike charges that concerne this Towne before the Select men are dismissed theire places & so to pfect theire aco^{ts} according to righteousness that ye Towne may understand True estate one way or other: what they owe or what is oweing them.

[I—180]

It is agreed that henceforth fro: yeare to yeare, all ye severall Inhabitants of this Towne, wth out expecting any further order, May & are hereby desyred to attend ye Generall Towne meeting day appointed on ye first Tuesday in ffeb^r yearly for election of Towne officers carying on & establishing matters of Generall Concernm^t to ye Towne. And for those psons who by Law are to vote in Towne affaires & act in ye choice of Towne officers if they shal not attend ye Generall Towne meeting day on ye first Tuesday in ffeb^r afores^d. It is ordered that every such pson absent at ye tyme of calling or that shall afterward absent himselfe wthout Consent of ye Moderator or Major part of ye assembly: shall pay Two shillings to ye Towne Treasurer, wch Penalty shall be exacted wthin one weeke after ye Towne meeting on all those psons whose excuse or reson for theire absence the Select men shall not Judge Sufficient.

[I—181]

And for ye Carying on of all (other) Towne meetings called at any tyme by the Select men: It is ordered:

That Whensoever there shal be notice given to the Inhabitants by the Select men on theire behalf of some necessary occasion wherein the Select men desire to advise wth ye Inhabitants: And ye Day, tyme, & place of meeting be appointed: It is expected that all ye Inhabitants attend psonally such meetings So appointed: But in case ye Inhabitants refuse to attend, if ye tyme & houer of meeting be Come, It shall be Lawfull if there be one and twenty of ye Inhabitants assembled for them to pceed in agitation of what so ever busyness is then & there ppounded to them: And what ye Major pt of ye Assembly then & there met Shall agree upon it shall be taken as ye act of ye whole Towne & binding unto all:—the words one and Twenty put in ffeb^r 3d, 162. The original words were, "but Seven."

Whereas it is found by Experience That some psons disorderly Doe Thrust themselves into this Towne, & agt ye Select men here Continue & abide notwth standing all former orders made to p^{r}vent ye same. It is therefore ordered That henceforth what pson So ever shall intrude himself into this Towne ag^t ye Consent of ye Major p^t of ye Select men, & shall p^{r}sume here to Continue & abide longer than one month or 30 days after notice given him by any of the Select men or theire order of theire unwillingness that he should abide in ye Towne: Such pson or psons hee or shee as shall so Continue ag^t ye Consent of ye Select men or Major p^t of them, shall for ye first offence pay 20s & if afterward they shall still continue in ye Towne wthout allowance fro: ye Select men, they shall pay 20s p Month for every month they shall so continue contrary to this order, wch Penaltys shall be duly exacted & pd into the Towne Treasurer:

[I—182]

The Select men at this Gen: Towne meeting in ffeb^r (59) before they went out of theire places made up theire aco^{ts}, & cleared it up before ye whole Towne, That theire last Rate did not Levell all aco^{ts}. But that there is still 2£ 17s 4d for ye Towne to allow, for ye clearing of all aco^{ts} & paying what is yet due to Mr Hooker: Namely to make up ye Sixe pounds & 4d wch was remaining due to Mr Hooker wch Two pounds 17s afores^d, the Towne doth thus allow & pay. There is of it in Tahan Grants land, wch he owes ye Towne for wheate

	£	s	d
he had to make nayles & made them not......	2	10	00
& Laurence Bliss is to pay for ye chaine of ye steele Trap wch he lost..................	0	05	00
And 2s 4d Mr Pynchon gives to cleare all......	0	02	04
	2	17	04

	£	s	d
And this cleares all Towne aco^{ts}: Mr Pynchon being appointed to look after & receive in the Sum afores^d of........................	2	17	04
And to pay it to Mr Hooker, wch wth 16 bush & halfe wheate in ye meeting howse, wch comes to	2	17	9

And 15d in hand in wampum................o 01 3
And John Riley Goodm: Sackuit & Blufield is behind on ye Rate with Mr Pynchon is to looke
   after ....o 04 0

                      6 00 04

all which cleares Mr Hooker. This is all p^d & to be p^d in to
Mr Pynchon (for Mr Hooker) who is ingaged & pmises to
allow & pay it to Mr Hooker: & so all the Townes Debts
are cleared & p^d: to this 7th day of ffeb^r 1659. All Towne
aco^{ts} cleared to this day.

Note.—On margin against the preceding paragraph is
this: "ye 8s 3d for mats & 5s 9d due G: Cooper viz 14s od &
Goodm: Dorchester his rate, wch is unpaid, cleares that, &
is set of y^t way & so all is quit."

[Page 183]

Rich ffellows is ingaged to ye Towne: (for taking off of
his forfeiture of his Land wch he sold contrary to order by
pmise) To supply ye Towne wth a sufficient horse for a Journey to ye Bay this next Spring or Summer, when ye Towne
shall please to call for it:

There is of ye Towne one Iron hooke & eye in ye Post &
gate goeing to ye Training place also ye Towne hath one
Iron hook & eye at Tho Coopers howse.

This aco^t ye old Select men gave in to ye Towne 7th ffebr:
1659.

Consideration being had concerning our way of Raising
rates whether to make any Alteration & what way to goe in
for future after much Debate about it: it was agreed upon &
Resolved by ye Towne That hence forward all Town rates
should be raised upon Land & Cattle: all Land & howsing
to be vallued by ye Select men in an equal & no indifferent
way according as they shal Judge most equal & right fro:
yeare to yeare if they so need of any new doeings w'soever:
& according to theire valluation of mens land to Reckne it
as so much estate wth mens estate in Cattle: & mens estate

of howsing & Land & cattle being put together to raise ye Rates thereby & cast up every mans Just pportion.

And it is ordered that all Cattle of all sorts shal be vallued or prized for making of Townes rates at ye same price & according to ye vallue wch ye Country Sets upon ye cattle by theire age. And that the Selectmen may know ye age & number of new cattle wherby to take ye right vallue of y^m when they are to make Rates thereby They shall make choise of one fit man yearly whom they shal appoint to goe thorow ye Towne to take an aco^t of mens cattle, ye age thereof according to law & to bring in to y^m a list of ye Number of mens cattle of such & such severall ages.

[I—184]

ffebr. 1659. Voted by ye Towne & ordered That y^e £60 to be allowed Mr Glover if he stay out ye yeare: The Rate shal be made by ye Selectmen according to this last order, & way of Rateing agreed on: And that Three quarters of ye Rate be gathered & paid in as soone as it is made: the other quarter only to remaine in mens hands till about michalstide next & to be pd then, when it is called for:

Voted to allow Rich fellows Ten shillings wch he pd to Gutteridge of wethersfeild for David Chapins horse (wch was imployed for ye Towne occasions about 2 yeares since.) The Towne granted to allow this Ten shillings to Rich ffellows upon his producing Gutteridge his receipt y^t he had Rec^d it of him, wch Receite was p^rsented & Showne in ye Towne meeting: Rich ffellows desyred a peice of Land in chikkuppy plaine in y^t wch is left in ye lot wch was Miles Morgans lying at ye end of p^t of ye same Lot which he hath lately purchased of John Sackut, & pmises to release ye Ten shillings due to him afors^d fro: ye Towne: wch psell of ground being about 15 or 16 acres is by ye Select men this 10th of feb^r 1659 Granted to Rich ffellows, pvided he set off & release ye 10s afores^d due to him fro: ye Towne wch he pmises to doe & accepts & receipts of ye land on these tearms.

The lot of Rich Maunds (being in Mr Pynchons hand) by Rich Maunds selling it to him though forfeited by his going

away it was by ye Select men confirmed to Mr Pynchon this
15th feb^r 1659 And by ye s^d Mr Pynchon it is [   ]
it is lying betwixt ye lots of Robert Ashly & y^t wch was Symon Beamon & Sold to Mr Pynchon.

[I—185]

March 5th 1659-60.   At a meeting of ye Select men: Miles
Morgan Benja Parsons, Tho Gilbert: John Dumbleton: It
is ordered, That swine wch are not shut up, & that keepe
about ye Towne, or w^th^in Two miles of ye Towne: All such
swine, shall be well & sufficiently Rungg, by ye owners thereoff: (or at theire Cost & Charge) To prevent (as well) the
rooting downe of ditches, & rooting up of ye Commons or
other hurts as ye spoiling of meddows pastures & Cornfeilds:
And if any swine above Three months old, shall be found
after ye 25th day of March yearley: w^th^out good & sufficient
Rings in theire Noses, to p^rvent theire Rooting: The owner
of such swine Shall pay Three pence a peice for every Swine
So found, though but in ye Commons or streetes. But swine
found in meddows, Pastures, Gardens, orchards or Cornfeilds w^th^out good & sufficient Rings as afores^d: The owners
shall pay Two shillings & Sixe pence a peice for every such
swine above Three months old besides Sattisfiing all damadges done to any pson by any Swine.   And though swine
be Rung yet if they damadge any: The owners shall pay for
such damadge or Trespase as theire Swine shall doe in Cornfeilds meddows orchards & gardens, pvided it be Judged by
2 indiffirent men: But ye owners of ye s^d ringed swine, shall
or may, (& are hereby enabled to) Recover what ever damadge they so pay, from them, whose insufficient fence, they
shall pve ye s^d Swine came thorow: And it is further ordered
That any Swine found in cornfeilds meddows,pastures gardens or orchards may be driven to ye pound, not only for y^e
Recovery of what damadges they shall doe, but also of y^e
forfeitures for theire being unrungg, unless ye owners of y^e
Swine shal either pay ye forfeitures & damadge, or ingage before witnesses to doe it, to ye ptys Sattisfaction: And for
Swine or any Cattle That are lyable to Poundadge who ever

[I—186] shall Pound them. They shall have foure pence a head, for yᵉ Poundage of them. And yᵉ pound keeper shall have 2d a head, for taking yᵐ in & letting yᵐ out of Pound. The Penaltys aforesᵈ, of 3d for swine found in yᵉ Comons or streetes unrung, to goe to yᵉ Informer, & if any shall refuse to pay it him So that he be put to call witness & to psecute it they shall then pay 6d a peice besides yᵉ charges: The other Penaltys of 2s 6d a peice for swine in meddows &c to goe halfe to yᵉ Informer & yᵉ other halfe to yᵉ Towne the informer being to Rec: it all & pay in halfe to yᵉ T. And all former orders about swine are hereby repealed except that for yᵉ Long meddow & yᵗ other for over yᵉ River:

Whereas divers offences arise, thorough defective ffences & different app'hensions Concerning yᵉ Sufficiency of fences betwixt pprietors It is therefore ordered that all outside ffences about meddows or Cornfeilds shall be substantially fenced, either wᵗʰ 5 railes, or Posts & Pales: or ditch foure foote & halfe broad wᵗʰ hedge on it, or otherwise according to yᵉ Judgment & sattisfaction of yᵉ veiwers, & that all ptitionall fences between lot & lot shall be ordered by yᵉ Select men in case of yᵉ disagreemᵗ of yᵉ pprietors & in case any damadge arise to others by yᵉ defect of fences, the pty whose fence is defective shal pay all damadges according as they shall be adjudged by yᵉ Select men or any deputed by them upon Complaint from any dammadged.

[I—187]

whereas there was an ancient order bearing date Jan. 24th 1638, requiring all that had ditches by yᵉ highway before theire dores to keepe yᵐ well scoured for yᵉ ready passadge of yᵉ water that it might not Pen up to flow the meddows. And after that in Decembᵣ 1641 it was ordered that every Inhabitant should make a ditch yᵉ breadth of theire lots before theire dores. & such as had ditches made should scour yᵐ by yᵉ last of May or Penalty of five shillings. & whereas the sᶜ orders have not bin attended by meanes of wᶜʰ neglect much damadge hath come to yᵉ Generalty if not to all yᵉ Inhabitants from yᵉ middle of yᵉ Towne upwards, thorough yᵉ

water penning up & flowing of theire meddows: for Prevention whereoff for future & in psecution of y̓ᵉ fore mentioned
orders, & according to an order made in December 1656: It
is further ordered That henceforward yearly, the severall Inhabitants or pprietors of y̓ᵉ meddows from Mr Pynchons
meddow downe to Henry Burts, shall keepe a good & sufficient ditch well cleared for y̓ᵉ free & ready passadge of water,
for w̓ᶜʰ end every pson the bredth of his meddow, (& from 6
or 8 rod up y̓ᵉ meddow betwixt Mr Pynchon & Mr Holyoke)
shal once every yeare sometime in May Scowre & cleare
theire s̓ᵈ ditches or water Passadges of Sand, dirt, wood, or
any rubbish. So y̓ᵗ y̓ᵉ water may have free Passadge away
w̓ᵗʰout penning up to flow y̓ᵉ meddows: And this to be attended at such tyme in May yearely as that it may be done by
the last day of May on penalty of [I—188] every pson neglecting to Pay five shillings to y̓ᵉ Towne Treasurer, if not
done yearly by y̓ᵉ tyme, & that sufficiently cleared acording
as shall be allowed of by Two of y̓ᵉ Select men appointed by
y̓ᵉ rest: Every pson to attend it when y̓ᵉ water shalbe turned
away fot y̓ᵗ end, by those that live uppermost or by agreem̓ᵗ
of y̓ᵉ Major p̓ᵗ: & in case it shal be found undone after y̓ᵉ first
weeke in June every pson whose ditch or water Passadge is
not then sufficiently cleared shall besides y̓ᵉ first five shillings
afores̓ᵈ pay Three shillings four pence p weeke till y̓ᵉ worke
be fully done to Sattisfaction of y̓ᵉ two Select men apointed,
all w̓ᶜʰ Penaltys shall be duly Levied by y̓ᵉ Constable p̓ᵈ in
to y̓ᵉ Towne Treasurer: The Select men appointed for this
yeare to se this done & to Judge of y̓ᵉ Sufficient clensing of
y̓ᵉ water Passadge are Serjant Morgan & Benj Parsons.

Serja: Stebbins & Reice Bedortha are chosen veiwers of
fences for y̓ᵉ upper p̓ᵗ of y̓ᵉ Towne from the meeting howse
upward.

George Colton & Jonathan Burt, for y̓ᵉ lower end, fro: the
meeting howse downeward.

Robert Ashly is chosen Sealer for weights & measures &c.

Sam: Marshfeild is allowed to keepe an ordinary or howse
for Comon entertaine, & to sell wine, Liquor &c.

Agreed to p^rsent these psons to ye next County Court, ye one to be licenced & ye other to be Sworne & to psecute ag^t John wood for staying in Towne.

[I—189]

March 5th (59) Lett out to Thomas Noble, the Thirty acres of Towne land in chikkuppy plaine on ye west side of ye greate River, for the terme & space of Nine yeares from this p^rsent 5th day of March 1659 upon ye tearmes hereafter mentioned (viz) That he shall cleare & Plow up fifteen acres of ground wthin five yeares: or at least before his tyme be expired, But he is not to deface or breake up any of ye meddow or mowing ground, but p^rserve it for Hay. And for the Two first yeares the s^d Tho Noble is not to allow or pay any rent: But ye Seven yeares following he is to allow or pay, yearly ye rent or Sum of foure Pounds, the wch Sum of foure Pounds a yeare he is to pay in, unto ye Select Townsmen or Towne Treasurer in good merchantable wheate, upon or before ye first day of March yearly till ye terme be expired: And in case ye land should come to be fenced he is to doe his share of fence wth other men. And he is to pay noe Rates, ye Land being Rate free. And to this ingagem^t & agreement he hath set to his hand, this p^rsent 5th of March 1659.

THO NOBLE.

Ordered that ye Surveighours shall make a foote Bridge, over ye Mill River in ye most convenient place betwixt ye Cartway y^t now is, & ye old mill of Two Trees Joined together & so fastened or secured, that ye floods may not Carry y^m away.

Also it is ordered that ye Surveighors shall make ye highway over ye grt River that goes betwixt John Clarks & Mr Smiths Pikle: Passable wth a Loaden Cart.

The Lower end of ye Towne have Liberty to make a cart Bridge over ye mill river above ye old mill, & such as Joine not in making of it, if they shall make use of it, they shall allow or pay to ye makers of it 3d p Load for Three yeares.

[I—190]

March 5th (59)

There is granted to Rowland Thomas 20 acres of upland at chikkuppe Rivers mouth, by his meddow there provided he continue 5 yeares in Towne.

Granted to Symon Beamon a wood lot of foure acres at ye east end of Ensigne Coop^s woodlot pvided he continue 5 years.

Granted to John Dumbleton a psell of meddow on ye other side of Pauccatuck brooke pvided it exceed not Ten acrs of meddow & that he continue in Towne 5 years.

Granted to Tho Stebbins the Pond in ye long meddow betweene wheele meddow & his fathers lot, the breadth of his fathers lot & ye ground there betwixt his fathers lot & wheele meddow. Also granted him Ten acres of land in ye plaine above next above ye Alotm^{ts} already granted there without ye fence.

Granted (likewise) to Miles Morgan Ten acres of land there in ye Plaine above.

There is granted to Laurence Bliss & Sam: Marshfeild & to each of them foure acres of Swamp over Agawam river in ye howse meddow that Spang of land twixt ye howse medo & Tho Mirick & Tho Bancraft to be y^t first & ye rest of it to adjoine to it & run fro: Agawam River to ye howse meddow.

March 26th 1660

At a meeting of Jno Pynchon J Dumbleton Benj Parsons Miles Morgan & Tho Gilbert. Henry Chapin is admitted an Inhabitant & Deacon Chapin acknowledges himselfe bound to ye Towne Treasurer in a bond of £20 to Secure ye Towne fro: any charge wch may arise to ye Towne by ye s^d Henry Chapin.

There is granted to Henry Chapin sixteene acres of land by Rowld Thomas on this side of chikkuppy river reserving full liberty to lay out highways & ye most Convenient Passadge.

Sam: Ely is admitted an Inhabitant & Mr Elizur Holyoke acknowledges himselfe bound in a bond of £20 to ye Towne

Treasurer to Secure ye Towne fro: any charge wch may arise to ye Towne by ye s^d Ely or his family.

Nath Ely is admitted an Inhabitant.

There is granted to Jeremy Horton & James Warriner a neck of land on this side of chikkuppy river at Skepmuck of about 20 acrs that is to say each of y^m 10 acrs: James Warrinar his Ten acrs lys uppermost next ye Comon passadge thorow ye river; & lys along by ye river side betwixt ye River & ye brow of ye Hill, only he is to leave out a Sufficient cartway above it (over ye river) or else to allow a Cartway thorow it, as shall be most convenient. Next to James warrinar, Westward downe ye River lys Jeremy Horton his Ten acrs Bounded by ye River North & Y^e brow of the Hill South: Also there is granted to each of y^m five acres a peice more, upon ye Brow of ye hill Homward, & adjoyning each of theire afores^d land, allowing a Common way most Convenient wch is granted y^m in lew of howse lots: this Grant confirmed 31 Decemb^r 1660, wth Liberty for each of y^m to Build there:

[I—191]

At a meeting of ye Towne August 27th 1660.

Mr. Holyoke was chosen Commissioner to Joine wth ye Select men for making ye Countrey Rates this yeare according to order.

At ye same Towne meeting Joseph Crowfoote ppounding his desires for Liberty to Build on his lot over ye greate River at ye Hay place, had Liberty granted him for erecting a Building or dwelling place there.

Also Tho: Gilbert hath Liberty granted him, for Building & dwelling on his Land, wch he hath bought of Benja Cooly at the Longmeddow Gate:

At a meeting of ye Towne Decemb^r 12th 1660: It was agreed that Mr Glover should have ye howse (wherein he now dwells) & Land belonging to it, during his Convenience among us to dispence ye word of God: And that ye Towne will repaire ye fences & Set all things in goodd repaire wch he is so to keepe, & to leave y^m in repaire to ye Towne when

P'vidence shall order his removall, by death or otherwise.
And for his maintenance yearly: The Towne agrees to allow
him £80 p anum: the getting his firewood, hay &c being to
be borne out of ye s^d £80 the yeare begins ye 29th of Septemb^r
1660.

And ye Towne agrees to pay for bringing up of his
goods &c.

[I—192]

Decemb^r 31th 1660: By ye Select men.

John Pynchon John Dumbleton Miles Morgan Tho Gilbert & Benja Parsons. Geo: Colton desiring liberty to
Build on his land at ye Long meddow: had Liberty granted
him for erecting a Building or dwelling place thare

Rowland Thomas had ye like liberty granted him, for
Building a howse or erecting a dwelling place on his land
at ye mouth of chikkuppy River, on this side of chikkuppy
River:

James Warriner, & Jeremy Horton have each of them liberty granted them, for dwelling, & erecting of buildings on
theire land at Skipmuck on this side of chikkuppe River:

Whereas there was one acre of meddow on ye mill river,
wch Goodm: Ashly in relation to his keeping of ye ordinary:
& he was to leave it into ye Townes hands when ever he
should cease to keepe ye ordinary: He having given over y^e
ordinary: & y^t acre of meddow more or less now falling into
ye Townes hands: It is ordered that Sam Marshfeild (who
now keepes ye ordinary) shall have y^t acre of meddow with
what overpluss belongs to it, if there be any, be it more or
less: Sam Marshfeild shall have ye use of y^t meddow for y^e
p^rsent & till ye Select men or Towne shall otherwise dispose
of it pvided he (ye s^d Sam) be at ye charge of measuring it
& bounding it out, sufficiently & this is granted to him in re-
lation to his keeping ye ordinary & yet wth Liberty to y^e
Towne or select men disposing it as they se cause.

There is Liberty granted for Quince Smith his tarrying 2
months in Towne fro: ye 18th of Decemb^r 1660 if he tarry
longer it must be by a new Liberty fro: ye Select men.

[I—193]

Decemb^r 31 (60) Observation being taken, of a greate neglect in many psons not bounding theire land by Sufficient marks wch neglect may occasion much Troble & disturbance in future tyme if not spedyly p^{r}vented: It is therefore ordered that every pprietor of land whose land is not fenced in pticular but lys in Common wth others, shall take care that before ye last of Aprill next, there be set on each side of his land at least two good stones, full an foote above ground, or else in ye stead of Stones a trench of three foote long & two foote wide & a foote & halfe deepe, (the Stones or trench to be set exactly ni ye front & reare) on penalty of paying five shillings for every distinct psell of land wch shall not be bounded as afores^d by ye last of April next ye 5s to be p^d by ye pty wch is defective, & if both ptys be defective in there neglect, then to be borne by both one to pay ye one halfe & ye other pty, ye other halfe according as ye Select men shall Judge: And that none may set theire bounds y^{mse} to ye offence of theire neighbour they are to require these y^t Joine upon y^m to goe wth them according to Country Law.

Octob^r 8th 1660 according to order By ye Select men, there was granted a psell of Land at fresh water brooke, to Mr Pynchon: Geo Colton & Benj Cooly in pportion according as they carry on theire designe of keeping swine there, at fresh water river, In all forty acrs of upland there: wch is to say Ten acrs to each quarter p^t & so to be pportioned to y^m to carry on ye q^r p^{ts}, & this upon condition y^t they doe wthin 2 years carry on theire designe of keeping swine there, if they faile in carrying on y^t designe of keeping swine there wthin Two yeares, or such of y^m as doe faile, they forfeit ye land & it remaines to ye other, or y^m who doe keep swine there, or else falls to ye Towne if none carry on y^t designe of keeping swine there. The designe of keeping swine there was accordingly carryed on & wthin ye tyme Limited, & continued till windsor cornfeilds eate up ye swine.

[Note.—On the margin of the preceding is this:] "To Geo Colton belongs 10 acrs & 30 acrs to Mr Pynchon who carryed on 3 qtrs."

[I—194 Blank—I—195]

At yᵉ Generall Towne meeting on yᵉ first Tuesday of ffebruary: (Being) ffebʳ 5th 1660.

There was a choice made of five Select Townesmen for ordering all yᵉ Prudentiall affaires of yᵉ Towne for this yeare ensueing: (viz) Mr Holyoke Deacon Chapin: Ensigne Cooper Serja: Cooly & Robert Ashly: who (by a full vote) have yᵉ same Power conferred upon them, as yᵉ Select men had last yeare:

Mr John Pynchon is chosen Moderator for all Towne meetings yᵉ yeare ensueing:

The Committy chosen for examening the Acoᵗˢ of yᵉ Select men are: Mr Holyoke & Ensigne Cooper:

Mr Holyoke is chosen Recorder or clarke for yᵉ Towne yᵉ yeare ensueing:

Mr John Pynchon is chosen Towne Treasurer for the yeare ensueing:

[In the handwriting of Elizur Holyoke.]

Thomas Merrick & Wᵐ Warrener are chosen surveyors for the High ways (belonging to this Towne) for the yeare ensueing.

Lawrence Bliss at this Same meeting is chosen to yᵉ office of a Constable for this Town for yᵉ yeare ensueing, who accordingly took his oath for the execution of his office:

And Benjamin Parsons is chosen for the Constables deputy to supply the Constables place in the Constables absence:

[I—196]

And at the same Towne meeting Thomas Merrick & Samuell Marshfeild were chosen Measurers of land for this Town (as need shall require) for yᵉ yeare ensueing.

Thomas Bancroft is chosen for a Searcher and Sealer of leather according to law for this Town for yᵉ yeare ensueing.

And whereas the Countrey Law enacts that noe house or cottage shall injoy yᵉ privelegges of any Comons wᶜʰ shall be Sett up in any Township without consent of the Town: This Town doth order and depute the Select men in the

name & on ye behalfe of ye Town to allow or disallow any
Such buildings.

Samuell Terry making claim before the Town to 10 acres
that appropriated Land in the playne on ye west side of y^e
great River called Chickuppe playne, for y^t there was a grant
to him of soe much land there, it was left to a Comittee of
6 men to consider what they should think convenient for y^e
Town to doe in the case: the Comittee chosen were Ensign
Cooper Nathaneell Ely George Colton Serjeant Stebbin
Samuell Marshfeild & Elizur Holyoke who are to make return of ye apprehension of ye Towne.

Alsoe the said 6 men & mr Pynchon Joyned wth them
are to consider what way they Judge most convenent for
raysing Town rates, for y^t the Town votes to alter from the
way that was observed last [I—197] yeere: & the said 7 men
are to make return of their app^rhensions to the Town:

ffeb^r: 12th 1660.

A Town meetinge being called to consider of & conclude
Some things not fully issued at the former meeting as concerning Samuell Terry his claime & the way of raysinge
rates for ye Towne. The Comittees chosen last meetinge
to consider of these things, delivering y^t app^rhensions. The
Town by vote concluded to leave ye busyness of Samuell
Terry his claime to ye Select men to consider of, & that if
they See cause to give Samuell Terry Some portion of land
they shall have liberty soe to doe, the Towne concluding
they condiscend to him herein more y^n they need to doe:

And concerninge the way of raysinge rates for bearinge
the Publike charges of the Town It is voted that such rates
shall be raysed on houses land & liveinge Stock accordinge
to their worth: houses & Lands to be prised by the Select
me; liveing Stock to be prized by men chosen by the Select
men from yeare to yeare. And the Towne concludes that
hereafter swine putt up for fatting & killing shall not be
prized for raysing Town rates: Alsoe that mens persons shal
be vallued as soe much estate; vizt all men from 16 yeeres

& upward wch vallue of [I—198] persons shal be at £12 £16 or £20 accordinge to the discretion of the Select men: all men to come under one of those prizes, except such persons as shal be found impotent by reason of lameness or sickness or infirmity to be judged by the Select men:

Alsoe the Town concludes that for raysing Town rates men shal be assessed for their merchandizing and trading suitable to w^t trade they drive in the Towne, wch also is to be judged by the Select men.

The day abovesaid vizt ffeb 12th 1660

Thomas Day & Thomas Noble makinge Suite for land behind Chickuppe plaine on the west side of the great River 2 or 3 mile more or less from the River. There is granted to them 20 acres a peece halfe meddow & halfe upland ye land lyinge together in those quarters where they can find it. this granted by ye Select men:

The Select men chose for prizers of cattell for this yeere where by to make rates these men: vizt Nathaneell Ely Samuell Marshfeild & Thomas Miller:

And for veiwers of fences for this yeere they chose for the higher end of ye Towne from ye meeting house Rowland Thomas & Griffeth Jones & Thomas Gilbert & Tho: Bancroft for ye lower end of ye Town, from ye meeting house.

[I—199]

ffurthermore there is granted by ye Select men to Anthony Dorchester 10 acres of land on ye backside of Chickuppe playne on the west Side of ye great River wch land is to lye at or neere the backerend of certayn lotts wch were his own in y^t playne: this 10 acres is said to be form^rly granted to him: wch grant is now renewed:

There is also granted unto Ensigne Cooper Robert Ashley Samuell Marshfeild & James Warrener All the meddow y^t lyes uppon the North Branch of the next brook y^t runs into the great River below Agawam River the said 4 persons are to share equally those meddowes amongst them: Themselves also are to aggree where each mans share shall ly.

There is also granted to Samuell Marshfeild that land that lyes between Pacowsick brook & the last of those lotts granted on this side the said land is bounded by ye great Riv^r west & the top of ye hill East: provided that the high way be not p^rjudiced by this grant: & y^t any person may have liberty to fetch Stones from the flatts in the great River.

There is granted to Tho: Gilbert 10 acres of meddow on fresh water brook if there be soe much there above former grants.

[I—200]

There is also granted to Thomas Miller Rice Bedortha & Edward ffoster 6 acres of meddow to such of them lyinge on the same meddow or over the Same brook where Tho: Noble & Tho: Day have meddows granted to them: the first grants to be first laid out:

At a Town meetinge ffebr. 15 1660.

It being propounded this day as a matter of importance & very Convenent for the Towne that bounds were sett to this Plantation & confirmed by the Genll Co^rte. It was by vote declared to be the desire of the Inhabitants. that the next Genll Cort be in humble wise petitioned to settle bounds for this Plantation: The Town desiringe that Our Northerly bounds may meet wth the bounds of Northampton on the West side of ye great River & wth ye New Town on the East side of the great River according as the bounds of ye said New Town were laid out by the Comittee appoynted thereunto & the Southerly bounds to extend 20 poles below the place where mr Pynchon had a ware house according to an Ancient Conditionall grant of ye Genll Co^rte: Dated...... & Soe to run the bounds East from the Great River ffive mile: & fro: ye Said Ware house place to [I—201] runn cross the great River, & to runne West as far as Woronoco is from Springfeild, takeing in also the Lands at Woronoco, (according the Genll Co^rtes conditionall grant concerning those lands) except y^t a plantation be sett up at or neere Woronoco: & then Worronoco to be dismissed fro: Springfeild: or if

Worronoco be absolutely taken away from us then to request the Corte to have ffoure miles in breadth granted
westward from ye great River: And in case ye Corte shall not
grannt five miles Eastward from the great River for y^e
Townes bounds then to gett ffoure miles Eastward: Or if the
North bounds wil not be granted as is above defined then to
gett the bounds to be granted wthin two miles thereof: But
the deputy is gott as much in all these respects as Co^{r}te may
be inclined unto: And Mr John Pynchon Ensigne Cooper
Elizur Holyoke & Rowland Thomas are appointed to make
a draught of ye lands to be presented to ye Co^{r}te:

Whereas by an Order of the 12th of this Instant ffebruary
It was concluded y^t for raysinge of rates for comon charges
of ye Town, mens persons should come under valluation w^{ch}
valluations are to be reckoned wth mens estates And y^r being
Three prizes pitcht on to Sett mens persons at vizt £12 £16
or £20 It is now concluded to add a fourth prize vizt £8, leaving it for to ye judgm^t of ye Select to Sett mens persons at
wch of those said prizes they judge most fitt.

[I—202]

ffebr 18th 1660.

Whereas Quince Smith had liberty of abode in this Town
for 2 months, his tyme being now expired he was by the Select men this day warned to depart the Towne:

John Keepe desiringe entertaynm^t in this Towne as an
Inhabitant his desires were granted by the Select men, y^e
day above said:

March 13th 1660.

There is by ye Select men granted to John Lambe ffoure
acres of land lyinge by & adjoyninge to the west end of his
lott in chickuppe playne on the West side of ye great River
the breadth thereof to be according to the breadth of his lott
there & Soe to runn west till his ffoure acres are made up:

Also y^{rs} grannted to John Lambe a certayne parcell of
meddow lying on the brook where Thomas Day & Thomas
Noble have Some grannted them: wch grannt is to be to the
number of ffoure acres if it be there & to lye Southward of

the meddow grannted to Thomas Day There were 2 acres
more granted Jn° Lamb in yᵉ Same place.

There is granted to Benjamin Cooley & Thomas Gilbert 6
acres a peece of the wett meddow & low land on the back
side & towards the lower end of yᵉ Long meddow if soe
much be there undisposed of:

[I—203]

There is granted to Nathaneell Ely a peece of meddow on
a gutter or little brook to 3 or 4 acres lying about a mile
from the long medow: provided this peece of meddow be not
form'ly grannted to any other: this meddow lyes by the path
to Moheage:

There is granted also to Nathaneell Ely 10 acr of meddow
lyinge on fresh water brook if soe much be there still undisposed of:

There is granted to John Keep ffive acres of meddow on
fresh water brook provided all former grants of meddow
there be first made good:

There is granted to Thomas Bancroft Abell Wright John
Lumbard & Richard Sikes a parcel of land lying on yᵉ West
side of yᵉ great River over agt yᵉ Long medow Something
below George Coltons: wᶜʰ Land hereby grannted lyeth between two brooks & is to runn westward fro: yᵉ River to a
hill about 40 rodd westward: Thomas Bancroft to lye next
to the Southermost brook Abel Wright next towards the
North John Lumbard next him & Rich Sikes next him: they
ffoure sharring there equally in threescore Acres of land if
there be Soe much there or if there be not Soe much they are
to divide the peece equally amongst them lyinge as is above
exp'ssed:

[I—204]

There is grannted to Nathaneell Pritchard certayne parsells of meddow lying by his meddow on Cow Seek brook
being in all the parcells about an acre: this upon measure
proves two acres wᶜʰ are granted him.

There is granted to John Bagg a parcell of land conteyning Six acres lying at the Reare of yᵉ 2d divission lotts neere

the cold Spring: A lott late of Symon Sackett lyinge on the South of it: & a lott of Obadiah Miller on ye West & ye Comons on the North: Also y^rs granted him a little narrow valley at ye north end of his lott for his more convenent passage fro: his lott.

There is granted to Obadiah Miller Six acres of land lying west on ye west side of the lott above said John Bagg:

There is granted to John Lumbard a parcell of meddow conteyning about an acre lyinge on Cow Seek above John Harmans meddow if it be there to be had:

There is granted to Henry Burt a parcell of Swamp land lying between the brook & his wett meddow Lot on ye back side of ye Long meddow.

There is grannted to William Morgan a parcell of land lyinge at ye higher end of ye playne over End brook between Miles.Morgans lott & ye great River: he is to have three acres of it bee there.—Will Morgan this land he surrendered to ye Town upon an after grant.

There is granted to Robert Ashly Six acres of meddow on the back side of Chickuppe Playne w^thin 2 or 3 miles of ye great River where he can find soe much undisposed of.

[I—205]

Also thereabout in the woods is grannted to Griffith Jones ffoure acres of meddow if he can find Soe much undisposed of.

Also there is granted to Richard Exell 3 or 4 acres in those quarters if he can find Soe much undisposed of.

There is granted to Thomas Merick ten acres of upland on Agawam River joyninge to his three corner meddow: wch land is to lye 30 rod in breadth by his medow & Soe to runn into ye woods to make up his ten acres.

There is also granted to Thomas Merrick a little parcell of meddow above the falls in ye East branch of y^c mill River beinge about an acr.

Also y^rs grannted to him that peece of ye Swamp y^t lyes between Agawam Riv^r & his own land & the brook y^t comes out ye middle meddow:

Also y^{rs} grannted to Benjamin Cooley thirty acres on ye East side of ye Swamp over ag^t his house at ye Long meddow wch Land lyes betweene two dingles & to runn from ye brow of ye hill backward into ye woods Eastward till 30 acres be made up.

Also y^{rs} granted to Thomas Gilbert tweelve acres on the North Side of Benjamin Cooleys grannt above said extending to another dingle Northward.

Theres liberty grannted to Charles fferry to build on Widdow Harmans wood lott wch he Sayth he hath bought.

[I—206]

There is grannted to Robert Ashley liberty to build on his land towards ye round hill:

Theres grannted to Thomas Day & Thomas Noble those little Spangs or peeces of meddow y^t lye adjoyning to y^r meddows lately grannted them behind Chickkuppe playne:

Theres granted to Elizur Holyoke twenty acres of upland adjoyning to his house meddow.

Theres granted to Thomas Bancroft about an acre of land more or less at the end of his wod lott to the top of ye hill by the pyne playne.

Theres granted to Samuell Chapin a parcell of land at Worronoco beinge between Twenty & Thirty acres lyinge on the East side of ye Second Brook y^t is on this side of Thomas Coopers farme there: & is to be bounded by the hills on the North & ye River on the South: provided those lands shall be confirmed by ye Co^{r}te to belong to this Town & y^t he purchase the said peece of land of ye Indians: & he is not to hinder passage thorow it to those other lands beyond it.

There is granted to Thomas Cooper Twenty acres of upland & Swamp over Agawam River vizt from the West side of Thomas Stebbins his meddow: begining at ye foot path y^t goes from John Leonards towards Wind Sor on the South part of the great hill & Soe to runn in length ffoure Score rod Westward. Also there is granted to him a little peece of meddow land on the west side of the Swamp wch bounds Jno Leonards land bought of [I—207] Thomas Merick:

Also y^{rs} grannted to him a parcell of land for a way up the great hill from the outside of his owne little meddow aforesaid.

Also there is granted to Rowland Thomas 24 acres of land lying on the west side of ye great River about halfe a mile below the highest falls in ye great River y^r wch land lyes by ye great River. Provided he pay for ye purchase thereof as ye Select men shall lott ye price & provided that the Corte confirme it to be wthin the bounds of this Towne: And he is to pay ye measurer for measuring it.

There is also granted to Samuell Terry Two little peeces of land above the brook at the head of chickuppe plaine on the West side of the great River wch parcells of land conteyne Seaven Acres more or less: (See below)—Memorandum that the above mentioned grant of land to Samuell Terry is upon condition that he doe quitt & release all or any right wch he p^{r}tends to have in any land which lyes toward the lower end of the said Chickuppe playne wch land he pleaded to have been granted to him by the Plantation:

There is granted to William Brooks a parcell of upland at the higher end of chickuppe playne on ye West Side of ye great River: on ye back side of the playne being the low land under ye hills & is to run from the brook on ye North to ye lotts on the South: about ffourteen or fifteen acres.

[I—208]

There is granted to Jonathan Burt a parcell of wett meddow lying on Cow Seek brook between Nath Pritchards meddow and ye meddow of Lawrence Bliss wch parcell of meddow contayne two acres more or less:

August 12th 1661.

At a Town meeting m^r John Pynchon was chosen for ye Commissioner to joyn wth ye Select men in making the Countrey rate & to doe therein as the Law enjoynes.

Jan: 3d 1661.

At a meeting of the Proprietors of the land on ye West Side of the great River:

It was agreed by the Proprietors of the land from the upper side of Abell Wrights lott to the Lower end of ye neck
to runn a fence from Agawam River to the great River for
the securing of that feild: the fence to be a good sufficient
fence of posts & rails, & this fence to be up & finisht by the
middle of Aprill next: hereto agreed the Major part of the
Proprietors of those lotts: vizt Samll Marshfeild, Nath: Ely,
Rich Sikes, Jonath Burt, Lawrence Bliss, Abell Wright,
Charles fferry, Nath Pritchard, Anthony Dorchester, John
Lumbard, Widdow Bliss, John Matthews:

And on the same day it was by vote concluded & agreed
by the Proprieto^{r}s of the land from that feild to the higher
end of ye 2d Divission & between [I—209] the said two Rivers to sett up a sufficient fence according to Order, from y^e
great River to Agawam River: the fence to be sett up by the
last of May next: and who soe shall be wanting in setting up
his proportion of fence by y^t tyme he is to make at the flatts
over Agawam River soe many rods of sufficient fence as
he is defective in: this as a penalty fr his neglect: & yet also
if he shal not sett up his proportion of fences as above said
w^{th}in a week after the last of May next he is to double that
proporton of fence on ye flatts: that is he is to doe twice soe
much fencing on ye flatts as is wanting in his proportion of
fencing between ye said two Rivers, in way of penalty for his
neglect.

And John Dumbleton & Thomas Miller were appoynted
to measure the length of ye ground between ye two Riv^{r}s
where the fence must run: & to cast up & tell every man what
their proportion of fence is: As also to appoynt where such
as are defective shall doe their fences on the flatts: as also to
see y^t all the fence be sufficiently done: And every man is to
sett up his fence, according as he dwells: they y^t live lowest
in ye Town, to begin first next the great River & Soe all y^t
live on this side are to take y^r proportons successively: &
then John Scott & Soe all upward to fall in according to y^r
Order of dwellinge.

[1—210]

At a Meeting of the Select men Jan. 9th 1661.

It is by them Ordered that the high way by Goodman Cooleys lott at the higher end of the Long Meddow shal be ffoure rodd broad from the top of the banke by the great River.

Also it is ordered that the high way to the Round hill shal be Six rod broad at the South end of y^t hill: that is to say Six rod broad from the top of ye bank or upland by the Hassoky meddow to ye end of the Vpland lotts: And the Westerly range of ye Said high way is to runn uppon a straight Course from ye Round hill to ye North end of the ditch fence of those lotts wch were Thomas Dayes.

Samuell Marshfeild propounding to & desiringe of the Select men for a confirmation of his deed of Mortgage from the Indians of theire lands wch deed ye Indians granted him for his security of certayn debts y^t the Indians owe him: The Select men doe approve of Samuell Marshfeilds deed to all intents & purposes in ye law in such case:

Theere is granted to m^r Hollyoke thatt small parsell off vacant land which Lyeth betwixt the small parsell off meddow which he bought off Thomas day Lyinge att the South end off 3 corner meddow what vacantt land Lyeth betweene thatt & the river off the upland lotts against the Same is granted to m^r Hollyoke.

[I—211 Blank]

[I—212]

At a Gen^{r}ll Town meeting ffebr: 4th 1661, being the first Tuesday in ffeb^r: the day Ordered for ye Gen^{r}ll towne meetinge every yeere.

Mr John Pynchon was chose Moderator for y^t meetinge & for all Town meetings if he be p^{r}sent for ye yeare ensueing:

Capt. Pynchon & Nathaneel Ely are chosen a Comittee to examine the acc^o of ye Select men y^t now expire. And The Select men y^t were chosen for the yeere ensueing were:

Capt John Pynchon, Nathaneell Ely Elizur Holyoke

George Colton & Miles Morgan who are to order the prudentiall affaires of ye Town:

Elizur Holyoke is chosen Town Clarke or Recorder for the yeere ensueing.

Capt. Pynchon is chosen Treasurer for ye Town for ye yeere ensuinge.

Lawrence Bliss Constable being desired to stand in his office till next August consented thereunto at w^t tyme he is to be dismissed of his office: And then another Constable is to be chosen for ye yeare ffollowing from that tyme, And so yearly at ye tyme of choosing ye Comiss for Court. And Benjamin Parsons is chosen Constable for this yeere from this 4th of ffeb^r 1661. And it is voted & concluded y^t theire shall always be two Constables in ye Town. One chosen every halfe yeere at the tymes above mentioned. And Benjamin Parsons took ye Constables oath at this gen^rll meetinge.

Samuell Marshfeild & Jonathan Burt are chosen Survey-^ors of ye high wayes of ye Town & p^rcinct y^r of:

[I—213]

Samuell Marshfeild & Jonathan Burt are also chosen Measurers of land for the yeer ensueinge.

John Dumbleton is chosen for a Surveyo^r of the high wayes to joyn wth ye two former.

Certayn proprietors of lotts in ye wett meddow on this side ye Round hill desiring that the Town lotts wth theire lotts may be Soe altered or remooved for ye Townes & y^r own convenience, that their lands may lye together: & that the Town lotts there in ye meddow may also lye together: Ensigne Cooper Deacon Chapin & Miles Morgan were chosen a Comittee to veiw those lands & make report to ye Town what they judge Convenient to be done therein for ye Town:

The Select men chosen for this yeere have the Same power conferred upon them as the Select men of the last yeere had wch was the same as was granted in ffeb^r 1659:

The Town by vote concluded that the Select men y^t went out of their places this 4th of ffeb^r 1661 shal notwith Standing ye expiration of y^t Office, make a rate for defraying such charges or debts, as are due fro: ye Town to this tyme: & y^t they shall gather it in & deliver their acc^o. to ye Select men chosen this day for ye yeere ensueing: And it was further voted that the said rate now to be made by the form^r Select men for charges already due Shal be made according to the acc^o of the last yeere prizing Stock & State for ye Ministers rate:

See ye next leafe for more Town Acts of this day vizt: ffeb^r 4, 1661.

[I—214]

At a meetinge of ye Select men, ffeb^r: 7th 1661.

Consideration beinge had in ye first place about the rate for m^r Glover:

In order thereunto there were chosen for the prizinge of the liveing Stock of the Plantation: Ensigne Cooper John Dumbleton & Tho: Gilbert.

William Brookes having felld a parcell of trees for fencinge stuffe (last winter) betweene the two brookes on this side Chicuppe playn, by reason of his weakness at the begininge of winter, he could not work them out, whereby the tymber is forfeited: It is ordered that such of ye trees as noe other man hath bestowed work on shall remayne firm to ye said William Brookes for two monthes from this tyme after wch Space of tyme it shal be lawfull for any man to take them in case he cleare them not away:

There is granted to Rice Bedortha Miles Morgan & Francis Pepper to each of them Six acres of land in y^t playne on this side Chickuppe playne: these lands are grannted for house lotts: also they are grannted upon Condition y^t the said Parsons build & dwell there or if they or eyther of them shall sell or any ways dispose of their lotts they shall not soe dispose of them but to such as will dwell there.

[I—215]

ffebr: 4th 1661.

And it is also Ordered & concluded that hereafter from yeare to yeare, the Selectmen shall cleare their accounts to ye Town uppon the Genll Town meetinge in ffebruary: And before they shall be accounted discharged of their trust, they shall soe performed such workes as for the Towne they have taken in hand though their yeere be expired: & y^t they shall take care to satisfy & pay such Debts as are due from ye Town to particular persons wch debts they are to discharge by making a Town rate for y^t purpose if they have not otherwise of ye Townes estate in y^r hands to doe it: And therefore they are also to gather in such debts as are due to ye Town & to be paid wthin y^r yeare:

And it was further voted & concluded that their shall be but one prizing yeerely of Stock & estate for making of all Town rates: That prizing in ffebr or March yeerly for makinge ye Ministers rate by, shall stand for those Select men to make the Town rate by, wch is to be made wth their yeere:

And it was further agreed y^t the way wch the Town the last yeere concluded of for making of rates, the Same shal be attended by the Select men this yeere & for future till ye Towne doe alter it.

[I—216]

At a meetinge of the Select men ffebr. 19th 1661.

vizt Capt Pynchon, Nathaneell Ely, George Colton, Miles Morgan & Elizur Holyoke.

Liberty is granted to Abell Wright to build on his land bought of Wm Branch on ye West Side of ye great River.

Likewise to Henry Chapin liberty is granted to build on his land on ye South Side of Chickuppe River.

There is liberty likewise grannted to Miles Morgan to build on his lott between ye two brookes below Chickuppe playne on ye west side of ye great River.

There is grannted to Sergeant Stebbin a parcell of land of Six acres over the pond on the back side of the long meddow wch land is to joyne to ye Southward of the meddow y^t was Samll Wrights, between the hills & the pond: if there be Soe much there undisposed of.

There is grannted to Robert Ashley a house lott of ffive acres between ye two brookes below Chickippe playne on ye West side of the great River provided that he build & dwell there, or that he dispose not of the lott but to such as shall build & dwell there:

There is granted to Thomas Miller two & twenty acres of land over Agawam River above the 2d brook that is above Goodm: Leonards: also Eight acres more in the same place: this 8 acres is granted on condition that he resigne into the Towns hand his lott in yᵉ playne that is above 2d brooke:

[I—217]

ffebr. 19, 1661.

There is grannted to Griffith Jones Twenty acres of land if he like to take soe much over Agawam River neere the land of Thomas Miller last mentioned this land lyes up the River fro: Tho: Millers land.

There is granted to John Dumbleton Richard Exell John Scott & Jnᵒ Henryson wᵗ land is between Agawam River & the 3d division & their lotts by yᵉ Cold Springe & the fence yᵗ is to be sett up from yᵉ great River to Agawam River. Jnᵒ Dumbleton & Richard Exell are to have three acres a peece to the others two acres apeece: Obadiah Millers lott neere yᵉ Cold Spring being the uttermost bounds Eastward of these grannts. John Dumbleton is towards yᵉ great River John Scot next him John Henryson next him Rich Exell next by Agawam River only high ways are to be allowed through these lands as need shall herein require in the judgmᵗ of yᵉ Select men.

There is granted to Charles fferry Six acres of land in yᵉ dingle called Tho: Thomsons dingle at the reere of Benjamin Parsons & Widdy Bliss their wood lotts:

There is granted to Goodman Colton along the Strappet of upland between the two ponds on yᵉ backside of the long meddow, lying on the West side of his own wett meddow there. Also there is granted him an acre & halfe or two acres of wett meddow lying over the pond at the Long Meddow, over the knap of the hill, that is by his own wett meddow, & it is to lye by Long meddow brook side.

There is grannted to William Morgan a house lott of ffoure acres, between yᵉ two brookes below Chickuppe playn

on ye west side of ye great River: provided he build & dwell on the lott, or that he dispose not of it but to such as shall build & dwell upon it.   Also theres grannted him 20 acres of land fro: ye River to the Hill. uppon this grant Wm Morgan surrendered his land in the playn above end brooke:
[I—218]

ffeb. 19th.   Rice Bedortha & Thomas Miller are appoynted to be veiwers of the fences for the higher end of ye Town from the meting house & over ye River: And Jno Clark & Samll Ely for ye Lower end of the Town & down to ye Long meddow:

Ensigne Cooper & John Dumbleton are appoynted to lay out the high ways from ye 2d division Lotts to Chickuppe playne according to their discretion they are to doe it for place where & for the breadth thereof: Also a high way thorow ye playne for convenency of ye Proprietors of the lotts in y^t playne: also they are to examine whether any high ways on that side ye River are p^rjudiced by fencing or plowing or otherwise: And they are to make return of their work to the Select men vizt of the wayes they lay out & how much they app^rhend any way is prejudiced as afore said:

It is Ordered that the high way from ye Town bridge by Thomas Bancrafts to Goodman Cooleys lott at the higher end of the Long meddow shall be ffoure rod in breadth: And the way is to lye where carts doe usually go: only it is to turne to ye right hand on this side the first bridge & Soe y^r is to be made a bridge ov^r that gutter to make ye way more Straight & to Save charge of repayring those bad places where ye way has usually been:

Also the high way from ye long meddow gate to ye lower end of ye Long Meddow shall lye where carts doe usually goe & is to be 4 rod in breadth from ye gate till it turne from ye River in to ye lotts & thence to the bridge running the way mens lotts it is to be two rodd in breadth: this way is apoynted to be there on Condition that any supposed grannt of a way all along by the River side shall be voyd: And every man is to have the priviledge of the herbage of the high way agaynst his lotts.

[I—219]

ffebr. 19th 1661. Benjamin Cooley & Benjamin Parsons are chosen to veiw & lay out a high way where they judge most convenient for a passage from ye Mucksy meddow bridge at ye long meddow to ye woods on the backside of the said Long medow: And they are to lay out ye way a sufficient breadth & to stake it out on both sides. Also they are to consider where George Colton may have convenient passage to his lott on ye back side of the pond & to Stake it out for him.

There is granted to Cap. Pynchon Robert Ashley & George Colton that share of upland & meddow at Worronoco that was form^rly grannted to Jonathan & John Gilbert who forfeited their grannt of the Islands: these lands thus grannted are all the low lands between ye River & the hills on ye Northeasterly side of woronock River. And this grannt is upon condition that those lands be confirmed to ye Town by the Genll Corte: & that the Grantees doe buy out the Indians right in the said lands here granted:

There is granted to Rice Bedortha a wood lott of ffoure acres adjoyninge to ye west side of his house lott grannted him between ye two brooks below Chickuppe playne: this being in leiw of a wood lott wch he challenges on this East side of ye great River.

It being necessary that tymber for Coopery ware be secured till it be Seasoned & dry: It is therefore Ordered that what tymber John Matthews shall provide for drying such tymber as aforesaid shal be allowed to lye in ye woods halfe a yeere longer before it is forfeited than other tymber may:

[I—220]

At a Town Meeting ffebr. 26, 1661

Vpon conference & Serious consultation, the Town by vote concluded it convenient & necessary that there should be all due consideration, concerning Settling the Townes in this Western part of the Collony into the forme of a County: In Order whereunto Capt Pynchon Leiut Holyoke & Ensigne Cooper..............

[I—221]

ffebr: 26, 1661.   At the same Town Meeting consideration being had of making more roome in the meeting house for better convency of peoples sittinge: It was voted & concluded y^t a gallery should be made in ye chamber & that therefore the middle row of boards & justs are to be taken up & Seates made on both sides wth as much conveniency as may be wch is left to ye Select men & for an increase of Seates on the South side of ye house the South doores are to be stopt up & two Seates made there for ye women.

At a meeting of ye Select men ffebr: 26: 1661 in ye Afternoone vizt Capt Pynchon George Colton Nath Ely Miles Morgan Elizur Holyoke

There is granted to Rich Sikes a house lott of 6 acrs between ye two brookes below Chickuppe playne, to lye next upper brooke together with a wood lott of 6 acres more these grannts being on condition y^t Rich Sikes doe build & dwell there or y^t he dispose not of ye land but to such as shall build & dwell upon it.

Also there is grannted him 60 acres of land in Chickuppe playne next above Willm Morgan & ye brooke

Next above Rich Sikes theres granted to Joseph Crowfoote 30 acrs fro: ye River to ye hill, if it be there to be had vizt between Rich Sikes & ye brooke:

There is granted to Edward ffoster a house lott of 4 acres between ye two brookes below Chickuppe playne on Condition y^t he build & dwell there or y^t he dispose not ye lott but to such as shall build and dwell there.

[I—222]

At a meeting of the Select men: March 12th 1661-1662 vitz of Capt John Pynchon. Nathaneell Ely George Colton Miles Morgan and Elizur Holyoke.

Whereas William Morgan had a lott of 4 acres grannted to him between ye two brookes below Chickupe playne on the West side of ye great River. This lott being laid out both inconveniently & contrary to ye intent of ye Select men in ye said grannt They do further Order that Wiliam Morgans lott of 4 acres shall ly in length from the Northward to ye Southward as the other lotts there laid out doe lye wch ffoure acres is to ly next to ffrancis Peppers lott & to range at the Northerly end of ye lott wth ye other lotts in y^t little plaine: & is to be 16 rod broad at that end next the brooke & Soe broad at ye River as to make up the 4 acres: & the Southerly end of this lott is to ly off from ye brook as ye other lotts doe y^t y^r may be a way to ye next lott.

There is granted to Richard Sikes the rest of ye land between William Morgans lott & ye River to runn fro: ye brook to ye Reer of William Morgans lott.

Also y^{rs} grannted to Rich: Sikes about an acre & 1-2 more or les being a little peece of lowland on the South side of ye first brook between the hil & ye brook provided ye high way be not p^{r}judiced by it: Also there is grannted to Rich Sikes five acres of land by the brook at the South end of Chickuppe playn the end of this 5 acres is to butt on the way by Edward ffosters land in the bottom & is to be about 10 rod broad: These grants are on condition that he build & dwel on one of ye lotts or y^t he dispose not of the land but to such as shall dwell on ye lott.

Theres grannted of the Swamp land over Agawam River over ag^t the Indian ffort to Lawrence Bliss 7 acres to Elizur Holyoke 3 acre [I—223] to Richard Sikes flour acres & to Miles Morgan 3 acres: provided there be soe much und'sposed of otherwise they are to abate according to each mans proportion: Lawrence Bliss his share to lye first next to Tho: Bancrofts land: Elizur Holyoke in ye 2d place Rich Sikes 3d Miles Morgan 4th: this grannt Lawrence Bliss is partly in-reference to a grant to him Dec: 1659.

What land remaynes in ye higher end of Chickuppe playn on ye west of ye great River above former grants is granted to Abell Wright & James Taylor provided it exceeds not 50 acres: This grant to Abell Wright is on condition he resign up his lot over the great River ag^t the long meddow, vizt his 15 acres there: wch if he doe that 15 acres is granted to John Clarke.

In these lotts at the higher end of Chickuppe playn high wayes are reserved wch are to be laid out for tyme & place as need shall require in the judgm^t of ye Select men:

It is ordered that there shall be a high way laid out to ye house of Correction y^t is to be built ov^r ye Meddow: & from thence to ye lott that is next to Tho: Thomsons Dingle: And Capt Pynchon & Nathaneell Ely are appointed to lay out the said way, for place & breadth as they shall See cause.

There is granted to Symon Bemon 6 acres of land at Skip-muck for house lott neere his own land in ye neck provided it be soe laid out as in the judgm^t of the Select men it doe not prejudice the laying out of other lotts in those lands there-abouts.

[I—224]

[In the handwriting of John Pynchon.]

June 4th 1662.

At a Towne Meeting Purposely to Settle Some things about ye Mill.

It is agreed that Mr Holyoke or his assignes shall well Grind wheat Corne of this Towne of Springfeild shall be brought to his Mill, & thereby furnish ye Towne with Good meale for Ten yeares: except Something extraordinary doe Intervene to hinder, as fire or floods or extreme drought that makes water to faile thereby when as ye defect is not by reson of ye Banks or ditches being faulty, or the like & in case People are damadge to get meale from other Places by reson of this Mill being defective he ye s^d Mr Holyoke to allow for it: In consideration whereoff ye Towne doth ingage to allow ye s^d Mr Holyoke ye twelveth part of whatever Corne shall be ground at ye s^d Mill for ye terme of Ten yeares as afores^d:

And heretoe Mr Holyoke did Ingage himself in ye Towne meeting viz to pforme what in this agreem^t concernes him-selfe his heires or assignes: And ye Towne did also by a full

& cleare vote declare theire asent to what in this agreem^t
Concernes themselves: Moreover ye Towne ordered this
Agreem^t to be thus entered in ye Towne book [I—225] And
that Mr Holyoke should set his hand to it, thereby ingage-
ing himselfe & his heires: And ye Towne Deputed Mr. John
Pynchon Geo: Colton: Robert Ashly Miles Morgan & Sam
Marshfeild to set theire hands to it in ye behalfe of ye Towne,
& theire hands being to it this Ingagem^t is firme to all intents
& constructions in Law. According hereunto ye aforementioned psons have hereunto Set theire hands this 4th day of
June 1662.

Elizur Holyoke

John Pynchon
Georg coulton
Robert Ashly, his Marke   In behalfe of ye Towne.
Miles Morgan, his Marke.
Samuell Marshfeild.

The Towne ordered & appointed Benjamen Parsons, Sam
Marshfeild & Robert Ashly the Sealer, to make a Tole dish
true & exact to ye twelfth p^t of ye bushell, & to Seale it wth y^e
Towne seale.

[I—226]

[In the handwriting of Elizur Holyoke.]

June 4th 1662

Thomas Mascall of Windsor being by the Commissioners
of this Town admitted into this Collony, is by the Select men
admitted to be an Inhabitant of this Town.

[In the handwriting of John Holyoke.]

August 14th 1662:

At a Towne meeting warned by ye Constable according to
law: Deacon Samuell Chapin was chosen for ye Commission-
er to Joyne wth ye Select men in making ye Countrey Rate,
& to doe therein as ye Law Injoynes.

The Towne having ordered that at this meting in August
yearly they would choose a Constable for ye yeare ensueing:
Did accordingly pceed to choise. And choose   Ensigne
Tho: Cooper Constable for ye yeare Coming:

In refference to ye order of ye Gen Cort last May That the Inhabitants of these Townes on Quinectticot should pay theire Corne to ye Countrey Rates not as ye Court sets ye price yearely but at such price as it passes among themselves The Towne conceiving it more hard for us than for other Townes in ye Collony, & not to be according to Law, voted to send a petition to ye next Gen Court for easing our Paym^t & y^t it may be according to Law: & Mr Holyoke is appointed to draw it up:

[I—227]

[In the handwriting of Elizur Holyoke.]

At a meeting of the Select Jan: 6th 1662

There was granted to Hugh Dudley a parcell of land contayning Six acres lying between the gen^rll fence y^t runs fro: the great River to Agawam River, & ye lott of Obadiah Miller y^t lyes neere the cold Springe provided y^r be Soe much land there undisposed of.

There is grannted to Benjamin Parsons one acre more or less of wett meddow joyninge to Jonathan Burts meddow on the brook called Small brook over ye mill River: this acr lyes up ward fro: Jonathan Burts medow the peece being granted him.

Theres granted to Benjamin Parsons 4 acres of the wett meddow on ye back Side of ye Long meddow joyning to Capt Pynchons meddow wch he bought of Alexander Edwards: this 4 acres runs to the hill on ye East to ye upland on ye west & is said to be form^rly grannted to the said Benjamin Parsons

Theres grannted to John Keepe ffoure acres of wett meddow on ye back side of ye Long meddow if there be Soe much there undisposed of by former grannts vizt to Goodman Cooley

Theres grannted to Peter Swink, Capt Pynchons Servant y^t vacant land y^t lyes between the gen^rll fence y^t runs from ye great River to Agawam River & Goodm: Muns lott Southward: this lott is to run 80 rod westward fro: the high way by ye River: & is granted on condition y^t he live till his tyme be expired & that he Settle his abode there vizt on ye Said lott:

[I—228]

Jan. 6 1662 Agreed wth Goodman Lamb to Ground Sill m^r Glovers barne: at 6d p foote: & for studd work 2d p foote: the Southerly grreat doore place is to be made up wth a wall, only a doore is to be sett up wide enough for 2 oxen to goe out: also he is to doe all the tymber work for closing ye walls & about the chamber floores till all be sett in good repaire wth ye great doores on ye East Side for wch he is to be paid 2s 4d p day for his own work he is also to clap board the ground Sills to keep y^m fro: ye weather: This work is to be done by the first of Aprill next if the frost shall not hinder.

Att a meting of ye Select men Jan. 9th 1662. The Select men haveing agreed wth Goodman Buell to sett up a Gallery in ye meetinge house: Capt Pynchon ingageth to defray all the charge that concerns ye work: To answer wch charge The Select men doe Order y^t Captayn Pynchon shal be paid by Such as shal be Seated there vizt 4s a pson wch is to be paid by those wch shal be Seated there wth in two yeares: Such as shall not within two yeares pay for their Seates together wth such as shall after two ycares be Seated there, shall pay twelve pence a peece each person for ye 3d yeare & for every yeare after eight pence a yeere by each person unless they shall buy their Seates of him at four shillings 6d per Seate for ye third yeare & five shillings p Seate for ye fourth yeere or any yeere after.

[I—229]

There is granted to Goodman Colton & Goodman Cooley thirty acres of land to each person between the brooks called fresh water brook & grape brook high ways to be reserved as the Select men shall appoynt: this grannt is on Condition that they or theirs build & Settle thereupon w^thin five yeeres.

And Capt Pynchon hath thirty acres of land grannted him on the South side of ffresh water brook by the brook: & he is to have the priviledge of ye said brook from ye great River to ye high way not p^{r}judicinge the high way: this grannt is on Condition y^t he build a Saw Mill here or wthin five yeeres fro: the date next before written:

There is liberty grannted to Nathaneell Burt to sett his fence on ye top of ye hill y^t is on the east of his meddow wch lyes on ye back side of ye Long Meddow: & ye land y^t he Soe takes in wth his Meddow is grannted to him for his property:

Theres grannted to Charles fferry three acres more adjoyning to his Six acres on ye dingle called Thomsons Dingle:

There is grannted to William Warrener, Thomas Noble Thomas Day Samuell Terry & Abell Wright Six acres a peece above ye fence that runs fro: the great River to Agawam River, leaving a high way of eight rod broad between ye great River & the lotts: There is also a high way to be laid out here the Select men think fitt to pass to ye Comon on ye Reere of the Said lotts: their lotts also are to run 80 rod fro: ye high way by ye great River. William Warreners lott to lye first towards ye generall fence ye rest are to lye as themselves shall agree: this grant is on condition y^t they or theirs build & settle there wthin five yeeres.

[I—230]

At a meeting of ye Select men Jan 30 1662. There is grannted to James Taylor an allotm^t of Six acres next adjoyning to ye northerly side of those lotts before mentioned abutting on ye high way by the great River & run back westward 80 rods provided he build & settle thereupon wthin five yeeres from this tyme:

There is also grannted to John Lamb an allotm^t of Six acres on ye South side of the great hill byond the lotts formerly granted: wch lott is to be 12 rod broad & to ly a little way upon ye side of ye hill: This grannt is on Condition y^t he build & Settle there upon wthin five yeares from this tyme according ye grannts above mentioned: This lott of John Lambs was allowed to Wm Hunter (as afores^d) to settle & Build on, who accordingly built & settled there wthin ye tyme afore mentioned, & so ye grant stands good & firme to ye s^d Wm Hunter & his forever.

[I—231]

At the Generall Towne Meeting ffebr 3d 1662 being the first Tuesday in y^t month ye day appoynted & Ordered for ye Genll meetinge of the Inhabitants for choyce of Select men & other officers

Capt Pynchon was chosen moderator for this meetinge & for all Towne meetings this yeere ensueing if he be p^rsent there at.

And the said Capt Pynchon, together wth Benjamin Cooley Robert Ashley Ensigne Cooper & Samuell Marshfeild were chosen for ye Select men for ye yeere ensueinge who have power to order the Prudentiall affaires of ye Town.

And Miles Morgan is chosen Constable to ye Towne for ye yeere ensueing & took his oath accordingly

And Elizur Holyoke is chosen Town Clarke or Recorder for ye yeere ensueinge.

Also Ensigne Cooper is chosen to be Clark of ye Writts who is to be p^rsented to ye next County Corte for y^r approbation.

And Lawrence Blis & John Lamb were chosen Surveyors for ye high ways for ye yeere ensueinge

And Samuell Marshfeild & Jonathan Burt are chosen & ordered to continue in y^r office of Measurers of land for ye Town this yeere ensuing.

[I—232]

At the Same Gen^ll Town meeting ffebr 3 (62) It is ordered & voted in reference to Ordinary Town meetings there shal be three days warninge thereof given to all the Inhabitants or proprietors of land in the Town that is to say the day of warning to be accounted for one & the day of appearance for another. And that men may not faile of haveing warning of Town meetings, Hugh Dudley being willinge is appoynted to give men warning thereof, by leaving word at mens houses or places of usual abode & if they are not at home he is to leave word for y^m at the next neighbo^rs: And for his paynes he is to have 3s a tyme for every meeting soe warned. And that Town meeting warned by ye Constable in August yeerely shal be accounted a **Legall Town meeting** for any Town affaires provided there are One & Twenty of yᵉ Inhabitants present: And for yᵉ Generall Town meeting in ffebruary yeerely men are not to expect any warninge.

There is by yᵉ plantation grannted to John Riley a house lott adjoyning to yᵉ South side of John Lambs house lott lying on yᵉ west of yᵉ great River by the great hill yᵗ is by the way to the playn called Chickuppe playne: this lott thus granntted on Condition yᵗ he build & Settle yʳ upon wᵗʰin five yeeres from this tyme:

And adjoyning to his lott Southerly there is granted to William Brookes a house lott of Six acres: 12 rod broad & fronting on yᵉ highway by yᵉ River & on yᵉ Same Condition as the last afore mentioned.

[I—233]

[In the handwriting of John Pynchon.]

At a meeting of yᵉ Select men J Pynchon: Tho Cooper: Robt Ashley Benja Cooly & Sam Marshfeild ffebr 23d 1662 The Constable being pʳsent Sam Marshfeild was chosen sealer for weights & measures for This Towne, for yᵉ pʳsent & till another shall be chosen & sworne: & Ensigne Cooper is appointed to prsent him to next County Court that he may be sworne according to Law:

[In the handwriting of Elizur Holyoke.]

At yᵉ same meeting of the Select men: William Hunter was admitted an Inhabitant of this Town and John Riley & John Henrison doe bynd themselves their executors & administrators to yᵉ Town Treasurer & Select men or eyther of them, in a bond of Thirty pounds, to secure the Town from the said William Hunter or any of his family. Witness their Hands this 23d of ffebʳ 1662-63.

The mark of   The mark of
John Henrison   John Riley

Witness to this engagemᵗ
    from John Riley & John Henri-
    son are Elizur Holyoke Recoʳdʳ
        Joseph Pynchon

[In the handwriting of John Pynchon.]

By ye Select men: ffeb^r 1662. p^rsent: J Pynchon: Tho Cooper Benja Cooly Robert Ashly Sam Marshfeild:

Anthony Dorchester: Jonath Burt & John Clark, are chosen prizers to prize ye Living Stock of ye Plantation for making ye Rates of the Towne, the yeere ensueing. ye estimates whereoff they are speedyly to bring in to ye Select men.

Nath Pritchard & Antho Dorchester are chosen Veiwers for all ye fences fro: ye meeting howse downe to ye Lower end of the Long meddow. And Wm Warrinar & John Riley are chosen Veiwers fro: ye meeting howse upward & over ye River:

[I—234]

May 11th 1663. At a Town meeting it was by the Inhabitants voted & concluded that whereas the Select men have formerly had power to make grannts of lands in the Plantation, Henceforward & till the Town shall otherwise Order it the lands of the Plantation shal be disposed of these Seven men hereafter mentioned vizt Capt Pynchon: Ens: Cooper: Benjamin Cooley: George Colton Rowland Thomas Miles Morgan & Elizur Holyoke & for ye p^rsent.

In reference to a form^r Order concerning Inmates it was now further Ordered that if any person shall entertayn any Inmate or Inmates after they have been in the Town one month w^thout consent of ye Select men they that soe entertayne them shall be liable to forfeit to ye Town 20s for ye first default & 20s p month for soe longe as they shall entertayne them: & besides if they shal neede releefe in the tyme of their abode in the Plantation then he or they that entertayne them shall be liable to be rated by the Select men for the releefe & mayntenance of such persons accordinge to ye judgm^t & discretion of ye Select men.

[I—235]

[In the handwriting of Elizur Holyoke.]

May ye 11th 1663. At a meetinge of the Comittee chosen by the Town for the distribution of the lands of the Plantation vizt both the lands at Worronoco & other lands belonging to ye Plantation: They granted as followeth:

Imprimis Thomas Miller desireinge that he may have in full possession that wett meddow over the great River at the backward end of the 2d devision wch meddow he hath the propriety only of mowinge & feeding but not to fence it from his neighbo^rs use: There is now grannted to him that soe much of the meddow as is on the Southward Side of the Comon fence wch runs from ye great River shal be his absolutely provided he relinquish his right in the rest of ye Meddow y^t is w^thout that fence by virtue of his form^r grannt:

There is grannted to Tho Noble & Abell Wright five acres apeece of Meddow lying in a wett meddow beyond ye Mill River about 3 qrters of a mile Southward of Thomas Bancrofts:

[I—236]

May 11th 1663. Also there is granted to Lawrence Bliss Six acres of Meddow wch was form^rly grannted to Deacon Wright: this meddow is in y^t meddow comonly called Watchuett:

Likewise to Richard Sikes Samuell Bliss & Edward ffoster there is grannted to each of them ffoure acres in ye Same wett meddow.

Also there is granted to Samuell Bewell of Windsor thirty acres of land at Worronoco wch land is to ly next beyond Ens: Coopers land there: & is to extend from ye River Southward to ye Brooke Northward: also theres grannted him ffoure or five acres of the wett meddow over that brook if it be there to be had:

The rest of the land y^t lyes between Samuell Bewells 30 acres & the hill Westerly is grannted to Tho: Day: this peece of land also is to extend fro: ye River South^rly to ye Hill North^rly:

These grants of land at Worronoco are uppon Condition that the Granntees doe build & Settle themselves & their famlyes there w^thin three yeere & continue uppon it foure yeere longer:

And whereas it is said that mr Whittinge layes claime to Some Lands at Worronoco, there is granted to ye said m^r Whittinge ffty acres of land there on the South side of the River. This grannt is on Condition [I—237] that m^r Whittinge doe quitt any further claime in any lands there about; alsoe y^t he cleare ye Land by purchase of the Indians of the Indians right, & that he or his doe settle there in five yeere fro: this tyme:

Also there is grannted of the lands at Woronoco on ye South side of the River:

To John Holyoke 50 acres, to Deacon Chapin 30 acres.

To Thomas Stebbins 30 acres, to John Horton 30 acres.

To John Bliss 30 acrs, to Samll Terry 30 acrs.

And to m^r Daniell Clarke of Windsor 40 acrs. This grant to m^r Clarke is on condition that he come & settle there in his own pson w^thin 3 yer from this tyme: & that he purchase his said portion of land of the Indians:

The rest of the grannts vizt to John Holyoke, Deacon Chapin Tho: Stebbin John Horton Samuell Terry & John Bliss are upon condition that they purchase ye land of the Indians w^thin 3 yeare & that it be not intanglem^ts to m^r Whiting or any others & that they goe thither to Inhabit & dwell on ye land for ye space of ffoure yeeres & if they or any of them shall dispose of their said parcell of land w^thin the yeeres premised it shalbe to such as the Selectmen of Springfeild shall approve off.

[I—238]

At a Town Meeting July 23, 1663. The Constable having received a warrant fro: ye Treasurer to assemble ye Inhabitants in the next Month to choose a Commisson^r to Joyn wth ye Select men for making ye Countrey Rate He ppounded it, to choose ye s^d Commission^r at this meetin wch was agreed too: And ye Towne choose Mr Elizur Holyoke for Comission^r to Join wth ye Select men for assessing ye Inhabitants according to Law: this p^rsent yeere:

August 1st 1663 Josias Chapin is by Select men admitted to be an Inhabitant of this Towne: And his father Samuell

Chapin acknowledgeth himselfe bound in a bond of twenty pounds to save the Towne harmless in respect of any charge y^t may accrue to this Towne by reason of his said Son Josias:

August 3 16663 At a meeting of ye Comittee chosen by the Town for the giving out of Lands belonging to ye Plantation:

There is grannted to Josias Chapin above mentioned twenty acres of land: wch land is to lye on the South Side of Rowland Thomas his land vizt in that little playne that is Southward fro: the said Rowlands land & house neere Chickuppe River: & it is to be bounded by the high way Easterly & the great River westerly & the Comons Southerly: & joyning to Rowland Thomas his land Northerly:

[Mistake in paging in original book.—I—241]

ffebr: 8th 1663   At a Meeting of ye Comittee chosen for ye grannting or destributing of lands vizt Deacon Chapin Nathaneell Ely George Colton Benjamin Cooley Rowland Thomas Thomas Miller & Elizur Holyoke:

Richard Sikes desiring Land on Pacowseek brook theres grannted him 30 acres lying downward from Benjamin Cooley: & ye Measurer vizt Nath Ely & Ben: Cooley are appoynted to bound ye land.

Also Severall of the Inhabitants appearing & desiring Some land in a certayne neck of land called by the Indians Ashkanunsuck by the north side of Agawam River neere halfe ye way to Worronoco there was grannted unto these as hereafter followeth: To Thomas Day the number of 20 acres.

To Abell Wright 40 acres: To John Bagg 30 acres.

To John Lamb 20 acres. To Samuell Bliss 40 acres.

To Charles fferry 20 acres.   To Samuell Terry 20 acres: [S. T. Surrendered ffeb. 1 64]

To John Harman 40 acres.   To Samuell Harmon 40 acres.

To Jonathan Taylor 20 acres: All wch said grants of Land in ye said neck of land are on Condition that within three yeeres from ye end of May next they fence ye land & improve one acre for each ten acres Soe grannted. These grannts of land are to altogether in one intire yeere Soe as not to hinder from coming to ye Comons about them: And the Grantees have liberty to fence y^r land Soe as be for their best advantage though the fence take in more yⁿ their grannts. [I—242] And if the Proprietors of that land cannot agree for the Order of the lying of y^r proportions they are to be determined by those who shall have the power of distribution of lands in ye Towne at the tyme when the Grantees shall goe to have their proportions laid out.

Thomas Mirack & David Ashley, Also Ensign Cooper in the behalf & at the request of m^r Timothy Mather of Dorchester desiring Some lands at Worronoco theres grannted to Thomas Mirack 30 acres; to David Ashley 30 acres & to m^r Mather 40 acres there. Those grannts are on the same tearmes & conditions as former grannts there y^t is to say that they purchase (or pay for the purchase of their proportion of) the Land of the Indians with in three yeeres tyme & that it be not und^r intanglements to m^r Whiting or to any other, & that the said Grantees go thither to Inhabitt & dwell ffor ye space of ffoure yeeres: And if they or any of them dispose of any of y^r pportions wth in ye yeeres p^rmised it shalbe to Such as ye Select men of Springfeild shall approve of. Also form^r grannts there are first to take place before these now grannted:

There is granted Thomas Miller 10 acres of land at Paucautuck towards Worronoco to joyne to that w^{en} was Jno Dumbletons Soe to be made up 10 acres on ye East^rly Side of that Brooke: not to hinder high wayes. Also theres grannted the said Thomas Miller [I—243] ffoure acres of land joyning to his form^r grants of thirty acres over Agawam this 4 acrs is to lye by ye River above ye form^r grannts:

Theres grannted to Jeremy Horton and James Warener upon y^r desires liberty to sett their fence where they may for y^r best advantage on the other side of Skipmuck when they fence their land there: And that they shall have the land that shall lye between ye said fence & y^r land in ye Meddow:

Theres grannted to Samuell Ely 3 or 4 acres of Meddow upon ye Long meddow brooke Easterly of the Cart way: lying in severall peeces: if it be there undisposed of.

There's grannted to Rowland Thomas 14 acres of land between his lott at Skipmuck & the hill on ye South East & the Swamp Easterly.

There's grannted John Mattthews 20 acres of land some where on ye plane neere Nath: Pritchards meddow on Pacowseek brooke.

There's grannted to George Colton & Benjamin Cooley 10 acr^s a peece of Meddow in ye woods beyond fresh water brooke East of Pequitt Path: Provided if it prove to be on fresh water brook or brookes or gutters y^t run into y^t brook: then former grannts on y^t brook shall first take place:

There is grannted to Rowland Thomas 6 acres of the low land on hog pen dingle below ye place where the hog pen was:

[I—244]

There is grannted to Goodman Colton 10 acr^s of land adjoyning to ye Norwesterly Side of his land between fresh water brook & grape brook & after that lyes Benjamin Cooleyes 30, & then if there be soe much land between those brookes not p^rjudicinge high wayes theres grannted to Benjamin Cooley & Nathaneell Ely 30 acres apeece: if otherwise yet soe farr as it will reach though less than 30 acres apeece: On the margin is this: "These 3 parcells of land vizt 30 & 30 & 30 acr^s are Ens: Cooleyes."

Theres grannted to John Horton 10 acres of land at Worronoco on the Same tearmes as the grannts on ye form^r leafe. And form^r grants there are first to take place:

Theres grannted to William Branch y^t land y^t lyes between ye side fence of ye playne above end brooke & ye hill by the cartway y^t leades from the Round hill to ye New bridge: the North^rly bounds to be from the higher side of Deacon Chap-

ins Lott in yᵉ playne & Soe wᵗʰ a straight Course to End
brook 10 rod below yᵉ place of yᵉ Old bridge:

Benjamin Parsons desires a little peece of Meddow a little
above the bridge yᵗ is in yᵉ way to yᵉ Swamp called John
Matthewes his Swampe Two acres is grannted him if there
be Soe much there undisposed of:

Theres granted to Abell Wright 4 acrˢ of meddow at those
Meddowes on yᵉ Mill River called the Worlds End in lieu of
yᵗ grant of meddow last yeere wᶜʰ he surrendered to yᵉ Town:

[I—245]

There is grannted to Deacon Chapin the land between his
low land at Worronoco & the top of the hill around the
North & Easterly Sides thereof Provided it be noe pʳjudice
to any wayes yᵗ may be laid out there:

There is grannted to Nathaneell Ely a peece of upland lying by Chickuppe Rivʳ Side a little above Rowland Thomas
his land & it is to be bounded Northʳly by the River from the
first brook above the said Rowland Thomas his land & Soe
downward the River to about yᵉ head of little Iland by yᵉ
Rivʳ Side: the South Easterly bound is yᵉ South Easterly
Side of yᵉ little Swampe: the East bound is yᵉ Side little
brook: twenty acres is here granted yᵉ Said Nath: Ely if it
be there to be had leaving a highway of 8 rod broad between Rowland Thomas his land & this grannt:

Theres grannted to Richard Exell about an acr of meddow
about a quarter of a mile above the block bridge in yᵉ way
to Worronoco.

Theres grannted to William Hunter yᵗ land yᵗ is betweene
his home lott & the top of yᵉ hill Northʳly to yᵉ first dingle
westward:

There's grannted to Henry Chapin an Addition (to his
home lott at Chickuppe) of 7 or 8 acres between the hill
South Easterly & his Lott if it be there to be had: & the high
way between Henry Chapin & Josias Chapins land from
Rowland Thomas his house to yᵉ Townward is to be ten rod
broad:

[I—246]

At a meeting of the Select men ffebr. 22th 1663 vizt Deacon Chapin Nathaneell Ely George Colton Rowland Thomas & Elizur Holyoke

The Select men considering the great damage done to ye glas windowes of ye meeting house by childrenes playing about ye meeting house. They doe Order y^t if any persons children or others Shalbe found playing at any sports about ye meeting whereby ye glass windowes y^r of may be endamaged Such persons shalbe liable to a fine of 12d a peece for each tyme they shalbe found soe playing, wch fine is to be paid w^thin 3 days after such default: & if the Governo^rs of any youth y^t Soe offend shall refuse to pay the said fyne such youths shalbe liable to be whipt by the Constable before 3 or more of ye Select men who shall determine ye number of stripes to be inflicted & if any other person Soe offending shall refuse to pay ye sayd fyne as aforesaid they shalbe liable to ye like punishme^t as aforesaid & all such fynes shall goe one halfe to ye Informrs & the other halfe to ye Select men for the use of ye Town in bearing publik charges.

At a meeting of ye Select men vizt Deacon Chapin Nath Ely George Colton Rowland Thomas & Elizur Holyoke on ye 2d of March being lecture day they chose veiwers of ye fences of ye Plantation: vizt Robert Ashley & Jonathan Burt for the home lotts & Meddowes before ye Town & the 3 Corn^r & the playne above 3 Corn^r Medd: & for the feilds over the River vizt right over & the playne called Chickuppe: John Dumbleton & Thomas Miller: & for the Long Meddow John Keepe & Nath: Burt. All whom are to attend the Order [I—247] of the Towne that concernes such officers as it is extant in ye booke:

Aprill ye 6t 1664. Received of Thomas Noble
     by J: Henrison for rent of ye land at Chick-
     uppe playne 6 bush of wheat laid in m^r Glo- £   s   d
     vers chamb^r......................................01   01   00
Reed of Tho: Noble by J Riley on ye same acc^o
     1 bu. wheat layd also....................00   03   06

Recd of him by his paying M: Morgans w^t was
due fro ye Town 1664.................00 14 00
& w^t was Due Tim: Cooper...............00 07 00
& w^t was Due from ye Town fro: W Warrener..00 04 00
Elizur Holyoke carted fencing Stuffe 1 day for
m^r Glover 00 06 00
ffor wch he accounts himself paid in stopping 5s
6d wch he owed Jno Henryson who was to
pay Soe much for Tho: Noble for rent of
the land at Chickuppe yet it is acc^oted as
Recd of Tho: Noble.
Recd of Tho: Noble 6s for y^t he paid Lawrence
Bliss Soe much for carting Stone for m^r
Glovers barne: 00 06 00
Recd by 1 fox killed by Tho Miller & 1 by Joseph
Warrener turned ov^r to Tho: Noble......00 02 00
Recd by his paying Rowl^d Thomas for ye Town
9s 2d wch was due to said Rowl.........00 09 02
Recd by his paying arest of Anth Dorch Town
rate..............................00 05 05
Recd by his payin Deacon Ch: wch ye Town
owed him.........................02 00 00
Recd by his paying E: Holyoke wch ye Town
owed him for writtinge...............00 16 00
Recd by his paying Ja: Chapin wch ye Towne
owed for 2 foxes.....................00 02 00
Recd by his paying Sam: Bliss for w^t the Town
owed him for 2 voyadges wth his horse....02 02 00
Recd by his paying Ens: Cooper for the Town..00 01 08
[I—248]
May ye 5th 1664. At a meeting of ye Comitttee chosen
for ye granting out of lands vizt Deacon Chapin, Nathaneell
Ely, George Coulton, Benjamin Coooley, Rowland Thomas,
Thomas Miller & Elizur Holyoke
There was granted to Richard Sikes Richard Exell John
Scott & John Riley ffoure acres of meddow to each of them
lying neere the great pond on ye back side Chickuppe playne

on ye West side of ye Great River. this grant is on Condition that they cleare ye purchase suitable to such proportion of land: the Measurer is to begin at the head of ye Meddow by the Pond & Soe to take it as it comes:

Theres granted to Samuell Marshfeild twenty acres of land on ye South Side of Agawam River joyning to Southside of Ensigne Coopers Land on the hill by ye Meddow & to run equall in length Eastward & Westward wth Ens: Coopers land Provided it doe not Hinder Ens: Cooper of a convenient way to his meddow that lyes Windsor ward:

Theres grannted to Griffith Jones ffoure acres of meddow about halfe a mile neerer Agawam River then the grannts above s^d to Rich Sikes Rich Exell & ye west & on like Condition he is to choose wch end of ye parcell to begin at:

[I—249]

Also theres grannted to Obadiah Miller ffoure acres of low lands Northwest^{rl}y from the logg bridge as it is called in ye way to Worronoco about halfe a mile above ye bridge; where he shall chuse it being to be in one peece:

Whereas Abell Wright had a grant of 17 acres of land at Chickuppe playne: wch was measured & recorded to him yet upon 2d measuring he was cutt off fro: having any there Therefore there is granted to him ye like quantity in any place where he can fynd it within ye bounds of the Town provided it be not in a place y^t may much hind^r ye pasturing of ye Townes Cattell

There was granted to Joseph Crowfoote foure acres of Medd neere ye great pond on ye back side of Chickuppe playn on the west Side of the great Riv^r if there be so much to be found after form^r grants:

June 1664 At a meeting of ye Comittee chosen by the Towne for distribution of lands vizt George Colton Benjamin Cooley Nathaneell Ely Rowland Thomas Thomas Miller & Eliz Holyoke

There is granted to Abell Wright & Thomas Noble a certayne peece of low land on the North side of Chickuppe River about 1-2 a mile or 3 q^{rs} of a mile below Schonunga-

nuck also a little Strappett of land neere it up the River: to
each of them [I—250] a like quantity: Provided their high
way to it, be where the Select men shal apppoynt. This
grant to Abell he requested & accepts in leiu of a former
grant of 17 acres of land at Chickuppe playne on ye West
side of ye great River, mentioned in ye former page. And it
is wth his consent y^t Thomas Noble is sharer wth him in this
peece of land:

Theres granted to Charles fferry 3 acrs of land joyning to
his Six acres in the swampe called Thomsons Dingle. Also
theres granted to Charles fferry Six acres of meddow if he
can fynd Soe much undisposed of on ye East^rly branch of y^e
Mill River above ye Sixteene acres.

Also theres grannted to Nathaneell Ely five acres of upland at Skipmuck wch is to lye next to Jeremy Hortons house
lott not p^rjudicing high wayes to be laid out by ye Select
men This lott thus granted is to be twelve rodd in breadth
from East^rly to West^rly:

There is also granted to Thomas Miller five acres of Vpland at the Meddows called Non Such on ye West Side of y^e
great River.

Also theres granted to Ensigne Cooper Eight or ten acres
of land upon ye hill Norwest^rly from his cellar over Agawam
River not p^rjudicing any high way that the Select men at any
tyme shal See cause to lay out through ye Said land:

[I—251]

June 1664. Att a meeting of ye Select men: vizt Nathaneell Ely Benjamin Cooley George Colton Rowland Thomas
& Elizur Holyoke:

It beinge observed & complayned of that Persons doe frequently take liberty to ride very swiftly wth y^r horses in y^e
Streetes to ye endangering of children & others: It is
Therefore Ordered that if any pson be observed to Run his
horse or to ride faster than an ordinary galloping in y^e
Streetes of this Towne except upon such urgent occasions as
shall by ye Select men be Judged warrentable soe to doe, he
shall be liable to a fyne of 3s 4d to be paid one shilling to

the Inform^r & the Rest to ye Towne: This Order not to extend to Troopers in ye Tymes of their exercise.

[I—252]

Decemb^r ye 8th 1664

At a Meeting of the Comittee for grannting of lands wth in this Township: vizt George Colton Benj Cooley, Nathaneell Ely, Rowland Thomas, and Thomas Miller & Elizur Holyoke:

The said Comittee considering that there are diverse Persons in this Town who have but little land for their improovmt who desire some land below the brook called ffresh water brook, & that there are div^rse young Persons in the Town for whom their Parents doe desire some land there also, And weighing this that the Gen^ll Co^rte hath apoynted & Ordered y^t the bounds of this Towne on the East side of ye great River towards Windsor shall extend as farr as the place where m^r Pynchon had a warehouse and Twenty poles lower: The said Comitttee also considering that fro the said brook to ye foot of ye falls in ye Great River doth conteyne such a portion of land as may be by good improovmt suffice for a small village. The said Comittee thought meet to declare And therefore doe now declare that the said lands vizt the said brook to ye foote of ye falls & 20 poles lower (according to ye Gen^ll Cortes grannt) shall be & is by them now grannted partly for lotts & partly for comonage for ye use & behoofe of such as shal transplant themselves thither & there dwell. Also the said Comittee doe further declare & Order that the said lands shalbe accounted as a part of the [I—253] Towne of Springfeild, & that such as shal remove thither & there Inhabit shalbe Ordered by the Towne of Springfeild except the Gen^ll Co^rte shall other wise dispose or till this Town shall see cause to sett them at liberty to order their own affaires, it being the desire of this Towne & of this Comittee to further Plantation work w^t may be:

And in reference to what is above specifyed the said Comittee have proceeded to ye grannting of sundry parcells of land for allottmts to sundry psons that desire land there for

their use: Which grannts of land there are on condition &
on ye tearmes hereafter mentioned, that is to say, That noe
Proprietor of land there shall sell or pass away such land or
any part thereof to any stranger except a Comittee y^t shalbe
chosen by this Towne to Order their affairs shall first ap-
proove of such stranger that shall appeare to purchase such
portion of land: Nor shal any Proprietor of land there, sell
his land there or any part thereof, to any person that hath
land now granted there, that soe noe person may ingross
more then One share of land there: Also All those Persons
to whom lands are now grannted as are hereafter mentioned
shall gett their lotts measured by the last of March next.
Their lotts are to run two hundred rod Eastward from the
high way, & Soe to lye Side by Side downward towards y^e
next brooke: The grantees being to cast Lotts for the Order how their lotts shall lye:

The Grannts follow:

[I—254]

Decemb^r 64. Vpon the request of Anthony Dorchester
there is granted to his own & to his Wives Sons:

To John Dorchester thirty acres.

To James Dorchester thirty acres.

To John Harman thirty acres.

To Samuell Harman thirty acres.

To Joseph Harman thirty acres.

[Note.—On the margin against the above is] "These 5
psons doe relinquish their right in this land resigning it up
again into ye hands of ye Towne Jan^r 1665."

To Charles fferry five & twenty acres.

To Jonathan Burt five & twenty acres.

To John Lumbard five & twenty acres.

[Note.—On the margin against Burt and Lumbard is]
"These 2 psons resigne up their grants Jan^r 1665."

To Thomas Bancroft thirty acres.

To Benjamin Parsons, fforty acres.—resigned for land at
Skeepmuck.

To Richard Sikes twenty acres—This he hath resigned up again Jan^r 1665.

To John Stewart ffive & twenty acres.

To Samuell Bliss Senr ffive & thirty acres.

To Reice Bedortha thirty acres.   resigned into ye Townes hand May 1672.

To Samuell Bliss Juno^r twenty acres on condition that his Mother or Some other satisfy all mann^r of charges y^t may come on the land before he or any other improve it.

To Obadiah Cooley ffive & thirty acres his ffather engaging to Satisfy charges y^t shall come on the land before it be improoved:

[I—255]

To Isaak Colton ffive & thirty acres his father engaging to satisfy charges y^t shal come on ye land til it be improoved:

To Samuell Stebbins thirty acres his father engaging to Satisfy such charges as shall come on the Land till it be improoved.

To Joseph Warrener thirty acres his father engaged to satisfy such charges as shall come on the land til it be improoved.

To Samuell Terry twenty five acres on condition he resign into ye Townes hand his grant at Worronoco:

To Nathaneell Ely thirty acres: Resigned into ye Townes hand Jan 67:

All these are grants of land at ffresh water brooke.

There is granted to Miles Morgan five or Six acres upon hog pen dingle of ye low lands there if he like to take it: being to lye above Rowland Thomas his land there:

Also theres grannted unto him ffour acres of land at the head of ye playn above End brook if there be Soe much there undisposed off.

There is grannted unto Ens: Cooper the North^ly & Westerly Sides of the hill at his farme over Agawam River vizt w^t land is between his own land & John Leonards.

[I—256]

There is also grannted to Richard Exell twelve acres of

land on the brook called block brook on ye way to Worronoco
to lye above the bridge on both sides the brook or how & he
& the Measurer shall determine.

Also there's grannted to Abell Wright Nine acres of land
at Chickuppe River on ye South side thereof in the lower
part of the neck of land below Schenunganuck.

Theres also grannted unto Symon Bemon ffourteene acres
of land joyning to his 6 acr lott at Skipmuck: Provided this
6 acr lott be ordered to lye as the Measurer & Thomas Miller
(Appoynted by the Comittee) shall determine who are to lay
it Soe as y^t other lotts that may be given them be not hindred
of conveniences of water: And the said two men are also to
determine how & where his 14 acr^s shall lye:

Also theres grannted to John Horton 8 acres of land at
Skipmuck, on the back side or South^{r}ly side of Jeremy Hortons & James Warreners land there, & to extend from Nath:
Eleyes land on ye West to ye brooke on ye East. Also 12
acres of land by chickuppe Riv^r at Skipmuck on the South
side of the River above the Vpper Wading place: beginning
at ye lower end of that little playne there:

Rowland Thomas haveing had sundry grannts of land w^{ch}
are not measured & recorded according [I—257] the Ord^r
of ye Towne whereby he is lyable to a fyne of the forfeiture
of his land whether he shall chuse, he chusing rather the
latter desires that the said lands vizt 14 acr at Skipmuck 6
acr at hog pen dingle & 24 acr at ye higher falls in the great
Riv^r may be confirmed to him: It is grannted to him y^t he
shall have full & cleare right to all ye s^d lands.

George Colton haveing had sundry grannts of land w^{ch}
are not yett measured whereby he is lyable to a fyne or the
forfeiture of his land he chusing ye latter & desiring that
the right & title to ye Said lands may be continued to him:
It is grannted to him y^t he shall have ye full & cleare interest
of ye said lands.

Benjamin Cooley having had sundry grannts of land in
the Town wch are not Measured whereby he is lyable to a
fyne or fynes for the forfeiture of his lands as he shall chuse,

he chusing the latter desires that the right in yᵉ lands may be continued to him: This Comittee doth grannt him the full right & title to all such lands yᵗ were his by grant.

Thomas Miller had sundry grannts of land wᶜʰ are not yet measured whereby he ls lyable to a fyne or fynes of the forfeiture of such lands whether he shall chuse, & he chusing the latter desires the said lands may be confirmed to him: This Comittee doth grannt him the full right & title to all such lands yᵗ were his.

There's granted to Henry Chapin about 16 acres of land on yᵉ West side of yᵉ great Rivʳ, above Sam: Terrys land above Chickuppe playne, Provided he pay the Indian purchase:

[I—258]

There is Grannted unto Samuell Marshfeild Thomas Noble Thomas Miller Elizur Holyoke upon their desires liberty for yᵉ Setting up of a Saw Mill on a brook below Ensigne Coopers farme over Agawam River: also theres grannted them about fforty acres of Land where they shal chuse it neere the place where the Mill shall stand not pʳjudicing any of yᵉ Inhabitants Propriety or the high way: Also theres grannted them thirty acres of Meddow wᵗʰin 2 or 3 mile of yᵉ place where they shall find it most convenient for their use, beginning at one end of the Meddow and Soe proceeding till 30 acres be made up: These grannts are on condition that they cause a saw mill to be sett up in the place above mentioned & sett to work in Sawing by the first day of Aprill wᶜʰ shalbe in yᵉ yeere: 1666. And in case the said Vndertakers when they have sett up such work shall see cause to desert the work wᵗʰin three yeeres from the said tyme, they shal yeeld up the place & lands hereby grannted into the hands of yᵉ Towne or such in the Town as shall carry on yᵉ work, Provided these undʳtakers be paid wᵗ charge they shal be at about the Work: Also they are not to be restrayned of the liberty of the Comons for all sorts of tymber for their use for Sawing or otherwise:

[I—259]

At a Towne Meeting warned by the Select men: Decemb^r 30 1664

It was voted concluded & Ordered that seeing this book wch from the foundation of this Plantation hath been the Towne booke is filled wth writing. And there beinge necessity of another booke for the Entering of Ord^{rs} & grannts of land & other things of Publike concernmt to this Towne & Township: That therefore a certayne Booke wch Capt Pynchon exhibited & p^{r}sented to the Towne for that use (& freely gave) Should hereafter be the Towne booke for ye ends aforesaid:

And Elizur Holyoke is chosen & appoynted to transcribe all the Orders y^t shalbe accounted of force into ye New booke: for wch his paynes he is to be allowed 6d p Order for every Order that he shall therein transcribe.

[L—260]

ffebr 1st 1664. At a Meeting of ye Comitte chosen for the disposing of or grannting out of lands wthin this Township: vizt Deacon Chapin Benjamin Cooley Nathaneell Ely Rowland Thomas, Thomas Miller & Elizur Holyoke

Theres grannted to Jeremy Horton a pcell of meddow on ye head of a Small brooke that is beyond ye head of Skipmuck brook: Eight acres is grannted him if it be there:

There's grannted to William Warren^r y^t pcell of Meddow wch is ag^t his own wett meddow at ye Worlds end provided he come not wthin Ten rod of ye turn of the Riv^r. Also he is to allow a high way thorough it as need shal require: This meddow thus granted lyes by ye River.

Theres grannted to Benjamin Cooley Soe much of the Pond as lyeth ag^t his own land at the higher end of the long meddow: wch grannt is to be bounded by ye brow of the hill over ye Pond.

There's grannted to Elizur Holyoke that p^t of the pond y^t lyes ag^t his own Meddow in the middle Meddow over Agawam River: vizt the whole breadth of ye pond:

Theres granted to Thomas Miller Six acres of land on ye South East^{r}ly side of that little brooke y^t is on this side Plant-

ation brook in ye way to Worronoco: this grannt of land is
to lye by ye brook & the River: & The Measurer is to lay it
out Soe as not to hinder convenient passage to other land
thereabout:

[I—261]

Theres grannted further to Thomas Miller 40 acres of land
at Ashkanunksuck in ye upper p^t of y^t neck of land: This on
Condition that he surrender his form^r grannts of 30 acr & 10
in y^t neck into ye Townes hands: wch he doth now acknowledge a surrender of to ye Towne.

Theres granted to Samuel Terry ffoure acres of wood
land next to ye upper wood lotts over ye Wett meddow:

Theres also granted to Samuell Terry ffoure acres at y^e
Worlds end by Abell Wrights meddow but opposite thereto
vizt on ye South East^{r}ly Side of the North^{r}ly branch of y^e
Mill River: this being grannted him he was willing to surrender his grannt at Ashcanunksuck: And he did surrender
it, wch was accepted:

Theres granted to Wilm Brookes 3 or 4 acres of meddow
at ye North^{r}ly end of ye great pond on ye backside of Chickuppe playne: if Soe much be there after form^r grannts there
about are laid out:

[I—262]

ffebr 6th 1664. At another Meeting of ye Comittee chosen
by ye Towne for disposing & grannting of lands vizt George
Colton Deacon Chapin Benjamin Cooley Nathaneell Ely
Rowland Thomas, Thomas Miller and Elizur Holyoke

Whereas Diverse of ye Inhabitants had grannts of land in
ye neck of land called Achkanunksuck towards Worronoco,
The Grantees concerninge the conditions to those grannts to
be Something hard: This Comittee doe now determine y^t
those Conditions shal be voyd: And y^t Thomas Noble
Thomas Day John Lamb Abell Wright & John Bagg who
first p^{r}sented their desires for land there shalbe first served
who for ye Order of the lying of their lotts are to agree
amongst themselves who also are to take their lotts together:
& the rest are to fall in after y^m, in case there be soe much

land there for them who are to cast lotts for Ord^r how their lands shall lye: After them Obadiah Miller is to have 20 acres & Japhett Chapin 40 acres if there be sufficient for them: & James Taylor 40 acres by Tho: Millers land there:

[I—263]

There's also grannted to Robert Ashley ffoure acres for a wood lot next beyond Samuell Terreyes wood lott mentioned on ye former leafe:

Theres grannted to Jonathan Burt & to John Keepe ffoure acres a peece at ye grape swamp by the Long meddow, only the small lotts ag^t that Swamp are to run thorow the Swampe then the remaynder to ffoure acres a peece is granted to them, if Soe much be there:

There's grannted to Nathaneell Burt ten acr of Wood land at the East end of his meddow y^t is on back side ye Long meddow provided this wood land be soe laid out as not to p^{r}judice any high way y^t may be laid out there: & George Colton & Benjamin Cooley are to goe wth ye Measurer to order in gen^{r}ll where this wood land shal lye. Also theres grannted to Nathaneel Burt a long narrow strappett of Wett meddow y^t lyes along the West side of y^t Swamp wch is by the side or end of his meddow: vizt Soe much of that strappett as lyes over ag^t his own meddow behind it, & between ye Swamp & ye high way: Also theres grannted him soe much of that Swampe as lyes between this starppet of meddow & his other meddow:

[I—264]

Febr. 6, 1664. Theres grannted to John Keep what land lyes at the east end of his own land below George Coltons house pvided he leave a high way by ye pond of 4 rod on firme land at the reere of all his land there.

There's grannted to Elizur Holyoke Senr thirty acres of upland ag^t the house Meddow to joyne to ye South East^{r}ly side of his form^r grannt of twenty acres of upland there. Se a meeting march 13th 1660 61

There's grannted to James Warrener the Iland in Chickuppe River at Skipmuck ag^t ye neck of land y^t is his & Jeremy Hortons.

Theres granted to ye Towne lott at Chickuppe playne on ye West side of the great River what land is ag^t ye said Town lott for Sixty rod to ye woodesward from ye said lott. As also what land is between those two brookes there or the same length of Sixty: Provided this grant is not to be to ye p^{r}judice of former grannts there:

Theres granted to Samuell Ely a little nooke of land about half an acre lying ag^t his own land at long meddow bridge: this nook lyeth ov^r ye brook a little above the bridge. Provided it p^{r}judice not ye high way:

[I—265]

Theres grannted to Rice Bedortha Ten acres of land joyning to his ten acres bought of Anthony Dorchester lying at Chickuppe playne on ye West side of ye great River: And it is to be bounded by the little brook that is a little Northward from his former ten acres, & w^t falls short there of ten acres it is to be made up on ye West^{r}ly side of the 10 acres y^t he bought as above s^d & to run equall in length wth the said ten acres:

Whereas George Colton hath paid many yeeres rates as is paid for meddow between ye hil & the pond at ye Long Meddow to about Eleven acres: & noe grannt can be found, The said Meddow is now confirmed to him:

Theres grannted to Rowland Thomas twenty acres more of land joyning to the upper side of his ffoure & twenty acres at the foot of the fals in ye great River on the West side of ye River:

[I—266]

Here follows an account of Diverse charges made by the Comittee for m^r Glovers house.

Feb: 1681.	£	s	d
To Tho: miricke for Carting clay..........oo		4	6
To Jonathan Bal for raising..............oo		6	0
To Henry Rogers & Jose. Bodurtha raising.oo		4	0

To Jnᵒ Dorchester 2 dayes & Oba: Cooley 1 day at raising ...... oo	6	0
To Hen: Chapin & Eliakim Cooley at raising ...... oo	4	0
To Henry Chapin for mending yᵉ cellar .... oo	2	6
To Jnᵒ Dorchester for worke about the Cellar & Laths ...... oo	11	0
To James Stevenson for work about the Cellar ...... oo	6	0
To David Morgan ...... oo	8	0
To Victory Sikes 71	oo	0
To Samll Bal for building the chimneys 10	10	0
To Tho. Day for carting Clay 01	02	0
To Jnᵒ Lamb for raising ...... oo	2	0
To 5000 of 8d nails 02	10	0
To 5000 of 6d nails 02	2	3
To 8000 of 4d nails 01	16	6
To bringing up the nails & Glass 0	12	0
To 1 bu: of Indian Corne ...... oo	02	0
To Glass for the house fro: Ensigne Cooley .. 02	15	0
To Ens: Cooley for 1-2 bush: wh. meale .... oo	2	0
To 3 day worke of Ensigne Cooley ...... oo	6	0
To Fran: Pepper for Cleansing yᵉ Cellar .... oo	5	0
To Ben. Knowlton & Edwd ffoster for raising ...... oo	4	0
To Tho Miller Jose. Leonard & Geo: Norton for raising ...... oo	6	0
To Incre: Sike for boards ...... oo	14	7
To Jose: Leonard for a Cellar window ...... oo	01	0
To Haw hes for raising ...... oo	02	0
To boardes about the cellar ...... oo	01	6
To serving two attachments ...... oo	06	0
To John Holyoke for hinges & 1 dayes work .oo	03	6
To Deacon Burt fetching corne fro: Dav:- Morgan ...... oo	03	0
To Glasse & lead & nailes 04	06	8

To Victory Sikes for fetching corne fro: the
    Major 00 04 0
To Sam. Bal for Brickes £5 16s. To Jn° Lamb
    for Carting & lime 5s mantletree 6sTo....
    is to Dan: Beamon is 6d...............06 09 6
                       Total is....108 15 0

[1—267]

Here followes an account of Divers Comon Charges for
    Towne, & paid by yᵉ Comittee

	£	s	d
To the major for paymᵗ to Lieut. Smith as messengʳ to Boston	00	10	0
To the major for purchase of Coes Medow	02	00	0
To Sam Harman for killing a wolfe	00	10	0
To Jn° Dorchester for Carying Down yᵉ bel	00	02	0
To formʳ Debts of the Town	06	19	0
To the Major for killing a wolfe	00	10	0
To the Town Debt Febr: 1676:	01	10	0
To the Sexton 1677	02	10	0
To Quuartʳmʳ Colton as Deputy	04	00	0
To Jose: Crowfoot for the mending the pound	00	01	3
To Samll Ely entertaining yᵉ Select men. 1675	00	10	0
To Samll Ely Entertaining 1676	00	04	0
To charges in taking down yᵉ bel	00	02	6
To charges about mʳ Younglove	00	04	0
To entertainmᵗ of the Select men: Dec:24th	00	04	6
To making a drum cord & mending the drum	00	02	6
To entertainmᵗ of Select men Jan: 1677	00	04	0
To making the Rates	01	00	0
To Selectmen & Comissionʳs dinner Aug. 1677	00	03	0
	24	07	01

more to ye majo^r for powd^r p^d by the

Comittee .... .01 07 10

26 04 11

An acount of what is still remaining to ballance the Pay-
ings out of the Comittee for m^r Glovers house & other Town
Charges that the Comitte chosen to ballance those accounts
do find

The layings out for the house & other Towne   det are
£135 oos & is received to satisfy those layings out.

£   s

by a rate of Anno: 1677:   122 10 0
& by a rate An° 1678   06 00 0   130 10
& by David Morgan: 02 00 0

So y^t y^r remaines to ballance the Comitte

Charges as neer as they can find......£4   10s   ood
[I—268 and 269 Blank—I—270]

[In the handwriting of Thomas Cooper.]

The order which parsons were Seated in the meeting house
by the Select men and Deacon Chapin in December 23 1659.
The Selectmen then was as followeth

Robertt Ashley Ben: Cooley Will: Warinar   Jonathan
Burtt Thomas Cooper

Henry Burtt in the little Seate by the Deacons Seate.

1st Seate—Robb: Ashley: Tho: Cooper: Rowld Stebbins:
George Coultton: Benjamin Cooley.

2d Seate—Rich Sikes: Tho: mericke: will: warrinar: Rich:
ffellowes:

3d Seate—Tho: Stebbins: myles morgan: John Harmon:
John Lenard: Ben: mun: Anto: Dorchester

4th Seate—Tho: Gilbertt Jonath Burtt Ben Parsons John
Dumbleton: will Branch Sam: marshfeild

5th Seate—John mathews: Rowld Thomas: Reese Bodor-
tha John clarcke John Lamb: Tho: Day

6th Seate—John Lumbard: Lawrence Bliss: Griffith
Joanes: Tho miller: Nath Pritchett: Rich Exell

7th Seate—Tho Bancroftt: Jonath Taylor: John Stewart John Scott will: Brooks James Osbourn:

[I—271]

8th Seate—Symon Bemon Tho: Noble James warrinar Francis peper Obadiah Miller: Nath Burtt

9th Seate—Abell wright: Hugh Dudley: John Bagg John Sackett David Ashley Sam: Bliss: John Riley

    and for order sake there weer placed in the

10th Seate—Japhat chapin: John Harmon: Sam: Harmon James Taylor John Henrison Edward ffoster peeter swinge the rest of the younger persons that wants yeares are to sitt on the other side of the alley in the Seate next to the stayers.

    [In the handwriting of John Pynchon.]

ffebr. 23 1662.   The order of Seateing psons in yᵉ meeteing howse, as followeth:

By Deacon chapin: & the Select men Tho: Cooper: Robert Ashley Benja Cooly John Pynchon, & Samll Marshfeild.

Goodwife chapin is to sitt in the Seate alonge with Mʳʳs Glover and Mʳʳs Hollyock.

In yᵉ first Seate—Robert Ashley: Benja Cooly: Tho: Cooper George Colton, & Rowld Stebins:

In yᵉ 2d Seate—Nathaneell Ely: Rich Sikes: Tho Mirack & Willᵐ Warrinar:

In yᵉ 3d Seate—Serja: Stebbins: Serja Morgan: Benj Munn: John Leanord: Anth: Dorchester: Sam Marshfeild:

In yᵉ 4th Seate—Benja Parsons: Jonath Burtt: Wᵐ Branch: Reice Bedortha: Jᵒ Dumbleton: Rowld Thomas

In yᵉ 5th Seate—John Mathews: Jᵒ Clarke: John Lamb Sam Bliss: Tho: Miller: Tho: Day:

In yᵉ 6th Seate—John Lumbard Griffith Joanes: N Pritchard: Rich: Exell: Tho Noble: Sam Ely:

In yᵉ 7th Seate—Jonath Taylor: Tho: Bancroft: John Scot Nath Burt: John Stewart: Wᵐ Brookes:

In yᵉ 8th Seate—Jer: Horton: Jᵒ Bag: Jᵒ Riley: Symon Beamon: Abell Wright:

In yᵉ 9th Seate—John Henryson: Sam Terry: Obadiah Miller: Hugh Dudley

In ye 10th Seate—J^o Crowfoote: Edw: ffoster: Charls ffery: James osborne Wm Hunter, Peter Swinck:

In ye forseate, of ye Gallery:

In ye upp^r part above ye Pillars on the North side, Henry Chapin: John Bliss: J^o Keepe:

In ye upp p^t above ye Pillars on the South side, ffraunces Peper James Warrinar: Sam Bliss:

Below ye Pillars on ye North side, Sam Holyoke: David Ashly: Japht Chapin Tim: Cooper Isaack Colton: Obadi Cooly:

On ye South side Below ye Pillars, Tho Cooper Jun: Jos Warrinar: John Leanord: John Harmon Sam Harmon, Increase Sikes: John Dorchester:

In y^t Seate in ye Gallery wch faces ag^t the minister, Ephraim Colton: Eliakim Cooly Jonath Morgan Sam Stebbins: James Dorchester:

In ye Backer Seate of ye Gallery on the North side at the upp end of it, James Taylor: John Horton: Hugh Mackey Wm Morgan:

On ye South side at upp end of ye Backer seate, Jonath Ball Sam Ball: Jos Harmon Nathanell Sikes: Tho: Thomson:

In ye Backer Seate, below the Pillars on the North Side, John Hitchcock J^o Clarke: John Lumbard: Sam Bliss

On th South, Jos: Thomas: Tho: Stebbins. Jos Bedortha:
[I—272]

[In the handwriting of Thomas Cooper.]

Charges layed outt of the towns stock in 16....

To Samuell marshfeild for fencinge..........00 05 00

to John Lambe for fensinge................00 01 06

to Thomas Stebbin for.....................00 01 00

To Rich Siks for Ringinge the bell.........01 06 00

to Griffith Joans.........................00 12 00

paid to goodman Sikes 2 bushell of indian corne

    for Ringinge...........................00 02 06

paid into m^r John pynchon treasurer.........00 03 03

paid goodman Sikes in his Rentt for worke....oo 04 oo
paid goodman Sikes in his Rentt for Ringinge..oo 04 oo
paid to goodman Sikes by the Rentt of the meet-
    inge house chamber for Ringinge........oo 19 06
to Robertt ashley for expenses.............oo 10 oo

              the charges layd outt is..04 08 09
  [I—273]
Receved by Samuell marshfeeld for Rent......o1 16 06
Receved by John dumbleton for Rentt.........oo 07 oo
Receved by Reess Bedortha.................oo 10 oo
Receved of John Stebbins for Rentt of the cham-
ber ....oo 07 06
Receved of good marshfeeld for Rentt........oo 08 oo
Receved in Rentt for this Rentt of the chamber.o1 oo oo
      the some of the Resaites is..........04 09 oo
Such pursons as are indebtted to the Towne in the yeare
               165..
Samuell marshfeeld for the Rentt of Land.....o2 08 oo
John dumbleton indebtted.................oo 03 oo
Richard Sikes ....oo oo oo
    29 octtober 1654 by the Selectmen

    Richard Sikes is to pay for the use of Housinge an Corne
Rooms till the 1st of may next 20s also Richard Sikes is to
pay the same Select men abated upon the Original of shil-
inge and clapbordinge the territts of the meeting house

                    £   s
and soe is ffreed from the clapbordinge........ 3 05 oo
by Richard Sikes in his Journey to the bay....o1 10 oo
also in wheatt............................o1 10 oo
Benjamin mun is to pay for Corne Roome......oo 05 oo
Symon Sackett is to pay for Corne Roome.....oo o1 oo
Griffith Jones to pay for Corne Roome........oo o1 oo
  [I—274]
        January 2th 1644

    It is ordered by yᵉ 5 men chosen by yᵉ towne yᵗ the upper
side of ffrancis Balls Lott shall be Sufficiently fenced by all yᵉ

neighbors y^t are in y^t division, fro: Goodman Pritchards upward, every man bearing a pportionable share in ye fence &
this to be done by the 20th of March next followinge

SECOND VOLUME OF TOWN RECORDS.

[In the handwriting of John Pynchon.]

The second volume of the Town Records opens with the
transactions of the Selectmen relative to highways on the
west side of the. Connecticut, granting the right to make a
landing place at the training field, and concerning street lines
in the town. Several pages have been so badly mutilated as
to make them unintelligible, and for this reason they have
been omitted from this printed volume. The record which
follows is without date and begins on page 3 of the original
book:—

. . . .

Laurence Bliss his fence, fro: James Osborns to Laurence
his woodpile, to be taken in straite wth ye rest of his fence,
wch wil make ye taking in to be about Three foote in the middle:

The fence ag^t old Goodm: Stebbins his howse to be set in
close to his cherry Trees And soe ag^t James Osborns land
there, & ag^t John Clarks all to be taken in & set straite wth it:
And John Clarks fence at ye upper side of his lot to be taken
in so far as to Range straite wth his whitethorne.

. . . .

At Thomas Nobles ye fence to Run close to ye North Corner or side of his howse & that to Range straice wth Goodman Warriners fence:

. . . .

At Mr Glovers Lower Corner, There Deacon Sam Chapin

is to take in his fence even wth it, and to Run straite from thence skewing off to N....at John Stewarts Corner:

. . . .

[II—8]

Some anoyances to ye way we find wch are hereby ordered to be Rectified & speedyly Removed, viz The Brush ag^t Goodm: Stewarts: The wood & other Lumber ag^t Nath Pritchards: The Tymber & Lumber ag^t Antho Dorchesters: This to be done spedyly or else to pay according to Towne order:

All these orders & acts of ye Selectmen aforesd were Published & declared to ye Towne at a meting 2 days after they were made, being a Lecture day:

Memorandum   That the Select men had a meeting ye weeke before this viz on y^e....day of this Instant March. wch day we spent in Considering how to order seatting of psons in ye meeting house, wch worke was this day perfected and is drawne up in a Page dated this day viz: March 13th 1664: & it was Published to Psons How they are to be Seated: ye wch is to be seene on ye afores^d Paper:

[II—9, number defaced]

March ye 20th 1664-65

By ye Select men, George Colton Benj: Cooly Sam Marshfeild Lawrence Bliss John Pynchon.

It is ordered that all psons who have any interest in Generall fences: Shall repaire & sufficiently close theire severall ffences in ye Comon ffeilds by ye last day of this Month of March, & shall carefully attend to keepe y^m in sufficient repaire all the Summer till all ye pprietors agree to lay y^m open, or till ye Select men shall appoint the Laying open of ye s^d feilds:. In wch interim of tyme viz: fro: ye last of March all ye Summer till the Select men (unles by consent of all the pprietors) doe order the opening of the Comon feilds, They are to be kept cleare from Cattle of all sorts, And if any pson shall lay open or let any part of his fence in ye Comon feild be defective, whereby Cattle may p^rjudice ye feilds, unles it be by consent of the whole that have interest in ye feild or by order fro: the Select men: he shall (besides paying all damadge done to any thereby) forfeit five shillings to ye Towne for such defect: only men have Liberty of Baite theire working Cattle on their owne Ground in ye tyme of their working of y^m, pvided they Secure y^m fro: doeing damadge to any pson;

[[II—10, unnumbered]]

It is ordered for ye p^{r}servation of ye feilds fro: the Lower wharfe to the head of the Plaine) That the Gate at the higher wharfe & ye Gate at ye Training place shall be well hung & set in good repaire by the last of March: & shall always be kept Shut till all ye feilds about them are by order broke open: And if any pson shal Throw open or leave open either of the s^d Gates fro: the 1st of Aprill till liberty of laying ye feilds Common such pson shall forfeite five shillings, halfe to the informer & the other halfe to the pprietors towards keeping ye s^d Gates in repaire: And the Proprietors of the s^d feilds are to meete & determine to whom the care of hanging those gates & keeping y^m in repaire fro: tyme to tyme shall belong: & in case of theire not agreeing then ye Select men to order ye same.

ffor ye Direction of such Persons, as are chosen & appointed by ye Select men, for veiwers or overseers of ye Comon & Generall fences belonging to the severall feilds of the Towne: It is ordered That ye psons chosen & appointed for ye service shall on the first day of Aprill next Surveigh all ye Common fences belonging to theire care & circumspection to see whether they be fully closed up & well repaired so as they shall Judge Sufficient to secure the ffeild [8—first numbered page] from hurt by Cattle: And if upon theire veiw they shall find any recall defect & insufficiencys they shall forthwth give notice thereoff to ye owner or owners of the s^d defective fence or fences warning him or y^m to amend ye same wthin 2, 3, 4, or 5 days time as according as ye veiwers shall pitch And if the pty warned shall not have amended his defective fence by ye tyme Limited & y^t to ye satisfaction of the veiwers Hee shall pay a fine of 12d for every defect under a Rod, & for all defects above a Rod 12d a Rod. wch fine shall increase 12d a day for every days neglect of amending any defect. And further ye overseers of fences shall always about ye beginning of July & about the beginning of Septemb^r veiw all ye Generall ffences under their Care to the Intent they may be kept up & in good repaire, & in case of any defect to give spedy Notice thereoff to ye owners who are at such times imediately to rep^r them upon notice thereoff: And if they shall be found unrep'd a day after notice given them of theire defects such pson to pay 12d for the least defect & 12d p rod for all ye Rods defective & to increase 12d p day for every days neglect as afores^d (besides w^t damages may accrew to any pson thereby) And tis further ordered that after ye veiwers giving men Notice of defects in their fences & setting y^m a tyme for amending of them: these s^d veiwers Shall [II—9] w^thin 3 days reveiw such fences to take notice whether ye defects thereoff be sufficiently amended: And at any tymes besides ye aforementioned tymes, ye veiwers observing defects in ye fences under theire charge. or having any information thereoff, they are spedyly to atend ye afore directions that they may be rep'd, And all fines or Penaltys incurred by this order, are one halfe of y^m to goe to ye Towne, ye other halfe to the overseers of the fences who may have warrant fro: the Select men directed to the Constable for Levying thereoff if ye pty upon demand refuse to pay it. And in case any Just Complt: Soe Judged by ye Select men shall be brought ag^t ye over seers or veiwers of fences, for neglecting theire Charge at any tyme, they shall be Lyable to a fine of five shillings for ye use of ye Town & in case of a greater Neglect Ten shillings according as they shall be Judged thereunto by ye Select men for any neglect:

These orders & acts of ye Select men were Published to ye Towne on ye 21th day of March 1664.

There being a Towne meeting warned on ye 11th day of Aprill 1665: severall of ye Inhabitants came not, to answer

to theire Names when called, who are to pay 6d a pce by
Towne order if there excuse were not Sufficient [11—10]
Here follows ye Names of those who not making of sufficient
excuses are lyable to pay 6d a pce, viz:

Henry Chapin: Griffith Joanes Edw: ffoster: Wm Branch
Deacon Chapin Robert Ashly Tho Mirick Anth Dorchester
Jonath Burt Wm Brookes Jos: Crowfoote John Leanord:
Ens: Cooper: Benja Munn John Clarke Nath Burt:

The Towne had all these psons fines: by ye Selectmens
adding them to theire severall Rates in January following as
p ye aco^t the select men gave in the Towne:

June 1st. 1665

At a meeting of ye Selectmen 1665, Geo: Colton Benja
Cooly Sam Marshfeild Lawrence Bliss & John Pynchon.

It is ordered that There be a Pound made on the west side
of ye greate River for ye Impounding of all Cattle y^t doe trespass: this worke to be gon about spedyly: the care whereoff
& the carrying it on to effect is left to John Dumbleton &
Thomas Miller: The Pound to be set about the Hay place:

At this meeting ye veiwers of fences viz John Bag & Rice
Bedortha declare agt John Scots fence over ye grt River being defective 20 Rod togither altogither deficient & 20 defects in other places, having given him warning yet upon a
2d veiw a month after they found ye aforesd defects & a 3d
Tyme found ye defects a fort Night after. This both the
veiwers afirme they being both togither at ye veiw:

The Select men doe Judge That after the first warning to
ye 2d veiw Should be aco^ted but one defect, y^t is to Say for y^e
tyme of it, But the 20 Rod is 20s, & the 20 other [11—11]
defects 20s more: After ye 2d warning when ye veiwers went
the 3d tyme to Se it a fortnight after, Being 12 days & 20
Rod at 12d p Rod, make 20s every day: wch comes to £12
the 12 days, togither wth ye 40s aforesd makes the whole £14
one halfe whereoff ye order gives to the veiwers & the other
halfe to ye Towne.

The Towne did by a cleare vote on a Training day discharge John Scot of this fine, freely releasing it to him so far as was yᵉ Townes due:

The veiwers also declare agᵗ Tho Noble for having 2 Rod defective: But he denying to be his fence, till it be made appeare to belong to him yᵉ Select men cannot Judge him faulty:

John Bag Complaining agᵗ Reice Bedortha his pᵗner for one Rod defective: Reice disowning it to be his fence: The Select men Judge yᵗ yᵉ fence must first be determined his before he can be Concluded defective or Lyabl to yᵉ fine.

Robert & David Asly being defective 4 Rod & one defect more, wᶜʰ yᵉ veiwers warned them to amend & yet on their 2d veiw thereoff doe find it still defective: They are Judged to pay 5s for theire defects according to order: halfe being to yᵉ veiwers: The Townes due is 2s 6d.

The veiwers declared agᵗ Some other psons for defects, but yᵉ psons being absent we could not at this tyme Judge of theire defects.

[II—12]

It is ordered that yᵉ veiwers of fences viz Reice Bedortha & John Bag for manifest neglect of their Charge, in not veiwing fences according to order, shall pay a fine of 10s to yᵉ Towne, that is 5s a peice:

It is ordered yᵗ yᵉ New fence over the River downe to Agawam river be forthwᵗʰ veiwed by yᵉ present veiwers of fences Reice Bedortha & John Bag & in case they find it not sufficient, they are forthwᵗʰ to give yᵉ owners notice warning yᵐ to make it sufficient wᵗʰin 5 days tyme, & when yᵉ tyme is expired then to Reveiw it & such as have not then sufficiently made up theire fence, having againe warneing by yᵉ veiwers, fro: yᵗ tyme to be Lyable to yᵉ fines wᶜʰ by former order is imposed on defective fences: And fro: thence forward this fence to be under yᵉ veiwers Care as other fences are:

And for yᵉ water worke viz the Joining of this fence to yᵗ over Agawam river, the veiwers are to give notice to all yᵉ pprietors that they attend to doe it in season.

July 28th 1665:

At a meeting of yͤ Select men: pʳsent John Pynchon Geo: Colton: Benj Cooly Sam Marshfeild Lawrence Bliss:

Thomas Powell yͤ Cooper was admitted an Inhabitant of this Towne:

Also John Petty of Windsor was at yͤ same tyme alike Admitted to be an Inhabitant of this Towne:

[II—13]

August 28th 1665.

By yͤ Select men, John Pynchon: George Colton: Benja Cooly: Lawr: Bliss & Sam Marshfeild.

It is ordered yͭ yͤ Long meddow feild bee cleared of all Corne, & be at Liberty for Cattle to be put in by those yͭ have an interest therein, on yͤ 29th day of Sept next: It is also ordered yͭ yͤ feilds over the River be cleared of all Corne & at Liberty for Cattle to be put there on yͤ 1st day of October next.

Sept. 27th 1665:

The Select men, John Pynchon George Colton Sam Marshfeild & Lawr Bliss

Vnderstanding that yͤ ffeilds are already as good as cleare of Corne wee Judge meete to allow Liberty for yͤ putting in of Cattle by those yͭ have Interest there, on yͤ 30th day of this Instant September.

Novembr 1665

By John Pynchon: Sam Marshfeild George Colton, Select men

Vnderstanding yͭ yͤ Bridge over yͤ Cawsey agͭ David Ashlys is defective, with some part of yͭ Cawsey, we doe hereby order yͤ Surveighours spedyly to amend & repaire the same:

[II—14]

June 1st 1665

By yͤ Select men, John Pynchon: Benj Cooly: Geo Colton & Sam Marshfeild

This day according to Towne order we Considered about

(making Rates &) takeing a list of ye estate of ye Plantation And for Prising the Living Stock of the Town we choose

> Robert Ashly
> Tho: Noble &
> James Warrinar

who are forth wth to goe about the worke & to bring in ye estate of ye Plantation to us spedyly And for the estimation of Land we considered y^t worke: meeting for y^t end also on ye 9th of January: & Likewise againe on ye 12th day of the same month: & then pfected the valluation of Land, Howsing &c: wch is to be seene in a writing or little longbooke for y^t Purpose dated January 9th 1665.

At this meeting we Judged it needfull to make a rate of £10 for Towne charges wch was raised on ye severall Inhabitants & each mans pportion Published on a Lecture day ye 17th of Jan 65. Every pson being desyred to bring in theire Rate y^t so we might defray & discharge ye Townes debts.

The aco^t of this Rate &c shall be given into the Towne at ye generall meeting next ffeb^r How it is disbursed for the Towne.

[II—15]

At a meeting of ye Comittee (appointed by the Towne) for Granting out of lands of ye Plantation Publike Notice having bin given of theire meting for y^t end, this day being ye 5th of January 1665 viz:

> John Pynchon:
> Natha Ely:
> Geo: Colton
> Rowland Thomas
> Sam Marshfeild

There is Granted to John Baker ye Carpenter eight acres of meddow over Agawam about 3 or foure Miles beyond Ensigne Coopers, upon or about ye North Branch of Stony River (in y^t psell of meddow wch Rowld Thomas guesses to be neere 30 acres) at ye South end of it John Bakers 8 acres of meddow is to lye wch 8 acres is granted him upon Comlition he do Settle in Towne, & continue in Towne five yeares:

[II—16]

There is Likewise Granted to Japhet Chapin: Tim Cooper: David Ashley & James Taylor ye rest of y^t psel of meddow there to be equally devided among y^m foure: And there is further Granted to y^m foure Twenty acrs a peice of upland, neere y^t meddow lying on this side of it neere about a mile to ye Northward of their medow, wch is to be pportioned amongst y^m ekually alike for ye goodnes of the Land.

Also James Taylor in leiw of former Grants wch were made to him, & yet ye land not found there for him, hath 30 acrs & in case it will hold out forty acrs of Land Granted him in a Low Peice of ground or Bottom havinge a brooke run thorow it about halfe a mile on this side Pakatuck: pvided it be noe ways p^rjudiciall to ye High ways:

There is Granted to Lawrence Bliss some smale Nooke & strappets of meddow & swamp, lying in ye Corners of his meddow laid out at Watchuit in case all besides his former Grant there exceed not Three acrs.

Granted to Tho Copley on the west side of ye grt River: A homlot of six acrs on this side of Wm Hunters: And Ten acrs under ye Hill at ye Reare of his Houselot & some distance from the fence. Also Thirty acrs at Ashkanuucksit: These Grants on Condition he settled in Towne five years:

Also there is Granted to Sam Marshfeild Ten acrs of Land under ye hill at ye Reare of the lots by Tho: Copleys.

Symon Beamon moveing that his six acres lot formerly granted him at Skepnuck & his former Grants of fourteene acres there may be laid out togither, his desire is granted him: And ye measurer is to lay it out for his best Conveniency, & upon his desire, There is further Granted him, eight acrs of land there adjoyning to ye former psells & all to be laid out togither by ye measurer, pvided it doe not hinder Rowland Thomas his coming to his land there:

Also there is Granted Symon Beamon five or Sixe acres of meddow over Chikkupy river beyond Jeremy Hortons meddow, ye best meddow he can find neere it on this side of Stony Brooke.

John Bliss hath liberty Granted him for mowing 8 or 10

acrs on fresh water river, where he Mowed last yeare, & this till y^t land shal be further Considered for disposing of it.

[II—17]

Nathanel Burt hath ye Pond ag^t his Two lots in ye Long meddow Granted him & So up to the Brow of the hill, if it be not already Granted him, pvided it be noe wrong to ye Indians & y^t he noe way hinder or molest ye Indians in gathering or coming to their Pease.

John Keepe also hath ye Pond ag^t his lands & so up to ye Brow of the hill Granted him, pvided it be noe wrong to the Indians:

Geo: Colton likewise hath ye Pond ag^t his Land there Granted him upon like Condition:

John Scot hath ye land at the west end of his Twenty acre lot in Chickkuppy plaine wch is betwixt his lot & ye fence Granted to him: viz That land fro: ye end of his lot to the fence:

Granted to Abell Wright a Homlot at Skeepnuck of eight or Ten acrs pvided it be on y^t plaine by James Warrinars land

Granted Tho Noble a lot there eight or Ten acrs on ye Top of ye hill ag^t Abell Wright:

Granted Charles fferry at Skeepnuck Thirty acrs in ye Plaine where he desires it if so much be there in y^t Plaine pvided he doe Build & settle upon it w^thin Three yeares fro: this day or else ye land to returne to ye Towne agayne:

Granted to the Inhabitants at Skeepnuck a highway fro: the Slow beyond ye Swan pond to ye higher wading place in chickkupy River.

[II—18]

There is Granted to Capt John Pynchon that those woodlots wch he bought of Miles Morgan, & Griffith Joanes, Should run in length Eastward, all ye breadth of them, So far further as to Paralell ye Equall & Just Length of his owne wodlot viz So as to be even at ye Eastward end, or further end in the Reare, wth his former Woodlots wch ly on ye South of this Grant:

Geo Colton hath Granted him in ye west meddow below ye Long meddow, that his meddow there may Run to the foote of ye hill, square wth y^t wch was Goodm: Harmons 2 acrs of meddow there:

Rich Exell hath Granted him y^t what land he hath already at Block Brooke shal be made up Thirty acrs there p^t of this is in Satisfaction for Land he hath laid Comon for ye fence to run to Agawa: river & the rest is an addition to his former grant.

Granted Obadiah Miller Twenty acrs of land at Block Bridge next to Rich Exell These Grants no to p^rjudice any Highways.

Joseph Chapin hath Granted him a strappet of meddow on ye mill River about one acre upon a little brooke y^t Runs into Goodm: Warrinars meddow.

[II—19]

ffrancis Pepper hath eight or Ten acres of Land Granted him in ye Plaine above End brooke at East end of Mr Holyoke & y^t wch was Mr Smiths Lot So to run Eastward towards ye hill but not quite to the hill that there may be sufficient walke & Pasadge for Cattle wth some scope for y^m under ye hill.

Sam Marshfeild desiring y^t the Highway over the River on ye Northside of ye Comon fence, may be caryed a little higher y^t So his lot wch he bought of Goodm: Warinar may ly next to ye fence, his desire is Granted pvided Charles ferry (whose lot is next) be contented to ly next ye highway & pvided also it may be noe detriment to ye highway to be caryed thus higher:

Thus far by ye Comittee for Granting out of Land:

30th January 1665.

By the Select men, John Pynchon: Benj Cooly: Geo Colton Sam Marshfeild & Laurence Bliss:

ffor as much as order is beautyfull & especially in ye howse of God, & ye want thereoff is displeasing to God & breeds disturbance among men: And whereas it doth appeare y^t Di-

THE FIRST CENTURY OF SPRINGFIELD.

vers young psons & sometimes others notw^{th}standing
there being called upon' Doe yet neglect to attend unto such
order as is prescribed them, either for theire sitting in y^e
meeting howse, or for their reforming of disorders in &
about ye meeting howse in tyme of Gods Publike worship:
It is Therefore hereby ordered That whosoever of This
Towneship shall not fro: tyme to tyme in respect of their Sitting in ye meeting howse submit y^mselves to the ordering of
ye Select men & Deacon^s, or such as are Impowered to Seate
& order psons in the meeting howse: All such Persons as
shall refuse or neglect to attend unto order as aforesd Shall
forfeit as is hereafter exp^rssed viz Hee or shee that shall not
take his or her Seate ordered y^m fro: Tyme to tyme. But
shall on ye days or tymes of Gods Publike worship Goe into
& abide in any other seate appointed for some other: Such
disorderly pson or psons for ye first offence shall forfeite
Three shillings four pence to ye Towne Treasury, wch shall be
exacted by warant fro: ye Selectmen directed to the Constable to Levy the same: And if afterwards Hee or shee shall
psist in such disorder, they shall pay Sixe shillings eight
pence as a fine to ye Towne, to be exacted as aforesd, & if a
3d tyme they shall still psist in such obstinacy, such pson to
pay Ten shillings to ye Towne: to be exacted as aforesd: And
if afterwards they shall still psist in such obstinacy, ye Select
men are hereby ordered to complaine of such psons to y^e
magistrate or County Court to deale wth them as they shall
Judge meete.

And whereas the Seate wch was made by ye Towne as a
Common Towne Charge (formerly called the Guard Seate)
is now appointed by the Selectmen [II—21] who pply have
ye disposing of that Seate for Boys to sit in: & ye Selectmen
having declared that the smaler Boys should sit there, that
they may be more in sight of the Congregation & having
warned all men out of ye s^d Seate both maryed & other
Growne psons, some whereoff doe still continue to sit there,
& seeme as if they did it wth a high hand: It is therefore
hereby ordered That noe Person of this Township above y^e

age of 14 or 15 yeares shall sit in ye Seate aforesd formerly
called the Guard Seate, unless he be ordered to sit there to
looke to ye Boys And if any pson hence forward shall p^rsume
there to sit Contrary to this order he shal for ye first offence
therein (after Publication hereoff) forfeite & pay to the
Towne Treasury Sixe shiling eight pence & if afterward y^e
same pson shall offend therein' Hee shall for ye 2d offence
pay to ye Towne Thirteene shiling foure pence, & for ye 3d
offence Twenty shillings: All the aforesd penaltys by warrant
under the hands of the Select men to be Levyed by ye Constable for the Townes use: And if after this any shall still psist
in obstinacy or contemptuous neglect of attending this order: The Select men are ordered to complaine of such Contemptuous pson to ye Magistrate or County [II—22] Court:
And it is further ordered That if such young men shall offend
ag^t this order as have noe estate, or are under theire Parents
or Governours Charge: If theire Parents or Governours shall
refuse to pay ye aforesd Penaltys' the Select men shall P^rsent
such psons to ye Magistrate to deale wth y^m as he shall Judge
meete.

This order was Published on a lecture day ye 31th of January 1665:

ffebr 1st 1665.

At a meeting of ye Comittee for Granting out of ye Lands
belonging to the Plantation: Publike notice having bin given
of this meeting: Also Geo: Colton: Benja Cooly & Lawrence
Bliss who belong to this Comittee all of y^m had notice of it:
& though absent, yet having had notice of ye Towne order
Impowers foure to act in such case. Present John Pynchon,
Nathan: Ely Rowland Thomas Sam: Marshfeild.

Robert Ashly desiring y^t ye foure acre woodlot wch was
Granted him, next beyond Sam: Terrys woodlot last febr
1664 may have an addition to it So as that he may have eight
or Ten acres there in all: his desire is Granted viz That his
woodlot there, shall be in al Eight acres to run in length 80
rod as ye other woodlots doe, & so to be ye more in breath:
only there is first to be Three rod broad left Common for a

highway, to be disposed for Passadge to ye woods either there, or Lower as shal be most convenient.

[II—23]

Benja Parsons hath ye Pond ag^t his land in ye Long meddow Granted him pvided it wrong not the Indians nor hinder theire taking of theire Pease:

John Bliss hath ye Pond ag^t his land in Long medow granted him pvided ye Indians be not wronged of theire Pease:

There is Granted to Benja Parsons & Tho Powel, between y^m forty acres of upland at Chikkuppy River side, below Schonunganick.—Resigned up.

There is Granted to John Horton eight acres of land on ye backside of his Homlot at Skeepnuck—resigned to ye Town before R Thomas & Jeremy Horton.

There is Granted to John Dumbleton Thirty acres of upland & swamp at Pacatuck on ye North side of Tho Millers: adjoining to it & to Mr Pynchons land wch he ye s^d Mr Pynchon bought of John Dumbleton formerly:

Also there is granted him over ye grt River Ten acrs of Land under the hills wthout the Common fence by Sam Marshfeild & Tho Copleys Land there.

There is Granted to Sam Marshfeild an Addition of sixe acres of land to ye Ten acrs Granted him last meeting under ye hills at the Reare of howse lotts wth out the Common fence: in all he is to have Sixteene acrs there togither (by Tho Copley) this is on Condition, he resigne up his sixe acre lot wch he bought of Wm Warinar wthout ye Common ffence, which Sixe acrs he doth hereby resigne up to the Towne to ly Common, & it hereby [II—24] ordered to ly Comon: wch sixe acrs being 12 Rod togither wth ye 8 rod formerly appropriated for ye high way there, makes in all 20 Rod: wch 20 rod broad wthout ye Common fence is to ly Comon for a Highway & for feed of Cattle: And so to Run thorow along by ye fence side to & over ye Muxy medow or further to be continued all ye way 20 Rod broad:

And it is ordered & Granted y^t there shal be 20 rod broad ly Comon at ye Reare of those howse lots w^{th}out ye fence: Ag^t y^m all: 20 rod wide to be left for a highway & for feed of Cattle:

Ther are certaine smale psells of meddow lying upon a Dingle on ye South side of ye Bay path ag^t the foure mile Pond, in al about Three acres wch are Granted to him y^t keepes ye ordinary in This Towne fro: tyme to tyme & at p^rsent Nathanell Ely who now keepes ye ordinary hath Liberty to Mow & make use of it till [II—25] ye Select men shall appoint it to any other y^t may keepe ye ordinary it being to belong to such as shall be by the Towne or Select men allowed & chosen to y^t worke.

There is a certaine psell of meddow beyond ye swan Pond on a Gutter wch ye Bay Path goes over, wch runs into ye swamp we go by: The which medow being narrow & So running up ye Gutter & to ye Northward of the Bay path & runs Compassing about: may Possibly be one acre & halfe or Two acres All wch is Granted to belong to ye Howse of Correction & to be Impved by ye Master of the s^d howse from tyme to tyme:

There is also Granted Ten acres of medow to belong to ye howse of Correction upon a Gutter or swamp wch runs into the mill River about 7 Miles of a little beyond where ye Tar kilne was by Bay path, to ye eastward of y^t Tar Kill This 10 acrs to ly at ye Lower end of it & to belong to the howse of correction, & be Impved by him y^t shall be master of y^e [II—26] s^d howse: for wch in after tyme there shal be allowed to ye Towne by the County or Master of ye s^d howse as the Select men of this Town shall condition for:

There is Granted Tho Noble a little beyond Skeepnuck 4 or 5 acres of medow where Symon Beamon hath medow, if so much there to be had.

There is also Granted to Tho Powell sixe acres of medow thereabouts if he can find it on this side of stony Brooke. Provided he continue five yeeres in Towne:

There is Granted to Joseph Crowfoote below Agawam River four acres of meddow in lew of a former grant (wch he hath not) where Joseph Leanord shal have some:

Joseph Leanord hath eight acrs of meddow granted him pvided it be there to be had besides Joseph Crowfoots afore-sd Also forty acrs of upland adjoyning to it.

There is granted to Joseph Crowfoote upon ye Brooke y^t Runs by Reice Bedorthas celar about ye head of y^t Brooke Two acrs of Low ground or meddow.

There is granted to Sam Terry Thirty acres of upland all along by his meddow (beyond Chickkuppy Plaine on ye west side of ye grt River) only a Highway is reserved all along thorow this Peice of Land wch this Grant is noe ways to p^rju-dice:

[II—27]

There is Granted Reice Bedortha & Edw ffoster each of y^m 30 acrs of Land in ye next hollow beyond Block bridge to ly a little on this side of ye Timber swamp below ye swamp to the Southward of it pvided noe highway be p^rjudiced by this Grant:

Serjant Stebbins hath ye swamp betwixt his meddow over Agawa: & ye hill, granted to him:

Nathanell Pritchard hath Granted him ye spangs or strap-pets of upland betwixt & about his medow at Pacowsick, to ye quantity of 10 or 12 acres.

Tim Cooper & Japhet Chapin have Granted y^m over Aga-wam River to ye Norwest of the meddow a peice to take it togither at ye Lower end of the meddow.

There is granted to Rowland Thomas by his howse at Chickkupy adjoining to his land, about Three acrs of Land to ye Northeast of his howse & so to Joine to his Broth Hen-ry Chapins land:

[II—28]

Here follows ye Returne of Nath Ely & Rowld Thomas appointed to Lay out a Highway to Chikkuppy river.

We underwrit being apointed & ordered By the Select men in October 1665 to consider of a Common way to & over chickkuppy River, neer Rowland Thomas & to lay it out doe make a returne of what we have done as followeth:

Wee doe Conceive That yᵉ Common way over Chikkup River should goe above the Islands about 20 rod, where the Indians Common wading place was formerly or a little higher, & so fro: thence to run up yᵉ River on this side of yᵉ River about 20 rod or more, And then to turne off in yᵉ vacant ground betwixt Rowland Thomas & Nathanell Elyˢ land, into yᵉ Pine Plain & so to yᵉ Towne. This Highway to be in breadth fro: chikkupy river to yᵉ brow of the Hill, wᶜʰ is about 7 or 8 rod: And where it turnes off fro: yᵉ River there is to be 20 Rod Broad, Given under our hands this 1st of ffebr 1665.

Nathanell Ely:
Rowland Thomas
R. T. his marke.

ffebr yᵉ 5th 1665

The Select men doe accept of this return & order the Highway above sᵈ to be as is there described, & appointed.

[II—29]

[In the handwriting of Elizur Holyoke.]

ffebruary 12th 1665

Att a meeting of the Select men vizt Ens: Cooper Robert Ashley John Dumbleton Benjamin Parsons & Elizur Holyoke.

The said Select men not finding any entry made of yᵉ high way that leades from the Hay place by the great River to Agawam ffalls by John Leonards, They doe order that the said high way shalbe two rod wide from yᵉ said hay place to Agawam ffalls before mentioned & that it shall lye as now it lyes & is used: Only Capt Pynchon is to remove part of his pasture fence to make it range equall wᵗʰ the front of yᵉ 3d division as it was at first layd out.

And further they doe order that there shalbe another common pound made in this Township vizt on yᵉ West side of the great River. Towards wᶜʰ John Dumbleton is to gett the posts & railes vizt 19 posts & 110 rayles: for wᶜʰ he is to be allowed 30s And that yᵉ old pound shalbe repayred:

[II—30]

Att this meeting of the Select men there was chosen for veiwers of fences Nathaneel Pritchard & David Ashley for the homelotts from the Meeting house downwards & the Meddow Lotts below y⁶ Causey & the Long Meddow.

John Scott & Richard Exell for y⁶ ffeild on y⁶ West side of the River & Chickuppe playne on the west side the River.

And Miles Morgan & Japhet Chapin for the house Lotts from y⁶ Meeting house upwards & the 3 corner Meddow & the playn above y⁶ Town from the Causey upwards:

And whereas upon the desires of the Inhabitants on y⁶ west side of the great River the Towne did Order & determine that Lotts fro: Thomas Millers to y⁶ Comon fence shalbe accounted house lotts:

It is now ordered that those lotts shal have a good sufficient fence in y⁶ front of them made by the Proprietors thereof wᶜʰ fence is to be sett up by the tyme limitted in y⁶ Towne Order for other fences.

John Matthews Jeremy Horton John Bagg being absent from y⁶ Genrll Town meeting in this month are according to Order to pay 2s a peece: to be added to yʳ next Town rate.

[11—31]

March 5th 1656.

At a Meeting of the Select Men vizt Ensign Cooper Robt Ashley Benjamin Parsons John Dumbleton & Elizur Holyoke.

Complaint being made that y⁶ ffeild on y⁶ West side of the great River hath not yet been fenced as to Some places & that others are burthened wᵗʰ more fence then their share: It is concluded yᵗ the Proprietors be called together on y⁶ 8th of this Instant to consider wᵗ is to be done in such cases:

It is also ordered yᵗ there shalbe a highway of 8 or 10 rod broad between Henry Chapins lott on this side Chikuppe River & the hill yᵗ is a little Southerly from y⁶ lott. This to run from the high way that leades to Rowland Thomas his house to y⁶ highway that lyeth betweene Nathaneell Elys land & Rowland Thomas his land.

[11—32]

March 5th 1665-6.

At a Meeting of the Comittee impowered for the grannting of lands: vizt Ens: Cooper Robert Ashley Benjamin Parsons John Dumbleton Rowland Thomas: Thomas Miller &
Eli: Holyoke.

There is grannted to John Bliss & Samuell Bliss Senior
Six acres a peece in a Meddow on a brook that runs into
fresh water brook (about a mile & halfe beyond Nathancell
Elyes Meddow) if there be soe much there: Samll Bliss his
share to begin at ye higher end next ye swamp y^t the brook
runs out of

Also to Samll Bliss Junior is granted three acres in ye same
meddow if there be soe much beside the form^r grants there

These grannts are on condition that the Land be undisposed of & y^t it be in ye liberty of ye Town to grant y^m:

Granted to Thomas Cooper Junior Twenty acres of the
high land Southward of ye Meddowes over Agawam River:
between Samll Marshfeilds land & Thomas Merricks land:
It is to lye in a Square peece & not to p^{r}judice any high way
y^t may be laid out thereabout:

[11—33]

Grannted to Griffith Jones ten acres of land Northerly
from ye Comon fence y^t runs from ye great River to Agawam
River, wch is to lye between John Dumbletons Land & the
high way & the hill: Provided soe much be there besides former grannts:

Also theres granted to Tho: Cooper Junior ffive or Six
acres of Meddow on ye most Easterly branch of Stony River
where he can it most convenient being 3 or 4 miles from his
fathers house ov^r Agawam River:

Grannted to Joseph Leonard Twenty acres of land above
the 2d brooke y^t is above his fathers house below Tho: Millers land: Provided he leave 20 rod in breadth between this
grannt & the bank of Agawam River:

Grannted to Rowld Thomas Six or Seaven acres of land
at the Easterly end of Henry Chapins Land on this side

Chickkupe River: being to Joyne to the said Rowlands owne land Northerly & to ye high way Southerly:

Grannted to John Dorchester a little pond contayning 2 or 3 acres more or less by ye way to watchuet Meddowes about 3 mile beyond the Mill River: Provided it p^rjudice noe high way thereabout:

Grannted to Widd Bliss soe much of the pond as is at ye end of her lott in ye Long medow: Provided the Indians be not wronged of their pease:

[II—34]

ffebr: 6th 65.

This Day being the Gene^rll Towne Meeting: It was considered y^t there is great necessity that a thorough be taken for the settlement of a Corne Mill that shalbe serviceable for a more comfortable supply for this town then of late there has been: This Town doth Order & appoynt Capt Pynchon George Colton Benjamin Cooley Ens: Cooper Nathaneell Ely Rowland Thomas & Samuell Marshfeild a Comittee to consider what course they judge best to be taken for ye supply of the Towne: They are to consider whether they judge it best to keepe up this Mill that is in p^rsent being for continuance or whether they judge best to lay this Mill aside & that preparation be made for another Mill in some other place: And the said persons are desired & earnestly intreated by the Town to consider seriously & speedily what they judge behoofefull in ye case: who also have power to call the Towne together as need shall require to declare w^t they apprehend requisite in the case:

ffebr 26th 1665. A towne Meeting being called by ye Comittee above mentioned, they declare their apprehensions y^t they judged it best for the Towne y^t a Mill be built on ye old Mill Streame & not that the Town should have dependance on this Mill y^t is in present being.

[II—35]

Whereupon the case being long debated Capt Pynchon did promise to the Towne y^t Hee will be at £200 charge for ye building of a new mill upon ye old Mill streame neere where yᵉ Old Mill stood: Provided the Towne will disburse wᵗ estate more must be laid out wᶜʰ £200 will not discharge for the effecting such a worke.

But the Plantation being not cheerfull to engage therein tryall was made what would be disbursed by particular persons: And divers psons did thereupon promise to allow Capt Pynchon towards yᵉ worke as followeth

	Shillings
Ens: Cooper	20
Elizur Holyoke	40
Benjamin Parsons	10
Joseph Crowfoote 2 days work	
Serjant Stebbins	20
Willm Branch	20
Jonath Burt	10
Thomas Day	5
Samll Bliss	10
Samll Terry	6
Rowland Thomas	20
John Matthews	20
John Lamb	10
Willm Hunter 3 d. work	
Nath Burt	10
Abell Wright 3 d. work	
Jonath Taylor	6
Thomas Bancroft	6
Miles Morgan	10
George Colton	30
Willm Warriner	10
Charles Ferry 3 day work	
Timothy Cooper 4 day work	
Richard Sikes	10
David Ashley 4 day work	
Encrease Sikes	5
Anthony Dorchester	12
John Dorchester 2 day work	
James Dorchester 2 day work	

John Lumbard 3 day work.............
John Leanord......................12

[II—36]

And further the Towne did vote conclude & agree (neminee contradicente) that the said Capt Pynchon shall have the twelfth part of the bushell of all such corne or grayne as shall ground at his said Mill.

March 8th 1665.

The Proprietors of the ffeild ov^r the great River meeting together to consider about the fencing it, & it being said that some have more fence than their share, Thomas Miller Samuell Marshfeild & Jonathan Taylor are chosen to proportion every mans share of fence warning every proprietors to goe & See their shares giving them notice of the tyme:

Also ye said Proprietors of the said ffeild doe judge & determine y^t the Pond about ye Middle meddow y^t the Swamp beyond Ens: Coopers barne under the hill shalbe accounted a sufficient fence, except it be needfull to fence a little by the Swamp at the end next Ens Coopers barne: And if the said Persons fynd any place a naturall fence in their apprehensions or well neere a good fence, they shall proportion how much any persons shall doe in such places.

[II—37]

At the Town Meeting abovesd ffebr 26, 1665. It was by the Plantation voted & granted that Capt Pynchon shall have 50 acres of Vpland & 30 acres of Meddow where he can fynd soe much undisposed of, Provided that he build a Saw Mill eyther on fresh water brook or on the Old Mill Streame wthin three yeeres from this tyme & that it be ready to be Sett a work wthin y^t tyme: Otherwise this grannt is to be voyd:

At a Meeting of the Select men March 5, 65, being the day that the Comittee mett for grannting of lands the said Select Men did consider of the absence of diverse Persons for ye Town Meeting in ffebr 26, 65 vizt William Brookes, John Bagg, Thomas Miller, Robert Ashley, Samuell Marshfeild, Griffith Jones, Edward ffoster, John Leonard, & Benjamin

Munn, All wch Said Persons are to pay 6d apeece to ye Town wch is to be added to y^r next Town rate:

[II—38]

At a Towne Meeting August 11th 1666. whereas Capt. Pynchon hath had & still hath intentions to sett up a Saw Mill within this Township eyther on ye Old Mill Streame or at fresh water brook: ffor his encouragm^t in the said work & upon condition that the Saw Mill be built on ye Old Mill Streame: To all other former grannts made to ye Said Capt Pynchon in reference to such work, There is further granted unto him by the Plantation the free use of ye said Streame for ye Said work as also free liberty for felling & Sawing what treees he shal please that are upon the Comons belonging to y^ePlantation except such trees as are between the Bay path & Chickuppe River Also the Plantation doth grant unto him & his heires & assignes thirty acres of land in the Southerly side of ye Said Old Mill Streame & neere his Said Saw Mill in the most Convenent place y^t he shall chuse reserving liberty for high wayes where the Select men of this Towne shall See meet to lay them:

Absent from a Town meeting August 29, 1666. William Brookes John Bagg Obadiah Miller Jonathan Taylor Joseph Crowfoote, Miles Morgan William Branch Wm Warren^r Benjamin Mun Thomas Mirack John Bliss: to be added to y^r next Town rate.

[II—39]

Sept. 7, 1666.

The Select Men haveing agreed wth ye Measurer of lands to meet in the house Meddow this day to lay out Mr Glovers 9 acres in ye Said Meddow. The Select Men mett all of them: but Nath Ely the Measurer not being able to attend y^t work, the Select Men proceeded in ye business & laid out 9 acres there for Mr. Glover, wch land is in length on the South-^rly lyne 53 road that is to say fro: a great tree marked that Stands by the Creek at or neere ye lower end of ye Meddow upon a Straight lyne to m^r Holyokes meddow: & from ye said tree the Southerly bound runs up into the said Meddow (keeping about 2 or 3 rod from y⁰ Swamp) to a round gutter cut in y⁰ ground by a small oake y' is marked & from there the lyne wch is the bound is drawn South'ly to y⁰ Swamp y' is under y⁰ great hill by a range of 2 other trees marked even in a row wth y⁰ said little Oake, Soe taking in that little peece of meddow over the gutter being about an acr: the Westerly bound is Mr Holyokes meddow, & y⁰ North'ly bound is ptly the Creek for y⁰ lower part of the Meddow, & partly a range of weedy land wch hath not been used to be Mowed, for y⁰ upper part of that Northerly side of the Meddow. The whole being Nine acrs lying mostly tryangular wise:

[II—40]

At a Meeting of y⁰ Select Men Dec: 26 1666, vizt Ens: Cooper Robert Ashley John Dumbleton Benj: Parsons & Eli: Holyoke

John Sackett & Ambrose ffowler veiwers of the fences of the feild at Worronoco have this Summer past p^rsented diverse defects in the fences of y⁰ feild there vizt Henry Glovers fence defective 12 rod John Williams fence defective 24 rod & Walter Lee his fence defective 10 rod for wch tho the fynes according to Order would rise high, the Select Men doe assess the Said psons as followeth vizt Henry Glover at 20s. John Williams at 3s. Walt: Lee at 18s. these fynes y⁰ Townes share & to be added to y^r rates to the Town this winter: And for y⁰ veiwers share It is left to them to moderate as they See cause:

Rice Bedortha David Ashley & Nath: Burt are chosen Prizers of the Stock of y⁰ Plantation for making rates this Winter.

The Day above said the Said Select Men together wth Rowland Thomas & Thomas Miller being the Comittee for grannting of lands did grannt To Obadiah Miller a little peece of meddow contayning 2 or 3 acres about 3-4 of a Mile fro: Non-Such meddowe upon a brook y' runs into the great River at the higher end of Chickuppe playne neere the head of the brooke.

[II—41]

Also theres granuted to John Clark 4 acres of Wett meddow on ye South side of ye Bay path about 4 miles from Town & neer the path: provided it be not already disposed of to Some other.

John Stewart requesting y^t his land in the third division may abutt on ye meddow lotts: y^t is to Say y^t if there be any Comon land between this land & ye meddow lotts he might have it: It is granted to him, provided he leave a rod broad from ye meddow lotts to ye high way y^t goes thorow the 3d division on that side of his land next James Warreners land: This rod broad being for a highway:

[II—42]

[In the handwriting of Samuel Marshfield.]

ffebruary the 11: 1666

at a meeting of the Select men viz George Colton benjamin Cooly nathanell ely roland Thomas and Samuell Marshfeild There was choise made off veuars off fences ffor the severall ffeilds.

John Kep & Samuell bliss veiwers ffor the long medo and the Home Lots of as ffar as the meeting house and downward.

ffor the Hiar end of the towne which is to say ffrom the meeting house and upward and three Cornar medow and the playne John Lamb and thomas day.

and for the ffeild over the west side of the rivar and chicabe playne Edward ffoster and Jonathan Taylor

in reffarance to the Caring on the work off long medo bridge the select men doe conclude that George Colton and roland Thomas shall as sone as the snow is offe the Ground shall Go down and se which ar the Stones may be had esiest and whether they must cart them or ffetch them by boat and that benjamin Coly and roland Thomas shall se to the Caring on the work.

[II—43]

The Select men Considering the ill Conveniaut pasage out off the meeting house ffor want off a dore for such as sit in the Gallari: thay do tharffor apoint nathaniell Ely to se that adore be made that so thay that sit in the Gallari may have passage out off the house without passinge out of the dore leading out off the ally but that adore be made ffor them to Go in and out by as also nathaniell Ely is to se to the new hanging off the bell.

The Select men with decon Chapin off seating off persons in the meeting house and taking a vew off the acts off the Select men the yeare before and ffinding no Cause to mak alteration nor ffinding rome ffor plasing off more persons do conclude that persons shall sit as thar ware plased the last year.

[II—44 and 45 Blank—II—46]

Springffeild ffebruary th 11: 1666.

At a meeting off the Comity: the Granting ye Lands of ye Plantation undisposed off viz

> Georg Colton
> benjamin Cooly
> nathaniell Ely
> roland Thomas
> Thomas Stebbins
> Thomas millar
> and Samuell marshfeild

[In the handwriting of Elizur Holyoke.]

There is Granted to John bliss ffour acars off medo som what beyond his six acars formarly Granted provided it be there to be had after that Gorg Colton and benjamin Colyes be measured out.

Theres granted to Peter Swink 20 Acres of land neere block bridge above Obadiah Millers land:

Also to John Baker 5 acres of land for a house lott by James Taylors or Thomas Copleys on the playne towards Willm Hunters.

Als yr grannted to Jonathan Ball ye peece of land yt lyeth between his land in ye 3d division & ye meddow lotts, yet not to prjudice any high way: this in reference to one acre & 1-2 yt is Said to be due to his mother on Some Old account this grant being in leiw y^r of & to Satisfy for it & no other-wise & soe accounted.

And theres granted to John Lamb two acres of meddow lying on a dingle or between ye hills or on a gutter y^t runs in-to ye easterly branch of the Mill River beyond the bridge called Goodm: Warriners bridge.

Also theres grannted to Rich Sikes a peece of land lying by his former grant of Swamp at ye lower end of Chickuppe playn on ye west side of the great River & for the convenent lying of it & the quantity thereof It is left to ye discretion of the Measurer & Thomas Miller.

Thomas Stebbins his desires for liberty to build on his lott neere Robert Ashleyes house, is granted.

[II—47]

There being certayne persons chosen & appoynted to con-sider of the necessitous Condition of some familyes in ye Plantation. The Said Persons did at this p^{r}sent meeting make report how they apprehended things & did declare that they fynd need for the raising of 4 or 5£ to help a little ag^t the want of some familyes: And the Town did mutually ag-gree y^t there shalbe a contribution called for the next Lords day to endeavor to rayse such a summe for ye end aforesd: And for the distribution of what shalbe Soe gathered It is left to ye discretion of Deacon Chapin George Colton & Ben-jamin Cooley to doe therein as they See cause:

At the said Town Meeting it is further mutually aggreed by the Inhabitants y^t whereas It is found y^t James Osborne doth p^{r}judice him self & his family by disadvantagious bar-gaynes It is therefore voted & concluded y^t none of ye In-habitants of this Town shall or will make any bargayne with ye said James Osborne without consent of 2 or 3 of ye Select men y^t shall amount to above 10s vallue: And that all such bargaynes with him shalbe voyd:

Att this Town Meeting Joseph Crowfoote John Clark & James Osborne were absent w^n y^r names were called: & Soe are to pay 6d a pson to ye Towne.

[II—48]

In reference to high wayes the Inhabitants that live on the West side of yᵉ great River declaring that there is great necessity of making & amending their high wayes: It was by the Inhabitants in genᵗˡl concluded & aggreed yᵗ those of yᵉ Inhabitants yᵗ dwell on yᵗ side of yᵉ River shall make & repaire their own highwayes for this yeere ensuing: In reference whereunto: There is remitted to them a dayes work (of each of those Inhabitants) of their working at yᵉ County way on yᵉ East side of the River. Provided their dayes works of each man be bestowed & spent in working at their own high wayes:

And in reference to such high wayes as are now private & not reckoned as the County wayes, but are to be repayred or made by particular Companyes The Town now doth appoynt certayne psons of yᵉ said company as Overseers of yᵉ works of such pticular wayes. Each one of wᶜʰ psons shall have power to call the Severall psons yᵗ belong to yʳ own company to the workes of their own high wayes

And it is further declared yᵗ if any pson shall have made such alteration exchanges or sales of land: that they have noe land to wᶜʰ such pticular wayes doe lead yᵗ then such psons shall not be called to such wayes to work but such psons as are yᵉ pʳsent owners of such lands upon wᶜʰ such alterations have been made from tyme to tyme

[II—49]

The Persons yᵗ are for this yeere chosen & appoynted Overseers of the Severaall companyes of workers at highwayes as aforesaid as are ffollows:

Benjamin Parsons for yᵉ way up the Long hill over the Mill River:

John Clark for yᵉ way to yᵉ 16 acres.

Rober Ashley for the way to the woods over the new bridge.

Japhett Chapin for yᵉ playne bridge:

Rice Bedortha for yᵉ way to Chickkuppe playne on the West side of yᵉ great River: And

John Leonard for the way to Agawam falls from the great River.

And the said psons are to call their severall companyes together when their yeere is expired to chuse other overseers in y^r roomes.

Liberty is granted to John Riley to build on his lott by Willm Hunters.

[II—50]

[In the handwriting of John Pynchon.]

ffebr 14 1666.

Robert Ashly (as p contra) was chosen overseer for ye Highway worke at upp end of ye Towne over the New Bridge into ye woods.

ffebr. 1667.

Wm Branch was chosen overseer to call ye Company to s^d Highways for repairing thereoff.

ffebr 25th 1668.

Wm Branch called ye Company togither to choose a new overseer for ye Highways: & accordingly the Company proceeded to choose & made choise of Jonath Ashly as overseer to take care for ye repairing of ye Highways & calling men to s^d worke as need shall be this yeare ensueing:

[II—51 and 52 Blank—II—53]

[In the handwriting of Samuel Marshfield.]

The account that the Select men Gave off the townes dets
—the holl Charges off Long medo bridg..17   9   6

To m^r holyok.....................4   10   0

To benjamin mun...................2   10   0

To Carnelius williams 00   6   3

to nathaniell Ely ffor nails & a hasp..00   00   06

To John hitchcock and Joseph harmon
   and thomas millar John Scot Jonathan morGan and Samuell holyok
   and Goeorge Colten and John Bagg
   all is 8 wolfs...................04   00   00

all is....28   16   3

The Towne yeilding to pay Joseph Lenard 10 shillings ffor a wolf that he
killed at worinok it maketh the dets
of the towne....................29)   6   3
[II—54]
The Towne Creditor in the year 1667:
    by a rate off.....................26   5   2
    by rent off Thomas nobell.......... 4   0   0
    by severall small fynes.............11   0   6
    by credit that the fformer Selectmen
    Gave the towne ....oo   17   8

                  the holl is....32   3   4

                    29   6   3
             rests 2   17   1

                   32   03   4

[In the handwriting of Elizur Holyoke.]

May 5th 1669.

The aco[t] abovesd, being overlooked by y[e] p[r]sent Select
men: together w[th] y[e] aco[t] the next yeare, 3 leaves on & also
in 4th leafe forward: we find y[t] this aco[t] above was not med-
led w[th] nor brought to aco[t] by y[e] next yeare select men, viz
in y[e] yeare 1668: So y[t] the £2 17s 01d above remaines due to
y[e] Towne: only y[e] Towne at the Generall meeting abated
Joseph Crowfoote what he was fyned for defective in his
fence, viz £0 6s 6d, So y[e] due to y[e] Towne is £2 10s 07.

This caryed to y[e] long book or Pap. of acot[s] where y[e]
Towne is Set Dr & Cr.

[II—55]

[In the handwriting of Elizur Holyoke.]

ffebr 10th 1667.

At a meeting of the Select men viz Leut Cooper John
Dumbleton Miles Morgan Benj. Parsons & Elizur Holyoke.

For veiwers of fences of the comon feilds & house lotts of
this Township Are chosen as followeth.

John Leonard & Edmund Pingridayes for the ffeild on ye West side of ye great River opposite to the Town & for ye playn called Chickuppe

And John Lumbard & Nathancel Burt for ye house lotts from ye Meeting house & downwards & for the Long meddow.

And Willm Warren^r & Timothy Cooper for ye house lotts from the meeting house & upwards & 3 Corn^r Meddow & playn above End brook.

John Matthews for his absence at the last Genll Towne meeting is to pay 2s to be added to the next Town rate.

There was granted to Abell Wright ten acrs of medow in that medow beyond Skipmuck where R Thomas had 10 acres granted him by the last Selectmen this medow is upon a brook y^t runs down to ye Stony brook on ye way to Hadley beyond haying well provided it free from former grants & y^t it be free for this Town to dispose of it & y^t if it be not purchased of ye Indians he cleare the purchases thereof.

Also Two acres more is granted to Rowland on ye same termes to be added to his former 10 acres.

Also grannted to Abell Wright about 2 acres at the South westerly side of R: Thomas his house lott [11—56] at Skipmuck pvided it p^rjudice not form^r Grannts on high wayes.

Granted to John Petty an addition of Six acres of meddow to his former 8 acres granted by ye Select of ye last yeere & on the Same termes & conditions & y^t it p^rjudice not former grannts.

Granted to Wm Hunter 20 acres of upland & 10 acres of meddow on or neere Stony river towards Windsor neere where John Petty hath land grannted & on the like tearmes & conditions

Granted to Thomas Day 4 or 5 acres above his meddow at Worlds end on both sides the brooke.

Also six acres for a wood lott or neere at ye reere of Capt. Pynchons wood lott lying from ye brow of the hill on the Northerly side of ye Garden Brooke & from thence the bound is bye Northerly or Norwesterly:

John Lamb hath granted him the land y^t is between his lotts in ye playne above End brook & the hills & ye land y^t is between the hills y^t was Griffith Jones & the hills there Eastward.

It is Ordered y^t every Proprietor of land in the comon ffeilds of this Towne Shall Sett up a stake at the ptition of his fence in ye comon fence vizt between himself & his neighbor &that they mark ye stake wth the first lres [letters] of their names this to be done before the veiwers goe to veiw fences in ye Springe under ye penalty of 12d fyne on each pson y^t shalbe defective herein wch fyne to goe half to the veiwers & the other Half to ye Towne:

[II—57]

m^r. J: Pynchon Junr & Jos: Hunwick killed a wolfe ffebruary 24 1667.

June 29 1668.

Att a Meeting of ye Select Men they being all p^{r}sent, for judging of diverse defects of fences in the Town feilds on ye West side of ye great River p^{r}sented & complayned of to ye Select Men:

Rober Ashley prsented for 2d   defects in his
    fence at Chick: for wch by ye Select Men

	s	d
fyned at	6	o
Goodm: Terry 1 defect fyned at	3	o
Tho: Mirack 2 defects fyned at	6	o
Rich Exell 1 defect fyned at	3	o
James Warriner 1 defect fyned at	3	o
Lawrence Bliss 1 defect fyned at	3	o
Miles Morgan 3 defects fyned at	9	o
John Bagg 2 defects fyned at	6	o

these fynes the half of wch belongs to ye Towne the other to ye vewers of he fences vizt: J: Leon: & Edm: Prin:

John Dumbleton 1 defect fyned at 3s od wch he is to pay to ye Veiwers who mended it:

Obadiah Miller 1 defect fyned at 4s od wch he is to pay to the veiwers who mended it.

[II—58]

Att a Meeting of ye Select men Jan: 11th 1668. Who mett to consider of ye Townes debts & Creditts And to make rates vizt a rate of £80 for Mr Glover & a rate of £15 00s 00d to pay ye Townes debts as follow:

The Towne is Dr

To Samll & Joseph Harman for   killing 6
   wolves this Summ^r past   3   00   00

To Charles fferry for killing 1 wolfe   0   10   00

To Timothy Cooper for his horse into ye Bay
   20s & his pasturing there 10s 6d this for
   ye Dept   1   10   06

for ye Deputyes Diet at the Co^rte May: 68 . .   3   10   00

   for his tyme at Co^rte & travellinge   1   10   00

to Elizur Holyoke for writings in ye Town
   book   10   00

for making rates this yeere   1   00   00

To Cornelius for worke about ye meeting
   house mending ye bell & hinges for the
   doore   1   00   00

To Capt Pynchon for nailes about ye Meet-
   ing house doore & windowes 00   02   06

To Jno Dumbleton for remaynder of pay for
   his work about ye pound over ye River . . 01   05   06

To Capt Pynchon for hire of his bull this
   Summer past to be raysed annually by
   ye neighbo^rs on ye East side of the River
   except ye Long Meddow (& Capt himself because he had another bull) according to ye number of the Cowes y^t every
   one had   1   02   00

To Ens Cooley for maynteyning ye water
   fence at long meddow gate to be raysed
   on ye land there y^t is w^thin ye fence vizt 3
   forth: on the £ as y^t land is prized he
   mayntayned y^t fence ye yeere at 5s p an-
   um & mending ye gates 1 yeere 2s in all . .   1   02   00

To Tho: Miller for making & mayntening
  ye water fence by his house this yeere £30
  raysed on ye land wthin y^t feild at half penny half farthing on y^e £ as y^t land is prized   1   10   00
To Benjamin Mun for ringing ye Bell &c..   2   10   00
To Mr J Pynchon & J Hunwick for killing
  a wolfe..........................   0   10   00

         16   18   06
To John Stewart for a branding iron......   0   4   00

         17   02   06

[II—59]
Jan. 11, 1668.

Att a meeting of ye Select Men vizt Eli: Holyoke T:
Cooper Miles Morgan & J: Dumbleton & Benjamin Parsons:

Granted to Samuell Ely ten acres of land below ye bridge
at N: Burts land adjoyning to ye lowe end of John Harmons
land there & the reere of long Meddow lotts by ye brook:
only there is to be left a sufficient high way for drift of cattell
to ye Comons below ye Meddowes.

Grannted to Lieut Cooper y^t if John Skinner doe not
come to inhabitt in this Township wth in two yeere fro: this
tyme y^n ye Said Leut Cooper shall have y^t 20 acres grannted
to ye s^d John Skinner.

Granted to John Dumbleton a peece of land about 6 acres
more or less next to the lott y^t was grannted to James Taylor above ye comon fence on ye west side of the River if Soe
much be there undisposed off:

Granted to Miles Morgan y^t peece of land y^t lyes above his
land on ye North side of ye Round hill between his land &
the 3 Corner Meddow brooke: only he is to leave 16 rod wide
between this land for grannted & Goodm: Branch his ditch &
soe forward 16 rod wide between this land thus granted & the
brow of ye hill y^t is on ye South Easterly side of the said
brook & this grantt is to extend Northerly to the brow or

top of ye next raising of land a little from ye brooke y^t runs out of the wett meddow vizt a little over ye Said brooke

Grannted to Edmund Pringridayes & ffrancis Pepper to keepe their fence by Chickkupe playne on the place where it now stands provided they doe the former themselves except Soe much as any of ye Proprieto^rs fall short of doing their share of fence there

[II—60]

Jan 11th 1668.

The Towne Cr

	£	s	d
By a Rate of £14 raysed on ye Town......	14	00	00
By Thomas Nobles rent due March next..	4	00	00

debt	17	2	6
rest	00	17	6

18	00	00

[In the handwriting of Samuel Marshfield.]

This account being examined by a Commiti Chosen by the towne namly nathanyell Ely and Samuell marshfeild find that thar remaineth du to towne............ 0 17 6

[In the handwriting of John Pynchon.]

the £17 2s 6d of ye Townes debt on ye former leafe being sattisfied & discounted: But in ye aco^t in ye former leafe there is charged £1 5s 6d as remaining due to J^o Dumbleton for worke about ye Pound, wher as ye whole £3 y^t he was to have was allowed & acot^{ed} by ye Select men in the yeare 1666: So y^t it is an error in charging this 25s 6d on ye Towne now & is to be allowed ye Towne................01 05 06

In all ye due to ye Towne fro: the select men, now goeing off is 43s 02 03 00

ffeb 2d 1668: By us

Nathanell ely
Samuell Marshfeild

This caryed to yᵉ long booke or Pap. of accoᵗˢ where yᵉ Towne is Dr & Cr

May 5th 1669.

[II—61]

Springfeild ffebr. 8th 1668. At a meeting of the Selectmen for yᵉ yeare ensueing: vizt John Pynchon: George Colton Nath Ely: Sam Marshfeild & Laur Bliss

At this meeting of yᵉ Select men: They chose & appointed veiwers of fences for the severall feilds for yᵉ yeare ensueing viz:

John Clarke & John Bliss ffor Long meddow & yᵉ Homlots up to the meeting house

Thomas Miller & Edw: ffoster for yᵉ feild on the west side of yᵉ River.

James Warinar & Tho: Day for the homlots fro: the meeting howse upward.

John Riley & John Bagg for Chickkuppe plaine.

The Select men considering the excuses of men absent fro: yᵉ Generall Towne meeting last weeke, doe allow of yᵉ Reson for most mens absence: only 4 psons who were pʳsent most of yᵉ day yet not attending to theire call, & being also absent some tyme after, we doe for theire neglect Judge yᵐ to pay 6d a peice to be added to theire next Towne Rate viz

	d	s
Abell Wright	6	
John Bliss	6	2
John Matthews	6	
John Harmon	6	

forward Three leaves are more dues to yᵉ Towne by some psons fines for Galloping in yᵉ Streetes contrary to order, To the Sum of 11s 8d.

The Publishing of who are chosen fence veiwers as above & wᵗ else is of publike concernmᵗ contained in yᵉ 3 next leaves was all publikely made known to yᵉ Towne on a Lecture day, all being read & declared to yᵉ Inhabitants after Lecture of yᵉ 24th day of ffebʳ 1668: all of publik to yᵗ date 3 leaves forward was then read to yᵉ Inhabitants.   J. P.

[II—62]

Febr. 8th 1668.

Lett out to John Bagg: Edm. Pringridays & W Brooke the 35 or 40 acres of Towne Land in chickkupy plaine on ye west side of ye greate River, for the Tearme & space of Seven yeares fro: this p^rsent 8th day of ffebr 1668: upon ye Tearmes hereafter mentioned, viz John Bagg: Edm Pringridays & Wm Brooke have free Liberty for Impvement of ye aforesd land to theire best advantage by plowing planting sowing & Mowing or breaking up any of ye New ground pvided they do not breake up any of ye meddow or Mowing Ground, wch they are noe ways to deface, but carefully to p^rserve all ye Mowing land for Hay: They are likewise to take care of ye fences belonging to this land, & carefully to repaire it, All ye fence wch from or for this land aforesd belongs to ye Common ffeilds, wch they are sufficiently to repaire fro. tyme to tyme for ye Security of ye ffeild fro: all or any damadge; And are likewise to leave the whole fence in good & sufficient repaire at ye end of theire aforesd Seven yeares: And for Rent the sd John Bagg Edm Pringridays & Wm Brooke, all as one party, are to allow or pay yearly the Rent or Sum of Seven Pounds Ten shillings p annum, they are yearly to pay in to ye Select Townsmen fro: tyme to tyme: And that upon or before ye first day of January yearly, one halfe in good merchantable wheate & the other halfe in Pease & Indian Corne, all good & merchantable: only for this prsent yeare now Coming in regard the fence is out of repaire & one acre & halfe of ye afore let land being Sowne wth winter wheate wch is reserved, they are to allow but seven pounds, for this yeare, And in case by the mere hand of Gods pvidence Inevitably blasting theire crop the land afore let Shall yeild but little wheate, in such case if they doe pcure 2 or 3 of ye Select men Sometime in July, or ye beginning of August at furtherest to veiw & take notice of such Blast, they shal then be abated of theire Rent such yeare, as ye sd select men shall Judge meete, always pvided they have Planted or sowne a considerable p^t of ye land at least halfe wth other granine then

wheate, otherwise they shall suffer for theire owne Impru-
dence in putting more to wheate, these uncertaine yeares,
And this Ingagem[t] & agreement the sd ptys all as one pty have
heretoe set theire hands this p[r]sent 8th of ffebr 1668.

William Brookes
John Bagg

the marke of   Edmund Pringridays
         E P

[II—63]

         ffeb 8, 68

By y[e] Select men all being prsent

Anthony Dorchester having a psell of Land granted him
in Chikkuppy Plaine on y[e] west side of y[e] grt River at the
back end or reer end of y[e] land Som[t] called Miles Murwins
lot, w[ch] grant was many yeares since, & he hath Posessed it
& Impved it severall yeares, & yet the Record of it thorough
some neglect is not to be found, The sd land is now confirmed to him viz sixe or seven acres, Robert Ashly his land
lying on y[e] Northside of it, & Miles Morgans land on y[e]
South.

Obadiah Miller having 20 acrs of land Granted him at
Ashkanuncksit in ffeb[r] 6, 1664, w[ch] was never laid out, & he
desiring y[e] place may be altered, and it may ly at block bridge
brooke: His desire is granted, And y[e] sd Twenty acrs of land
he is to have it on y[e] west side of his other land there: &
hereby y[t] grant at Ashkanunksit is void.

Edmund Pringridays desiring one or two acrs of meane
land to be granted to him w[ch] lyes at y[e] Reere of his land in
chikkupy plaine, & was taken in wth his land only for conveniency of fencing: The aforesd acre or 2 of Land is Granted
to him.

Likewise there is Granted to ffraunces Pepper y[e] land at
the end of his Lot there:

The Proprietors of y[e] 3 corner meddow plaine on this side
y[e] Round hill & plaine above the 3 Corner meddow, agreeing
to ly togither in one feild & intending to keepe it intire Propounding theire desires that they may have liberty as to or-

der theire owne pprietys according to Law, So in pticular, to choose theire owne Hayward & veiwers of fences & to make orders for Regulating of theire owne fences & Improvem^t of theire land there from tyme to tyme, & that the Select men would not Impose upon them, as to y^t ffeild, from ye upp end of Reice Bedorthas John Lams & That wch was Tho Days Homlots to ye Head of the Plaine: Theire desire is accordingly Granted & y^t they take in Wm Branch wth y^m: Provided they doe agree among themselves, y^t is to say ye Major pt of ye pprietors according to law, & y^t they doe choose theire fence veiwers & fro: tyme to tyme or else be lyable to ye same penalty y^t ye Select men are for neglect, And so they have Power & Liberty & have hereby appointed fro: tyme to tyme to make orders about theire fencing & repairing thereoff & may Impose Penaltys according to Law, wch shall be to ye use & behoofe of theire owne Company & they are to have ye whole advantage of theire feild intire to y^{m}selves only it is ordered y^t in case complaint be made Justly ag^t ye fence veiwers of this feild aforesd, That they allow of fences sufficient then other veiwers in such ye Select men shal rectifie as is most Just & right to y^m.

[II—64]

At a meeting of ye Select men: ffeb^r 12th 1668.

Present viz John Pynchon Nath Ely Geo: Colton Sam Marshfeild Laur Bliss

A Bay Stone horse of Mr Pynchons, foure yeare old in ye Spring, being veiwed and measured by ye Select men & found according to law, is allowed to goe at Liberty for a Stonehorse:

Also a whiteish Stonehorse of Laurence Bliss: 3 y old & full ye height reqred is allowed to goe at liberty for a Stonehorse:

Likewise Capt Pynchons white lock horse is allowed off to goe at liberty but tis only for this yeare Coming in regard of his age:

The order about Swine in pa. 15 (of ye Towne book) That all Swine runing at Liberty & keeping ordinarily wthin 2 mile of ye Towne shal be rung, & if found on medow Pastures or gardens unrung to pay 2s 6d. This Penalty being thought a little to high & y^t ye neglect if psecuting ye s^d order is occasioned by ye grtnes of ye Penalty: It is Therefore ordered y^t the Penalty for Swine above 3 Mo. old in meddows Pastures orchards & gardens or Inclosed ffeilds shall henceforth be but 8d a peice for being unrung one halfe to ye Informer & ye other halfe to the Towne & in case swine y^t Doe ordinarily keepe in ye woods shall by accident get into Inclosed ffeilds in such cases to pay but 3d a pce as those are to doe y^t goe on ye Comons, unless it be knowne y^t they have got a haunt of lying about ye Towne or about inclosed feilds: & in all other respects the former order about swine to stand good, only whereas by sd order Swine may goe at Liberty till ye 25th of March: It is now ordered That it shall be left to ye Select men fro yeare to yeare to shorten the tyme if ye earlyness of ye Spring req it:

The order about ffences as in the 4th leafe in the begining of this booke made ye 20th March 1664-65 being considered, wee Judge it meete to Continue it wth a little alteration, namely where ye Title in the Margent is (ffences Vp for ye last of March) we put in 10th of March unless the frost be in ye ground to hinder doeing up ye fence (In Title wharfe gate & T^r to shut) Instead of, to ye head of ye plain (It is to be) to the further end of John Lambs Reice Bedorthas lots & Mr Holyokes land & for last of March, there to put in ye 10th of March: (In directions for veiwers, instead of Aprill 1st. To be, ye 15th of March, (And adde) That ye increasing 12d p day shall extend but to 3 days The veiwers being to see y^t defects run noe longer: However 3 days shall [II—65] terminate ye increase of ye 12d p day unless upon the veiwers reveiwing y^t fence & giving new notice to ye pprietor he shall continue to neglect ye amending it after y^t notice, And in all cases about fines for defective ffences it is left to ye Select men to mittigate y^m, both ye veiwers p^t &   ye Townes p^t, where they Judge it apparent equity or other considerations doe req it:

There being Complts of grt damadge like to ensue to many psons by Swine & cattle goeing at liberty this forward Spring, especially where there is winter wheate. It is therefore ordered that all feilds that are fenced shall be cleared of Swine & cattle to p^rvent damage what may be by ye 10th of March next upon penalty of paying 5s for every head turned or left in, either of swine or other cattle. And for all cattle found, in ye owners to pay 6d a head for all cattle & 8d p head for swine unrung according to orders.

The want of a Bull for ye use of ye Towne being considered It is left to Nathanell Ely & Laur Bliss to take care for to Provide one:

Also ye care of mending ye Pound is left to y^m, to agree wth the Pound keeper about it, who shall be pd for his Paines out of ye Townes estate, And they are to pcure locks for each Pound.

The Seating of psons in ye meeting howse was now considered, but obstructed by want of ye list thereoff fro: ye former Select men wch at p^rsent cannot be found.

Whereas there was a Highway over ye grt River w^thout ye comon fence, laid out 20 Rod wide by ye Common fence towards Agawam river & ordered to be continued till it came over ye Muxy medow or further: It is now ordered y^t ye sd Highway shall be continued beyond ye muxy meddow Twenty Rod wide all along by ye comon fence as far as to Agawam River: ptly for Highways sake & ptly for Comonage for cattle 20 Rod wide is to be always continued Common, fro: ye grt River to Agawam.

Ther is granted to J^o Dumbleton, Sam Marshfeild, Griffith Joanes & Tho Copley That for conveniency of fencing theire lands under ye Hills at ye Reare of the Howselots w^thout the comon fence They shal have Liberty to set theire fence toward the Brow of the great Hill:

[II—66]

Peter Swink desiring some land to make meddow off lying over ye Brooke on ye Northerly side of his land at Block Brooke There is sixe or seven acres of Low meddowish land

Granted to him, wch is to be laid out to him on ye Northerly side of Block brook ag^t his former grant of Thirty acres of Land there, & adjoyning to it: Provided it may be Lawfull for ye Inhabitants to make use of Timber Trees, that grow in his 30 acrs formerly granted him, While it lys Comon, or till it shall be Impved or fenced in, in p^t, some acres, at least Two, till then ye Timber to be common for ye neighbors there & upon this condition y^t he allow of the taking of Timber out of his former 30 acrs till Impvm^t as aforesd: he hath the grant of ye 6 or seven acrs of meddowish land as abovesd And he is spedyly to declare whether he acept this grant on the condition specified, That ye Liberty for ye Inhabitants to make use of the Timber Trees y^t are growing there may be known. ......He accepted of this Grant on ye Tearmes mentioned for ye Inhabitants to make use of Timber till he fence in pt.

There is Granted to Symon Beamon, an acre & halfe or Two acres of medow upon a smale brooke northward, a little beyond Skeepmuck, wch runs down toward Stony River: this meddow being a litle off of Rowld Thomas his meddow there:

Granted to John Riley an adition of Two acrs of land to his former Ten acres by ye grt River above chickup: plaine.

There is Granted to Tho Day: John Clarke, Nath Ely & Charles fferry ye Land at ye end of theire Lots over the meddow (where Tho Day dwell by the Prison house) for 20 Rod long fro: ye Reare of theire lots, wch were 80 Rod long & now this adition of 20 Rod long at theire Reares makes all those Lotts to be 100 rod long: this 20 rod long added all theire breadths besides theire first grant being made good 80 rod Long & then this 20 rod taking place at ye end, is in lew of land wch is taken fro: these lots for ye Highway in ye front, is in ful sattisfaction for ye land taken for sd Highway:

There is likewise granted to Laur Bliss ye land ag^t his lot there for 20 rod long fro: Reare upon ye like condition as ye former y^t is to say in sattisfaction for land taken for ye Highway: The like grant is made to the lot belonging to the howse of Correction & to yᵉ lot yᵗ belongs to ye howse & land wᶜʰ John Mathews is now in.

[II—67]

Tho Stebbing Junʳ last wednesday in yᵉ forenoon fcircely Galloping, & running his Horse, in yᵉ streete fro: Godm: Miricks upward, & wᶜʰ was seen by many psons & he acknowledged it before yᵉ Select men, it being expʳsly agᵗ yᵉ Towne order, He was accordingly sentenced to pay 3s 4d (the Informer taking 12d according to Towne order) The 2s 4d is payable to yᵉ Towne:

Tim: Cooper & Jonath Ashly: likewise Jo Hitchcock & Sam: Bliss Junʳ being complained of for running theire horses in yᵉ Streete on yᵉ same day (But being absent) It is ordered that they be required to appeare before yᵉ Select men, next Lecture day Imediately after Lecture, to give an acoᵗ of theire so doing:

ffebʳ 24th 1668 The select men met, & yᵉ psons afore mentioned appearing & desiring they might not be condemned wᵗʰout xse. Thereupon Serj Tho Stebbing & Laurence Bliss Testyfied that they Saw John Hitchcock & Sam: Bliss Junʳ running theire horses this day fortnight as fast as well they could run, & yᵗ in yᵉ streete: Likewise: Nath Ely & Laur: Bliss Testyfied that they saw Timothy Coop: & Jonath Ashly gallop & Run theire Horses in yᵉ streete last Lecture day in yᵉ forenoon & yᵗ as fast as they could Run. Whereuppon Timothy Cooper & Jonathan Ashly: also John Hitchcock & Sam Bliss Jun for Running theire Horses as aforesd, it being expressly agᵗ yᵉ Towne order: are adjudged each of yᵐ to pay yᵉ order Injoynes viz: 2s 4d a peice to the Towne:

At this meeting: A Black Stonehorse of Tho Coltons 4 y old in yᵉ Spring being measured & found the height the Law reqʳs wᵗʰin a very smale trifle & being a handsome comly horse well Limmed: is alowed of to goe at liberty for a Stone Horse.

Also a Brown Bay Stonehorse of Robert Ashlys 4 y old in yᵉ Spring being veiwed & found acording to Law, is allowed off for a Stonehorse: Likewise A Bay horse of Tim Coopers 5 y old & full ye height required, is alowed for a Stonehorse to goe at Liberty:

Aprill 21th 1667.

A Roane horse of Symon Beamons of 10 y old is allowed to goe at Liberty for a Stone horse for this yeare now coming:

[II—68]

At a meeting of ye Select men: Aprill 7th 1669.   Present J. Pynchon G. Colton X: Ely: S: Marshfeild L Bliss:

Miles Morgan & Jonath Burt are ordered to sit up in ye Gallery to give a check to disorders in youth & young men In tymes of Gods worship: Anthony Dorchester to sit on ye Guard Seate for ye like end:

The veiwers of fence over ye River p'sent John Baker for 4 rod of fence defective 3 days for wch sd Baker is Lyable to 4 s p day fine But John Baker pleading noe damadge hath come to ye feild, & it being at ye first closing of the feild: we abate the fine to Sixe shilings, To be to each veiwer 2s viz Edw: ffoster & Tho Miller, & 2s to ye Towne.

They also complaine of ye Indian Cattonis & his company for not doeing up ye water fence belonging to theire land in ye feild they having had warning & neglecting it: about 4 or 5 rod being defectve upon ye land next ye River, besides the securing of ye River, for wch neglect they are fyned to pay 2 bush: & 1-2 of Indian Corne or other pay so much vallue, Halfe to belong to ye veiwers & halfe to ye Towne.

There is granted to Benjamin Parsons about an acre of meddow Three Miles of ye Towne, on ye right hand of the way to watchuit, on a Gutter running downe to John Harmons Pacowsick meddow.

Joseph crowfootes request for halfe an acre of land at chickkuppy lying Cornerwise, next ye highway at ye southerly Corner, & so will bring his lot square at the front, as also about 4 acrs more at ye flank of his lot toward ye easterly end: is Granted to him accordingly:

Jeremy Horton hath about halfe an acre of land Granted to him at yᵉ west end of his howselott (next to Symon Beamons) to lay his lot square as also a triangle peice of about halfe an acre at yᵉ Southeast Corner to bring his lot up to yᵉ Highway there:

There is Granted to Capt Pynchon about a quarter of an acre of land in yᵉ further side of yᵉ 3 corner medow brooke above yᵉ plaine Bridge, to cary yᵉ Brooke straite next to the plaine land under yᵉ hill there, thereby taking 2 or 3 smale spangs of Land, wᶜʰ are now lying on yᵉ North side of yᵗ Brooke, all being about a quarter of an acre or but litle more, & is adjoyning to Capt Pynchons other Land wᶜʰ he hath lying at yᵉ Northwest end of yᵉ Round hill;

Eliakim Hitchcock of New Haven, desiring to be admitted into This Township to dwell, hath Liberty, pvided he bring certificates fro: New Haven yᵗ he is an orderly Liver there, & yᵗ his father there desires it, & assist him on his remove, & pvided also that he pcure 2 sufficient men of this Towne to enter into £30 Bond to secure yᵉ Towne fro: any charge yᵗ may any way arise to this Towneship by sd Hitchcock or any of his family.

[II—69]

At a meeting of the Selectmen Jˡ: G C. N E. S.M: & L B. April 21, 1669.

John Baker being pʳsented for defect in his ffence that wᶜʰ he was fyned for last meeting yᵉ whole 4 rod was not mended, & he owning it yᵗ it was neglected a day after he Ingaged it should be done, though the veiwer Tho: Miller says it was above a day undone after he had veiwed But we take notice of only yᵉ days neglect: for wᶜʰ he is fyned 4s according to order: halfe to yᵉ Towne.

Edw: ffoster for one defect is ordered to pay 12s.

Leiut Coopers pʳsentmᵗ is taken off, the water being up yᵗ he could not doe his fence he is freed fro: first taking care of it.

Rich Exells, (he not being pʳsent) is left till friday one of ye clock. He not appearing on friday & not knowing whether he had notice, it is referred to next Lecture viz ye 5th of May. He then appeared & was quitted.

The Indian ffence into Agawam River being still defective to ye grt damadge of ye feild: It is therefore ordered that the veiwers shall amend it, at least y^t into ye water, & make it sufficient ag^t cattle to secure ye feild, for wch they shal have double recompence according to law & have warant fro: ye Select men to ye constable to Levy it: & also to Levy the 2 bush: & 1-2 of Indian Corne wch they were fyned last meeting of ye Select men for ye defect:

The Homlot feild not being in a secure Pasture by reson of alteration of fencing (& some having fenced y^m se. in pticlar) & thereby ye veiwers being at a loss what to doe about defects, as also who should secure ye upper wharfe gate, or whether it should be laid downe: It is therefore ordered that ye pprietors of land of all the Homlots, Shall be warned to meet togither next friday being ye 23th of this Aprill: at Three of ye clock, that so there may be a meete Settlement of ye fencing, to p^rsent dammage, as to ye whole so also to pticular psons.

[II—70]

Aprill 23th 1669 The Proprietors of ye land in the Homlots met according to appointm^t, also the Select men met togither ye same tyme:

At this meeting it appearing that ye Homlots from James Warinars upwards were in pticular Inclosures It was therefore considered concerning y^m y^t ly in comon fro: James warinars downwards to John Harmons: And ye sd Proprietors lying togither in Common, they have now agreed & determined to fence at ye Reare of their lots next to ye River for securing of y^mse. & theire feilds:

And for securing ye Gate way or Bars by ye meeting howse, Benja Mun, Serj Stebbing: Wm Warinar & James Warinar, are to take care & charge thereoff, & doe the same:

The Gate at ye Higher wharfe being Judged needfull to be kept well hung & Shut, for a Generall good to ye whole, to p^rvent cattles p^rsing upon ye feild at ye Reare of mens lots, or goeing over the River: therefore that cattle may be kept from goeing to the River & also fro: damadge to corne or Hay brought thither in ye season of it: It is ordered By the Select men that for ye p^rsent (til other order be taken) all the Neighbors fro: Deacon chapins, taking in Deacon chapin & fro: him all upward, shall take care of ye sd gate that it be well Hung & also that ye fence aqjoyning ye Highway be done up close to the sd Gate: And whosoever shall leave open the sd gate such pson shal pay as a fine 2s 6d for neglect one halfe to go to ye informer & ye other halfe to go to the psons y^t keepe ye gate up for securing ye feilds. The psons aforesd are to meete to agree for carying on this worke: all whom Deacon chapin in some convenient tyme, is to cal y^m togither for y^t end:

And that something may be done at or toward ye Lower wharfe, for a Generall good & securing, as to p^rventing cattle fro: p^rseing ye feilds either by making up a gateway if a lane can be contrived, or otherwise to run a fence into ye River & put a stop to cattles goeing on ye Backside or Reare of ye lots. Anthony Dorchester is appointed & ordered to call ye Neighbors at ye Lower end of the Towne togither from Cornelius Wiliams, taking him in, to consider & take order there about to doe what may be advantageous & good for ye whole therein:

[II—71]

In answer to the veiwers for their direction: ffor setling where the veiwers shal have charge, It is declared, (ye Range now apearing to be at James wariners & not at ye meetinghouse) That John Clarke & John Bliss theire veiw of fences shall reach thither, & Tho Day & James warinair, there veiw of fences shall be from thence upward.

Severall psons complaining that they cant get theire Neighbours, where theire fences is in pticular, to make up theire fence sufficient, & all bec: ye veiwers are not requirable to veiw pticular & Ptitionall ffences: And whereas the Towne order says that ptitionall ffences betweene Lot & Lot in case of disagreem[t] betwixt y[e] pprietors shal be ordered by y[e] Select men:

The Select men doe now (therefore) Order That where there are Complaints ag[t] Neighbours, that any one of y[m] doth not make good fence, in such Case, where either Neighbour desires it, The veiwers yearely appointed, shal veiw such ptitionall ffences fro: tyme to tyme, & shall have Power to allow or disallow of y[m], according as they do, or may, y[e] Generall & Comon ffences of corneffeilds, w[ch] ffences disallowed, or declared defective by any veiwers Shall forth w[th] by y[e] pprietor or owner of it, be amended, & made sufficient to secure his Neighbour from any damadge, according to y[e] Judgmt of y[e] viewers:

At this meeting Consideration being had about p[r]venting y[e] wetness & flowing of y[e] medows before the Towne on the east side of y[e] street & by y[e] orders on the Towne Booke for ditching & Clearing the Brooke being read & Judged Sufficient for y[t] end, if attended: The xsecution of them is therefore desyred & ordered, only y[t] order being a litle to Short in seeming to leave y[e] clearing y[e] Brooke at the medow w[ch] was Henry Burts, It is therefore declared & ordered that each pprietor of meddow as far as Benja Parsons, shall make a sufficient ditch before his meddow and cleare it yearly as far as the Lower side of Benja Parsons Lower meddow, And the Recorder [II—72] ordered in pa. 17, of the grt Towne Booke, line 14. (Instead of) (That was Henry Burts deceased) To put in To y[e] lower side of Benja Parsons lower meddow:

At this meeting there was Granted to Jonathan Burt a smale psell of meddow about an acre or Two uppon a branch that comes out of y[e] hither wachusit & runs into Pacowsick brooke, pvided it be not already granted to any other:

There is foure acrs of meddow Granted to Deacon Chapin, on y[e] hither branch of fresh water River pvided it be not already Granted to any other.

May 5th 1669.   At a meeting of y[e] Select men JP GC: NE SM: & La Bliss.

Wm Brookes Complaining of John Bagg for Letting 3 of his Cattle last friday ye 30th of Aprill to be in Chickkuppy feild wthout a keeper, Also on Edm Pringridays for 3 there wch were in or under his Impvent, & of Jos Bedortha for 2 of his fathers cattle there at ye same tyme, all wch cattle were turned in over night & left in ye feild: Wm Brookes affirming that they were there wthout a keep: & y^t as conceive all Night & that he was bringing y^m to a Pound but that they were taken fro: him: Bag & Pringridays also owning y^t they left y^m there over Night, & though they say they then left a keep: wth y^m yet Wm Brookes afforms there was none wth them in ye morning & they not pveing or saying y^t a keep: was then wth y^m otherwise the calling on Brookes to pve that he found y^m wthout a keep: wch were vaine, for theire grt neglect & breach of Towne order: The sd Bagg Pringrydays & Bedortha are ordered & Cast to Pay 5s a head for each beast to ye use of ye Towne, wch for the 6 beasts comes to 30s.

June 3d 1669.   By the Select men: Present

John Pynchon

Geo: Colton

Nath Ely

Sam Marshfeild &

Laur Bliss:

This day according to Towne order wee considered about making Rates & taking a list of ye estate of ye plantation, & for Prizing the Living stock of the Plantation we chose & appointed Sam Ely: Edw ffoster & Jonath Ashly who are to goe about ye worke spedyly & bring in ye estate of the Towne to us, for ye spedy making ye Rates:

At this meting we Judged it Needfull to make a Towne Rate off £60 neere about £10 of it, in reference to severalls due fro: the Towne to discharge & y^e £50 toward ye carying on of the new Building for Mr Glovers house, although we find all this will be to little to defray ye Townes debt upon y^t aco^t yet considering ye Inability of of the Towne this yeare by reason of ye hand of God on our crops, we know not well how to doe y^t wch we are necessaryly Inforced too, & therefore shall determine upon only y^e £60 to be raised on ye Inhabitants for the whole of all Towne charges: ye Ministers Rate being besides, this wth countrey & county Rates.

At this Meeting a Motion being made in Writing by Joseph Parsons of Northampton for Liberty to Purchase a psell of land belonging to this Township. of Tho Coply: wch land lyes at ye foote of the higher ffalls, his desire is granted, & also Liberty to build &c: according to his desire:

[II—74]

At a meeting of ye Select men: January 14th 1669. Present:

J Pynchon:
G: Colton
Nath Ely
Sam Marshfeild
Laur Bliss:

At this meeting we considered ye Compl^t of y^m y^t tooke ye Towne Land at chick: what to abate y^m according to agrem^t ye hand of God having bin very heavy Blasting their wheate as also by ye floods but most excedingly by ye wormes eating up their Ind Corne, so that their loss & damadge there by is exceeding much since Capt Pynchon & Sam Marshfeild veiwed it, who then Judged an abatem^t of halfe to be made But upon certaine understanding of what further damadge ye wormes did y^m afterward whereby they have not as they say to pay for their Labor wee Doe Judge meete to make y^m a further abatem^t: & so order theire Payment of Rent to be as followeth viz each of y^m to pay 3 bush. of wheate & one bushell of Indian Corne apeice wch is in all 9 bush of wheate is.............................I   11   6

& 3 bush of Ind: Corne is....o   07   6

————————

I   19   0

And this to goe for theire whole Rent this yeare past: pvided they pay in their fines for cattle in ye feild viz: 10s pce. J^o Bag & Edm: Pringridays.

There being as is sd by severall psons, need of a Highway

over yᵉ wet meddow so into yᵉ woods, toward the Lower end of the Towne about Benja Parsons: the Select men doe therefore appoint: Serjant Stebbings Rowland Thomas & Jeremy Horton to veiw & consider & where yᵉ sᵈ way may be most Conveniently laid out & to make report thereoff to yᵉ Select men what they Judge thereabouts & how far they Judge such a way necessary for yᵉ use of the Inhabitants thereabouts: & theire returne to be made to some of yᵉ select men some time next week.

[II—75]

Jan. 14th 1669. At this meeting:

Granted to Anthony Dorchester about Ten acres of Swamp & low land lying beyond Agawa: River where his wet meddow is betwixt yᵉ hills agᵗ his wet medow there.

Granted to John Clarke Ten acres of land by his medow on yᵉ Mill River in severall spangs to lay his meddow & that togither.

Granted to John Bagg Twenty acrs of Land on yᵉ west side yᵉ grt River beyond chickkuppy Plaine next above John Rileys land, Convenient Highways being reserved or else to be laid out afterward. Also Granted him five acres of swampy Meddowish land hemmed in wᵗʰ Hills, wᶜʰ is lying about 60 rod above chikkuppy Plaine fence:

Granted to Capt Holyoke over yᵉ grt River on this side of yᵉ higher ffalls alittle below Tho Coplys land wᶜʰ he hath sold to Joseph Parsons: eighty acres of Land to ly fro: thence downeward by yᵉ great Riverside to yᵉ Land abovesᵈ Granted to John Bagg: reserving Liberty for Highways thorow it as there shall be occasion if they cannot conveniently be laid by yᵉ side of it.

Also there is an addition Granted to Mr Holyokes wet meddow by yᵉ 3 corner meddow wᶜʰ formerly was not to come quite to yᵉ foote of the Hill, it is now granted that his land there shal come not only to yᵉ foote of yᵉ Hill, but also that he shal have the land all along on the side of the Hill up to yᵉ edge of yᵉ Brow so as to set his fence there if he so cause, pvided he doe not Intrench upon the ends of any of the homlots that were granted there. al wch are to goe to y^t Brow of y Hill wch Runs all along by the Three Corner meddow side.

[II—76]

Severall psons desiring Grants of Land at toward or about Stony River on ye west side of ye grt River toward Windsor: Having taken the same into Consideration togither wth what is sd by many psons that if it were well ordered & managed aright, it might make a fine village or smale Plantation, wee therefore Commend it to ye Towne to consider how far they may se cause to order or settle ye Same: And in the meane tyme in refference to those that desire Grants there: we Judge meete that Sam & Joseph Harmon have 30 acres of land a peice there & 6 acres apeice of wet meddow.

Also that John Lamb have 30 acrs there & 6 acrs of meddow

Benja Parsons 30 acrs & 6 acrs of medow.

Sam Bliss Senr 30 acrs & 6 acrs of medow.

Griffith Joanes for his 2 sons 20 acrs apece & 4 acrs of medow apeice.

All on condition they attend such termes as shal be concluded on by any Comittee appointed ye ordering the same:

Granted to Wm Brookes 40 acrs of land on ye west side & North end of land which Tho Coply hath sold to Jos Parsons at ye foote higher falls, convenient Highways being reserved. Also by way of exchange Granted to Sam Marshfeild Sixty acrs of land there, by Wm Brookes they agreeing in laying of it out, this of Sam Marshfeilds is in Lew of Sixty acrs wch he had over Agawam River & upon condition he resigne up hereby declaring it & acepting this he to alow . . . . . Highways allowed to be laid as . . . .

[In the handwriting of Elizur Holyoke.]

[II—77]

Springfeild ffebruary ye 7th 1669. At a meting of the Select Men vizt Elizur Holyoke Leu^t Cooper, Ens: Cooley Benj: Parsons & Henry Chapin:

The Select Men chose John Matthews & Nath Pritchard

for veiwers of yᵉ fences vizt for yᵉ Long Medow & the home Lotts to the upper wharfe Lane.

Wᵐ Brookes & Wᵐ Hunter for yᵉ feild caled chickuppy playne.

John Dumbleton & Obadiah Miller for ffences on the west side of yᵉ River oposite to yᵉ Towne.

Granted to Lawrence Bliss 2 or 3 acres of Medow land on yᵉ North branch of yᵉ Mill River above his Medow bought of Rowl Stebin: pvided it be not granted to any other pson.

Graned to Symon Bemon & Jeremy Horton 3 acres a peece of land agᵗ the great bar of yᵉ higher falls in yᵉ great River on yᵉ east side of the River to be laid together in one peese provided the Indians are wiling to sell & that he cleare the purchase thereoff.

Granted to John Matthews 30 acres of land the swamp called J Matthews his swamp.

Granted to Thomas Miller 3 acres of land at Askanunsick by his other land there provided it pʳjudice not the laying of yᵉ high way to Westffeild wᵗʰin conveniency in yᵉ judgmᵗ of the Select Men or others appointed by them.

Granted Tho Mirick 2 or 3 acres of Medow land & Swampe by his land at 16 acres pvided it be not granted to any pson already.

Samuell Marshfeild hath granted unto him 40 acres of land above or by his & Wᵐ Brookes land grannted at yᵉ higher falls in yᵉ great River to be laid out soe as not to hinder highways...........

[II—78]

ffebr 7, 69. Jonathan Burt Jonathan Ball Charles fferry for himselfe & Nath Hermon also Lawr Bliss all these desire accommodations of land at Stony River: Consideration whereof is referred to another Meeting of yᵉ Select Men:

May the 14th 1670

At a Meeting of yᵉ Select Men: pʳsent Ens Cooley Benj: Parsons Henry Chapin & Elizur Holyoke. It is Ordered yᵗ yᵉ veiwers of yᵉ fences (appoynted by the Select Men) for the Severall genʳll corne feilds shall about yᵉ beginning of July

& about ye end of August next ensueing veiw the Severall fences under their charge: & in case of defects in ye fence they shall give notice thereof to the Owners of such deficient fences & warne y^m immediately to repaire them & if they be found unrepayred one day after such notice given them ot their defects such pson shal pay (besides all damage that shall accrue to any pson by such deficient fences) 12d p defect for ye least defects & 12d p rod for al the rods defective & the fynes to encrease 12 both p day & p rod for 6 days after such notice given to amen them: And if any pson shall neglect to amend his fence for ye 6 days the veiwers of such fences shall amend y^m & have double recompense: the like Od^r shalbe observed for ye such fences as now deficient or shalbe till they be veiwed in July as aforesd: And the fynes incurred upon this Od^r shalbe gathered by ye Constable by warant fro: the Selectmen upon complaynt of the veiwers.

Cornelius Wiliams desiring a smal pcell of Meddow betwen the 4 mile pond & chickuppe [II—79] River there is grannted unto him 2 acr or 2 acr & 1-2: if there be soe there undisposed of:

John Lamb hath liberty granted him (uppon his desire) to build on his land in ye playne above End brooke.

August 19th 1670

Att a meeting of ye Select Men vizt Leut Cooper Ens Cooly Ben parsons He: Chapin: E: Holyoke

Thomas Miller, Hayward of ye feild on the West side of the great River p^{r}senting John Petty John Scott Edw ffoster Ja: Tayle^r Tho: Mirick Jo: Clark Lawr Bliss Antho Dorchester Jon: Burt & J: Lumbard for turning or keeping their Cattell wthin ye sd feild contrary to Ord^r. Vpon hearing ye case the six last their offence being for y^t ye 18th of May their teemes were found in ye neck wthout a keep: but it being declared y^t y^r cattell were impounded & the poundage paid by ye owners of ye cattell they were dismist & Soe were the rest on other considerations

[II—80]

There is grannted unto Rice Bedortha that 5 or 6 acr of

wett land wch was firmly grannted to Joseph Crowfoote & resigned into ye Townes hand lying about 1-2 a mile fro: his house upon y^t brooke y^t comes out of ye woods & runs by Edm: Pringridays cellar.

Oct 12 1670. At a meeting of ye Select Men they being all p^rsent.

Whereas in Aprill last there was grannted to Mr Glover an addition of £20 p anum to his £80 p anum: his first begining at Michltide last the £20 for this yeere should be raysed thus: vizt y^t Mr Glovers fire wod for this yeere should be gotten for him as pt of ye pay & £10 to be another pay & it was left to ye Select men to pportion each man his share: that is to say who should gett ye fire wood & how much & who should pay y^e £10 & how much: now the Select Men doe judge y^t he will need for ye yeere 70 loads of fire wod wch they Order this to be gotten for him: the psons undernamed to get it & cart it.

	Loads
Rowland Thomas	2
Jeremy Horton	2
Henry Chapin	2
Joseph Crowfoote	1
Robert Ashley	3
Jonathan Ashley	2
Samuell Terry	2
John Lamb	2
Miles Morgan	3
[II—81]	
Serjean Stebbins	2
Thomas Day	2
Charles fferry	1
John Clark	2
John Matthews	1
Nath Pritchard	2
Samll Bliss Senr	2
Richard Sikes	3
John Lumbard	1

ffrancis Pepper & Tho: Stebbins Junr......1
William Branch.........................1
Elizur Holyoke......................4
Deacon Chapin 2
Timothy Cooper................2
John Hitchcock 2
John Stewart.........................1
James Warrener 2
William Warrener 2
Cornelius Williams..................1
Symon Lobdell......................1
Thomas Merrick....................2
Lawrence Bliss 2
John Harmon 1
Benjamin Parsons 2
Anth Dorchester..................4
Jonathan Burtt 2
Jonathan Ball 1
Samll Ball 1
Samll Harmon & Joseph Harmon.........1
Samll Bliss Junr....................1

And the £10 is to be pd thus

	£	s
Capt Pynchon	4	0
John Keepe	0	6
Samll Ely	0	5
Ens: Cooley	0	14
John Leonard	0	05
Edw: ffoster	0	03
Quart'master Colton	1	0
Nath Burt	0	5
John Bliss	0	5
Leiut Cooper & Tho Cooper Junr	0	11
Thomas Miller	0	5
John Scott	0	3

pd wheate

John Dumbleton	0	03
Obadiah Miller	0	2

Edm: Pringridayes...........................0   2
William Hunter 0   2
John Bagg 0   2
Richard Exell.........................0   2
Samll Marshfeild.......................0 07
John Riley............................0   2
Rice Bedortha.........................0   5
Nathanell Ely........................0 10

Theres grannted Nath Pritchard 10 acr of land neere ye foote path in ye way to watchuett not to hinder high ways to those quarters in place most convenient.

[II—82]

Theres granted to John Stewart 3 acres of medow neere ye 4 mile pond by ye Bay path in y^t med where Cornelius Willms hath some granted him: if Soe much be there undisposed of.

Theres grannted to Lieut Cooper 16 acres of lowland on the most Southerly branch of ye 3 mile brook: below his house about half a mile up ye brook, provided it be wthin this Towne bounds when ye bounds are sett.

Theres grannted to Ens: Cooley w^t vacant land lyes between the Rere of his land in ye Long medow & the fence where it stands by the pond.

There is grannted to Serjeant Stebbin the dingle ag^t his meddow called wheele meddow for 80 rodd up ye dingle & of ye high land by the upper side of ye dingle the Same length & 20 rod broad.

It is ordered y^t there shalbe a highway of 5 or 6 rod broad fro: ye way that goes to ye mill up to the cart bridge y^t is over the mill Riv^r & so fro: that bridge up into the pine playne: to be laid out in place most convenient by Benj. Parsons Jonath. Burt & Nathaneell Pritchard.

Complaynt being made of ye deficiency of the bridge called the new bridge Jonathan Ashley is to call ye company together y^t are to repaire it to chuse one to see it done wch if he have done already the Select Men doe appoynt Serj to call ye company to ye work.

[II—83]

It is ordered that there shalbe a highway by the fence on ye back side of the long meddow, (vizt wthin ye fence) 2 rod broad from Nath Burts upper lott to the bridge on the way to Nath Burts said upper lott, to the backer fence: this way being for passage into y^{re} woods y^t way:

There is grannted to Samll Ely 6 acres of ye high land below long meddow brooke neere ye great River.

Grannted to R Sikes 2 or 3 acr of wett meddow & low land on a little brooke y^t runs into ye mill River about a mile above y^e. Saw mill if it be not already grannted to some other.

There is granted to Symon Bemon 5 or 6 acr of Swamp & low lands under ye hill on the South side of his other land.

[II—84]

Decemb^r 19th 1670　Att a meeting of ye Select Men they being all p^{r}sent:

There is grannted to Symon Lobdell 3 acres of medow about 1-2 a mile beyond ye medow y^t was granted to Cornelius Williams towards Skipmuck (northerly fro: Cornel: his meddow:) lying in 2 pcels: if it be undisposed off: this is y^t wch is also grannted by ye next Select men Aug 28, 71.

Theres grannted to Eliakim Cooley 6 acr of wett medd & lowlands upon fresh water brooke below Pequitt path: lying in 2 or 3 pcells provided it be not already otherwise grannted & y^t it be disposable by this Towne.

Dec ye 3d 1670　Att a Meeting of ye Select Men al p^{r}sent

Granted to Symon Lobdell 3 acrs of wet meddow neer or by goodman Thomas his medow about 1-2 a mile fro: ye Bay path: provided it be not disposed of already:

The Select determined y^t a rate of £34 shalbe levyed on ye Inhabitants of this Town.

II—85]

December 1670 The Towne Dr

To Samll & J: Harman for killing 4 wolves.. 2　00　00

To ye Recorder for writings in Town book . o 10 oo
To J: Hitchcock for his journey to ye Bay
wth Mr Glover in May last............ 1 oo oo
To J: Clark for mending ye pound........ o o2 oo
To J: Stewart for hookes & hinges for y^e
To E: Holyoke for work & nayles about y^e
Meeting house win 'owes............. o 06 oo
Meeting house windowes....:........ o o1 oo
ffor 18 foot of boards for Meeting house
windowes .... o o1 oo
To John Harman & J: Osbern for killing 1
wolfe .... o 10 oo
To Benj: Mun for ringing ye Bell &c...... 2 10 oo
To Nath Ely from charges of ye Select Men,
&c at his house..................... 2 03 oo
To E: Holyoke for making ye rates...... 1 oo oo
To Richard Sikes 5s for assisting J: Hitch-
cock .... o 05 oo
To Miles Morgan for ferrage of 3 men y^t
went upon pambulation between Springfeild & Westfeild.................... o 05 oo
To Anthony Dorchester for ferrage of 2
men y^t went to lay out bounds to Westfeild Southward of Worro: River....... o o2 oo
To £4 for ye Deputyes diet for next yere... 4 oo oo
To Capt Pynchon for hire of his bull this
summer last past to be pd by pticular
persons .... 1 oo oo
To ffrancis Pepper for 2 dayes digging clay
for m^r Glovers house................. o 03 04
To Jno Stewart for a lock 6s & bolt 18d &
plate 6d for ye lock for the meeting house
doore & keyes & cotters for ye bell 1s.... o 11 oo
To Richard Sikes for mending ye bell...... o o2 oo
To Serj: Stebbins for................... o 10 oo
To John Lamb: 3s for work for J: Hitchcock.............................. o 03 oo

memente J Petty about ye water work for
  this yeer............................   o7
Memente ye hire Capt Pynchons Bull 20s to
  be raysed on all in ye Street except Capt
  Pynchon at 3d p cow.
[II—86]

1670:   The Town Cr.

                                         £   s   d

By rent of ye land at Chickkuppe vizt from
  Wm Brookes 30s, from J. Bagg 30s & fro:
  Edm: Pringridayes 30s in all.......... 4   10   00
By 1 bush 1-2 of Ind: Corn due fro: E Holy-
  oke Pd Indian C....................   o   03   09
By a rate of £37 7s to be raysed on ye Town
  to pay ye debts p Contra & the remaynder
  to be expended on m^r Glovers house next
  spring 37   07   00
Edm: Pringridays pd 2 bush & 1-2 wheat &
  1 bush Ind corne these towards his rent.. o   08   09
Edm: Pr ye rest of his rent..............   o   02   06
[II—87]
             [In the handwriting of John Pynchon.]
                  ffebr 13th 1670.

At a meeting of ye Select men for the yeare ensueing viz:
Capt John Pynchon Geo: Colton Sam Marshfeild John Dumbleton Rowland Thomas All being present

At this meeting the Reson mens absence fro: ye last Generall Towne meeting was Considered & alowed off wthout
finding any of them.

Veiwers of ffences for ye yeare ensuing were now chosen
& apointed as followeth:

Tho Mirick & Laur Bliss for ye feild on the west side of the
greate River ag^t ye Towne:

Robert Ashley & Miles Morgan for ye ffeild called chikkuppy feild on ye west side of the River.

Sam Ely & Ephraim Colton for the Long meddow ffeild.

Tho Day & Sam Terry for ye Homlots fro: the wharfe lane
downe to Obadiah Cooly taking him in. And these veiwers

are also to veiw Lots on ye North side of the wharfe Lane water fence

Jeremy Horton & Symon Beamon for Skipnuck & chikkuppy feild on this side of ye River.

The order about fencing being Considered: The Select men doe order the same as was 2 yeare agoe on ye 12th of feb^r 1668. Title fences, only for ye tyme wee now appoint & set ye 15th of March next unles ye frost be in the ground And all feilds what ever to be cleared of Cattle by the 15th of March next unless·ye frost doe Indeed hinder men fro: fencing: on Penalty as is there, Title, cleare feilds. ffor seating Persons in ye Meeting house, we had it under consideration but could effect nothing for want of a list:

[II—88]

Feb^r 13th 1670

Whereas Sometimes mens yards adjoyning uppon Common feilds are an occasion of dammage to ye ffeilds by reson of defective fence about such yards: It is therefore ordered That ye fence next to ye Common feild shall be lyable to the veiwers Care to see y^t they be sufficient to secure ye feilds & to p^rvent damage to ye pprietors.

There is Liberty Granted to John Bliss to Build upon his Land in ye Long meddow at ye end of his lot next the Pond, & ye Land there at ye end of his lot to the Pond side is now granted him to be his, If it was not his by former grant.

Aug: 28th 1671. All ye Select men present viz

Mr Pynchon: Geo: Colton
Sam Marshfeild: J^o Dumbleton
Rowland Thomas

Symon Lobdell desyring a strap of meddow alitle beyond y^t Granted to Cornelius Wiliams & Eastward of it There is granted to Symon Lobdell five acres of meddow if so much be there in ye place desyred pvided he take it fro: upland to upland & y^t it be not already granted to any other pson.

Granted to Mr Pynchon y^t if he set up a Barne upon his Ground at ye hither end of ye Round hill: That for Convenience & advantage of ye wind wch ye Hill deprives him off.

He shall have Liberty to set it out into ye Highway there, not exceeding 2 Rod at ye hither Corner of it, & so to slope of ye fence to nothing running it fro: y^t Corner of ye Barne into ye Range where he Joines to Serja Stebbings: And he hath Liberty Granted him to Build on his Land for Dwelling there, when he shall see cause so to do:

[II—89]

Aprill 5th 1671.

James Osborne Brought a wolfes head & I cut of his eares according to Law: he says it is betweene him & J° Harmon

May 6, 1671.

Sam & J°s Harmon killed a wolfe ye head of wch they Brought to G: Thomas & he cut of ye eares.

Octobe^r 16th 71.

John Harmon & James Osborne killed 2 wolves, of wch Goodm: Marshfeild cut of ye eares of both.

October 20th.

John Harmon kiled one wolfe: & G: Marshfeild cut of ye eares.

Octob^r 24.

Sam & Jos Harmon kiled one wolfe & G: Thomas cut of his eares.

John Harmon & James Dorchester killed one wolfe & G: Thomas cut of his eares

Rowland Thomas killed one wolfe.

Dec. 27, 71.

Sam & Jos Harmon brought one wolfes head of which I cut off ye eares.

[II—90]

At a meting of ye Selectmen Janu: 1st 1671. Present all, viz: Jo Pynchon: Geo Colton John Dumbleton Sam Marshfeild & Rowland Thomas.

John Petty moveing that the land Granted to Edward ffoster of 30 acrs beyond Block Bridge wch was measured out, & since excepted agt as not being laid out according to ye grant, might yet notwthstanding be allowed off as it is laid out Edw: ffoster having sold it to him: & manifesting his like desires: The select men doe now Confirme it to y^m & allow of ye sd acrs acording as it was measured out & Bounded. And doe moreover at ye desire & request of John Petty Grant to ye sd John Petty Seven acres more, there, as an addition thereto viz 14 Rod wide on ye west side of ye former 30 acres wch is to Run 80 rod Long as ye former 30 acres doth & so makes ye whole 37 acres.: The Timber & wood growing on ye whole psell being to be free for any of ye Neighbors to make use off, till he shall Impve it or ffence it in.

Granted to John Lamb 5 or 6 acres of land for a homlot wth Liberty to Build on it, in ye Plaine beyond End Brooke from ye side of his owne & Goodm: Muns Land there, to ye grt hill, & so lying by ye side of ye hill: Liberty for wood & Timber being free for all Inhabitants till he shall Impve it.

Granted to George Colton (for conveniency of ffencing) 10 or 12 acrs of land, adjoyning to & by his owne Land wthout ye Long meddow, beyond Nathanell Burts Land there:

[II—91]

Sam^{ll} Barber (of windsor) is admitted & his Brother John Barber becomes Ingaged & doth hereby Bind himselfe in ye sum of Twenty Pounds to ye Selectmen of Springfeild fro: tyme to tyme: to Save ye sd Towne of Springfeild fro: any charge that may arise to ye sd Towne by ye sd Sam Barber. or any of his: as witness his hand this 1st of January 1671.

John Barber.

January 1671.

Granted to John Barber & to Sam Barber his Brother (if he come to dwell in this Towne) To each of y^m 16 acres of Land by Agawam River side alitle below Ashkanunksit in a bottom there, alitle beyond block Bridge. If the Bottom will afford it they have Liberty to have 17 or 18 acrs a Peice there: John Barber to choose wch land he please to take for his pt of it

Granted to Abell Wright 2 acrs of Land by his house Lot formerly granted him at Skeepnuck, wch is an adition theretoe pvided it hinder not ye Highway: Also he is alowed Liberty to Build on his Lott there:

There is granted a Highway there To ye Towne of 3 or 4 Rod broad fro: ye w^t oake marked by ye Comittee, To a Pine Tree wch is at ye west Corner of Mr Pynchons Land there.

Granted to Sam Holyoke a psell of land at ye further end of ye Round hill betweene Crooked Point & Serja M^organs Land there: wch was formerly left 16 Rod wide for a Highway there, but there being noe necessity of such a Highway that Peice of Land fro: ye Round hill all along Northward to ye Brooke wch ye New Bridge goes over is now granted to Sam Holyoke, reserving only 2 rod wide for a Highway if there shall be any need or occasion thereoff

[II—92]

Granted to Pelatiah Morgan ffive or Sixe acres of Land for a homlot beyond his fathers Land, y^t is beyond ye Round hill: on ye east side of ye Brooke & east end of his fathers Land there this is to ly: & so to be laid out as not to p^rjudice ye clay pits not far off it, nor ye way or Passage to y^m: nor any Highway out into the medos there, & this grant is p^rvided Pelatiah doe Build or Imp^rve there wthin five years: hereby having Liberty granted him for Building there accordingly:

Granted to Wm Brookes on ye other side of the Highway fro: his howselot at chikkuppy, alitle above ye gate goeing into ye feild 2 or 3 acres of Land for to Build a Barne on, upon ye hill there p^rvided he p^rjudice noe Highway there Needful:

At this Meeting ye Select men Considering ye Dues fro: ye Plantation to severall psons ordered a Rate of £20 to be Raised on all ye Inhabitants for defraying thereoff:

[II—93]
[In the handwriting of Elizur Holyoke.]

ffeb^r 12 1671. At a Meeting of ye Selectmen, all of y^m being p^rsent vizt: Ens: Cooly Nath Ely Anth: Dorchester Benj Parsons & Elizur Holyoke Senr. Veiwers of fences for ye yeere ensueing there are now chosen & appointed.

Jonath Taylor & Richard Exell for ye feild on ye West side of ye River over ag^t ye Town.

Rice Bedortha & John Riley for Chickuppe ffeild on ye West side of ye River:

John Clark & Samll Bliss for ye Longe Meddow:

Serj: Stebbin & James Warrener for the house lotts from ye Lower wharfe to ye upper wharfe & for the North^rly fence of ye wharfe lane, & to ye lower gate y^t opens to 3 corner Meddow.

Granted John Holton 6 acrs of land by Pelatiah Morgans grant not to p^rjudice high wayes in most convenient place reserving ye wood y^ron till it be fenced in.

Granted Joseph Leonard what vacant land lyes between William Warr: medd: in Middle meddow & Benj: Muns meddow in ye next medd. also soe much of ye pond as lys agt Wm Warreners medow.

Granted Samll Ball 6 acrs of land at or neere w^r the old brick kilne was provided he come to dwell in this Town not to p^rjudice high ways.

Granted Tho: Stebbin Junr 6 acrs of land by or neere the grannt of Samll Ball not to p^rjudice high wayes:

[11—94]

Granted John Stewart 6 acres of land at or neere ye reere of Maj^r Pynchons upper woodlotts over ye medow.

Granted Samll Bliss Junr 2 or 3 acrs of Medd: in ye Medd: w^r he had a form^r grant in march 65-66 if there be soe much there & on like Cond: as y^t Also 3 acrs more of wett medd is granted to him behind long meddow below N Burts Medd.

And next to Samll Bliss is granted to Obadiah Cooley & Eliakim Cooley Isaak & Ephraim Colton 5 acres apeece in y^t wett Medd: if there be soe much undisposed of: they to agree among y^m selves how to lye.

Granted to Charles Ferry 40 acres of land neere ye Bay path about ye two gutters wch are about 6 mile off provided it be not purchased of ye Natives he cleare ye purchase y^t be disposable by the Town.

Granted Tho Day 2 or 3 acrs of land at Ashcanunksitt ioyning to his own land there at y^e......

Granted Ja: Warrener 20 acres of land beyond block bridge

on ye West side the great River next beyond John Pettys land there if it be not already granted.

[II—95]

Whereas Diverse psons y^t dwell on the East side of ye great River haveing land in ye playne called Chickuppe playne on ye West side of ye great River are liable to be called to reparation of ye way fro: y^t playne to ye Lower brook they accounting themselves opp^{r}ssed y^t seeing they make little or noe use of y^t way they should be called to repe: that way or bridges in y^t way equall with those y^t dwell there: The Select Men considering the case determine & order that such of those Proprietors of land there who dwell on ye East of ye great River shalbe liable to be caled to ye reparing that way only one day a peece to each of theire three dayes apeece that is to say w^n each of y^m y^t live on y^t side ye River that have land there wrought 3 dayes a peece in y^t way then those y^t live on ye East side of ye River shall be called each of y^m 1 day a peece to y^t way & soe fro: tyme to tyme.

As for fences about corn feilds meddowes &c the Select Men order all fences to be made up by the 1st of March next & all feilds to be cleared of cattle by y^t tyme: & in other things concerning fences the Order made by ye Select men ffebr -2 1668 is to be attended:

[II—96]

March 20th 1671-2 At a meeting of ye Proprietors of ye ffeild on ye West side of ye great River It is voted & concluded that ye water work fence y^t use to be below Tho: Millers shall be set there agayne this yeere & Jonathan Ball undertakes to make & maynteyne a fence there sufficient to secure the feild he is to fence fro: ye top of the bank down to & unto ye water soe farr as to secure the feild fro: damage that way this summer for wch his soe doing he is to have 30s raysed on the Proprietors according to y^r land in the feild:

And Joseph Leonard hath undertaken to make the water fence at Agawam River & to maynteyne it sufficiently to secure the feild fro: damage that way this yeere for wch he is to have 30s raysed on ye Proprietors who are to pay each man his share of it according to w^t land he has in ye feild: & Josephs tearmes were to have his money pd in to ye Majo^r tho yet there was noe asent to any such tearmes.

[II—97]

May 21 1672   Att a Meeting of ye Select men they being all p^rsent.

Rice Bedortha & John Riley veiwers of ye fences of Chickuppe playne feild on ye west side of ye great River: John Riley being sick Rice Bedortha present Samuell Terry & Serj: Morgan for deficiency of y^r fences of ye said feild: Samuell Terryes fence proved 4 rod defective 3 weekes at least & he being warned to amend it refused bec: he said he had more laid to him than his due to maynteyne but whether y^t be soe or noe is doubtfull but it is proved y^t y^t part wch he refused to mend is out of doubt his fence: soe the veiwers were fayne to mend it for wch labo^r they req double recompense as ye law allowes they reckon y^r labor well worth between man & man at 2s. also the veiwers pleades other trouble & charges as his attendance to psecute & for witnesses &c:

The Select men uppon hearing ye case Judge Goodm: Terry Culpable & Soe determine him to pay to ye Veiwers double recompense for y^r labo^r in mending   ye fence

vizt	o	04	00
for 2 witnesses 1s & other trouble 18d.	o	02	00
for 1 of ye Veiwers attendanse to psecute.	o	01	00
for deficiency of ye fence 3s 1-2 to ye veiwers & 1-2 to ye Town.	o	01	06
	o	08	06

Samll Terry owes ye Town on ye acco. . . . . o   01   06

[II—98]

And Serja Morgans fence proved defective   in   diverse places wch he has refused to mend pleading it was not his right to maynteyne it: the Veiwers mended it wch their labo^r they acco well worth 4s 6d the first penny but they require double recompence as the Law in such cases allowes: & their other charges

The Selectmen upon hearing yᵉ case Judged Serj Morgan culpable & acordingly called him to pay yᵉ veiwers their cost & charges vizt

	£	s	d
Double recompense for mending yᵉ fense....o	9	o	
One of yᵉ Veiwers attendance to psecute......o	3	o	
4 witnesses attendance....................o	I	o	
deficiency of yᵉ fence 3 dayes at 12d p day 1-2			
whereof is yᵉ Veiwers pt.................o	I	6	

o   15 6

And yᵉ other 1-2 is due to yᵉ Town.........o   o1 o6

At this meeting there was granted to Richard Exell 8 acres of land to joyn all along his land at block bridge on yᵉ East side of yᵗ brooke.

Grannted to Thomas Miller Jnʳ 20 acres of land by or neere his fathers land West side: not to hinder high wayes to be laid in most convenient places:

Granted to Wᵐ Warener wᵗ vacant land lyes between his land in yᵉ middle Meddow & Jos: Leonards late grant if there be any such vacancy & yᵗ it was not his by formʳ grants:

[II—99]

Granted to Rice Bedortha 30 acres of land on yᵉ West side yᵉ great River betwen yᵉ great pond & Samll Terreyes land above Chickuppe And hereuppon he resignes into yᵉ Townes hand his grannt of yᵉ like quantity of land at ffresh-water brook.

Granted to Joseph Bedortha twenty acres of land about 3-4 of a mile beyond his fathers house westward or a little to yᵉ Northward of yᵉ West:

Granted to Joseph Leonard the swampe between Agawam River & his fathers land over that River if it were not his fathers by formʳ grants: or by purchase fro: Goodm: Mirack highwayes not to be pʳjudiced.

John Lamb hath granted unto him a high way of 3 or 4 rod wide fro: his land towards the Towne vizt his land by the great hill towards Chickuppye River beyond End Brooke.

August 20th 1672. At a meeting of ye Select men, being all present.

Granted to Ob: Miller 7 acrs of upland on the west side of his lott at Achcanunksitt to lye all along the side of his land there vizt the land he had of R: Bedortha, & 8 acrs at ye ffront of his land there not to p^{r}judice laying out high wayes in most convenient place.

Granted Nath Pritchard 8 acres of upland at Cowseek.

Granted Anth Dorchester 20 acrs of land of & about ye dingle ag^t his land at Cowseek brook:

[II—100]

Granted to Nathaneell & victory Sikes 30 acrs of land by the Northerly side of their fathers land at Cowseek brook yet not to p^{r}judice passage that way over y^t brook in tymes of floods in ye great River: for y^t the floods in ye great River setts up soe as to hinder passage in ye River way ov^r ye bridge.

Grannted to Ob: Cooley for conveniency of cellar roome liberty of setting his fence 5 or 6 foot into ye way ag^t his house vizt soe far along ye way (as the cellar may extend) if he shall see cause to make a cellar there by his house also liberty to run his fence from ye west^{r}ly corn^r of such cellar 2 rod askew to met wth his other fence by ye way to ye wharfe

John Stewart haveing form^{r}ly a grannt of 3 acres of wett meddow in y^t medd where Corneli: Williams had a grannt it being not there to be had theres grannted him his 3 acres in a little stripe or stripes between ye medow granted to Cornelius & Skeepmuck vizt westerly fro y^t Meddow grannted to Cornelius: on a gutter y^t runs into Chickuppe River above Skeepmuck.

Granted to John Dorchester the rest of Meddow where Cornel: W had some granted him:

Grannted Tho: Day 4 acr of ye garden brook valley ag^t his woodlott y^t is over ye brooke.

Granted to Anth Dorchester what land is yet undisposed of in ye further meddow over Agawam to ye quantity of 2 or

3 acres lying at yᵉ South end of his own land & betwen the land John Leonard bought of S: Marshfeild & the upland.

Granted Peter Swink 6 acres of land adjoyning to his other land at Block bridge.

[11—101]

There is grannted to Benjamin Mun Junioʳ 6 acars of land by his brother Balls at the old brick killn to ly all along his brothers land there not pʳjudicing high wayes in most convenient places.

Grannted Samll Holyoke that peece of land wᶜʰ lyes betwen his formʳ grannt by the round hill & the fence or new ditch End brook to be yᵉ bounds fro: yᵉ ditch to the brook yᵗ runs out of yᵉ Meddowes.

Dec: yᵉ 30th 1672.   Town is Dr.

To Serj Stebbin for help & tymeber about yᵉ Meeting house Staires & pound.......................0 4 0

Jan 3 72 At a meeting of yᵉ Select men all pʳsent except Ens: Cooley:

Grannted to Nathaneell Burt ten acres of upland to lye joyning to yᵉ East end of his other 10 acres on yᵉ hill (where he lives) formerly grannted unto him to run fro: brook to brook pvided it pʳjudice noe high way yᵗ may be had there:

Vppon this grannt he allowes of a high way of 1 rod & 1-2 wide fro: yᵉ river to yᵉ pond through his upper lott in the long Meddow vizt on yᵉ side of yᵉ lott.

Also yʳˢ grannted him a little Strappet of land vizt Lowland being betwen a quarter of an acr & half an acr lying on yᵉ west side of his wett Meddow wᶜʰ is on yᵉ west side of his swampe land behind yᵉ long meddow on condition yᵗ there be roome for a high way Sixe rod wʳ yᵉ small lotts in yᵉ long meddow have their full pportion:

[11—102]

Jan 1 72 At a meeting of yᵉ Select Men all prsent.

Theres grannted to yᵉ Neighboʳs on yᵉ West side of the great River yᵗ ingage to set up a Saw mill neere block bridge 10 acr of land on that brook in yᵉ most convenient place for yᵗ work: provided it pʳjudice noe mans ppriety of land thereabout & that they doe wthin two yeere fro: this tyme carry on such a work there to effect.

Granted to Tho Miller about half an acr of land neere his cellar at Ashcanunksett to make his rang for fencing a little straiter provided it be noe hinderance for laying out a high way in most convenient place.

Grannted to Charles fferry for conveniency of fencing 4 acres of land by his Meddow on ye Mill River bought of Nath Ely.

Grannted to J^o: Keep 4 acr of wet meddow at ffresh water brook by his own meddow there:

Grannted Samll Holyoke 10 acres of land between Robert Ashleyes wood lott & the wood lot of Tho: Stebbin Junr wch is by ye old brick kilne.

At a Meeting of ye Select Men all p^rsent, Jan 31, 72.

There is grannted to Nath Burt that his first grannt of land vizt of 10 acr not yet measured w^r he dwells shall run fro: brook to brook.

Theres grannted to Rich Exell 4 acres of land lying all along the South end of his lott at Block bridge.

[II—103]

Jan 31 72

There is grannted John Bag 10 acr of land by his own land above Chickuppe playn not to p^rjudice laying out high wayes in most convenient place.

Nathaneell Burt hath grannted unto him Six acres of wett Meddow in the great meddow above Pequitt path provided it belong to this Township & that it be free for this Town to dispose of & that he pay ye Indian purchase if not already pd & that y^r be soe much undisposed already.

Serjant Stebbin hath grannted unto him Six acres of land lying between Majo^r Pynchons Longer wood lotts & John Stewarts wood lott & at ye reere of ye Majo^r shorter wood lotts.

Majo^r Pynchon hath grannted unto him ffoure acres at Paucatuck towards Westfeild to lye by Tho: Millers land

there, not pᵣjudicing the laying out high wayes in most convenient place:

Also yʳˢ grannted to Major yᵗ little peece of land at the
Southeast end of the round hill of farr as yᵉ Northᵣly side
of yᵉ causey vizt John Stewart Rayle fence on his ditch: provided a high way be left of a rod & half wide soe through
toward Goodm: Branch his land & yᵉ like for passage to yᵉ
playne gate & that the way be not encumbered wᵗʰ gates or
bars:

[II—104]

Jonath Burt hath Six acres of land grannted him vizt wett
medd: in yᵉ great Meddow above Pequitt path: on like conditions as his Brother Nathaneell grant of Meddow there:

Theres grannted to John Keepe 4 acres of wett meddow
on ffresh water brook below Pequitt path to joyne to his
owne meddow on the hither branch.

[In the handwriting of Samuel Marshfield.]

January 9th 1673 Att a meeting off the Selecktt men
(viz) George Coulton John Dumbleton Henry Chapin Samuell Marshfeild and Thomas Cooper The ffarmers off The
Townsland att cheeckapee making complaintt off The mean-
ness off There cropp The Selecktt men abated Them off This
yeares rentt £3

[II—105]
[In the handwriting of Elizur Holyoke.]

At a meeting of yᵉ Selectmen All pʳsent Jan 31 1672

Theres grannted to yᵉ Neighboʳs on the West side of yᵉ
great River about ffifty acres of land upon yᵉ most Southerly
Branch of yᵉ 3 mile brook below Leut Coopers, they desiring to Set up a saw mill there: This grannt is on condition yᵗ
they give up there interest in yʳ former grannt of land at
block bridge brook wᶜʰ was for yᵉ like designe: And pvided
it be not pᵣjudiciall to yᵉ high way, nor to any mans ppriety
by ponding up of water wᵗʰout reasonable satisfaction &
pvided it fall wᵗʰin the bounds of this town wⁿ our bounds are
stratened & settled: & that they pay their reasonable share
for yᵉ purchase of lands in these quarters: And it is to be un-

d^rstood y^t this grannt is only to such as shall cary on y^r work to effect that a saw mill there be sett on work wthin 2 yeeres fro: this tyme.

The Veiwers of ye fences of Chickuppe ffeild complayning of the deficiency of the fences of Robt Ashley & Jn° Scott 9 or 10 rod a peece & Jonath: Ashleyes: about 16 rod: All defective 4 dayes & they warned to appeare before ye Select Men Robt Ashley & Jonathan Ashley appeared: The case being heard they were all found culpable & were fyned 6s a peece vizt 3 shillings a peece to ye veiwers & 3s a peece to ye Towne.

[II—106]

feeb: 9th 1673. At a Meeting of ye Select Men there being 4 p^rsent vizt E: Holyoke N: Ely Ens Cooley & John Keepe

The Select according to Town order considering how to seate Such Persons in ye Meeting house y^t have not been seated there doe reckon that there being not neere enough to seate all y^t want seates they judge it not convenient to doe any thing in it till more roome be made there:

Veiwers of ye fences of ye gen^rll feilds these new chosen for Long Medd: Ephraim Colton & Sa Stebbins.

ffor ye feild on ye W side of the Riv^r: John Leonard & Thomas Miller.

ffor Chickuppe ffeild Sergant Morgan & John Bagg:

ffor house lotts fro: ye upper wharf to ye gate y^t goes to the Lowest wharfe Serjant Stebbins & John Matthews.

At a meeting of ye Select Men March 9th 74 p^rsent N Ely Ens Cooley Ben Parsons & Eli: Holyoke. It is Ordered y^t the Gen^rll termes of the gen^rll feild above Samll Terryes pasture shalbe closed by ye 12th day of this Month & yet the fences of all other ye gen^rll feilds of this town shalbe closed by the 20th of this Month And in refence to ye fences of the comon or gen^rll feilds It is ordered that the fences thereof shalbe sufficiently made up & repayred by ye tymes above limited & that the veiwers of ye fences shall wthin a Day or two after veiw the fences of ye Gen^rll feilds. And where they fynd defects therein they are to give ye owners of such fences pticular notice to amend them wthin 2 or 3 dayes: And such fences as are not amended according to such warning given The [II—107] Owners thereof shal pay as a fyne 12d a peece for each defect under a rod & 12d p rod for every rod defective wch fynes shal encrease 12d p day for every day thay shall lye wthout being sufficiently made or repayred vizt for 3 or 4 dayes after the tyme they are soe warned to repayer them: the veiwers being to se that the defcts run noe longer: however 5 dayes is to terminate the increase of 12d p day unless upon the veiwers reveiwing such fences & giving new notice to ye pprietor he shall continue to neglect to amend such defects after y^t notice: And all fynes incurred by this Order shalbe One half to ye Townes use & the other halfe to ye veiwers of the fences And in all cases about such fynes It is left to the Select Men to mitigate them; both ye veiwers pt & ye Townes pt where they shall judge they may rationally soe doe:

Whereas there is noe record extant of the grant of any high way to Mr Holyokes 3 corner Meddow only the Select Men fynd y^t in ye record of the lott wch was ffra: Peppers It is said ye sd lott is bounded by the highway to m^r Holyokes 3 corner Meddow North, by Symon Bemons lott bought of m^r Pynchon & Serjant Stebbins affirming that he many yeeres synce laid out the highway there: & ffrancis Pepper affirming that he was wth Serj: Stebbin w^n he both layd out that high way 2 rod wide & m^r Pynchon 15 acr grannted for a sheep pasture at ye Round Hil upon those considerations the Select Men doe order that m^r Holyoke shall have his way 2 rod wide in ye Said place & doe Order him at least give him liberty to enter ye same accordingly:

The Select men doe also order that a former order concerning swine made by ye Select Men ffebr 12 1668 written before in this book shall stand good & be ye Towne Order ior ye yeere ensueing concerning swine Only ye tyme for restraynt of swine is not to take place till March 25th now at hand.

[II—108]

Aprill 15 1674   Att a meeting of the Select Men: y^r were p^rsent E: Holyoke Ens Cooley N. Ely & John Keepe:

Compl^t being made form^rly vizt on ye 8th instant by Tho Miller & Tho: Cooper Junr veiwers of ye fences of y^e [   ] ye feild on ye West side of the River opposite the Town, agt diverse psons for deficiences in their fences of ye feild the Select men issuing out warrants the persons p^rsented should appr this day at 7 o'clock in ye Morning the Select wayted at least till 10 o'clock & neyther ye veiwers apped to prsent their complt nor any supposed delinquent to answer any complt: only Jno Matthews who was to mend some of ye Majo^rs fences appd who sayth he had no warning to amend the fence & the Majo^r also saith y^t he had noe warning of any place of his fences y^t needed repaire till the said 8th day of this Instant w^ras by ord^r ye owner of any deficient fences ought to have 3 or 4 dayes warning to amend them before they are p^rsentable for such deficiencyes: & soe they were dismist: yet also It is now said that the fences were repaired 4 or 5 dayes agoe: others also were p^rsented by ye veiwers for deficiencyes of fences vizt John Scott Edw: ffoster Jno Petty Eli: Holyoke & Tho: Merick who could have nothing said to y^m for ye reasons above exp^rsed:

[II—109]

Aprill 29th 1674:   Att a meeting of ye Select Men of w^m were p^rsent E: Holyoke N: Ely: B: Parsons: J: Keep:

There being compl^t made by Miles Morgan & Jo: Bagg: veiwers of ye fences of ye ffeild called Chickuppe on the West side of ye River agt Jonathan Ashley for deficiency of his fence belonging to that feild: the said Veiwers testifying that he hath 30 rod of fenceing there It is bad & insufficient to this day: but 3 places in ye said fence they specially com-playne of concerning wch they testify they have given him warning severall tymes to amend them wayting severall dayes between each warning y^t soe they might if possible avoyd p^rsenting him but they testify those extreme bad places are yet not sufficiently repayred: The Select Men upon hearing the case on both sides judged y^t the said Jonathan Ashley shall pay as a fyne 18s vizt 9s to ye Veiwers & 9s to ye Towne.

June 30th 74. Att a meeting of ye Select Men being all p^{r}sent. Samuell Ely complaynes ag^t ye veiwers of ye fences of ye long meddow feild for that they have eyther neglected the work of y^r place or at least they have not taken an effect-uall course for the amending of the fence vizt the lower water fence wch being as he reckons insufficient was the occasion of cattell coming into a ffeild last Sab: & doing him much dam-age in his corn & grass, wch he have gott judged by N: Burt & Nath Harman the judge it at 10s wch G: Ely demands satisfaction for: the Select Men upon hearing ye case doe not fynd a way how to pcure him satisfaction for ye damage done him: Ptly bec: It is not p^{r}sented to us whos cattle did ye damage: & ptly because one of ye vewers vizt Eph^r Colton very lately wth diverse others of Long Meddow did make up ye said water fence & did then reckon it sufficient for the end for wch twas made & ptly also for y^t it is in some measure uncertayn whether they came in through ye water fence or no: But for asmuch as ye s^d water fence is held up in a kind of un-certayne way w^{r}by y^{rs} grounds to suspect it is not [II—110] very well done the Select have aggreed wth Ephraim Colton & Saml Ely to make up the said fence well & sufficient if it be not soe already & well to maynteyne it this summ^r till ye ffeild open & that then they give an acount of w^t labo^r they have bestowed about it & they shalbe paid next winter by ye pprietors of land in ye feild:

[II—111]

[In the handwriting of John Holyoke.]

Dec. 29, 1674:   The Town is Dr.

	£	s	d
To Rowland Thomas for killing 1 wolf....	0	10	00
To Saml Holyoke & Charles fferry for 1 wolf	0	10	00
To Anth Dorchester for 4 wolves........	2	00	00
To Ens Cooley for 1 wolf.............	0	10	00
To Jno Stewart for irony for ye pound....	0	05	03

To David Morgan for ye pound gate.... 0 05 00
To Benj: Mun for ringing ye bell &c...... 3 00 00
To Nath Ely for use of his house at ye Gen^rll
    Town Meeting in ffeb^r the 3d 1673 3s 6d
    & for another Town Meeting at his house
    ffebr 16 last the like summe of 3s 6d: & y^e
    Townesmen dinner August 18th 1674 5s. 0 12 00
To Capt Holyoke for his 2d & 3d journey to
    Genll Corte as deputy 1673.......... 5 00 00
And for making ye rates this December
    1674 .... 1 00 00
And for writing in the Town book this yeere
    past 0 05 00
To Jonath Ashleyes pambulation between
    us & Westf. 3 yeeres agoe........... 0 03 00
To Robt Ashly scouring ye trench of ye Town
    Medd: in 1673..................... 0 03 00
It £4 for ye Depty for ye Gen^rll Co^rte next
    Spring 4 00 00
To Goodm: Ely for 2 dayes roome & dyn-
    ners for ye Select Men meeting to prize
    ye lands of ye Town w^rby to make rates
    in Jan: 74......................... 0 10 00
To Eliz: Holyoke for writing a deed for y^e
    land bought of Wequagam & Wecombo. 0 10 00
for entering a list of the Voters & ye ffree-
    mens confirmation of grannts in ye Town
    booke 0 03 00
[II—112]
        Dec: 74.   The Towne is Cr.
By rent of ye land at Chick: summer 1674,
    their crops being veiwed by ye Select Men
    all the Select judge y^t they shalbe abated
    one halfe of ye rent Soe y^t now they are
    to pay 3 15 00
By Jonath Ashley for deficient fence at
    Chickuppe this last Summer.......... 0 09 00

By a rate on the Town Jan. 74..........10 00 00
May ye 1st 75
Received of Goodm: Bagg 15 bush of Ind:
   corn & 3 bush of wheat wch is in part of
   paym^t for his 2 last yeeres rent: the whole
   was to be, 55s.................... 2 08 00
[II—113]
Jan 74.
Att a Meeting of ye Select Men they being all p^{r}sent

The Comittee y^t are chosen for ordering matters concerning building a new meeting house declaring to ye Select Men that there is need of raysing £150 on ye Inhabitants of this Town for that Work, the Select Men have Ordered that such a rate be made towards ye carrying on of ye work:

[II—114 Blank—II—115]

[In the handwriting of Samuel Marshfield.]

at a meeting off the Select men ffebuary the 8, 74 namely Quarter Colton John Dumbleton Henry Chapin Jeremi horten and Samuell Marshfeild.

Choise was made off vewars of fenses ffor the severall ffeilds also The Constabell being present choise was made off a sealer for weights and mesurs and John Lamb was chosen and the Constabell apointed to present him to the Court to be present.

ffor Long Medo feild nathaniell burt and Samuell Ely

ffor the house lots in the Towne nathaniell prichard and

ffor the ffeilds over the rivar right ovar mils morgan John dorchister richard Exell.

ffor Chicabe ffeild one the west sid the rivar John bagg and Joseph badartha.

agreed with Samuell Marshfeild to mak a Good paire of Stockes of eight ffoot in length with ffive holes in them ffor which worke he is to have ten shillings payd by the towne.

The Select having Consideration about swine & ordar in the towne book page 15 and with the abatement of the penalty in this book made ffebruary 12: 1668 do ordar the sad ordar to stand in fforce in all respects as it is in this book ffor this yeare.

The select men apoint John dumbleton and Samuell Marshfeild to take care that some things be done to the repairing of the pound one the west side of the rivar

Complaint being made ffor want off vewars off fences about the feild at Skipmuck The Select men have chosen John Clark and Charles ffery to vew the ffences off the ffeilds both at Skipmuck and Chicabe.

[II—116]

Having Consideration off the Great damage which is done in the severall ffeilds belonging to the towne in Cattels being suffared in the ffeilds lat in the springe which is a great wronge to wintar Corne The Select men doe ordar that all Cattell and swine shall be cleared out off the genarall ffeilds by the tenth of march next: and it is expected that all ffences be made up by the 10 of march if the season of the year will pemit and at ffarthest by the 25 of March.

ffinding an ordar in the Town book that doth require the Select men to Consider off seating parsons in the meeting house yearly: The Select men meting this 8 of ffebruary 74 and ffinding no rome or not sufitient to seat all we Concluded to mak no alteration till more rome be found.

The Select men Taking it into Consideration of the Causey at thomasdayes how that often Complaints have been made for want of its due breadth we have set out 2 rod ffinding that Goodman miricks ffence is within the 2 rod at both ends and we apoint him to set his ffence in to the stakes set up and so the Casey will have its due.

[II—117]

The towne detor January the 31 1675

To Sweeping the Meting house and ringing
the bell.............................2 10 0
by one wolf to Samuelll Jones and Jonathan
Taylor 0 10 0
by one woolf to Maj^or Pinchon which william
brookes killed.......................0 10 0

by one wolf to nathaniel bliss.............o   10   o
by the Select mens expences.............o   17   o
to Samuell Marshfeild 3 shiling...........o   03   o
by laying out the bounds betwene South ffeild
   and Springfeild.......................o   03   o
roland thomas..........................o   03   o
the quarter mastar ....o   03   o
to encine cooly........................o   03   o
To Samuell Holyoke for a woolf..........o   10   o
by making of the rates..................1   00   o

The holl is...6   19   o

The Towne dettor ffebruary 5: 1676

To ringing The bell and sweping the meting
   hous 2   10   o
To making The rates...................1   00   o
To enter tain ment of the Select Men 5 dayes,
   nothing alowed......................1   10   o

4   10   o

The Select men this yare are encine Cooly Jonathan burt Anthony dorchister John Hitchcock Samuell Marshfeild.
   [II—118]

The Towne Credit is

by rent of Chicabe land................05   06   oo

ffebruary 5: 76   the Select men Grant phillip matone liberty to abide in the towne: also Isack Gleason and Isack Cakebread are admitted inhabitants off This towne

This Samuell Marshfeild had

Received off wido pringridays one bushel off ry oo   03   o
   [II—119]

[In the handwriting of Jonathan Burt.]

this was concluded on by us the Select men Beniamin Cooly John Keepe John highcock Jonathan Burt.

[In the handwriting of John Holyoke.]

June: 2d: 1679.

At a meeting of the Select men, being p'sent: Deacon

Benja: Parsons Jnᵒ Dumbleton Henry Chapin Jnᵒ Holyoke.

It haveing been formerly at a Town meeting propounded to yᵉ Town, that they would set up a school house for the Town, they concluded that such a house should be erected, & appointed the Select men to bargain with any meet person to build such an house for such use: accordingly they have bargained wᵗʰ Tho: Stebbin Junʳ to get timber for such a building & frame it, whose length is to be 22 foot; & breadth 17 foot: & stud 8 foot & halfe & he the said Thomas Stebbin is to carry the frame to place & to naile the clap boards close on both sides & ends, & to Lath & shingle the roofe, & to make three light spaces on one side & two lights on one end, & to set up a mantletree, & set up a rung Chimney, & to daub it, & the said Thomas is to have for his work so done fourteen pounds paid him by the Towne, & in case it so prove that the said Thomas Stebbin have an hard bargaine, it is hereby agreed that he shal have 10s more of the Town.

Thomas Stebbins

[II—120]

[In the handwriting of Jonathan Burt.]

At a meetin of the Select men ffebuary the 7th 1675.

Theyr was made of vewers of ffences for the feilds for the Longe meadow Isaack Coulton Samuell bliss Junyr; For over the great ryver Jonathan Ball Joseph Leanerd. for Chicopy feild Rees Bothorda John Scot.

for the home lots Thomas Day John hermon.

the Select men doe order that al thos fenses be made up by the tenth of march next.

[II—121]

[In the handwriting of John Pynchon.]

At a Towne Meeting: ffebr. 23th 1675:

This meeting being called to make Supply of a Select man & also of one to enter things: God having taken away Capt Holyoke: Sam Marshfeild was by a cleare vote chosen a Select man, to make up yᵉ Number for the yeare ensuing.

Jonathan Burt is chosen Towne Clarke to enter all writings, & to take care for yᵉ Recording Towne affaires & keeping yᵉ Records of yᵉ Towne:

Samll Holyoke is made choice of for Clarke of yᵉ writts to be ppounded to yᵉ County Court for confirmation in sd office:

[In the handwriting of Jonathan Burt.]

nathanyell ffoot was voated an inhabitant of the Towne Also mʳ Denton voated an inhabytant.

also it was voated that the Town would fortyfy and garyson the mill a long with the gayrson solders.

[I—122]

At a Town June 8th 1676. god in his providence having taken away John Keep by death Anthony Dorchester was Chosen by a Cleare voat of the plantation a Select man to supply that want for the yeere ensuing.

At a Town meetin June 21 1676 John Dumbleton was Chosen by a voate of the Town a comysyner to Joyne with the Select men for to make the Country rats both for the present an allso for the yeare ensuing.

[In the handwriting of John Holyoke.]

march 1681-82

At a meeting of the select men, vizt: Joseph Parsons, Jonathan Burt Tho: Day Jnº Hitchcock Jnº Holyoke The said Select men did bargaine or Indent wᵗʰ Jnº Miller & Tho: Tailor to set up a pound on the West side of the River, & to do at the Carpenters workes fro: the beginning worke to the Compleat finishing thereof, That is to say they are to set up four Lengths of railes on the four sides, six good substantial railes in a length, & ten foot Long between the Postes, being white oke. Posts mortized, & a braced Gate wel hung wᵗʰ a Cross peice on the top of the gate postes, They also to pin the upper raile of Each Length, by the Tenth of April next in such place as the said Select men shal appointe, & the said Select men do covenante to give the said Miller & Tailor fifty & five shillings, which is to be paid by the next Town Rate.

[II—123]

[In the handwriting of Jonathan Burt.]

October 2th: 1676

The Select men have let out to John Pety that parsell of

land in Chicopy plaine 35 to 40 acors more or les for the terme of five years this land lyeth on the west side of the great ryver and the said John Petty doth promis and ingage to pay into the Select men five pounds for the first yeare and make up the fenses and yearely afterwards he is to pay six pound ten shillings yearely and for the maner of payment if in case the land shall produce sutable Crops of wheat then the saide John Petty is to pay three pound ten shillings in wheate at a curent prise yearly but if god in his providens shal blast his Crope of wheat then he shal pay the full sume in indyan Corne pease and rye at the Curant prise as it paseth from man to man in the Town and the said John Petty is to secure the ffense from year to yeare al the tyme of sixe years and to leave the fense in good repare at the end of his terme of sixe years.

To this agreement the said John Petty hath set to his hand. The mark of John

pety.

[In the handwriting of John Holyoke.]

April 1: 81.

Anna Petty the Relict of Jn° Petty abovesd deceased doth Covent & pmise to & wth the prsent Select men, that she wil fulfill the Conditions above mentioned wth her husband to the end of ye abovesd terme of yers, & accordingly doth here set to her hand. Anna Petty

her marke

Feb: 13, 1681.

Samuell Owen doth Covenant wth ye prsent Select men to fulfill ye conditions above mentoned about payment for The Towns Land at Chickuppi, & in Special that he engages the crop for security for ye ful satisfaction of ye rent, but as he shal need for ye family bread, the Select men to allow him what they Judge meet for necessary bread.

Samuel owen his Mark.

[II—125]

[In the handwriting of Henry Chapin.]

ffebruary 12: 1676

Atta meet of the Seleck men, Gorg Coulton John Dumbleton, Ben Parsons, John Dorchester, Henry Chapin, Survaiors of fences for the longmedo Nathanel Burt and Samuel Stebin. for the homlots Samuel Bliss Senior Thomas Stebing Juner. for the feldes ofer the great rifer and agawam Jams Tayler and Thomas Miller. for chipapy feild on the west side of the great rifer Sarjent morgin and John Bag. wher of wee find that fences are much demolished and cannot be so spedily Sutup therfor it is ordered that Swin Shall be run by the 10 of march and to be kept run until the 10 of november. for this Present yer [II—125] and there is chosen Samuel ball to ring the swin on this side of the rifer and Samuel Taylor on the west side of the rifer and to have 8 pens p swin for Ringing of them in cas the oners ring them them selfs.

it is ordered that all comen fences be made up by the 10 of march next in case the frost henders not and that everi man Sut up Staks with his nam apon it and in caus any man negleck suting up his stak wit his nam apon it he shall pay 6 penc for his defeck.

At a meeting of the Seleck men Aprel the 23: 1677, they being all present ther was an acount taken of defecks of seferal mens fenses:

At a meeting of the Seleck men the desember 21, 1677 ther war chosen for Prisors Jafet Chapin Jams warener Samuel ely.

[II—126]

the toun detor Juneri the 7: 1677.

by on woolf to Samuel harman	00	10	00
to John Dorchester for caring doun the meeting hous bel	00	02	00
by the toun deter in Junary the 31 1675	06	19	00
& more for one wolfe ye Majors black man killed	00	10	00
by the toun debtor in ffebuary the 5. 1676.	04	10	00
by ringing the bel and sweping the meeting hous 1677	02	10	00
to quartermaster Coulton being debity	04	00	00

to on bushel Indian Corn to Gorg coulton	00	02	06
to inckrs Sicks for building the toun hous	70	00	00
for building the chimlis................	10	00	00
by glass to the toun hous.............	06	00	00

	115	02	03

[II—127]

to insin cooly for 1-2 bushel of wheat meal	00	02	00
to 3 days work to Insin Cooly about the town hous........................	00	06	00
to Josep Croofut for mending the pound..	00	01	03
to Sam ely intertaining the tounsmen in 75	00	10	00
mor to intertainment in 76............	00	04	00
mor to the charg of taking doun the bel...	00	02	06
by chargis about m^r Younglif..........	00	04	00
by entertainment of tounsmen desember the 24:...........................	00	04	06
to making a drum cord and mending the drum	00	02	06
to intertainment of Seleck men Junari the 7: 77	00	04	00
to making the rates.................	01	00	00
To the Major ffor nailes and other thing for and about Mr Glovars house......	01	01	02
to m^r Glovers rate..................	80	00	00
to thomas day for carting of clay........	01	02	00
to John Lam one day raisng at the toun hous	00	02	00
to John Dorchester to too days raisin....	00	04	00
to nayls by quarter master coulton and insin Cooly: 5 thousand of 8.........	02	10	00
mor to 5 thousand and of 6is and 5 hunder	02	02	03
mor to 8 thousand of 4...............	01	16	06
to Gorg Coulton and ben Cooly for bringing up the nayls..................	00	08	00
ffor the Select mens and Commitionars dinar in August 27: 77..............	00	03	04

	4	5	3
	115	2	3
	119	7	3

[II—128]

[In the handwriting of John Holyoke.]

Feb^r. 5th: 1677:

The Town is Creditor by a rate of £122 10s as also some-thing for ye Rent of ye Towns land at Chickuppi:

The Account of ye Townes debts........119 7 3

& the account of ye Towns Credits........122 10 0

£ s d

Examined by us Samuel Marshfeild &
   John Holyoke & we find ye Town Creditor by £3 2s 9d.................... 03 02 09

---

ffeb^ry 11th: 1677:

At a meeting of the Select men: viz: Samuel Marshfeild, Japhet Chapin John Hitchcocke. Nathaneel Burt, Jn° Holyoke:

At this meeting of ye Select men Veiwers of fenses for Genll feilds were chosen Charles Ferry:

for ye long medow Charles Ferry Nathll Bliss.

for Chikuppi feild Jos Bodurtha Jonath Ashley

For the feilds on west side ye River: Samll Tailor Abel Leonard

For ye house Lots, Samll Ely Jam: Dorchester

Whereas not wthstanding al Laws or orders to p^rvent Damages by Swine, much Damag & trouble is done, It is now ordered [II—129] That al Swine above 3 months old Shalbe both ringed & yoked from ye 20th of march: & so Continued to ye 20th of october, And in case that any mans swine from ye 1st of April shal be found in ye streets or commons in or about the Towne unringed or unyoked, for al such defects ye owners of such swine shal pay 6d P swine, & in case that such swine shal be found in ye Hom lots meddows orchars Gardens Comon feilds unringed or unyoked, ye own^{rs} shal pay 8d P swine, whereof halfe shal go to ye Informer, & the other halfe to ye Town & shal be added by ye Select men to such persons next rate....And Luke Hitchcocke & Henry Gilbert are appointed to se to ye performance of this order.

And it is further ordered that these persons so appointed shal have power both to yoke & ring such swine, & for ye encouragem^t they shal have paid y^m 10d P swine by ye owners of the swine.

And for the west side of ye River Jonath Tailor Junr & Ebenezer Jones are appointed for to se to ye performance of this order And seing this order waches not for swine under 3 months old, It is now ordered y^t for al swine above one month & under three months age that shal be found trespassing as aforementioned ye owners of those swine shal be to ye same penalty above mentioned. It is also further ordered that ye fences of common feilds be set up by ye 10th of march ensuing, & that every person set up a stake wth ye first letters of his name thereon, at one end of his portion of fence, those letters facing to ye other end of his proportion of fence.

The names of such persons were absent at ye General Town meeting feb. 5th, 1677, & p^{r}sent noe reason for y^r absence viz: Robert Ashley & Jonathan Ashley: whose penalty is two shillings apeice according to town order:

[II—130]

The names of such persons as did afterwards absent y^{m}selves in ye town meting wthout Leave fro: ye moderator or ye major part of ye Inhabitants, & present no reason for y^t absenting themselves, vizt: Henry Chapin, John Riley, Obadiah Miller, Edward Foster Joseph Leonard, Jno Clarke, Jno Bliss, Jno Matthews, Quart^{r}m^r Colton, Ephraim Colton, Samll Bliss Junr: Samll Stebbins whose Penalty is two shillings according to Towne order. The Towne abated 1s P virtu of these fines: the next general meeting febr: 4, 1678.

April 26, 1678

At a meeting of ye proprietors of ye Genll feild on the west side of ye River, at this meeting for the Doing of the water fence at Widow Millers, Jonathan Ball Engaging to make

& maintaine the same a sufficient fence It was voted & Concluded by yᵉ proprietors to whom that water fence belongs
to give the same Jonathan: twenty five shillings for this yeer
wᶜʰ 25s the Worshipful Major Pynchon promises to se him
paid, The select men taking care that a Rate be made for the
Collecting of the said sum: now yᵉ proprietors yᵗ are to pay
this 25s are those on yᵉ East side of the River, the proprietors on yᵉ west side being to make & maintain yᵉ water
fence on yᵉ Agawam River.

It was further voted & concluded yᵗ the Genll fence of yᵉ
said feild shal be kept up in sufficient repair thorowout the
yeer, as also that al Cattle that shalbe found in the feild from
the beginning of februᵗy (next ensuing) shalbe Accounted as
trespassing & be empounded.

At the same time, It was by the Select men agreed that
Goodman Dumbletons yard be accounted & made use of as
a pound for the loest side of the Great River til such time as
a new pound be made.

May 3: 78:

It is agreed that Samll Ely's yard shalbe esteemed & made
use of as a pound until such as yᵉ Towne's Pound be repayred.

[II—131]

may 8th: 78:

At a meeting of yᵉ proprietors of yᵉ Genll feild on the west
side of yᵉ great River, the proprietors being warned to appeare by the veiwers of yᵉ same feild to answer their Complaints wᵗʰ reference to defects in yᵉ fences, & of stakes: yᵉ
underwritten proprietors did meet according to warning after Lecture: viz: Samll Marshfeild: Tho: Mirricke Jnᵒ Barbʳ
Senʳ: John Holyoke: James Sikes Jonathan Burt: Widow
Blisse:

June 3d: 1678:

At a meeting of the Select men at wᶜʰ Meeting Samll
Marshfeild Japhet Chapin Jnᵒ Holyoke were pʳsent upon
the desire of yᵉ Worshipful Majoʳ Pynchon to have the Lib-

erty to set up a flanker into the street at the east end of his new house y^t is now building on the North side of his own homelot the which flanker he desires he may have liberty to set into ye street five foot broad & ten foot in length: the wch his desire they do hereby grannt unto him soe long time as y^r may be need of a flanker: as also they do admitt his building there to the priviledges of the comonage of this Town:

Sept: 2d: 1678. At a meeting of the Select men being presen Samll Marshfeild: Japhet Chapin Jn° Hitchcocke Jn° Holyoke: The fence veiwers Complaining ag^t severall persons for ye Defectivenes of their fences belonging to ye Genll feild on ye west side of ye gr^t River: viz Jn° Scott: Ebenezer Jones 4 rod, Joseph Stebbin Edward Stebbin 8 rod. The case being heard Joseph Stebbin alleged he had not particular notice & was accepted promising forthwith to make his fence good: Edward Stebbin was found culpable, & having agreed wth fence veiwers for y^r parts, was fined 5s to ye Town, soe was Ebenezer Jones, who agreed wth ye fence veiwers for y^r parts, and was fined [II—132] 2s 6d to ye Towne: & Jn° Scott for Defaults was fined 10s to ye veiwers & 5s to ye Town:

Dec: 26th 78:

At a meeting of the Select men, y^r were al p^{r}sent. At this meeting Samuel Ely Samuel Terry, Luke Hitchcocke were chosen apprizers of Town stocke.

Luke Hitchcocke desiring Liberty to entertain Thomas Brissenton untill the next may, its accepted herein:

Rolland Thomas Japhet Chapin Abel Wright Charles Ferry Tho: Cooper Jonathan Bush, have y^r buildings allowed off, as also al those persons who have builded up ye ruines, have y^r buildings allowed off.

Janu^{r}y: 1678.

The Towne is debter

To the ministry or minister............ 80   00   00
To the Comittee for ye new meeting house 50   00   00
To the Comittee for m^r Glovers house.... 06   00   00

To the schoolmᵣ £6 fro: yᵉ Town: & £6 10s
  fro: Chickupi...................... 12   10   00
To yᵉ sweeping the meeting........... 02   10   00
To Sam: Ely for expences at his house & 1
  qu: Rum for Perambulators.......... 01   13   06
To G: Parsons for his team 1 day for yᵉ
  Flanker 0   05   00
To make a pound: &....must be money.. 2   00   00
To make yᵉ rates 20s to Incr Sikes for a
  plank 1   01   06
To Sam: Marshfeild for making yᵉ stockes. 0   05   0

                              156   04   00
The Town is creditor by a rate made for mᵣ
  Glover, ... 80   00   00
by a rate made for yᵉ new meeting house.. 50   00   00
by a Town rate...................... 20   00   00
It by a sale of the old meeting house.... 05   00   00
It by boards of yᵉ same house.......... 01   00   00
It. by yᵉ Town Land at Chickuppi £6 10s.. 06   10   00

                              162   10   00
[II—133]
The Account of the Townes Credits on yᵉ
                               £   s   d
  other page 162   10   00
& The accounts of the Townes debts in yᵉ
  same page........................ 156   05   00

                              006   05   00
being examined by us Quarter mᵣ Colton & Henry Chapin
we find that there remaines to yᵉ Town, 06 05 0 giving yet liberty to such persons as have ought due to yᵐ fro: yᵉ Town,
to bring in an account of what is yet remaining due to yᵐ.

Six pound above mentioned was set off with Leifftenant
Stibings for sweeping the meeting house the year 79 and 80.

Feb. 10th 1678

At a meeting of the Select men when were pʳsent Jnᵒ
Dumbleton Benj: Parsons: Henry Chapin Jnᵒ Holyoke.

At this meeting veiwers of fences to ye genll feilds were chosen

For the Homelots Tho: Mirick: Increase Sikes.

For Chickuppi Jno Bag Joseph Ashley

For ye west side of the Rive: Jam: Warrener Jno Dorchester.

For Longmed. Obad. Cooley Sa. Bliss Junr.

The Inhabitants are desired to take notice that the former order for making or repayring of all the fences to al the general feilds remaine still valid, viz: al be substantially done by ye 10th of march next & that each person set up a stake wth the first letters of their names to their portion of fence.

For the preventing of Damages & troubles to & between neighbo^{r}s that is wont to be by reason of swine, It is ordered that al swine above 3 months old be ringed by the first week in march & so to continue til the latter end of october & In case that any such swine shalbe found fro: ye first weeke in march in the streets or comons in or about the Towne unringed for al such defects the owners of such swine shall pay 3d p swine: & In case such swine shalbe found in comon feilds on lands medows gardens homelots unringed the owners shal pay 8d p swine: & In case any Persons swine shalbe found in homelots on lands gardens medows or comon feilds unyoked after due notice is given to ye owners of such Swine so breaking into inclosures, the owners to pay 6d p swine for such defects; wch money shalbe granted to ye Informers. And Joseph Stebbin & Benja Knoolton are ordered to se to the performance of this order. & they shal fro: ye 10th of march have power to ring such swine as they shal find unringed in ye Comons or streets, as also to yoke such swine as shalbe found breaking into inclosures after notice given to ye owners & these persons so appointed shal for satisfaction for y^r paines have 3d p ring, & 3d p yoke paid him by ye owners of such swine.

Rolland Thomas is by the constable & ye forenamed Select men chosen sealer for the weights & measures of this Towne.

It is further ordered that no persons henceforth wthout liberty fro: ye Towne doe clog up cumber ye highway or street fro: ye upper wharfe to ye bridge by Obadiah Cooleys wth firewood, Clay timber unles it be for building of fencing & that such as have filled the streets or Lanes wth clay Timber & remove not the same by the middle of June next shal be Lyable to forfeit the same, as also that no persons dig holes or pits in the streets wthout leave, upon the penalty of 5s, & that such as have already digged pits in the streets & do not fil y^m up by ye 10th of April shal be lyable to ye penalty of five shillings: & the surveio^{r}s of the highways to see to the performance hereof:

Feb: 16: 78:

At a meeting of ye proprietors of ye Genll feild on the west side of ye River It was voted & agreed by ye proprietors of ye said feild, for good agreem^t sake & ye security of the feild, that each proprietor thereof shall (according to his number of acres) fence the west side of the new high way, provided, that the proprietors make no alteration in their portion of ye Comon fence of the feild, yet understanding or it is to be observed that we are not so wel satisfyed that ye proprietors of ye East the River should ([II—135] be brought to ye fencing of this highway, or that we do not hereby engage to maintain the fence or any p^t of it alwayes [   ] to come but doe refer ourselves to ye Judgm^t of ye County Court next at Springfeild or else of Indifferent men.

It was further voted that Samll Marshfeild & Jno Barber Senr: & Edward Foster should attend to the Laying out or measuring of this new highway.

may: 28: 1679:

Att a meeting of the proprietors of the long medow, togather wth the Select men, P^{r}sent: Benja: Parsons Jno Dumbleton: Henry Chapin & Jno Holyoke.

1. At this meeting it was voted & concluded that each particular mans fence, or portion of fence on the brooke below the sd medow should ly al at one playne.

2. That if so be in this ordering of the brooke fence, any

of the ppriete's portions of brook fence there which form'ly
was in two places, being now laid together, should happen to
be where there is no fence, y' then such persons as happen to
have such fence on the brook, shal make an equal proportion
of new fence for them.

3. It was voted & agreed, that Ensigne Cooley, Jn° Blisse
& Ephraim Colton be the persons to lay out this fence on the
brooke.

4. It was voted & agreed that in this new model of fence
y' that they should lay out or begin to Lay out mens particular porton at & fro: the lower end of the brooke. onely w'th
respect to Ephraim Colton & Danll Cooley, because they
have engaged to do the water fence at the lower end of the
medow, fro: the top of the bank into the River, for [II—
136] the security of the feild for ever, the proprietors did re-
engage to them that this fence this water fence should be acount-
ed to y'm as thirty rod of fence on the brooke y' is fifteen rod
apeice, As also that if they prove to have any more portion
of fence on the brooke, the Proprietors promise that it shal
ly next to the water fence there.

5. It was further agreed to Lay out or order each particular mans portion of fence upon this brooke by the way of
casting of Lotts: The lot being cast the disposition thereof
fel 1. To Jn° Clarke. 2. To Samll Blisse Jun': 3. To Ensigne
Cooley. 4. To Samll Blisse Sen': 5. To Samll Stebbin.
6. To Quart' m' Colton: 7. To Benja. Parsons. 8. To Jonathan Burt Sen' & Widow Burt: 9. To Thomas Merrick.
10. To Harmon. 11. To Obadiah Cooley. 12. To Jn° Blisse.
13. To Nathanll Burt. 14. To Nathanll Pritchard. 15. To Jn°
Keeps Land. 16. To Isaac Colton. 17. To James Osborne.
18. To Charles Ferry.

6. It was also voted & Agreed & consented to on both
parts y' Ensigne Cooley would & should doe, make, & maintaine the gate & the water fence at the upper end of the Long
medow for ever, & that this worke should be accounted to
him as the doing of twenty rod of the upland fence belonging
to the long medow feild. As also that he shal have liberty, if

he sees meet to translate that gate & ye water fence & whole cross fence to the lower side of his Son Eliakim Cooley's Lot there pvided it be no p^rjudice to the feild.

[II—137]

7. It was further voted & concluded that ye Vpland fence belonging to the s^d long medow should be a new measured & laid out to each proprietor, as neer as may be, in the particular places, where they have al along made & maintained ye portions of fence there. And that Isaac Colton Samll Bliss Junr: & Samll Stebbin shal be to measure this upland Fence

Aug: 4th 79:

At a meeting of the Proprietors of ye feild on the west side of the River.

It was voted & agreed by ye Proprietors of that feild wch sit down on the East of the River to allow fifteen shillings for satisfaction for the damage the feilds portion of ye water fence blow Thomas millers pasture.

It was further voted & agreed that Samll Marshfeild, Miles Morgan, & James Taylor, should do their proportion of theire fence that they used to doe out between the feild & Tho: millers pasture:

November: 3 d. 1679

At a meeting of the Select men This 3d of Novemb^r. Rolland Thomas his bul was hired for the use of the upper end or part of the Town, for which they engage him by the Inhabitants of the s^d upper part of the Towne & that they wil see him paid. his cowes being exempted fro: the rate that shalbe made to levy this 20s hire.

Dec: 18th: 79. At a meeting of the Select men Thomas Stebbin Junr: Charles Ferry Jno Harmon were chosen for to be the apprizers of the Towns stock:

[II—138]

Dec: 29, 1679:   The Town is Dr:

	£	s	d
To Goodm: mirrick for his house for ye schooling	00	10	00

To Goodman Pasons for Settin nailes for y^e
school house 29s 6d & 1s 8d for ferriage
of his horse, & his own time & horse 2
dayes 2s pr day 4s.................... 1 15 02
Ite. to Goodm: Parsons for worke about the
pound 9s 6d & for worke about the
school house. viz: carting stone 7s.... 0 16 6
Ite. to Benja. Knowlton for helping about
the pound & a gate.................... 0 06 0
To Jn° Steward for making an eye for the
gate 0 01 0
To David Lumbard for killing 1 wolf.... 0 10 0
To Sam: Ely for Select men Feb. 1, 78,
Aug. 79. Dec: 79 & for entertaining the
schoole house raisers................ 1 05 0
To m^r Denton for his Labors in schoole
work ....'..................... 10 0 0
To Tho: Stebbin Junr: for his worke about
ye school house...................... 10 0 0
To m^r Glovers stipend.................100 0 0
To Samll Ely paying to Goodm: messen-
ger 1s & entertaining Qua^r colton 1
night: 14d & by eighteen pence forgot:
Anno 1678.......................... 0 3 8
To Goodm: Marshfeild by mending the
stockes & staple.................... 0 1 0
To major Pynchon for flints 10s........ 0 10 0
To making rates...................... 1 00 0
To Recorder for recording 4 Deeds fro:
the Indians ....,.................... 0 10 0
To the Worshipful majo^r Pynchon for 4 lbs
of pouder for the use of the Guard..... 0 14 0
by 2s 6d allowed to Jn° Holyoke for his
making of severall rates Ano 1678, w^{ch}
should have been made divers yeers
before 0 02 6
To Goodman Lamb carting 1 day Clay for
ye school house...................... 0 05 0

[II—139]

Jan: 14th: 79   Town C^r

              £ d s

by our ministers rate.................100 00 00

by the Town Rate 029 12 00

Feb: 3, 1679.

We whose names are underwritten being appointed to
Examine ye last Select mens accounts of the Townes debts

              £ s d

& credits & we find ye Townes credit is.........01 04 2

        Samuel Marshfeild

        Samll Ely

Feb: 7th 1679:

The Towne is debter to majo^r Pynchon for the freight of
3 barrells of powder fro: Boston to Hartford the last sum^r
wch was not brought to account 6s: & by Paym^t to Tho: Miller 3s 9d for bringing those 3 barlls of powder fro: Hartford

              £ s d

              00 9 9

The £00 9s 9d above specified was payed out of ye 1 04 02
above mentioned.

[II—140]

[In the handwriting of Jonathan Burt.]

ffebruary 9th 1679

at a meeting of the Select men whear were present Beniamin Cooly Samuell marshfeild John hitchcock Jonathan
Burt Japhet Chapen. at this meetin veiwers of ffence weare
chosen.

for the hom lots David Lumbard John norton

for Chicopy Jonathan morgan Samuel Bothorda

Long meadow Thomas Coulton Obadyall Cooly.

The Select men doe order that al generall feilds be inclosed & fensed by the 25 of march next unles the seson be
such that the ffence vewers shal give notis for sooner mending of the same fence

it is also ordered that al swine shall be ringed & yoked
that are about 3 months old from the 20th of march to the

20th of october next and in case any swine shal be found in
the streets Comons or Corne feild in or about the Town unringed and unyoked they shall pay six pens per hog or swine
and in case such swine be found in the home lots meadows
orchards gardens Cornefeilds unyoked and unrunged the
owners shal pay 8 pence for each such swine whare of half
shal goe to the informer and halfe to the Town Beniamin
Knowlton and Richard waight to se to the performans of this
order and the persons have power to yoke and ring such
swine and for incouragment they shall have paid them by the
owners ten pens per swine.

[II—141]

at a meetin of the Select men ffebruary the 9th it is ordered that all male persons that are above fourteen years of age
and under seventy years of age shal and are required to atend
the work of Clearing the brush or what may anoye the Highways and Comons about this Town to acomadate the keeping of sheep as the Country Lawe prescribs al such persons
are injoyned atend this work ether personaly or by a sefysent
hand in ther roome on day in June and another in agust next
when they shal be Called by the Select men and he that shal
not atend when he is warned shal pay as followeth from 16
years of age to 60 years shal pay 3s a day and under 16 and
above 60 shal pay 2s and this to be improoved to Cleare the
Comon: and heare are only exemted the worshipful maior
Pinchon and our Reverent Teacher m^r Peltyah glover.

it is also ordered by the Select men that al youths or boys
under the age of twelve years of age sit on that seat under the
deacons seat and also on that seat against it and on the stars
only they must not Block up the stars when m^r glover coms
and seats thar about and all parents doe order thare Boys
and Children to sit thare unles such as sit with thare parents
under this age a bove mensyned Josyas marshfeild henry
Burt Samuel parsons Samuel Chapen ar ordered at the end
of the Deacons seat against the stars to sit the Select men
doe request our ffreinds Beniamin Cooly and Deacon Parsons to have an eye to the boys [II—142] whar as there have

ben for a long tyme great disorder in our assembly by many
young persons steeling out of the meeting house before the
blessing be pronounced many of them canot be thought to
have any nesesyty so to doe and thare being a Country law
that doth comend it to the Select mens care and it being a
greife to seryous minds we doe declare and order that no
person so doe exceptin thare shall be a nesesary ocasion: And
we doe request and order Incres Sicks to keepe the east
doore and Isaack gleson and Beniamin Thomas to looke to
the South doore, and we doe request Liftenant Stebins to
apoynt on of the guard to see to the youth thare about that
thare be no disorderly practis by the youth and doe apoynt
Samuell Bliss Snyer to looke to the youth about the east
doore which men are seryously to admonish any disorderly
persons and if they will not be reformed then to mak returne
of the persons to the Select men

[In the handwriting of Samuel Marshfield.]

We ffind that The Towne debts being payed the yeare 79
by a rate and athar wayes as may apeare by the Select mens
account and by the Cammity apainted to examine their account the Town was Credit one pound four shilling 2 penc
which is in the hands of Samall tery Canstabell that yeare and
reseived the towne rate; but the Towne being indetted to
majar pynchon 9s an 9d far freight of 3 barrils of powdar
from boston to hartford and from hartford to springfeild the
townes due when this is payd the majar will be 14 shilling
and 5 pence.

[II—143]

[In the handwriting of John Holyoke.]

Aug: 20th 1680: At a meeting of the Selectmen:

The Select men have let out the Townes medow in the
boggy medow on the East side of the high way to the round
Hill, To mr Daniel Denton & his heirss for the ful Terme of
Twenty & one yeeres. The first Eleven yeeres the said mr
Denton is to have ful power & liberty to occupy & improve
the whole said medow, provided he do bog & clean the said
medow & bring it to be mowable medow; & fence it wth good

sufficiet fence front & rear & flankes and so Leave it: & the After Ten yeers the said m^r Denton is to occupy & improve the said medow conditioned he pay to the Town forty shillings p annum & maintain the said fence, & Leave the same in good repair, yet giving leave to the said m^r Denton that In case he Judge this bargaine of allowing forty shillings p annum & fensing the said medow as abovesaid too hard for him that he shal have liberty to desert the aforesaid bargain at any time between the begining of ye Twelfth yeer & the end of the one & Twentieth yeer of this Lease. In witnes whereto the said m^r Denton hath hereto set his name, this 20th of August, 1680.

Danll Denton

Benjamin B C Cooley
  his marke
Jonathan Burt
Samuel Marshfeild
John Hitchcock
Japhat Chapin
[II—144]
    [In the handwriting of Jonathan Burt.]

September 4th 1680

The vewers of fenses making presentments to the Select men of several defects of fenses in the feild on west side of the great ryver and the Select men have hard the cause and doe fine persons as followeth

the Worshipfull major Pinchon	0	2	0
John Dumbleton	0	2	0
Widow miller	0	1	6
Benjamin Leanerd	0	8	0
Joseph Stebins	0	2	0
Thomas myrak	0	1	6
Samuell & nathanell Bliss	0	3	0
John Warner & nathanyel Sicks	0	3	0
Widow Bliss	0	2	0
	1	5	0

Samuel Graves off hatfeild propounding to the Select men

that he might be admited an inhabitant the Select men do
Grant him his desire and Quartar Mastar Colten doth in
Gage in the sum of twenty pounds to secure the town from
any charge.

[In the handwriting of Henry Chapin.]

Springfeild the 3 of January 80

Liftenant Stebing hath payd the year 80 3 Jan ffor the old
meeting house which was set off in what should have bene
payd him ffor his sweeping the new house.

decon burts bull is hired by the Select men for the use of
the loar end of the towne for the yeare 81 he is hired till
michallmass next and he is to have 1 pound payd him by
those neibors of the loar end.

[II—145]

The Towne dr desembar the 30: 1680

To repairing the Long medo bridge.......03	5	6
To the deputy.........................04	0	0
To mr denton.........................10	0	0
To money to pay the remaindar of the Scoll house 08	0	0
To Samuel Marshfeild for killing a wolf....oo	10	0
repairing the drum for the Saboths use....oo	05	0
to Jonathan Taylor for killing a wolf......oo	10	0
To Obadiah Millar Ju for killing 2 wolfs....o1	oo	0
to Lifftenant Stebings for sweping the meeting house & beating the drum he desiring part of his pay we concluded to raise only.o1	10	0
To Samuel Blisses acount for the Constabell what at times when he reseived the rates..oo	o1	4
To Select mens expence..................oo	16	0
To housing and firewod to entertaine the Towne at the Genarall meeting ffebruary 79 ....oo	04	0
To making the rates...................o1	oo	0
To Luk hitchcock ffor ffetching mr Younglove in 76.........................oo	05	0
To Jonathan Taylor Ju for kiling a wolf....oo	10	0

To m^r holyoke for wrighting............oo 04 o
To maj Pinchon ffor nails for the Scool
    house ....oo 11 6

                                        32 13 6

also having not wheat to pay the deputy but
    taking indian Corne at 2s per bushell it
    addeth 15 shillings to the towne det....oo 15 o
also benjamin Knowlton for [   ]
    to scoole in.........................oo 05 o

                                        33 18 6

Samuel bliss Junar for killing a wolf........oo 10 o

                                        34 033 6

[II—146]

The Towne Crd January the 20: 1680

by a rate of 3.........................35 oo o
by ffines ffor deffects of som men that ware
    presented by the Vewars..............o 12 6
ffeb^r: ye 1st 1680
Received off ye Select men in ye year 1680 Ten Pounds
    ffor Schooling   Danll Denton.

Wee whose names are underwritten being appointed to
examin ye Select mens accounts of ye Townes Debts &
Credit wee find ye Townes Credit to bee..........I 9 0
more not allowed by ye Town to Goodm: Terry..o 2 6

                        Danll Denton
                        Samll Ely

men not answering to their names at ye Town Meeting
ffeb^r 1st 1680: Henry Chapin John Bag Rice Bedortha Obadiah Miller Edw: ffoster Samll Terry Ensign Cooly Quart
Coulten Eph Coulten Isaack Coulten.

memoranim: due to ye Town, in Goodm Terrys hand,
upon ye Country Rate in David Morgans hand. In Samll
Elys hand 8 14 6 of ye Town Rate.

[II—147]

ffeb^r: ye 7th 1680.

At a meeting of the Select Men present Quartermaster Coulton Mr Holyoke Deacon Parsons John Dumbleton Danll Denton

ffence viewers made choice off: ffor ye Home lotts, Charles fferry Thomas Merrick. ffor ye field over ye River Thomas Miller Nathaniel Sykes. ffor Skidmuck Jeremiah Horton Joseph Thomas. For ye Long Meddow Eliakim Cooley nathaniell Bliss: ffor Chickapee Rice Bedortha John Bag.

The first day of ffeb^r A wolf killed by Isaak Coulten ye head brought in according to Law.

The Select men doe Ratifie the order made by the townsmen in ye year 79: about ye yoaking & Ringing off Swine & doe appoint John Clark Senr: & Beniamin Knowlton to see after ye performance off y^t order.

It is ordered by ye Selectmen That all ffences about ye corn ffeilds shall bee set up & repayrd by ye 7th of march next & The fence viewers shall have liberty & are impowered to view ye ffences & to proceed against all defective fence according to Law & ye orders of ye Town.

[II—148]

It is ffurther ordered by ye Towns Men That the propriotours off ye ffeild on ye other side of the River Shall provide either a pound or a strong Substantiall yard ffor ye securing off such Cattell or Swine as shall bee ffound in ye ffeild Contrary to order: Likewise y^t ye propriotours in ye ffeild at Long Medow shall doe ye like. And it is ffurther ordered y^t John Dumbleton shall take Care y^t ye abovesayd order bee performed on ye other side of ye River: & Quartermaster Coulton at ye long Medow.

At a meeting of ye Select men March ye 2d 1680 present Mr Holyoke Deacon Parsons John Dumbleton Danll Denton.

Agreed upon y^t James Brown shal have notice given him y^t hee is not admitted as an inhabitant in y^s Town. And that hee is to leave ye Town unless hee produce Some approved person That wil enter into a bond off Twenty Pounds

To ffree ye Town ffrom any charge y^t shall by him or his happen to ye Town. John Dumbleton is desired & ordered to give James Brown notice off ye order:

[II—149]

This writing witnes and agreement betwene The Select-men of Springfeild for the year 1673 being Leiftenant Coapar quartrmastar Colton John Dumbleton henry Chapine Sam-uell Marshfeild and Joseph Crofoot the said Crofoot doth Covinant and promis to and with the said Select men To get stufe as good substantiall whit oke post and good railles and the pound is to be of the same bignes as the formar and to be six rails in height The said Crofoot is to get the stuf draw it in place frame it and set it up eviry way well finished by the 25 of March next insuing and so to take of the holl Care and Charge of the said work and what evar damage may acrue to the said Select men for the not doing it: and the select men doth promise to the said Crofoot payd: 3 pound for the said work so finished this pound is to be set up by the meting house whare the ould pound standeth and to the tru proform-ance the said Crofoot hath set to his hand this 3 of febuary 1673.

Witnesses are   The mark of
Beniamin Parsons   Joseph Crofoot.
John Barber:

[In the handwriting of John Holyoke.]

March 16: 1881-82

The p^rsent Select men have agreed wth Jno Miller & Thomas Tailor to make or set up a pound on the west of the River do al that shal belong to the compleat finishing of it (unles Iron worke) which pound is to be made of four Lengths of rails on each side or the 4 sides: & 10 foot length between. Se backward at p. at a meeting June 21: 1676.

[II—150]

[In the handwriting of Daniel Denton.]

March ye 4th 1680 James Brown making application to ye Townsmen & desiring liberty to stay in ye Town y^s Summer The Townsmen did give him leave to Continue in ye Town till Michalmas next ensuing.

At a meting of ye Selectmen ffeb^r: ye 7th 80 Tithing Men made choice of (viz) Serieant Morgan Thomas Day & John Warner ffor this side & Jonathan Ball ffor ye other side of the River:

March ye 8th 1680 David Morgan & Samll Lamb brought a wolffs head into ye Constable wch ye Constable atested under his hand:

Samll Marshfeild 2 wolves Anno 1680

[II—151]

At a Town Meeting of ye Select Men being present Mr Holyoke Quartm Colton Deacon Parsons & Daniell Denton: July ye 25th 1681 Agreed upon y^t a stanger y^t for some tyme hath had his Residence at ye Widdow Pettys & also Mr Brice have both of them notice given them to depart ye Town

July ye 29th 1681.

At a meeting of ye Selectmen present Mr Holyoke quartermaster Coulton Deacon Persons & Danll Denton

Whereas ye Townsmen at ye fformer Meeting Arthur Dudly was according to order warned out off ye Town & now making his application to ye Townsmen they give him a months liberty to answer his ingagement to ye Widdow Petty:

Goodman Merick & Charles fferry ffence viewers for ye home Lots bring in deffects as followeth James Warriner 2 deffects ffor 3 dayes six shillings. Goodman Clark 2 deffects 6 shillings. John Hitchcock one deffect 3 shillings Samll Bliss one 3 sh Increase Sykes one 1 sh: which ye Townesmen p order to be payd according to law & Samll Jones ffind 12s damage to John Dorchester by his defective fence.

[II—152]

August ye 29th 1681

David Morgan appearing beffore ye Select men & Comittee appointed ffor Calling former Constables to an account ffor overpluss mony Did Compound & agree to pay to yᵉ Town fforty shillings as overplus Mony in his Country Rates when he was Constable.—Febr 7, 81: wʳas there is due to Countrey Treasurer £3 for transporting Country Corne fro: Hartford to Boston this yer the Town give David Morgan to pay £3

Samll Terry Senʳ also appearing on yᵉ Same account did agree to pay six bushells off indean Corn (being overplus mony in his Country Rates when hee was Constable) to yᵉ town.

At a meeting of yᵉ Selec men December yᵉ 7th 81 present Mr Holyoke Deacon Persons Danll Denton. Prizers made Choyce off this present year (viz) Samll Ball Obadiah Cooly & Nath: Bliss:

January: 1681: The Townes charges appearing to be £32 or upward the rate was made to the sd sum.

[II—153]

[In the handwriting of John Holyoke.]

Dec: 31: 1681:   The Town is Dr.

	£	s	s
by £100 for our Reverend Teachʳ	100	00	00
by what is Due to the worshipl Major	01	05	02
by what is due to he schoolmr	10	00	00
by what is due to Deacon Parsons	01	02	03
by Jnᵒ Holyoke for making rates & for hook & for 1 dayes worke of Jnᵒ Crowfoot	01	08	06
by Tho: Day for bolts	00	01	06
by David Morgan his making a door for yᵉ school	00	01	06
To G: Lamb 1 dayes work 2s 6d: & Richd waite 2 dys 4s	00	06	06
To Roland Thomas for boards	00	01	06
To Samll Ely for entertaining about making rates & the Comittee when they called the Constables to the examining country Rates	01	10	09

It. To Jnᵒ Pope for what yᵉ Comitte in
part promised him, & for what loss he
sustained in making yᵉ pulpit Mʳs Glov-
ers pue & yᵉ Deacons seat......... 04 04 06
To Obads: Cooley for 1 day at raising, Mr.
Glovˢ 00 02 00
To fr. Pepper for 3 dayes worke 5s To Ja:
Stevenson 3 day 6s................. 00 11 00
To Ben Knowlton 1 day to Edwd Foster
& Ja: Darby 1 day p mem............ 00 06 00
To Tho: Miller & George Norton Jose
Leonard day ap.................... 00 06 00
To Increase for boards 14s. To Harry
Rogors 1 day 2s................. 00 16 00
To Jnᵒ Dorchester for 4 dayes & Lathes
11s 00 11 00
To Henry Chapin for 2 dayes 4s 6d...... 00 04 06
To Jose Leonard for a Cellar Window.. 00 01 00
To Goodm: Marshfeild for killing 2 wolves 01 00 00
To Joseph Bodurtha for a journey Ano
1676 to N. H. Northampton wᵗʰ yᵉ Com-
ision'' 00 06 00
To David Morgan Sam: Lamb: for killing
1 wolfe........................... 00 10 00
To Leiut Stebbein for sweeping yᵉ meet-
ing house &c 03 00 00
To the deputy..................... 04 00 00
To the comittee for mʳ Glovers house.... 07 00 00
To Samuel Ball for worke about mʳ Glovers
house 00 16 06

[II—155]
[In the handwriting of Daniel Denton.]

Due to our Landlord ely £1 10s 9d off which 9 shillings
ffor a school in his house, Anno 1680.

a bottle of Rum for perambulators six shillings ffor yᵉ
Comittee in 78 for yᵉ Constables in 81. the Rest ffor yᵉ Select
men in 81

[In the handwriting of John Holyoke.]

Jan: 1681:

To Samll Ely—This to S. Ely pd Indian Corn by Select men	1	10	9
To the worshipful major	1	5	2
To what is due to the Schoolmr	10	0	0
To Deacon Parsons wt worke about the scholh	1	2	3
To Jno Holyoke for making rates & for huges: & for a dayes work of Jno Crowfoot	1	8	6
To Tho: Day for bolts 1s 6d to Richd Waite for Two dayes work 4s To G: Lamb £, 2s 6d	0	8	0
To Rowld: Thomas for boards for ye Schoolhouse	0	1	6
To David Morgan making a door to scholeh.	0	1	6
To Deputy	4	0	0
To the Sextone	3	0	0
To Goodm: Marshfeild for killing 2 wolves	1	0	0
To Dav: Morgan & Sam: Lamb, killing 1 woolfe	0	10	0
To Isaac Colton for killing 1 woolfe	00	10	00
To the Comittee for mr Glovers house	7	00	0
To Samll Ball for worke about mr Glovrs house	0	16	0
To Jose Bodurtha Anno 1676 for a journey to X. H. wth Comisionr	0	6	0
	33	00	2

march 17 87

more to David Morgan for layg ye School Chamber to be paid by ye next Town rates.	00	10	0

[II—155]

Feb: 3 1681:

The Constable Joseph Stebbein Informes of a wolfe killed by mr Samuel Glover & Samll Bliss the Third:

as also of Two wolves killed by Benjamin Sebbein & Jno Mirrick:

Febr. 7: 1 81: also one wolfe more was killed by Ben. Stebbein & Jnº Mirrick: also one wolfe by Edward Stebbein: Feb. 10. march 28 82. one wolf more killed by Benj. Stebins & Jnº Mirricke: 81.

Feb: 7th: 1681

The Comitte chosen to examine the Select mens acounts for the pʳsent yeer doe find the Townes Debt: £32 15s 2d & the Towne Credit by

	£	s	d			
by J Hol.....................	oo	o5	o			
& by Troopʳs money wᶜʰ is						
Rate	32	10	9			
to be paid in Country pay.	o6	18	o			
So yᵗ the Townes Debt is but				o	4	3
& the Towne Credit is in						
Country pay...........				6	18	o

Joseph Parsons
Jonathan Burt Senyʳ

March 10: 1681-82

The Select men chosen Then subscribed persons to run the bounds between us & Westfeild: viz Tho: Miller Abel Leonard John Dorchester wᶜʰ is to be done the first Monday in march next, & in case of foul weather the next fair day, & westfeild men to met at the bounds & line defining the N. H. path.

[II—156]

Febr: 13: 1681:

At a meeting of the Select men being pʳsent Cornet Parsons, Deacon Burt: Tho: Day, Jnº Hitchcock & Jnº Holyoke:

At this meeting fence veiwers were chosen for the Comon feilds. for home lotts, Samll Bliss Senʳ Tho Stebbein Junʳ for Long medow Nathll Burt Ephr: Colton for the feild over the River Edwᵈ Foster Samll Miler. for Chickuppi Jose. Bedurtha Nicho: Rust.

Tithing men Rolland Thomas James Warrener & James

Dorchester for this side: Samll Marshfeild for the other side
yᵉ River & Nath Burt for Long Medow.

It was ordered that no swine, from the first..........
be permitted to go up & down the streets bet............
& that Isaac morgan & Danll Beamon do see to..........
......of this order, & that they do Ring such swine as.....
find not Ringed, & that they shal have 4d p swine for their
paines paid yᵐ by yᵉ owners of such swine.

It was furthed ordered that a pound be made on yᵉ......
side the River, & that Tho. Day & Jnᵒ Hitchcocke, do consult the neighboʳs yʳ where to set this pound & that the said
Select men doe bargaine wᵗʰ any met persons in their discretion what the Town shal allow yᵐ for this worke.

It is ordered that the order for setting up or repairing
of fences be as was ordered yᵉ yeer 1679:

It was agreed wᵗʰ Deacon Burt to give him 15s for his bul
& yᵗ the neighbors fro: Jnᵒ Harmons Downward do pay this
15 shillings by a rate made according the number of Cowes
Deacon Burts Cowes being not taken Into the number:

received on his rat   4   9   2
......his son Isacks 1   2   6 all is......... 5   11   8
due to Samuell Marshfeild rest due to him.... 4   8   7

S ely old account for entertaining the Selectmen in 75 17
shillings

the going the bounds between the town & Suffield
by making the rates 76 1 pound
entertaing the select men 5 dayes 76 1 pound
....1 pound 14 shillings and 8 pence...4   14   2
........agreed wᵗʰ Samuel Ely that he should........

Quarter Master Coultens due to the Towne as deputy 4
pound

ffor [   ] 5 pound 1 shillings 7 pence
one bushell of indian Corne 2sh 6 pence
to setting nails 4 shillng
to going the bounds between Suffield and this towne 3s
payd victory Sikes 9 shiling 2 pence, all is.....10   00   3
acquite the Towne of yᵉ money quartʳ rate The Town ac-

quitting or discharging him of ye seven pounds........the Towne upon the account of Troopers money......him 10s in Corne at Town prices & this is paid viz 4 bu: Ind: 10s mar. 2, 82.

Oct. 13th 81 one wolfe killed by Jose: Ashley.

Febr. 27 81 one wolfe killed by L. Hitchcock & Obadiah Miller jun^r:

Feb. 28 81: one wolfe m^r Glover & his partn^{r}s.

These four wolves Informed by Constable Jose: Stebbein.

April....82: one wolfe killed by Ben: Stebbein & Jno Hitchcocke.

INDEX OF TOPICS.

Thomas Cooper buys the Cable lot of the town, 154.

Unmarried men to be compelled to work on the highways, 214.

Unmarried of Springfield settlers, 20.

Unworthy persons excluded, 53.

Unwelcome intruders excluded from the town, 269-70.

Use of meeting-house chamber granted, 227, 228.

Wages of laborers fixed, 166, 171.

What constitutes the early records, 20, 21.

When chosen to any office or service in the town, those who refuse to act to be fined, 210.

William Pynchon's sealed measure the standard for buying and selling, 165.

William Pynchon's book, Meritorious Price of Our Redemption, etc., 89-125.

William Pynchon's career in New England—his Book of Heresy burned in Boston; his return to England, 79-121.

Woronoco lands for six years to be rated at half the rates of other lands, 249.

Work for building the meeting-house, 176.

Wood for Mr. Glover—the number of loads for each person, 387.

INDEX OF PERSONS.

ALEXANDER.

Alexander, George.—
When settled, 44.

ALLIN.

Allin, John.—
Laths, nails, etc., for house, 160.
Minister's rate, 161.
When settled, 41.
Witnessed deed, 41.

ALLIS.

Allis, John.—
Builds new meeting-house, 150.
To lay out road to Windsor, 140.

ASHLEY.

Ashley, Robert.—
Appraiser, 340.
A cartway and toll gate over his meadow, 53.
Breaking law about selling canoe, 167.
Collector of a rate for flooring the meeting-house, 200.
Constable, 68, 268.
On committee to make and seal "Tole Dish," 301.
On committee to bind the town concerning toll at mill, 301.
On committee to floor the meeting-house, 50.
On committee to grant land, 351.
On committee to set off swamp land, 173.
On committee to apportion land, 179.

Defective fence, 338.
Fence viewer, 187, 217, 314, 392.
Fined for defective fence, 364, 405.
Fined for absence from town meeting, 337, 354, 419.
Fined for selling his canoe, 178.
For his mare, 225.
Granted land, 167,171, 172, 173, 221, 225, 238, 240, 283, 287, 294, 297, 345.
His stone horse, 375, 376.
Keeping the ordinary, 185.
Land for a cartway, 196.
Land for keeping the ordinary, 279.
Leave to build, 288.
Minister's rate, 161.
Overseer of highway work, 360, 361.
Rate for Indian purchase, 175.
Rate for purchase of lands, 190.
Scouring trench, 409.
Sealer of weights, 256, 275.
Seat in the meeting-house, 127.
Seat in the meeting-house, 329, 330.
Selectman, resigned, 25, 26.
Selectman, 27, 127, 251, 255, 259, 305, 306, 307, 329, 330, 349, 350, 356.
Surveyor of highways, 219, 223.
Townsman, 199, 227, 235, 242.
Townsman,—refused to serve, 242.
When settled, 41.
Wood for minister's salary, 387.

Ashley, David.—
Appraiser, 356.
Defective fence, 338.
Fence viewer, 350.
Land granted, 311, 341.
Subscription for Mill, 353.

Seat in meeting-house, 127, 128, 129, 330, 331.

Ashley, Jonathan.—
Appraiser, 381.
Accused of fast riding, 375.
Defective fence, 407, 409.
Fence viewer, 418.
Fined for fast riding, 58, 375.
Fined for absence from town meeting, 419.
Overseer of highways, 361.
Perambulating town line, 409.
Seat in meeting-house, 128.
To call meeting concerning new bridge, 389.
Wood for minister's salary, 387.

Ashley, Joseph.—
Fined for fast riding, 375.
Fence viewer, 423.
Killing wolf, 442.

ATHERTON.

Atherton, Capt. Humphrey.—
Deputy, 37.

BAGG.

Bagg, John.—
Absent from town meeting, 433.
Cattle fine, 382.
Defective fence, 364.
Fence viewer, 55, 407, 410, 416, 423, 434, 437, 468.
Fined for neglect of duty as fence viewer, 56, 338.
Fined for letting his cattle trespass, 381.
Fined for not attending town meeting, 350, 354, 455.
Granted land, 310, 324, 345, 383, 386, 403.
Killing wolf, 361.
Lease of land, 369.
Rent of land, 392.
Rent, 40.
Seat in meeting-house, 127, 128, 330.
Selectman, 31, 405.
When settled, 44.
Wheat for minister's salary, 389.

BALL.

Ball, Francis.—
Allowance of land for training field, 163.
Builds shop for the smith, 63, 145.
Land for burying ground and training field, 50, 51, 144.
On committee to view Longmeadow, etc., for division, 178.

Making cartway, 196.
Minister's maintenance, 192.
Rate for Indian purchase, 175.
Rate for purchase of lands, 190.
Sale of land for cemetery, 174.
Surveyor, 193.
To build shop for the smith, 185.
When settled, 42.

Ball, Widow Francis.—
One of owners of toll gate and way over Ashley meadow, 53.

Ball, Jonathan.—
Appraiser, 437.
Bricks for Glover's house, 328.
Contract to maintain water fence, 398.
Fence viewer, 413.
Granted land, 174, 358, 385.
Raising Glover's house, 326.
Seat in meeting house, 129, 331.
Selectman, 29.
Tithingman, 436.
Wood for minister's salary, 388.

Ball, Samuel.—
Chimneys for Glover's house, 327.
Land granted, 397.
Seat in meeting-house, 129, 331.
Selectman, 29.
To mend Widow Miller's fence, 419, 420.
To ring swine, 416.
Wood for minister's salary, 388.
Work at Mr. Glover's, 438, 439.

BAKER.

Baker, John.—
Defective fence—fined, 376, 377.
The carpenter—land grant, 340, 358.

BANCROFT.

Bancroft, Thomas.—
Fence viewer, 242, 283.
Grant of land, 230, 241, 286, 288, 319.
Sealer of leather, 281.
Seat in meeting-house, 127, 128, 330.
Subscription for mill, 353.
To present for breaches of order, 255.
When settled, 44.

BARBER.

Barber, John.—
Complaint concerning fence, 420.
Land grant, 395.
Selectman, 29, 30.
Surety for brother Samuel, 395.
To lay out new highway, 424.

Witness to Crowfoot's contract, 435.
When settled, 45.

Barber, Samuel.—
Land grant, 395.

BEAMON.

Beamon, Simon.—
Fence viewer, 393.
Grant of land, 236, 239, 241, 248, 300, 321, 341, 374, 385, 390.
His stone horse, 376.
Leave to dig cellar, 256.
Purchase of land, 233.
Seat in meeting house, 127, 128, 330.
When settled, 44.

Beamon, Daniel.—
Sundries on Glover's house, 328.
To enforce order concerning swine, 441.

BEDORTHA.

Bedortha, Reice.—
Absent from town meeting, 433.
Appraiser, 356.
Complained of for having defective fence, 56.
Fence viewer, 56, 242, 275, 296, 337, 397, 399, 413, 434.
Fined for neglect of duty as fence viewer, 56, 338.
Grant of land, 221, 233, 240, 284, 293, 297, 320, 326, 348, 386, 387, 400.
In trouble over fence, 338.
Lease of land, 176.
Matter of fences, 371, 372.
Minister's maintenance, 192.
Overseer of highway work, 360.
Rate for purchase of lands, 191.
Seat in meeting-house, 127, 128, 329, 330, 331.
Surveyor of highways, 255.
Wheat for minister's salary, 389.
When settled, 43.

Bedortha, Joseph.—
Fence viewer, 410, 418, 440.
Fined for letting his cattle trespass, 381.
Grant of land, 400.
Journey to Northampton, 438, 439.
Raising Glover's house, 326.

Bedortha, Samuel.—
Fence viewer, 428.

BLAKE.

Blake, William.—
Granted land, 159.

Settled, 143.
Signed agreement, 160.
When settled, 40.

BLISS.

Bliss, Widow Margaret.—
Complaint concerning fence, 420.
Defective fence—fined, 431.
Granted land, 220, 241, 253.
To fence land over river, 290.
When settled, 43.

Bliss, John.—
Absent from town meeting—fined, 355, 368, 419.
Cash towards minister's salary, 388.
Fence viewer, 368, 379.
Granted land, 309, 341, 342, 351, 358.
Granted part of pond, 346.
Liberty to build, 393.
Seat in meeting-house, 128, 331.
To lay out brook fence, 425.
When settled, 43.

Bliss, Lawrence.—
Cattle complained of, 386.
Committee on town bull, 373.
Constable, 281, 292.
Defective fence—fined, 364.
Deputy Constable, 68, 268.
Fence viewer, 251, 259, 333, 392, 440.
Grant of land, 231, 235, 241, 252, 263, 290, 299, 308, 341, 374, 384, 385.
Highway surveyor, 305.
His stone horse, 371.
On committee to grant land, 345.
Seat in meeting-house, 127, 128, 329.
Selectman, 27, 28, 277, 334, 339, 343, 368, 371, 376, 377, 380, 381, 382.
To pay for chain he lost, 270.
Witness before Selectmen, 325.
When settled, 43.
Wood for minister's salary, 388.

Bliss, Nathaniel.—
Appraiser, 437.
Defective fence—fined, 431.
Deputy, 35, 38.
Fence viewer, 196, 418, 434.
Granted land, 221.
Highway surveyor, 219.
Killing wolf, 412.
Minister's maintenance, 192.
Rate for purchase of lands, 191.
Selectman, 29.
When settled, 43.

Bliss, Pelatiah.—
Selectman, 30, 31.
Town recorder, 47.

Bliss, Samuel.—
  Constable, 432.
  Defective fence—fined, 431, 436.
  Due him for two voyages with his
    horse, 315.
  Fence viewer, 357, 397, 416.
  Granted land, 308, 310, 320, 351.
  Portion of brook fence, 425.
  Seat in meeting-house, 127, 129,
    330, 331.
  Selectman, 29, 31.
  Subscription for mill, 353.
  To stop noise at east door of meet-
    ing house, 430.
  When settled, 43.
  Wood for minister's salary, 387.
Bliss, Samuel, Jr.—
  Absent from town meeting—fined,
    419.
  Fence viewer, 413, 423.
  Fined for fast riding, 58, 375.
  Granted land, 320, 351, 397.
  Portion of brook fence, 425.
Bliss, Samuel, 2d.—
  Killing wolf, 433.
  Selectman, 31.
  To measure upland fence, 426.
  Wood for minister's salary, 388.
Bliss, Samuel, 3d.—
  Killing a wolf, 439.
  Selectman, 30, 31.

BLUFIELD.
Behind in rate, 271.

BRANCH.
Branch, William.—
  Concerning fences, 371.
  Fence viewer, 227.
  Fined for not attending town meet-
    ing, 337, 355.
  For his mare, 225.
  Granted land, 312, 313.
  Minister's maintenance, 192.
  Overseer of highway committee, 361.
  Rate for purchase of land, 191.
  Seat in meeting house, 127, 128, 129,
    330.
  Subscription for mill, 353.
  When settled, 42.
  Wood for minister's salary, 388.

BRIDGMAN.
Bridgman, James.—
  Fence viewer, 187, 188, 195, 219.
  Land grant, 171, 172, 173, 221.
  Making cartway, 196.

One of the owners of toll gate and
  way over Ashley meadow, 53.
Rate for purchase of lands, 190.
Rate for Indian purchase, 174.
Surveyor of highway, 196.
When settled, 42.

BEWELL.
Bewell, Samuel.—
  Land granted, 308.

BREWER.
Brewer, Daniel.—
  Minister, 22 and 23.

BRECK.
Breck, Robert.—
  Minister, 22, 23.

BRICE.
Brice, Mr.—
  Notice to depart, 436.

BRISSENTON.
Brissenton, Thomas.—
  Granted entertainment, 421.

BROOKS.
Brooks, William.—
  Complains against cattle trespass-
    ing, 381.
  Fence viewer, 385.
  Fined for not attending town meet-
    ing, 337, 354, 355.
  Granted land, 235, 238, 240, 284, 289,
    306, 324, 396; at Worronoco, 250.
  Killing wolf, 411.
  Lease of land, 369.
  Order concerning his fence stuff,
    293.
  Rent of land, 392.
  Seat in meeting-house, 127, 128, 330.
  When settled, 43.

BUELL.
Buell, Goodman.—
  To build gallery in meeting-house,
    147, 303.

BURRHALL.
Burrhall, John.—
  Granted land, 179.
  When settled, 42.

BUSH.
Bush, Jonathan.—
  Building allowed, 421.

BUTTERFIELD.

Butterfield, Samuel.—
Granted land, 159.
When settled, 40.

CABLE.

Cable, John.—
Land measurer, 166.
Minister's rate, 161.
Sale of land to town, 153, 154.
Land grant, 159.
Sawing boards, locks, nails, etc., for house, 160.
Setting bounds to Plantation, 163.
Signed agreement, 160.
Settler, 143.
To lay out lots in Plantation, 144.
To set bounds to Plantation, 144.
When settled 40.

CATONIS.

Catonis (Indian).—
Fined for neglect of fence, 57.
Defective fence—fined, 376.

CLARK.

Clark, John.—
Absent from town meeting—fined, 359, 419.
Appraiser, 307.
Cattle complained of, 386.
Defective fence—fined, 436.
Fence viewer, 217. 296. 333. 368, 379, 411.
Fined for not attending town meeting, 337.
Mending pound, 391.
Overseer of highway work, 360.
One of owners of toll gate and way over Ashley meadow, 53.
Making cartway, 190.
Portion of brook fence, 425.
Purchased land, 221, 242, 250, 263, 356, 374, 383.
Rate for purchase of lands, 191.
Seat in meeting-house, 127, 128, 129, 329, 330, 331.
Surveyor, 193.
Tar burner, 187.
To enforce order concerning time, 434.
When settled, 43.
Wood for minister's salary, 387.
Clark, Daniel.—
Granted land, 309.

CLARKE.

Clarke, Lieutenant William.—
Deputy from Northampton, 36.

CHAPIN.

Chapin, Samuel.—
Bondsman for two sons, 54.
Commissioner, 25, 27, 59, 178, 223, 301.
Conducts services, 125, 126, 146, 147, 242, 250, 254, 256.
Due him from town, 315.
Fence, 333, 334.
Fined for not attending town meeting 337.
Granted land, 171, 172, 173, 198, 221, 231, 240, 280, 309, 313, 380.
Has charge of poor, 359.
Minister's maintenance, 192.
On committee to consult with Mr. Hooker, 262.
On committee to lay out meadow and upland, 144.
On committee to purchase Mr. Moxon's lands, etc., 146, 222.
On committee to obtain minister in Thompson's place, 247.
On committee to grant land, 170, 180, 310, 315, 323, 324.
On committee to apportion land, 179.
On first Board of Selectmen, 144.
One of Prudential Committee, 175, 187, 193, 195.
Purchase of land, 237.
Rate for Indian purchase, 175.
Rate for purchase of lands, 190.
Seat in meeting-house, 127, 329 330, 429.
Selectman, 21, 26 27, 57, 281, 314.
Townsman, 217 219, 223.
To report concerning wet meadow, 292.
When settled, 42.
With Selectmen arranges seats in meeting-house, 126, 358.
Wood for minister's salary 388.
Chapin, Mistress.—
Seat in meeting-house 330.
Chapin, David.—
Grant of land, 240.
Money received for use of his horse, 272.
Sealer of weights, 251.
When settled, 42.
Chapin, Josiah.—
Admitted an inhabitant, 54.
Admitted, 309.
Granted land, 310.
When settled, 42.
Chapin, Henry.—
Admitted an inhabitant, and father was bondsman, 54.

Colton, Isaac.—
  Absent from town meeting, 433.
  Due him, 441.
  Fence viewer, 413.
  Granted land, 321, 397.
  Killing a wolf, 434, 439.
  Portion of brook fence, 425.
  Seat in meeting-house, 128, 331.
  Selectman, 29.
  To measure upland fence, 426.
Colton, Thomas.—
  Fence viewer, 428.
  His stone horse, 375.
  Selectman, 29, 30, 31.

COOLEY.

Cooley, Benjamin.—
  Absent from town meeting, 433.
  Cash towards minister's salary, 388.
  For maintaining water fence, 365.
  Granted land, 220, 230, 233, 237, 241,
    248, 261, 280, 286, 288, 289, 291,
    303, 312, 321, 322, 323.
  Grant of land to raise pork, 59, 60.
  Has charge of poor, 359.
  Killing wolf, 408.
  Neglect to record his land, 34.
  On committee on corn mill, 352.
  Committee to lay out road to Wind-
    sor, 140, 143.
  One of committee to obtain min-
    ister in Thompson's place, 247.
  On committee to build new meet-
    ing-house, 149.
  On committee to enforce fencing
    fields in Longmeadow, 228.
  One of committee to grant land, 307,
    310, 315, 316 318, 323, 324, 345,
    358.
  On committee to grant land at
    Woronoco, 245.
  On committee for formation of
    county, 298.
  On Prudential Committee, 186, 187,
    193, 195.
  Portion of brook fence, 425.
  Rate for purchase of lands, 191.
  Rents part of meeting-house cham-
    ber, 227.
  Refused to serve, 242.
  Report of committee on Woronoco,
    249.
  Seat in meeting-house, 127, 329, 330.
  Selectman, 25, 26, 27, 28, 30, 251,
    259, 281, 305, 306, 307, 317, 329,
    330, 337, 339, 343, 357, 384, 385,
    386, 396, 405, 407, 412, 428, 431,
    434.
  Sundries, 412.

Sundries for town house, 417.
Townsman, 223, 227, 235.
To "have an eye to the boys" in
  meeting, 429, 430.
To lay out brook fence, 425.
To maintain water fence, 425, 426.
To lay out highway, 297.
To have charge of building Long-
  meadow bridge, 357.
Use of meeting-house chamber, 251.
Work on town house, 417.
Work, etc., on Glover's house, 327.
When settled, 42.
Cooley, Daniel.—
  Selectman, 29.
  To build water fence, 425.
Cooley, Eliakim.—
  Fence viewer, 434.
  Granted land, 390, 397.
  Seat in meeting-house, 128, 331.
  Selectman, 29, 30.
  Raising Glover's house, 327.
  Water fence, 426.
Cooley, Joseph.—
  Selectman, 30, 31.
Cooley, Obadiah.—
  Appraiser, 437.
  Fence viewer, 423, 428.
  Granted land, 320, 397, 401.
  One day raising, 438.
  Raising Glover's house, 327.
  Portion of brook fence, 425.
  Seat in meeting-house, 128, 331.

COOPER.

Cooper, Thomas.—
  Appraiser, 293.
  Appraiser of estates and cattle, 225.
  Builds meeting-house, 49, 176, 177.
  Building allowed, 421.
  Cash towards minister's salary, 388.
  Constable, 301.
  Clerk of Writs, 32, 46, 305.
  Concerning pay for building meet-
    ing-house, 184.
  Contract to build the meeting-house,
    145.
  Deputy, 37.
  Due him, 271.
  Fined for not attending town meet-
    ing, 337.
  Granted land, 171, 172, 173, 220, 221,
    231, 238, 240, 250, 265, 283, 288,
    317, 320, 366, 389.
  Handwriting, 21.
  Iron hook and eye at his house be-
    longing to town, 271.
  Judge as to repairs on meeting-
    house, 200.

Day, Samuel.—
Deputy, 39.
Selectman, 30, 31.

DARBY.

Darby, Jo:—
One day's work, 438.

DAVIS.

Davis, William.—
Deputy, 34, 37, 38.
Objected to as deputy, 35.

DENTON.

Denton, Daniel.—
Admitted, 414.
His labor in school work, 427.
Due him, 437, 439.
Examines Selectmen's accounts, 433.
Receives land at Round Hill, 430, 431.
Concerning his salary, 432, 433.
Town Recorder, 47.
Selectman, 28, 434, 436, 437.

DIBBLE.

Dibble, John.—
Granted land, 172, 173, 179.
Rate for Indian purchase, 175.
Rate for purchase of lands, 191.
When settled, 42.

DORCHESTER.

Dorchester, Anthony.—
Appraiser, 307.
Cattle complained of, 386.
Deputy Constable, 255.
Due on rate, 271.
Fence viewer, 227, 251, 307.
Fined for not attending town meeting, 337.
For ferrying, 391.
On committee to build new meeting-house, 148.
Ordered to remove lumber, etc., 334.
Ordered to sit in guard seat to check disorder at church, 59.
Grant of land, 219, 220, 233, 236, 242, 252, 270, 283, 383, 401, 402.
Killing wolves, 408.
Selectman, 28, 396, 412, 414.
Seat in meeting-house, 127, 128, 329, 330.
To sit in guard seat at meeting-house, 376.
To fence land over river, 290.

To call meeting concerning the lower wharf, etc., 379.
Town rate, 315.
Subscription for mill, 353.
When settled 43.
Wood for minister's salary, 388.
Dorchester, James.—
Granted land, 319.
Killing a wolf, 394.
Seat in meeting-house, 128, 331.
Subscription for mill, 353.
Tithingman, 441.
When settled, 45.
Dorchester, John.—
Fence viewer, 410, 423.
For carting the bell, 328.
Four days' work, 438.
Granted land, 319, 352, 401.
Raising town house, 417.
Raising Glover's house, etc., 327.
Seat in meeting-house, 128, 331.
Selectman, 28, 29, 416.
To run town lines, 460.
When settled, 45.
Work on meeting-house bell, 416.
Dorchester, Joseph.—
Seat in meeting-house 129.

DOVER.

Dover, John.—
Granted land, 172, 173, 179.
Rate for Indian purchase, 175.
When settled, 42.

DUDLEY.

Dudley, Arthur.—
Warned out of town, but given a month's liberty to stay, 436.
Dudley, Hugh.—
Granted land, 236, 238, 240, 241, 302.
Seat in meeting-house, 127, 330.
To serve summonses for town meeting, 148.
To warn people to attend town meetings, 305.
When settled, 44.

DUMBLETON.

Dumbleton, John.—
About rating three-corner meadow, 245, 246.
Appraiser, 293.
Appraiser of estates and cattle, 225.
Bill, 332.
Claims exemption from taxes on three-corner meadow, 69, 70.
Commissioner, 414.
Committee to grant land, 351.

Defective fence—fined, 364, 431.
Due for labor, 367.
Fence viewer, 235, 314, 385, 418.
Grant in relation to fence, 373.
Granted land, 221, 226, 233, 236, 240, 277, 205, 346, 366.
Has charge of pound, 337.
Highway surveyor, 292.
Repairing pound, 411.
Seat in meeting-house, 127, 128, 329, 330.
Selectman, 25, 27, 28, 29, 138, 255, 266, 273, 277, 279, 349, 350, 356, 362, 366, 392, 393, 394, 404, 410, 413, 415, 416, 422, 424, 434, 435.
Townsman, 242.
Town pound in his yard, 420.
To lay out highways, 296.
To get posts, etc., for pound, 349.
To measure land, 290.
To enforce order concerning swine, 434.
Wheat for minister's salary, 388.
When settled, 43.
Work on pound, 365.

EDWARDS.

Edwards, Alexander.—
Appraiser of estates and cattle, 225.
Fence viewer, 196, 223.
Granted land, 171, 172, 173, 179, 180, 191, 198.
Rate for Indian purchase, 175.
Rate for purchase of lands, 191.
When settled, 42.

ELY.

Ely, Nathaniel.—
Admitted inhabitant, 278.
Appraiser, 283.
Bill for nails, etc., 361.
Committee to grant land, 310, 323, 324, 345.
Committee on town bull, 373.
Committee on corn mill, 352.
Committee to consider Terry's claim, 282.
Committee to build new meeting-house, 148.
Committee to examine town's accounts, 367.
Entertainment for Selectmen, 409.
Granted land, 286, 313, 317, 320, 330, 347, 374.
Seat in meeting-house 128, 330.
Selectman, 27, 28, 57, 291, 292, 294, 298, 314, 317, 357, 368, 371, 376, 377, 380, 381, 382, 396, 405, 407.
To lay out highway, 348, 349.

To lay out way, 300.
To hang the bell, 358.
To make a door for meeting-house, 358.
To fence land over river, 290.
To examine Selectmen's accounts, 291.
Use of land for keeping ordinary, 347.
Wheat for minister's salary, 389.
When settled, 44.
Witness before Selectmen, 375.
Ely, John.—
Selectman, 31.
Ely, Samuel.—
Admitted inhabitant, 54, 277.
Appraiser, 381, 416, 421.
Cash towards minister's salary, 388.
Complains of fence viewers, 408.
Entertaining Selectmen, 328, 391, 417.
Entertaining school house raisers, 427.
Entertaining Goouman Messenger, 427.
Examines Selectmen's accounts, 428, 433.
Due him for entertainment, 437.
Due the town, 433.
Fence viewer, 296, 392, 410, 418.
Granted land, 312, 326, 366, 390.
Rum for perambulators, 422, 438.
School at his house, 438, 439.
Selectman, 30, 31, 128, 330.
Sundries due him, 441.
Town pound in his yard, 420.
When settled 44.

EVERETT.

Everett, Richard.—
Chapman for Gregory, 32.
Land for road, 166.
Measuring land, 162.
Minister's rate, 161.
Refused as chapman, 170.
Setting bounds to Plantation, 163.
To set bounds to Plantation, 144.
When settled, 40.
Witness to Indian deed.

EXELL.

Exell, Richard.—
Acquitted of defective fence, 377, 378.
Detective fence—fined, 364.
Fence viewer, 219, 221, 235, 350, 396, 410.
Granted land, 240, 287, 295, 313, 315, 320, 321, 343, 400, 403.
Rate for purchase of lands, 191.

Seat in meeting-house, 127, 128, 329, 330.
Wheat for minister's salary. 389.
When settled, 43.

FELLOWS.

Fellows, Richard.—
Forfeiture of land. 67.
Land granted, 265.
Land purchased. 265.
Seat in meeting-house, 127, 329.
To furnish horse, 271.
To pay for Chapin's horse. 272.
When settled, 44.

FERRY.

Ferry, Charles.—
Appraiser. 426.
Building allowed, 421.
Fence viewer, 411, 418, 434, 436.
Granted land, 288, 295, 304, 310, 374, 397, 403.
Killing a wolf, 365, 408.
Seat in meeting-house, 128.
Selectman, 29.
Subscription for mill, 353.
To fence land over river, 290.
Wood for minister's salary, 387.
Ferry, John.—
Selectman, 30, 31.

FOSTER.

Foster, Edward.—
Absent from town meeting, 419, 433.
Appraiser, 281.
Cash towards minister's salary, 388.
Cattle complained of, 386.
Defective fence—fined, 377.
Defective fence. 407.
Fence viewer, 357, 368, 376, 440.
Fined for not attending town meeting, 337, 354.
Granted land. 284, 298, 308, 348.
Makes complaint about fence, 57.
On work one day, 438.
Portion of brook fence, 425.
Raising Glover's house, 327.
Seat in meeting-house, 127, 128, 330, 331.
To lay out new highway, 424.
When settled, 44.

FOOT.

Foot. Nathaniel.—
Admitted as an inhabitant, 414.

FOWLER.

Fowler, Ambrose.—
Fence viewer, 356.

GILBERT.

Gilbert, Thomas.—
Appraiser, 293.
Fence viewer, 283.
Granted land, 284 286, 288.
Liberty to build. 278.
Selectman, 27, 255, 273, 279.
Seat in meeting-house, 127, 329.
When settled, 44.
Gilbert Henry.—
To enforce order concerning swine, 419.
Gilbert, John.—
Granted land, 44.
Granted land at Woronoco, 249, 250.
Grant forfeited, 297.
Gilbert, Jonathan.—
Granted land, 44.
Granted land at Woronoco, 249, 250.

GLEASON.

Gleason, Isaac.—
Admitted, 412.
To look to south door of the meeting-house. 430.

GLOVER.

Glover, Pelatiah.—
Granted land in house meadow, 355.
Salary, 365, 387, 422, 437.
Second permanent minister, 23.
To have use of the house and land, 278.
Glover, Pelatiah, Jr.—
Selectman, 30.

GRANT.

Grant, Tahan.—
Did not remain here, 44.
Nails that he did not make, 270.

GRAVES.

Graves, Samuel, of Hatfield.—
Admitted, 431, 432.

GREGORY.

Gregory, Henry.—
Allowance of land for the meeting-house. 164.
Breaking law about selling canoe, 167.
Land for meeting-house, 49.
Location of his lot, 144.
Granted land, 168.
Sale of land. 170.
Sells land. 32.
Value of estate, 153.
When settled, 41.

Granted land, 309, 312, 321, 346.
Seat in meeting-house, 128, 331.
When settled, 45.
Horton, Jeremy.—
Fence viewer, 393, 434.
Fined for not attending town meeting, 350.
Granted land, 311, 312, 323, 328, 377, 385.
Highway Committee, ?83.
Liberty to build, 279.
Seat in meeting-house 128, 331.
Selectman, 28, 410.
When settled, 45.
Wood for minister's salary, 387.

HUBBARD.

Hubbard, Samuel.—
Appointed to keep ordinary, 168.
Granted land, 167, 171, 172, 173.
Land measurer, 166.
Leave to sell canoe, 169.
Rate for Indian purchase, 175.
To lay out lots in Plantation, 144.
When settled, 41.

HUNTER.

Hunter, William.—
Admitted as an inhabitant, 306.
Fence viewer, 385.
Granted land, 304, 313, 363.
Seat in meeting-house, 128, 331.
Subscription for mill, 353.
Wheat for minister's salary, 389.
When settled, 45.

HUNWICK.

Hunwick, Joseph.—
For killing wolf, 364, 366.

JONES.

Jones, Griffith.—
Bill for, 331.
Defective fence, 421, 436.
Fined for not attending town meeting, 337, 354.
Fence viewer, 223, 242, 283.
Granted land, 233, 239, 240, 287, 295, 316, 351, 384.
Grant in relation to fence, 373.
Minister's maintenance, 192.
Old Katherine's (this may mean Katherine, widow of Morgan Jones) maintenance, 246.
Rate of purchase of lands, 191.
Rent of corn room, 332.
Seat in meeting-house, 127, 128, 329, 330.

To present breaches of order, 235.
When settled, 42.
Jones, Ebenezer.—
To enforce order concerning swine, 419.
Jones, Samuel.—
Killing a wolf, 411.
Jones, Morgan.—
Granted land, 171.
Rate for Indian purchase, 175.
When settled, 42.
Jones, Katherine.—
Rate for purchase of lands, 191.

JESSE.

Jesse, William.—
On committee to appraise property for minister's rate, 177.
When settled, 42.

JOHNSON.

Johnson, John.—
Deputy, 34.

KEEP.

Keep, John.—
Cash towards minister's salary, 388.
Death of, 414.
Fence viewer, 314, 357.
Granted entertainment, 285.
Granted land, 286, 302, 325, 403, 404.
Granted pond and land, 342.
Portion of brook fence, 425.
Seat in meeting-house, 128, 331.
Selectman, 28, 405, 407, 412.
When settled, 44.

KNOWLTON.

Knowlton, Benjamin.—
Concerning "scoole," 433.
One day's work, 438.
Raising Glover's house, 327.
Raising a pound, 427.
To enforce order concerning swine, 423, 434.

LAMB.

Lamb, John.—
Bill for fencing, 331.
Clay for the school-house, 427.
Concerning fences, 371, 372.
Contracts to groundsill minister's barn, 303.
Fence viewer, 227, 357.
For work, etc., 391.
Granted land, 221, 223, 233, 238, 240, 259, 285, 304, 310, 324, 325, 364, 384, 386, 395, 400, 437.

On committee to build new meeting-house, 149.

On committee to bind the town concerning toll at mill, 301.

On committee to make and seal "tole dish," 301.

On committee for a corn mill, 352.

On committee to consider Terry's claim, 282.

On committee to examine town accounts, 367.

One of the owners of toll gate and way over Ashley's meadow, 53.

To keep ordinary, 275.

Sealer of weights and measures, 306.

Surveyor of highways, 251.

Seat in meeting-house, 127, 128, 329, 330.

Selectman, 27, 28, 29, 127, 305, 306, 307, 330, 334, 337, 339, 343, 357, 368, 371, 376, 377, 380, 381, 382, 392, 393, 394, 404, 410, 412, 413, 418, 420, 421, 428, 431, 435.

To fence land over river, 290.

"To do his portion of fence," 426.

To lay out new highway, 424.

To make the stocks, 410, 422.

Town measurer, 281, 305.

To repair pound, 411.

Tithingman, 441.

Wants his Indian mortgage confirmed, 291.

Wheat for minister's salary, 389.

When settled, 43.

Marshfield, Josiah.—

Seat in meeting-house, 429.

MACKCRANNY.

Mackcranny, William.—

Allowance for killing four catamounts, 71.

MACKEY.

Mackey, Hugh.—

Seat in meeting-house, 128, 331.

When settled, 45.

MASCALL.

Mascall, Thomas.—

Admitted, 301.

When settled, 45.

MATTHEWS.

Matthews, John.—

Absent from town meeting—fined, 350, 363, 368, 419.

Beat drum for Sunday meetings, 48.

Fence viewer, 256, 384, 385, 405.

Granted land, 230, 236, 242, 312, 385.

Mending Pynchon's fences, 407.

Minister's maintenance, 192.

Privileges as cooper in respect to timber, 297.

Rate for purchase of lands, 191.

Seat in meeting-house, 127, 128, 329, 330.

Subscription for mill, 353.

To beat drum for Sunday meeting, etc., 145, 183.

To fence land over river, 290.

When settled, 42.

Wood for minister's salary, 387.

Matthews, Pentecost.—

Killed at the burning of Springfield,

MATHER.

Mather, Timothy.—

Granted land at Woronoco, 60, 311.

MATTOON.

Mattoon, Philip.—

Liberty to abide, 412.

MAUND.

Maund, Richard.—

Granted land, 248.

Purchase of land, 230.

His land sold to Pynchon, 272, 273.

When settled, 44.

MESSENGER.

Messenger, Goodman.—

Entertainment, 427.

MERRICK.

Merrick, Thomas.—

Carting clay for Glover's house, 326.

Cattle complained of, 386.

Complaint concerning fence, 420.

Committee to lay out meadow and upland, 144.

Defective fence, 407.

Fence viewer, 195, 392, 423, 434, 436.

Fixing the school-house, 426.

Fined for not attending town meeting, 337, 355.

Fined for defective fence, 364, 431.

Granted land, 167, 171, 172, 173, 179, 198, 220, 221, 223, 231, 233, 241, 287, 311, 385.

Highway surveyor, 183, 184.

Land measurer, 243, 268.

On committee to grant land, 170.

On committee to view Longmeadow, etc., for division, 178.

One of committee to apportion land, 179.

Town vote concerning his making bargains above 10s, 359.
When settled, 42.

OWEN.

Owen, Samuel.—
To carry out Petty's lease, 415.
Seat in meeting-house, 127, 128, 330, 331.

PARSONS.

Parsons, Benjamin.—
Committee to grant land, 351.
Constable, 292.
Deputy Constable, 281.
Due him, 437.
Fence viewer, 219, 256.
Grant of land, 241, 302, 313, 319, 376, 384.
Granted part of pond, 346.
Granted land which founded Suffield, 148.
One of committee to make and seal "Tole Dish," 301.
Overseer of highway work, 360.
Portion of brook fence, 425.
Repairs on school-house, 427.
Seat in meeting-house, 127, 128.
Selectman, 27, 28, 29, 138, 266, 273, 277, 279, 349, 350, 356, 362 366, 384, 385, 386, 396, 405, 407, 413, 416, 422, 424, 434, 436, 437.
Subscription for mill, 353.
Surveyor of highways, 235.
"To have an eye to the boys," in meeting, 429, 430.
To lay out highway, 297, 389.
To measure land, 72.
To have charge of cleaning brook, 275.
When settled, 44.
Witness to Crowfoot's contract, 435.
Work about schoolhouse, 439.
Work about school-house, 439.
Wood for minister's salary, 388.
Parsons, Joseph.—
Committee to examine Selectmen's accounts, 440.
Bill for hour glass, 225.
Deputy, 38.
Fence viewer, 217.
Highway surveyor, 183, 184, 227.
Overseer of highways, 228.
Permission to buy land, 382.
Rate for purchase of lands, 191.
Selectman, 25, 27, 28, 31, 414, 440.
Townsman, 223.
When settled, 40, 41.
Witness to Indian deed, 18.

Parsons, Ebenezer.—
Selectman, 30, 31.
Parsons, Samuel.—
Seat in meeting-house, 429.
Parsons, Hugh.—
Fence viewer, 195.
Rate for purchase of lands, 191.
Witchcraft, 73, 79.
Witchcraft examination, 146.
When settled, 43.
Parsons, Mary.—
Witchcraft examination, 146.
Witchcraft trial in Boston, 73, 79.

PEPPER.

Pepper, Francis.—
Cleaning Glover's cellar, 327.
For work at minister's house, 391.
Three days' work, 438.
Granted land, 179, 220, 236, 241, 293, 367, 370, 343.
Seat in meeting-house, 127, 330, 331.
Wood for minister's salary, 388.
When settled, 42.

PETTY.

Petty, John.—
Admitted, 309.
Cattle complained of, 386.
Defective fence, 407.
Granted land, 363, 394, 395.
Leases land, 415.
Water work, 392.
When settled, 45.
Petty, Anna, widow of John.—415.
Stranger at her house, 436.

PHILLIPS.

Phillips, Lieutenant.—
Keeper of ship tavern at Boston, 35.

POPE.

Pope, John.—
Making the pulpit in Mrs. Glover's pue, 438.

POWELL.

Powell, Thomas.—
A cooper. Admitted, 339.
Granted land, 346, 347.

PRINGRIDAYS.

Pringridays, Edmund.—
Fined for letting his cattle trespass, 381, 382.
Fence viewer, 363, 364.
Granted land, 367, 370.
Lease of land, 369, 392.
Wheat for minister's salary, 389.

STEVENSON.

Stevenson, James.—
  Work on Glover's cellar, 327.
  Three days' work, 438.

STILES.

Stiles, John.—
  When settled, 44.

SWINK.

Swink, Peter—negro.—
  Granted land, 302, 358, 373, 402.
  Killing wolf, 416.
  Seat in meeting-house, 127, 128, 330, 331.
  Settled, 44.
Swink, Susannah.—
  Death, 22.

TAYLOR.

Taylor, Jonathan.—
  Fined for not attending town meeting, 355.
  Fence viewer, 354, 357, 396.
  Granted land, 221, 239, 242, 310.
  Killing wolf, 411, 432.
  Seat in meeting-house, 127, 128, 330.
  Subscription for mill, 353.
  When settled, 43.
Taylor, James.—
  Cattle complained of, 386.
  Fence viewer, 416.
  Granted land, 299, 300, 304, 325, 341.
  Seat in meeting-house, 127, 128, 330, 331.
  "To do" his portion of fence, 426.
  When settled, 45.
Taylor, Jonathan, Jr.—
  Killing wolf, 432.
  To enforce order concerning swine, 419.
Taylor, Samuel.—
  Fence viewer, 418.
  To ring swine, 416.
Taylor, Thomas.—
  To build pound, 414, 435.

TERRY.

Terry, Samuel.—
  Appraiser, 421.
  Absent from town meeting, 433.
  Bill against town, 433.
  Claims land, 282.
  Constable, 437.
  Defective fence—fined, 399.
  Due the town, 433.
  Fence viewer, 392.

  Granted land, 236, 240, 244, 262, 289, 304, 309, 310, 320, 324.
  Report on his claim, 282.
  Seat in meeting-house, 330.
  Subscription for mill, 353.
  Wood for minister's salary, 387.
  When settled, 44.
Terry, Thomas.—
  Selectman, 30.

THAYLER.

Thayler, Faithful.—
  Witnessed deed, 41.

THOMSON.

Thomson, Mr.—
  Granted land, 237, 241.
  Maintenance, 244, 240.
  To enjoy town land, 243.
  Rate for purchase of land, 191.
  When settled, 43.

THOMAS.

Thomas, Rowland.—
  Boards for school-house, 439.
  Building allowed, 421.
  Due for boards, 437.
  Fence viewer, 227, 283.
  Granted land, 220, 248, 257, 259, 277, 289, 312, 321, 326, 348, 351.
  Killing a wolf, 394, 408.
  Money due him, 315.
  Leave to cart stones from Pecowsic, 226.
  Liberty to build, 279.
  On committee to grant land, 307, 310, 315, 316, 318, 323, 324, 345, 356, 358.
  On committee for highway, 383.
  On committee for corn mill, 352.
  Selectman, 27, 28, 57, 314, 317, 357, 392, 393, 394.
  Sealer of weights and measures, 423.
  Seat in meeting-house, 127, 128, 329, 330.
  Subscription for mill, 353.
  Sundries, 412.
  To view grant of land to Pynchon and Holyoke, 233, 234.
  To have charge of building Longmeadow bridge, 357.
  To make draught of land at Woronoco, 285.
  Tithingman, 440.
  Rate for purchase of lands, 190.
  Town hires his bull, 426.
  To lay out highway, 348, 349.
  To measure land, 231.
  When settled, 43.

Wood for minister's salary, 387.

Thomas, Benjamin.—
"To look to south door" of meeting-house, 430.

Thomas, Joseph.—
Fence viewer, 434.
Seat in meeting-house, 129, 331.

THOMPSON.

Thompson, Thomas.—
Complained of for fighting Sunday, 59.
Seat in meeting-house, 129, 331.

TOWNES.

Townes, John.—
Witnessed deed, 41.

TILTON.

Tilton, Peter.—
Deputy, 36.

WRIGHT.

Wright, Abel.—
Building allowed, 421.
Deputy, 38.
Fined for not attending town meeting, 368.
Granted land, 237, 241, 251, 252, 263, 286, 299, 300, 304, 308, 310, 313, 316, 321, 324, 325, 342, 363, 395.
Liberty to build, 294.
Seat in meeting-house, 127, 128, 330.
Selectman, 29.
Subscription for mill, 353.
To fence land over river, 290.
When settled, 44.

Wright, Samuel.—
On committee to obtain minister in Thompson's place, 247.
Deacon—conducts religious services, 126, 146, 248, 250, 254.
Granted land, 167, 172, 173, 179, 198, 236, 241.
Making cartway, 196.
Minister's maintenance, 192.
One of owners of toll gate and way over Ashley's meadow, 53.
Rate for Indian purchase, 175, 191, 248.
When settled, 41.

Wright, Samuel, Jr.—
Fence viewer, 223.
Granted land, 220.
When settled, 41.

Wright, Benjamin.—
When settled, 41.

Wright, James.—
When settled, 41.

WAITE.

Waite, Richard.—
Two days' work, 437, 439.

WALKLEY.

Walkley, Henry.—
When settled, 43.

WARNER.

Warner Andrew.—
Committee to lay out road to Windsor, 140, 143.

Warner, John.—
Defective fence—fined, 431.
Selectman, 29, 30.
Tithingman, 436.

WARRINER.

Warriner, William.—
Constable, 251.
Committee on gate way on meeting-house lane, 378.
Fence viewer, 107, 217, 223, 256, 307, 363.
Fined twice for selling canoe, 178.
Fined for not attending town meeting, 355.
Granted land, 167, 171, 172, 173, 221, 240, 304, 323, 400.
Leave to cut canoe tree, 168.
Making cartway, 190.
One of owners of toll gate and way over Ashley's meadow, 53.
Rents part of meeting-house chamber, 226, 227.
Rate for Indian purchase, 175.
Rate for purchase of lands, 190.
Seat in meeting-house, 127, 128, 329, 330.
Surveyor, 187, 196, 281.
Subscription for mill, 353.
Selectman, 27, 259, 329.
Selectman—arranges seats in meeting-house, 127.
Townsman, 199.
Wood for minister's salary, 388.
Witness to Stewart agreement, 64.
When settled, 41.

Warriner, James.—
Appraiser, 416.
Committee on gate way on meeting-house lane, 378.
Defective fence—fined, 364, 436.
Fence viewer, 368, 370, 397, 423.
Tithingman, 440 .